INSIDE STORY

A NOVEL BY

MARTIN AMIS

JONATHAN CAPE

LONDON

1 3 5 7 9 10 8 6 4 2

Jonathan Cape, an imprint of Vintage,
20 Vauxhall Bridge Road,
London SW1V 2SA

Jonathan Cape is part of the Penguin Random House group of companies whose
addresses can be found at global.penguinrandomhouse.com.

Penguin
Random House
UK

First published by Jonathan Cape in 2020

penguin.co.uk/vintage

A CIP catalogue record for this book is available from the British Library

ISBN 9781787332751 (hardback)
ISBN 9781787332768 (trade paperback)

Printed and bound in Great Britain by Clays Ltd, Elcograf S.p.A.

Penguin Random House is committed to a sustainable future
for our business, our readers and our planet. This book is made
from Forest Stewardship Council® certified paper.

INSIDE STORY

STORY

How to Write

ALSO BY MARTIN AMIS

FICTION
The Rachel Papers
Dead Babies
Success
Other People
Money
Einstein's Monsters: Stories
London Fields
Time's Arrow
The Information
Night Train
Heavy Water: Stories
Yellow Dog
House of Meetings
The Pregnant Widow
Lionel Asbo
The Zone of Interest

NON-FICTION
Invasion of the Space Invaders
The Moronic Inferno
Visiting Mrs Nabokov
Experience
The War Against Cliché
Koba the Dread
The Second Plane
The Rub of Time

EDITOR
Philip Larkin: Selected Poems

To Isabel Elena Fonseca

Contents

INSIDE STORY

Preludial

Welcome! Do step on in – this is a pleasure and a privilege. Let me help you with that. I'll just take your coat and hang it up here (oh, and incidentally that's the way to the bathroom). Sit on the sofa, why don't you – then you can control your distance from the fire.

Now what would you like? Whisky? Common sense, in this weather. And I anticipated, I divined your needs . . . A blend or a malt? Macallan's? The 12 Years Old or the 18? How do you like it – with soda, with ice? And I'll bring in a tray of snacks. To keep you going until dinner.

. . . There. Happy 2016!

My wife Elena will be back around seven-thirty. And Inez will be joining us. That's right – stressed on the second syllable. She'll turn seventeen in June. We've been pared down to just the one child for now. Eliza, her slightly older sister – Eliza's been doing her gap year in London, which after all is her home town (she was born there. As was Inez). Anyway, it so happens that Eliza was planning a visit – and she's just touched down at JFK. So it'll be the five of us.

Elena and I, we're not there yet, but the next phase in our lives is already in plain view. I mean Empty Nest . . . There are only about half a dozen real turning points in an average span, and Empty Nest looks to me like one of them. And you know, I'm not sure how worried I ought to be about it.

Several contemporaries of ours, having watched their last fledgling flutter off into the distance, succumbed within minutes to passionate nervous breakdowns. And at the very least my wife and I will start to feel like that couple in *Pnin*, all alone in a big and draughty old house that 'now seemed to hang about them like the flabby skin and flapping clothes of some fool who had gone and lost a third of his weight' . . . That's Nabokov (one of my heroes), writing in 1953.

*

Now Vladimir Nabokov – *he* had every right and warrant to attempt an autobiographical novel. His life was not 'stranger than fiction' (that phrase is very close to meaningless), but it was wildly eventful, and shot through with geohistorical glamour. You escape from Bolshevik Russia, and seek sanctuary in Weimar Berlin; you escape from Nazi Germany, and seek sanctuary in France, which Hitler promptly invades and occupies; you escape from the Wehrmacht, and seek – and find – sanctuary in America ('sanctuary' in those days being part of the American definition). No, Nabokov was a very rare case: a writer to whom things actually happened.

By the way I warn you that I'll have a few things to say about Hitler in these pages, and about Stalin. When I was born, in 1949, the Little Moustache had been dead for four years and the Big Moustache (still called 'Uncle Joe' in our household *Daily Mirror*) had four years to live. I've written two books about Hitler and two books about Stalin, so I've already spent about eight years in their company. But there's no escaping from either of them, I find.

I never had the – no doubt terrifying – pleasure of meeting VN himself, but I had a memorable day with his widow, Véra, beautiful, goldenskinned, and Jewish, it is relevant to add; and I got to know his son, Dmitri Vladimirovich (a flamboyant prodigy and prodigal). It was a double sadness to me when Dmitri died, without issue, three or four years ago. Dmitri was the Nabokovs' only child – born in Berlin in 1934, and officially a *Mischling*, or 'half-breed' . . . At lunch, in Montreux, Switzerland, Véra and Dmitri were very fond and sweet with one another. There'll be more about them later, in the section called 'Oktober' (it starts on page 235). I sent Véra a photo of my first son, and received a charming reply which of course I've lost . . .

In general? Oh, I'm a ridiculously lax and indulgent parent – as my children have had occasion to point out to me. 'You're a very good father, Daddy,' Eliza confided at the age of eight or nine, on a day when I was in sole charge: 'Mummy's a very good mother too. Though sometimes she can be just a little bit *strict*.'

Her meaning was clear. I'm incapable of embodying strictness, let alone enforcing it. You need genuine anger for that, and anger is something I almost never feel. I tried being an angry father, but just once and only for six or seven seconds. Not with my daughters but with my sons, Nat and Gus (who are now about thirty). One day – when they too were eight or nine – their mother, my first wife, Julia, came to my study in despair and said, 'They're being unusually impossible. I've tried everything. Now *you* go in there!' Now you go in there, the suggestion was, and apply some masculine fire.

So I dutifully shouldered my way into their room and said in a raised voice,

'*Right*. What the *hell* is all this?'

'. . . Oh,' said Nat, with a languid lift of his eyebrows. 'Taste the wrath of Daddy.'

And that was that as far as anger was concerned.

The thing is I just don't hold with it – anger. The Seven Deadly Sins ought to be revised and updated, but for now we should always remember that Anger rightly belongs in the classic septet. With anger – *cui bono*? Pity anger; pity those who radiate it as well as those on the other end of it. *Anger*: from Old Norse, *angre* 'vex', *angr* 'grief'. Yes – grief. Anger is almost as transparently self-punitive as Envy.

In the parenting sphere I am innocent of anger, but the deadly sin I do own up to is Sloth – moral sloth. Giving the mother more to do . . . I warned Elena about this, slightly pleadingly (after all I was fifty by the time Inez was born). I said, 'I'm going to be an emeritus parent' (i.e., 'retired but allowed to retain the title as an honour'). So in general a slothful father, though I'm quick – and eager and grateful – to accept the honour of it.

Three years ago I gave a talk at my middle daughter's school, here in Brooklyn, at St Ann's (where Inez also goes). Eliza was fifteen.

'This could be embarrassing, Dad,' said Gus (son number two), as I prepared to describe the occasion, and his older brother Nat said, 'Definitely. Plenty of room for embarrassment here.'

'Agreed,' I said. 'But it wasn't embarrassing. Eliza wasn't embarrassed. And I can prove it. Listen.'

The auditorium the school chose was an adjacent or maybe an adjoining house of worship – a real church (Protestant), with polished hardwood and stained glass. I stood at the pulpit facing a large congregation of humid young faces (I think attendance was compulsory for all in the ninth grade); these faces had an air of 'sensitive expectancy' (as Lawrence says of Gudrun and Ursula in the opening pages of *Women in Love*) when I tapped the microphone and greeted them and introduced myself, and asked: 'Now. How many of you have ever thought of being a writer?' And I'll tell you the number of hands that went up in just a minute. I continued,

'Well it so happens that you of all people know almost exactly what it's like – to be a writer. You're in your early-middle teens. The age when you come into a new level of self-awareness. Or a new level of self-communion. It's as if you hear a voice, which is you but doesn't sound like you. Not quite – it isn't what you've been used to, it sounds more articulate and discerning, more thoughtful and also more playful, more critical (and self-critical) and also more generous and forgiving. You like this advanced voice, and to maintain it you find yourself writing poems, you keep a diary perhaps, you start to fill a notebook. In welcome solitude you moon over your thoughts and feelings, and sometimes you moon over the thoughts and feelings of others. In solitude.

'That's the writer's life. The aspiration starts now, at around fifteen, and if you become a writer your life never really changes. I'm still doing it half a century later, all day long. Writers are stalled adolescents, but contentedly stalled; they enjoy their house arrest . . . To you the world seems strange: the adult world that you're now contemplating, with inevitable anxiety but still from a fairly safe distance. Like the stories Othello tells Desdemona, the stories that won her heart, the adult world seems "strange, passing strange"; it also seems "pitiful, wondrous pitiful". A writer never moves on from that premise. Don't forget that the adolescent is still a child; and a child sees things without presuppositions, and unreassured by experience.'

In closing I suggested that literature essentially concerned itself with love and with death. I didn't elaborate. At fifteen, what do you know about love, about erotic love? At fifteen, what do you know about death? You know that it happens to gerbils and budgies; maybe you know already that it happens to older relatives, including your parents' parents. But you don't yet know that it's going to happen to you, too, and you won't know for another thirty years. And not for another thirty will you personally face the really hard problem; only then will you be required to assume the most difficult position . . .

'And why are you sure', asked Nat in due course, 'that Eliza wasn't embarrassed?'

'Yeah, Dad,' asked Gus, 'and how can you prove it?'

I said, 'Because when it came to question time, Eliza wasn't the first to speak but she wasn't the last. She did speak, clearly and sensibly . . . So she didn't disown me. She owned me, I'm proud to say. She claimed me, I'm proud to say, as her *own*.'

Oh, and when I asked my listeners how many of them had ever thought about being a writer? What proportion raised their hands? At least two-thirds. Making me suspect, for the first time ever, that the urge to write is almost universal. As it would be, wouldn't it, don't you think? How else can you begin to come to terms with the fact of your existence on Earth?

———————

Now you're a close reader, and you're still very young. That in itself would mean that you too have thought about being a writer. And perhaps you have a work in progress? It's a sensitive subject, and it deserves to be sensitive. Novels, especially, are sensitive, because you're exposing who you really are. No other written form does this, not even a Collected Poems and certainly not an autobiography or even an impressionistic memoir like Nabokov's *Speak, Memory*. If you've read my novels, you already know absolutely everything about me. So this book is just another instalment, and detail is often welcome . . .

My father Kingsley had a nice introductory formula on sensitive subjects. It was: 'Talk about it as much as you like or as little as you like.' Very civilised, that, and yes, very sensitive. Perhaps you'll want to talk about your stuff, perhaps you won't. But you needn't feel shy. You said in your remarkably pithy note, *I don't want this to be about me.* Well I don't want this to be about me either; but that's my task.

In any case I'll be giving you some good tips about technique – for instance, about how to compose a sentence that will please the reader's ear. But you should take any advice I might give you very lightly. Take all advice about writing very lightly. It's expected of you. Writers must find their own way to their own voice.

*

I attempted this book more than a decade ago. And I failed. At that point it was provisionally and pretentiously entitled *Life* (and coyly subtitled *A Novel*). One weekend, in Uruguay in 2005, I strong-armed myself into reading the whole thing, from the first word to the last: there were about 100,000 of them. And *Life* was dead.

That I'd apparently wasted about thirty months (thirty months spent plodding around a muddy graveyard) was the least of it. I thought I was finished. I really did. As if seeking confirmation – this was in Uruguay, in the northerly village of José Ignacio, near Maldonado, not far from the Brazilian border – I walked down to the shore and sat on a rock with my notebook, as I quite often did: the inrushing South Atlantic, the boulders the size and shape of slumbering dinosaurs, the lighthouse solid against the babyish pale blue of the sky. And I wrote not a syllable. The scene prompted nothing in me. I thought I was finished.

A horribly unfamiliar sensation, a kind of anti-afflatus. When a novel comes to you there is a familiar but always surprising sense of calorific infusion; you feel blessed, strengthened, and gorgeously reassured. But now the tide was going the other way. Something within me appeared to be subtracted; it was receding – with its hand at its lips, bidding adieu . . .

Naturally I confessed to Elena about the demise of *Life: A Novel*. But I confessed to no one about being finished. And I wasn't finished. It was just *Life* I couldn't write. Still. I'll never forget that feeling – the outsurge of essence. Writers die twice. And on the beach I was thinking, Ah, here it comes. The first death.

Any minute now I'll tell you about a perverse mental period I went through in early middle age. And I often wonder whether it had much to do with that nadir or climacteric, on the shore, that vertiginous plunge in self-belief. I think not. Because the perversity predated it, and went on beyond it. Yes, but these things take a long time coming, and a long time going.

My oldest child, Bobbie. I didn't get to know her till she was nineteen. She was already at Oxford (reading History).

'Yes, that's the way to go about it,' said my pal Salman (oh, and I apologise in advance for all the name-dropping. You'll get used to it. *I* had to. And it's *not* name-dropping. You're not name-dropping when, aged five, you say 'Dad'). 'Don't get to know them', said Salman, 'until they're already at Oxford.'

A nice remark, but that's *not* the way to do it, as we were both aware. And I often feel regret, sometimes uncomfortably sharp, that I never knew Bobbie as an infant, a toddler, a child, a pre-teen, and an adolescent. But there it is. There won't be much about her here: she already starred in a book I wrote after my father's death in 1995, and now she's a whole ocean away . . .

So I helped raise two boys, and I helped raise two girls. I know about boys and I know about girls; what I don't know so much about is how they mingle. In recent years Bobbie has 'presented' me, as they say, with two grandchildren, a perfect boy and a perfect girl. So maybe I'll learn something – at one remove, through the wrong end of the telescope.

On the other hand, I grew up as a middle child: with an older brother, a younger sister. Nicolas was and is a year and ten days my senior (my Irish twin). But Myfanwy (pron. Mivvanwee), four years my junior, died in the year 2000. That event, too, took a long time coming, and a long time going.

A word about the unnatural interest I started taking in suicide – my extended period, in fact, of what they call 'suicidal ideation'.

It officially began on September 12, 2001. I wasn't reacting to the suicidal events of the day before (though I suppose I was feeling unusually porous and susceptible). It was not Osama bin Laden who threw me. It was an ex-girlfriend, a woman called Phoebe Phelps (and Phoebe will not allow herself to be kept offpage much longer).

. . . The poet Craig Raine said of Elias Canetti that he had 'a swarm in his bonnet' about crowds (his best-known book was called *Crowds and Power*). Oh, and by the way here's an intriguing bit of gossip: Canetti, the Nobel-winning *Dichter*, was a lover of the young Iris Murdoch (and you wonder about the quality of their pillow talk). Phoebe Phelps put a bee in my bonnet – but it felt like a swarm.

You won't believe this, but turning sixty, for men, is a great relief. To start with, it's a great relief from your fifties. Of the seven decades: the thirties constitute the prince, the fifties the pauper. I assumed that my sixties would differ from my fifties only in being much, much worse, but I'm finding the gradient unexpectedly mild; in fact it embarrasses me to say that the only time I've ever been happier was in childhood. True, you have to deal with an uncomfortable new thought, namely: *Sixty . . . Mm. Now this can't* possibly *turn out well*. But even that thought is better than nearly all the thoughts of your fifties (an epoch to which I will bitterly return).

More recently I've been wondering, *How exactly am I going to get out of here? By what means, by what conveyance?* Not that I'm at all keen to be gone (even at the height of my suicidal-ideation period I was never keen to be gone). You just feel the exit coming closer – as you're drawn (in the dignified phrase of an American writer we'll be meeting very soon) towards 'the completion of your reality'.

And coming closer with ridiculous haste. In fact you start to feel a bit of a dupe every time you open your eyes and get out of bed. The psychic clock (people have written about this) definitely accelerates . . . After I turned sixty my birthdays became biannual, then triannual. The *Atlantic Monthly* gradually became a fortnightly; and now it's the *Atlantic Weekly*. Just lately, I shave, or feel as though I shave, every day (and I provably *don't* shave every day). In the *New York Times* the op-ed columnist Thomas L. Friedman used to appear on Wednesdays only, but now he writes a piece every twenty-four hours (following the example of Gail Collins and Paul Krugman); and when it's bad, I seem to be settling down to these authors, over a leisurely breakfast (fruit, cereal, softboiled egg), every forty-five minutes.

You feel a schmuck and a patsy because it's somehow as if you're colluding in your own demise. A certain poet, who will also appear before long, put it more sombrely, in 'Aubade' (aubade – a poem or piece of music appropriate to the dawn):

> In time the curtain-edges will grow light.
> Till then I see what's really always there:
> Unresting death, a whole day nearer now.

Time has come to feel like a runaway train, flashing through station after station. But back when I was climbing trees, playing rugby football, and giving the girls in the schoolyard an occasional game of hopscotch (and all three activities now strike me as appallingly dangerous) – the runaway train was moving no slower. Nabokov even gives the speed: 5,000 heartbeats per hour. Life moves towards death at 5,000 hph.

*

You must be aware of it – and you must've been tempted by it: the huge sub-genre now known as 'life-writing'. It spans everything from Proust to the personal ads, from *Sons and Lovers* to the travel piece, from *Does My Bum Look Big in This?* to . . . I was going say to Mystic Meg's astrology column; but at least Mystic Meg has gone to the trouble of making it all up.

In a way I'm excited by the challenge, but the trouble with life-writing, for a novelist, is that life has a certain quality or property quite inimical to fiction. It is shapeless, it does not point to and gather round anything, it does not cohere. Artistically, it's dead. Life's dead.

Only artistically, that is. In down-to-earth realist and material terms, of course, life is bright-eyed and bushy-tailed and has everything to be said for it. But then life ends, while art persists for at least a little while longer.

Are you worried about the Great Pretender? I mean that high-end bingo caller who occupies pole position in the GOP? Every few years the Republicans feel the need to valorise an ignoramus (you may remember Joe the Plumber). They *like* the fact that their new champion, that trafficker in beefsteaks and dud diplomas, has no experience and no qualifications; if he wins, the first-ever political office he will hold is the leadership of the free world. Until recently, he was no more than a reasonably good sick joke. But I'm afraid we'll have to keep a pained and rheumy eye on him for a little while longer.

I saw Trump in the flesh just once, about fifteen years ago, and Elena and I had an excellent view. It was at a tiny airport in Long Island. He walked very slowly from plane to car (not *his* plane, just some open-prop shuttle), followed at a respectful distance by two beauty queens wearing sashes: Miss USA and Miss Universe. He looked put-upon and longsuffering; the limousine was inconveniently distant; and the flatland wind was having a day at the races with his hair.

———————

As I said, I couldn't write this novel back in Uruguay, but I think I can write it now – because the three principals, the three writers (a poet, a novelist, and an essayist), are all dead. The poet went in 1985, the novelist in 2005, and the essayist in 2011. The essayist was my closest and longest-serving friend and my exact contemporary. Whatever else it did to me and for me (a very great deal), his death gave me my theme, and meant, too, that *Life* could earn its subtitle. There was more room to manoeuvre, more freedom; and fiction *is* freedom. *Life* was dead. Life *is* dead, artistically. Death, on the other hand, is in this respect very much alive.

I'll show you to your room. Or to your floor. This house used to consist of separate apartments. On every landing there's a thick door with a chunky lock and a spyhole – separating private space from public. Around here we call your floor Thugz Mansion, with a zed. Or, more simply, Thugz. It got that name when Nat and Gus were both here. You can change it if you like but that's what it says under your bell on the doorstep – Thugz. So notify any visitors.

We'll be eating in around half an hour, and you'll have time to wash or lie down or unpack or just get your bearings. Thugz consists of a bedroom with an alcove study off it, a sitting room, and a kitchen. And two bathrooms. Yes, two. In Cambridge, England, I lived in an eight-bedroom house with one (cramped) bathroom just above the groundfloor boiler. But this is the United States, after all. There'll be a fair amount to say about what it's like living in it, this country, America.

It's basically a female set-up here: at mealtimes I join Elena, Eliza, and Inez – and frequently Betty (mother-in-law) and Isabelita (niece). My only comrade and bro, my only home boy, is Spats, who's the cat.

And here he is. He's a pretty decent little guy, you'll find. And exceptionally handsome, according to Elena. When I accuse her of spoiling Spats, she says, 'If you're that good-looking, being spoiled is what you get.' We'll return to the question of looks: a profoundly mysterious and irksome human sphere.

Here he comes . . . Have you noticed how *entitled* cats seem to be? Entitled, and coolly self-sufficient. That's the main difference between cats and dogs. That, and the fact that cats are *silent*.

Oh, thank you very much, Spats!

He timed that very wittily, don't you think? Yes, Spats, you did. He won't bother you much. If you're down here and we're all somewhere else and he's complaining, he either wants to be let out or . . . I'll show you where we keep his dry food and the tins – the Fancy Feasts. And you'll be as pleased as I am to know that he has his shits in the garden.

He'll be gone soon, Spats. He's retiring to the Hamptons, where he has family. Elena has family there too – a mother, a sister, and (sometimes) a brother . . . Now I hope you won't find your stay here wholly unstimulating. You and I will have our sessions, and you're always very welcome at the table, but otherwise take this place for what it is – an apartment block. Where you have your own keys.

By the way, this final draft will take an incredibly long time – at least two years, I reckon. You see, unlike poems, novels are limitlessly, indeed infinitely improvable. You can't *finish* them; all you can do is put them behind you . . . So for now, most afternoons, there'll be an hour or two of what Gore Vidal used to call 'book chat', until you move into your own place. And then, too, you'll be off and away for long stretches, and so will I. We can do a lot of it by mail. Let's just see how we go.

The book is about a life, my own, so it won't read like a novel – more like a collection of linked short stories, with essayistic detours. Ideally I'd like *Inside Story* to be read in fitful bursts, with plenty of skipping and postponing and doubling back – and of course frequent breaks and breathers. My heart goes out to those poor dabs, the professionals (editors and reviewers), who'll have to read the whole thing straight through, and against the clock. Of course I'll have to do that too, sometime in 2018 or possibly 2019 – my last inspection, before pressing SEND.

Meanwhile, enjoy New York. And once again – welcome to Strong Place!

Now, you take your drink, and I'll take your bag.

It's no trouble. There's a lift . . . Oh, don't mention it – *de nada*. The honour is all mine. You are my guest. You are my reader.

PART I

Chapter 1
Ethics and Morals

Could you put me through to Saul Bellow?

The time was the summer of 1983, and the place was West London.

'Durrants?' said the hotel telephonist.

I cleared my throat – not the work of a moment – and said, 'Sorry about that. Uh, hi. Could you put me through to Saul Bellow, please?'

'Of course. Who shall I say is calling?'

'Martin Amis,' I said. 'That's eh em eye ess.'

A long pause, a brief return to the switchboard, and then the unmistakable 'Hello?'

'Saul, good afternoon, it's me, Martin. Have you got a moment?'

'Oh, hello, Marr-tin.'

Martin, in very early middle age, would for some reason try his hand at a polemical work entitled *The Crap Generation*.* It would be non-fiction, and arranged in short segments, including 'Crap Music', 'Crap Slang', 'Crap TV', 'Crap Ideology', 'Crap Critics', 'Crap Historians', 'Crap Sociologists', 'Crap Clothes', 'Crap Scarifications' – including crap body piercings and crap tattoos – and 'Crap Names'. Well, Martin thought that 'Martin' was a crap name if ever there was one. It couldn't

---

* By 'the crap generation' I meant the one that came after the baby boomers – those born around 1970 (the Generation Xers). I couldn't be sure, of course, but the generation that came *after* the crap generation (those born around 1990 – the Millennials) seemed more or less okay . . . *The Crap Generation*, as a project, was put out of its misery by Elena. 'You're not serious,' she said. 'Who do you think'll review it, fool? Crap sociologists and crap historians and crap critics.' This stirred my fighting spirit, and I said, 'Yeah, well, they'll have to take it on the chin and move on.' Elena said, 'Everyone'll think you're as bad as Kingsley. And they'll be right. You're having one of your dizzy spells. Forget it. *The Crap Generation*'s a crap idea.'

even get itself across the Atlantic in one piece. Nowadays, true, most Americans naturally and relaxingly called him *Marrtn*. But those of Saul's age, perhaps feeling the need to acknowledge his Englishness, came up with a hesitant spondee: Marr-tin. In Uruguay (where 'Martin' was *MarrrTEEN*, a resonant and manly iamb), Martin had an attractive friend called Cecil (mellifluously pronounced *SayCEEL*). And 'Cecil', similarly, was unable to ford the Rio Grande intact, and became a ridiculous trochee. 'In America, man,' said Cecil, 'they call me *CEEsel*. Fuck that.' Martin, on the phone, wasn't going to say 'Marr-tin? Fuck that' to Saul Bellow. For the record we should additionally concede the following: 'Martin', in plain old English, wasn't any good either. It was just a crap name.

I said to Saul, 'Uh, you know the Sunday paper I wrote about you for last year?' This was the *Observer*. 'They generously said I could take you out to dinner anywhere I liked. Would you be able to fit that in?'

'Oh, I think so.'

Bellow's voice: he gave it to the dreamy, prosperous, but somewhat blocked and inward narrator of the spectacular fifty-page short story, 'Cousins'. *[M]y voice had deepened as I grew older. Yes. My basso profundo served no purpose except to add depth to small gallantries. When I offer a chair to a lady at a dinner party, she is enveloped in a deep syllable.* Thus enveloped, I said,

'Now I happen to know you like a nice piece of fish.'

'That's true. It would be idle to deny it. I am partial to a nice piece of fish.'

'Well this place specialises in fish. It might even be fish-only. And it's near you. Have you got a pen? Devonshire Street. Odin's – like the Norse god.'

'Odin's.'

I said, 'Would you mind if I brought my serious girlfriend?'

'I'd be delighted. Your serious girlfriend – do you mean that she's serious or that you're serious?'

'I suppose both.' That was the point: we were both serious. 'She's American – Boston – though you wouldn't know it.'

'Anglicised.'

'More Europeanised. American parents, but born in Paris and grew up in Italy. Adulthood in England. She's got an English accent. She's such an absentee that they won't even give her an American passport.'

4

'No?'

'No. Not unless she goes and spends six months in an army camp in, I don't know, Germany. They won't give her one, she says, until she's screwed enough GIs.'

'Well she doesn't sound *too* serious.'

'She's not. She's just right. Her name's Julia. Is there anyone you'd like to bring?'

'My dear wife Alexandra is in Chicago, so, no, I'll be alone.'

The American Eagle

It was to Chicago that Martin had flown, in December 1982, to interview the man whom even John Updike – an unusually generous critic, but unusually tightfisted, unusually *near*, when he dealt with his obvious living superiors – acclaimed as *our most exuberant and melodious postwar novelist*.* Much would turn out to hang on this meeting.

I checked into my hotel: big and cheap and by Midwestern standards implausibly old (it was now a Quality Inn but the more senior locals still called it the Oxford House), downtown, between the IBM Building and the El, in Chicago, 'the contempt centre', as Bellow called it, of the USA. I was in an exhilarated state, a state of evolutionary excitement – because my life was about to change, and as profoundly as a young life can ever change† . . . The next morning I breakfasted early,

---

* Updike's obvious living superiors did not form a numerous company, consisting at the time of Bellow and Nabokov. In his *New Yorker* reviews Updike was consistently impertinent in his evaluations of Bellow, and in my opinion slackly wayward and off-target in his evaluations of Nabokov (though wonderfully expressive about the prose). Having saluted Bellow's exuberance and melodiousness, Updike adds, in more or less the same breath: 'at this point of his career, Bellow has sat atop the American literary heap longer than anyone else since William Dean Howells'. William Dean Howells? This is, and was meant to be, slyly insulting. Unmasked by the passage of time as a bloated mediocrity, Howells lived from 1837 to 1920. In any serious critical sense, the man who sat atop the American literary heap during this period was Henry James (1843–1916) . . . There'll be more to say about Updike, and more to say about James.
† Oh, and my fifth novel was just a few months away from completion. My first four novels, like all the British novels published in the 1970s and early 1980s, consisted of 225 pages (and took eighteen months to write); my fifth took twice that long and nearly twice that length (it seems that I'd taken a leaf out of Bellow's book and trusted to *voice*) . . . But anyway, the arrival of my fifth novel was about fifth on my roster of imminent amplifications.

and showered and spruced myself up for our lunch, and then walked boldly out into the Windy City. Risibly so named, by the way, because of its reputation for boosterism and 'hot air' – and not because the city was and is really fantastically windy, with a glacial blast (known as the Hawk) veering in over Lake Michigan . . .

Bellow was sixty-eight and I was thirty-four, exactly half his age (a conjunction that would of course not recur). But I was already an old hand at processing American writers, having done Gore Vidal, Kurt Vonnegut, Truman Capote, Joseph Heller, and Norman Mailer. Still, this was different: when I read my first Bellow, *The Victim* (1949), in 1975, I thought: This writer is writing just for me. So I read him all.

The only other writer who turned out to be doing this – composing each sentence with me in mind – was Nabokov. (He and Bellow had one other thing in common: they both derived from St Petersburg.) In my immediate circle there were no convinced Nabokovians with whom I could crow and gloat. But I had a convinced Bellovian close by; at that stage he was just a journalist and a 'meteoric Trotskyist', and not yet the much-loved essayist, memoirist, and blaspheming polemicist he would eventually become. I mean Christopher Hitchens. Christopher had left England in 1981 and was now living in what he proudly and affectionately called 'the projects' in Washington DC . . .

So at twelve-thirty I left the Oxford House and strode to the Chicago Arts Club. In my mind I was already sketching out some preliminary passages for the piece I would soon write, one of which went as follows (and I know it's very bad form to quote yourself, and it won't happen again*):

> This business of writing about writers is more ambivalent than the end-product normally admits. As a fan and a reader, you want your hero to be genuinely inspirational. As a journalist, you hope for lunacy, spite, deplorable indiscretions, a full-scale crack-up in mid-interview. And, as a human, you yearn for the onset of a flattering friendship.

Three wishes, then. The first came true. And so did the third – but not yet, not yet. That didn't happen until 1987, in Israel, and it relied on the intercessionary figure of Bellow's fifth and final wife, Rosamund. In the end it was she who put me through to Saul Bellow.†

He had cheerfully told me on the phone that he would be 'identifiable by certain signs of decay'. But in fact he looked scandalously fit – he looked like the American Eagle. And as he began to talk, I felt an acrophobic dizziness, and thought of the description of Caligula, the eagle in *The Adventure of Augie March* (1953):

> [He] had a nature that felt the triumph of beating his way up to the highest air to which flesh and blood could rise. And doing it by will, not as other forms of life were at that altitude, the spores and parachute seeds who weren't there as individuals but messengers of species.

*

* I won't be quoting myself, but I will be repeating myself (in paraphrase). This long novel is almost certainly my last long novel, and some of it – about 1 per cent – has the character of an anthology. Self-plagiarism is not a felony; I would agree, though, that I am open to the charge of authorial misconduct. Much of the time I'm simply relaying necessary information. As for the rest, I'm usually turning again to an unanswered question, one that refuses to leave me alone.
† Me, and others too. Having spent time with the Bellows in I think Vermont, Philip Roth (until then a probationary intimate) wrote: 'Dear Saul: At last you've married a woman who understands me. Love, Philip.'

They can hear your medals shake

But let's keep a sense of proportion and context: first things first. My character was about to reveal itself in the form of destiny; I was moving on to a further and a higher phase of adaptation to the adult world; I was about to get married; and not only that . . .

And it was all secret, for now. Still posing as a friendship (our mothers after all were expat neighbours in Ronda, Spain, and we'd known each other for years), our affair itself remained unacknowledged. On pain of death I was forbidden to tell anyone; so I only told Hitch.

'Julia and I are having an affair,' I said.

'. . . I'm overjoyed to hear it. Though I had my suspicions. Bring her to dinner at my place. Just the four of us. Don't worry, I won't let on I know. Tonight.'

This happened, and was a riotous success.

' Hitch,' I said when he and I were briefly alone (the girls had gone down on to Portobello Road – it was Carnival weekend in Notting Hill). 'I think the quest is over. I think she's the . . . I think she's the other half.'

'Oh, without a doubt. Bind her to you with hoops of steel, Little Keith. Very clever, very attractive, *and*,' he said (this settled it), '*and* a terrorist.'

Christopher was about to marry a terrorist of his own, the fiery Greek-Cypriot lawyer Eleni Meleagrou . . . A terrorist, in Christopher's application, meant a woman with a strong personality – strong enough to inspire fear (when roused, terrorists became ungainsayable); and there weren't all that many of them in the early 1980s, with the sexual revolution in only its second decade. I said,

'Well Eleni's definitely a terrorist. And yeah, I suppose Julia's one too.'

'All the best ones are.'

'They're feminists, which goes without saying, but not even feminists are all terrorists. Or not even all feminists are terrorists. Christ. What I'm trying to say is it's not the same thing.'

'No, not yet. Let's go down. Bring your glass.'

And the four of us danced to the reggae on Golborne Road, as in an urban fertility rite, the boys shufflingly (and drunkenly), the girls with abandon and panache, again and again flinging their hands gracefully backwards above their heads . . .

———————

Martin flew to Chicago, 'huge, filthy, brilliant, and mean', in the words of its tutelary spirit (and the only American city that, like a terrorist, was frightening and proud of it, with those subterranean metal chutes on the way in, like a delivery system to the urban future). But Chicago admitted him, and let him out again. He flew back, and delivered his long piece to the *Observer*. Soon afterwards he happened to have a transatlantic conversation with Saul's agent, Harriet Wasserman, who said,

'Your piece. I read it out to him on the phone.'

'On the phone?' The piece ran to over 4,000 words. 'The whole thing?'

'The whole thing. And guess what he said when I finished. He said, "Read it again."'

In 1974 the unofficial shortlist for the Nobel Prize ran as follows: Bellow, Nabokov, and Graham Greene.* That year the joint winners were two Swedes of profound and durable obscurity, namely Eyvind Johnson and Harry E. Martinson. But Saul, unlike Greene and Nabokov, won it later, in 1976. He was sixty-one. And the Nobel was more or less the only prize (or award or medal or orb or gong) that wasn't already his. Yet he sat there, on the phone, for well over an hour, listening to praise.

———————

* Whose shade, by the way, warily awaits the destiny of William Dean Howells. I was a late developer, and Greene was the first serious writer I ever read; and I revered him, I think, largely for that reason. Forty years later I incredulously revisited *Brighton Rock* and *The End of the Affair*, and it became quite clear to me that Greene could hardly hold a pen. His verbal surface is simply dull of ear (a briar patch of rhymes and chimes); and his plots, his narrative arrangements, tend to dissipate into the crassly tendentious (because they're determined by religion. See below). The Stockholm Prize is adjudicated by a standing committee, so it is less scattershot than some; still, there have been many famous absurdities (and the great Borges said that *not* giving him the Nobel was 'an old Scandinavian tradition'). A Laureate Graham Greene would have been as historically embarrassing as the Laureate Eyvind Johnson . . . I interviewed Greene, in Paris, on the occasion of his eightieth birthday (1984), and came out with the rudest question I have ever asked anyone. It was a sort of accident: my question was in fact kindly meant (and at that stage I still thought he was some good). As we'll see in about twenty pages' time, he took it rather well.

So when Bellow came to London in the spring of 1984, and I went to the welcoming party thrown by George Weidenfeld, I (indirectly) brought it up with him, the writer's susceptibility to praise and dispraise (does it ever end?). We were out on the balcony, looking down at the Embankment and the Thames, and Saul said,

'It's an occupational vice. You fight it, and you don't want to admit to it, but you're never free of it. Do you know this story? . . . There was a girl in a village who was very good at everything and she won all the medals. She was covered in medals from head to foot. And a wolf came to the village, and the trembling children all ran and hid and kept as quiet as they could. But the wolf found the little girl and he ate her. Because he could hear her. He could hear her medals shake.

'That's what happens when you've won everything and imagine you're safe at last. Really you're more vulnerable than ever. They can hear your medals shake.'

Cocktails at Odin's

I was always going on about Bellow, so my secret fiancée was to some extent prepared. Unlike most of my close girlfriends Julia was a reader. So she read *Henderson the Rain King* (his least typical novel) and liked it. A few days later, though, she looked up from page 30 of *Augie March* and said,

'Does anything actually happen in this book?'

'Well the title mentions his adventures. There's development but no real plot.'

'Ah,' she said. 'So it's a babble novel.'

'A babble novel?'

'You know. Him just going on.'

Rather than expatiating on the babble novel, rather than defending the babble novel (as a route to self-liberation), I just said,

'It's the calibre of the babbler that counts. Anyway. You're okay about the dinner?'

'Don't worry about me. I'll probably be quiet at first. Pretend I'm not there. Talk to Saul. You don't have to worry about me.'

*

The Arts Club in Chicago had featured a de Kooning, a Braque, and a drawing by Matisse – 'but as you see,' Saul had commented, 'it's *not* an arts club. It's just an exclusive grillroom for elegant housewives.' In the same kind of way, Odin's flirtatiously acknowledged the appeal (and the expense) of high culture – it was practically panelled with modern masters, Lucian Freud, Francis Bacon, David Hockney, Patrick Procktor. In this setting, then, Julia and I were already ensconced on our velvet chairs when Saul Bellow was shown to the table.

I saw him come in. Fedora, checked suit with a crimson lining (not loud exactly, but *a bit sudden* as the English say); just below average height (he once complained that time had shortened him by at least two inches); resolutely and handsomely full-faced, and solid-looking. Half a decade from now it would be my habit to embrace Saul on meeting and parting; and I never failed to register his density of chest and shoulder: the build of a stevedore. At the age of seven, the ghetto child in Montreal lost a year of his life to tuberculosis; one of the many changes this wrought in him was the determination to become strong . . . In 1984 Bellow was in the middle of his third marriage – or was it his fourth? To tell the truth, I was not a keen student of Saul's private life (in literary matters I was far too earnest for that); no, I was a keen student of the prose, the tone, the weight, the disembodied words.

Julia was introduced, and was duly enveloped in a deep syllable. For a minute or two they had a genial exchange about *Henderson* ('Oh, you liked that one, did you?'). Then I said,

'We've ordered cocktails. And for you?'

And Saul surprised me – and pleased me – by consenting to a Scotch.

Looking around for a waiter I said, 'The owner isn't here tonight.' I meant Peter Langan, the controversial Irish restaurateur. 'Unless he's asleep under one of the tables. He's a Celt, you know, and what they call *a roaring boy*. But a nice chap. They say he can get three bottles of champagne down him before lunch.'

Saul asked, 'And how often does Peter accomplish this?'

'Oh, daily, I think.'

There naturally followed a discussion about drunkenness and drunkards (with Saul describing the two drunkards he'd known best, the poets Delmore Schwartz and John Berryman). Saul had not yet come up with one of the great observations on drunkenness and drunkards (it appears in the late story 'Something to Remember Me By'): *There was a convention about drunkenness, established in part by drunkards. The founding proposition was that consciousness is terrible.** And then there was the mysterious American tilt to the nexus between writers and suicide . . .

I said, 'There's a paragraph in *Humboldt's Gift*. I loved it and assented to it at once but I don't really understand it. Maybe you have to be American.'

'Let's see if I understand it,' said Julia.

'Okay. Then we'll know how American you are and whether you deserve a passport . . . That bit, Saul, when you say America preens itself on the suicides of its writers. *The country is proud of its dead poets.*† Why? Because it makes Americans feel virile?'

'Well yes. I meant business America, technological America.'

'Somebody wrote that you could count on the fingers of two hands the American writers who didn't die of drink. I suppose he meant the moderns, because Hawthorne didn't die of drink, did he? Melville didn't. Whitman didn't.'

---

* I naturally had an encyclopedic knowledge of drunkards and drunkenness. 'Now and then', wrote my father in his *Memoirs*, 'I become conscious of having the reputation of being one of the great drinkers, if not one of the great drunks, of our time.' In addition, Myfanwy, my little sister, would drink herself to death (2000); and so would Robinson, my most long-established friend (2002). By then I felt I could add a modest corollary to Saul's Law. Consciousness is terrible; and tomorrow, moreover, is neither here nor there, because tomorrow, for drunkards, doesn't exist. There: consciousness is terrible, and tomorrow is crap. Suicides, on the whole, climactically subscribe to both propositions. John Berryman, a suicide, wrote about the struggle to forgive his father, another suicide, and recalled the 'frantic passage' of Berryman Sr, 'when he could not live / an instant longer' (*The Dream Songs*) . . . My brother Nicolas and I were teetotal until our early twenties – because we associated alcohol with louts, hooligans, and tramps. This was unaccountable. We grew up in literary bohemia. Why didn't we associate alcohol with all the poets, novelists, playwrights, and critics we saw every other day, slurring, weeping, singing, declaring war, professing love, and falling crunchily down the stairs?
† Later I regaled Julia with the following quote. The country 'takes terrific satisfaction in the poets' testimony that the USA is too tough, too rugged, that American reality is overpowering. And to be a poet is a school thing, a skirt thing, a church thing. The weakness of the spiritual powers is proved in the childishness, madness, drunkenness and despair of these martyrs . . . So poets are loved, but loved because they just can't make it here. They exist to light up the enormity of the awful tangle and justify the cynicism of those who say, "If *I* were not such a corrupt, unfeeling bastard, creep, thief, and vulture, I couldn't get through this either."' And Julia understood.

'Whitman was a temperance-leaguer. With episodes of frailty.'

'Henry James didn't. But nowadays, I bet, it's only the Jews who don't die of drink. Because they don't drink at all. What does Herzog's father say about his hopeless lodger? "A *Jewish* drunkard!" So it's an oxymoron. Even their *writers* don't drink.'

'With exceptions, like Delmore. I'm wondering. Roth hardly drinks.'*

'Perhaps that explains the dominance of the Jewish American Novel.'

'Yes. We just lay in our hammocks till the field was clear.'

I too wondered. 'Heller drinks a bit. *Mailer* drinks.'

'He sure does.'

'Mm. I like old Norman.'

'So do I.'

'It's strange. No one behaves worse or talks more balls than Norman, but he's widely liked . . . The question remains. Why don't Jews drink?'

'Well, it's the same with Jewish achievement in general,' said Saul (as his drink arrived). 'And that achievement is disproportionate.† Einstein put it pretty well. The great error is to think it's somehow innate. That way anti-Semitism lies. It isn't innate. It's to do with how you're raised. All good Jewish children know that the way to impress their elders is through application. Not sports, not physical strength or physical beauty, and not the arts. Through learning and studying.'

'When did Einstein say that?'

'I think just before the war. In 1938 . . . You know, Einstein lived in Princeton, and in 1938 the incoming undergraduates were polled on the question "Who is the greatest living person?" He, Einstein, came second. And Hitler came first.'

'Christ,' I said. 'And wasn't American anti-Semitism very strong before the war?'

'During the war – that was its historic apogee.'

'I confess I just don't understand it, anti-Semitism. You copped some more of the same, didn't you, with *The Dean's December*.'

---

* For Roth in his comic novels drunkenness is a goy thing, an Irish thing (the owner, Peter Langan, would be very much on the premises, would be fatally in situ, when he burnt his house down in 1988), a Polack thing – those people, as Alexander Portnoy puts it, whose names 'are all X's and Y's'.

† The Nobel Prize, first awarded in 1901, gives us a useful index. Twenty-two per cent of its recipients are Jewish; and Jews comprise just 2 per cent of the world population.

13

'Yes, but from a different quarter. Not from the world of primitive superstition but from high academe.'

'From Hugh Kenner, wasn't it?'

'Uh. Hugh Kenner. He tormented Delmore and now he torments me. He managed another hissy fit in defence of uh, "traditional culture".'

'Meaning non-Semitic culture?'

'Meaning anti-Semitic culture, in this case. The traditional culture of Pound and Wyndham Lewis and T. S. Eliot.'

'Mm. Well, two nutters and a monarchist. And Wyndham Lewis did at least come up with that wonderful phrase . . . How do you think it went, by the way? I mean the moronic inferno?'

'I thought the moronic inferno went rather well.'

'Me too. The moronic inferno went very smoothly.'

'What', asked Julia, 'is the moronic inferno?'

The moronic inferno

Two or three days earlier Saul and I had taped a TV programme entitled (with a glance at Freud) *Modernity and its Discontents*, chaired by Michael Ignatieff; and that had been Michael's first question. 'I'm wondering what you meant, Saul Bellow, when you picked up that phrase from Wyndham Lewis': the moronic inferno. And Saul answered:

> Well, it means a chaotic state which no one has sufficient internal organisation to resist. A state in which one is overwhelmed by all kind of powers – political, technological, military, economic, and so on – which carry everything before them with a kind of heathen disorder in which we're supposed to survive with all our human qualities.

And the question before us, Saul went on, is whether this is possible . . . So we talked about that, bearing in mind that writers, as he said, are expected to have 'a fairly well-organised individuality', and are therefore able to put up some opposition – some internal opposition to the moronic inferno . . .

It lasted about an hour, and then the car dropped Saul and me off in Gower Street, and we strolled through Bloomsbury – the garden squares, the plaques and statues, the museums, the houses of worship and the houses of learning. As we crossed Fitzroy Square I talked scornfully about the Bloomsbury Group (in my view a disgrace to bohemia); and we moved on to the major class antagonisms that were only now beginning to fade . . . Saul needed no goading to think ill of what he called Bloomsbury 'patricianism', though he was surprisingly relaxed about Bloomsbury Judaeophobia.

'But Saul, it was so fierce and it was *all* of them.'

'Yes, even Maynard Keynes. But they were only reflexive anti-Semites. Not visceral. Being anti-Semitic was just one of the duties of being a snob.'

'. . . Maybe also one of the duties of being second-rate. The only one who wasn't was Forster – not anti-Semitic and not second-rate. As for Virginia Woolf . . .'

'But bear in mind she was married to a Jew. Leonard . . . That kind of drawing-room anti-Semitism – it's mostly just a posture. They'd've been horrified by anything serious.'

'True. I suppose. But that Virginia though . . . Imagine reading *Ulysses* and mainly coming away with the notion that Joyce was *vulgar*.* You know, *common*. And that's what strikes her most . . . Unbelievable.'

'Well it's a hard life, being a snob. You can't relax for a moment . . . You know, a decade ago I spent six weeks in the Woolfs' country house. East Sussex. It was very cold, and I expected Virginia to haunt me and punish me. But she never did.'

Next, the full English tea at the hotel, crustless cucumber sandwiches, quite possibly, and maybe even scones and cream, with the two of us swathed in the lace and chintz of Durrants. Saul was quietly *tickled* by all this, I realised. And at one point, that afternoon, he did actually say (revealing a fondness, too, for Anglicisms),

'You know, they treat me very well here. Because they think I'm a toff.'

---

* 'An illiterate, underbred book . . . the book of a self-taught working man, & we all know how distressing they are, how egotistic, insistent, raw, striking, & ultimately nauseating.' This was a diary entry, admittedly, and not a published statement – but still. 'A queasy undergraduate scratching his pimples', she says elsewhere: and this is at least fleetingly sane. When she returns to the pimples motif, though, she writes: 'the scratching of pimples on the body of the bootboy at Claridges'. I wonder if Woolf was slightly thrown by the fact that *Ulysses* is, among its other strengths, a masterpiece of anti-anti-Semitism.

And in general how pleasant, how touching, how humorous it was to re-experience London through the eyes of one's older American friends, who saw the place as a bastion of courtesy, rootedness, and imperturbable continuity (and, through them, I could see it too); but otherwise, in everyday life, London felt to me like discontented modernity, stoked by subterranean powers . . .

The conversation with Michael Ignatieff was reprinted in a BBC publication, and so that longish quote from Saul is verbatim. The transcript tactfully omits my final remark – when I startled myself with a quavering *cri de coeur*. I said that Bellow stood above the moronic inferno, and could survey it from on high, whereas I was still in it, still under it, pinned and wriggling, and looking out.

What I was referring to, I later realised, was the erotic picaresque of my early adulthood. This was one of my hopes of Julia: that she would emancipate me from the moronic inferno of my lovelife (best encapsulated in the person of Phoebe Phelps) . . .

Honour

Odin, god of poetry and war . . . Fortified by a second round of cocktails, we had moved on to America – America and the religious Right, and the erring clerics of the Bible Belt.

Saul was telling us about a reverse recently suffered by the Born Again community in West Virginia. An unusually puritanical video vicar (he hoped to criminalise adultery) was under federal investigation for swindling his flock (he peddled miracle cures, they said, and preyed on the ill and the old). In addition, the troubled divine had just been found under a stack of hookers in a de luxe Miami sex club called the Gomorrah, a visit he paid for with church funds . . .

'We'd better leave aside the question of hypocrisy,' said Saul. 'As for relieving Christians of their jewels and disability cheques, he'll just say, *Well everyone else does it* – which is no kind of defence, of course, though it happens to be true. As for the hookers and the church funds . . . You've got to understand that in America there are two distinct spheres of wrongdoing.'

'Which are?'

'Ethics and morals. Going to the Gomorrah – that's morals. Paying for the Gomorrah out of the donations bowl – that's ethics. Morals is sex and ethics is money.'

. . . Now Saul had a famous laugh: back went the head, up went the chin, and then you heard the slow, deep, guttural staccato. And Saul, by the way, loved *all* jokes, without exception, the feeblest, the dirtiest, the sickest. But the line about ethics and morals hardly qualified as a joke to Saul Bellow: it was just a sober statement about America (and is a fact confirmed every day).

So it wasn't Saul's laugh that now turned all heads, that stilled the tables, that made the waiters freeze and smile – it was Julia's. An orchestral laugh, eruptive, joyous, with a note of pure anarchy that I never dreamt she had in her.

Saul and I looked at each other in wonder . . . And then we all cheerfully frowned over the menus, and ordered our nice pieces of fish and our costly white wine, and the dinner at last began.

She was my age and she was a widow. Her first husband, a handsome and vigorous philosopher, died of cancer at the age of thirty-five. More than this, she was a pregnant widow; and I was the father.

You know, when my erotic life got going, in the mid-1960s, I pretty soon decided that I wouldn't encumber myself with worries about *honour*. Given the historical situation (what with the sexual revolution and so on), honour, it seemed to me, would be nothing but trouble.

And the human being who would go on to set me straight about all this – not by suasion but by example – was already present, that night at Odin's. A tiny amphibian, less like a newt than a tadpole, scudding and skittering about in there, enwombed. It was Nathaniel, my first son.

In conclusion: Memoir of a Philo-Semite

June 4, 1967, was a Sunday.

In the Middle East the armies of three nation states seemed poised to attack Israel – in a campaign that Gamal Abdel Nasser, their de facto generalissimo, promised 'would be total'; and 'the objective will be Israel's destruction'.

In London W9, on the afternoon of June 4, I was watching a Zionist getting dressed. She reached for an item of clothing I now knew was called a *panty girdle*. It was as white as bridal satin; then she reached for her skirt, which was as black as mourning ribbon; then for her blood-red shirt.

She was called . . . oh, my fingertips are impatient to type it out, the sonorous double dactyl of her real full name. But I have written about her twice before (in a novel, in a memoir), and her pseudonym is here preserved: Rachel.

The black skirt, the red shirt.

'I've got to rush,' she said.

Rachel looked about herself, as if she might have left something behind. And she had: she had left it between the sheets, where I still lay . . . Even in the 1960s you occasionally heard that tender euphemism for virginity: 'unawakened'. What Rachel had left behind that Sunday afternoon was her unawakened self, her unawakenedness.

I was pushing eighteen, she was a year older – the same age as Israel. It was first love, our first love, my first, her first.

'It's half past *four*,' she said.

'You'll be in time. It's only two stops.'

'But it's Sunday. On Sundays it takes longer because they insist on watching you recover. I don't know why. They watch you having your cup of tea and your ginger biscuit. And they close early too. Sometimes they turn people *away*.'

I knew exactly what she was talking about. And I was already sitting up and getting dressed. 'I'll put you on the bus.'

'Hurry up then.'

We embraced and kissed and sank on to our sides; but not for long. Rachel, a Sephardi, with her ebony hair, her fine tomahawk nose, her wide lips the same colour as her complexion (like damp sand at the seashore). I was seventeen, I read poetry, and I reckoned I knew an epiphany when I saw one.

Rachel had to go to the institute, she had to hurry to the institute on a Sunday, in time to give her blood to Israel. And there was no escaping the simple truth that she had just given her blood to me.

Which would have been enough, more than enough, to activate something durable. But it was already activated, it was already there.

A flying visit to Christmas Day, 1961. After a four-hour lunch I am playing Scrabble with Kingsley and Theo Richmond (an innermost family friend). My father takes two tiles from his rack and for a teasing moment, before withdrawing them, forms the word YID. I am twelve.

Do I even know what that word means? Anyway, Kingsley gives a shrugging laugh, and Theo gives a laugh of a kind (it is not his real laugh), and I woodenly do enough to seem to smile. Even as I write I can remember how my cheeks felt: like cardboard.

During that moment I must have made several quite strenuous deductions. That Theo was Jewish;* that *yid* was a hate word for Jew; and that hatred of Jews was something that existed, and was well established. And was dark and hot and insidious and *violent*.†

What did I have to go on? Only some photographs I'd seen in the *Daily Mirror*, back in Swansea when I was nine or ten, and this exchange with my mother.

'. . . Mum.'

She could see I was worried. 'Yes, Mart.'

'Hitler, and all those starved people.' I was thinking of the railtracks, the smokestacks. 'Why was Hitler . . . why was he –?'

'Oh, don't worry about Hitler,' she said (very characteristically). 'You've got blond hair and blue eyes. Hitler would have loved *you*.'

From that reassurance – that Hitler would have loved me – two whole novels would eventually emerge. Because novels come from long-marinated and unregarded anxiety, from silent anxiety . . .

---

* 'Richmond', I now know, was an Anglicisation of 'Ryczke' (pronounced Rich-ke). Thirty-four years later Theo would publish *Konin: A Quest*, his reconstruction (through oral testimony) of the Polish *shtetl* of that name. Konin, the Ryczkes' home town, was wiped off the map by the Germans in 1939.

† My father's anti-Semitism was of course reflexive and non-visceral, and far less insistent than the anti-Semitism of Virginia Woolf. It belonged, not to the drawing room, but to the parlour or the lounge: it was in origin suburban and lower middle class. That it was inherited and largely unexamined was shameful enough, I think; but Kingsley seemed to accept it as you would a birthmark. It was mild and idle, and had no public aspect. When he went into print on the matter he knew the difference between right and wrong. 'Anti-Semitism in any form', he wrote in a letter to the *Spectator* the following year (1962), 'must be combated', 'including the fashionable one of anti-anti-Semitism'. Nietzsche coined 'anti-anti-Semitism', which was his own position, just as Hitchens's Communism (seemingly) resolved itself into 'anti-anti-Communism'.

Rachel gave blood on Sunday. The next morning, at 07.10 Israeli time, the June War – now known as the Six Day War – began. Rachel's anxiety too was silent, or mostly silent; it had eased by Wednesday; and that following weekend she was quietly and calmly stunned with relief.

I now ask myself, How much did she know? Did she know of Nasser's pledge – that he would 'totally exterminate the Jewish state for all time'? Did she know about extermination? Her tiny, witty grandmother, who lived in the family house high up on Finchley Road, was orthodox, to the extent that even her instant coffee, her green-labelled Gold Blend, was stamped *Kosher* ('proper'); *she* knew about extermination. Rachel's uncle, Uncle Balfour, knew about extermination . . .

And I, what did *I* know? Nothing. I was seventeen, and politically detached; more than this, I felt that history couldn't reach me, somehow, that it couldn't reach me. Invulnerable to Hitler, thanks to my colouring, I was also an irrelevance to Nasser, for the same reason. Both men might have found me guilty on a lesser charge: I was a Zionist sympathiser and I was a Jew-lover.

And I was. I loved Rachel, of course (as who would not?), but the point is I loved Theo, too, loved him anyway, from early childhood. I loved looking at his eyes, which seemed almost kaleidoscopic, like a mobile above a crib. In his case a living, stirring pattern of all the gentler human impulses. The intelligent gentleness of those eyes.

'What is it, five hundred millilitres every six weeks? You give so much,' I said, 'I keep worrying you'll disappear. And you don't eat. Or sleep.'

They were at the bus stop and he had his arms round her middle. 'You're so slim anyway. That panty girdle – why d'you wear it?'

'Because my stomach sticks out.'

'It doesn't stick out. It curves forward. It's beautiful, and I love it.'

They embraced and kissed as the double-decker pulled up with an indulgent sigh.

A theory – floated here with all due diffidence.

The philo-Semite and the anti-Semite do not stand in diametrical opposition, not quite. They are, alike, incapable of responding neutrally to what Bellow has called 'the Jewish charge', the stored energy of the

Jew. *Charge*: 'the property of matter that is responsible for electrical phenomena, existing in a positive or negative form'.

The stored energy, the stored history, existing in a positive or negative form.

Guideline
Things Fiction Can't Do

Before we go on to the next chapter do you mind if we take a short break? I want a rest, just now, from 'the fury and the mire of human veins' (Yeats). My conscience, when I train it on Phoebe, is reasonably clear, but it's still a – she's a –

Oh quiet, Spats. Stop it at once. Excuse me, I'll have to attend to him for a moment, and while I'm at it I'll make some more tea . . . Oh that's very thoughtful of you. Thanks. Yes, black, please. No sugar.

. . . Anyway I want to go on for a while about the things fiction can't do – and its blindspots are in themselves illuminating. I'll have to generalise with some shamelessness, as usual, so bear in mind that a generalisation, in these pages, isn't meant to have the force of an axiom; it merely draws notice to a marked tendency. And it follows that a generalisation is not dismayed by the unearthing of one or two exceptions – or one or two thousand exceptions.

It is sometimes said that Coleridge (d. 1834) was the last man to have read everything. But not even a veteran mythomaniac would dare to claim that title in 2016, no, not even the studious Mr Trump. Thus the blandest possible generalisation must now coexist with an unknowable multitude of anomalies. So let's forget about the anomalies and concentrate on the generalisations – about what fiction can't do.

Oh, on the stranger-than-fiction front . . . Actually nothing is stranger than fiction. You may well have 'troubling dreams', these days, but you're not going to wake up 'transformed into a gigantic insect'. And such lines as *no writer could invent a character more outlandish than our would-be president* and *our would-be president has made satire redundant* are almost touchingly naive. One thing literature *can* do, and has always done and will always go on doing (with no particular exertion), is conjure up characters stranger than Trump. As for satire: while turning him into art, would Swift, Pope, Dickens, Evelyn Waugh, or Don DeLillo, say, feel that there was nothing to add?

———————

. . . In real life – in society, in civilisation – we bow to the old rule, No freedom without laws. Novels and stories aren't like that: in fiction there are no laws and at the same time freedom is limitless. Fiction *is* freedom. Mm, I suppose that's what some people find so terrifying, early on, about the blank sheet of white paper: write anything you want; no one's stopping you.

Still, I've come to an awkward conclusion: there are certain things that fiction must broach with extreme caution, if at all, certain sizable and familiar zones of human existence that seem naturally immune to the novelist's art. At the least, fictional successes, in these areas, are dismally rare. Just the three things, by my count (though there may be more) – and that's not many things.

One. Dreams. This would be the least controversial . . .

'Tell a dream, lose a reader' is a dictum usually attributed to Henry James (though I and others have failed to track it down). Dreams are all right as long as they exhaust themselves in about half a sentence; once they're allowed to get going, and once the details start piling up, then dreams become recipes either for stodge or for very thin gruel. Why is this? Any dream that lasts a paragraph, let alone a page, is already closing in on another very solid proscription, Nothing odd will do long (Samuel Johnson). But it's even more basic than that.

Dreams are too individualised. We all dream, but dreams are not part of our shared experience. Oh, we've probably all had the one where you're sitting a major exam in a crowded public space, and your pen doesn't work and for some reason you're in the nude. And there are a couple of others – the aeronautic dream, the dream where your legs turn to liquid as the demon draws near, and so on. Mainly, though, and fatally, dreams are plucked from the random world of the unconscious, the subterranean perverse, reducing the dreamer–author to an agglomeration of quirks – a trait it shares with our next customer.

Two. Sex. This would be the most controversial . . .

I used to say that *Pride and Prejudice* has only one serious flaw: the absence of a thirty-page scene involving Mr and Mrs Darcy on their wedding night (in which Lizzie is irresistible and Fitzwilliam, too, acquits himself uncommonly well). A futile notion: where would Jane Austen find the language or even the thought patterns of sex? Even so, there's a startlingly worldly exchange, very close to the wedding day and the festive conclusion, when Elizabeth is called in to her father's library, and the very intelligent but very cynical Mr Bennet identifies her as a young woman of forceful and perhaps transgressive erotic range . . .

It takes almost the length of the novel for Elizabeth's dislike of Mr Darcy to evolve into love (and he has certainly earned it). Unaware of the recent sea change, Mr Bennet has rather woundingly decided that she's about to stoop to the 'disgrace', as Jane Austen habitually calls it, of marrying for money. 'I know your disposition, Lizzie,' he tells his favourite daughter:

> I know you could be neither happy nor respectable, unless you truly esteemed your husband . . . Your lively talents would place you in the greatest danger in an unequal marriage. You could scarcely escape discredit and misery.

In other words, Lizzie's 'disposition' would cause her to take those 'lively talents' elsewhere – she would stray, she would *fall*. Just for a moment, listening to Mr Bennet, I miss the chapter-length sex scene even more . . .

Mr Bennet's brief speech is probably the dirtiest thing in all Jane Austen. I am now going to quote what is probably the dirtiest thing in the entirety of mainstream Victorian fiction. It comes in Dickens – *Hard Times* (1854). Thomas Gradgrind, the pinched, the parched utilitarian schoolmaster (who thinks that the first thing you need to know about a horse is that it's a 'granivorous quadruped'), is urging his beloved child, Louisa, to marry his friend Josiah Bounderby, a bumptious minor industrialist who is three times her age.

> 'I now leave you to judge for yourself,' said Mr Gradgrind. 'I have stated the case, as such cases are usually stated among practical minds . . . The rest, my dear Louisa, is for you to decide.'
>
> Removing her eyes from him, she sat so long looking silently towards the town, that he said, at length: 'Are you consulting the chimneys of the Coketown works, Louisa?'

'There seems to be nothing there, but languid and monotonous smoke. Yet when the night comes, Fire [note the superstitious capital] bursts out, father!' she answered, turning quickly.

'Of course I know that, Louisa. I do not see the implication of that remark.' To do him justice he did not, at all.

And so saying, Charles Dickens, perhaps the most headstrong writer in English, shyly shuffles from the room.

In the West the mainstream novel got going around 1750.* And for a couple of centuries it was simply *illegal* to write about sex. Then something happened.

> Sexual intercourse began
> In nineteen sixty-three
> (Which was rather late for me) –
> Between the end of the *Chatterley* ban
> And the Beatles' first LP.
>
> Philip Larkin, 'Annus Mirabilis' (1967)

D. H. Lawrence is unquestionably the bridging figure – indeed, the putative father of the sexual revolution. *Lady Chatterley's Lover* was privately printed in Italy in 1928, and then – heavily self-censored – in England in 1932. The unexpurgated version was grudgingly acquitted thirty years later, in the UK, the US, and Canada (though still found guilty in Japan, India, and Australia). Thereafter, in the anglophone world, novelists were suddenly allowed to write about sex – to write about sex without fearing the siren and the policeman's knock.

---

* The very first mainstream novel came well over a century earlier, and it wasn't in English . . . Restlessly searching for prototypes, literary historians have tried to enlist Petronius, Apuleius, St Augustine, and Rabelais (or some antique satire or icicled Norse saga), but I see no reason to push it back any further than *Don Quixote*. Even now the reader feels the awe and apprehension of being present at a birth – the birth of a new genre. *Don Quixote*, Part 1 (1605) is instantly recognisable as a modern novel. And, not content with that, Cervantes gives us Part 2 (1615), instantly recognisable as a post-modern novel (this may be the greatest double-coup in all literature) . . . There is of course no sex in *Don Quixote*, and not only because our hero's love-object, the glamorous Dulcinea del Toboso, is just another delusion.

And so they all had a go at it. Of course they did (I fondly imagine them crouched at their desks in the *on your marks* position, raring to take it on). In the past, they couldn't write about sex. Now they could. And guess what. They still couldn't. They were free to write about it, but they couldn't write about it with the necessary weight, they couldn't write seriously about it; they couldn't find – and they still haven't found – the right voice.*

It is a startling and baffling lacuna – possibly the strangest of all strange things having to do with literature on the one hand and, on the other hand, life. Physical love is the force that peoples the world; and yet novelists get nowhere with it. They can't find a tone for the transcendental element, which most of us know to be there. Lawrence spent a very long time trying (a huge fraction of his forty-four years), and he couldn't find a tone for it either.

The collective failure is complete – and truly abysmal. *Dreams* are a spume that dances on the surface of a troubled pond or puddle; but *sex* is oceanic, and covers seven-tenths of the globe. A force so fundamental, so varied, so grand, so rich. And yet its evocation on the page is somehow beyond us.

Writers will just have to grin and bear it, and look for comfort where they may. Well, I suppose it magnifies our respect for the act, the act that peoples the world. It does do that. We can bow with honour to what is ineffable, and follow Dickens to the door. But why can't we describe it? What makes our hands loth and cold?

Just as human beings are not yet intelligent enough to understand the universe (we are at least six or seven Einsteins distant), we are also not yet sensitive enough to render physical love creatively, on the page.

---

* Things go rather more smoothly when the novel in question is *all* about sex (as in *Lolita*, say, or *Portnoy's Complaint*). Here the sex scene is no longer a divagation: thematically it earns its keep, and doesn't just drain the unities. (Notice how, at the end of an interposed sex scene, the writer suddenly has to snap out of it and ask, *Uh, where was I? . . . Ah, yes.*) In addition, any signs of specialised interests, marked preferences (and any signs of authorial excitation) bring to mind Kurt Vonnegut's one-sentence parody: 'She let out a cry, half pain, half pleasure (how do you figure a woman?), as I rammed the old Avenger home.' Sexual *failure* – the dreaded fiasco – can be written about, but in such cases there isn't a great deal to describe. In his gentle book of essays, *On Love*, Stendhal treats the fiasco as 'tragedy' (which is certainly how it feels at the time), but all one's writerly instincts assign it to comedy. Sex is itself assigned to comedy. What is our reaction to sex written about earnestly? Laughter.

The attempt has been going on for only fifty-odd years, I concede. But the weight of the past is for the time being insurmountable. Centuries of inhibition and euphemism and embarrassment (and furtive chortling) have conspired to keep us underevolved.

So avoid or minimise any reference to the mechanics of making love – unless it advances our understanding of character or affective situation. All we usually need to know is how it went and what it meant. 'Caress the detail,' said Nabokov from the lectern. And it is excellent advice. But don't do it when you're writing about sex.

Three. Religion. This would include all ideologies, all institutionalised networks of committed belief . . .

People who talk at any length about dreams, or about sex, will soon find themselves standing alone at the bar. And the same goes for faith.

That outrageous impertinence I served up to Graham Greene – in Paris, if you remember, in the headmasterly mist of greys and greens (and browns) that pervaded his spacious but unairy apartment on the boulevard Malesherbes, during a visit-interview-lunch on his eightieth birthday in 1984? It really was outrageous: a comprehensive and quite detailed insult packed into a single sentence. And I swear I never meant it that way . . . A few minutes after arriving, with a look of sincere friendliness on my face, I said,

'Now that you're passing this milestone, your religion must be more of a comfort to you than ever – don't you find?'

In other words: you're going to be dead quite soon, so your gullibly self-interested expectation of heavenly reward must be a welcome sedative as you . . .

Greene took it well, I hasten to repeat – he rose to the occasion. With a marked yodel in his voice he replied,

'Oh no! Oh no! Your faith *weakens* as you age. In common with all your other powers.'

Faith as a *power* (a power that weakens). That's good.

But to speak truthfully . . . Reading a Graham Greene 'theological' (the Bollywood name for the genre) can be likened to a train journey, a train journey of a curious kind. You have boarded and settled, and with a soft lurch you leave the station; you have opened your book and you're pretty happy, entering a different mind and a different world, and occasionally glancing out to see a landscape set in motion (and you too are trusting in the impetus of a confident narrative); then, after half an hour or so, with a clack and a clatter the tea trolley enters the compartment and starts to rattle down the aisle.

And by then you may well feel like a cup (and a pause and a think) before going back to Greene's tale – but that's the end of your reading experience, because the tea trolley will clack, clatter, and rattle away for the rest of the ride. That tea trolley, in Greene, is religion.

The importation of a completely extraneous value system: the miracles, the conversions, the monotonous negation of free will, the commandments (adulterers must be punished, the apostates must either disintegrate or tremulously 'return'), the obedience to an inherited architecture of belief (and to a vast cliché), et cetera. In a theological, most crucially, death ceases to be death (it is sapped of its energy and force). No, fiction can't be doing with religion, because fiction is essentially a temporal and rational form – a social-realist form, as we'll see.

English literature is imbued with the Bible, and would be unrecognisable if shorn of those rhythms. And all that. But the poem, and not the novel, is the natural home of religion; and the religious poets hovered around the centre of the canon for a millennium. Poetry and religion are in some sense co-eternal, having to do, perhaps, with pre-literate longings . . .

This is not to suggest for a moment that writers aren't desperately interested in the spiritual self, in the psyche (a key word, that, because it includes the soul), and in questions of morality.

But Phoebe awaits, so can we leave morality out of it for a little while longer?

———————————

Universality: it appears that all three no-entry signs – Dreams, Sex, Religion – warn of a deficit of universality. We have seen how dreams and sex confine the writer to an unshared consciousness; religion does it differently, because it claims, at least, to have universal application. In fact, the main monotheisms explore a dully partial view of the cosmos, whatever the sect or sub-sect. Greene's faction was Roman Catholicism. So he might have commanded a plurality in fifteenth-century Europe. But not now: in an intellectual age that has grown used to quasars, singularities, and curved spacetime, Greene's novels are still inviting us to gape at the burning bush.

We have been begging a question – a big question and a very pertinent question. How can an autobiographical novel possibly attempt, let alone achieve, the universal (though Saul found a way)? But let's go on begging it for now.

As you see, I'm stalling for time. Yes, yes, Phoebe. Christ, she's as bad as Spats . . .

Remember that homily of Saul's about ethics and morals, about ethics being money and morals being sex? In a civilised society on a good day morals and ethics are part of the same thing, which is integrity – though it must sometimes be soothing to compartmentalise them, as Americans do. Then you can say to yourself, Well, my ethics may not be too clever, but my morals seem to be holding up. Or alternatively, My morals are admittedly not of the very finest, but my ethics . . .

Morals and ethics, money and sex. Dear oh dear. Julia would have laughed with far greater abandon if she'd known the half of it, the tenth of it – the penultimate truth about me and Phoebe Phelps.

Novels produced by people in their early twenties are more or less bound to be loosely autobiographical. *Write about what you know and what you've lived* has become a widely circulated and valuable piece of advice; but that's what you'd be doing anyway, willy-nilly, because you're clueless about everything else.

So I put 'Rachel' in my first book – I even put her in the title. When it came out she read it, and rang me up, and we met, and that night the affair resumed. I was astonished: all the gross indiscretions, all the painful secrets laid bare – and that deliberately but repulsively cold-hearted final chapter! Oh, life-writing (as Churchill said of Russia) is 'a riddle wrapped in a mystery inside an enigma'. But somehow the very act of composition is an act of love.

Now imagine for a moment that Phoebe was herself imaginary: only very glancingly true to life, a made-up character in a made-up novel. As I set about fashioning her, how would I proceed?

Well, first I would take Phoebe and stylise her looks and her emotional presence – largely through gross exaggeration (this part is always fun). Next I would cumulatively burden her with qualities that answered to the general design of the novel I was trying to write (its arguments, themes, patterns, imagery, and all the rest). She would then have to behave herself, never deviating from her designated role. And by then, after all that, the original Phoebe would have disappeared, buried like a fossil under the sediment of invention.

This novel, the present novel, is not loosely but fairly strictly autobiographical. And to qualify for an appearance in such a work all you need is *historicity*. You just need to have happened – and you're in.

Chapter 2
Phoebe: The Business

Although we won't even consider doing this point by point and blow by blow, we may as well start with the first date. Everything was decided on the first date.

It was 1976.*

Kontakt

Martin met Phoebe – no, he picked her up, he pulled her – one April afternoon on a side street near Notting Hill Gate. The hub of the operation was a phone booth.

There was the quiet road half full of writhing shadows (bristly elms all asway in the weather), and there was the phone booth, slobberingly coated in thick red paint, and massively seized into the paving stones. Within, behind the glass, giving silent instructions to the black club of the mouthpiece, was a slender young woman with henna-coloured hair. She wore a tailored business suit – pale yellow.

Taking this in, he walked on for a few seconds, then hesitantly turned back, and stood there, a one-man queue (patting his pockets as if for loose change). She looked out and their eyes met and he made a gesture of reassurance, dismissing the very notion of hurry. From then on he gazed at the trees and the shadows, but he was continuously aware of her shape and mass, continuously aware of the exact space she filled . . .

---

* Hence all the anxiety about social class. Which is no more than period verisimilitude, like all the smoking.

He wondered at the strength of the attraction, because slenderness was not in itself compelling to him (the girls he liked usually had a few extra pounds on them – and now and then a few extra stone). She wasn't beautiful. Was she pretty? He couldn't quite tell. If good looks had to do with symmetry, as was being widely claimed at the time, then it was a test she failed. She wasn't ugly-beautiful either. Was she perhaps ugly-pretty? Or something else, something other . . .

Anyway he realised, with near despair, what he was going to have to do. He was going to have to *try* . . . At that moment his confidence fell away, as he readied himself for an interlude of stark vulnerability – but girls, women, very seldom actually laughed in your face, and besides when you feel like this, he told himself, there's no choice: you've got to try, you can't not try, you've got to at least *try*.

You do it nice, mind – and then you throw yourself on their mercy . . .

He waited. The breeze had died, disclosing a settled humidity that now crept up into his armpits. Martin seldom seemed to go out with girls from his own niche or echelon (bookish bohemia), but now he felt, with a rush of real glandular daring, that the woman in the booth was very much not like him, was from an alien moral sphere . . .

She shouldered the door open.

'Oof.'

Then she paused (to make a note in what looked like a pocket diary). All right: she was lightly bronzed, the auburn hair had been recently and professionally primped (it now lay in moist coils and runnels), and there was the business suit and the business shirt (and the business shoes). But the face itself was not businesslike: not cunning, not even particularly shrewd, just sensible and amused. She took four or five steps in his direction, and her walk, with its looseness and ease, told him something new about her body: *she* liked it (which was a very good start).

'Oh I'm so sorry that took as long as it did.'

'Well,' he said in a thickened voice (and this wasn't a line of his – it was helplessly untried), 'I'll forgive you if you'll have dinner with me.'

'What? Repeat that please? . . . Yes, I thought that's what you said. Now why would I mind whether or not you forgive me? What do I get out of it?'

He said, 'Oh come on, it's nice to be forgiven. Then you won't be tortured by your conscience.'

'Mm, well, that's an incentive.'

This human engagement was already pleasant, meaning also humorous, and there was a cautious levity in the air between them. For a moment he thought that her eyes were perhaps fractionally misaligned. But it wasn't that. Her eyes were just unforthcoming, and colluded not at all (it seemed) in the candy-like glow of her smile. The mouth was wide but the lips were economically lean. He said,

'And it's your own fault. You're very compelling.' Was it her figure? 'You forced me to find the courage to ask. I mean that. You did. Go on, have dinner with me. I so want you to.'

'. . . D'you do a lot of this? Trolling round street corners on the off-chance?'

'Christ no. It's much too nerve-racking.' Her flesh, he decided, was bronzed from the inside, and faintly red-tinged (Cheyenne, Choctaw, Mohawk). 'That's all you've got to do. Have dinner with me. Then you'll regain your peace of mind.'

'. . . I'm considering it. You're a bit young. Can you even *afford* dinner? I'm thinking of the donkey jacket.'

'It's not a donkey jacket! . . . It's an overcoat.'

'And the girl-length tresses. And you're also on the short side, aren't you.'

'Yes. And I've got a crap name too. Martin. But I can afford dinner. Don't forget that short men try harder.'

The asymmetry – it wasn't in the eyes. It was in the mouth. Buck teeth? No. A slight awkwardness in the palate? When she grinned she looked frankly loutish, even feral – which, we're afraid, awoke some unworthy atavism in him. She said,

'Martin. Well it could've been worse I suppose . . . Now first and foremost, Martin, what is it you do?'

He felt no vulnerability here. About how he looked, certainly, and about how he dressed, certainly (like all the boys he dressed very hideously in 1976, and the less said on this shaming subject the better), but not about what he did.

'I'm the assistant literary editor of the *New Statesman*.' There was also the question of his two published novels – but he wasn't going to bother a businesswoman with fiction (not yet). 'And I write for the papers.'

'Where were you before the *New Statesman*? Or is it your first job?'

'Second job. My first job was at the *TLS*. The *Times Literary Supplement*.'

She straightened up. 'Well I suppose you must be one of those people who're very much cleverer than they look. Uh, listen. It would have to be tonight.'

'Tonight is perfect.'

'You see, tomorrow I'm off to Munich. D'you mind if we make an early start?'

'The earlier the better.'

'Okay,' she decided. 'I'll book the place on the corner . . . So! Come to my apartment for drinks around five-fifteen?' She gave him her card. 'What it says on the bell's *Contact*, with kays. Kontakt.'

So I went round there

'So I went round there,' I told Christopher the next morning (we were in his office on the political floor of the *New Statesman*; it was not much bigger than a sentry box and known as the Hutch of the Hitch).* I continued, 'Mansion flat in Hereford Road. Sort of traditional but quite flash. In a grown-up way. Like a Harley Street waiting room. Very much not a bedsit.'

'Or a hippie hell.'

'Very much not a hippie hell. No. And she answered the door in *another* business suit. Tea coloured.'

'Ah. A whole new episode of *Peyton Place* is opening up before me. What have you gone and done now, Little Keith?'

---

* A couple of years later, I read (or heard) somewhere that there were essentially two types of human being, the organised and the disorganised, and you could tell which was which from their 'work stations'. So I went on a fact-finding tour of the *New Statesman*. The desk of Julian Barnes (literary auxiliary and novelist) was bare except for a fountain pen; the desk of James Fenton (parliamentary correspondent and poet) was bare except for a lone paperclip. Christopher's desk, like my own, was an action sculpture entitled 'Haystack'. This was somehow very bonding.

'Hang on. Her parlour. No books. Well, a few financial thrillers – oh yeah, including one called *The Usurers*. She's not a reader, which is odd, because she sure talks like one. Fluent . . . A couple of old *Economist*s and a *Financial Times* on the ottoman. And Phoebe. I began to think that her business suit looked like a uniform. Issued by someone else. I liked it. Uniforms are good.'

'Erotically good, so they say. Why?'

'I'm not sure, but they are . . . The apartment didn't make you think of the future but Phoebe did, somehow. I kept imagining a kind of air hostess on a spaceship.'

'A space hostess.'

'Something weird like that. And the set-up . . . I really didn't know what to expect. For a while I thought we were just going to sit there and have a pep talk about careers. Motivation. Office methods. Then she led me to this bar. You'd've very much approved of this bar, Hitch. In its own closet – a full bar and a *wet* bar too. With a sink and a little fridge.'

'That bar', he said, 'fetches my respect. And what did you have, Little Keith?'

'She advised me to join her in a Campari and soda.' I shrugged.

'A business drink.'

'And a weak one too. Then we went and sat on the balcony and talked about nothing much till she said . . . all casual and conversational, *This flat used to be on indefinite loan. Such a generous old friend. Alas he died rather suddenly just after Christmas. And it's rented. I'm loth to move out, but as you can imagine it's a sudden drain on my disposable. Whatever that is. It's far too big. I won't force the full tour on you, but you might like to see* . . . And I still thought we'd shortly be having a chat about property values in W2. But then she gave me a different kind of smile.'

Yes, a different kind of smile. It featured the same touch of off-centredness, the mouth mis-angled as if by an overbite. It was not a smile so much as a very interested sneer. And unmistakably vandalous, too: there was a defiant, willed ignorance in it, and a kind of asociality; there was outlawry in it. And again my swamp-dwelling brain was transmitting a sick static, like a Geiger counter.

'And she said, *But perhaps you'd like to have a look at the master suite . . . Come on then. Bring your drink.*'

'. . . My dear Little Keith.'*

———————————

And within a matter of seconds Martin heard himself murmur, 'Phoebe. What a very unexpected figure you have.'

'I know. That's what all the men are forever saying. Tits on a stick.'

'No,' he said. 'Tits on a wand.'

'. . . Thank you, Martin, that's a clear improvement. Tits on a wand. Plus the decent-sized arse of course.' She went on dreamily, 'That's the *second* reason why women all hate me.'

'Well it is a bit much.'

'Yes it *is* a bit much.'

'What's the first reason? Or are the tits the first reason and the arse the second?'

'No. The tits *plus* the arse are the first reason. The second reason's this. I eat like a pig and never gain an ounce . . . Okay.' At this point she had nothing on but her skirt and her shoes, which she now kicked off. As she raised the top sheet she consulted the (digital) bedside clock, and said, 'No more talking. It's five forty-five and the table's booked for nine . . . Oh yes. Here's another uh, surprising protuberance. Give me your hand.'

A moment passed. 'Gawd,' he said (it was originally *gaw*, with the *d* added to seem less juvenile). 'It's like a – a fist in a mink mitten.'

'. . . Thanks again, Martin. Another improvement. Most men just notice how it sticks out and then say something impossibly vulgar about how gooey it soon gets.'

He said, '. . . It's your boner.'

'How extraordinary. That's what I think of it as. My boner . . . Right. No more talking, but let me just give you a bit of advice, my young friend. A bit of advice that will stand you in good stead for the rest of your active life.'

---

* There's no help for it: I find that I can't, after all, avoid explaining about Little Keith. Little Keith, Keith Whitehead, is an ensemble player in my second novel (1975), and the most programmatically repellent character I have ever tried to create. He is four foot eleven, and fat with it, and very nasty (scowling away under his pizza of acne) . . . Little Keith Whitehead made me realise how much human sympathy readers bring to fiction, because quite a few of them were saddened by his unpleasant fate. Sorry for *Keith*? I used to think – Who cares about Keith? But readers do care . . . Quite a few people called me Little Keith, including girls. To this day Eleni Meleagrou, the first Mrs Hitchens, calls me Leedell Keith.

'That's nice. Your *active* life. And a timely reminder, Little Keith, of your inevitable . . . So what was it?'

'What was what? Oh. Well the advice didn't sound all that marvellous when she spelled it out . . . Hitch, have you ever watched a girl climb out of a business suit?'

'Of course not.'

By now it was late morning, so we were in the Bunghole, the wine bar across the street, drinking hard liquor (screwdrivers for me, double whiskies for him). I said,

'Or better, much better, have you ever *helped* a girl climb out of a business suit?'

'Of course not. Why would I? I have no truck with business suits.'

Christopher was very attractive to women but remained, in my view (considering that this was London, in the mid-1970s), inexplicably unpromiscuous. He was an internationalist and a universalist, but his standard girlfriend was a Marxist and preferably a Trotskyist (and these affairs were durable, dutiful, and, it seemed, grimly dialectical). At first I used to think, Yeah, that's all fine for now – the girls will win you round . . . But Christopher was strafed by propositions from various pampered beauties, all in vain. *My* lovelife he called *Peyton Place*, intending to evoke a series of coarsely repetitive encounters between members of the petty bourgeoisie. *His* lovelife I regarded as something drawn up not by Grace Metalious but by Rosa Luxemburg.* There would be one famous exception (but not yet, not yet): Anna Wintour.

'You're interested in the wrong revolution, mate. Free love, Hitch.'

'Mm. Listen. Before you expatiate on the business suit, tell me what her advice was . . . Mart, you're tranced. The advice that will serve me all my active life.'

---

* Red Rosa (1871–1919), imprisoned many times by Kaiser Wilhelm II, was eventually beaten, tortured, and shot dead by a gang of *Freikorps* (monarchist bitter-enders and proto-Brownshirts). Christopher would sometimes define himself as a Luxemburgist – meaning, I now suppose, a revolutionary who rejects violence (on the whole) and embraces freedom of speech. He never relinquished Luxemburg (similarly and far more controversially, he never relinquished Trotsky). 'To me, the most brilliant – and the most engaging – of these Marxist intellectuals was Rosa Luxemburg,' Christopher wrote in June 2011, six months before he died.

'Oh yeah. Sorry. Well. She said, and she said it in the tone of a patient agony aunt, she said, *When you've got a real session in front of you, Martin, then this is the key. Don't come.* Those were her words.'

'. . . Don't come?'

'Don't come. *Not till the very end. It's the answer. I swear you'll have a much better time.*'

We both ordered fresh drinks.

'And not coming till the end, Hitch – it transforms the whole experience. Three hours. A few rests and cigarette breaks, but no fucking around with *recovery* times or anything like that. And it improves your concentration. You steady yourself and you pace yourself. You settle down to it.'

'I think I see . . . Is she older than you, d'you think?'

'She's taller than me. By a couple of inches. And yeah, she might have a couple of years on me too. Maybe thirtyish. She definitely had uh, seniority.'

'Let me impress that on my memory. Just in case. Don't . . . come.'

'Don't come. And I wasn't going to come after dinner either. Not till the end. And I was thinking about the next morning, too, and worrying whether the not-coming rule would still apply. But then . . . She was surprising enough before dinner. And during. But after dinner she . . .'

Quality control

After dinner – Phoebe had soup with plenty of bread, potted shrimps with plenty of toast, a gurgling, farting beef stew, a crème brûlée with brandy snaps, and a double helping from the cheeseboard with plenty of oatcake – Martin proudly walked her back to Hereford Road, and looked on with some complacence as she marshalled her keys . . . The moral atmosphere Phoebe imposed was partly familiar to him; and that atmosphere was one of normlessness, of obscure improvisations and compromises, and rippled by counter-currents and different ways of going about things. Who cared, though, at this stage?* Awaiting ingress

* In the second half of 1972 I paid regular calls on a gentle and grateful fifty-year-old called Marybeth, who happened to be a proletarian *demi-mondaine* ('half-worlder'). Vividly scalene individuals passed through or hid out in Marybeth's loftlike apartment in Earls Court: burglars, blaggers, madams, molls. One night I spent several hours making myself as unobjectionable as I possibly could to two savage and rancorous young Scots – who were on the run from a celebrated borstal in Newcastle. The half-world, I already knew, was only half sane. The point being, I suppose, that none of this ever came close to putting me off.

to Phoebe's mansion flat, he was vibrantly intrigued. Now he moved closer and smoothed his hands over her hips, then her waist, then her midriff, cherishing great schemes and projects, huge exertions and initiatives, epic undertakings . . .

'Is that your middle name?' he mouthed into her brown nape. 'Kontakt?'

'That's there for business reasons.' She turned. 'I'm plain old Phoebe Phelps. Well. Goodnight!'

It was something more piercing than disappointment (it felt like a thrust, it felt like a spear through his very soul). But he at once regrouped and said lightly, 'Oh, that's a shame – but I understand. Munich tomorrow.'

'Yes, tomorrow night . . . Come here a second.'

She stepped back out through the arch and into the firmly replenished breeze and the amber lamp. With an unlit cigarette poised between her fingers she slowly stretched her arms at shoulder height.

'I'll just have a lazy day and won't even get out of bed before three. So it's nothing to do with Munich . . . Even now I'll be staying up for a while. And I won't be washing my hair.' She kissed his neck. 'And it isn't that I'm not . . . But no!'

He said, 'In that case I don't understand.'

She considered him. 'Ah, you're looking all *brave* . . . Not what you had in mind. What you had in mind isn't hard to guess. Mm, and then you'd round it all off with a sweaty one in the morning where you come as fast as you can. Then off to work on the tube with your bacon sandwich. Or am I completely wrong?'

He could have said she was wrong about the bacon sandwich; but he just waited.

Sadly, slowly, she shook her head. 'The idea of that', she said, 'makes me think, God, what a waste, what a tragic waste. To me that seems truly feckless, just frittering it away like that.'

'Frittering what away?'

'The element of – of surprise. Why d'you put perishables in the fridge? So they don't go off, they don't "turn". As you see I've got very firm views on how to keep things good and fresh. Based on principles I picked up, Mr Amis, from what I do.'

'From the entrepreneurial sphere.'

'Really obvious stuff like *don't* live off your capital. And quality control.' She was looking at him with general benevolence, diluted by amusement and some pity. 'Why doesn't *everyone* do it my way? . . . Well! Have you enjoyed our date?'

'Oh yes. Very much.'

'You may want to retire while you're winning, Mart. You should – if it's a quiet life you want. There are loads of girls who can give you a quick smelly one in the morning. Withdraw, retire. If you choose not to I'll tell you what lies ahead.'

And she told him . . . To proceed with this, he already felt sure, would be to invite many varied hardships. Then she added,

'And it's even worse than that. I used to have "affairs", when I was young and innocent, but now I only do it with the same man once. That's why I'm so thorough. Once.'

'Once?'

'Once. With a few rare exceptions. And it's even worse than *that*.' And she told him. 'So then, Martin. I'll see you around.'

He was thinking. 'Actually,' he said, 'the even worse thing isn't as bad as the worse thing. I'm sorry, Phoebe, but I'm going to pursue this. Withdraw, retire? Where to? No, I'm not giving up. So. When do you get back from Germany?'

'*Enfin*, Little Keith. The business of the business suit.'

It was nearly two by now, so we were in Luigi's, the Italian caff on Red Lion Street, ordering our meat breakfasts and the first carafe of Valpolicella. I said,

'For a start it's not just the business *suit*, is it. It's the whole ensemble. You know it's not like she's taking off a denim miniskirt and a fucking tank top.'

'Or a pair of tracksuit bottoms and a fucking sloppy joe.'

'Yeah. Or even the fragrant wisp of a summer frock. No . . . See, she spends a lot of time and money on it, gussying herself up like that. And it obliges you to meet the uh, the challenge of her investment.'

'Her outgoings and her overheads and her running costs.'

'Exactly. The removal of a business suit is somehow transactional. When I was finally allowed to come, and we were lying there, I had a sudden sense of danger. I suddenly expected Phoebe to say, All right, that'll be five hundred quid.'

'Mm. Remember the paranoid headlines in *Portnoy*? Asst Lit Ed Found Headless In Go-Go Girl's Apt.' Christopher looked around for the waiter. He murmured, 'It's time, or so it seems to this reviewer, for an alerting *digestif*. Grappa?'

'Oh go on then . . . And afterwards, when I walked her home, she cooled me! She wasn't having it.' I explained. 'She calls it quality control.'

'Well, *control* anyway. She's obviously mad about control.'

'Mm.' Just then I had a presentiment that on this subject I might cease to confide in Christopher. Either that, or my confidences would become inauspiciously terse. 'But the gimmick of the self-imposed purdah. I'm hoping she'll relax about that.'

'Probably. You'll wear her down. A bold and tender lover like yourself, Little Keith. Sensitive but strangely masterful. Caring and empathetic, and yet, withal, excitingly bold. Adventurous? Yes. Disrespectful? No. At once athletic and –'

'Yes yes, Hitch.'

He sat back. 'Oh well. For the record she sounds like a – like an uneconomical use of your energy, Mart. But there's no point in telling you that, now you've got the scent of her. So. When does she get back from Germany?'

The bill came. We would be the last to leave.

I said, 'Whose turn is it?'

'Oh yours without question.' He passed me the tray. 'This shouldn't present any undue difficulties. Who paid last night?'

'Me of course and happily. She said, *You know, if I paid, or even if we went Dutch, I'd have to hate you for all eternity. Yup. Until the conversion of the very last Jew.*'

'. . . Is she religious by any chance?'

'As she was sending me on my way she said, *And on top of everything else I'm a believer. She's Catholic. It's very important to me, but utterly private. I don't go on about it.* But at dinner she went on about – or kept returning to – a certain Father Gabriel. My mentor, my second father. All this.'

'Catholicism. The far right at prayer. And her politics?'

'Her politics?' And I thought (as usual), What's that got to do with anything? 'She doesn't have any politics. What she has is current affairs.'

41

They were gathering their things. 'Mao hasn't got long, et cetera. And oh yeah. She loathes Mrs Thatcher.'

'Does she now. Phoebe can't be Labour. So it's personal.'

'Oh, from the gut. By no means everyone fancies Mrs Thatcher, Hitch. Like you do.'

'Ah come on, she's a minx.'

'Miss Dairy Product 1950. No erotic content whatever.'

'False, quite false! And I can prove it.' He started leading the way to the door. 'In this day and age I suppose it should really be *Ms* Dairy Product. And Ms Universe.'

'Mm. Why's Miss Universe always from Earth?'

'Why not Miss Neptune.'

'She sounds nice. You can almost visualise her. Long eyelashes. Miss Neptune . . .'

'But how about Miss Pluto? D'you like the sound of her? No, you're wrong, quite wrong, about Maggie. The Leader of Her Majesty's Opposition? She *stinks* of sex.'*

We swung ourselves out on to the street.

Now how in fact did the first date end? On what terms?

Let me think, let me consult memory, let me consult – the truth . . .

And the truth was he kissed and praised her and stroked her hair and weighed its runnels in his hand for six or seven minutes. And made it clear how ready he was to learn more – to learn more, at the feet of

---

* From *Hitch-22: A Memoir* (2010): '"Care to meet the new Leader?" Who could refuse? Within moments, Margaret Thatcher and I were face to face.' Christopher goes on: 'I felt obliged to seek controversy and picked a fight with her on a detail of Rhodesia/ Zimbabwe policy. She took me up on it. I was (as it chances) right on the small point of fact, and she was wrong. But she maintained her wrongness with such adamantine strength that I eventually conceded the point and even bowed slightly . . . "No," she said. "Bow *lower*." Smiling agreeably, I bent forward a bit farther. "No, no," she trilled. "*Much* lower!" . . . Stepping around behind me, she . . . smote me on the rear with the parliamentary order-paper she had been rolling into a cylinder behind her back . . . As she walked away, she looked over her shoulder and gave an almost imperceptibly slight roll of the hip while mouthing the words: "Naughty boy!"' . . . Under Thatcher, as one commentator put it, Britan felt 'the smack of firm government'. And it is on *le vice anglais* (and the deliciously tingling bottom) that her erotic allure, such as it was, entirely relied. Christopher was susceptible to it, and so was Kingsley, and so was Philip Larkin.

Phoebe Phelps. He stood back as she entered the little conservatory of the vestibule. Behind glass once again. The way she was when he first saw her, safely encaged in glass.

He lingered under the arch for a valedictory cigarette. Meanwhile his male intuition was telling him that even if he won the privilege of a second date, and a third, it was unlikely to last long – this thing with Phoebe. 'Time', says Auden, 'that is intolerant / Of the brave and innocent / And indifferent in a week / To a beautiful physique . . .' Her physique, it seemed to him, was an embarrassing, even an accusatory godsend (put together, inch by inch, with all his susceptibilities in mind). That body, in combination with that face: an image of middle-class probity, till slit by her lawless smile.

But the trouble was, or the trouble would soon be . . . Time, long-term time, what does it hold dear? It 'worships language and forgives / Everyone by whom it lives'. What this would come down to, in the here and now, was everyday discourse; and when they talked there were few shared registers and associations, and so the words seemed to hang in the middle air somehow, keeping themselves to themselves. Clearly, the thing with Phoebe was bound up with the life expectancy of his carnal awe. It was a trite question, of course, but how long does lust last – all on its own?

. . . Was she watching him now, from the shadows of her balcony, as he enjoyed his husky smoke under the lamplight? There were moments, during the kissing and praising, when it seemed possible she might relent. Would she now call down for him – in aching languor? . . . He waited. Then as he buttoned his overcoat he raised an arm to her in tribute and farewell. Farewell – until May Day.

Then I turned with a flourish and walked back to Bayswater. I was not yet twenty-seven. It was 1976.

Mind over matter

'Oh, Phoebe, is it always going to be like this?' he asked in the dark – in 1977.

'Ew, Phoebe, eez eet ohlways going to be like theece? . . . You've been saying that, in your poncy accent, every night for eleven and a half months. Did you go to Eton or somewhere?'

'No, I told you, grammars and crammers. And no I haven't been saying it every night. And how d'you mean, poncy?'

'You know . . .' She shrugged. 'Poncy. And yes you have. Every night since that time I got back from Germany.'

'Okay, yes, I said it then. Because I thought you'd be pleased to see me.'

'And I was pleased to see you.'

'But not pleased enough.'

And this was what he was going on about. On average (he had recently paged through two pocket diaries), just under 85 per cent of their dates were *anticlimactic* in at least two senses.

She said, 'But it works, doesn't it. Come on, concede. It works.'

He gave no answer. Tonight, on this special occasion, there'd been an exchange of gifts and an unprecedented dinner for two, by candlelight, at Hereford Mansions (a cold collation from the corner deli – but those candles were mounted and torched by Phoebe alone . . .). And tonight, too, had been chaste. She said,

'The ingratitude. It's extraordinary, it's absolutely *extraordinary*. Here you are, still snivelling with lechery after how long? When was the last time you felt like that after a whole year? And do I get any credit? . . . Own up, Martin. It works.'

With a silent sigh he said, 'It works.'

'There. Finally . . . And as you know, it isn't that I'm not tempted. Give me your hand.' He obeyed. Then she whispered, 'See? No – *listen*. You can hear it . . . I suppose you think', she said (slowly unsticking his fingers), 'that this is just an extra tease, but I'm trying to instruct you, Martin. Mind over matter.'

'Mm. Is that what it says on your Buddhist symbol?'

'Stop *whining*.' She settled herself. Contented grunts punctuated the silence. A silence that lasted till she said, pensively, sleepily, half yawning as she turned over on her side, 'An entire year. This is madness.' Her voice again became a whisper. 'One of the things is, sex terrifies me. Haven't you noticed? It'd be fine if I didn't enjoy it.' She turned away again and her tone renormalised. 'This comes under the heading of religion, Mart, so I'm not going to labour the point. I just keep feeling there must be repercussions. For me enjoying it. There.' Yawning now without restraint she said, 'Anyway. It might a good idea to move on to a different regime. Sexually. And you'll have to meet my parents at last.'

'. . . Different in what way?'

'Less permissive. That's right, Martin – *less* permissive. But not yet. Well it's a logical step. Just think of it as the next thing.'

The eleven developments

So what else surfaced, in the course of that first year? The main developments are listed below – in no particular order, and certainly not in order of importance. He didn't know what was important, at that stage, and he didn't discover the core truth about Phoebe till July 15/16, 1978 – thereafter iconically known as the Night of Shame . . .

(1.) 'Marry me!' he cried out one night, at a very dire moment. And this was pitifully early on – just two weeks after he sped to the airport to meet her Lufthansa flight. 'Please. Marry me.' 'Nope,' she said distinctly in the dark. 'I don't want a husband. Let alone a child. Ever . . . This subject is now closed.'

(2.) Her age. Phoebe had always dismissed with a flip of her hand his occasional enquiries (as if finding them simply very dull); but in the spring of 1977 she accompanied him to the south of France,* and at the little hotel she looked on with apparent unconcern as he paged through her passport. Phoebe was born (in Dublin) in 1942. Which made her seven years the elder – thirty-five. He approved. The older the better, he thought, within sane limits. Older women impressed him and moved him with their greater share of lived life, of time and experience.

(3.) She wasn't metropolitan middle class, as he'd assumed, but something more exotic. Phoebe spent her childhood in South Africa, and her youth in the London dormitory belt (where her parents remained). Twice Phoebe had got him in the car to go to Sunday lunch at the Phelpses', and twice the mission was aborted ('I suddenly don't *feel* like it, okay?'). On the other hand, Phoebe was often made welcome at the huge freestanding house in London NW3, shared by Martin's father and his second wife – the award-winning novelist Elizabeth Jane Howard . . .

---

* I was writing a colour-mag feature about the Cannes Film Festival. All the attendees and all the locals looked rich (even the innumerable beggars); and beyond La Croisette, where the sky met the sea, each and every female (child, teen, starlet, young mother, *grand-maman, arrière-grand-mère*) swam and sunbathed topless – except Phoebe, who loftily retained her racing one-piece.

Phoebe had two much older sisters, Siobhan (pron. Shuvawn), and Aisling (pron. Ashlin). Her dad, Graeme, was Scottish-English, and her mum, Dallen, was Irish. Phoebe idealised Graeme and demonised Dallen; she gave the impression, too, that the family had known better days, much better days – and that it was all Dallen's fault.

(4.) Oh yeah. He had glimpsed it regularly enough, but four months passed before Phoebe let him take a proper look at it (under a reading lamp): the tattoo on the taut slope of her left buttock. *Jungle Book* and *Kama Sutra* colours (bluey-green with dots of garnet), roughly rectangular, and about the size of a folded butterfly. A *mandala*, she said, a cosmic Buddhist symbol – the lone vestige of her brief spiritual period (*c.*1960). Tattoos, to him, only looked nice on non-white flesh; and Phoebe's looked nice, louchely nice on her Amerindian glaze; it had a tiny rubric in an unfamiliar alphabet; she had forgotten what the words were supposed to mean.

(5.) Lightfooted Phoebe had the gift of silence, of equable silence. She occupied herself for hours and hours while he read or wrote. She banged about in the kitchen and squirted out fizzy drinks at the bar, but she was otherwise silent. After a while she repaired to the phone in her bedroom and got on with her vendettas. She hounded office-furniture suppliers, accountants, utilities bureaucrats, and the owners or managers of betting shops (this last point will be clarified) . . . He couldn't hear the words but he sometimes attended to her tone: either sarcastic, incensed, haughty, or quietly spiteful. She had an ever-shifting roster of vendettas.

(6.) There was a strange disconnection – strangely hard to describe – in her response to humour. When amused by others, she laughed throatily and often. But when others were amused by her, when she made others laugh (his friends, her friends), she never joined in, she never laughed along; her mouth, her eyes, maintained neutrality, as if she was only funny by accident . . .

(7.) Every now and then her combative buoyancy ebbed away from her: these episodes were called her *slumps*. She would ring him and postpone the next visit, her voice somnolent and weirdly hollow. This happened patchily. Nothing for months and then once a week. After a day or two her combative buoyancy returned. They were seeing each other about every other night plus most weekends. She went on business trips, and he too had occasional assignments (mainly in America).

(8.) Phoebe's workplace was in a freshly gilded medium-rise just off Berkeley Square. Quite often he left the *New Statesman* around midday and rode the Underground westward a couple of stops to Green Park, and collected her in the infinite atrium, and took her to the Fat Maggot, an early gastropub, for an elaborate Ploughman's Lunch (and three bags of crisps); and then he returned her – to Transworld Financial Services (or TFS), whose HQ was in Threadneedle Street, EC1.

(9.) Once, at the Fat Maggot, the young couple were hurriedly and alarmingly joined by Phoebe's parents. 'They're shopping in town and I asked them along. And by the way,' said Phoebe, looking at her watch, 'he likes to be called *Sir* Graeme.' 'Why? For fun?' 'No, it's inherited. So it's Lady Phelps too, but you can just call Dallen Dallen. Ah here they come.' Martin went on full alert . . . Sir Graeme was slim, almost scrawny, with flowing caramel hair and shapely bones – an artistic face, but one ruined by a disgracefully small nose. Bibulous, flat-topped, and tubular, it looked like a scarlet thimble. His voice was ultra-refined (far posher than the Queen's) and as flowery as he could make it with his lazily pretentious vocabulary ('And how was it received, Martin – your latest oeuvre?') . . . Dallen, being Irish, talked with real fluency, and Martin quickly decided he liked her; she was darkly neurasthenic, but a fairly comfortable valetudinarian by now, despite her hot flushes and her migraines . . . Phoebe paid, in cash. 'You must come to Sunday luncheon, dear boy,' stressed Sir Graeme in parting. 'Nearly a year, eh? *Chapeau!*'

(10.) Phoebe was, she said, 'appalled' by her own handwriting. When she told him this, one weekend, as they wandered along the Serpentine, he gradually realised that he had never seen any examples of it – her calligraphy, her penwomanship. If she left him a note (get milk, back in an hour) she resorted to her antique typewriter or to toiling block capitals.

(11.) In bed . . . Time had only deepened and simplified his respect for her body: to him it was something like the hard proof of his own heterosexuality (it was the smoking gun); everything he needed was there. And in bed – on those occasions when she didn't just get into it and go to sleep and then get out of it – she was both busy and businesslike, energetic, unsqueamish, shockingly inventive, and at the same time curiously detached, conscientious, even painstaking (she left nothing undone) . . . Never entirely naked, she wore stockings, a sash, a boa, a shirt, a skirt, and once or twice her whole office ensemble, not excluding her shoes – her high-heeled shoes, sliding in over the bottom sheet. But her defining peculiarity, or so it seemed to him, had to do with her *hands*.

Her peccadilloes, her weaknesses, her friends

As for Phoebe's little vices (this bulletin is technically datelined April 1977): she was not a serious drinker, not a drinker at all by national standards, and she was an utterly frivolous smoker (she didn't even inhale; like his mother, Hilly, with her menthol Consulates, Phoebe instantly expelled the smoke over her shoulder or straight up in the air). What she was was a *gambler* . . . *

A gambler, and not a reader. After a year, the only literary development at Hereford Mansions was this: her pile of unread *Economist*s now included two unread *New Statesman*s and, further down, an unread *TLS*. In February she paid her maiden visit to his flat off Queensway (14c, Kensington Gardens Square: very small and very cheap but just about presentable in its studenty way, sitting room, bedroom, kitchen, bathroom, all clumped together with no passages in between); she came through the door and stood still. 'Too many books, man,' she sorrowfully decided.

A couple of weeks later Phoebe primly spent the night, and when he brought her tea in the morning she was propped up in bed with a thin paperback – *The Whitsun Weddings* (1964). This wasn't entirely

---

* She bet on the horses, on athletics, cricket, and football, but it was mainly on the dogs (accumulators and reversible forecasts). Phoebe said that now she was in administration (Personnel), and no longer 'on the floor' (actually trading), she missed the physical sensation of risk ('That's why they call a bet a *flutter*, Mart'). Her stakes were substantial, twenty quid, thirty, sometimes forty – which was my net weekly wage. The betting shops she ducked into during our Saturday strolls reminded me of the commissaries and common rooms of London prisons (fresh in my mind from recent visits to my self-tormenting old friend Robinson – at Pentonville, at Brixton, at Wormwood Scrubs): sullen men, sullen, stubborn men who, not unlike Phoebe in a way, bloodymindedly moved against the social flow, like the ragged bore of a river . . . In this setting Phoebe mingled with burly male shapes filling in forms on the wall-side ledges or grimly queuing in front of the meshed till; their common aim was to predict the future. Phoebe also had an account somewhere and dealt with a certain bookie (Noel) by phone.

unexpected.* As he positioned the cup in her grip he saw she was reading the title poem, but he made no comment and just settled himself beside her. Minutes passed. Every now and then he ventured a peripheral glance: she was moving her lips to the words (which she did not do with newspapers or menus or betting slips), and he clearly saw her mime the phrase: *we slowed again.* Soon she put the book aside with a lift of her eyebrows.

'Humph,' she said.

'. . . Humph?'

'Yeah. *Humph.*'†

Later in the morning they performed their first act of love in a week; and for him, as always, it was like the tearsoaked reunion which marks the end of a long romantic melodrama about the Second World War. But the act of love, that morning, was probably a frail coincidence, or so he thought in 1977.

Sometimes she called him Martin, and sometimes she called him Mart. This was useful, because it gave sure notice of her mood: *Martin* prepared him for a certain solemnity, stringency, and (often) reproach;

---

* Phoebe's interest in Larkin – mainly human interest – had been stirred by a TV rerun of an interview, in black and white, with John Betjeman. I watched it at Hereford Road, with Phoebe looking doubtfully over my shoulder.

† And Phoebe, philosophically, saw eye to eye with this poem. 'The Whitsun Weddings' describes a 'frail travelling coincidence'. The poet is taking the train from the north of England to the capital on Whit Sunday, the Christian festival of early summer, traditionally a propitious time for marriage. And '[a]ll down the line / Fresh couples climbed aboard'. The eighth and final stanza ends when the train is approaching a London 'spread out in the sun, / Its postal districts stacked like squares of wheat'. And here it comes: 'We slowed again, / And as the tightened brakes took hold, there swelled / A sense of falling, like an arrow-shower/ Sent out of sight, somewhere becoming rain.' That isolating scepticism about love and marriage, in the face of time, was part of an inner argument that Larkin often gave voice to, but never as tellingly as here: the arrows of desire, as the poet sees it, are doomed to deliquesce in impotence and tedium – becoming as dull as rain. Phoebe was in profound sympathy with such a view. So it wasn't the paraphrasable content of 'The Whitsun Weddings' that provoked Phoebe's *humph*; it must have been the form itself, he thought – the poetic form . . . The actual practitioners they were always running into socially (James Fenton, Craig Raine, Peter Porter, Ian Hamilton) she regarded quizzically, suspiciously; and whenever I talked about poetry she looked at me as if I was nuts. This would be explained, or roughly accounted for, in 1978.

Mart meant friendliness and high spirits and even on occasion led the way to eros, as *Martin* never did.

'Correct me if I'm mistaken, Mart,' she announced, about six months in, 'but when I'm *noli me tangere* like this your thoughts must often turn to uh, to infidelity. Well, you're a man.' She told him that for years she had tried her hand at infidelity. 'And I didn't have the knack. Girls don't seem to be very good at infidelity. To their extreme discredit. But you're a man.'

'This is true, Phoebe.' It felt anachronistic, even counter-revolutionary – the notion that certain allowances should be made for men (of all people). 'So you're saying?'

'Well. If I happen to find out you've spent the odd afternoon with a trusted ex-girlfriend . . . you might just be forgiven in the end. A deeply trusted ex-girlfriend. And a compulsively hygienic ex-girlfriend. Because if you ever give me a nasty surprise, Martin, then you won't just be spurned, I promise you. You'll be *sued*.'

He watched as her smile disappeared, leaving no trace on the lean lips.

'Now you've said you want children.'

'Yes I do, in principle. But I'm not in any rush.'

'Then you'll also be prospecting for wives. And, Mart, honestly I approve – because it sets a natural time limit. Let me know, immediately, if you think you've found one, and that'll be that. With no hard feelings.' Another smile. 'In the meantime I issue this warning. If you ever, if you *ever* publicly compromise me with another female, then . . . Then, Martin, *woe betide you*. Do I make myself clear?'

He was used to strongminded eccentricity, or adamantine whimsicality, and none of this was altogether foreign to him – apart from the purdahs and the gambling. Still, the sense of an additional, an ulterior strangeness persisted, and was regularly topped up by her so-called friends. Barely worth describing, Phoebe's friends were at least very few in number. There were three.

Comprising Raoul and Lars, who sometimes showed up for an hour in the late evening, two tall young men (a paunchy Austrian and a wiry Dane) with suntans and layered hair, whose talk was unswervingly footling and plutocentric (and eloquent, despite their waisted pinstripe suits, of truly boundless free time) . . .

Comprising Merry, who had a flat in one of the terraced houses further up the street. Perhaps ten years older than Phoebe, frizzy, flustered, ladylike in manner, slapdash in appearance (the offwhite tackle of her bra always peeping through the misbuttoned gaps of her blouse), this neighbourly visitor was Phoebe's only associate of the gentler sex . . .

Martin asked Phoebe about Merry, Raoul, and Lars. Phoebe explained that they were people who had happened to attach themselves to her and then time passed, until it became a question of loyalty and habit. He acknowledged that this was how things often turned out (look at Robinson). But even so he thought that Phoebe's friends were meaningless. They didn't add up to anything.

By now he could tell when her episodes of lassitude were looming. She would sometimes go silent in the middle of a conversation, seeming not vacant but concentrated, and then both angered and fearful, as if listening to a voice within herself, a voice that sharply criticised or cruelly mocked . . .

The view of the elders

I said, 'The only other girlfriend of mine you seriously fancied was Denise.'

Kingsley lifted his glass (Scotch and water) and said over the top of it, 'What makes you think I fancied Denise?'

'Oh nothing much. You went slightly intent whenever you talked about her. It wasn't your Sex Life in Ancient Rome face, no. But your eyes widened. Or lengthened. Intently.'

'Balls,' he said.

'I only mentioned it because it's so rare. And now with Phoebe you've come out into the open. You freely admit as much.'

It was after dinner. My car was outside but I would be staying here this Saturday night. Not that long ago the Amises had moved house, from the northernmost fringe of London, and there were still stacks of books on the floor and half-empty tea chests . . .

'I can see why you fancied Denise.' Yes, because she looked like a gorgeously soft-hearted barmaid (very gentle with her hungover regulars). 'But why d'you fancy Phoebe?'

'You know, apart from just liking the look of her I'm not . . . She reminds me of an illustration I saw in a children's book. A little fox dressed as a forest ranger.'

'What was the little forest ranger wearing?'

'Green skirt and green tunic,' he said. 'And brown shoes. *Bob* was very taken with Phoebe. Remember last time? Very taken. He even asks after her in his letters.'*

'So. Bob too.' Nodding, and half to myself I said, in vindication, 'There you are you see, it's the business suit. I keep telling Hitch it's the business suit.'

'How do you mean?'

'Sorry, Dad, I've been wondering. And you won't like it, but it's to do with your age and your work ethic. And I have that too. In weaker form, diluted by time.'

'Get on with it.'

'Well, there she is, Phoebe. A looker, and a probable goer, but also an *earner*. That means you and Bob can fancy her without feeling haunted by the poorhouse.'

Kingsley was wearing his inconvenienced expression, and was about to say something gruff – but then his wife entered the room . . . Things had got to the point where tension entered with her (a false stillness); on the other hand, tension was already there, waiting. That was what the two of them were doing these days: directing tension at one another. I got to my feet and said,

'Ah. We were talking about Phoebe. You quite approve of her, don't you Jane?'

She sat, and took up her sewing (another huge and heavy patchwork quilt – swirling squares of velvet and slanting trapezoids of silk and satin; all the beds in the house were bedizened in Jane's patchwork quilts).

'I, I admire Phoebe. All right, she's undereducated, but then so was I. She's a striver and she's come a long way, and good for her.'

---

* Bob was Robert Conquest (1917–2015), poet, critic, and historian – specifically a Sovietologist, best known for *The Great Terror* (on the purges of 1937–8) and *The Harvest of Sorrow* (on Collectivisation, and the terror-famine of 1932–3).

I could feel an impending proviso. Jane looked up frowning and said,

'She's not an orphan, is she?'

'. . . No. No, she's got parents. I've met them. No, she's not an orphan.'

Thereafter the evening seemed to lose its shape. But the next day, as I was leaving, I went up to Jane's study to thank her and hug her goodbye. First I said,

'What made you think she's an orphan? Phoebe.'

Jane's study window used to look out on the vernal expanse of Hadley Common (giving on to Hadley Woods) – with the small circular pond, the size of a helipad, just on the other side of the road; and at her disposal, back then, was a five-acre, three-lawn garden topped by an extravagantly imposing and ancient Lebanon cedar. She missed it all. Now Jane's study window looked out on the steep and jumbled chunks of Hampstead as it reared up towards the Hill and the Heath.

'Yes, why *did* I say that?' Jane had turned in her swivel chair and now slipped off her glasses.

These glasses had a history and I asked, 'Are they the ones that make you look like a career-mad cockroach?'

'They're the ones.'

'Put them back on a second. Christ. They really do.'

'I know, it's the curly bits up here.' Resignedly she lit a herbal cigarette, with its unenticing scent. 'Yes, why *did* I say that? . . . When I was eleven or twelve I shared a governess with an orphan. Hattie. And Hattie put on a good show. She was always pretending things were all right, but they weren't all right. Because her parents had both died in a hotel fire. Hattie – a good show, but she seemed to exist in another dimension. Always slightly glassy and preoccupied. One step behind.'

'. . . And Phoebe reminds you of Hattie? Giving a good show?'

'She gives a very good show, a very advanced show. It's a show of normality. Well I suppose we all do that, a bit. I'm not trying to put you off, Mart. I understand the attraction . . . What is she, thirty-five? She's going to want –'

'No, she doesn't want that, she says. No husband, no child . . . I must go.'

'Mm. Then she has decided views.' We embraced and Jane swivelled round to face her desk and the window. 'She's also got a wound, I think.'

The drive back in the Sunday twilight, with the days of the working week stacked up ahead of me. It was eerily daunting, that Sunday drive. Knowing how far I was from the child, the halfmade pupa, and how far I was from the adult – the finished imago.

Beset by small fears

That same Sunday night he rolled up late and parked on a yellow line outside the mansion flat on Hereford Road.

As she undressed in the bathroom (yes, yes: 'in solitary', 'in splendid isolation', 'up the ivory tower', etc.), he lay in bed, stoically reminiscing about their last act of love, 164 hours ago . . . With some girls, with many girls, with most girls, no, with all girls, even the most energetic and proactive, there came a point when their hands would float down to rest on the pillow – palm up on either side of the face, in what did happen to resemble an attitude of surrender; but the point was that their hands were finally still. Phoebe's hands were never still; they never rested, right up to the very end . . . How to account for the attentiveness of the hands? Busying themselves down there, in the little menagerie, her hands were *meticulous*: 'careful and precise' but also 'wary or timid' (from L *metus*, 'dread'). Her hands were beset by small fears . . .

When it was over, that time, and Phoebe prepared herself for sleep (struggling to untangle her garter belt and *two* sets of pants), she said,

'One of these days I'm going to dress up as someone. Guess who. Eve.'

'How can you dress up as Eve?'

'Eve *after* the Fall.'

Next door, a light and two taps were thrown off, and she emerged, in her nightdress (white, opaque, knee length). Which reminded him.

'Uh, Jane's a fan of nightdresses – she thinks they're good because if you . . .'

Phoebe gave him a look of the sourest exasperation, as if he'd been going on about Jane for at least an hour. It was one of those times when her feelings were very close to the surface – there to be read.

'Sorry, I forgot,' he said lightly. 'Jane's a woman.'

'I'm a misogynist, okay?' This wasn't the first time that Phoebe had laid claim to that noun (seldom heard in the 1970s, and certainly never laid claim to, and only ever directed at men). 'Can't a girl even . . . And don't blame me, Martin. Blame – blame that sick bat in Morley Hollow!'

This was Phoebe's mother. He said, 'You're a bit too hard on Dallen, Phoebe.'

'Oh am I. When I was seven you know what she did? She upped and went to bed for ten years!' Phoebe reached for her hairbrush, and after a while the rhythmical motions had the effect of siphoning off her anger and replacing it (he thought) with sorrowful perplexity. 'Not ten years. Eight. See, she had me in her forties and it completely did her in. First a heart attack and then she broke both her legs. Brittle bones. And after the hysterectomy she doubled her weight, so she was sort of trapped. All to do with "the Change" – don't you think that's a beastly word for it?'

'Yes, beastly. That must've been hard on you. How did Graeme cope?'

'Luckily Father Gabriel stepped forward.' She opened the bed and let herself into it. 'Father Gabriel's very organised.'

'Good,' he said as he unemphatically embraced her. 'You know, Phoebe, a misogynist hates women. All women. You don't. You don't hate Merry.'

'You're right. Blind loyalty, you see. The thing is I'm beholden to the old slag. Do the light . . . Do the light – so I won't see your hurt face. I told you *not* to be hurt. How *dare* you be hurt? What about me? Give me your hand.'

He did her bidding. With the hand and then with the light.

About fifteen minutes later she murmured,

'As it happens, Mart . . . Tomorrow I'm not going in till nearly noon.'

He felt a thrumming in his chest. It would be wiser, now, not to say anything at all. He kissed her palm and pressed it to his cheek and turned over.

'. . . Mm. Now you can have a lovely sleep! And lovely dreams about tomorrow morning . . . I'm setting the alarm', Phoebe said sternly, 'for eight.' She yawned and licked her lips. 'We'll need showers and a proper breakfast first of course. And you've got to dash down and do the Mini. So seven-thirty. No. Seven . . . fifteen.'

Courtesy car

Out on the balcony, clad in Y-fronts and donkey jacket, his hair chilling in the needles of cold rain, he smoked a delicious and seemingly endless hand-rolled cigarette, and, with that achieved, he slid inside, poured two cups of coffee from the steel jug on the stove, and got back in time to see Phoebe emerging from her second shower of the morning, with a white towel round her waist and another one hanging loose from her shoulders like an unfurled scarf (and of course he kissed her and praised her) . . . She now attended to her day clothes, pre-assembled on a straightbacked chair, as if ready for school. (He similarly, if less pleasingly, had an arm out for his socks.) With a forbearing shrug Phoebe said,

'Jane *isn't* so bad I suppose. She can't help being a know-all. And a snob . . . What was that about the nightdress, Mart?'

He was thinking, he was languidly deciding that this was yet another reason for the marked popularity of the sexual act: you also got the ease and freedom that nearly always bobbed along in its wake. And you could also talk freely about sex. He said,

'Between you and me, Phoebe, the nightdress thing was really pretty lame. But let me tell you what she says about . . .' He hesitated. Anglosaxonisms didn't really sit well with Phoebe (and Sir Graeme also had a horror of rude words). 'About, you know, men's *things*. Men's arrangements. Ready? See if you agree.'

Phoebe gave a tolerant lift of the chin as she positioned her snaps and stays and leaned down from the chair to start scrolling up the white stockings.

'Well. Jane says it's not size that matters. Within reason of course. It's *hardness*.'

'. . . Jane said that to you? About penises?' Phoebe's tall neck lengthened. 'She's your stepmother for goodness' sake.'

56

'Yeah. She's Dad's wife. And it can be a bit awkward. Listen, I want your opinion. Now weigh, with your practical mind, Phoebe, weigh these two items of evidence.'

'I'm listening.' She looked at her watch and reached for her coffee. 'Quick though.'

'Number one, she stops me on the stairs and says, *Your father hasn't fucked me in three months.*'

'She said that?'

'Yes. And indignantly too. And years ago. In 1973 or something.'

'That's disgusting . . . That's abuse of trust, that is.'

'No. No it's not, Phoebe. I've known her half my life. We're pretty close. Anyway.' He felt an obscure unease pass over him. 'Anyway, item number two . . . Dad, *Dad* told me, just the other night, he's been going in for sex therapy . . . I can't believe it.'

'There. See? That's what Jane's reduced him to.'

He went on wanderingly, 'I couldn't believe it, because he loathes all that. Viennese innuendoes, anything *personal*. I said, *Bad luck, old man*, and he just shrugged and said, *Well, in a case like this you have to show willing.*'

With a faraway look Phoebe rose to her feet, like a girl in church slowly straightening up for the hymns. '*Now* will you admit I'm right.'

Phoebe was at this point fully primed for the outside world, hugging her business jacket close as she strode towards the door. 'Oi. Chop chop. So tell me, Martin. Do you want to follow in his footsteps? So, so dulled they send him to a bloody *lab*?'

'. . . No. You show me how, Phoebe. Show me the way.'

'I will,' she said. 'Stick with me, kid.'

'I will.' As they were shuffling round the front door she said, 'What kind of therapy?'

'I've no idea. Just Dad and Jane sitting there with the guy or the girl and discussing how they feel about each other.'

'Oh, well. Once they start doing that it's all over very quickly.'

'Is it? Why?'

'Because it's more of what you hate.'

She did the bolts and they stepped out on to the landing. 'You show me how. I *like* you, Phoebe. You're great. I like you very much. You show me how . . .'

'All right. Deal.'

'You know, Dad said you looked like an adorable woodland creature in a children's book. And Jane said, oh yeah, Jane wondered if you were an *orphan*. She –'

Now Phoebe faltered as they started down the stairwell, half sliding towards him on the moist tiles; he easily steadied her; she regained her height and gave him an ordinary glance, but he saw that her eyes had freshened and her upper lip had a numb and puffy look to it.

'Sorry,' he said. 'Maybe I shouldn't've passed that on.'

'What on? Oh. It's nothing to do with *Jane*. When you said those nice things . . .'

'Come on, I've said nice things before.'

With her head up she took his arm and said sensibly, 'I know you have, Mart. I know you have.'

Under the archway they waited in the light rain for Phoebe's car, her courtesy car (this sometimes happened).

'Will you call me later? Of course you will, you always do. Oh dear. *Oh* dear. We've been together for twenty months, Martin. It's the longest I've . . . It's ridiculous. What do I have to do to put you off?'

He said, 'I know. Let me make love to you every night.'

'Oh, and betray my deepest convictions? No. Time for the new regime. Sorry!'

She gave him a kiss on the lips, in consolation; he nodded fatalistically and bowed as her delicate legs, clenched together, slid smoothly into the back seat. They waved.

He already knew a fair amount about the new regime, which she called the Next Thing (the two words had long been fearfully capitalised in his mind).

Would it be sudden, the next thing? No. It's not one big idea. It's more like a package of measures. *How'll I know when the next thing's begun?* You'll know after a bit, Martin. The realisation will steal up on you. . . . *Is there another thing* after *the next thing?* Yes, but I've never had to use it. The next thing has always been enough. Actually the *first* thing has always been enough. Except with you.

The thought of being an exception flattered his vanity. So did her otherness, with its weird cinema (the atrium at TFS, the business trips to Prague and Budapest, the courtesy car). So did the evident fact that he had the gravitational weight to attract someone from such a distant system, to draw someone in through so many voids from so very far away.

She's also got a wound, I think, Jane had said. Martin thought that too; and it made him vulnerable to the fantasies of rescue and redemption – fantasies of honour – that had been part of his imaginative life since the age of five or six. Redeem her how? Through love. He wanted her to love him. If he could achieve it, he knew, then he was ready to take the enormous risk – commit to the outlandish gamble – of loving and honouring Phoebe Phelps.

'What is honour?' asks the inglorious Falstaff. 'He that died o' Wednesday. Doth he feel it? No.' Can honour 'take away the grief of a wound? No.'

Where was that wound? Where was that grief?

Guideline
The Novel Moves On

What's the difference between a story and a plot? you ask.

According to E. M. Forster (whom Jane used to refer to by his middle name, as did everyone who knew him), 'the king died and then the queen died' is a story, but 'the king died, and then the queen died of grief' is a plot. Not so, Edward, not so, Morgan! 'The king died, and then the queen died of grief' is still a story. To mutate into a plot, a story needs a further element – easily supplied, here, by a comma and an adverb.

The king died, and then the queen died, ostensibly of grief is a plot. Or a hook. Plots demand constant attention, but a good hook can stand alone and untouched, like an anchor, and keep things fixed and stable in any weather. Plots and hooks yield the same desideratum: they set the reader a question, with the implicit assurance that the question will be answered.

Those amiably vague remarks about the king and the queen come from Forster's stimulating little book, *Aspects of the Novel*, which appeared in 1927. At that time it went without saying, in polite society, that plots – and hooks – were beneath the dignity of serious writers, and that the Great Tradition consisted of stories: long stories. 'Yes – oh dear, yes – the novel tells a story,' wrote Forster; and it is probably his most-quoted line (apart from 'Only connect!') . . . He died, aged ninety-one, in 1970, when the novel, the Forsterian novel, so sane, so orderly, was in quiet retreat. Because the literary vanguard was starting to say, *No – oh God, no – the novel* doesn't *tell a story. Because times have changed.*

As early as 1973 Anthony Burgess was floating the notion that there are, in fact, two types of novelist, which he called type 'A' and type 'B'. 'A' novelists were interested in narrative, character, motivation, and psychological insight, said Burgess, while 'B' novelists were interested above all in language – in the play of words.

That statement seemed precipitate back then, but within a few years it was no more than a fair description of the status quo. While the 'A' novelists were carrying on as normal, the 'B' novelists (who had long been hazy presences on the fringe) were suddenly everywhere, composing novels as structureless as alphabet soup and as wayward as schizophrenia.

We saw novels that did without paragraph breaks or punctuation, or did without monosyllables, or polysyllables, or common nouns or verbs or adjectives; one assiduous daredevil thought it worth putting together a prose epic that did without the letter *e*. There was also much stream of consciousness, much self-referential friskiness, and – in a broad variety of styles and registers – much overwriting.

The surge in experimentalism ran alongside the sexual revolution, and sprang from the same collective eureka: the unsuspected flimsiness of certain venerable prohibitions. As it turned out, the 'language' novelists slowly peaked and then slowly plunged, and the whole thrust was over in two generations . . . So the stream of consciousness – to take the least attractive innovation – raved and mumbled on for sixty years; looking back, reading back, one is amazed it lasted sixty minutes. Nowadays, anyway, the 'B' novel is dead.*

Detectable too has been a reordering of the relationship between writer and reader (in the plainest of times a relationship of inexhaustible

---

* And leaves behind it, so far as I can ascertain, only one long-term survivor (apart from *Ulysses*): Burgess's *A Clockwork Orange*. This is a language novel, written in a futurised farrago of Romani, rhyming slang, and Russian; and it can still be read with steady engagement and admiration. It is, in addition, appropriately short . . . The most iconic 'B' novel by far is *Finnegans Wake* (1939). Nabokov hailed *Ulysses* as the novel of the century, but called the *Wake* 'a tragic failure', 'dull and formless' – 'a snore in the next room' (that last phrase captures not only its tedium but also its extraordinary indifference to any likely concern of the reader's). *Finnegans Wake*, which famously took seventeen years to write, resembles a cryptic crossword clue that goes on for more than 600 pages. And the pithiest thing ever said about it, satisfyingly, appeared in a cryptic crossword clue: 'Something wrong with *Finnegan's Wake*? Perhaps too complicated (10)'. The solution is an anagram (signalled by 'complicated') of 'perhaps too': *apostrophe*. This clue involves general knowledge (which slightly diminishes it) but remains almost as perfect as 'Meaningful power of attorney (11)', whose solution is *significant*: sign-if-i-cant.

complexity and depth). 'We like difficult books,' *littérateurs* used to claim; and this supposed preference turned into a rallying-cry for the cause of High Modernism. Perhaps we did indeed once like difficult books. But we don't like them any more. Difficult novels are dead.

We no longer court difficulty partly because the reader–writer relationship has ceased to be even remotely cooperative. Whatever you do, don't expect the reader to *deduce* anything. I learnt that the hard way with my eleventh novel (2006): one of its protagonists, an American girl called Venus, is black, and her ethnicity is shored up by so much internal evidence that somehow I felt it would be ham-handed to spell it out (surely Venus Williams was doing the job for me). The result? Not a single reader I'm aware of has ever doubted for a moment that Venus is white.*

Mark my words: every piece of vital information has to be clearly stated in plain English; when it comes to inferring and surmising, readers have downed tools. The unreliable narrator (once a popular and often very fruitful device) has given way to the era of the unreliable receptor. The unreliable narrator is dead; the 'deductive' novel is dead.

There used to be a sub-genre of long, plotless, digressive, and essayistic novels (fairly) indulgently known as 'baggy monsters'. *Humboldt's Gift*, with its extended asides on such things as theosophy and angelology, is a classic baggy monster; and when it was published in 1975 (before Bellow's Nobel) it spent eight months on the bestseller list. Forty years on, the audience for such a book has dwindled, I would say, by 80 or 90 per cent. The readers are no longer there – their patience, their goodwill, their autodidactic enthusiasm are no longer there. For self-interested reasons I like to think this sub-genre retains a viable pulse; but broadly speaking the baggy monster is dead.

In brutal summary, then, the 'B' novel died, the deductive novel died, and the sprawl novel, the baggy monster, died. They are fondly remembered, at least by novelists, who by definition revere all diversity.

---

* I fixed this in the paperback edition, where I spelt it out (almost in italic capitals) on page 3. And I did so rather resentfully – and rather furtively, I admit. Venus's ethnicity was structurally crucial. I'd done wrong (how could I be so out of touch?), and now I was ham-handedly covering my tracks.

Still, tucked away among these literary obituaries we glimpse the proud announcement of a birth. Actually the new arrival has been with us for some time – since around the turn of the century – and the child has steadily thrived. I mean the aerodynamic, the streamlined, the *accelerated* novel. More in a moment.

You know, it was only when I was revising the two chapters devoted to her ('The Business' and also 'The Night of Shame', which is forthcoming) – only then did I realise how 'novelistic' Phoebe was: a being of strong lines. If she ever woke up and found herself in a *roman-fleuve*, say, or a comedy of manners, she would effortlessly find her place and hold her own. Because in her person she contained themes and patterns, and she had the necessary energy, the binding energy, and the vehemence (and the mystery – the ever-present question mark). These were all qualities she was destined to lose, over the course of a single season in 1980 . . .

As a character she did what so few of us do: she cohered. Consider the following item in her CV (dramatic enough but comprehensively dwarfed, at the time, by three far more startling disclosures). It concerned itself with the apparently blameless sphere of poetry; and you need that wilfulness, that self-exaggeration – if you're going to combine poetry and *prison*.

Aged fifteen, a class-topping pupil at Spelthorne High School for Girls (*It was good, too*, she often stressed. *A proper grammar*), Phoebe had an affair with her English master – her poetry master (his name, misleadingly, was Timmy). And before that got going she became *a terrific memoriser of verse. I did it to please him, naturally. But I could do it. And I liked doing it.*

Their half-year affair included orgies of quoting and reciting. *And he fancied himself as a poet, too. He wrote me love poems, Martin, that were quite frankly obscene* . . . Timmy was thirty-six and had a wife and two toddler daughters. One spring Sunday he and Phoebe were spotted – by the deputy principal – as they frolicked together on Richmond Common. *Timmy had a blind panic. And he ended it.*

Now Phoebe, in shirt and tie and bobby socks, though *shattered, completely choked and gutted*, did manage to accept this loss – out of love for her Timmy. Ah, but then the following term he began to move in on *one of my classmates! Not at all pretty and an utter hick. Well of course I went straight to the headmistress. I made a detailed statement and the next day I handed over all the rhymed filth he'd sent me.* Timmy was first sacked (and instantly banned from the family home), then arrested. He got thirteen years. *Serve him bloody well right. Moving in on another one like that. I ask you. I mean the* nerve . . .

All this happened in 1957. *Category A – for his own protection. Yeah, they banged him up with all the other nonces*, she said, adding (with some licence), *and they only let him out the other day. Serve him bloody well right.* Phoebe then, as an addendum, punished the yokel classmate. *How? Oh, nothing much. I just made her have a crush on me. And then I dropped her cold. In public, mind – in the yard during break.*

1957. In Swansea, South Wales, clad in short trousers, I celebrated my eighth birthday. And fifteen-year-old Phoebe Phelps, school-uniformed in the Home Counties, banged up Timmy, her pastor of poetry . . .

Vengeance was hers – vengeance was always hers. Phoebe prosecuted her feuds to the point, perhaps, where the average Corsican cut-throat would throw up his hands, roll his eyes, and call it quits. Or so I came to believe when she took her revenge on me: September 12, 2001. And to be fair, Phoebe had another reason for blowing the whistle on Tim – and a very terrifying reason . . .

As for poetry, Phoebe renounced it: not so much as a single word, a single iamb or trochee, for two decades – till she opened *The Whitsun Weddings* in my bedroom.

'You see how it'd go. If I let you have your way. It'd be like that poem. Your desire would be sent out of sight. Yes, Martin. Somewhere becoming rain.'

––––––––––

The accelerated novel is a literary response to the accelerated world.

September 11 verified what many had already sensed: the world was speeding up, history was accelerating, time was flying faster and faster. An accelerated world: no human being in history had experienced even a murmur of this feeling until, say, 1914 – and in 1614 (to paraphrase something of Saul's) it was an idea that would be as likely to occur to you as it would to the dog sleeping at your feet. The other accelerant is of course technology.*

Serious fiction could respond to the accelerated world; but serious poetry couldn't. Naturally it couldn't. A poem, a non-narrative poem, a lyric poem – the first thing it does is stop the clock. It stops the clock while whispering, *Let us go then, you and I, let us go and examine an epiphany, a pregnant moment, and afterwards we'll have a think about that epiphany, and we'll* . . . But the speeded-up world doesn't have time for stopped clocks.

Meanwhile the novelists subliminally realised that in their pages the arrow of development, purpose, furtherance, had to be sharpened. And they sharpened it. This wasn't and isn't a fad or a fashion (far less a *bandwagon*). Novelists aren't mere observers of the speeded-up world; they inhabit it and feel its rhythms and breathe its air. So they adapted; they evolved.

The world won't be slowing down, either, and so poetry will give ground (as the literary novel may sooner or later do), becoming a minority-interest field – more shadowy and more secluded . . . We can if we like fondly imagine Phoebe, in a cheap hotel, on a certain half-deserted street, in a sawdust restaurant with oyster shells: Phoebe reviewing the discomfiture of poetry – serve it right – and giving a contented smack of the lips before showing the ferocious finish of her teeth.

———————

What doomed them, the unreliable narrator, the stream of consciousness, and all the other dead strains? What was the morbidity they shared?

A rational form, a secular form, and a moral form, the novel is in addition a social form. That's why social realism, always the dominant genre, is now the unquestioned hegemon. A social form – you might even say a sociable form. And the fatal character flaw of experimentalists?

* 'Intel engineers did a rough calculation of what would happen had a 1971 Volkswagen Beetle improved at the same rate as microchips . . . Today, that Beetle would be able to go about three hundred thousand miles per hour. It would get two million miles per gallon of gas; and it would cost four cents . . .' Thomas L. Friedman, *Thank You for Being Late* (2016).

They're introverts, they keep themselves to themselves, they prefer their own company. They're antisocial, in a word.

I don't want to sound too alchemical here – but did you know that 'guest' and 'host' have the same root? Though 'reader' and 'writer' are less tangibly interconnected, the affinity is there and it is both strong and strange. Now you're a naturally sensitive reader, and a naturally sensitive guest . . . So while you're away I want you to imagine novelists as *hosts*, as people who answer the door and let you in.

And I want you to think about the desperate importance of the opening pages. That's your greeting to the reader, that's your generous *welcome* to the reader. And remember the warning a wise friend put to Christopher Hitchens in 2003. It was during a talk they had about the failing occupation of Iraq. He said,

You never get a second chance to make a good first impression.

Chapter 3
Jerusalem

Seeing is believing

Without Israel, Saul Bellow said to me (in Israel), *Jewish manhood would've been finished*. I could get his drift, but it took me a while to get his meaning.

He said it in Jerusalem – Jerusalem, 'the terrestrial gateway to the divine world' (Sari Nusseibeh), 'the shortest path between heaven and earth' (Nizar Qabbani) . . .

Jerusalem would come later. First, though, Saul and I (and a couple of hundred others) had to do our duty in humble Haifa, a merely temporal city ninety-five miles to the north-north-west. It was the spring of 1987. I was nearly thirty-eight, and Saul was nearly seventy-two; I would be there with my first wife, and Saul would be there with his fifth.

But wait. Were she and Saul actually married? Was she his wife or was she his fiancée, his cohabitee, his 'friend'? And who was she, anyway? As the journey to Jerusalem took shape, I had meetings in London with an Israeli novelist and an Israeli academic, and none of us knew anything about her. Just two semi-verified facts emerged: her name was Rosamund and she was younger than he was. So she was younger than seventy-one . . . Of course I wished them well with all my heart, but at that stage I was still innocent of curiosity about Saul's private life (it was his private life. It happened somewhere else).* What attracted

* He and I had exchanged a few letters by then, but I was only distantly aware that Saul had had an *annus horribilis* in 1985: the deaths, one after the other, of his two elder brothers (Maury and Samuel), followed within weeks by the sudden decampment of his fourth wife, Alexandra.

me was his prose – to be exact, the *weight* of his words on the page) . . . And you could argue that Bellow's fiction was in any case abrim with his private life; and you'd be right. He wrote about other things, but he wrote short stories, novellas, short novels, novels, and long novels about people he knew and things that had actually happened.

England came into being, as a unified polity, in 937 CE, whereas Israel was barely a year older than I was (and eight months younger than Pakistan).

'Well I'm basically on their side,' he said to Julia as they were packing their bags. 'Why? Because they're surrounded by countries that want them dead.'

'Then why'd they go there? Couldn't they *see*? And it's not just the surrounding countries, is it. What about the country they're actually in? Palestine. Why there?'

'Religion. It was religion, Julia, that led them to the Promised Land.'

She made a nauseated face. 'Promised by who.'

Of course he had other reasons for sympathising with Israel, namely lifelong predispositions, and Rachel – his first love . . . Love, in Martin's experience, greeted you head-on and face to face, and so it had been with Julia; but now, after three years of marriage, he felt something misaligned, aslant, athwart . . . He said,

'In my opinion you're too English about Israel. Arabophile and easily annoyed. You should be more American about it.'

'Like an evangelical. Thinking we need it for a proper Judgment Day.'

'. . . Oh come on, Julia. You'll love it once you're there. I did.'

Twelve months earlier, along with four other British writers (Marina Warner, Hermione Lee, Melvyn Bragg, and Julian Barnes), I was a guest of the Friends of Israel Educational Trust. And so we visited the Knesset, lunched overlooking the Lake of Galilee, had audiences with rabbis and diplomats, played ping-pong in a kibbutz on 'the Golan', floundered about in the Dead Sea, and – like novitiates in the Israel Defense Forces – circled Herodion and climbed Masada.

The only Arab I knowingly said hello to was a showpiece Bedouin in whose tent we drank tea and whose camel we all in turn clambered up on. Marina, certainly, and perhaps Hermione had semi-clandestine meetings with Palestinian activists, and the Palestinian 'question' was on everyone's lips (there is no small talk in Israel); but back then I was still politically incurious, and didn't really see the Palestinians.*

Was there a special difficulty in seeing the Palestinians?

This question isn't *faux naïf* and it isn't rhetorical; it is non-figurative and it expects or at least hopes for an answer.

An answer to an enquiry about the condition of Israeli eyesight.

———————

I had this idea that people were like countries and countries were like people.

Do you remember the literary convention whereby countries were *feminised*? 'England's might depended on her navy', and so on. That convention – always a quavering false gallantry – was silently abandoned during the first half of the twentieth century. Historians and politicians started calling countries *it*.

. . . If Israel were a person, what kind of person would Israel be? Well, male, anyway – male, for a start.

'She' was never any good; 'it' is a tenable compromise; really, though, it should have been 'he', all along. Without exception, countries are men. That's the trouble.

Getting to the other planet

'And is your father still a Communist?'

'No. He stopped about thirty years ago.'

'Why did he stop?'

'Hungary, 1957. And general disillusionment.'

'. . . Was *his* father a Communist?'

El Al, even then, long before the days of shoe bombs and toothpaste bombs and Y-front bombs, distinguished itself from other carriers. Instead of showing up at the airport, a trifle flustered perhaps, forty-five

———

* It was not a sin of omission, in my case. It was an error of inclusion. I didn't omit them; I included them (along with everyone else I saw), because I couldn't tell them apart. They're all Semites, aren't they – Arabs, Jews? Semite: 'a member of a people speaking a Semitic language, in particular the Jews and Arabs'.

minutes before take-off, you had to be there three hours early. What came next was a solemnly detailed interrogation. James Fenton, in his formidable poem 'Jerusalem' (1988), does this with it:

> Who packed your bag?
> I packed my bag.
> Where was your uncle's mother's sister born?
> Have you ever met an Arab?

By the time my cross-examination was over (it was polite and not without a certain warmth, but softly intense and hypnotically eye to eye), I wondered whether anybody in my entire life had ever been quite so interested in me.*

Approved for transfer by El Al, you feel shriven and cleansed. And also surprisingly well-qualified in rectitude and high seriousness (eligible, say, for a key role in the priming of Israel's nuclear warheads) . . . Julia and I, two travellers of stainless reputation, took our seats. Her in-flight reading would be *Daniel Deronda*. Mine would be *To Jerusalem and Back* (Bellow, 1976). Some reviewers of Saul's memoir/travelogue complained that the author hadn't 'seen' any Palestinians ('seen' in the journalistic sense, and not in the sense I am trying to define). There were other books on Israel in my luggage. I was beginning my trek along the foothills of Mount Zion – or Mount Improbable.

The Amises had been together for six years, three of them as husband and wife. And there was a pair of Millennials back in Ladbroke Grove, W11: Nat (two and a half) and Gus (one). But now, like a tide, the marriage was beginning to turn.

Dangling men

The two-hour quiz, the five-hour flight, the late arrival at Ben Gurion International Airport, the three-hour drive, the business hotel, the

---

* To gain entry to the US (in those days), all you had to do was fill in the form and say No to the questions that only the odd lunatic has ever said Yes to. No, I am not a fatally and contagiously diseased terrorist who's spent the last six months immersed in pig troughs and sheep dips. This could change: the 2016 US election looms as I write . . . El Al still stipulates three hours, so it hasn't become more rigorous since September 11; what has happened is that the world has caught up with Israel. Perhaps, one day, a neighbourhood bus ride will be like flying El Al.

extraction of a tomato and an apple from the closed kitchens, the wholly wakeful night under the panting AC, the unsolicited wake-up call telling me that, even now, the conference minibus was revving in the forecourt. Dinnerless, sleepless, and breakfastless, I climbed aboard and was ferried with others to the University of Haifa . . . The campus, perched on Mount Carmel, seemed to consist of mammoth bomb shelters and pillboxes and watchtowers, reminding some visitors of the illegal Israeli settlements (whose 'new concrete buildings have a grim Maginot Line look about them'*). After a smoke in the sun I went inside and wandered along the strip-lit corridors, and finally succeeded in dozing my way through two or three fifty-minute dissertations.

In the common room I at once linked up with the novelist Jonathan Wilson (a Jewish Londoner whose academic base was now in Boston). His expression as he surveyed the crowd was almost succulently ironic, brimming with guarded, hoarded amusement. The mayors and ministers, the duo of famous Israeli novelists, the many escorts and facilitators, plus local and national journalists and a radio team and perhaps a TV team, and there through the windows the sky-god blue of the Levant; but Jonathan was gripped in particular by the huddled delegates and dons, crouched over their coffees and stolidly dealing out inch-thick typescripts to one another . . . In a tone that presupposed the answer No, I said,

'Any sign of Saul?'

'Yes. In fact he looked in on the opening ceremony. With his girlfriend. She's uh, younger than he is.'

I nodded. 'I assumed she'd be younger than he is.'

'She's appreciably younger than he is.' Jonathan paused. 'Oh, look at the crazy professors . . . You know, Bellow calls himself a *comic* novelist. And this isn't the setting for a comic novelist, is it. They're all stucturalists and semiologists and neo-Marxists. And dogged careerists. And they haven't forced a smile in years.'

Apparently Saul the day before had writhed his way through a paper called something like 'The Encaged Cash Register: Tensions Between Existentialism and Materialism in *Dangling Man*'. Now I already knew

* From *To Jerusalem and Back*, in common with all the other unattributed quotes in this chapter. I was in Haifa for what billed itself as the First International Saul Bellow Conference; it was set in motion by the Saul Bellow Society, and coordinated by the genial Israeli novelist A. B. Yehoshua.

that this was the kind of literary pedagogy, or one of the kinds of literary pedagogy, that Saul despised with every neutrino of his being. Jonathan continued,

'Oh, he was suffering. Somebody heard him whisper, *If I have to listen to another word of this, I think I'll actually* die.'

'Mm. The last thing he ever wants to be told is what Ahab's harpoon symbolises.'

'Well, here he'll be told what Herzog's hat symbolises . . . Did you hear about Oz?'

I had been to Israel before so I knew the process (as inexorable as having your passport stamped): the immediate baptism in a riptide of urgencies . . . That day the multinational Bellow buffs, the Israeli scholars, and all the others were still recuperating from Amos Oz's introductory address, entitled 'Mr Sammler and Hannah Arendt's Notion of Banality'.* Israel's most celebrated novelist had opened up three controversies, two of them familiar and digestible enough, the other disconcertingly arcane.

'He was in a weird mood, all driven and defiant,' said Jonathan. 'To begin with, he asked, he demanded to know – first in Hebrew, then in English – why the conference wasn't bilingual. He said English-only, in an Israeli university, was a disgrace.' And Oz somehow went on from there to suggest that Jewish 'passivity', in the face of Auschwitz, had

---

* Although there are many hyper-intelligent pages in Hannah Arendt's *Eichmann in Jerusalem* (1962), her central conceit – 'the banality of evil' – has over the years been steadily debunked. Artur Sammler, the hero of the Bellow novel of 1970, *Mr Sammler's Planet*, played his part: 'The idea of making the century's great crime look dull is not banal,' says Sammler on page 20. 'Politically, psychologically, the Germans had an idea of genius. The banality was only camouflage. What better way to get the curse out of murder than to make it look ordinary, boring, or trite? . . . [D]o you think the Nazis didn't know what murder was? Everybody (except certain bluestockings) knows what murder is. That is very old human knowledge' . . . And consider Eichmann's statement in 1945 (quoted at the trial): 'I will leap into my grave laughing because the feeling that I have five million human beings on my conscience is for me a source of extraordinary satisfaction.' What is banal, what is tediously commonplace, about that? I think Robert Jay Lifton, in *The Nazi Doctors* (1986), comes very close to the truth (and bear in mind that in the course of his research Lifton, a Jewish doctor himself, spent many hours face to face with twenty-eight such Nazis): 'Repeatedly in this study, I describe banal men performing demonic acts. In doing so – or in *order* to do so – the men themselves changed; and in carrying out their actions, they themselves were no longer banal.'

something to do with the *showers*; subconsciously the Jews themselves craved ablution, Oz argued, to wash away the calumnies of millennia. 'I know – very odd. And all this was said *scathingly*.'

'And metaphorically.'

'Hard to tell. He's an impressive man and it was all quite compelling. Anyway, the showers weren't banal either, according to Oz. They were the manifestation of a devilish insight.'

'Will this stir things up?'

'For a while. What writers say here really matters. Writers have power.'

We frowned at each other. Only English writers, perhaps, would find this notion quite so bizarre. I said,

'Maybe it goes to their heads. It'd go to mine.'

'In Israel writers aren't just entertainers. They're prophets. This isn't the diaspora. This is the pointed end.'

. . . I moved around the common room looking for the door to the open air and the minibus. By now the tabletalk had moved on from Amos Oz – to Bellow's 'muse' (as she herself, in the papers, spiritedly called herself); the speculations were indulgent and mildly and enviously salacious; they found it reassuring that Saul was cleaving to type, that of the sensual intellectual. Somebody claimed that the muse was Bellow's junior by half a century.

Sheen

Julia and I mingled and explored, and at some point Jonathan drove us to Tiberias, where we sat on the shore of the Sea of Galilee and ate St Peter's fish . . .

But I still had to complete my essay or lecture, and I had a raw throat and a dry cough. So Julia sat in the garden with George Eliot, and I sat in our room and wrote and smoked and read while, in my peripheral vision, an attaché case quietly gleamed on the glass table; it was complimentary (issued to all delegates); it was made of soft matting and Naugahyde; and it seemed to embody the surface of Israel and its pseudo-normality – the business-class interiors of the modern state, the market state, the business state. And here we were in this business hotel, a business hotel like any other, in a port city like any other on the northerly littoral of the Mediterranean. Haifa seemed innocent, in 1987, to my innocent eye.*

Inside – in the cafés, bars, and eateries, and in the corridors and commissaries of the university – you felt the steady gush of earnest debate: 'exposition, argument, harangue, analysis, theory, expostulation, threat, and prophesy . . . [And] the subject of all this talk is, ultimately, survival.'

Outside, the extraordinary air with its tang of lemon-grove antiquity, the rounded hillocks, the orchards – and the stones. 'Many times cleared, the ground goes on giving birth to stones; waves of earth bring forth more stones.' All day you heard the mad ratchetings of the crickets (or were they *locusts*?) and the bedraggled yawns of the goats.

Beyond, down there, the bay, the sand, even the tame and tideless wavelets of the Med, look silently ominous. This is the Promised Land, after all, this is utopia, this is Byzantium, this is the City on a Hill, this is Jerusalem. And how do you reach it, the land of the golden bells? On a dolphin's back they come, 'spirit after spirit':

> Marbles of the dancing floor,
> Break bitter furies of complexity,
> Those images that yet
> Fresh images beget,
> That dolphin-torn, that gong-tormented sea.

'Byzantium', W. B. Yeats, 1932

The muse

In the presence of Julia and Jonathan, of Saul and his travelling companion, in the presence of novelists Alan Lelchuk and A. B. 'Booli'

---

* The historian Martin Gilbert, not content with being preternaturally prolific, goes so far as to assemble, and sign, his own indexes. Gilbert's *Israel* (1998) is 700 pages long; and this is what you'll find, in its index, under 'Haifa'. Even in my shortened version it has a certain gothic flair (the page references are omitted). Haifa: 'and "gangs of criminals"; Jews murdered in (1938); an internment camp near; a death in; sabotage in; a Jew murdered on the way back from; Jewish terrorist attacks near; an Arab act of terror in; and the War of Independence; bombarded (1956); and the October War; Scud missiles hit . . .' And this was Haifa, which, from the crest of Mount Carmel, looked as artless as dew. I now find myself wondering if there is a single acre of the Holy Land that is free of recent memories of blood and grief. And what does this do to the man called Israel?

Yehoshua and the impeccably courteous Amos Oz, and in the presence of several dozen professional Bellovians, I croaked out my lecture. It had nothing to do with Marxism, or Israel, or even Judaism. Today I think that my words (given the location and the ambient mental temperature) could be regarded as offensively unprovocative. I talked about fictional effects, and about love – love in the setting of American modernity.

My assignment was *More Die of Heartbreak*, the Bellow novel published later that year. And I began by saying that I was the only person in the room who had read it; those who had not read it, I went on, included its author. He has written it, I argued, but he has not *read* it, as I have.* While I talked, and coughed, I stole the odd glance at the Nobelist and at his young friend, who sat demurely beside him, under an effusion of dark brown hair . . . The talk ended, and Saul gave a short and generous response; then the crowd churned and intermingled. I collected my wife, and we made for Rosamund – the muse.

Academic gossip had imagined her as someone like Ramona (*Herzog*) or Renata (*Humboldt's Gift*). Both these characters are endearing in their way, but Ramona is a sophisticated man-pleaser, and Renata is a mixed-up gold-digger; and Rosamund was something else again. With her oval face and elliptical eyes, she could have been the kind and clever stepsister in a fairy tale. Rosamund was indeed very young – not just Saul's junior, but mine too, by eight or nine years.

There was fresh commotion, as the entire crowd started funnelling down from the twenty-ninth floor to the first, to hear Shimon Peres (a Foreign Minister who knew his Flaubert) introducing Saul's public lecture, 'The Silent Assumptions of the Novelist'. The auditorium was full; listeners seemed to be up there cooing and fluttering in the rafters like pigeons, or like doves. There were no hawks: all were of one spirit – the unanimous reverence for learning.

Saul began. The voice was resonant, it carried, but with the beginnings of a new (and near-elderly) lightness of pitch. By my side, Rosamund sat rapt and intense . . . I knew then that I had been quite wrong, upstairs, claiming that I was the only one present who had 'read' *More Die of Heartbreak*. Rosamund would have read it, at least

---

* What I meant was: writers cannot 'read' their own books (in any normal sense of the word) until a year or two after publication. They are still correcting, they are still haunted by alternatives and missed chances. For them, the prose needs time to settle into something fixed and tamper-proof.

once. And she would have noted this passage (which I had recited an hour earlier). 'Towards the end of your life,' says Benn Crader (a world-renowned botanist, a 'plant clairvoyant'),

> you have something like a pain schedule to fill out – a long schedule like a federal document, only it's your pain schedule. First, physical causes . . . Next category, injured vanity, betrayal, swindle, injustice. But the hardest items of all have to do with love. The question then is: So why does everybody persist?

'Because of immortal longings,' answers Benn's nephew and intimate, Kenneth (a teacher of Russian literature). 'Or just hoping for a lucky break.'

Filling out the pain schedule, then, is something you do in your head, weighing the wounds, and the lucky breaks, that will decide your destined mood.

The next morning, after fruit, coffee, and breadrolls, the Bellows and the Amises journeyed to Jerusalem, the numinous city.

The sun can do no more with them

'I gather you've been reading Philip Larkin,' I said (which was no great inferential feat, because Larkin is cited twice in *More Die*). And by the spring of 1987, it should be remembered, Philip Larkin, my father's exact coeval, was already dead – dead for seventeen months, dead at sixty-three, and not of heartbreak . . .

'Yes I have,' said Saul, 'and with great pleasure. His poems make you laugh but all the time you're sensing the heavy melancholy, like a medieval humour – what they used to call black bile. And maybe the comedy gains from that. The melancholia – it's pointless to look for causes, but what was his background and his family?'

'Blaming the Parents?* These are just impressions. His mum was supposed to be a great nag and whiner, but his dad, his dad sounded

---

* We had already talked about the widespread habit of Blaming the Parents, which Saul sharply identified as a 'vice' (and if he wanted to cultivate it he had more to go on than most: when roused, his father used to strike his sons with a closed fist; and his mother died when he was fifteen) . . . For my part I said that I had hardly anything to reproach my parents for, and what little there was vanished with a shriek when for the first time I changed my first son's nappy.

really unusual. Unusually right-wing Middle England. Yeah, I seem to remember he was a Germanophile – of all things. I think he even took Philip there. In the mid-thirties. For a *holiday*.'

We were having tea on the rooftop terrace of the government guest house, which lay just beyond the walls of Jerusalem; meanwhile, Mount Carmel, as gracefully as a mountain could manage it, had stepped aside in favour of Mount Zion. The guest house was called Mishkenot Sha'ananim, or 'peaceful habitation'. And this was the spring of 1987, seven months before the end of one of Israel's quiet times.

'That poem . . . *In everyone there sleeps A sense of life lived according to love*.'

'Yes,' I said, 'and they dream of *all they might have done had they been loved. That nothing cures*.'

'Was he not loved?'

'I think his parents loved him. You mean later on?' Whereas Saul's tea was enliveningly laced with a slice of lemon, mine was qualified with milk – with the milk of concord. I lit a cigarette. 'My father couldn't believe how unambitious he was, how uh, *defeatist* he was about girls. To hear my father tell it, he worked his way through a tiny coven of weird sisters.' Sympathetically Saul leant his head sideways. 'And it's odd, because poets get girls. As we know. What does Humboldt say when he bangs on the girls' door? *Let me in. I'm a poet and I have a big cock*.'

'. . . Did you meet any of these sisters?'

'Only the main one – Monica. And it was just the other day. Well. 1982. So not long before he started to ail.'

'What was it in the end?'

I told him the little I knew. 'And Monica was . . .' How to put it? Never mind, for now, her room-flooding quiddity. 'She looked like a trusty in drag.'

'Oh. I'm sorry to hear that.'

The colour of the day was changing. *Late afternoon light on the stones*, Saul had written ten years earlier, *only increases their stoniness. Yellow and gray, they have achieved their final color; the sun can do no more with them*. I said,

'Well, he took Yeats's advice. Seek perfection of the work, not of the life.'

'Yeats doesn't always talk sense. Like his advice to writers – *never struggle, never rest*. And you won't find perfection in anyone's life. Or in anyone's work.'

78

'I know. In another poem the poet steps back from himself and sees *Books; china; a life Reprehensibly perfect.* Well there was no danger of that.'

'Anyway there must *be* a life. Yeats certainly had one.'

'Mm. And so did Primo Levi.' Until just the other day: on April 11 Levi threw himself down the stairwell of his apartment block in Turin. 'Sincere condolences, Saul . . . I'm trying to see his suicide as an act of defiance. A way of saying, My life is mine to take, mine and mine alone. But that's . . .'

'Primo Levi – he never wasted a single word.'

A silence. Then I told him about the new apparitions – my sons . . . But as the day withdrew Mount Zion seemed to glow and glower (yes, a yellow light, but powerful: tiger-yellow). What was the matter with us, the mountain seemed to ask – how could we go on neglecting the only possible subject? Which was Israeli survival.

'It's a garrison state,' said Saul, 'but it's here. And without Israel, Jewish manhood would've been finished.'

I at first took him to mean that the Jews would stop feeling the desire to reproduce. That was literal of me. There was another way of disappearing.

'Assimilation,' he said, 'abject assimilation, and the end of the whole story.'

The story that went back 4,000 years.

But now we had to go and find Julia and Rosamund, and Saul's sidekick Allan Bloom (author of *The Closing of the American Mind*), and get ready for our dinner in the Old City with (among others) Saul's old pal Teddy Kollek, Mayor of Jerusalem.

Encrustation of curses

'Stone cries to stone,' writes James Fenton.

> My history is proud.
> Mine is not allowed.
> This is the cistern where all wars begin.
> The laughter from the armoured car . . .

From the same poem, 'Jerusalem': 'It is superb in the air . . .'

Bellow and Kollek in 1987

And it is. Many, including the Sages themselves, have claimed that the air of Jerusalem is thought-nourishing. Saul, in his book, is 'prepared to believe it':

> . . . on this strange deadness the melting air presses with an almost human weight . . . the dolomite and clay look hoarier than anything I ever saw. Gray and sunken, in the thoughts of Mr Bloom in *Ulysses*. But there is nothing in the brilliant air and the massive white clouds hanging over the crumpled mountains that suggests exhaustion. This atmosphere makes the American commonplace 'out of this world' true enough to give your soul a start.

As you pick your way from tomb to tabernacle, from shrine to icon, from cave to chasm (each consecrated to a different monotheism – so it's hats off here and shoes on there, and hats on here and shoes off there), you gradually absorb the fact that you are wandering in the graveyard of at least twenty civilisations (their rise and fall punctually enriched by massacre, with blood flowing *bridle deep*). The earth 'acts queerly on my nerves (through the feet, as it were), because I feel that a good part of this dust must have been ground out of human bone'.

*

80

The air feeds thought, but it also feeds one of the opposites of thought – which is faith, which is religion: the belief in a supernatural patriarch, together with a desire to win his favour (through worship). And Jerusalem remains the planetary HQ of idolatry. It is a low-lying babel of confessions.

Look. In the Old City a black-haired man with sidelocks topped by a wide-brimmed black hat, in a black frock coat, walks at speed down this or that blind alley (his face drained of all colour by secluded study, by epic memorisations, among other causes, possibly including the sin of Onan); and he progresses quite unseeingly, like a frantically inspired poet homing in on his desk and his writing pad. The black-clad ghost is halted in mid stride by the upraised palm of a tanned and cuboid middle-aged American in a hot-pink T-shirt and polka-dot Bermudas.

'My friend!' the American cries. 'My friend! Time to think anew! Oh, time to feel *Jesus* come into your heart. Come into your heart with such love . . .'

The Hasid pauses long enough to form an expression of concentrated, of distilled incredulity, and then, with a bristling flourish, strides on. Watching him go, the American sorrowfully shakes his head and mutters to himself about Israeli narrowmindedness . . . You see, he is a born-again fundamentalist, and his goal is modest enough: all he's trying to do is speed up the Second Coming, which can't get started until every single Jew has been Christianised.

Only literal evangelicals take the conversion of the Jews as a necessary precondition (for Apocalypse and then Rapture); everyone else takes it as a metaphor for the end of time. 'I would love you ten years before the flood,' Andrew Marvell assures his coy mistress, 'And you would, if you please, refuse / Till the conversion of the Jews.' And the Jews too will tarry, as will their own Messiah . . . That hill up there, Megiddo, is earmarked for Armageddon – the last battle between good and evil. Then the dead will eventually be kicked awake by furious angels, to face the Day of Judgment.

Hitchens had recently spent time in Israel, and I wished we were there together in Jerusalem that spring – to wonder at this fantastic entrepôt of wild goose chases, snark hunts, and fool's errands. Here the faithful use up nearly all our metaphors for futility. Look at them, grasping at shadows, writing on water. No one is visibly trying to extract blood from a stone; but if you want to see an endless press of people beating their heads against a brick wall then go to the Wailing Wall itself, on the western flank of the Holy Mount.

Seeing the worshippers slowly jerk back and forth in their rockinghorse rhythm (also strikingly onanesque), Christopher would have felt contempt, with perhaps a garnish of pity; me, I felt a weaker resistance – say bafflement and exasperation; and Saul, without question, would be feeling something else again.

In him the religious impulses survived. Wistful, tentative, diffident – but still there; you could sense it in the restlessness of the eyes: and it was an indispensable component of who he was. What other modern master, describing a sunshot New England landscape, would write 'Praise God' and unironically refer to 'God's veil'?

Like Christopher, Saul was an old Trotskyist, and temperamentally anti-clerical (sympathy was almost wholly withdrawn from religion once it got itself organised and collectivised); but even the pilgrim, scraping his pale brow against the slabs and boulders of the Wailing Wall, would not be uncongenial to him.* It seems that what he valued was the same thing Christopher despised: continuity, rote continuity. Rote continuity, to Saul, was still continuity. Continuity by heart, he might have said . . .

Bellow was alive to all that was maddening and impossible about Jerusalem, about Israel. It was he who redirected our attention to Herman Melville's travel notes of 1857. Melville (a most interesting and attractive case) was recovering from some kind of psychosomatic breakdown, considering himself 'finished' after *Moby-Dick* had uneventfully come and gone (back in 1851, when he was thirty-eight). He was still physically vigorous. After Jerusalem (the 'color of the whole city is grey and looks at you like a cold grey eye in a cold old man'), he rode to the Dead Sea: 'A mounted escort of some 30 men, all armed. Fine riding.' And then Judea:

. . . whitish mildew pervading whole tracts of landscape –
bleached – leprosy – encrustation of curses – old cheese – bones

---

* 'The children of the race [the 'bootlegger's boys reciting ancient prayers'], by a never-failing miracle, opened their eyes on one strange world after another, age after age, and uttered the same prayer in each, eagerly loving what they found.' The scene is Napoleon Street, Montreal – 'rotten, toylike, crazy and filthy, riddled, flogged with harsh weather' – in the early 1920s. From *Herzog* (1964).

of rocks, – crunched, knawed, & jumbled . . . *No moss as in other ruins – no grace of decay – no ivy – the unleavened nakedness of desolation . . . Wandering among the tombs* – till I begin to think myself one of the possessed with devels.

That is the phrase, that is exactly what you writhingly thrill and shiver to in the Holy Land. The encrustation of curses.

The actual

'One day when he saw me in the library he asked me to come to dinner. And I said yes, with a shrug. I thought, I know – pizza and dictation.'

Rosamund must've told me this later on, but I helpfully insert it here . . . She was a grad student in Chicago. And when professors invited you over after dark it was for exactly that: pizza and dictation.

'But when he opened the door to me he was in an apron. He was cooking.'

There was wine and there was dinner; there was no pizza and no dictation.

That dinner was in 1984. 'And since then we haven't spent a night apart.'

I keep disclaiming any interest in Saul's personal life, but of course I already knew a great deal about it – and on terms of the most searching intimacy – from his fiction. And as I gazed at Rosamund, I no doubt slightly protectively wondered how it would go. I seemed to remember that wife number two or number three wrote a piece entitled 'Mugging the Muse' . . .

Because Saul wrote fiction about real men and women. Even as I type those words (on page 83 of a novelised autobiography) I haven't lost the suspicion that writing fiction about real men and women is an extraordinary thing to go and do.

And the first serious life-writer – come to think of it – was someone Saul and I always argued about (Saul having the higher opinion of him): David Herbert Lawrence (1885–1930). D.H.L. started it, and he started much else. In actuarial terms Lawrence (like Larkin, one of his greatest admirers) died without issue; culturally, though, he left behind him two of the biggest children ever to be strapped into highchairs: the sexual revolution and life-writing . . .

When a writer is born into a family, Philip Roth has fondly but slyly said (more than once), that's the end of that family . . . Ah, but only if that writer is a life-writer. It is life-writing, not writing, that is the homebreaker. In fact, life-writing goes so far as to flirt with criminality: throughout his career Lawrence was bedevilled by the law, and they went after him on two main counts – obscenity and *libel*.

In Saul's case, auto-fiction gave rise to weeklong bouts of sleepless anxiety about lawsuits (he made last-minute proof changes, he asked people to sign waivers) – plus family troubles (with father and eldest brother), broken or suspended friendships, the deepening rancour of ex-wives and ex-lovers, and above all the indecipherable disquiet of children. It is morally treacherous ground, and Bellow himself thought the question 'diabolically complex'.* Diabolically complex, and – I would've thought – fatally self-shackling. Fiction is freedom? Well, the life-writer seems to be crying out for boundaries and impediments and restraints. Crying out for them, or crying out against them – but nevertheless inviting them in.

And Amos Oz was shackling himself, by being a public voice, and so were Yehoshua and David Grossman and others, and they knew it and complained about it, expressively describing this burden – but they could not do otherwise.

In Israel, Yehoshua has said, the writer cannot attain the 'true solitude' that is the 'prerequisite' of art. 'Rather, you are continuously summoned to solidarity,' summoned not by any 'external compulsion' but 'from within yourself'.

---

* James Wood, I think, got close to the nub of it when he wrote that 'an awkward but undeniable utilitarianism' needs to be applied: 'the number of people hurt by Bellow is probably no more than can be counted on two hands, yet he has delighted and consoled and altered the lives of thousands of readers'. In other words, right-and-wrong must bend to an author of sufficient quality and reach . . . Clio, the muse of history, and Erato, the muse of lyric poetry and hymns, might express unease at such presumption. But fiction is a young form (b. 1600), and auto-fiction is younger still (b. 1900), and there is, anyway, no muse to stick up for fiction – or to inspire its practitioners with the purity of her example. Perhaps that's why fiction has always been a rougher barrio than any of the others.

You cannot do otherwise. And the same went for Saul: if it comes from within yourself, then you cannot do otherwise. No novelist can.

D.H.L. failed to get anywhere much with 'direct experience', in my view. No one gets anywhere much with 'life'. Its limitations are life's limitations: poverty of incident, repetitiveness, imaginative thinness, and shapelessness.

And there is something too *democratic* in it. Why surrender so much initiative and autonomy – so much power? Of writers, novelists are the most tyrannical. A playwright menially bows to practical logistics, a poet is menaced by tradition and formal constraints. But Lawrence wasn't wrong when he said that the great thing about the novel was that you could 'do anything with it'. Novelists are power-crazed usurpers; they are presidents-for-life who have illegalised all opposition . . .

If I had to define writer's block, I would say: It is what happens when the subconscious, for whatever reason, has become inert or has even absented itself. With auto-fiction, the subconscious is nearby and available; it is just woefully underemployed.

But Saul Bellow did get somewhere with the real, the actual; he found in it an uncovenanted freedom. His way of doing this was completely instinctive, and blindingly radical.

Divorce

To the British, serial matrimony is 'very American' (not utterly unlike serial murder): a national enthusiasm to which writers show no obvious resistance. We associate it with Americans, but it is not something that anybody associates with Jews: divorce, let alone recurrent, recidivist divorce, is surely a goyish indulgence, like dipsomania. The big bearded WASP Ernest Hemingway might have had four wives; but Saul Bellow had five – and Norman Mailer had six, like Henry VIII.

There was, I felt, something *voulu* about all Norman's marrying and divorcing, as there was about all his drinking, his drugging, his loudmouthing and showboating, his slumming, his brawling . . . It was as if he had set himself the goal of becoming, not only the iconic anti-hero and anti-citizen ('I am an American *dissident*'), but also the perfect anti-Jew. All this marrying and divorcing verged on the parodic: as if to prove the point, Mailer divorced one wife, married and divorced another, and married yet another – all in the space of a week. Bellow wasn't like that.*

Still, five marriages meant four divorces. And even one divorce, my father wrote, 'was an incredibly violent thing to happen to you' – because you're now in a war (and it's usually a dirty war) with someone you loved. I had felt divorce from the vantage of a child, and I always feared it – as an admission of failure, above all. In Israel I was bathed in wavelets of a helplessness that I thought might precede defeat – not constantly, or even often, but every now and again.

Rosamund would not experience divorce. I soon knew what she was: one of nature's straight arrows. Like my mother, Hilary Ann Bardwell. Straight arrows can come from any source and any direction. And they are very thin on the ground, these people with no deviousness and no airs. And another thing: Rosamund was not just thoroughly committed – she was also thoroughly in love.

In Vermont on their wedding day, 25 August 1989

* He wasn't like this, either. During a marital clash at a riotous party (November 1960), Mailer stabbed his second wife, Adele Morales, in the chest and in the back. As she lay haemorrhaging on the floor, Mailer reputedly muttered, 'Let the bitch die.' And she nearly did die: the blade had pierced the membrane enclosing her heart. Mailer

I already knew, as any reader of *Herzog* would already know, that Saul was a suitor with 'an angry heart', a suitor both sore and tender, the product of a collision: 'At home, inside the house, an archaic rule; outside, the facts of life.' He was like the poet in Peter Porter's volume *Once Bitten, Twice Bitten*: often bitten, but never shy, and still coming back for more.

Years later Rosamund would say, of this persistence, that Saul wanted and needed physical love at the centre of his life. And I thought of my father, back in 1987, sitting by the fire, unattached at sixty-five, and saying, yes, yes, he was 'basically all right. But it's only half a life without a woman'.

Asked to name the Walt Disney character he would most like to meet, Andy Warhol selected Minnie Mouse. Why Minnie? 'Because she can get me close to Mickey.'

Now, Rosamund is not Minnie, and Saul is not Mickey, and it never crossed my mind until after the friendship was long established. But that was what Rosamund did: she got me close to Saul. She did it in her person, and with the transfusional power of her youth. She was not just his Muse and his Eros, she was also his Agape.*

Rosamund was a woman whose atavisms became visible only in her virtues: savagely protective, barbarically loyal. She would need that atavistic fire (though not yet, not for more than a decade), and then those virtues would be fully stretched.

*

was arraigned for attempted manslaughter (in the end his lawyer bargained it down to simple 'assault'). What tipped Norman over the edge, as Adele screamed back at him? Not the scurrilous doubts she cast on his manhood and sexual orientation. No, the husband cracked when the wife questioned his talent, intolerably suggesting that Norman was inferior to Dostoevsky . . . Mailer's iconoclasm had many targets, probably including the notion of the good Jewish son. But we should be grateful that the notion of the good Jewish mother was fully embraced by Fanny Mailer: 'My kids are tops,' she summarised. And of her controversial son, Fanny settled for saying, 'If Norman would stop marrying these women who make him do these terrible things . . .' Matrimonially, Norman and Saul had one thing in common: the best came last.

* The sister of Aphrodite, Agape (pronounced like *canapé*) symbolises many kinds of love, 'divine love', 'sacrificial love', but her meaning seems to have settled on 'social love', or comity. The social-realist novel needs Eros, of course; but it also needs Agape.

We live this way

Visiting Jerusalem in the late 1920s, the young Arthur Koestler found its beauty 'inhuman': 'It is the haughty and desolate beauty of a walled-in mountain fortress in the desert, of tragedy without catharsis.' Catharsis: the processing and the purgation of pity and terror.

'I pass the little coffee shop', wrote Saul in 1976,

> outside which the bomb exploded a few days ago. It is burnt out. A young cabdriver last night told . . . me that he had been about to enter it with one of his friends when another of his pals called to him. 'He had something to tell me so I went over to him and just then the bomb went off and my friend was there.* So now my friend is dead.' His voice, still adolescent, was cracking. 'And this is how we live, mister! Okay? We live this way.'

When the time came we all safely disbanded – a good six months before the (First) Intifada, which would start in December . . . Getting to the other planet, via El Al, is arduous, but getting back from it is just a slightly worse-than-average airline experience. The Bellows returned to America, and the Amises returned to England. In London I continued to read up on Israel – though my question about Zionist eyesight went unanswered for another twenty-six years. I'll come to that answer in a page or two; it is shockingly stark.

. . . There was a terroristic incident – in the Hitchensian sense – on our flight home. We were in the business-class cabin, which as well as being unusually garish was unusually empty. A lone pair of Hasids sent over the stewardess to tell Julia that they objected to her presence, on grounds (it was conceded in a regretful whisper) of possible menstruation . . . In Julia's long and loud response I saw and heard not only rightfully appalled indignation, but also a) decisive

---

* 'The bomb in the bar will explode at thirteen twenty. / Now it's just thirteen sixteen. / There's still time for some to go in, / And some to come out.' This is the opening of 'The Terrorist, He's Watching' by Wisława Szymborska. It occurs to me that the second couplet would be even darker if the lines were transposed, reading, 'There's still time for some to come out, / And some to go in.'

antipathy to Israel, and b) renewed contempt for religion and patriarchy, and c) disappointment (or so I imagined) in a second husband who had failed to fill the void left by the first.

Zeal

I later found out that 1987 witnessed the convergence of certain historical lines, a convergence that would change the Middle East and (for an indefinite period) change the world . . .

On May 27 of that year there was a gala dinner in New York, organised by the American Friends of Ateret Cohanim ('Crown of the Priests'). In his address the leader of the movement, Rabbi Shlomo Aviner, summarised its aims:

> We must settle the whole land of Israel, and over all of it establish our rule. The Arabs are squatters. I don't know who gave them authorisation to live on Jewish land. All mankind knows that this is our land. Most Arabs came here recently. And even if some Arabs had been here for two thousand years, is there a statute of limitations that gives a thief a right to its plunder?

The main speaker at the event was the Israeli Ambassador to the UN (a successor of the redoubtable Abba Eban), Benjamin Netanyahu, destined to oust David Ben Gurion as Israel's longest-serving prime minister.

Eight months later, on December 9, after several violent incidents (the precipitant was a car crash that killed four Gazan workmen), the First Intifada began. *Intifada*: literally 'a jumping up in reaction'; 'to shake oneself', 'to shake off'. Over the following five years, Israeli deaths numbered 185; as always in these intramural conflicts, Palestinian deaths were very roughly ten times higher (estimated at 1,500). And of course the First Intifada, compared to the Second, now seems implausibly tame.

On February 11, 1988, a new political party was established in the Holy Land. Drawing on the inhabitants of the twenty-seven refugee camps within Israel and the million-strong population of Gaza, it called itself the Movement of the Islamic Resistance, *Harakat al-Muqawamah al-Islamiyyah*, and was soon known by its Arabic acronym, Hamas, or *zeal*; it was thus a key element in what some call the Islamic Revival, and others call political Islam, or Islamism, and yet others call *takfir*. This was a movement that was reaching critical momentum, and this was its founding idea: *Islam huwa al hali* – Islam, far from being the problem, *is the solution*.

Islamist policy on Israel was maximally rejectionist and maximally Judaeocidal. Hamas itself quotes from *The Protocols of the Elders of Zion* – that long-exploded Tsarist fabrication – in its *charter*, if you can believe. Yes, but if you can believe . . .

Is believing seeing, or is it not seeing?

Ninety years earlier, in April 1897, a man called Herbert Bentwich, accompanied by twenty other Zionists, went on an exploratory pilgrimage to a certain province of the Ottoman Empire. Bentwich and the group he led were not from the ghetto or the shtetl; they were unbuffeted by White Guards and Black Hundreds. Affluent professionals, they sailed in style from London (the trip was catered by Thomas Cook, with carriages, horsemen, guides, servants). Their mission, assigned to them by the founder of political Zionism, Theodor Herzl, was to assess the feasibility of settling in Palestine, and to submit a report to the first Zionist Congress (November 1897). Herzl's Zionism was secular, even atheistic; but Bentwich was a believer.

Ari Shavit is a modern Israeli, an author and veteran *Haaretz* columnist; he is also a great-grandson of the Right Honourable Herbert Bentwich. In *My Promised Land: The Triumph and Tragedy of Israel* (2013) Shavit retraces that Cook's Tour. We remember Bentwich's task: to decide whether the Jews should spurn this land or settle on it. Shavit feelingly but unsparingly interjects:

> My great-grandfather is not really fit to make such a decision. He does not see the Land as it is. Riding in the elegant carriage from Jaffa to Mikveh Yisrael, he did not see the Palestinian village of Abu Kabir. Travelling from Mikveh Yisrael to Rishon LeZion, he did not see the Palestinian village of Yazur . . . And in Ramleh he does not really see that Ramleh is a Palestinian town.

And so it continues, as Bentwich trundles on, crisscrossing the entire region:

> There are more than half a million Arabs, Bedouins, and Druze in Palestine in 1897. There are twenty cities and towns, and hundreds of villages. So how can the pedantic Bentwich not notice them? How can the hawkeyed Bentwich not see that the Land is taken? . . . My great-grandfather does not see because he is motivated by the need not to see. He does not see because if he does see, he will have to turn back. But my great-grandfather cannot turn back.

He believes, so he cannot turn back. He believes, so he does not see. As a case of selective blindness this would be sufficiently remarkable. But Bentwich is in the vanguard of something far more extraordinary.

One member of his group was Israel Zangwill, the internationally celebrated writer known as 'the Dickens of the Ghetto', who at the turn of the century would popularise the Zionist slogan, 'A land without a people for a people without a land'. By 1904 Zangwill had changed his mind (or regained full consciousness); he delivered a speech in New York which startled his audience and scandalised world Jewry (and for this 'heresy' he was pressured out of the movement for a decade). Palestine, he let it be known, was populated.

Zangwill added, again controversially, that the Jews would have to learn the arts of violence, and claim the land with fire and sword.

The spirits of the shady night

And I went on reading Bellow, too . . . Regular novelists, non-life-writing novelists, how do they go about it? Typically they assemble their cast of individuals and then engage in a struggle for coherence; and the more ambitious of them, having long ago assumed universality, are now also struggling to achieve it on the page.

With Bellow the process seems to operate in the other direction. He stares his way into the individual with a visionary power, a power that adores and burns, and so finds a way to the universal.

'The rapt seraph that adores and burns' is a line from Alexander Pope. In angelology, with its nine orders, the seraphim are one rung down from the cherubim; and whereas the sovereign cherubs are equipped with 'the full, perfect, and overflowing vision of God', the seraphs are engaged in 'an eternal ascension toward Him in a gesture both ecstatic and trembling . . .'*

Bellow is a seraph, aspiring up, up (and as a Chicagoan, impatient with eternity, he quietly hopes for due acceptance on the uppermost tier). He is a nature poet almost rivalling Lawrence (who could tell you what this or that plant looked like in any given week of the year), and when he turns to society he is a nature poet now dealing in humans.

He is a sacramental writer; he wants to transliterate the given world. He pirates the real; he is something like a plagiarist of Creation.

If countries are like people, then people are like countries.

In common with most inhabitants of the free world, I am a liberal parliamentary democracy (one with certain grave constitutional flaws).

I have known human-sized despotisms and theocracies. I have known oligarchs and anarchs and banana republics. I have known failed states . . . My oldest friend Robinson was a failed state. My younger sister Myfanwy was a failed state . . .

Saul was a regional superpower – like Israel. Saul wanted and needed Israel to exist and survive; he identified his manhood with it, compelled by the events in Eastern Europe between 1941 and 1945. But he was a social realist, and saw things as they really were.†

Bentwich was actuated by a sense of religious homing. The result, half a century later, would be Israel – a land chosen and duly settled

---

* The commentary is provided by the non-believer Jorge Luis Borges in one of his most charming and informative essays, 'A History of Angels'. Angels outnumber us mortals, and by a wide margin: every good Muslim 'is assigned two guardian angels, or five, or sixty, or one hundred [and] sixty'. Borges (like Bellow) formed a spiritual alliance with angels: 'I always imagine them at nightfall,' he writes, 'in the dusk of a slum or a vacant lot, in that long, quiet moment when things are gradually left alone, with their backs to the sunset, and when colours are like memories or premonitions of other colours.'

† In *To Jerusalem and Back* Bellow quotes a leftist as saying, 'We came here to build a just society. And what happened immediately?' Bellow's stance, here, was centre-leftist: along with Oz, Yehoshua, and Grossman, he supported the *two-state solution*. The left had a plurality in 1987; by 2013 it belonged to the fringe, or the past, polling at 7 per cent. And the two-state solution was dead.

by hallucinators . . . And today they are in the bind described in the closing couplet of Andrew Marvell's 'An Horatian Ode upon Cromwell's Return from Ireland'. In the course of a partly sectarian war, Puritans v. Catholics (1649–53), Cromwell brought to Ireland conquest, famine, plague, and death (eliminating 20 per cent of the population).

'March indefatigably on,' Marvell nonetheless urged the Lord Protector:

> Still keep thy sword erect;
> Besides the force it has to fright
> The spirits of the shady night,
> The same arts that did gain
> A pow'r, must it maintain.

But power corrupts, and maintaining power corrupts; and violence corrupts.

Guideline
Literature and Violence

So. From the Lord Protector to the Great Pretender . . .

Exactly a year has gone by since Donald J. 'announced' (I'm sure you recall the scene on the burnished chariot of the Trump Tower escalator: June 2015), and now's a good time to pause, take stock, and get our bearings.

In my struggle to assimilate Donald Trump – and as you see *The Art of the Deal* (1987), *Think Big and Kick Ass in Business and Life* (2007), and *Crippled America* (his campaign manifesto, released last November) are there on the table – I've found some guidance in two oddly undervalued hypotheses, namely 'The Barry Manilow Law' and 'The Maggot Probability'.

Let's begin with the Barry Manilow Law (promulgated by Clive James). When faced by the inexplicable popularity of this or that performer or operator, apply the Barry Manilow Law, which states: *Everyone you know thinks Barry Manilow is absolutely terrible. But everyone you don't know thinks he's great.* And bear in mind that the people you know are astronomically outnumbered by the people you don't know . . .

As with Barry, so with Donald – but there's an important difference. The Barry Manilow fans cannot increase my exposure to Barry Manilow, but the Donald Trump fans can certainly make me watch, hear, and otherwise attend to Donald Trump – maybe until February 2025 (when I'll be well over seventy and, more to the point, he'll be nearing eighty . . .).

If that happens then the Maggot Probability (formulated by Kingsley Amis) will come into play. It would work as follows: faced day after day by the senseless notions and actions of an elderly madcap, I won't bother to parse and analyse. I'll simply shrug and say to myself, *It's probably just the maggot*, or alternatively, *The maggot's probably acting up*. The maggot is the virus or bacterium – or actual grub, with antennae and maw – that devours an ageing brain; and the maggot acts up whenever it finds a patch of relatively healthy grey matter, and settles down to a square meal.

. . . I adopt this facetious tone more or less willy-nilly, because Trump's candidacy is in itself a sick joke. It began as a business venture – an attempt to boost his tarnished brand (mineral water, neckties). Then someone like Steve Bannon told him that his only imaginable route to Pennsylvania Avenue lay in white supremacism. And Trump, perhaps recognising that whiteness (endorsed by maleness) was his only indisputable strength, limply acquiesced.

Next, having registered the stupendous welcome given to this approach, Trump began underscoring it with the moronic sincerity of violence – inciting his crowds to 'beat the crap' out of protestors, and openly thirsting for mass deportations and collective punishments (plus more torture and more police brutality) . . . Doing harm to the defenceless: it seems to be a recent enthusiasm, an urge awakened or unleashed by his political rise. And on the way he has discovered something about himself. He likes it. He is one of those people who finds violence exciting.

Which surprised me, I confess. In his memoir *The Art of the Deal* (heavily and cleverly ghosted by Tony Schwartz), Donald, then aged forty, comes across as a man instinctively averse to the rough-and-ready aspects of his trade (coercive rent-collections, coercive evictions, etc.), associating 'that kind of thing' with his rags-to-riches father, the gnarled and mottled Fred C. Trump; and while Fred was applying himself in the outer boroughs, the young Donald, his gaze on Manhattan, was tonily nourishing 'loftier dreams and visions'. We therefore presume that Trump's sudden liking for violence is just another corruption: violence vivifies his proximity to power.

Joe the Plumber never got anywhere. As against that, next month in Cleveland, Ohio, Don the Realtor will be anointed as the . . . But wait. I'll return to Trump at the end of the section, if there's time (as you know, tomorrow morning we're off to England), and after that you'll also be away for a while. So let's get on. And we won't be changing the subject. The subject will still be violence.

What is the good of the novel, what does it do, what is it for?

On this question there are (as so often) two opposed schools of thought, in the present case the aesthetes versus the functionalists. The aesthetes would wearily and indeed pityingly explain that the novel serves no purpose whatever (it is just an artefact – nothing more). The functionalists see it as earnestly progressive in tendency: fiction is (or should be) involved in improving the human condition.

Well, the progressivists may indeed be wrong, I have always felt; but the aesthetes can't possibly be right. We can, if we like, sophisticatedly agree that a certain kind of novel can be purposeless. But can a novelist be purposeless, be monotonously purposeless, for an entire adult lifetime? Can anybody?

It's a matter of pressing interest, I find. What is the purpose of my average day?

If you'd asked me that five years ago, I would've equably cited John Dryden, who said that the purpose of literature is to give 'instruction and delight'. That verdict goes back three centuries, and in my opinion has worn pretty well.*

You hope to delight, and also to instruct. Instruct in a way that you hope will stimulate the reader's mind, heart, and, yes, soul, and make the reader's world fuller and richer. My ambition is summed up by a minor character in the late-period Bellow novel *The Dean's December*: a stray dog, on the streets of Bucharest, whose compulsive barks seem to represent 'a protest against the limits of dog experience (for God's sake, open the universe a little more!)'.

And that's what I would have answered in early 2011. Then I read Steven Pinker's massive and authoritative *The Better Angels of Our Nature*, in which the author – a cognitive scientist, a psychologist, a linguist, and a master statistician – fully earns and justifies his subtitle, which is *Why Violence Has Declined*.

Violence has declined, has drastically declined. You frown; and on first hearing this I too frowned. Because it certainly doesn't feel that

---

* 'Delight is the chief if not the only end of poesy. Instruction can be admitted but in the second place, for poetry only instructs as it delights' (*An Essay of Dramatick Poesy*). So the pleasure principle had an eloquent champion even then, in 1668.

way – partly explaining why Pinker's book has yet to bring about a real shift in consciousness: his thesis and its conclusions are jarringly counterintuitive, and provoke much natural resistance. My nerve ends insist, as do yours, that the world, with its steady accumulation of weapons of every grade, has never been more violent. But it isn't so.

As measured by Pinker, 'violence' is the probability of sudden death at the hands of others (and includes deaths on the battlefield). Now let me ask you a question: Which was more violent, the England of *The Canterbury Tales* and Richard the Lionheart and the Crusades, or the England of *The Waste Land* and the two world wars?

Professor Pinker ran a survey. The typical respondent 'guessed that twentieth-century England was about 14 per cent more violent than fourteenth-century England. In fact it was 95 per cent less violent.'

Violence has declined. Why and how? And what, you might ask, has this got to do with writing novels?

In his book Pinker presents what he takes to be the decisive influences.

1) The rise of the nation state, which in effect demands the monopoly of violence.* Pre-state societies were basically warlord societies, and they were up to ten times more violent than societies of the later phase. 'Leviathan' wields a police force, and the word *politics* (the art or science of governing) derives from *police*.

2) The rise of *doux commerce* – 'soft' commerce, grounded on cooperation and mutual advantage (and not on cheating, gouging, welching, and sueing).

3) The rise of a modestly generalised prosperity. What used to be called 'a competence' settled on more and more people, giving them more to lose from disruption and more to fear from it.

4) The rise of science and the rise of reason; this included the retreat of superstition and the retreat of that evergreen *casus belli*, religion.

5) The rise of literacy, which gradually burgeoned into a mass phenomenon – roughly 300 years after the invention of printing (1452).

6) The rise of women. Violence is almost exclusively a male preserve, and cultures that 'respect the interests and values of women'

---

* America flexes its exceptionalism in neglecting to disarm its citizens; in Pinker's words it has 'never fully signed on to this clause of the modern social contract'.

are destined to become not only much more peaceful but also much more prosperous.

7) The rise of the novel.

At first number 7 looks like an interloper, don't you think? In terms of efficacy it is no doubt the last among equals; but the novel shouldn't be shy to find itself in such grand geohistorical company. The novel has other reasons for embarrassment, true, but these are minor and comical, having to do with the messiness of its birth.

Rousseau's *Julie, or the New Heloise* (1761) was hugely influential, but the totemic anglophone book, here, is unfortunately Samuel Richardson's *Clarissa* (1748). I own the four-volume Everyman edition, and over time I have put in about a dozen hours with it. And it is terrible. *Clarissa* is terrible, and Richardson is terrible: fussy, prissy, finicky, and batted about the place by anxieties connected to religion, class, and above all sexual repression (pious Clarissa is finally drugged and raped by the brooding anti-hero Mr Lovelace, and dies of shame, all alone). It is in addition unforgivably long – the longest novel in the language.*

But we have to note that early admirers of *Clarissa*, a vast company, felt themselves connected to the heroine with unprecedented intimacy and warmth; they identified, they sympathised, they shared and understood her feelings; a new and quite unexpected stage of the reader–writer relationship had been reached – one that pressed home the elementary lesson about doing to others as you would have them do to you . . . So we feel grateful to Richardson; and never mind, for now, that literary – or literate – England, in the late 1740s, found itself passionately rooting for a prig, and a prig dreamed up by a philistine.

---

* Literary history conclusively humbled *Clarissa* by following it, a year later, with Henry Fielding's *Tom Jones* (and how thuddingly democratic that name must have sounded – cf. Charles Primrose, Tristram Shandy, Peregrine Pickle, Sir Launcelot Greaves) . . . Fielding was already a committed tormentor of Richardson, whose bestselling first novel, the bourgeois penny-dreadful *Pamela, or Virtue Rewarded* (1741), was instantly answered by Fielding's *Shamela* (a contemptuous parody). But it is the example of *Tom Jones*, with its easy candour and humour and sexual straightforwardness, that provides the real refutation. In due course the Richardson-type novel (after a nervously extended stay in the genre mocked by Jane Austen and others, that of the Gothic) died out, while the Fielding-type novel, backed up by *Don Quixote* (thrillingly translated by Tobias Smollett in 1750), went on to constitute fiction in English.

Everything has to start somewhere. And, besides, this deep-sea wave of enlightenment has already rolled through villages (and now extends, as Pinker shows, to our treatment of sexual minorities, of children, and of animals) . . . It seems there was an evolutionary readiness to be more *thoughtful*, in both senses, thinking more, and thinking more considerately.

To return for a moment to the Pinker paradox. 'In 1800,' he writes (in a later book), 'no country in the world had a life-expectancy above forty.' And what is it now? 'The answer for 2015 is 71.4 years' – worldwide. If progress has been made, and it has, why do we persist in feeling it hasn't?

Well, there's the news media of course ('if it bleeds, it leads', etc.); there's the inherent difficulty (as all novelists know) of writing memorably about well-being; and, perhaps most perniciously, there's the intellectual glamour of gloom. The idea that sullen pessimism is a mark of high seriousness has helped to create an organic (perhaps by now a hereditary) resistance to the affirmative and a rivalrous attraction to its opposite – the snobbery of one-downmanship.

Optimists are quickly exasperated by pessimism (I know I am), by the habitual lassitude and disgust we associate with adolescence – early adolescence. So I tell you what: I'm going to leave all that for another fifty pages, and wait till I visit the world HQ of ennui, cafard, and nausée – yes, France.

So for now I'll say au revoir to the counter-Enlightenment spirit, only pausing to glance at Goya's famous etching of 1798. This shows a slumbrous *philosophe* against a background of bats and screech-owls. *The Sleep of Reason*, runs the title, *Brings Forth Monsters*.

On July 21, as we're all aware, that strictly non-combatant bruiser, that chicken-hawk, that valorised ignoramus, that titanic vulgarian (dishonest to the ends of his hair) will be anointed as the Republican contender for the 2016 presidential election.

But tomorrow the Amises fly to London, in good time for the Brexit referendum. Elena has dual nationality, so that'll be two sure votes for Remain . . . And take my word for it, this won't be a close-run thing. As with Scotland and breakaway 'independence' – once you get in that booth, you stop fancying a leap in the dark. No: the Brits are going to stick with the devil they know.

As for the USA . . . In *Crippled America* Trump says that he faced much discouragement along the way – until, that is, 'the American people spoke'. By *the American people* he means, of course, registered Republicans. En masse the American people have their fluctuations, but they're essentially practical, don't you find? Americans respond to leaders who they think will get things done. And I can't believe that a plurality of voters, come November 8, will solemnly reject the most qualified candidate of all time in favour of the least.

So we only have to blush our way through another four months of this before Trump gets booted and hooted out of town on November 9. And then we'll be able to relax, and look forward to putting the memory (at least) of this tragicomic excruciation further and further behind us.

After lights out . . .

After lights out Elena said, 'I stole one of your Valium. In case I fret. About Spats.'

'About Spats? Not Nigel Farage, not Trump. Spats. Elena, let me put your mind at rest. Spats is as happy as a pig in shit out there. Midnight prowls. Birdlings and baby rabbits to rip apart. We'll see Spats soon enough.'

'That's true,' she said. 'Mart. I may be wrong, but you seem to have stopped agonising about your book. Is that true too?'

'Yeah,' he said, 'I have to own up to something.'

'Uh-oh.'

'It's nothing bad. It's good . . . Very early on this year I had a kind of . . . I wasn't at my desk. I was reading on the sofa. I closed my eyes and imagined a visitor had come to the house. Entirely benign. A gentle ghost – a gentle reader, in fact. And guess who it was. My much younger self, come to me with questions. Only I felt more like a girl this time round. It was like receiving a child of mine. Kind of Nat plus Bobbie.'

'Jesus Christ. Were you having one of your episodes d'you think?'

'Probably. Anyway, then I wrote ten pages – fast. Something became undammed. It was me at eighteen, when I used to say to myself, *I don't want to be a writer (or not yet). I want to be a reader. I just want to be a part of it*. Humbly resolved, Elena. Devotional. I just wanted to be a part of it.'

'. . . Okay. Bye now. D'you realise how early we've got to get up? In about half an hour!' She yawned. 'Well if you do go crazy, I'll stand by you. Up to a point.'

'I know you will, my dearest. Up to a point.'

Martin was eighteen, and he was walking just after dark through a distant and neglected suburb of North London when he saw a lit window on the second-lowest floor of a council medium-rise. All it showed were the dark-blue shoulders of an unoccupied armchair. And he thought (this is word for word),

That would be enough. Even if I never write, complete, publish anything at all, ever, that would be enough. A padded seat and a standard lamp (and of course an open book). That would be enough. Then I'd be a part of it.

Chapter 4
The Night of Shame

She's scaring me, Hitch

'Ah, you're opening up at last. Go on, Little Keith. Sob it all out.'

'Well,' I said. 'Whatever else I might like about her, and there's plenty I like about her, I haven't got to the end of her physically. There's still a long way to go.'

'How's she managed that? After – after two years . . . Is it all the purdahs?'

'They help, I suppose.' I had never confessed to Christopher about the true extent – and the true durations – of all the purdahs. 'Have you ever dated a religious chick?'

'No. Or not knowingly. Of course,' he said, 'you've dated whole nunneries and priories of religious chicks.'

'Yeah – there wasn't any way round it till I was sixteen or seventeen. All my ones were working class or lower middle, and that lot were all religious. Gaw, what you had to go through, to get a kiss on the cheek.'

'Mm, I'd like God to know before he dies just what a huge geohistorical *turn-off* he's been. Think, Little Keith. Not just the prohibitions but the guilt. Think of all the fiascos, all the no-shows, and all the hairtrigger ejaculations. And don't forget all the consoling handjobs – tearfully aborted for fear of blindness and insanity . . .'

'All true, O Hitch. When Dad was a kid the school vicar took them round the chronic ward of a madhouse saying one wank and you'll be just like them. But every now and then – and you may not know this –

every now and then old Nobodaddy bestirs himself and cooks you up . . . one hell of a fuck.'

'Really?' Christopher's *intent* look: not so much a frown as a bulging stare. 'This is a real gap in my religious knowledge. In my RK. Please continue.'

It was seven-fifteen on a Wednesday morning, so we were on the train bound for Southend and the printers' plant (it was our turn to help check the final page proofs and put the *Statesman* to bed). We never uttered a word of complaint about the six o'clock start, the artistic misery of Liverpool Street Station, the sopping scud of the eastern shore, the reeking hot metal: all this felt to us like honest toil . . . On our laps we now nursed trembling Styrofoam cupfuls of weak milky coffee. Reduced for now to the blandest of beverages, we were, on the other hand, exercising our civil right as travellers in a smoking car. I said,

'With ninety-nine per cent of religious chicks, sex comes at them like a horror film. Saturated in dread. Then time passes, and they slowly ease into it, getting less religious along the way. But this little minority, Hitch, this one per cent, they find out very early on that they've got a real appetite for it, and a real talent for it too. So of course they start putting themselves about. And guess what. Along the way they get *more* religious.'

'As a means of . . . extenuation? And what's the result? I mean in the bedroom?'

'Well. It's not like the usual Home Counties fuck, I can tell you that. You know, when they, where you . . .'

'Where you both bounce around for a bit, then it's over, and she makes a joke.'

'Yeah. It's not like that. It's no joke for a start. It's . . .'

I turned and looked out – through the diagonal rivulets slowly jolting their way down the glass. Beyond, the east of the city crept past (always in my memory under a wet blanket of ashen grey, whatever the season); and then the stops would glide towards us in their turn, Manor Park, London Fields, Seven Kings . . .

'It's like this. As well as being tremendously carnal and dirty and everything, it's suddenly got all hushed and eye to eye, and glazed, and hypnotic. With an edge of doom to it.'

Christopher said, 'That sounds . . . absorbing.'

'Oh it is. But see, Hitch, and this is the difficult thing to imagine. She doesn't just think it, she knows it – she knows for a fact she's going to Hell. Father Gabriel said so. And it's like the Fall, every time she does it. Full of woe. *All* our woe.'

'Mm. Correct me if I'm wrong, Mart, but this must involve her in some strain.'

'Oh a great deal of strain. It's all right for me. *I* don't think I'm going to Hell.'

'*You* don't think you'll be scorched and peed on for eternity.'

'. . . Eternity's weird, don't you find, as an idea? It's not that it never ends – it never even begins.'

'No. A trillion years into it and it's not a heartbeat nearer to being over.' We lit fresh cigarettes and he went on, 'When faced with eternal torture, it's very hard to look on the bright side. And if she really *believes* it, as billions do . . . Maybe that's why she needs her rests. All her poor little purdahs. If it scours her out like that.'

'That's exactly what I used to whimper to myself – during purdahs. Anyway. It's suddenly getting critical. And crises can't go on being crises. *They're* finite.'

'And this one's whisking itself to the boil.'

'Yeah, and bubbling over. You should see her at the parties she drags me to. *Flirting's* a fucking useless word for it.* Any old arbitrageur, any old ski bum, and her gaze fills with – as if she's never even imagined there could ever be anyone quite so heavenly.'

'. . . Aw, terrible she've been.'

'Yes, terrible she've been. *Terrible*. You know, she's always had a grievance. Before I came along. And now it's all directed at me, because I'm nearest. So what do I get? Torture. What kind of torture? The sexual kind. I've had my cock teased in the past, but I've –'

'You've had it teased clean off. That Melinda.'

---

* Now, with a dictionary and a thesaurus on my lap, I scroll through the indulgent synonyms ('captivate', 'tantalise'), seeing no connection at all to the practices of Phoebe Phelps, till I arrive at the following: '(of a bird) flap or wave (its wings or tail) with a quick flicking motion'. And again with *coquette* (a feminised 'dimin. of *coq* "cock"'): '1. a flirtatious woman 2. a crested Central and South American hummingbird'. And that was Phoebe: a quickly flickering hummingbird, diffusing an agitation that looked obscurely purposeful, as she pollenised her garden moving from stem to stem . . .

'Compared to Phoebe, Melinda was a wallflower. Melinda teased it – she never *taunted* it. Let me try and give you some idea.'

The cold sea mist – the brume, the haar – of Southend was drooling all over the train by the time Christopher said, '. . . It pains me, Mart, but I have to ask whether you think she's trying to make you – lose heart. Lose heart and retreat.'

'Mm, well that's always been her style. More or less from the first date. *Why are you still here?* And now suddenly it's a good question.'

'And what would be your answer?'

'. . . I suppose I'm just hanging on for the odd religious fuck, but part of it's plain vulgar curiosity. No – plain human interest. She's like a character in a novel where you want to skip ahead and see how they turned out. Anyway. I can't give up now.'

'Having come this far, and so near the end?'

'There's that. But I can't give up when she's all raw like this. Jesus, it's like having the care of a toddler. What if she hurts herself on my watch? Who can I entrust her to?' We started gathering our things. 'On the way back I want you to tell me all you've ever learnt about mad chicks.'

'Oh. I'm supposed to know a thing or two about mad chicks am I?'

'Yeah,' I said. 'Yeah, mad chicks flock to the Hitch. I don't mean the ones you end up with, I mean the ones you spurn. The crazed beauties who lash your grim rock. Tell me about mad chicks.'

'All right. What about them?'

The train was now slaked of motion. We stood and I said, 'Christ, I hate crazy people. They make *me* crazy. They do. I'm nuts too now. I am.' And I reached up and scratched my scalp with both hands. 'She's scaring me, Hitch.'

Solzhenitskin

Some dates might be useful (this was a dislocating time).

The night of shame, with all its unwelcome wonders, would unfold on July 15/16, 1978 (a Saturday, a Sunday). That particular ride to Southend with Christopher was back in late March. And in early June

Phoebe's postal address changed – from The Hereford, Apartment One, Hereford Road, to Flat 3, 14 Kensington Gardens Square. She moved in.

It was temporary, she said – 'Just part of the new economy drive.' The new economy drive was made necessary by Phoebe's wager of mid-May.* Hereford Road was immediately, and illegally, sublet to three immigrant families – with Phoebe retaining a back bedroom wedged solid with her worldly goods.

It was now May 4, a Friday, and on the phone she was saying,

'Still at Merry's. Who's very sweetly going to drive me over. When she's ready, that is. We've got a minute, so go on. And no, it's *not* too painful for me to talk about.'

'Okay. Just curious, but why d'you keep betting against Mrs Thatcher?'

'I told you. Because I don't want to be ruled by a woman, okay?'

'Yeah, but *betting* against her doesn't make that less likely.'

'It's the principle, Martin. You wouldn't understand. It's a matter of being true to your convictions and your . . . Ah, Merry's emerging at last. Right. I'll be on your doorstep in five minutes.'

There was only the one suitcase – unliftably heavy, but only the one. She stood there on the porch, in her oldest black business suit (with the worn patches and missing buttons).

'Ask me in then,' she said. And he obliged with a twirl of his hand. 'It's like with vampires, Mart,' she went on with a stare of sudden clarity. 'And it's a good vampire rule, this – like them being invisible in mirrors. You see, vampires can't cross your threshold unless you ask them to.'

*

* A long footnote, this, but one that will serve as a short guide to Phoebe's mental state . . . In a party political broadcast of April 15, 1978, Mrs Thatcher referred to Solzhenitsyn as 'Solzhenitskin'. *I heard it! They said she mixed him up with Rumpelstiltskin!* cried Phoebe that night (she had the radio on in the bathroom); and early the next morning she was on the phone with Noel: her forecast was that Thatcher would be ousted as leader (by April 30), and Noel got good odds . . . Of course, Thatcher's error made not the slightest impression, and Phoebe herself only knew it was 'Solzhenitsyn', and not Solzhenitskin or for that matter not Rumpelstiltskin, because all three volumes of *The Gulag Archipelago* were on display in my flat (and I sometimes talked about him and his rural exile in Vermont) . . . *How much was your bet?* I asked her on May 1. She looked away and said, *Well that's the thing. Um. About the same as your advance for the last one.* The advance for my third novel amounted, by the skin of its teeth, to four figures. *Plus about twice your salary.* I was by then full literary editor of the *New Statesman*. So Phoebe had lost £11,000. *In short, Martin,* she said, *I'm ruined.*

Which he definitely had done – asked her to. She did the prompting and the hinting, but he did the asking. This should be noted. Martin certainly noted it: it astonished him. The Next Thing was in its early days, but he was already wondering if in all his life he had ever suffered so . . .

'Martin, I'm ruined,' she'd said in the Fat Maggot on May 2. 'Penniless, and homeless. I'm on the street! I don't even know where I'll lay my –'

'That's all right,' he said. He gave an emphatic nod. 'Move in. Move in with me.'

Unsummoned, and very much against the run of his conscious mind, the invitation just formed on his lips: the words said themselves. And as he sat there, eating bread and cheese in the burbly pub, he wondered why he felt proud, why he felt he had done the right thing – the bold thing, the manly thing, the interesting thing.

Move in with me, he said. And now she was here.

'You know, Mart,' she called as she unpacked in the other room (the only other room), 'we must have our housewarming. One of our Blue Moons.'

Cautiously he stirred. That was the current name for their interludes of passion, Blue Moons (in triple reference to their impurity, their melancholy, and above all their rarity). She said,

'But first I've got to recover from all this insane rushing about. I'm shattered. And how'll we fit it in? It's the party season and my diary's about to burst.' The disembodied voice resumed; and she sounded (he thought) like a hearty aunt in a radio play. 'I was thinking perhaps Sunday. But no! Cohabitation, my friend, isn't all beer and skittles, not by any manner of means. On Sunday, Martin, you'll have to squire me to Morley Hollow – there to seek the paternal blessing. Oh yes. Sir Graeme'll have to forgive us for living in mortal sin. Now – now what have we here?'

. . . If he leant forward, which he did, he could see her, watch her: her reflection in the long mirror on the face of the wardrobe (so no, she was not invisible). And framed in that way, she moved with the temporary innocence of the unknowingly observed . . . Phoebe had in front of her the wrenched-open suitcase; its contents lay at her mercy. With quick fingers she was sorting and grading her smalls and separates, flicking some items away towards the pillows yet seeming to cherish others, at one point raising to her cheek a purple scarf and briefly communing with it . . . Still in the remains of her officewear, Phoebe: the loose blouse, the dark skirt cinched but half unzipped with a white bloom of slip or camisole sprouting out from the haunch. She stopped dead. Staring into nothing, her eyes hardened. Then she steadied, and went on in a private murmur,

'One pair, two pairs, three pairs, four . . . Oh, my clothes, my clothes, my loathsome clothes.'

Over the next few days, while the realignment settled (and while her musky, smiley, gauzy, rumpy, nipply presence thickened round about him), he continued to feel he had something to celebrate. And he continued to wonder why.

Perhaps there were grounds, at least, for some primordial Mesozoic satisfaction, in that it was to him, Martin, mandrill number one, that she gravitated (and not to Lars or Raoul, or to any old arbitrageur or ski bum). No great triumph, clearly, but why disdain a silent grunt of simian support?

Perhaps he was still fantasising that as her champion, guardian, and regent (and as her ruthless slum landlord) certain seigneurial privileges would inevitably begin to come his way. And they did, too, in a sort of sense. In Kensington Gardens Square she was almost constantly naked, or more often practically naked, or at the very least (to use a word she liked) thoroughly déshabillé. He very soon found out that this was not meant as any kind of invitation.

The nudism was new. He remembered Phoebe saying that the Next Thing 'would be a package of measures'; and *display* was clearly one of them, joining *applied flirtation* and *stingey foreplay* (as well as the ever-lengthening purdahs) . . . Now it got complicated for him. At first he liked the idea of her being broke and homeless and above all vulnerable, but now she was actually present, with her toothbrush and her pillowslip of laundry, he soon saw that her vulnerability made her – that her very vulnerability made her invulnerable to unworthy designs . . .

Perhaps, in the end, it was because she was a cryptogram he very much wanted and needed to solve. He had the answer trapped here at Kensington Gardens Square. It was cornered; it couldn't get away.

So let it reveal itself, he thought, let it all come down. What's next is next.

And yet there were moments – the moments in between the other moments – when he knew for a certainty that he was in an alien medium, and out of his depth, and going under. If he closed his eyes he was once again seven years old (the sailboat off the Welsh coast, the bang on the head from the loosened boom, the cartwheeling drop overboard); and, once in, he sank. Is this the way to death then? he wondered. But it was not an unhappy memory. He continued his leisurely descent, too stunned and winded to swim or even struggle; and he seemed to be watching a pretty cartoon, a silent *Fantasia* – sinking through the fathoms of the Bristol Channel, and hoping to witness as much of this blue-black world as he survivably could before someone (his Uncle Mick or one of his older cousins) hoisted him out again.

Morley Hollow

'Father Gabriel will be looking in. Keep left. Now he's sort of nonconformist for a priest in two respects. For a start, he's not poor. Now signal right. In fact he's very lavish. Normally I'd be bringing tons of food and drink but I can save a few quid because Father Gabriel'll be doing all that. Now turn. He adores spending money. He's actually far less pious than my parents. What they adore is poverty.'

'They what?'

'Didn't you know this about Catholics? In a minute the road forks and you go straight ahead. They adore poverty. And cold and damp and discomfort. And dirt. One mustn't forget dirt. It's called *mendicity*. It's meant to uh, to relieve you of distractions from your full devotion to God. Poverty doesn't relieve *me* of distractions. Does it you?'

'No. But I don't mind being distracted from my devotion to God.'

'Oh very droll. Keep going. It's in the cul-de-sac at the end on the right, and it's the one with its own sludge driveway and not just a concrete slot for a Ford Cortina. Ooh look. Clever him, he's beaten us to it. Well at least you'll get a proper drink. They usually serve an oloroso called Folkestone Dew. Eighty pee from Safeway's. Get me close to the grass but leave him room to back out. Mind your shoes.'

The bungalow was called Morley House, even though it was if anything slightly smaller than the other very small bungalows in Morley Hollow, where every bungalow had a name – Dunroamin', HiznHerz, Journey's End, Shangri-La . . .

'Don't be deceived by the exterior. It's not a suburban villa. It's more like a cowshed with the odd stick of furniture in it. You expect to see stacks of sleeping sheepdogs.'

They climbed out and edged past and around Father Gabriel's car, a Mark IX Jaguar, perhaps twenty years old but fiercely burnished. It looked like a hearse but one with artistic lines and contours; the interior with its leather and walnut had the sealed fixity of a confessional. He said,

'What's the other heretical thing about Father Gabriel? He's not poor . . .'

'Uh, oh sorry. And he's not queer.'

———————

I held up my furred toothglass to receive more champagne. The three Phelpses were still in the kitchen unpacking the hamper, and Father Gabriel was genially saying,

'So, Martin – I may call you Martin, mayn't I? – you're here, no doubt, to see Sir Graeme. And to clarify your relationship with his youngest child. A testing moment.'

I shrugged and smiled. 'So will there be a little inquisition?'

'Mm. There's such a scene in one of your father's fairly recent novels. What *is* the title? Anyway, it's most amusingly done. The father, a Mr Cope, asks his daughter's suitor four questions, the first of which is – I take it you're sleeping with my Vivienne?'

'Would you like a seat,' I said and shuffled sideways along the ankle-high sofa.

'No, I'll remain perpendicular for now, thank you – having crouched all morning behind the wheel. You know, going about my rounds.'

He stood over me, sixtyish, sleek, still solid, with thick pewtery hair fringing his clerical collar (a tight black band almost entirely concealing a tight band of white); he also wore a silk-backed waistcoat, striped City trousers, and succulent galoshes.

'Mr Cope asks four questions, all of which the young suitor answers with an indignant negative. Are you sleeping with my Vivvy? The second

110

is, Then I take it you're sleeping with some other young lady – or young ladies? The third is, So perhaps you prefer your own kind? And the fourth is, Ah, then you must surely rely on those solitary practices they warned us about at school?'

'I remember. And when he says no to that, Mr Cope disqualifies him as unnatural.'

Father Gabriel laughed – we both laughed. 'He means no harm, Mr Cope. It's really just a tease, isn't it, or a rhetorical snare. The trick is to say yes to the first question.'

'Or failing that to say yes to the second question. And then go on about how your feelings for Vivvy are on a far higher plane.'

'Very good, Martin. And very filial too.'

'The novel is *Girl, 20*,' I said. Which soon left both of us rather staring at the fact that Phoebe was girl, thirty-six. 'So I suppose Sir Graeme won't ask whether . . .'

'No, he won't. Nor will he ask whether you intend to make an honest woman of her. Because he of course knows that Phoebe's gone her own way – she doesn't *want* to be made an honest woman of. And she's honest already, by her lights, God bless her.'

Crockery and cutlery were being laid out on the Fablon-decked table in the corner. Phoebe and her mother started gathering an assortment of kitchen chairs, and Sir Graeme, jerking upright with a corkscrew in his hand, called out,

'Oh Martin! Would you care to wash your hands before we sit?'

Having followed directions to the lavatory (and found it, and used it), I then followed directions on how to flush it. These were handwritten, and gummed up on the flaking ballcock: 'Pull the chain very slowly downwards, sustain your grip on it's handle, wait at least a minute, then release. Then tug it sharply. Repeat 'til sucess is your's!'

I rinsed my hands under the arctic trickle of the basin, dried them with Bronco toilet paper, and retraced my steps, past gumboots, detergents, groundsheets, a broken hockey stick, a child-scale tin bathtub, a stringless tennis racket . . .

'. . . no Jews or Muslims or Buddhists,' said Phoebe, trailing off.

'It seems, Dallen,' said Father Gabriel with amused regret, 'that "ecumenicism", among the young, has come to stand for a kind of metaphysical BYOB. Whereas all it's ever meant, my dear Phoebe, is good relations between Christians. To avoid such setbacks as for example the Thirty Years War. Gustavus Adolphus . . .'

As he talked on I marked him, I tried to grade him, the very white whites of his clean blue eyes, his full, lineless, and studiously barbered face (Sir Graeme, hunched over at his side, seemed physically benighted, almost medieval, with his craters and orbits and the divots sprouting from his ears and nostrils) . . . Also, Father Gabriel was the only ecclesiarch I'd ever come across who had no twinkliness in him, no unconscious theatricality, no offered excuse for his lifelong commitment to something so elaborate and so flimsy (and so intellectually null) . . . The outward man was worldly, serious, decided, intent.

'Now Grae,' he said, 'before I go, which I must, I want to help you through the uh, the purely formal aspect of our gathering here today. Forgive me, but Romans are such *ninnies* when it comes to their daughters' care. And I –'

'It's all right!' cried Sir Graeme, wagging an agitated finger while he chewed and swallowed. 'I trust him! It's all right!'

'You trust him – that's good. But tell us, Martin, is Sir Graeme being . . . wise?'

'Uh, yes.' I sat up and said, as I'd intended to do if it came to it (but now feeling as coldly fraudulent as I always did whenever I set foot in church). 'Certainly. It'll be as if she's my best friend's sister. An honourable friend, one I'd be ashamed to sadden. She's safe with me.'

Father Gabriel said, 'Why, 'tis a loving and a fair reply.'

And Dallen leant forward and said pleadingly, 'Ah now, and I'm sure he'd be knowing that the girl's a little frailer than she –'

'Oh, *Mum*. Don't *start*.'

Father Gabriel rose to his feet. 'Well I'm off – to visit a woman. And before you set the tongues flapping in the village, she's a spinster of ninety-three.' He went around the table, impressing his goodbyes on everyone including me, and saying, 'Unfortunate word that, *spinster*. With none of the festive associations of *bachelor*. She keeps a "spinster pad" in town? A "gay" spinster?'

Phoebe stood and offered her cheek. 'Well I'm a, I'm a "confirmed" spinster.'

'I know you are, my dear. I know you are.'

During the hour that remained Sir Graeme finished the gull's eggs and the potted shrimps and the beef sausages and the huge game pie and the second bottle of claret, and then went and rocked on his heels with his back to the room's only source of heat. Comfortably muttering to himself, he rocked and twanged away – the one-bar electric fire, the slimline shirt, the shiny old flares.

'Of course it's uninhabitable in winter,' said Phoebe. 'Really terrifyingly cold.'

'Why don't they sell it and get a nice little flat?'

'Sell it? It's worthless. Negative equity. Mortgaged to death.'

'. . . Who was the first Sir Phelps?' Placed in the passenger seat (no better for drink than Graeme), Martin thought of the baronets in Trollope. 'Some soldier or bureaucrat, I suppose, under Queen Victoria . . .'

'Rodney Phelps was uh, *semi*-ennobled in 1661. By Charles II. Sir Rodney's the only one who ever did a stroke or earnt a bean. His son, Sir Reginald, pissed it away. And all the others inherited nothing but debt.'

'Has he got any income, your dad?'

'Yes. He rents out his name for letterheads. Pools firms, casinos. Payday Loans Inc., chairman – Sir Graeme Phelps. Don't imagine the baronetcy helps. It doesn't. It's a deadly secret. He wants people to think he actually *got* it for something. Services to this or that.'

'What did Sir Rodney get it for in 1661?'

'He ran a plantation in Barbados. He got it for services to slavery . . . Uh, how did you hit it off with Father Gabriel? Did you take to him at all?'

'Mm, I did, quite. He has a certain, I don't know, a certain persuasiveness.'

'Yes. He does.'

Dallen – not long before they left (Phoebe was in the lavatory and making the ballcock honk and bray) – laid her hand on Martin's arm and said, 'Phoebe's sisters, they're like Grae. They take the world as it comes. Phoe, though, she's more like myself. It happens sometimes that her mind . . . it goes away, you know? The dear help her, but it does.'

That was all. And it came just as he was warming to the realisation that for the last span of time (with its encumbrances and its patches of awkward new ground) Phoebe had at no point seemed less than sane.

The night of shame: Foreplay

Morning.

On the day of the night of shame all was innocent. And all would remain innocent – for as long as the light held.

'Good morrow to you,' she said, opening her eyes as he brought in her tea. 'Milk! What's this? . . . I hate milk.'

'No you don't.' He assessed her glare, which contained sincere reproach (as if saying, Don't you even know *that* about me by now?). 'Not first thing. It's in the afternoon you like it black.'

'. . . I *hate* milk. But never mind.' She drank her tea. 'Ah, that's better.' She lay back. 'Mart . . . Give me your hand.'*

Having woken around nine, they were washed and dressed by ten. They then made their way to Normann's, the local café. Here he had the still-reliable pleasure of watching his elegantly flutelike girlfriend apply herself to a huge bowl of sugary porridge, a full English breakfast including chips and fried bread, followed (over two pots of coffee), by several rounds of buttered toast thickly lashed with marmalade. Does she get that from her father? he wondered. Unlikely. With Graeme it was mere hunger, with Phoebe it was greed . . .

Together they strolled around for an hour in the unnatural humidity, under a nauseated sky (coppery twilight colours on a felt of blackness so deep that it made everything – trees, buildings, their own faces –

---

* In calmer and happier times, bouts of *heavy petting* were an occasional feature of our weekends. Protracted and strenuous (everything-but and not for the queasy), those sessions used to end with Phoebe – holding a bouquet of paper tissues in her free hand – granting him brisk relief, in the manner of a therapist or, more exactly, a dairymaid. These days it was different: she simply waited for the phase of maximum engorgement, then just stopped, desisted, without a word or a glance. When I eventually rolled out of bed I still had a little diving board (recently bounced on and vacated) attached to my pelvic saddle. You couldn't call it foreplay; nothing followed from it . . . In this chapter, I notice, much that is pertinent but embarrassing has been confined to the footnotes: a sort of internal exile or house arrest.

seem electrochemically pale. And he thought, These are the colours loved by the mad). From his wallet he offered up three, no, four, no, five tenners, and went home to write.*

———————

Afternoon.

She returned around three and disappeared into the bedroom; around five he heard the bare-flame *whump* of the gas water-heater and the rush of the taps. Around six she emerged with a towel turbaned over her hair, wearing a pleated dress shirt (*One of Raoul's cast-offs*, she'd earlier explained. *It's newish but he was already too fat for it*). By this time Martin had reached the end of his effectiveness at the desk and was to be found on the sofa, reading.

'You must get a proper shower fitted, Martin. I can't rinse my hair.'

He said inattentively, 'Isn't there that uh, that rubber tube?'

'But it takes ages because it's all flabby and warped. You just get dribs and drabs . . . Oh, so he's got his nose in a book now, has he.'

'That's right. No fresh air and ruining my eyes.'

He went on reading or at least looking at the page.

'. . . Oh, "poetry",' she said. 'You're such a hypocrite!'

———

* Those spare tenners. Life goes on, after all; and it became clear, a week or two after the cohabitation began, that my monthly income would for a while increase by a factor of twelve. And 'writing', for now, meant humouring Kirk Douglas and Harvey Keitel (who were always in venomous opposition). But that's another story – some of which is told in my fifth novel (1984) . . . The film was presided over by Stanley Donen, who in his twenties co-directed *On the Town* and *Singin' in the Rain* with Gene Kelly . . . One night after work Stanley invited me to dinner at his 'local place'; Phoebe was in Belgrade, so without hesitation I went along to his plush and panelled sanctum in St James's . . . Now at that time Stanley was married to Yvette Mimieux, wife number four (and his past lovers included Judy Holliday and Elizabeth Taylor). Having picked Christopher's brains about girls and madness, I took the chance to pick Stanley's brains about girls and coquetry – a subject that was on its way to becoming my chief concern. Stanley talked discreetly, naming no names, but otherwise with boundless candour, and for almost two hours my ears hummed to tales of Hollywood's most famous vamps (some of them famous actresses, some of them just vamps and famous for nothing else – chorus-liners, body doubles). And even in this company, I reckoned, Phoebe could hold her head high . . . By the way (a footnote to a footnote), nearly forty years later I ran into Harvey Keitel at a Christmas party in Manhattan (December 9, 2016). We agreed that this was one of life's little epiphanies: it was Kirk Douglas's one hundredth birthday.

'Oi,' he said lightly. 'Hark at the pot calling the kettle black. I saw you in there yesterday. Having a sly look at *High Windows*.' P. Larkin, 1974. 'I saw you.'

'Well if you will leave them lying around . . . Shove up then!' He straightened his back and Phoebe eased in beside him. 'And they're meant to be great mates, isn't that right? Him and Kingsley? Lifelong mates.'

'. . . Yeah. Supposedly. Not lifelong. They met at Oxford. During the war.'

'Oh. So he must've pinched your cheek and tousled your hair when you were little.'

'Yeah, he was around, a bit. Maybe once or twice a year he'd come and stay.'

'So he'd have you on his lap. Give you your baths.'

'My baths? Christ no. He really didn't like children. My *baths* . . .'

'Oh, that's funny. Because to me he looks like a classic . . . you know, the kind of bloke that hangs around the parks? I bet, I bet if you went into a copshop with your nippers and lodged a complaint, and they opened their album of local fiends and flashers, that'd be the first face staring up at you. The pasty dome and the specs. Don't you think?'

'Uh, what did Timmy look like? Fresh as a daisy, you said. Apparently there's no real physical type. They come in all shapes and sizes.'

'Still. When you were little, uh, did he ever uh . . . ?'

'No.' He was starting to feel unnerved; but he was used to that by now and he said, in the supernormal tone he seemed to have developed for her, 'No. He didn't just fail to warm to children – he actively disliked them. It's even there in a poem. *Children, with their shallow, violent eyes*. To him they're like aliens . . . But he was all right, Larkin. Solemn but benign. Benign. And children can tell.'

'Not at first they can't. Often. Warm my feet! . . . No, he's more than solemn, that one. *Man hands on misery to man. It . . .*'

'*It deepens like a coastal shelf.*'

'*Get out as early as you can,*' she said. '*And don't have any kids yourself.*'

'Mm. So he says.' Of course Phoebe had never drawn attention to the thing she shared with the poet: their common recusancy from the sway of common life. She couldn't talk about it; but she could sometimes talk around it . . . Martin leant his head on her shoulder (the smell of talc and limey shampoo). 'He doesn't always feel like that. It's a kind of poetic bravado. Or real bravery at least on the page. It's just a mood, but poets have to go to the end of the mood.* To explore.'

'Oh they explore, do they. Explore the mood. What's the point of that?'

'I don't know – to contain it, the grievance. Whatever quarrel you pick with life, whatever it is that chafes you. You have to see it through.'

'Yes, well that's what I'm doing – seeing it through. Haven't you noticed? . . . You say it's just a mood, with him. When his mood changes, what's he going to do? Up and start a family? At his age?'

'Mm. Mm, a comical thought, I agree. No, you've got me there, Phoebe.'

'. . . Now who's *this*? Ooh, "Stevie Smith" no less.'

'I think you'd take to Stevie Smith. Little girl lost in the woods – that kind of thing.'

She slid the book from his hand and leered at the back flap. Yes, this was very bad: not only poetry but poetry written by a woman. 'Cor, you can pick 'em, Mart. Her and that other old boot. Begins with a B . . .'

'Elizabeth Bishop.'

'Yeah. Boiler Bishop. You're *such* a hypocrite . . . I'm going to ring the papers and tell them what a dirty little bastard you really are. Underneath.'

'The papers wouldn't be interested.† Anyway, I'm reformed. I haven't been a dirty little bastard for nearly three weeks.'

* Phoebe's evident favourite, 'This Be the Verse' ('They fuck you up, your mum and dad'), has a technically near-identical sister poem, 'The Trees', which ends: 'Yet still the unresting castles thresh / In fullgrown thickness every May. / Last year is dead, they seem to say, / Begin afresh, afresh, afresh.' At the foot of the manuscript Larkin wrote, 'Bloody awful tripe'. But he let the lines stand; and rightly. 'The Trees' represented a very different kind of mood; but in both cases the poet has to explore it and get to the end of it. As Auden writes in another context (with accidental but complete appositeness), 'Follow, poet, follow, right / To the bottom of the night . . .' *Larkin comes to London once a year,* I said that same afternoon. *There's usually a party. I'll introduce you.* The meeting did in fact take place; and it was eventful, too.

† In fact Phoebe's prompting was only marginally ahead of its time. In the UK in the very early 1980s, the newspapers were getting thicker and thicker – first the Sundays, then the Saturdays, then all the days in between; and what filled these extra pages was not additional news stories but additional features. Soon the featurists were running out of people to write about – running out of alcoholic actors, depressive comedians, ne'er-do-well royals, jailed rockstars, defecting ballet dancers, tantrum-prone fashion models, reclusive film directors, adulterous golfers, wife-beating footballers, and rapist boxers. The dragnet went on widening until journalists, often to their palpable irritation and dismay, were reduced to writing about writers: literary writers.

'What about this morning? Oh, I suppose that doesn't count because you didn't . . . Well one thing's for certain. You won't be being a dirty little bastard tonight. Either.'

His shoulders went slack and he said, 'Look at it out there, Phoebe. *Listen* to it out there.' Listen to it: the hissing, the seething. 'It's a mess. Do we honestly have to go to this do? It's for a nude magazine for Christ's sake.'

Nude magazines

She said affrontedly, 'You like nude magazines!'

'Nude magazines, Phoebe, have their place.* But I don't want to go to *functions* for nude magazines. Why'd they invite you anyway?'

'Oh, I expect they're asking all their . . .'

Her face shone out at him. And he was freshly startled by her eyes. Normally Phoebe's snuff-coloured eyes seemed to address you through a lens of detachment, as fixed and unrevealing as damp brownstone. Now they had a glisten and a crackle, like caramelised sugar. She went on,

'All their past stars, Mart. All their pets and playmates.' She jolted to her feet and surged outward. 'Don't move a muscle. I've got an offering for you.' And as she left the room she gave vent to a glissade of laughter . . .

He heard her next door – the snaps of the suitcase, the rummaging. Phoebe strode out of there and offered it to him like a waitress with a tray (and she curtsied when he took it). The nude magazine was called *Oui*.

'My bit's under a false name,' she said. 'You've got to keep some things secret . . .'

---

* Pornography has become a sorry business all round (though I ask readers to ponder a remark I heard from the amiable Art Spiegelman, cartoonist and graphic novelist: 'Banning pornography would be like killing the messenger') . . . In the era under review, pornography had not yet revealed itself as an intensely misogynistic form, and nude magazines were admired, amassed, and exchanged by – among countless others – Philip Larkin, Kingsley Amis, and also by Robert Conquest, who went as far as to publish a poem in praise of them.

For a moment he thought she was about to sneeze; but now the head went back and she laughed again. And the sound of it, vaguely surprisingly, made him feel exhausted, physically exhausted; and he even felt that if she laughed again he might have to curl up and fade away, just from physical exhaustion . . .

'Concentrate, Martin.'

Very much as if in an uneasy dream (the succession of strange challenges, the strange weakening of cause and effect, together with the proximity, well known to male dreamers, of a strange and equivocal woman), he mustered his urbanity . . .

The nine-page section bore the title 'Tycoon Tanya'. And there she was, Phoebe, in the year – he checked the cover – 1971. So she was twenty-nine, but not looking qualitatively younger: the angular bonescape fully formed (fully and interestingly evolved and completed). Tycoon Tanya was to be seen methodically removing her businesswear in a narrow variety of settings: a penthouse roof garden, a softly lit boardroom, a brass-bright City office. *Tycoon Tanya*, ran the text, *is a stratospheric financier who is also versed in the more intimate skills and arts. Sometimes she likes to cast off her burdensome responsibilities and relax in the* . . . And what struck him and held him was her face. All along the way, unconcernedly shedding this or that article of clothing until there was nothing left to shed, Phoebe went on looking as though she had just punished the weak yuan, or approved that astronomical loan to the Argentinians, or pulled the plug on General Motors.

'Mm. I thought you'd like that one.'

He had reached the page immediately following the centrefold (where Phoebe was up to her knees in an executive Jacuzzi). In the photo now before him she was in a luminous steel-ribbed kitchen wearing only a pair of white tights; and her pubic shield was the shape and size of a halved apple. *Getting the picture?* ran the text. *Tanya has curves in places where other girls don't even have places! Small wonder she's decided to spearhead the much ballyhooed 'Ess Es'* (turn to page 5).

'And what d'you think you're doing?'

'Turning to page five.'

'You certainly are *not* turning to page five. Hand it over. Now.'

'. . . Well that was a classy shoot, Phoebe. Your expression is very good. Not all bashful or dreamy – or witchy. Serious. Mm. Serious.'

'And you're shocked.'

'Hardly.' Hardly, because even this wasn't a new one on Martin: two earlier girlfriends, Doris and Aramintha, had posed in nude magazines.* Yes, but he wasn't living with Aramintha, he hadn't devoted two years of his life to Doris, and with neither were there presentiments of love . . . This last consideration pained him and made him jealous of other men's eyes. But he wasn't shocked.

'Do I sound or look shocked? I'm not. I'm curious though. Was it just an impulse, or did you have a reason?'

'Yes. There was a reason. I was under massive pressure at Ess Es.'

'What is this Ess Es business?'

'I'll explain later.' She turned to the window. 'There won't be any taxis – not in this muck. And if we took the Mini, where would we stick it? Anyway! Time to get ready. For the function for the nude magazine! . . . Now what type of pants shall I wear?'

Phoebe had two types of pants, which she called *cheap* and *dear*: she bought her cheap pants in Woolworth's, and her dear pants at a place in Mayfair called Mirage. Both had their own charm. He said,

'Your very dearest. Tonight you'll have some real competition for once.'

'Ooh. I know what it is. You just don't like it when I'm being friendly.'

'No. When you're being friendly, you're not being friendly to me. It's torture.'

'Huh.' She leaned into him and quickly and wetly licked his lips. 'What makes you think you know the first thing about torture?'

She went next door and reappeared almost naked. 'How about these?'

---

* So when I characterised Phoebe's shoot as 'classy', well, I knew whereof I spoke . . . In a sombrero and frilly bikini bottoms, and larking around in a studio sandpit, Doris had graced a cheerful little sauce-sheet called *Parade* (late 1960s, and costing one shilling and three grim and grimy old pence); Aramintha, by contrast, wholly and pallidly and uneasily naked, wandered the racks of a shadowy wine cellar, in the pages of a short-lived glossy called something like *Atelier* (mid-1970s, and costing an outrageous £3.50) . . . Among the young at least it was silently accepted that posing in nude magazines was just another thing girls could do. Doris and Aramintha did make me wonder about their personal reasons for taking this step – but not for long: Aramintha did it to spite and sully her father (a prominent Tory MP), and Doris, Doris McGowan, did it because that was more or less her job (she also featured regularly in *Fiesta* and *Razzle*) . . . *Oui* was a British cousin of *Playboy* and cost just over a quid.

'They're not dear. They're your very cheapest.'
'Yeah. That's right.'

They were close, the two of them; he was there and she was there; they were near.

And tonight, he knew, he would get closer to that part of her which he had never been able to broach or breach – what was unnearable in her.

The Inn on the Park

Evening.

Now they splashed their way south from Marble Arch Underground, moving through shift after shift of hot rain – sultry, sticky rain. Sweaty rain: the black Saturday dusk was sweating, heavily sweating, in the form of rain. Under its shunting curtains they ducked and hurried; and all along Park Lane the wedged traffic, red-eyed or yellow-eyed, trembled and steamed. Martin had a soaked copy of Friday's *Evening News* plastered over his hair, while Phoebe wielded her single-occupancy umbrella – a polythene sheath with a rectangular slit at chin height, like the mouth of a postbox, and through it she said,

'Look at them. Already written off.'

She meant her high heels. Courtesy of which she was five foot eleven. To his five foot six (and a half). He was yawing along beside her.

Now wait. Suddenly there is an exchange of words (unstrident but earnest) and the man halts. The woman walks on, then swivels and lingers, like a mother with a sullen child; she reaches out a hand, and with hesitation he reaches out to take it.

'Phoebe. What d'you mean? You were an escort girl. What d'you mean you were an escort girl?'

'I was an escort girl. At Ess Es – Essential Escorts. You know what that means.'

'Yes,' he said. 'You went on dates with strangers and slept with them for money.'

'Yup. Sometimes. Now pull yourself together, Martin. Stop carrying on like a bloody . . . Ah, good evening to you! We're here for the –'

'Quick! Ooh, you get yourself out of the filth, my lovely. Come on in here, the pair of you. That's it! Quick!'

The vast puddles were aglow with the bone-white reflection of the pale hotel, whose beefeater doorman, a dark purply slab in his greatcoat, beckoned and then led them into a kind of sentry booth (with its fug of fagsmoke, Bovril, and BO).

'This is more like it, eh? Now,' he said. 'How can I help you, young lady?'

Phoebe's carapace (transparent but as steamy as the window of a fish-and-chip shop) was now unzipped and stepped out of . . .

'Sweetheart, you've barely a stitch on!' said Bumble the Beadle wonderingly. 'You'll catch your death.'

And both propositions seemed true . . . The pop-art umbrella, tradenamed the Drolly (which would go on being fashionable for another couple of weeks), had obvious design flaws, and Phoebe, with her frizzed hair, and her ridiculously short flower dress clinging to her torso in pockets of damp, looked leggy, wiry, and crazy, like a ravished rag doll. Martin thought that she also looked driven, or cruelly coerced, as if she hated all this even more than he did.

'And dear oh dear – you're soaked through!'

'What nonsense. I'm as sound as the mail. Now. We're here for the *party*. The party for the nude mag called . . . Shit. The party for the periodical called *Oui*.'

'Uh, let's have a look.' As he frowned over his clipboard (and as Phoebe frowned over his shoulder), Martin stepped back out.

Only three years earlier he had spent a couple of hours in this hotel: an interview with Joseph Heller. Just around the corner, on Piccadilly, loomed the hotel where, three years later, he was destined to interview Norman Mailer. Life would go on, and literary life would go on; Martin's fourth novel was currently under way, and there was that long essay he had to write on – what was it? – 'diversity and depth in fiction' . . . But for now here he stood, in full ordeal readiness (and additionally weighed down by his dripping corduroy suit). Once inside, he confidently foresaw, as Phoebe went about her work and as he himself short-arsed around trying to get himself drinks and then more drinks, he would be smelling of damp dog and chickenfeed.

'Are you sure you've got the correct venue, love?'

'Positive. I mislaid the actual invitation but this is definitely the place.'

While this exchange continued on its way, Martin was free to receive two complementary thoughts: Phoebe dressing up as Eve *after the Fall*; and something from *Humboldt's Gift* – *I never saw a fig leaf that didn't turn into a price tag* . . .

'A party for a magazine,' Phoebe insisted. '*Oui*. French for *yes*. Christ, how many parties for magazines can there be? *Oui*.'

'There's a party for a magazine,' said the doorman. 'But it's not called *We*.'

'. . . What can you mean?'

'It's called *IOU*.'

Having taken this in, Martin bowed his head and followed her through the revolving doors.

Cocoa

Night.

It had been waiting in their future, perhaps inexorably. Perhaps for a certainty. Phoebe herself might have placed money on it. And here it was – the night of shame.

At one o'clock in the morning, London, as seen out of the windows of the black cab, was trying to look tranquil and blameless; it looked rinsed and brushed, too, as if the city trucks had just come and sluiced it all down; a wispy breath of mist now seeped from the terraced buildings, from the rooftops with their vague crenellations . . .

The first thing Phoebe did, on her return, was surge virtuously towards the cooker and the cocoa. After a while Martin came out of the bathroom and through the bedroom and across the sitting room and into the kitchen and said, defeatedly, and as he saw it reasonably drunkenly, deservedly drunkenly (and of course he said what he said tritely too, because the idiom of anger is always trite),

'Phoebe, you surpassed yourself. That was your worst yet. How could you?'

'What's all this? I was just being sociable. God.'

'Mm. And now – yes. After that kind of evening, what with so many changes of temperature,' he said in the wheedling tone he knew she hated, 'and you didn't dress sensibly, as you yourself, Phoebe, were prepared to admit, and, after all that, what could be more wholesome, more restorative, than a nice cup of something *hot*?'

'. . . No, don't have another one, Mart.' She had the kettle's steam in her hair; she folded her arms while he clacked about in the high cabinet. 'When I saw you on your fourth glass I thought, Well, *he'll* go home singing.' She looked him up and down with her blokeish sneer. 'Sing? You can barely . . . It's like you're phoning me long distance. *Hello*, caller? I can't hear you, caller. Is there anybody *there*?'

'What the fuck were you doing down in that grotto? With that, with that, with that Californian *wretch*? What was his name?'

With her neck held straight she said, 'Carlton.'

'Okay. *Carlton* had your dress hoicked up over your ribcage!'

With quiet matter-of-factness, taking rightful warmth from her cup with both palms, Phoebe said, 'He wanted to see it. So I showed him.'

'Yes, completely straightforward. And logical. Carlton wanted to see it, so you hoicked up your dress and showed Carlton your . . . ?'

'My mandala. Luckily these pants are see-through so I didn't have to take them down. I'll explain,' she said. 'Now Carlton's a corporate raider, but you have to understand that he finds himself drawn, he finds himself increasingly drawn, Martin, to Buddha.'

The *Oui* party had been ideal for Phoebe's operations, an Ottoman-themed labyrinth of cushions and low sofas and lanternlight. The men were all European varieties of Carlton, and the women . . . the women were off the human scale, either radiantly enormous, like thoroughbreds and steeplechasers, or guardedly petite, like much-groomed toy poodles or papillon spaniels. It was among such that Martin roamed . . .

'That tattoo of yours must've been on seventeen different laps tonight. And why were you down on your knees in that alcove?'

'Perfectly innocent. I'd accidentally spilt powder on Jean-Paul's trousers. And I was just brushing it off.'

'Oh, why d'you do it, Phoebe? What's it *for*?'

'What's it for? I collected, oh I collected a whole wodge of phone numbers. So I'll be a busy girl when you're off with that little poof in . . . What's his name?'

'Truman Capote.'

'Yeah. When you're off oiling up to that little poof Truman Capote in New York.'

'That's not you,' he said, and took a defiant pull on his (weak) whisky and water. 'And stop going on as if this is like any other night. You just told me you were an *escort* girl for Christ's sake.'

Phoebe smiled dangerously and said, 'I heard you in there, turning on the taps. Sniffling and mewing . . . You want to go back in that bathroom, mate. And take Tycoon Tanya with you. And don't have a weep, this time. Have a wank.' She looked startled, and took a sudden step back – as if wanting a better distance to gauge the effect of her blow. 'That's what I've done. I've turned you into a wanker.'

She seemed about to laugh, and he flinched, and Phoebe's hand flew to her mouth. As if remembering herself. He said as steadily as he could,

'No, no laughter, Phoebe.' He waited. 'Jesus. Finally I see it. You want me to leave you, don't you. Well instead of torturing me to death,* why didn't you just *say*?'

'Because it's not in my power.'

'Your power?'

'That's right. And it's sad, it really is.' She bowed down and bestowed a sisterly kiss on the side of his head. 'It really is. And now, we two, you and I, must go to sleep . . .'

Aubade

At least an hour later in the dark he heard her sigh – and yawn – and he said,

'Phoebe.'

'What.'

'A question . . . Tycoon Tanya.' He was quite impressed to discover that his voice had cleared up – no longer the echoic croak. 'Did Tycoon Tanya, did she get any other offers? Back in 1971?'

---

* I never expected to forget the sexual terror-famines imposed by Phoebe Phelps, and I never have. Well, the *famines* proved indelible. The *terror* element (the antic hummingbird) turned out to be more evanescent. The only time I can't help reliving it, funnily enough, is when I'm acutely jet-lagged. Acutely jet-lagged, I look at my watch – and its hands seem cruel and crazy: saying not two forty-five but a quarter to nine, saying not half past six but twelve-thirty. Phoebe was like that. Her hands, her arms, her legs: in the wrong position. And there was this element, too. All her eroticism capsized: from lover to hater. Because I knew, in detail, the quality of what seemed to be on offer, on offer to every man but me.

She half rolled over. 'Oh, loads. Loads. Guccione, all of them. They wanted to fly me to the Playboy Mansion. First-class.'

'Then why aren't you driving down Rodeo Drive', said Martin (who in 1985 – literary life continuing – would interview Hugh Hefner), 'in a pink convertible?'

'Yes, it's baffling . . . Well. The thing is, they vet you. And they couldn't have it come out, could they. That I was an escort girl.'

'Bob Guccione couldn't have it come out?'

'Of course not. Are you serious? I'd be like one of those beauty queens who're suddenly disgraced. Miss Paraguay, was it – the white-slaver? And around then I decided to go straight. I retired.'

'You decided to become a retired escort girl.'

'Yes,' she said plainly. 'A retired escort girl. It was a long time ago.'

'In those far-off days, then, Phoebe, when you were an escort girl . . . How much did the agency pay you per date?'

'The agency? Ess Es? Well, the blokes pay the agency direct, and you only get your seven and a half per cent.'

'How much was seven and a half per cent?'

'Oh, sod all. A fiver.' She moved closer and he could feel her radiation on his back. 'Now don't be bloody insulting and say a fiver was all it took. Things didn't work like that. You made your own arrangement with the client. If they were all right . . . And a few of them were all right. Now shut up and go to sleep.'

He lay there in the dark. 'A tenner for a kiss.'

She gave a sigh of the weariest disgust.

'Plus the flat-rate fiver of course. Okay. Twenty-five for a proper snog. With tongues.'

She violently resettled herself.

'Okay. Fifty quid for a wank. With you doing it.'

'. . . Hah. Go up to Soho, mate. Windmill Street. You'll find an old trout who'll give you a wank for fifty quid.'

'Two hundred for a blowjob.'

Silence.

'Five hundred for a fuck. Six hundred.' He sensed a stillness. 'Seven-fifty. Okay, a thou.'

'. . . Done.' The bedside light came on. 'Now how long for, Martin?' she said as she glanced at her watch. 'And what else? I warn you. Extras are extra.'

During the act there were little shouts of laughter as the values dipped and climbed, like the price of crude.

———————

The bedroom curtains were only half drawn, and he could make out a streak of pale light against the rosy tint of the sky. That pale streak reminded him of the scar, the snag, he occasionally thought he saw somewhere in Phoebe's face, a disequilibrium giving that lawless slant to her smile. Her smile, her sneer, her snarl, with its defiance, its pain, its grief . . .

Martin thought he was old friends with the sad animal, with the creature in its tristesse; but the animal had never been quite as sad as this. And for only the third or fourth time in his life, he felt like a dirty little bastard (and one whose recent exploits might very well spark interest in the papers, even in 1978). He prepared and put a match to a cigarette in the accumulating dawn.

A couple of seconds later Phoebe turned to him saying,

'Now how much did that set you back . . . I make it fourteen hundred and twenty. You know, Mart, you reminded me of someone. Haggling away in bed nineteen to the dozen. *If you do that, you'll get this.* Et cetera. You reminded me of someone.'

She reached for his handrolled burn, and dragged, and, for once, inhaled . . .

'You know who?' She expelled smoke. 'He got around to money in due time, of course. But at first he used sweets. Father Gabriel.'

Transitional
The Sources of the Being

. . . Poor Phoebe. This is the first thing that needs to be said. Poor, poor Phoebe . . .

After what we've just been through, though, I think a cleansing thought experiment – or thought exercise – is in order, don't you? And there's more confessional stuff to come, including the Worst Thing I Ever Did. So let's take a break and briefly repair to the cool symmetries of art.

1. The four seasons

A great philosopher of literature – the Reverend Northrop Frye – suggested that the four seasons correspond to the four major genres. I think that's a sweet and lyrical notion (though I admit that nothing really hangs on it). Now I suspect you know what the four seasons are. And here are the four major genres: tragedy, comedy, satire, romance. So the question is: Which genre corresponds to which season?

Tragedy, in its shape, follows the mouth on the tragic mask. Picture that ominous grimace: a starting point (on the lower left-hand corner), a steep rise, a flattening out, then a steep decline. The tragic hero is simultaneously transcendent and earthbound – human, all too human in the end: only human. That monumental individuality is one of the reasons why tragedy is now so seldom seen – a rare bird in the grey sky of post-industrial modernity.

Comedy, classical comedy, is similarly obedient to the line of the mouth on its mask. In this case it's a smile: a deep descent that levels out and gathers into a fresh resurgence. The logistics of classical comedy are touchingly straightforward: a young man and a young woman fall in love and eventually get married (overcoming the obstacles cast in their way by the more hidebound society that surrounds and frustrates them). All Shakespeare's comedies, and all six of Jane Austen's novels, strictly adhere to this form (and my own father's *Lucky Jim*, considered so rowdily iconoclastic in the mid-1950s, shows lamb-like submission to it). Comedies end happily, tragedies unhappily. The tragic hero is conspicuously distinguished; the comic hero is an everyman, the comic heroine an everywoman, and they are distinguished only in their charm.

Satire is best understood as militant irony. Vice, affectation, and stupidity are exposed to ridicule and implicit moral correction but also to anger and contempt. Whereas comedy tends to run only a light fever of subversion (off with the old), the mood of satire is revolutionary and hotly roused.

Romance, classical romance, only incidentally includes sentimental or idealised love stories; neither is it confined to medieval tales of chivalry. Romance, with its delirium and voodoo, identifies itself as being largely indifferent to the cause-and-effect of everyday life. For example, science fiction of the 'star tsar' variety (Nabokov's anagrammatic phrase) is pure romance. Harry Potter et cetera is romance. Anything that reifies fantasy is romance.

I'll give you a few minutes to think. Tragedy, comedy, satire, romance; spring, summer, autumn, winter. If, say, tragedy is winter (and it isn't), what are the affinities?

2. Disgrace

While you consider that, consider this.

George Orwell famously said that 'autobiography is only to be trusted when it reveals something disgraceful' ('a man who gives a good account of himself is probably lying'). By that measure at least, what follows is gospel truth.

Unintellectual girls (including avowed philistines and bibliophobes) are one thing, and girls who pose in nude magazines are another, and girls on the borders of criminality are yet another – but not even escort girls, non-retired escort girls, escort girls going about their business, lie beyond my experience (or make that *his* experience. In this context the words come much more willingly when you wear the loincloth of the third person).

In the early–middle 1970s Martin himself contributed to *Oui* magazine, and under his own name (unlike the prudent Phoebe). There were two pieces: the first was about decadent London nightclubs; the second was about escort girls. And the second piece was a pack of lies. More than that, it aspired to the stout condescension of an old Fleet Street exposé, along the lines of *I made my excuses and left*. In reality, of course, the present writer did nothing of the sort; he made no excuses, and he stayed.

At that time Martin was fresh from a summary eviction. He had been told to leave the flat he shared with his longterm sweetheart (arraigned for infidelity). So by the time he began his research on the question of escort girls, he was already to be found in a hotel – a decadently welcoming little place in South Kensington. Although the published piece claimed to describe his engagements with three escort girls, in reality there were only two: Ariadne and Rita.

Ariadne was from Athens; Rita was from Whitechapel in the East End. These were atypical escort-girl experiences, he assumed: the subject of money never came up. In fact, when he casually offered Ariadne a fiver for cab fare (it was raining), she said, 'A taxi does not cost five pounds.'*

Why did Ariadne and Rita go to bed with Martin for nothing? A brief trance of self-satisfaction would seem to be in order. As against that, though – well, he was anomalously young (twenty-five), and he was anomalously respectful and unpresumptuous: he treated them not like escort girls – and how would you go about that? – but like blind dates whom he naturally wished to please with his inquisitive and undivided attention. Anyway, go to bed with him they did . . .

Meanwhile, as he wondered what he was about, his whole being, his history, his childhood, his Ribenas at Sunday school, his particular elders, his heroes and heroines in poetry and prose: his entire inner life was saying to his inner ear, You can't possibly get away with all this – and nor should you.

---

* Yes, this all took place a very long time ago. Forty-odd years later, London taxis persist in not costing £5: they now cost £88.80. But back then the sum of £5 was only seen on the meter of a taxi bound for the airport. (And £5, as Phoebe reminded us, was what the agency would have paid Ariadne.)

He agreed (quite right), and bowed his head, thinking, Come *on*. What was the world waiting for?

. . . The quote that opened this segment is one of Orwell's more limited epigrams. He was writing about a memoir by Salvador Dalí, the kind of man who was far more likely to belittle his virtues, if any, and aggrandise his sins. It is not for nothing that Orwell is regarded as quintessentially English; and the English literary tradition, unlike those of the mainland, is quintessentially moral, never having come up with many exponents (or many readers) of the perverse. There is only Lawrence, that perennial exception . . . With just a single novel under his belt, Martin knew very well that this was the tradition he belonged to. 'You've done wrong,' his mother used to say all her life, humorously (and nearly always referring to herself). 'So now you've got to be punished.'

3. Genghis Khan

Satire is winter, wintry, bitter; the frost has its teeth fast in the ground.

Romance is summer, a time of freedom and adventure, and dream-strange possibilities.

Comedy is spring, the burgeoning of the flora, the Whitsun weddings, the maypole.

Tragedy is autumn, the sere, the yellow leaf . . .

While every death is a tragedy, Stalin famously observed, the death of a million is just a statistic. The second half of this statement is untrue. In giving voice to it, the big moustache laid bare his hope for some historiographical leniency – as did the little moustache when he said that the court of time listens exclusively to the victors, and so for example 'history sees in Genghis Khan only the great founder of a state'.*

---

* Genghis Khan is revered today only in Mongolia (whose premier airport bears his name). Elsewhere and always – even in Nazi Germany – he is remembered as a blood-smeared genocidaire. He killed about 40 million: close to 10 per cent of the global population in 1300. We remember him too, now, as a hyperactive satyr and rapist: 16 million people alive today are not being at all deluded when they claim to feel the blood of Genghis coursing through their veins . . . Hitler's declaration – part of a morale-stiffening lecture to his military brass – was made on August 22, 1939, when the immediate prospect was the 'depopulation' of Poland; and Genghis, said Hitler (getting slightly carried away), 'hunted millions of women and children to their deaths, consciously and with a joyous heart'. We may incidentally note that the

A million deaths are at the very least a million tragedies (to be multiplied by the children, spouses, and immediate family of each victim). Every death is a tragedy; but then so is every life. Every life is a slave to the curve, the upended U, the woeful gape of the tragic mask.

4. The gravamen

In the decadent hotel Martin typed out the piece on his Olivetti (*now was the moment, Leonora was clearly suggesting, when I should conjure up the 'gratuity' or the 'little present', i.e., the carnal bribe, to call it what it was; but with a smile of regret, etc., etc.*), placed the folded sheets in the addressed envelope, and went downstairs to give it to the desk clerk; then he returned to his room and smoked and waited.

Retribution was surely impatient to come his way – and from so many angles. Let him think: a dramatic intervention from Ariadne's mountain-dwelling, junta-loving father (and all his male clan); or a surprise visit from one of Rita's many ex-convict ex-boyfriends; or an invasion of passionately mercantilist pimps armed with baseball bats and straight razors . . . At the very minimum (what was keeping it?) he hourly foresaw a targeted nemesis, one brewed by Mother Nature.* In the end even his dealings with the nude magazine would advance smoothly; *Oui* at once accepted and processed his perjured report (and duly printed it without challenge), and remitted him £200 . . .

---

liberal thinker Alexander Herzen, in one of his extraordinary premonitions, said in the 1860s that a Russian post-revolutionary power might resemble 'Genghis Khan with the telegraph'. Khan is Turkic for 'ruler, lord, prince' (and when Churchill heard the news on March 11, 1953, he said, 'The great khan is dead'). At that point Stalin was revered as 'the father of the peoples' by about a third of humankind (China, et al.). So you could say that Stalin got away with it (i.e., his personal toll of 20-odd million), in the West at least, until the publication of Conquest's *The Great Terror* (1968) and more comprehensively Solzhenitsyn's *The Gulag Archipelago* in the early 1970s. Today, in 2018, Stalin's approval rating in Russia is over 50 per cent.
* Specifically 'a real dilly of a VD', in the words of William Burroughs. One of the books I was reading at the time was *The Naked Lunch*. 'The disease in short arm hath a gimmick for going places . . . And after an initial lesion at the point of infection [it] passes to the lymph glands of the groin, which swell and burst in suppurating fissures, drain for days, months, years . . .' Elephantiasis of the genitals is 'a frequent complication', as is gangrene, to the point where 'amputation *in medio* from the waist down [is] indicated'.

Thus the world did nothing. Society, equity, law, God, the Protestant ethos, common justice – all these spirits and entities stood down and sat on their hands. In the end only one precept applied. If you want something done (i.e., punishment), you have to do it yourself.

It started in the hotel room as he was packing his bag: a marshland, illumined by marshlights and fireflies and phosphorescent earthworms, was opening up beneath his feet. The sudden sickness felt mortal; in somatic synergy, organ after organ, one after the other, would be apologetically shutting down. At no point did he connect this horrible turn with his recent trespasses; it was perfectly simple: he had reached the end of his span. There was the phone on the bedside table. Should he dial 999? . . . When you're young, and you find yourself in sole charge of the bodily instrument, you may be infinitely hypochondriacal, of course; but you're also much too fatalistic to squander your last breaths among *doctors*. He sank back and dialled o.

'Good morning – this is room twenty-seven. I'll soon be checking out.' And he asked them to prepare the reckoning.

. . . I will arise. I will arise and go now, with a suitcase to the callbox. A phone call will I make there . . . All he wanted was somewhere to lie down and, if at all possible, the extreme unction of a pliant palm on his brow.

5. Florence Nightingale

Let us stand back for a moment.

Question: Who would present herself as his carer and redeemer, who would deliver him from this bottleneck of sexual opportunism and abuse?

Answer: The world's most glamorous and celebrated feminist. That's who.

He made the phone call and steered himself to the broad deep house off Ladbroke Grove, up near Portobello. Of course Germaine had no knowledge of his latest doings; to her he was only an occasional friend and visitor. But she took him in.

He slept on a mattress in a nook just beyond her bedroom door, so she could hear his groans, his piteous cries; she tended him and soothed him until one morning, after about a week, having brought his usual cup of tea and settled herself down to cradle him in her arms, as she did every morning, Germaine said, . . . *Oh. You really are feeling better, aren't you. I'll just go and brush my teeth.**

The planetary forces of retribution, the local genies of justice, we can assume, were inactive in that precinct of West London during a certain month in 1974. All they could come up with was Germaine Greer – to minister to me in my trial.

6. Freedom and Ariadne

Now you probably wouldn't mind hearing more about the author of *The Female Eunuch* (1970), my host and my nurse, and there is plenty more to say; but if you'll bear with me I'm thematically obliged to concentrate on whatever it was she nursed me out of.

I have not stopped thinking about that little packet of my life – those five or six nights in the complicit South Kensington hotel (I only remember the Regency caddishness of the striped wallpaper in its single public room); and I have gone on thinking about those two young women. The unanswerable malaise that overtook me clearly derived from an awareness of transgression. But which transgression?

No trawling of the conscience has ever presented me with a single reservation about what went on with Rita. With Ariadne, though, I sometimes feel about myself an inner rumour of parasitism. It was I hope a gentle encounter – in mid-afternoon, beginning with tea and biscuits (brought to us by room service). Still, I felt a deficit of volition in Ariadne; and I feared I was the beneficiary of something outside myself. Something like an indoctrination. Ariadne was nowhere near as experienced as Rita, and I now wonder what kind of tuition she was given as she acclimatised herself to the culture of escort work.

---

* Germaine was unwaveringly kind and gentle, and in every way – but the amatory demeanour of the world's most glamorous feminist is surely of scant general interest in this day and age . . . I don't think she and I ever talked except glancingly about the situation of women. Germaine's strength was wild brilliance, not sober instruction; she certainly infused her influence, but the job of turning me into a true believer devolved upon the world's second most glamorous feminist, Gloria Steinem, with whom I spent a not especially relaxing but highly educational day, as an interviewer, in New York State in 1984 . . . It was said of Florence Nightingale that she was 'very violent' – tacitly. All the great feminists of my era had moral menace in them. And they were almost invariably childless. They had to harden their hearts: such was the historical demand.

But in truth there was plenty of that in the 1970s: the exploitation of cultures, of currents of thought. To put it more crudely, men ponced off ideology. I ponced off anti-clericalism, I ponced off rejectionist ageism, and most generally of course I ponced off the tenets of the Sexual Revolution – meaning I applied peer pressure and propagandised about the earthy wisdom of the herd.

Ariadne was what is now known as an outlier. In her modest way she represented a reactionary force, that of female submission. And, given the chance, I (silently) ponced off that. She wasn't acting in perfect freedom. Who ever was, back then? Who ever is?

Anyway, that wasn't what laid me low.

7. Revolutions

Now. What do you do in a revolution? Very broadly, three things. You see what goes, you see what comes, you see what stays.

In the Sexual Revolution, what went was premarital chastity; what came was a gradually widening gap between carnal knowledge and emotion; what stayed was the possibility of love. The Sexual Revolution made no particular demands on writers; all it did was grant them a new latitude. They could now busy themselves with subjects that were previously forbidden, by law; and nearly all of them tried it (without success).

But imagine for a moment, that you are a poet or a novelist in a *real* revolution, and a very violent revolution – like the one in Russia (incomparably more violent than the one in France). For the novelist or poet, what went was freedom of expression; what came was intense line-by-line surveillance;* what stayed was the creative habit of putting pen to paper. So how was a writer to adapt and adjust?

Well, you could be like the novelist and dramatist Alexei Tolstoy (distantly related to the author of *Anna Karenina* and also, through marriage, to the author of *Fathers and Sons*). Alexei was a venal cynic

---

* 'He could feel quite tangibly the difference in weight between the fragile human body and the colossus of the State. He could feel the State's bright eyes gazing into his face; any moment now the State would crash down on him . . .' The extreme asymmetry in mass defines the 'fear that millions of people find insurmountable . . . this fear written up in crimson letters over the leaden sky of Moscow – this terrible fear of the State'. Vasily Grossman, *Life and Fate*.

who confessedly 'enjoyed the acrobatics' of trimming his work to 'the general line', or to current Bolshevik orthodoxy (a protean contraption). This is also the man who said that one of the things he hated most in life was windowshopping with inadequate funds . . .

Alternatively you could be like Isaac Babel, the writer of sharply expressive short stories, who at a certain point declared himself to be 'the master of a new literary genre, the genre of silence'. It was a noble intention. But even if you stopped writing, you could hardly stop talking; Babel said enough, and was shot in a Moscow prison in 1940.

'Of the 700 writers who met at the First Writers' Congress in 1934,' writes Conquest, 'only fifty survived to see the second in 1954.'

The choice, then, was active collaboration or mutism. There was also a third way, involving what we might call a delusion of autonomy. Writers of the third way persuaded themselves that they could proceed, could get on with their stuff (quietly and yet publishably), without grave internal compromise. Alexei Tolstoy could flourish because he had the thick skin of artistic indifference – in common with all RAPPists (members of the Russian Association of Proletarian Writers); privileged and decorated, they lived well; more basically, they lived on. It was the idealists who were culled, one way or the other. The lethal element here was literary authenticity; if you had it within you, you were doomed.

A glance at the fate of two poets.* The talented Vladimir Mayakovsky wrote obligingly gruff-voiced hymns to bayonets and pig-iron statistics; and he put a bullet in his brain in 1930, aged thirty-six. The talented Sergei Yesenin wrote obligingly soft-voiced hymns to rural toilers and reapers; and hanged himself in 1925, aged thirty. What these two men had done was betray their gift and their avocation; and therefore they fell afoul of the sources of their being.

Me, I wrote a bit of hack reportage about escort girls in a nude magazine. But to compare little things with large is a salutary habit; the little

---

* And one senses that the third way attracted more poets than novelists. Obviously it did. Poetry by definition a) tends to be oblique, b) resists paraphrase, and c) can find refuge in extreme brevity. It is the work of a moment to imagine an opaque haiku about (say) the collectivisation of agriculture (1929–33); it is very hard to imagine an extended socialist-realist narrative on the same subject with not a thought in its head about the annihilation of several million peasant families.

thing tells you a little about the large thing. In miniature, little things, like exceptions, prove the rule – using *prove* in the older sense of 'test'.

Yesenin and Mayakovsky told what they knew to be lies in their *poems*. Me, I wrote lies about escort girls in a nude magazine. Consequently I didn't kill myself. I just had the third cousin of what Solzhenitsyn had when pressured (unsuccessfully) to denounce, to delate, to 'write', as they said ('Does he/she write?' was a common, and anxious, enquiry). He said to himself: 'I feel sick.' Yesenin and Mayakovsky were self-denouncers, in their verse.

All the writers whose last decision was suicide were killed by the State. Their situation affected them like a slow-acting poison, delivered (perhaps on the point of a phantom umbrella) by 'the Organs', as the secret police were popularly known; or like a course of mind-altering drugs, administered over months or years, in national psychiatric wards specialising in the ideologically insane.

But the poet-suicides had to have something within them to make the spell firm and good. Demyan Bedny, the obese 'proletarian poet laureate', lived complacently (until the later 1930s); he had a town named after him, his face appeared on postage stamps, and he was the only writer in the USSR to be honoured with an apartment in the Kremlin. None of this seemed to bother Bedny, and why would it? He was *manqué*, and could say of any of his poems, *I didn't really mean it*. The writers who really did mean it ended differently; in their own souls they were playing with fire.

8. Ever at the lips

My thing with Phoebe Phelps went on until Christmas 1980. The night of shame was merely the halfway point; and for a while, for a year, for two years, there was love, there was unquestionably love. But after that she attenuated, gradually receding from me. Today, when I think long enough about her as she was then, as she faded, I end up with a version of Keats's line about 'Joy' (capitalised, like Pleasure and Delight, in 'Ode to Melancholy'): those hands of hers (moving languidly now) seemed to be ever at her lips, bidding adieu. And she lost her quiddity and solidity, no longer novelistic, merely lifelike . . .

Phoebe will not tend to dominate these pages, as she would in a work of unalloyed fiction; but she will periodically resurface. There was her bold move in the summer of 1981, and her even bolder move on September 12, 2001. And, much later, there was the meeting in London in 2017, when she was seventy-five.

———————

Before we sign off on the nice idea about the genres and the seasons, I will suggest that the progress of a human life can also be evoked in genres and seasons. In this minor thought experiment, chronology is reversed (do you think that's significant?): the three-score-and-ten begins around August 31, moves backwards through summer and spring and then winter and autumn, and comes to an abrupt halt around September 1. I'll be brief.

Life begins, then, with summer and romance. Childhood and youth constitute the phase of the fairy tale – with domineering fathers, wicked stepmothers, vicious half-siblings, etc., to be included ad hoc. The time of quests, dragons, and hidden treasure. The Brothers Grimm, and *Alice in Wonderland*.

Then comes spring and comedy. The problem comedy of one's twenties and thirties, the phase of the love story, the picaresque, and the bodice-ripper, the sentimental education and the *Bildungsroman*, leading one way or another to marriage and probably children, *Love in the Haystacks* leading to *All's Well That Ends Well*.

Then comes winter and satire. Maturity and middle age, the phase of the brackish *roman-fleuve* and the increasingly sinister Aga saga, with sour whispers gathering in the kitchen dusk. For some, the great losses and injustices of life can be tamed and borne; for others, the debit ledger breaks free and burgeons. It is the time of *Can You Forgive Her?* (yes, you can) and *He Knew He Was Right* (no, he was wrong).

Then comes autumn and tragedy: decline and fall, the *roman noir*, the Gothic ghost story, the book of the dead.

9. Identity crisis

Until September 2001, when I was fifty-two, I'd never given my 'identity' (my *what?*) a moment's thought. Why would I? I was white, Anglo-Saxon, heterosexual, non-believing, able in mind and body . . . Identity crises were for the rest of the world to worry about, the present world (the extant, the actual), fluid and churning and chameleonic, with its array of syndromes, conditions, disorders, and its burgeoning suite of erotic destinies (I'm bi, I'm trans, I'm chaste). In short, your identity sleeps inside you, unless or until it is roused.

Yet it occurred, my crisis, it took place – it elapsed. Not that I would dare to claim any kind of parity with the outliers, the anomalies, those singled out for questioning in the planet-wide identity parade. My case was peculiar. There were no models or patterns, no support groups or integration programmes, no experts or counsellors, no newsletters, no 'literature'. I was all on my own.

. . . As Larkin wrote (in a letter of 1958, complaining to a woman friend about the banal irritations of the Christmas season, and briefly comparing her trials to his): 'Yours is the harder course, I can see. On the other hand, mine is happening to me.' There. It even rhymes; it may not scan – but it rhymes.

And the poet's comment is a useful check, perhaps, on the ambitions of the sympathetic imagination. *Mine is happening to me* – a factor of incalculable weight. The identity crisis in question was a humble thing; but it was exclusively and indivisibly mine.

PART II

Chapter 1
France in the Time of Iraq
1: Anti-américain

Invisible ink

There's no doubt about it: this is the life.

St-Malo, on the north-west coast of France, in March 2003. The name of the seafront hotel was Le Méridien . . .

Freshly showered, and wearing only a pair of kitten-heeled red shoes and an attractive lower undergarment (arguably her coolest pants), she came out of the bathroom and into the bedroom and stood quite still with her back to the bright bay window. There was a one-page single-spaced typescript in her hand . . .

Beauty is in the eye of the beholder. So wrote the Irish novelist Margaret Hungerford (1855–97; typhoid) in her best-known novel *Molly Bawn* (which earns a friendly mention in *Ulysses*). It is a generous thought, and memorably expressed; its spirit is inclusive and egalitarian (*there's hope for us all*, it murmurs); and it has the further merit of being broadly true. But 'beauty', here, is a misnomer or an example of poetic licence: Mrs Hungerford means physical charm, or appeal, or the power to attract and endear. Her aphorism doesn't really apply to the beautiful.*

* Although etymology is a notoriously poor guide to meaning, it makes its contribution to the weight, feel, and flavour of a word. 'Cute' is a shortening of 'acute' (shrewd). And as for 'pretty': 'ORIGIN: OE *praettig* (in sense "cunning, crafty", later "clever, skilful"), from a W. Gmc base meaning "trick"'. By contrast, 'beauty' regally proceeds – via 'OFr *beauté* – from Latin *bellus* 'beautiful, fine' . . . There is something remarkably undesigning about beauty. Although no one really understands it (and I include scientists who study nothing else), everyone knows it when they see it. Beauty isn't shrewd or crafty and it is not a trick. Beauty, perhaps, is more like a force of nature.

You see, in the case of the woman with her back to the window – it wasn't just him. In her case there was more than one beholder; there was in fact something like a beholder consensus. To take one concrete example, in the mid-1990s *Vogue* magazine ran a feature called 'The World's Hundred Most Alluring Women'; and she came thirty-sixth . . . She was half Uruguayan and half Hungarian-American Jewish – a very *good* mixture, that: and just look at it all. Behold the moist brown flesh, the graceful power of the legs, the thick black hair wet and gleaming. Her figure, by the way, had been variously described in print as 'hourglass' and 'pneumatic'.

Just for a moment she tipped her head back and sneered at him, the scrolled upper lip slightly skewed to the side – Presleyesque. This porno sneer was in fact a respectful acknowledgement of his performance, half an hour earlier, in the bed where he yet sought his ease . . . In the porno version he would've been, say, a local cat burglar who, once within the hotel, is surprised in mid-theft by the elegant lady guest – but succeeds in reassuring her, to such effect that before very long . . .

'Who's paying for this?' he said.

'I am,' she said. 'They are.'

Now she dipped down and took a gulp of orange juice from the breakfast tray.

She said, 'Are you ready? Have you got your watch?'

'*Oui*. Right . . . Go!'

Exactly two minutes later he said, 'Exactly two minutes.'

'Perfect.'

'Perfect.'

What was she doing, standing there near-naked with the typescript in her hand? She was rehearsing and timing her acceptance speech for the Prix Mirabeau (category: Non-Fiction). Her speech was in French.

And she was his wife.

And this was the life.

Yes, perfect, perfect. Still, his recurring thoughts, the recurring questions posed in his mind, even when he was half asleep, all had to do with suicide. Not his own suicide, not exactly, but suicide.

Why? What was eating Martin Amis?

Oh, he had his troubles. And on top of everything else, in a planetary beauty contest – a real-life Miss World – with approximately

1,800,000,000 bobbing hopefuls up there on the stage, his wife only came thirty-sixth. Hence, conceivably, his obscure cafard. Or was there more to it than that?

———

So what about this couple (we ask, while they ready themselves for the outside world)? How can one possibly address them in print? They had been together for nearly a decade, and their union was blessed not only with children (those two young daughters of theirs) but also with happiness.

And happiness, in literature, is a void and a vacuum, an empty space. *Happiness writes in white ink on a white page*, said a certain poet, novelist, and playwright, namely Henry Marie Joseph Frédéric Expedite Millon de Montherlant (1895–1972). And it's true. You can take a blank sheet of paper and cover it with fine prose; but the sheet is still blank. What can the pen do with happiness – with the invisible ink of happiness?

The struggle for coffee

'I want my *grand crème*,' she said.

He said, 'And I want my *double espresso*.'

Making their intention quite plain, this enviably – indeed nauseatingly – compatible pair stepped out of Le Méridien and turned right towards the *croisette* and the Atlantic Ocean. She said,

'Oh my God,' she said. 'The heat! The people!'

It was certainly a warm day, a warm day on the coast of Brittany. And there were certainly people, people, people – everywhere. Festival-goers, and writers and publishers and representatives of the media, and also families, large families, pressing coastward . . .

'Yeah, we've had it relatively easy so far, El.' El was short for Elena – and also for Elvis, whom she did resemble when she had her hair up in a quiff. 'Now things could start getting really rough. And I want you to make me a promise. That you'll watch yourself here in France.'

'We're getting no nearer to the sea . . . Why, particularly?'

'Because it's a sensitive time – with your tanks revving up, even now, in the deserts and marshes. You're an American. And you a Jeeew.

And you know what France is like. Promise me you won't take any of France's shit.'

It was barely more than a party game I sometimes played with Elena: the aforementioned notion that people were like countries and countries were like people. And we have already drawn one obvious conclusion: countries are like men.

Seagoing vessels are often feminised in spoken and written English. Are boats like women? Admirers of Melville and Conrad will need no persuading that sailing ships, at least (galleons, yachts, schooners), have qualities that might be considered feminine. But what made anyone think for a moment that *countries* were like girls?

For instance, how clearly absurd it would be to write: 'Prerevolutionary China considered that it was in her interests to maintain the status of women at about the level of livestock.' Or, more relevantly, try this: 'A year after her victorious campaign in Western Europe in 1940, Nazi Germany turned her attention to a war of annihilation in the USSR.'

Historically countries are men; they have always behaved like men.

In St-Malo I was trying to imagine France as a person, France as a bloke, in 2003 . . . Well, contrary to popular belief, France has made substantial and still-evolving efforts to come to terms with those 'dark years' of his: the Occupation, from the summer of 1940 to the autumn of 1944. During this period, to quote the historian Tony Judt, France 'played Uriah Heep to Germany's Bill Sikes' (and he was an unusually energetic Uriah, as we know). In trying to face up to his sins and crimes, France was and is encumbered by the persistence of a certain superstition: that of anti-Semitism.*

What immediately concerned me here was how he, France, was feeling about this venture in Mesopotamia, this thrust by the US-led Coalition of the Willing. Because the imminent Iraq War brushed up

---

* The Anti-Defamation League has produced a compelling world map of anti-Semitism. Some scores for Europe: 4 per cent of Swedes are anti-Semitic; in Britain the figure is 8 per cent (though in Ireland it is 20), in Germany the figure is 27, in Austria 28, and in France 37 (and in Greece it is a near-Middle Eastern 69). The ADL's findings are dated 2015; in that year over 8,000 Jews left France (mostly for Israel), compared to 774 from Britain and a mere 200 from Germany.

against another French neurosis: anti-Americanism . . . In the coming days my wife would be often in the public eye; and she was an American Jew. So how would he take to her, France?

'*Finally.*'

Yes, here at last was the North Atlantic with its rollers and combers and breakers. And, yes, an abnormally, a freakishly warm day, and there were citizens, down on the sand, who were cautiously availing themselves of it. French parents and grandparents on towels and blankets, French boys and girls with buckets and spades and beach balls, and dozens of French dogs jumping and digging and running their laps and loops . . .

'*The miniature gaiety of seasides,*' he said. 'Larkin.'

'I can't believe you're still going on about that.'

'Surely I'm allowed to quote him aren't I?'

'All right,' she said longsufferingly. 'Go on then.'

'*Steep beach, blue water, red bathing caps,* Elena. *The small hushed waves' repeated fresh collapse.* What's wrong with that? I used to quote him before.'

'I can't believe you're bending over for her. For Phoebe Phelps.'

'How am I bending over for Phoebe Phelps?'

'By letting yourself get . . . bedevilled. It was such an obvious attempt to spook you. And it worked. Look at you, you're cooperating, you're collaborating with that mad bitch . . . And all that was *years* ago.' (It was eighteen months ago: September 12, 2001.) 'It's why you've been so quiet, so . . .'

'Mm.'

This was true and it was a grief to him. Elena, he guiltily noted, had taken to ending many of her declarative sentences with a plaintive *don't you think?* or *wouldn't you say?* or, more simply, *right?* It was a gentle and a just reproach. He too was exasperated by it: why this silence, why this unwelcome seclusion? And it was worse than unfriendly. It was unhusbandly. But it was real.

'I'm very sorry. A temporary condition, and it's lifting. I don't feel quiet today.' No, in fact he felt uncontrollably garrulous. Realising this, he jumped to a new conclusion: So now I'm bipolar . . . His relationship with his sanity was becoming self-conscious, or going back to being

147

self-conscious – the way it was in his teens. 'I'm feeling talkative, and I'll tell you for why. I'm thinking of starting a smirk novel.'

'What's a smirk novel?'

'A novel of self-congratulation, of unalleviated self-congratulation. There aren't many of them but they do exist – smirk novels. The one I read gloried in the author's literary fame and stupendous success with women. We're in the land of the scowl novel. *Le roman de grimace*. Just the place to get going on a *roman de* . . . What's French for smirk?'

She considered. 'I don't think they have a word for smirk. It would be something like *un petit sourire suffisant*.'

'Really? Not just *smirque* with a q? All right. A *roman de petit* . . .'

'*Sourire suffisant*.'

'A *roman de petit sourire suffisant*. A smirk novel. Now what the *fuck* is all this?'

Their pace had slowed – in forced deference to an unusual concentration of pedestrians. Unusual demographically, that is. One often saw children en masse, but Martin wondered if he had ever seen such an army, such a serried host of seniors. These ancient parties, these Decembrists, were inching their way along the narrow strip between the housefronts and the kerbside barriers. All this was clearly going to take a very long time. He said,

'How'd it happen? We stepped out for a simple – an honest – cup of coffee. And now we're trapped in this incredible operation with all these elderly.'

Yes, his *Concise Oxford Dictionary* was behind the game with *elderly*, confining itself to '*adj*. old or ageing'; future editions would be forced to add '*n*. (*pl*. same) an old or ageing person'. In America nowadays they confidently used *elderly* as a noun: *The guy freaked out in the hospital*, for example, *and gunned down three elderly*.

'I want my cappuccino,' said Elena. 'And I keep wondering how old I'm going to be when we get there.'

'Me too. But you, you'll still be reasonably young. I'll be an elderly.'

It could have been worse – much worse. Martin wasn't ninety-three, he wasn't eighty-three, he wasn't seventy-three, he wasn't even sixty-three, not yet; he was fifty-three (a slightly vampiric fifty-three to Elena's forty-one), and just crossing the line, just turning the corner and beginning to make out, in the grey twilight, the shapes and forms of what lay ahead of him. Sensory adjustments to the new order of being were already well under way. For some time he had been aware that, in his outward guise, he was physically undetectable by anyone under the age of thirty-five. In the year 2000, in Uruguay, he walked around a crowded nightclub (in search of a young cousin) and he realised something: he was the Invisible Man.*

The young had stopped seeing him; and now, in dubious recompense, he saw afresh that hitherto invisible population, the seriously old.

'I encountered Jed Slot,' she said as they stood there waiting.

'So did I.' Jed Slot was the mystery-man writer at Le Méridien. 'When I saw him I thought his huge bestseller must be about computers or video games. What was he doing when you saw him?'

'Being interviewed. By an incredibly brainy-looking old lady with a lorgnette. What was he doing when you saw him?'

'Being interviewed. By two incredibly brainy-looking students or post-grads.'

'His book's fiction, Mart, and it's not just a bestseller. It's a *succès d'estime.*'

'I'm sorry to hear that. Nah. Good luck to Jed. All power to Slot. He seemed nice enough . . . Jesus, *c'est incroyable, ça* – these old wrecks!' He said, 'Mark it well, kid. The future is going to look like this. In twenty years or so. And I don't just mean me. They say it's the gravest demographic change of all time. The *silver tsunami.*'

'I'm preparing myself for it. That'll be when all you filthy baby boomers get sicked on us.' She smiled. *'You're* the crap generation.'

The continuing struggle for coffee

Nothing had changed.

'What we're in', he said, 'is no longer just an emergency. It's a humanitarian crisis. A deepening humanitarian crisis. I want my coffee.'

---

* Meaning the H. G. Wells creation so thrillingly serialised on TV when I was a boy. And now that same boy looked like the Invisible Man – not as you saw him in company or in public (a tweed-jacketed and roll-necked mummy in dark glasses), but as he was when he went on his missions, invisibly naked except for a pair (or so Martin, aged eleven in South Wales, had automatically supposed) of invisible underpants. In the nightclub it was as if I wasn't there. It was a moment that broke the illusion described by Tolstoy: our feeling that time was something that just moves past us while we stay the same . . .

'*I* want, I want my coffee,' sang Elena (to the tune of 'I Want My Potty'). 'I want my coffee. I've just thought. If Robinson was North Korea, what's Hitch?'

'Good question. Suggest somewhere.'

'Israel.'

'I was going to say Israel. Yes, like Saul in a way, Hitch is Israel. He has chosen the most difficult position. And the most difficult position for *him* – for him in particular. An anti-Zionist who turns out to be Jewish.'

'He didn't *choose* to turn out to be Jewish. But I see what you mean about difficult positions. And now Hitch, the Marxist hawk, is going to get his war. I saw him on CNN while you were having your shit.'

'Elena . . . Uh, and how did he look about his war?'

'Very steely.'

'Mm. Did I tell you he rang the day before we left? To "encourage" me, as he put it. "What are your doubts, Little Keith?" Well we'd been through everything else so I just said, "Two things. In the war on terror, is this the best use of resources? And, second, lack of legitimacy."'

'Is that all? And?'

'He pooh-poohed the first, but the second gave him pause. He acknowledged a certain deficit of legitimacy. But you know what he said to Ian – a couple of weeks ago? Hitch said, "It's going to be a wonderful adventure."'

'An adventurist war,' they both said at once.

Actually Martin was starting to think it was something even more capricious than that: it was an experimentalist war. He said, 'While you in your turn were powdering your nose, Elena, I too had a look at CNN. They'd moved on to Bush. And I didn't like the way the president was playing with his dogs. With Barney and Spot. I didn't like the way he was playing with Barney and Spot.'

His wife shifted her weight from foot to foot. 'Have you *told* Hitch?' She gave him a few seconds until he understood. 'Or didn't you want to bother him with Larkin at this stressful time.'

'No, I haven't. But I do want to bother him. Because he understands something about Larkin that I know I'll never get. I won't get it because I don't want it. The love of *that* England, you know, all those muddy little villages with fucking stupid names like Middle Wallop and Six Mile Bottom. And Pocklington.'

'Wait. What's the Phoebe business got to do with Larkin? I know it's *ostensibly* about Larkin. But what it's really about is Phoebe and your father. And about you. *Christ.*'

She meant all the oldsters – the slowly and tremulously bobbing coachloads of oldsters . . . Their numbers had at last begun to thin, and there was a loose sense of calibrated delay – as in a stacked aircraft groaning around high above the tarmac, with the captain coming on to say they were ninth in line for landing. The coachloads of oldsters continued to filter through the gap, stiffly upright, the feet moving in soft-shoe shuffle (no space admitted between cobble and sole); every few seconds they glanced at one another, to give encouragement or to seek mutual recognition – or mutual verification; on they edged, their faces flickering not just with discomfort, difficulty, and mistrust but also with innumerable calculations, every step measured on a scale of soreness, effort, and jeopardy. Looking beyond them, beyond their denim-clad shoulders, their pinions of cloud-white hair, their ears furry in the sun, Martin saw that the next stretch of road seemed reverse-telescoped, and the next junction felt implausibly remote, like gate 97E in a Texan airport. The elderly were making him think of planes – planes, and the poetry of departures. Here we are on our journey. Is it far? Are we nearly there?

Old age kills travel . . .
    I interviewed Graham Greene (1904–91) in Paris on the occasion of his eightieth birthday, and I interviewed V. S. Pritchett (1900–97) in London on the occasion of his ninetieth. 'Old age kills travel,' said Pritchett.
    Greene talked about failing powers, but only in the context of his religion, his faith. Faith was a power, and faith weakened with time. His listener, who was thirty-five, was far from terrified by this prospect: if it made you less inclined to crave the good opinion of supernatural beings, I reasoned, then old age wasn't all downhill. Pritchett talked about failing powers in the context of putting words on the page. And *that* was frightening. His verdict was often on my mind, in 2003.
    'As one gets older,' he said, 'one becomes very boring and longwinded to oneself. One's thoughts are longwinded, whereas before they were

really rather nice and *agitated*. The story is a form of travel. As I go across the page my pen is travelling. Travelling through minds and situations that reveal their strangeness to you. Old age kills travel. Things don't come suddenly to you. You're mainly protecting yourself.' He meant protecting yourself physically and emotionally: no surprises, please. 'Stories come up on you almost by accident. And now one tends to live a life in which there are no accidents.' Pritchett paused, and then added with a smile of pain, 'It's nothing to do with that really. It's just getting older.'

Martin said, 'You mean . . . ?'

'I mean one can't travel any more. And one's pen can't travel any more. So one can't write any more.'

Now they were suddenly on the move. His wife stepped forward, and he followed.

Is Europe an elderly?

'*Merci beaucoup*,' she said. '*Cela va bien.*'

And it is now the novelist's pleasant duty to report that the cappuccino, and indeed the double espresso, were at last on their way.

'*Écoute*, Elena. I understood bits of your speech but not all of it. I hope it's nice and tactful. You know how sensitive France can be.'

'Sensitive. You mean touchy and vain.'

The two of them were seated side by side at a table in the market square, facing the town's dominant hotel (which had an Alpine, cuckoo-clock look to it); above their heads striped awnings faintly clacked and rattled in the ozonic gusts. He said,

'All right, you know how touchy and vain France is. How sensitive Jean-Jacques can sometimes be. And your Secretary of Defense, Mr Rumsfeld, is already being impossibly rude – in all directions. Typical German.'

'Why, what's he done now?'

'Well, this isn't the main thing, but he said, if you please – he said he could easily do without my help in Iraq! After all that trouble I went to.'

'You don't want to be there anyway.'

'No, *I* don't. I personally don't want us to be there. But Blair does. And Rumsfeld taunts him like that – his best ally.' Martin carefully lowered his face towards the coffee cup (he had become suspicious, after innumerable spillages and breakages, of the stability of his hands). 'I don't want to be there. But Bush does. And so does Hitch. Hitch has *gone on the road* for this war. What he calls a media burn. Like the one he did on Princess Di and Mother Teresa. Remember?'

'No.'

'When was it? 1996 or '97. They died in the same week, and Hitch was much in demand – for "balance". He said he was the only human being in America who was perfectly ready to dump on the pair of them. Especially the nun.'

'Okay, but why's he doing a media burn for Iraq? It was that sex breakfast he had with Wolfowitz.'

'It was more like a sex snack. In the Pentagon. Hitch wants regime change. What he's after is the end of Saddam. Who grew up as a bucketboy in the torture corps.'

'. . . And what was the main thing Rumsfeld did?'

'Herr Rumsfeld?' For effect Martin took his time. 'He called Jean-Jacques an elderly . . . That's right. He called me one too. That reference to "old Europe". According to him, we're just a load of old elderly. I happen to find that very hurtful.'

'Yes, and a bit snide too – considering your demographic troubles . . . *My* birth rate is sound. Yours is crap. So is Europe's. That thing we saw about Italy. *Italy.*'*

Additional coffees were gracefully served. Martin said,

'Jean-Jacques' crap birth rate has tormented him for centuries. *Dénatalité.* But he got to work on that and his birth rate's now better than Mario's. Or Miguel's. Jean-Jacques isn't touchy about his birth rate. But don't say anything about his war record. That's a tender spot.'

'I'll bet. If it wasn't for me, they'd still be here.'

Even when they weren't playing party games, he often wanted to ask Elena to recast certain sentences using proper nouns (in this case, *If it wasn't for America, the Germans would still be in France*), but he hardly ever needed to: after a couple of seconds he always knew what she

---

* By the year 2060 (we had read) most Italians will have no sisters, no brothers, no aunts, no uncles, and no cousins. Yes, Italy.

meant. The point being that she reflexively felt that her thoughts were his thoughts – and after a beat or two they were. It was that inestimable thing, never complete of course and for good reason: co-identity.*

'After all,' she said, 'I won the war.'

'Not so, El. If it wasn't for you, you claim, Fritz would still be here. In 1940, after the fall of France, who still *stood*, who stood alone? Me. I. *I* stood alone against the fascist beast. For well over a year. While you, you quailed before Lindbergh and what was it, "America First".'

'But then I rode to your rescue.'

'Then you came in – but not until Fritz called you out. By declaring war on you, my dearest. It's true that once you joined me in the struggle I knew we couldn't possibly lose.† Uh . . . hang on, what does GI stand for in GI Joe?'

'General Issue. Or Government Issue.'

'Really?' he said. 'So that was the earlier version of *grunt* . . . GI Joe didn't win the war. Nor did Tommy Atkins. It was Ivan who won the war, Elena. Ivan *absorbed* Fritz. At the cost of twenty-five million lives.'

She thought about this. 'But you can't say that if it wasn't for Ivan, Fritz would still be here. *Ivan* would still be here . . . Well, we'd have won in the end, you and I.'

'Mm, I suppose. But yes, Elena, we'd have seen off Fritz, you and I. And Yukio. And Mario. In the end.'

'Precisely . . . Look at you. You talk about not offending the French. And look at you.'

He saw what she meant. Martin had before him, at chest height, an eyecatching paperback called *France and the Nazis*.

'Quite right too,' she continued. 'I'm going to take that book and brandish it on stage. Why should I mollycoddle Jean-Jacques? He hates *me*. So why the hell should I humour Jean-Jacques? Fuck him.'

---

* For an evocation of co-identity, I again turn to Tolstoy. In the novella 'Family Happiness' (sometimes called 'Happy Ever After') Tolstoy gives us the nocturnal imaginings of the orphaned seventeen-year-old Marya as she reviews the attentions paid to her by her guardian, Sergei: 'I felt that my dreams and thoughts and prayers were living things, living there in the darkness with me, hovering about my bed and standing over me. And every thought I had was his thought, and every feeling his feeling. I did not know then that this was love – I thought that it was something that often happened . . .' Tolstoy is the presiding spirit of this chapter. Who else has made happiness swing on the page?
† On the night after Pearl Harbor, Churchill said that for the first time in years his insomnia withdrew, and he slept the sleep of 'the grateful and the saved'; he said he hoped that the sleep of eternity would be as soft and as pure.

America hates France back

Christine Jordis, Martin's editor at Gallimard, briefly stopped by, and in her wonderfully *finished* English enlightened them about the meteoric Jed Slot – and all the huge prizes and genius awards that were sure to come his way . . .

As it progressed the afternoon was getting ever warmer. Elena naturally and eagerly wanted a long stroll on the beach, plus a real hike on the cliffs and the headlands; but she had a media burn of her own to deal with, starting at four . . . They looked up. A solitary senior, somehow detached from his friends and minders, veered around in harmless disarray, coming so close to their table that they could read the address he had pinned to his shirt: *C/0 Dr Priestly, 127 Marine Parade, Brighton, Sussex.*

'Jesus. I went to school on Marine Parade. That boarding crammer, remember? . . . Uh, let me try some counselling, some guidance here, Pulc.' Pulc was short for pulchritude. 'I want to help you and France work it out.'

'France started it.'

'Quite true,' he said (and he registered, as he often did, the bare fact of Elena's birth order: the youngest of four). 'Because you, my bride, represent soulless modernity, you're mechanised, standardised – according to son-of-the-soil Jean-Jacques. Okay. Now you're entitled to resent his anti-Americanism. But back home, you're letting Francophobia get out of hand.'

'I know I am.'

'You're having one of your funny spells. One of your neurotic episodes.' One of your 'orrible turns. Yes – like the time you tried to give up drink, like the time you feared Reds under your beds, like the time you test-drove your domino theory in South East Asia. 'And now you're coming down with a nasty case of –'

'It's true. You've seen all this about freedom fries . . .'

'I have.' At the present time – mid-March, 2003 – cafeterias in the House of Representatives were offering 'freedom fries' and 'freedom toast', served no doubt with freedom mustard and a garnish of freedom beans, and (let's clunk on with this for a while) congressmen in their hotel rooms were dispensing freedom kisses before peeling off the freedom knickers of their secretaries or interns and before peeling on their own freedom letters . . .* He said,

'Will I still be able to say, "Excuse my French"?'

'Excuse my French? Meaning sorry my French is crap?'

'No. As in, He's a rotten little prick, if you'll excuse my French.'

'I don't see why not. Sure.'

They read their books. Elena had another coffee; and he took the opportunity to order a modest beer . . . Actually America, at present, would by no means excuse your French, in the literal sense. Francophobia was playing so well that it was on course to decide the 2004 general election. ('Hi,' began one Republican bigwig as he opened a meeting, '– or as John Kerry might say, *Bonjour.*') . . . Martin received his beer and lit a cigarette to go with it. Most American politicians had foibles and episodes they wanted to play down: that ten-year relationship with the very special (if somewhat troubled) Times Square rentboy; that billion-dollar big-oil kickback for thwarting the environmentalists. And so it was with Kerry, who as a child had learnt to speak French. The rentboy was morals, the kickback was ethics, but speaking French was something like treason. Martin said,

'You seem to have forgotten that France was your crucial ally in the Revolutionary War. Jean-Jacques helped Uncle Sam – to spite Tommy Atkins. Yorktown, Elena. If it wasn't for France, I'd still be there. In America.'

'No. I'd've crushed you and swept you out long ago.'

'All right. But you know on prize day they're going to hate your fucking guts.'

'Of course.'

'Because you're an American Jew.† This is the land of the anti-Semitic *riot*. Our George Steiner says that *at any time* you can get an "explosion" of French chauvinism against Jews.'

---

* America went through exactly the same routine after the First War, targeting the Germans, and we had 'liberty cabbage' and even 'liberty measles'. Except that Germany was a foe, while France, now, was just a carping ally. This freedom–liberty business, I later discovered, predates the birth of America. The domestic alternative to the heavily taxed tea of the Boston Tea Party was an 'unappetising potion called Liberty Tea', writes Barbara Tuchman in *The March of Folly*.

† At one point in Ron Rosenbaum's classic *Explaining Hitler*, Yehuda Bauer, the dean of Holocaust studies, tells the author that French anti-Semitism was 'far worse, far more virulent, deep-rooted and bitter than Germany's in the pre-World War I period'. Bauer cites the highly regarded historian George Mosse, who said that 'if someone

'Not up here, surely. It's like America – for that kind of thing you have to go south. Anyway, if there's so much as a *whisper* of dissent on Friday, then I'll . . .'

He said, 'Now now, Pulc. Now now.'

Oradour

He sat back and sipped his beer and inhaled his fill of smoke. *Oh*, as Christopher often said, *the miracle of the cigarette* . . .

'Are you going to stop?'

Stop what? he thought – but only for a moment (he knew very well what was coming, but as usual he sought to delay it or divert it). Stop what? Stop being a sap for Phoebe's depth-charge *venganza*, stop brooding about Larkin, about Hilly? Stop thinking about suicide? Stop boning up on war and dearth and megadeath?

'Stop what?' He raised his eyes from the page. 'Stop reading about massacres?'

She said, 'I saw the books you brought along. What were they?' Sadly Elena shook her head. '*The Rape of Nanking* and uh, the one about Rwanda.'

'*We Wish To Inform You That Tomorrow We Will Be Killed With Our Families.*'

'There was one about an endless battle. Verdun. And a huge biography of Genghis Khan. Why? Why read about massacres?'

'I don't know.' And he wondered, Why do we read what we read? Because it answers our state of mind? 'There were plenty of massacres in wartime France. *France and the Nazis* deals with two of them. Tulle and Oradour.' Elena seemed attentive (and unimpatient), so he continued. 'In Tulle the SS ransacked people's attics and cellars – looking for rope. They hanged ninety-nine men on the Avenue de la Gare. Off lamp posts and balconies. That was a reprisal for forty Germans killed by the

had come to me in 1914 and told me that one country in Europe would attempt to exterminate the Jews, I would have said then, "No one can be surprised at the depths to which France could sink." Bauer and Mosse are both serious men, but I find myself starting back from this and shaking my head. For one thing, I can't imagine the Holocaust translated into French – a language without tonic stresses. '*Sortez! En dehors! Vite! Plus vite!*'; these words have none of the plausibility and menace of '*Raus! Raus! Schnell! Schneller!*'

partisans. But the next morning the same SS division went to Oradour and murdered absolutely everyone. The –'

'Christ, well you're not quiet any more . . . Would your mum like to hear all about Oradour?* Would your daughters?'

He frowned and said, 'I think I read about violence because I don't understand it. It's the thing I hate more than anything else on earth and I don't understand it . . . I'm like the memory man in Saul's novella.' This was *The Bellarosa Connection* (1997). 'He has that Holocaust dream, and he's shattered to discover that he doesn't understand it. He doesn't "understand merciless brutality". Me neither.'

'I don't know, maybe that's as it should be. Who does understand it?'

'In the months before Liberation there were lots of little Oradours all over France . . . In your acceptance speech, Elena, don't dwell too long on 1940 to 1944. Spare France that. Mm, I suppose it's not especially considerate of me, reading this in the town square. The cover . . .'

He pushed the book across the table. There was the famous stock photograph (one of the most gruesome ever taken): Hitler at dawn in Paris, as conqueror (with the splayed calves of the Eiffel Tower in the background), sauntering around at the head of his aides, all of them in collar and tie, in leather greatcoat (and nearly toppling over backwards with power and pride); and there he is, his pale and pouchy face under that crested cap, wearing an expression of imperturbable entitlement.

'Imagine if that was Big Ben. I don't know, if that'd happened, I wouldn't . . .'

'What?'

'I wouldn't have been fit to marry you, El. Seriously. I would've choked even as I begged for your hand.' Her face showed clemency as well as curiosity, so he continued, 'Well, think. Let's tick them off. Great Britain easily crushed in battle by the Wehrmacht. A fascist regime installed in uh, Cheltenham. With its militia sworn to combat democracy and "the Jewish leprosy" and defend Christian – i.e., Catholic – civilisation.

---

* The toll was 642. The Germans machine-gunned 190 men in sheds and barns; 247 women and 205 children were confined to the church, which was set on fire. The village was looted and razed; there were six survivors. This happened in Oradour-sur-Glane, and it was the wrong village, with no connection to the Resistance. Apparently the SS wanted Oradour-sur-Vayres – just under twenty miles away.

Meanwhile, SS massacres in Middle Wallop and Pocklington. And Jews being rounded up – by English bobbies following English orders – and carted off to Silesia.* *Ferries* from Hull to Hamburg . . . Given all that in my past, would you consent to be mine?'

Being alone freely

When I say he thought about suicide, I don't mean he was sizing it up as his next move. He just went on thinking about it: suicide. And he seemed to believe that everyone else was thinking about it too: he was aware that they weren't, but he seemed to believe that they were. This kind of mental tic was known in the trade as 'suicidal ideation' (and was considered an unpromising sign). But there it was: he kept asking himself, Why aren't there more suicides?

'The time has come for you to change your ways,' she said. 'It's time.'

'What ways? This book's good, you know, thoughtful, well written. But there's no index. If it *did* have an index, one entry would go Hitchens, Christopher, page 204.'

She asked for the bill and said, 'Why? What's Hitch up to in *France and the Nazis*?'

'It's weird. He's singled out for praise by an inhabitant of present-day Vichy, Robert Faurisson. The nation's premier negationist – Holocaust denier.† He met Hitch at some dinner and says he admires his stuff. Probably just fancied him – fell for the velvet voice and the Oxford charm . . . Uh, is that what you mean, Elena? Has the time come to stop reading books like *France and the Nazis*?'

'No, that's not what I mean. I mean the thing in your other hand. The thing with smoke coming out of it . . . Do you *want* to stop?'

---

* The coralling – its manner, its dot-the-i cruelty – also followed the Nazi example. Before being herded on to cattle cars bound for Auschwitz, 13,152 people, including 4,051 children, were held for several days at the Vélodrome d'Hiver (a bicycle track in the middle of Paris, unventilated for the occasion) in July 1942; according to some reports, all the toilets were sealed and there was only one tap.
† It would be some years before Christopher wrote, 'A Holocaust denier is a Holocaust affirmer.' Though not nearly as rhetorically satisfying, 'Holocaust endorser', I told Christopher, would make the point less ambiguously.

Years ago Christopher said to him, 'I don't *want* to be a non-smoker.' And Martin said, 'I couldn't agree more' or 'Exactly' or even 'Hear hear' (or even 'Hear him, hear him!'). Their attitude to nicotine – and to benzene, formaldehyde, hydrogen cyanide, and all the other ingredients – seemed to be incurably adolescent.* They just couldn't connect it to life and death.

'You had one after breakfast,' said Elena. 'You had two after breakfast.'

'Ah, but I was smoking for a worthy cause.' He had managed to put it about that he needed a salutary cigarette or two after breakfast. To bring on the thing that Larkin called the daily 'contact with nature'. With *what* nature? Human nature? Animal nature? 'I was smoking in the furtherance of a noble dream.'

'And how did it go?'

'A disappointment. It was a crap shit, Elena, between you and me.'

'What are you smoking for now?'

'Uh, to steady my nerves. There's your speech on Friday. And the Iraq War on Saturday. I'll go on smoking for the duration, then quit when it's over.'

'I could be out of there in less than a month.'

'We, you mean we. I'm going in there too.'

'Yes, but I'm the one with all the power. I'm so powerful – why would I even bother to be anti-French?'

'And that's why you're so loathed. Hating you was government policy in postwar France. And you know who made hating you respectable? Sartre. Terrible guy.' In fact Martin had a soft spot for old Jean-Paul. Advised not very late in life that unless he gave up smoking he faced imminent quadriplegia, Sartre said he would need a while 'to think it over'. 'Him and Simone. They made hating you chic.'

'Look,' she said and nodded towards an owlish gentleman at the facing table, who was bent over a book (by Jean-François Revel) entitled *L'obsession anti-américaine*.

'Well there you are. Come on. You've got *Le Monde* in ten minutes.'

The two of them stood and gathered their things. He said,

---

* One day, in about 1997, I was confronted in a kitchen by two glass bowls of white crystals, sugar and salt, and it took me quite a long time to establish which was which. Another day, in about 2000, I noticed that my tongue had gone black. It turned out to be nothing that half an hour with a toothbrush and a bar of soap couldn't put right. But it did occur to me that pretty soon I'd probably have to start thinking about cutting down.

'An American *juive*. Who comes over here and wins all their literary prizes . . .'

'Not *all* their literary prizes. Only one.'

He didn't wake up happy in St-Malo – but very generally he resumed being happy in St-Malo. Why? He thought it might be the fact that he was never alone.

Very close to a hundred per cent of his working life was spent in unrelieved solitude: the room, the chair, the flat surface, the page. All day, every day (and especially Christmas Day) . . . And what was it he did for a living, in that annex at the back of the garden in NW1? A disembodied observer might conclude, after an hour or so, that all he did for a living was smoke. Oh yeah, and pick his nose and scratch his backside and stare into space. What he did was becoming more and more mysterious to him; and so was solitude. Larkin again ('Vers de Société'):

> Only the young can be alone freely.
> The time is shorter now for company,
> And sitting by a lamp more often brings
> Not peace, but other things.

And for Martin this was existential. If he couldn't be alone, if he couldn't be alone freely . . . What *was* writing? Writing was a soliloquy: *solus* 'alone' + *loqui* 'speak'. So what would happen if he couldn't be alone?

'Let's go.' She shouldered her bag. 'Okay. Stop smoking. Stop reading so much about massacres. And stop brooding about Larkin and that hellhag Phoebe.'

'Will do. Uh, remind me, Pulc,' he said as he rose. '*Why* are we invading Iraq? I really can't remember.'

'Uh, weapons of mass destruction.'

'Ah yes. Well we know for sure that Iraq hasn't got any – otherwise we wouldn't be invading it. WMDs make you unassailable . . . I suspect Bush is doing it just to get a second term. Americans never fail to re-elect a president at war . . . You don't have *raison*, Elena. And guess what a majority of your compatriots take to be their *casus belli*. I saw a poll. They think it's vengeance.'

'Vengeance for what?'

'No one who knows anything about it thinks so. But most Americans believe it's retaliation. Invading Iraq constitutes rightful *payback* for September 11.'

As it turned out, the levelling of the Twin Towers – together with the mauling of the Pentagon – did find a place in the strained rationale for the war in Iraq: *raisons d'état* demanded it, to assert American *resolve* and *credibility*. After September, Kissinger reportedly told George W. Bush in 2002, 'Afghanistan is not enough'; and a second Islamic nation would have to be made to yield.

You'd have thought that March 2003 was perhaps rather late for a wild overreaction to September 2001. Most of us got our wild overractions to September 2001 out of the way in September 2001. And as mere civilians we did it with no investment of blood or treasure; we did it in seclusion, in the privacy of our hearts and minds.

Chapter 2
September 11
1: The day after

Wound

We begin with the day after – September 12, 2001.

I was in my rented workplace (kitchen, study, bedroom, bathroom, in a mews off Portobello Road), standing at the sink and attending to a wound. It was on the back of my right hand – just beneath the knuckle of the middle finger; about the size of a thumbnail, it was a wound upon a wound (there was a wound there already – sustained in mid-July). I gazed at it, I listened to it (I sometimes imagined I could hear the faint fizz of traumatised tissue), and I dabbed at it with a ball of cotton wool drenched in disinfectant . . . That morning, when I awoke in the marital bed, my pillow was haphazardly badged with blood; instantly I thought of three, no four possible outlets (mouth, nose, ears, *eyes*) until I remembered, with shallow relief. Of course: it was my right hand.

Now I crossed a doorway and activated the answering machine. Using the rewind button I found the message I wanted, which was logged at around eight o'clock that morning. *Martin. It's your old friend Phoebe here. I have something to tell you. Something to pass on to you. It's been bothering me for twenty-four years and I don't see why it shouldn't start bothering you. Expect a communication. Goodbye.*

It was her vendetta voice: not wholly unamused, but seriously embittered, with authentic grievance in it, something narrow-eyed and white-lipped (seldom the case when she taunted shifty suppliers of office furniture, evasive bookies, and the like). So authentic, indeed, that I felt the urge to consult my conscience about Phoebe Phelps. But before I could consult it, I would first have to find it . . . *Twenty-four years*: 1977. I thought for a moment and wondered, Was it that business with Lily? Surely not: that business with Lily was something I got away with. Wasn't it?

Well, I would find out.

The coffee cup, the ashtray, the open exercise book . . . He sat slumped at his desk. To repeat, it was September 12, 2001; and for the time being his work in progress (a novel) seemed neither here nor there – nor anywhere else. The way he now saw it, this particular fiction, and for that matter fiction itself (*Middlemarch*, *Moby-Dick*, *Don Quixote*, etc.), was demoted to nonentity – by World War III or whatever it was that announced itself the previous day.

He would soon learn that all the novelists (and all the poets and dramatists) were being asked by the Fourth Estate to write about September 11. Ian had already written about it (and Christopher, of course, had already written about it). Salman and Julian would be writing about it. All of them were asked, and all of them said yes. What else was there to write about? What else was there to do?

Asked that morning by the *Guardian* to write about September 11, he said yes. And so he turned to a fresh page and scrawled 'September 11' at the top of it. He wrote his fiction and his journalism in the same exercise books, so he just turned to a fresh page and began to unearth his parallel self: the one that wrote about reality, in editorial (or op-editorial) mode.* He usually made this switch with reluctance, even with some self-pity; but that morning he went about it with numb resignation. Then he just sat there, numbly smoking.

The part of him that produced fiction, he felt, was in any case shutting down for ever. And how did it feel? If you took its pulse, that day, it felt like a very minor addition of grief, to be tacked on to the grief that was due to the thousands of dead (no one yet knew how many

---

* A technical point. Poetry and fiction are silent. As J. S. Mill put it, the literary voice is not 'heard'; it is 'overheard'; it is a soliloquy addressed to no audience; it has no designs on anyone . . . All opinion journalism, including literary journalism (and most literary criticism), is an argument that seeks to persuade; coming *ex cathedra* (from the pulpit), it is pedagogic, it is 'interested', and it demands the loan of your ears . . . This rather exalted distinction is not so much purist as idealist in tendency; it doesn't apply to those who sit down with the express intention of producing a Bestseller, or a Masterpiece.

thousands – eight, ten?) and most particularly, most essentially, to those who found themselves leaping from the Towers: leaping out into the blue, and dropping seventy, eighty, ninety floors rather than stay for another instant within. They fell at the rate of thirty-two feet per second squared, and, as we later heard with our own ears, exploded like mortar shells when they hit the ground; they were not suicide bombers; these people, they were suicide bombs; and some of them were themselves already on fire . . .

So no fiction, thank you (he couldn't be doing with fiction), because fiction was partly a form of play – and reality was now *earnest*.*

With his stiffened (and throbbing) right hand he reached out and wrote *1) all over again the world seems bipolar*. And, yes, it really did . . . One day in the very early 1990s Martin made an announcement to Nat and Gus (they were perhaps seven and six). 'I'm so glad you won't have to live out your childhood under that shadow. As I did.' He meant what he said and they peered up at him, all meek and grateful . . . The shadow he had in mind derived from the Cold War and the equation $E=mc^2$: in other words (in Eric Hobsbawm's words), the forty-year 'contest of nightmares'. And that shadow did go, or it receded – to be replaced, yesterday, by another shadow. And what did that shadow derive from?

'It's an ideology within a religion,' said Christopher on the phone. 'This is fascism with an Islamic face.'†

---

* Later that week I compared notes with a much younger novelist, and I asked her, I asked Zadie, 'Do you feel the pointlessness of everything you've ever written and everything you'll ever write?' And she said, 'Yes. Yes, at first I did. But then your fighting spirit gets going . . .' This was true, and there was much to fight against: the opposition of forces and goals could hardly be plainer, could it – a matter of 'everything I love' versus 'everything I hate' (as Salman wrote in the *New York Times*). I could fight in the pages of the *Guardian*; but what could anyone fight for in (or with) fiction? . . . Christopher, incidentally, wrote about September 11 on September 11, September 12, September 13, September 20, October 8, October 15, October 22, and November 29, and went on writing about it in *Hitch-22* (2008) and *Arguably* (2010) and elsewhere.
† 'I know what fascism is,' I might have answered him, 'but what's Islam?' Everyone had at least heard of Islam, of course, but no non-specialist had heard of Islamism. And over the next weeks the bestseller lists of the First World hurriedly filled up with books on Islam (more than one of them by Bernard Lewis), as we very logically sought illumination about our new enemy. Far from ever wanting to 'destroy' Islam (as its leading voices claimed), the West needed to find out what Islam was . . . In media usage 'fascism with an Islamic face' became 'the unsatisfactory term "Islamofascism"' (*Hitch-22*).

In any event one thing was plain enough. The twelve-year hiatus – beginning on November 9, 1989, with the abdication of Communism – the great lull, the vacuum of apparent enemylessness (during which America could cosily devote a year to Monica Lewinsky and another year to O. J. Simpson), came to an end on September 11, 2001. And he already sensed that the new hatred, like the old, was somehow inward looking and self-tormented, and that its goals were unachievable and therefore unappeasable. Planetary agonism had resumed; and all over again the other half of the world (very roughly speaking, but so it felt) was out to kill his kids.

The doorbell sounded.

Special delivery

The doorbell sounded. Which would be a shattering development at any time. He wasn't expecting anyone (he very seldom expected anyone); and besides London on that Wednesday morning, yes, distant London, an ocean away, had an inert and abject air to it, sparse, silent – in fact sick to its stomach (even the buildings looked squeamish and tense), with few people in the streets, and all of them going where they were going because they had to, not because they wanted to (the idea of pleasure had withdrawn, had gone absent. It was not yet clear that the assailants were in general the armed enemies of pleasure).

When he didn't expect anyone and the doorbell rang, he crept to the window in the disused bedroom; here you could look down at an angle and see your callers on the doorstep as they stood there erectly blinking and composing themselves . . . He had often been struck by the fact that people who are monitored in this way tend to diffuse an aura of innocence. Now he thought he knew why: they are at that moment comparatively innocent, innocent compared to their furtive observer. And the woman outside did indeed seem innocent, considering she was Phoebe Phelps.

. . . And not Phoebe as she would be now, in 2001 (getting on for sixty), but Phoebe as she would've been then – in say 1978, or even 1971 (Tycoon Tanya), before he ever knew her. Seen from his vantage, seen from above: the slanted profile, the straight no-nonsense nose, the level chin out-thrust. But it was her shape, her form, her outline that ignited his recognition: she and Phoebe displaced exactly the same volume of air.

He went down and opened the door and said,

'Hello – I know you. You're Siobhan's girl.' There was an easing, and he continued, 'Maud. We took you out to tea at Whiteley's when you were ten.'

'Yes, that's me all right. I remember. You had very long hair.' For a moment she smiled unreservedly; but then the smile was quickly shelved or put aside, and she straightened up. 'Uh, Mr Amis, sorry to bother, but Aunt Phoebe asked me to pop this round, person to person. She doesn't trust the post. She says what they don't lose they steal. Or burn. Or in this case sell.'

'Sell? Who to?'

'There was mention of the *Daily Mail* . . .'

She held out the envelope and he took delivery – just his name (scornfully dashed off). 'Ah,' he said. 'This'll be my anthrax.'

'Sorry?'

'Anthrax. It's just hearsay. Last night I talked to a friend who lives in Washington DC, but for now he's stranded in Washington State. Seattle.'

'No flights?'

'No flights. Every non-military plane in America is grounded. And he says anthrax. You know,' Martin went on (it was a grey morning but harmlessly mild), 'the first thing they did, yesterday in New York, was test the air for toxins. Chemicals and spores. Anyway it's just hearsay, but anthrax is meant to be next.'*

'This isn't anthrax. It's just a letter.'

'Well, thanks. Thanks for your trouble.'

---

* '9–11-01. THIS IS NEXT,' began the note included in the first of the anthrax letters, six days later (September 18): 'TAKE PENACILIN NOW. / DEATH TO AMERICA. / DEATH TO ISRAEL. / ALLAH IS GREAT' . . . The anthrax letters killed five people and infected fifteen (and they cost the government $1 billion in cleanup and decontamination). Furthermore, they suffused the heart of every First Worlder with another sepsis of impotence and dread . . . It eventually turned out that the perpetrator was a man called Bruce Ivins, who worked in the national biodefence labs in Maryland. Ivins had a long history of mental 'episodes', suffering from a paranoia of pride as much as persecution (a committed threatener and feuder); he was thoroughly mixed-up all right, but he was neither foreign nor especially religious ('penacilin' and 'Allah is great' were mere chaff). Unapprehended by the law, Ivins went on a one-man suicide mission in July 2008.

'It's no trouble. My office is just round the corner. But . . .' She gave a soft wince. 'The thing is I'm supposed to wait while you . . . She expects an answer.'

'. . . Oh.' This was a forcing move, he later realised. He said, 'Well come on up.'

It was lovely and warm in his flat but it was warm for an unlovely reason. Each September he put the heating on a few days earlier in the month. The flesh thins, the blood thins; the horizons slip their moorings and drift a little nearer; and the creature slowly learns how to cover up and 'creep into its bedding' (Saul).

So his kitchen was tepid with the aroma of Cold Old Man – or so he resignedly presumed as he watched Maud slide off her leather jacket and hook it over a chair and blow the fringe clear of her brow. The white shirt, the soon unbuttoned charcoal waistcoat, the mauve skirt – businesswear for another kind of business (she worked for the PR firm called Restless Ambition in All Saints Road). Yes, she was very like Phoebe, very like Phoebe in her movements and address, the light, quiet step, the way she seemed to coast through the air . . .

He said, 'I'll read this next door. How long will I be gone would you say?'

'Oh no more than ten minutes. Fifteen. But then you'll have to do your reply.'

'. . . I'm sorry – there's some fresh coffee there.'

'Ooh, that'd be brilliant.'

'Take a seat. And here are the papers.' Headlines were spread out on the kitchen table. TERROR IN AMERICA . . . A NEW DAY OF INFAMY . . . ACT OF WAR . . . BASTARDS! 'Have you read it? The letter?'

'I've listened to it. A couple of times. There were uh, different versions.'

'Go on, give me a hint.'

'Well, the names didn't mean much to me. But I could see why she was worried about the media getting wind of it.'

He left the room holding the envelope between finger and thumb.

What was he expecting Phoebe to tell him? About the slow-acting but fatal social disease he had unknowingly transmitted, about the college-age triplets he had unknowingly sired . . . He took out the two stiff sheets and read. And reread. And emerged from his study saying,

'Maud, Phoebe *doesn't* expect an answer. There's no answer to this. She just wants you to tell her how I took it.'

'. . . Your hand.'

'Oh, *Christ.*'

The plaster on his knuckle, loosened (again) by the mobility of the joint, now dangled like the tongue of a dog while blood dribbled on to his palm and down his wrist. He woodenly moved to the sink and engaged the cold water, and flapped around with his other hand for the box of Band-Aids. She said,

'Let me do it . . . Mm, that looks quite nasty.'

Maud came up and stood close; she scrolled the dressing over his graze, scrolled it tight. Girls' hands, each finger with its own intelligent life; and his own hands, webbed, quivering, undefined . . .

He thanked her, and she took half a step back and asked him with a new kind of brightness, 'Do I remind you of her?' When he nodded she went on, 'People say we're very alike. The figure too, don't you think? Slim, but . . .'

'Vaguely,' he said – though for a moment he had definitely felt Phoebe draw near (her body weight, her force field with its orbs and planes).

'What was it you once said? About the wand?'

He turned his head away in a sort of shrug. 'Now Maud, tell your aunt I won't be writing back, or not yet anyway. I'll see what my wife says.'

She smiled now, with relief (and even approval), 'Oh, Phoebe said you might be one of them. A good husband. She *will* be disappointed. I'm afraid she slightly revelled in your divorce. Your new wife, she's very beautiful.'

'Thanks. And not only that . . . Apart from sending you here today with her, with her message, is Phoebe more or less all right?'

'Oh yes. She's rich suddenly. She sold her business.'

'What business? Oh never mind.' He offered his left hand, his good hand, which she took. 'Give her my . . .'

'Well thanks for the coffee. Personally I can't see the point of vengeance, can you? I mean, who benefits? And it's so much trouble.'

'Mm. Mm. But I bet vengeance was great fun in the old days. If you're the type and in the mood.'

'I'll walk myself down. I apologise for that nonsense about the wand. But I promised Phoebe. She just wanted to know. Anyway, again – sorry to bother.'

Loth and cold

Before I could see what my wife said about it (everything would be laid before her), I was asked to absorb two lessons, two readjustments, bequeathed by September 11. Both involved a subtraction of innocence.

Lesson number one. They would never look the same – those things up there in the firmament, those A-to-B devices, those people carriers: airbus, skytrain. On my way home that evening, at a traffic light, I saw one of them glinting in over the tower blocks . . . Already and unalterably associated with mass death, a commercial aircraft did not, perhaps, have that much innocence to lose; but only now did it look like a weapon.

Lesson number two. Planes would never look the way they used to, and neither (strange to say) would children.

Or my children. Who did not look the same. At the evening meal that Wednesday night in the house on Regent's Park Road all five of them were present: Bobbie (twenty-four), Nat (sixteen), Gus (fifteen), little Eliza (four), and tiny Inez (two).

In the L-shaped kitchen/dining room on the ground floor I gave everyone drinks (Eliza ordering milk), laid the table – six places plus a high chair – and did odd jobs for my wife at the stove, and chatted away as convincingly as I could . . .

My feeling for my daughters and sons: it was more than a change, it was a capsizal. The sensory pleasure they gave me when all of them were gathered had its core in their strength of numbers, the amount of them, all the flesh and bone and brain they added up to; but now it was that same multiformity that made my heart feel loth and cold. Because I knew I couldn't protect them. Actually you cannot protect your children, but you need to feel you can. And the delusion was quite gone, replaced by a bad-dream sensation, not a nightmare, quite – more like a dream of nudity in a crowded public place . . .

The connoisseur of vengeance would savour just this – the taste inside our mouths, the mineral sourness of a lost battle, the ancient, the Iron Age taste of death and defeat.

'Will there be a war?' asked Nat. Nobody answered.

In the crook of the room there was a miniature TV wedged into a low cupboard (with folding doors). For the last couple of weeks it had often been tuned to the US Open at Flushing Meadows (and only three days ago, on Sunday, Lleyton Hewitt had in the end thrashed Pete Sampras 7–6, 6–1, 6–1). At that moment, I saw, the little set was silently rescreening the clips – the first plane, the second plane . . .

Inez staggered over there and took the two white panels in her hands ready to slam them shut. 'No . . . *tennis,*' she said scathingly, as the North Tower (the first to be hit, the second to drop) folded in on itself; and there was New York under its soiled sheepskin of chalk-thick smoke.

Parfait Amour

'Okay.' He took the envelope from his breast pocket. 'Now you're going to have to be a good sport about this, Elena, and you're going to have to be wise, too. I know you're a good sport and I know you're wise. I need your guidance. Your counsel.'

This was 2001, so his wife was even younger than she would be in St-Malo.

She said, '. . . Go on then.'

He remembered a piece of advice in a novel of Kingsley's. What it amounted to was this: *In conversations with women, never even mention another woman's name – unless it's to report her (very painful) death.* Yes, but that was in the second of the two forthrightly misogynistic novels he wrote after Elizabeth Jane Howard walked out on him ('I'm a bolter,' Jane once levelly told her stepson). To be honest Martin thought that Kingsley's advice had its applications; but he wasn't worried about Elena, so advanced and evolved (almost a generation on), and he said with perhaps a touch of complacence,

'Elena, when it comes to ex-girlfriends, I know there are three or four you take a dim view of, but there are some you broadly tolerate. And some you even like. Isn't that the way of it? You like some and dislike others?'

'No. You hate them all.'

'Do you?' he asked and laughed quietly (at the instant rout of all his expectations). 'You've heard me speak of Phoebe Phelps . . .'

'The sex one.'

'Roughly speaking.' Although now he came to think of it, she was, on balance, more like the no-sex one. 'It's from her.'

Elena said, 'The one that didn't want to get married or have kids. Would you call that a real love affair? Phoebe?'

Man and wife were still at the table. Bobbie, who shared a flat with her (half) brother, had been put in a taxi, and the four others, all supposedly asleep, were in the four bedrooms just beneath his attic study. He poured more wine . . . Unlike Julian (who wrote a whole novel about it), and unlike Hitch (who had found himself increasingly prey to it), Martin did not suffer from retrospective sexual jealousy; and nor did Elena. They were not inquisitive about each other's anterior lovelives. He was aware of certain male preponderances (certain weights on the fabric of her personal spacetime), and very much alive to any suspected ill-usage; but he was not inquisitive, and asked few questions. And Elena was the same.

'A real *love* affair?' Well, we never exchanged the three words, Elena (he said to himself). As you and I so often have and do. You know the three words: first person singular, verb, second person singular. 'Not in the strictest sense.'

'So just a detour.'

'As you might say. A dalliance, a digression.'

'Mm. How long did it last?'

'Five years.'

'Five *years*.' She went still. 'I had no idea.'

'Yes you did. I told you at least twice. 1976 to 1980. On and off.' Almost entirely on. He waited. 'Now – the matter at hand, if you would, Elena. Here. Read, *recite*, as Allah instructed the Prophet. Jesus, listen to him.' He was referring to one of the talking heads on *Newsnight*. 'He's saying it's all our fault. And serve us fucking well right.'

'Quite a few of them are saying that. As Hitch said they would.'

'Mm, that lot think Osama did it for the Palestinians . . . Now proceed, dread queen.'

She sat back and straightened the stiff sheets out in front of her. 'Ready? *Dear Martin. I'm going to tell you something that . . .*' Her eyes focused, then dilated. 'My God, what truly hideous handwriting.'

'She thought so too. It mortified her.'

'There's no consistency to it. It's like one of those blackmail letters that's patched together from different strips of print . . . Something really ghastly must have happened to her when she was very young.'

Indeed, Elena. Starting when she was six, an old priest called Father Gabriel bribed her into bed three times a week for eight years . . . He, Martin, had never told this story to anyone, ever, not even Hitch. All afternoon he had considered telling Elena – for its explanatory power; but as ever he found its violence unmanageably and unusably exorbitant, like nuclear fission. It was just too big.* Elena said,

'So. *Dear Martin, I'm going to tell you something I think you ought to know. Now I'm sure you remember a certain day in 1977 – November 1 – because by the standards of the "literary world"* in quotes *it had its moments. Let me jog your memory!* exclamation mark.' Elena visibly honed her attention. '*Just after lunch your old flame Lily rang up in hysterics and you chose to rush off and join her for the night. I prepared dinner for Kingsley . . .* For Kingsley? What's all this?'

'See, I was doing a spell of Dadsitting so Jane could have a holiday.† Greece. Phoebe consented to come over for the weekend. Lily, Lily was organising a literary festival up north. Some old poet chucked or got sick or actually dropped dead at the last minute, and she had a big gap

---

* Beyond establishing the bare outlines, I had never really talked about it with Phoebe, either – and wouldn't do so with any candour until 2017 (at which point she was seventy-five); as I had always subliminally supposed it must, the case history involved an additional and ulterior element of moral horror.

† Kingsley, whose third novel was called *I Like It Here* (1958), was never much of a traveller. In addition he couldn't fly, he couldn't drive, he couldn't take a train or a subway unescorted, and he couldn't be left alone in a house after dark without the company of close family or very old friends. Hence 'Dadsitting': his three children managed it by rotation. The system was institutionalised after Jane left him in December 1980.

in her programme. Saturday night. She was desperate. And I couldn't say no, could I.'

'Yes you could. Very rash not to, I'd've thought. Very rash indeed. Are you nuts? *I prepared dinner for your father, and that was fine, but then he . . . invaigled me into drinking a glass of Parfait Amour.* Can't spell inveigled. What's Parfait Amour?'

'That's significant. See, alcohol didn't agree with Phoebe and she very rarely touched it. But she had a weakness for Parfait Amour.'

'What's Parfait Amour?'

'Parfait Amour is a disgustingly sugary liqueur. It's the same colour as that notepaper and it smells like cheap ponce. Eliza might fancy a dab of it behind her ears. And it's *Mum's* favourite drink too. By far. One glass of that and her whole personality changed. I mean Phoebe's did.'

'Her whole personality changed. You mean she became less of a slag.'

He said, 'Very good, Elena. No. She became more of a slag. She became *something* of a slag. And she *wasn't* a slag.' He thought for a moment. 'True, she had a tendency to flirt, but that was later on. Phoebe was in many ways rather proper.'

'Oh was she. Did your father know that drinking made her more of a slag?'

'Uh, yeah. But it had to be Parfait Amour. He was always fascinated by people who didn't drink. He asked, and I told him.'

'*That's why*', Elena continued, '*I was so ill when you got back from your mission of mercy.* Did you tell him that drinking made her ill?'

'No.'

'You just told him that it made her more of a slag.'

'Jesus. I didn't put it quite like that. I think I just told him it made her, you know, unusually easygoing. More amenable . . . Now how did Kingsley get hold of a bottle of Parfait Amour? – that's what I want to know. I've never seen it on sale here. He must've called one of his vintner friends. He must've gone to a fair bit of trouble.'

'. . . New para. *So as you can imagine I was feeling pleasantly languid, sitting there in front of the fire.*'

'Romantic, isn't it. The marmalade light, the Parfait Amour . . .'

'*Your father then made a verbal pass at me that went on for half an hour.*'

On the table in front of them the baby monitor politely cleared its throat; and there came the first notes of protest and distress. These

174

opening cries always seemed to tell them how long the visit would need to last. Ten minutes, he thought.

'You do the next one,' said Elena as she rose.

He poured himself more wine and remembered.

It was a recent (and temporary) development in Phoebe's life – the Parfait Amour. She got her first taste of it the year before, in 1976, sitting opposite Hilly and her third husband at an outside table in a restaurant in Andalusia. Hilly asked for a glass, and drank it with every sign of near-unbearable enjoyment. 'Go on, dear,' she said. '*I* hate the taste of drink too. But I love Parfait Amour. Mmm.'

Phoebe acceded. And that night, at the hotel, Martin was suddenly in complete possession of a smilingly acquiescent stranger (of sharply reduced IQ). She was somewhat indisposed the next morning, admittedly, but it was a thing of the past by lunchtime . . . Four nights later it happened again – the damson *digestif*, her meandering gait along the shadowline of the bullring and up the slope, the dazed and breathy succubus in the Reina Victoria; but this time she spent all the following day groaning and sweating in the darkened bedroom. Nonetheless he found himself unobtrusively buying a litre of Parfait Amour at duty-free in Malaga Airport . . .*

After that he inveigled Phoebe into a Parfait Amour only once, and she was so very poorly, for nearly a week, that he reluctantly swore off Parfait Amour – sobered, or so he thought, by the interminable business with the trays and the tomato soups and the lightly buttered toast, and by all the recriminations. But as he poured the Parfait Amour down the kitchen sink he felt pleased and proud in an unfamiliar way. His sense of honour – or of minimal decency – was not quite defunct; it could still twitch and throb . . .

Martin got up from the dining table and fetched a bottle of Scotch, and then, reckoning he still had a few minutes, went out through the

* In Spain, at least, Parfait Amour enjoys a folkish reputation as an aphrodisiac. Whenever Hilly ordered it her husband was jovially nudged and elbowed by the waiters . . . That third husband of hers, my beloved and long-serving stepfather, was called Ali and he would later work as a postman. Which sounds promisingly egalitarian. Ali had no money or land or anything like that, but his full name was Alistair Ivor Gilbert Boyd and he was the seventh Baron Kilmarnock . . . A few months after Jane bolted, Hilly and Ali moved in with Kingsley as housekeepers, and this unlikely arrangement stood firm until his death in 1995.

back door for a stoical cigarette. He could hear Elena veering off into another room on her way down.

. . . As he was getting himself ready to fly to Newcastle (and take a train on to Durham) Phoebe caught up with him in the hall and said,

'So you're off are you then.'

'Phoebe, I can't possibly not do this. She's my oldest friend.'

'I see. I see. You're going all the way to Hadrian's Wall for a thankyou fuck.'

'What?' She was one step ahead of him. 'How d'you mean?'

'*Come* on. You've gone to John o'Groats to save her bacon. You'll be up on stage seeming chivalrous and clever. There'll be a dinner. She's an ex-girlfriend. You're both in hotels. Beyond any doubt there'll be a thankyou fuck.'

He said, 'Lily and I broke up at university. There won't be a thankyou fuck, I swear. Anyway, thank *you* for tending to Dad tonight. He trusts you, Phoebe.'

'. . . I can't believe it! You've trapped me here just for a thankyou fuck!'

She refused his kiss and he turned and pulled open the door and went down the garden path with his bag.

The storyteller

'Eliza,' he now said (he had naturally recognised Eliza's cry).

'Eliza,' said Elena. 'She just wanted her water refilled and a chat. All fine. You'll have to do Inez.' His wife settled. 'When was this? How old was he?'

'Uh, Kingsley was in his mid-fifties.'

'How old was she? How old were you?'

'I was twenty-eight. Phoebe was thirty-five.'

'Oh. An *old* slag. No wonder she didn't want children,' said Elena (who was the same age when she had Inez). 'She didn't dare . . . At what point was it? I mean in your eon together?'

'About eighteen months in.'

'How attractive was she? Wasn't she a ginge?'

'No – dark auburn. At first glance you'd say she was a brunette. Not pale. She had a kind of rusty colouring.'

176

'A ginge, in short. Right. *Your father then made a verbal pass at me that went on for half an hour. I've never known anything like it. It was like a flood of praise, and he was very eloquent, being a poet of course and not just a storyteller.*' Elena gave a comfortable grunt and said, 'So, a poet's pass. Not just a novelist's. *As these things go it was pretty painless. No bullying and no whining. I always liked your father – he, for one, knew how to be attentive to a woman.* New para. *Well I don't need to tell you how "tolerant" that particular drink makes me, and I have to confess I was quite tempted in a way. He was still fairly slim and handsome, then, and beyond all else by far it would have been a reasonably good way of paying you back for Lily.*

'New para. *I can't remember how he phrased the actual proposition, but I'll never forget how he rounded it all off. He said, "It's a faint hope, I realise. But I do want you to feel secure in my admiration."*'

'That's Kingsley, that is. I can hear him saying it. That's his style.'

'And was it his style', asked Elena, 'to drug, rape, and poison his sons' girlfriends?'

'. . . When he was younger, there was no limit to how reckless he could be with women. *Much* more reckless than I ever was. Here's an example. You'll have to concentrate, Elena.'

'I'm listening,' she said and reluctantly raised her eyes from the page.

'Okay. I'll be quick. Hilly and Kingsley are asked to dinner by some old friends – call them Joan and John. Now Kingsley's been having an affair with Joan and nobody knows. And there's another couple there – Jill and Jim. You'd think Kingsley'd have his hands full, keeping Mum in the dark and giving Joan the odd stroke. But guess what. He goes and makes a pass at *Jill*.'

'That's . . . that's ambitious. And Jill's keen?'

'Yeah. So he ups and has an affair with Jill. As well as Joan. He goes on about it in the novels – with girls, he says, he was like a frantic adolescent. See, they tended to say yes. He must've felt infallible – inerrant. Like the Koran.'

'Never mind the Koran . . . *In the end I just said, "Look, Kingsley, come on. This is all very well but you're Martin's father!"* New para.' Elena's eyes widened. '*Then he* really *shocked me. He said –*'

The baby monitor again sounded – not with the preparatory cough but with a convulsive splat of alarm. Immediately followed by the ratcheting wail.

'Inez. *"D'you think I'd be talking to you like this this if I were Martin's father?"*'

'Stop! Wait,' he said as he made for the stairs.

'Why? You already know what she's going to say.'

'I still need to watch your face,' he called out . . . But Elena had already settled into it, looking ahead to see how much more there was to go.

It was indeed Inez, and she had started as she meant to continue; but I sensed that she lacked the stamina to detain me for very long. And she soon quietened in my arms, only giving the occasional weak quack (just meant to keep me there) . . . The younger son, Gus, had had childhood asthma, and every other night for two or three years I administered the dose with the electric nebuliser, sessions in a blacked-out room that went on for an hour and sometimes twice that, with the threadily wheezing boy on my lap. So this was nothing; and in those days I was seldom bored or daunted by the company of my own thoughts – nor was I now, even on September 12. With Elena, the act of full disclosure always brought a measure of relief: the difficulty, the confused order of things, was now under competent supervision . . . As I lay there holding Inez my mind even felt free enough to indulge a hard-wearing memory from the time of my earlier marriage: repeatedly circumnavigating the little roundabout at the end of the street in twilight, holding hands with Gus (also, then, a two-year-old), who was trying out his first pair of real shoes, proper shoes of the kind someone older and taller might wear; every couple of yards he stopped and smiled upwards with eye-closing exultation and pride.

Inez's swaddled body gave a pulse (a silent hiccup), and went still.

'This is bullshit,' Elena was already saying as he re-entered the kitchen. She had loaded the dishwasher and was drying her hands with a tea towel. 'It's *all* lies. No. It's *nearly* all lies.'

There was a certain shaky levity in her voice that put him on his guard. 'Tell me what to believe. Let's go through it, and you tell me what I'm supposed to believe.'

She sat. 'If we must . . . *Then the whole story came out*, writes Phoebe. "Story" is correct. *It all went back to the Christmas of 1948 and a place called "Mariners Cottage"* quotation marks *near a town called Ainsham. Have I spelt that correctly?* Has she? A-i-n-s-h-a-m.'

'Almost. It's Eynsham with an E-y. And Marriner's Cottage is double-r with an apostrophe. I checked. Otherwise accurate. She could've got all this from the biography, but if she'd done that you'd think she'd spell the names right.'

'Not necessarily. Not if she's really clever. *Kingsley and Hilly were going through a very rocky patch. He was in love with a student of his called Verna David. Ring a bell?* Does it?'

'Oh yeah,' he said. 'Maybe an ex-student by that time. Still. And yes I know. A grave abuse of trust. But you were more or less allowed to, in 1948.'

'Not just in 1948. All my professors made passes at me and all my friends,' said Elena. 'Thirty years later.'

'. . . I knew Verna.' His early years were full of Verna, and her husband too (and they were both warm and welcome presences). 'Verna was bright and very pretty. It was a big thing, but she somehow never fell out with Mum. Verna came to Kingsley's memorial service. I introduced you. Remember?'

'No. *On the day before Christmas Eve your parents had a blazing row and he went off with a suitcase to Verna David. So there was your mother left alone for the "holiday", left alone with the baby in a wasteland of village idiots.* The baby was Nicolas, right? How old?'

'Four months. And in those days, Elena, right through to New Year's Day the world just curled up and died. You'd get the creeps if it happened now – no open shops, no lit lights. At Christmas England just curled up and blacked out.'

Elena was studying the envelope. His name – no stamp, no postmark. 'Did she hand-deliver this? . . . You know, maybe she *is* really clever.'

'How d'you mean?'

'She knows as well as I do how credulous you are.'

'Oi.'

'Now you listen. How impressionable you are. How easily swayed.'

'Oi.'

'How obsessive. You *are*. Especially when something like this happens – a world event. That you think only you are really registering. If I'd been her *I* would have struck today. To get you while you're in shock. All wobbly and doomed.

'New para. Ah here we are. All alone with the baby over Christmas. In a hayrick somewhere. Having been dumped by her husband. *So, not surprisingly, your mother decided to retaliate. Good for her!* exclamation mark. *She sent a telegram to the poet from Hell.*

'Yeah,' said Elena. 'Your Phoebe picked the right day for it. The day after.'

Chapter 3
September 11
2: The day before the day after

The second plane

Look, now, at the filmic record of that morning. The live coverage starts just before 8.46 a.m. and what you see is a shockingly, a chasteningly bright blue sky. Yes, a strong blue sky – but an innocent sky.* An innocent sky, one that even in its worst dreams had never imagined anything like . . .

Until 8.46 that morning, or more precisely until 9.03, travellers were arriving at American airports with leisurely tardiness; and they were all right. For domestic flights, at least, they needed no photo ID; they kept their shoes and jackets on, their quarts of shampoo went unconfiscated; they strolled to the gate with non-travelling family or friends, paring their nails (if they felt like it) with Swiss Army knives, unfrisked, unblessed by the security rod . . . They were on the old schedule, and they were all right.

The sky humming in its blue, the leonine sun ('Heat is the echo of your / Gold', Larkin, 'Solar'), the first of the two planes (they are both Boeing 767s out of Boston) – its unignorable roar, its apparently frictionless disappearance into the North Tower, 'Holy *SHIT!*' Is it an accident? This possibility, this 'theory', had a short life: it was noisily and gaudily refuted seventeen minutes later. And soon we see the second

* This was 2001, and of course everything seen from a distance in time looks innocent, and *is* innocent, comparatively (because the opposite of *innocence*, when it's not *guilt*, is *experience*, and experience just accumulates, like age). That was an unsuspecting sky in the hours after dawn on September 11.

181

plane homing in like a cartoon hornet over the stocky black skyscape of downtown.

The public archive has only one shot of the impact of the first plane (hand-held, sudden, veering); by contrast, there are thirty different angles for the impact of the second (this was a component of Osama's plan). Some are network-professional, some are semi-amateur, some are soundless, some erupt in shrieked obscenities, some just falter on . . .

'Then it must be – deliberate,' says a female voice; 'So it's – on purpose,' says another female voice . . . 'That's *terrorist* shit, man,' says a male African American with decisive conviction. He said this on the dot of 9.03 – twenty-eight minutes before President Bush, speaking from Florida, rather more cautiously gave voice ('an apparent terrorist attack') to the same opinion. No, not happenstance, and certainly not double happenstance . . .

And one other thing. What you're watching is mass murder, but it is also multiple suicide. We are often shown death or its aftermath (*warning: some viewers may find . . .*), but we are never shown suicide. We were not shown the atomisations of the 'skydivers'; we are never shown suicide bombers as they self-detonate – we are not shown 'martyrdom operations': over suicide a veil is quietly drawn.*

There were many suicides on September 11. The overwhelming majority were the jumpers, the leapers (roughly 200 of them) – and they were only nominal suicides; they were people who very suddenly had to choose between one form of death and another. Those plummeting figures represented the outer limits of pathos and despair. And meaninglessness, too: they were not dying for any reason they knew

---

* Suicide missions are no doubt as old as human conflict, and you and I may have actually glimpsed the grey and grainy footage of the *kamikaze* (the word translates as *divine wind*) going about his work over the Pacific, in 1944–5. But Japan, at that stage, was fighting for national survival, and the tactic was partly an effect of what Churchill called 'the moral rot of war': as a war grows older, it also grows crueller. September 11 was not the last act of a drama but its prologue; the suicide mission is what it *started* with . . . Some points of general comparison. The kamikazes' 'success rate' (hitting a ship) was 19 per cent; they killed 4,900 sailors at the cost of 3,860 pilots. Al-Qaeda's success rate (hitting a building) was 75 per cent; they killed just under 3,000 for the loss of nineteen. The kamikaze operation lasted for ten months, al-Qaeda's for just ninety-one minutes. And while the suicidaires of 1944–5 killed uniformed enemy combatants, those of 2001 killed men, women, and children who were dressed for the office or for the airport.

about . . . Those at the controls of the fourth plane, its black box tells us, spent their last seconds (before they ditched United 93 in some pastureland in Pennsylvania) hesitantly chanting *God is great*. They hadn't found their appointed target. Imagine, then, the fervent chorus in the cockpit of United 175, whose immolation (seen from thirty vantage points) was unmistakably triumphal and ecstatic.

. . . So here was a new kind of enemy: preternaturally innovative, daring, and disciplined, and not at all afraid to die. So it seemed to us, in September 2001.

GMT

It was 08.46 Eastern Standard Time (EST) when the first plane struck the North Tower. At that moment, over in London, it was 13.46 Greenwich Mean Time (GMT) – or, more grandly, Coordinated Universal Time (UTC) – and I was gazing admiringly and proudly and relatively innocently at the discoloured knuckle on my right hand. Yes, that wound of mine, received as I said in mid-July (through unemphatic contact with a brick wall), was doing wonderfully well: take a good look at the dime-sized scab (don't stint yourself), with its resilient ridges; in a few weeks it would surely wither away or just drop off, putting me well on the road to perfect manual health. Yes, my wound was set to disappear more or less without trace by Christmas or even as early as Halloween . . .

Someone working in the yard at the rear of the house had his radio on, and the gaily babbling voice abruptly modulated into a tone of mature concern. I went to the window and listened. Reports were coming in that 'a light plane' had 'collided' with a building in Lower Manhattan. At that point the words were overwhelmed and scattered by two rival city noisemakers (chainsaw, car alarm), and after a while I went back to the desk and the exercise book. But my mood was wrong – meaning I couldn't seem to get in touch with the novel I was trying to write.

So I went to the kitchen and activated the kettle, and the TV. It had just gone two. Now before me, on the screen, was a thing I'd never encountered before – an aircraft looking and behaving like an animal, like a cross between a carnivorous bull and an ink-black shark, seeming to rear up in greedy anticipation before putting its head down for the urgent rush of the charge . . . It was of course the second plane, and that jolt it gave (I later thought) was a reflex of the pilot, Marwan al-Shehhi, as he saw the achievement of his predecessor, Muhammad Atta. In the very last second before contact with the South Tower, with a quixotic flourish the second plane tipped its wings from the horizontal to the near-vertical – an angle of perhaps forty-five degrees.* And soon both buildings would wear lantern-jawed grins with oily black smoke frothing out of them.

Seconds later the telephone rang. It was Dan Franklin, my editor–publisher at Jonathan Cape, with some queries about the paperback of a collection of essays that had appeared earlier in the year. And why would anybody want to know anything about that? The collection – dismayingly it now seemed – was called *The War Against Cliché*. And who cared about cliché?

'Are you happy with the quotes? I wanted the *LRB* on the front cover, but they –'

'Dan,' I said. 'Two passenger jets have just crashed into the World Trade Center . . . Thousands dead. Nobody knows how many thousand.'

I called home as I watched the first Tower coming down. Elena was calling home too – the house of her childhood, her mother's house in Lower Manhattan (and there was also Elena's sister and brother, both nearby). We talked at length about organising the girls, and about shopping, and about having what used to be known as a quiet night in.

I called Washington DC, and got the machine – but Christopher, I remembered, was on the road somewhere in the west. Washington DC had also been attacked, by the third plane, which was flying so low, a witness said, that it seemed to be *driving* to the Pentagon (and driving at

* The angle was in fact twelve degrees – confirming the marked distortion of one's senses on that day (with the pathetic fallacy also showing its presence). But the mind was not deceived about the aircraft's *speed*. In the thicker air of the troposphere, planes observe set limits, and must not exceed 230 mph below 2,500 feet (stacked above an airport, you are wallowing around at 150 mph). Muhammad Atta hit the North Tower at 494 mph (floors ninety-three to ninety-nine); Marwan al-Shehhi hit the South Tower at 586 mph (floors seventy-five to eighty-five) and his 767 was close to breaking up in the air. Partly for this reason, the North Tower stood for just over a hundred minutes, the South Tower for just under an hour.

500 mph). I had another look at New York. Manhattan was barely visible beneath the fouled sky. Manhattan had gone under.

I called a couple of friends in SoHo and got dead lines.

All off

It was Tuesday. And at four o'clock every Tuesday (and every Thursday) I attended an exercise class in Notting Hill Gate. So I thought I might as well act normally, and there seemed no point in not going . . . On my way out I had another brief session with my scab; whereas the carapace, the protective crust, gave no pain when I prodded it, the ambient area, I found, was still stringently tender to the touch.

Then I walked down the cobbled mews and under the arch and out into the street. Early autumn, and no weather to speak of, no weather one way or the other. As I passed the primary school on Elbury Avenue I slowed and slowly rocked to a halt. The children were being given a final flail in the playground, and I was abruptly riveted by the texture of the noise they made. This was the noise of ingenuous energy and excitation; but it now sounded like mass panic – a ragged crackle as loud as their lungs could make it . . .

At the crossroads again I paused, and stayed there for two or three cycles of the traffic lights. It seemed a curious arrangement – with the cars: how they stopped and patiently crouched in position when the lights went red, then crept meekly forward when the lights went green.* From where I stood on the kerb it felt waywardly literalistic, almost whimsically quaint, to heed the dictates of the lime, the gold,

---

* Much later I would learn that British Islamists, lifelong residents of (say) Bradford or Luton, habitually disobeyed traffic lights, on principle, as a way of showing their disdain for the norms of an alien and impious land. The deeper urge, perhaps, is to free yourself from reason. This is really a *sine qua non* for the jihadi ideologue: free yourself from reason, and anything seems possible (at least for a while), including world domination and a global caliphate . . . I cannot refrain from quoting *Lolita* – three pages from the end. Humbert is in his car, having just murdered his rival Clare Quilty: '. . . since I had disregarded all the laws of morality, I might as well disregard the laws of traffic . . . It was a pleasant diaphragmal melting, with elements of diffused tactility, all this enhanced by the thought that nothing could be nearer to the elimination of basic physical laws than deliberately driving on the wrong side of the road. In a way, it was a very spiritual itch.'

the rose. An anoraked youth on a bicycle was approaching with an arm trustfully out-thrust, dramatising his firm intention of turning left . . .

The users of the thoroughfare had not yet absorbed the other lesson of that particular day. That lesson was about the pitiful flimsiness of all prohibitions.

When I'd done my pilates, when I'd waved my arms about and flexed and wiggled my legs in the air and performed 'the sock stretch' (*so you can still get shod when you're eighty*), I headed for the Sun in Splendour, as normal, to join up with my pubmates Mike and Steve, to drink beer and smoke cigarettes (a process that Steve, the older of the two, forgivingly called 'retox') and play the Knowledge. Nothing much was said when I joined them, on September 11; we communicated with flat smiles and with little upward jerks of the chin. Then we shrugged and ordered our pints and (as we normally did) moved to the brick-red slab of the Knowledge.

With the Knowledge, you insert the pound coin, and the screen flares into a map of the world (vividly modelled on Risk – one of the most addictive boardgames of my childhood); you advance from your assigned starting point, Poland, say, or Peru, and you try to invade contiguous countries by answering three multiple-choice questions (and getting on the road to winning a small cash prize). After half an hour, and after much failure, we were poised to complete the conquest of Irkutsk (worth two quid), and had only one more question to go. Now the screen said:

When in Islamic history did the Sunni–Shia schism take place?
a)   After the Sykes–Picot Agreement in 1916
b)   After the Alhambra Decree in Spain in 1492
c)   After the death of the Prophet Muhammad in 632 AD

None of us had any idea. What schism? What was Shia and what was Sunni? And remind us – who exactly was the Prophet Muhammad? As the clock ticked we hurriedly conferred: 1916 looked too recent, 632 too ancient, so we opted for 1492. Wrong . . . Quite a while later, when we were on our third round of drinks (and about £25 down), the question reappeared (questions quite often reappeared); and this time we went for 1916 and Sykes–Picot. Wrong again.

'. . . So quite a while back,' concluded Steve.

'Yeah, they must've done it first thing,' said Mike. 'They didn't hang about.'

The TV on its perch above the mirrored bar was not silently devoted to snooker or golf or darts, as it normally was. On the screen we saw the sulphurous hole in the flank of the Pentagon. This image was then supplanted by the priestly and prissy beauty of Osama bin Laden.

'Well. One thing we do know,' said Mike. 'It's all off now.'*

'Now it's all off,' said Steve.

And I agreed that now it was definitely all off.

Hanif and the great sea

On my way back to the mews (to freshen up before going home) I stopped at Hanif's Service Store on Portobello Road for a fresh wallet of Golden Virginia. Hanif, the owner–manager, had come to Britain four decades ago from the city of Gujarat (there were, and are, more Muslims in India than in the Islamic Republic of Pakistan, and Hanif's father was one of them). He and I had regular exchanges, in the warm, courteous, rather literary, no, in fact strikingly high-style English characteristic of the Subcontinent, so I was planning to say something like *Well, Hanif? It seems, does it not, that yet again the violent have borne it away?* But there were other customers to be served, and while I waited I reached down for an *Evening Standard* (whose front page confronted you with 09.03, September 11, 2001, and the moment of climactic kinesis, as the second plane hits the South Tower in ballooning parachutes of flame), not the copy on the top of the stack, which was wet and frayed, and not the copies immediately under it, which were curled and damp; no, I boldly seized the spine of a copy about halfway down, and tried to ease it free . . .

Now it was already a family joke, the promptness – the instantaneity – of my reaction to any resistance whatever on the part of inanimate

---

* The phrase 'all off' derives, I assume, from the sphere of spontaneous brawls and broils and ruckuses. It means something like 'now anything goes' or 'now all hell can break loose' or 'now all bets are off'. In Bill Buford's book about football hooliganism, *Among the Thugs*, a tracksuited capo rallies his troops by weaving among them and potently repeating the words *It's going to go off*. In this context violence 'goes off' in the way a bomb goes off. Mike and Steve were applying 'it's all off' to international relations – and informally prefiguring the wars in Afghanistan and Iraq.

objects. Just the other Sunday I came down to breakfast and my wife and daughters (trying not to laugh) presented me with a fresh item of evidence. Exhibit A, this time, wasn't a bent door key or a scragged toilet roll. It was an allegedly resealable ice-cream carton that I had briefly struggled to open the night before. The rectangular plastic lid bore the crosswise gashes of a carving knife. Even Inez, at twenty-five months, had come to see this sort of thing as extremely funny. In other words, at the slightest show of dumb insolence from the non-organic world, I turned at once to uninhibited force.

So now I am reaching down for that stacked *Standard*, and pulling on it. And encountering recalcitrance – followed by intransigence. My internal mutter was as usual *Christ – what's in it for YOU?* and with fingers that were always impatient, always tremulous (Eliza called them 'too wobbly'), I tensed myself in a half-crouch and tugged with maximal strength.

My grasp slipped and my hand flew wildly up and drove its knuckle into the rusty iron bracket of the shelf above – scab first.

Hanif hurried over, tearing at a little packet of paper tissues. The *Standard*'s front page was being steadily and audibly dotted with blood.

'Here, my friend.'

'Thank you. Thanks.' I sighed. 'So I add my drops . . .'

'. . . to the great sea.'

'Yes, Hanif. To the great sea.'

For twenty minutes in the kitchen of his workplace he wearily sluiced his wound under the cold tap. Outside, high, high up in the sky, a dark shape cleaved its way through the colourlessness.

Was it a Bird? No. Was it a Plane? No, not really. Was it Superman? Or perhaps one of Superman's enemies – the Joker, Black Zero, Mr Mxyzptlk . . . ?

Osama had unveiled a new target: human society (in all its non-Koranic forms).

. . . Martin knew that for the rest of his life he would never see a low-flying aircraft with his original eyes. And what lay beneath? A place where every building was a vulnerability and every citizen was a combatant. A place where everyone was dreaming they were naked.

Which they were.

Chapter 4
September 11
3: The days after the day after

Don Juan in Hull

Elena yawned lavishly and said to him, 'It's midnight.'

'That's true, El. It is now September 13.'

'And I'm tired . . . Why does she call Larkin the poet from Hell?'

'. . . It's not in the sense of, I don't know – the neighbour from hell. He was the poet from Hell, capital aitch. Hell was where he lived. Hull. A port city in Yorkshire, Pulc, where the constant mist reeks of fish.' With his sound hand Martin got hold of the Scotch bottle and poured himself a big one. 'He wasn't from Hull yet, mind, not in 1948. He was still pulling his wire down in Leicester.'

'How old was he then? Was he just a librarian?'

'Mm, and he wasn't a poet yet either, not mainly. He was Kingsley's age, so twenty-six. But he was a red squirrel all right. He'd already published two novels.'

She said, 'Like you.'

'. . . Uh, yeah, now you mention it.' He drank. 'You know, at that stage it looked as though Larkin would be the novelist and Kingsley'd be the poet. If anything.'

'Your wound's seeping. Use the roll.' She took up the pages. 'PL as she now calls him *got to Ainsham in time for Christmas Day. And he was still there when Kingsley crept back with his dirty laundry on New Year's Eve. So there was an awkward but in the end "very jolly" Hogmanay.* In quotes. I see. They all got pissed.'

'Yeah, assuming they had the cash. They were very poor. I was a penniless baby.'

'*Kingsley said he knew at once that something had happened. He was frankly relieved because it sort of equalised the guilt. PL took his leave on Jan 2 and K and Hilly, after a cagey interlude, got back to normal. At which point they discovered Hilly was pregnant. With you, Martin. And Kingsley hadn't laid a finger on her since November.*

'*They agreed that they'd never say anything to PL. Who would've been* horrified, don't you think? Being a child-hater? . . . *And life went on.*

'*Anyway, such was Kingsley's account. And of course he swore me to absolute secrecy. Well, that vow I considered void the moment I saw his obituary. For six years I've been wondering when it would be best to tell you and so free myself of this awful burden. Oh, sure . . . I feel better already.* Yeah, I bet you do.

'New paragraph. *I heard him out and I told him quite firmly, "I've always thought of you as Martin's father, so the taboo is still there and I can't pretend it isn't. Sorry to disappoint, but there we are." He was a perfect gent about it, as I said. Then we watched the news and he played some jazz, you rang, and I went to bed (I was already ailing from the Parfait Amour).*

'We're coming to the last bit. God, this – this calligraphy's positively gruesome. *So bad luck, mate. Rather confusing, no? Still – not the milkman!* exclamation mark. *Not the milkman. Just the wanker from Hell. Yours, Phoebe Phelps. PS. It broke my heart to hear about poor dear Myfanwy. You must feel so horribly guilty . . .*

'Dot dot dot. The end.'

They sat for a time in silence.

'Elena, which one is lying? Was he lying? Or is she lying?'

'. . . Most likely they're both lying. He lied to get her into bed. Which he no doubt did anyway, without lying, without exerting himself in any way. She lied about that. And now she's lying about this.'

He waved his bandaged hand in the air. 'Wait. Give me a moment to . . .' Just then the dishwasher churned into life. 'You know, some of this is plausible – the stuff about 1948. Okay, circumstantially plausible. But psychologically plausible too.'

Elena was sceptically considering him. He went on,

'See, Mum always admired and respected Philip. I've been looking at the *Letters*. Kingsley's. She'd dress up – she needed some persuasion but she'd dress up in sort of babydoll outfits, and Kingsley took photos and sent them to Hell. Hull. No. Leicester. Oh yeah. And Mum woke up once saying she dreamt Philip was kissing her. I don't know. The jolly Hogmanay rings true. Kingsley wouldn't have minded that much. If at all.'

'Because he was drunk.'

'No – because he was queer. Kingsley was a bit gay for Larkin. And you know how that works. Like Hitch approving of me sleeping with any girl he'd slept with.'

'. . . Why does Phoebe have it in for you?'

'Hull hath no fury . . . There're others like that,' he vacantly continued. 'Hull is other people. Don Juan in Hull. The road to Hull is paved with good intentions.'

'*Did* you ever scorn her?'

'Phoebe? Turn her down, you mean? No.' Certainly not. Are you kidding? But then of course he remembered – the stairwell, the bathroom, the swollen breasts. 'Yes I did. Once. Very late on. After it was over.'

'Well there's that. And there was Lily. You're not seeing the obvious with Lily. You *confine* Phoebe for a night alone with your father, while you go off to Durham to rescue an ex. Jesus. And don't tell me she didn't reward you. No need to ask. In general, though, your conscience is clear.'

'More or less. Over the five years. But I did end it – to get married to someone else.'

'Was there any overlap?'

'No. There would've been if I hadn't turned her down. That one time.'

'All right.' Elena gave a shiver of dismissal. 'What this shows, at most, is the lengths your father would go to for the chance of a fuck. Now you get this straight.' And her glass came down on the tabletop, like a gavel. 'I'm serious, Mart. This girl knows you and thinks she can toy with your head. Like you're a lab rat. *Don't let her.*'

He raised his palms and said, 'I'll try.'

'You'll try? Listen. Ask your mother! Ring her tomorrow and ask her.'

'I can't ask her over the *phone*.' Or in person, he thought. 'Nah. Mum didn't have a go at adultery for another ten years. And it never sat well with her. She was a country girl. She was twenty. No. The idea of her being uh, consoled by Larkin with Nicolas sniffling in his cot. No, I don't believe that part for a moment.'

'Promise? Do you realise that not once've you . . . You always call him Dad. But you haven't done that once tonight. You've called him Kingsley.'

'Is that so?' He shifted in his chair. 'And what about *his* father, Larkin's, that filthy old fascist Sydney? I'm giving myself cold sweats just imagining the horror of being a Larkin male. You'd have to look quite like him too. Imagine that.'

'There you are then. You're the spit of your father. *Identico.*' Those were her words. But now she was frowning and gazing at him – with her aesthetic eye, her genealogical eye, feature by feature (and Elena, in speaking of cousins and old family friends, had been heard to say such things as *She's got her grandmother's lower lip* or *He has his great-uncle's earlobes*). 'No. It's her you look like. Your mother.'

The hidden work of uneventful days

I felt its concussive magnitude: September 11 looked set to be the most consequential event of my lifetime. But what did it mean? What was it for?

'The main items of evidence', said Christopher on the phone from DC, 'are the fatwas issued by Bin Laden in '96 and '98. And both are blue streaks of religious parrotshit, with a few more or less intelligible grievances listed here and there.'

I said, 'From now on Osama should let the intellectuals state his case. What the fuck is going on with the American left?'

'Yes I know. What does it like about a doctrine that's – let's think – racist, misogynist, homophobic, totalitarian, inquisitional, imperialist, and genocidal?'

'Maybe the Marxists like its hard line on usury. Christ, let's have some light relief. Tell me about Vidal and Chomsky. I know Gore, but you know them both.'

'Mm, well, Gore's got this side to him. Remember that guff about FDR being in on Pearl Harbor? If a conspiracy theory traduces America, then Gore'll subscribe to it. With Gore it's just a fatuous posture. With Noam, I'm sorry to say, it's heartfelt. He just doesn't like America. As he sees it, it's been a sordid disaster starting with Columbus. He thinks America's just a bad idea.'

'A bad idea? We can argue about the practice, but it's a good *idea*.'

'Agreed. If Gore's addicted to conspiracies, Noam's addicted to moral equivalence. Or not even. He thinks if anything Osama's slightly more moral than we are. As proof, he reminds us that we bombed that aspirin factory in Khartoum. Killing one nightwatchman. I had to point out to him that we didn't bomb crowded office blocks with jets full of passengers.'

'. . . Well keep it up, Hitch. You're the only lefty who's shown any mettle. It's your armed-forces blood – the blood of the Royal Navy. And you love America.'

'Thank you, Little Keith. I do, and I'm proud that I do.'

'You know, what I can't get over is the dissonance. Between means and ends. The intricate practicality of the attack – in the service of something so . . .'

'Benthamite realism in the service of the utterly unreal. A global caliphate? The extermination of all infidels?'

'The whole thing's like a head injury. Last question – I'm being called to dinner. Will there be more?'

'Maybe that's it for now. But it's probably just the beginning. We'll see.'

What we saw the next day was the delivery of the first of the anthrax letters. And at that point the occult glamour of Osama reached its apogee. It was as if his whisperers and nightrunners were everywhere, and you could almost hear the timed signals of his hyenas and screech-owls, and rumours were skittering about like a cavernful of bats.*

There would be a war – no one doubted that.

. . . 'The silent work of uneventful days': this prose pentameter is from Saul Bellow's autobiographical short story 'Something to Remember Me By'. He means the times when your quotidian life seems ordinary, but your netherworld, your innermost space, is confusedly dealing with a wound (for Saul – he was fifteen – the wound was the imminent death of his mother), and has much silent work to get through . . . The populations of the West were for now otherwise occupied, with the coming intervention in Afghanistan; they were busy; and the silent work it very much needed to do would have to wait for uneventful days.

An act of terrorism fills the mind as thoroughly as a triggered airbag smothers a driver. But the mind can't live like that for long, and you

---

* Christopher told me there was a WMD scare in Washington: it got around that a rogue nuclear weapon was poised to vaporise the capital. Some friends were urging the Hitchenses to leave town – urging in vain.

soon sense the return of the familiar mental chatter – other concerns and anxieties,* other affiliations and affections.

Like everyone else I processed a great many reactions to September 11, but none proved harder to grasp than the reaction of Saul Bellow. Somehow I just couldn't take it in.

There was no difficulty in understanding Pat Robertson and Jerry Falwell (those Chaucerian racketeers of the Bible Belt), who said that September 11 was due punishment for America's sins (especially its failure to criminalise homosexuality and abortion). It was rather harder to tell what Norman Mailer was going on about when he said that the attack would prove salutary, because only ceaseless warfare could maintain the virility of the US male . . . And more routinely I attended to all the appeasers, self-flagellators, defeatists, and relativists on the left, as well as all the pugnacious windbags on the right; and I could see their meaning. Even Inez's struggles I could faintly make out.† But not Saul's.

'He can't absorb it.'

'What?' I was on the line to Mrs Bellow in Boston. 'Can't absorb it?'

Rosamund was confining her deep voice to a throaty whisper, so I knew Saul must be somewhere in the house – the house on Crowninshield Road. She said,

'He keeps asking me, *Did something happen in New York?* And I tell him, in full. And then he asks me again. *Did something happen in New York?* He just can't take it in.'

And I couldn't take it in either – the news about Saul.

---

* For instance, I was secretly spending a lot of time with Philip Larkin: the *Collected Poems*, the *Selected Letters*, and Andrew Motion's authorised Life. Although I knew these books well (I had written about them at great length in 1993), two main themes came at me with all the force of discovery . . . First, Philip's father. Not many pages ago I called Sydney Larkin a fascist. That word was often used loosely in my time (parking wardens were called fascists), so it might help to be more specific. Sydney wasn't a fascist, or only secondarily. He was something much more advanced. What he was was a Nazi. This remains a startling – and startlingly underexamined – truth: Philip had been raised and mentored by an adherent of Adolf Hitler . . . But what I kept thinking about, what I kept returning to, was the destitution – the irreducible church-mouse penury – of Philip's lovelife.

† Inez was two; so in her infinite book of secrecy only a little could I read. Maybe she seemed vague in distinguishing the falling towers from the US Open (or maybe she thought 'tennis' meant 'television'), but she certainly registered the new atmosphere, the sudden congealing of mood in everyone around her . . . Eliza, almost five, was more

Two years earlier Saul had personally fathered a child (setting some kind of record) and his somatic health seemed imposingly sound (Rosamund still described him as 'gorgeous'); but the fact remained that Bellow was born in 1915.

For some while there had been an uneasiness having to do with his short-term memory; and in March 2001 Saul was tentatively diagnosed with 'inchoate' dementia (whose progress would be gradual and stop-start). I went to Boston that spring and was present on the morning of an important test or scan; the three of us then had lunch in a Thai restaurant near the medical centre, and for the first time I heard mention of Alzheimer's.

She disguised it but Rosamund, I thought, was (rightly and prophetically) alarmed. Saul was reticent but seemingly untroubled; it was as if he'd made a resolution not to be cowed. He would be

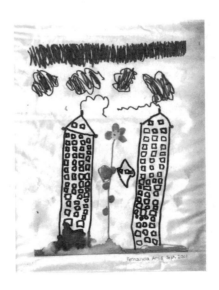

transparent (see above): the plane, hauntingly, looks more like a Stealth Bomber (or a flying saucer) than a 767; and notice how the black smoke is leniently attributed to the WTC's chimneys. That flower is all her own (with perhaps a nod to 'Jack and the Beanstalk') . . . When they spoke of the event, Bobbie, Nat, and Gus, all three of them respectful students of history, lowered their voices and their gazes, no doubt already aware that the political consequences would dominate much of their early lives. The Amises were all doing what they could with September 11. Elena, protective and also pugnacious in the name and the spirit of New York City, where she was born and raised, wanted to 'go home soon' (and soon did).

eighty-six on June 10 . . . A little later, in July, the Bellows came to stay with us on Long Island. I convinced myself that 'all marbles' (to quote the title of a novel he would never finish) were 'still accounted for' – until I watched our home movie of that visit, which was full of portents.

My habitual response to disastrous diagnoses of close friends, as we'll see, was one of studied insouciance: fatal diseases, in this world view, were hollow threats, scarecrows, paper tigers . . .

All the same, back in London after Labor Day, I made an effort to discover what all the fuss was about: I got hold of a couple of books and tried to settle down to them. But I found myself immediately unnerved: Alzheimer's clearly meant what it said; Alzheimer's *followed through*. And I, I, who cruised through whole libraries devoted to famine, terror-famine, plagues, and pandemics, to biological and chemical weaponry, to the leprous aftermaths of great floods and earthquakes, was quite unable to contemplate dementia – in its many variants, vascular, cortical, frontotemporal, and all the rest.

Why? Well, call it the universal cult of personality, call it the *charismatic authority* of the self – the divine right of the first person. And this particular numero uno wasn't going to wake up one morning in the Ukraine of 1933 or in the London of 1666; but anybody can wake up with Alzheimer's, including the present writer, including the present reader (and most definitely including about a third of those who live beyond sixty-five). As ever, I was Saul's junior by three and a half decades. Even so and even then, reading about Alzheimer's brought me close to the onset of clinical panic . . . The death of the mind: dissolution most foul, internal treachery most foul – as in the best it is, but this most foul, strange, and terrifying.*

Iris

Now it happens that life (normally so slothful, indifferent, and plain disobliging) had gone out of its way, in this very peculiar situation, to

---

* The rebel angel Belial, consigned to Pandemonium ('place of all demons'), puts it simply enough (*Paradise Lost*, Bk II): 'For who would lose, / Though full of pain, this intellectual being, / Those thoughts that wander through eternity . . . ?' Alzheimer's, like populism, is decidedly philistine; it hates the intellectual being.

provide me with a 'control', a steady point of comparison: if I wanted to know what Alzheimer's could do to a brilliant, prolific, erudite, lavishly inspired, and excitingly other-worldly novelist, then I needed to look no further than the example of Iris Murdoch.

Iris was a very old friend of Kingsley's. As undergraduates they were both card-carrying Young Communists – they marched and agitated and recruited, heeding the diktats of Moscow. And in later life they continued to fraternise as they crossed the floor (more or less in step) from Left to Right . . .

So Iris had been an intermittent presence since my childhood. The last time I saw her was at a party or function in 1995 or 1996. It was being put about in the press, around then, that she was suffering from nothing more serious than writer's block; I had no reason to doubt this polite fiction, and I said,

'How awful for you, Iris.'

'It is awful. Being unable to write is very *boring*. And lonely. I feel I'm somewhere very boring and lonely.'

'Writer's block – I get that.' Yes, but only ever for a day or two. 'You can't do anything but wait it out.'

She said hauntedly, 'And I already have a waiting feeling.'

We talked on. Present as always throughout was Iris's one and only husband, the distinguished literary critic John Bayley (who was crooked forward in gentle commiseration). As I was leaving I laid a hand on her wrist and said,

'Now Iris. Don't let yourself think it's permanent. It isn't. It will lift.'

'Mm. But here I am somewhere dark and silent,' she said, and kissed me on the lips.

That at least hadn't changed. With Iris (who was Irish), if she liked you she loved you. It was the way she was – until February 8, 1999, when she ceased to be.

Not satisfied with giving me a control experiment in the example of Iris, life, in September 2001, was suddenly giving me a detailed crash course on the further decline of Iris: earlier in the summer Tina Brown (then editor of *Talk* magazine) had asked me to write a piece about Iris, and to this end I read John Bayley's two memoirs (*Iris* and *Iris and the Friends*) and arranged to go to a preview of Richard Eyre's biopic, *Iris*. So I was in no position to echo Harvey Keitel's line in *Taxi Driver*: 'I don't know nobody name Iris.' In principle, I knew a fair amount about Iris, and about Alzheimer's, or so you might suppose.

. . . Towards the end of the morning of Friday, September 14, I went to the screening room off Golden Square. In the thoroughfares the pedestrians, the comers and goers, still gave off an impression of tiptoe or sleepwalk, a flicker of contingency, as they moved past the boutiques and bistros of aromatic Soho . . . John Bayley was standing at the door; with a dozen others we took our seats as the lights were going down.

Kate Winslet plays the younger Iris – all hope and promise and radiance. Judi Dench plays the older, incrementally stricken Iris: her growing apprehension, and then the shadowing and clouding over as her mind starts to die. And before very long you are the witness of an extraordinary spectacle: Britain's 'finest novelist' (John Updike), or 'the most intelligent woman in England' (John Bayley), sits crouched on an armchair with an expression of superstitious awe on her face as she watches . . . as she watches an episode of the preschooler TV series, *Teletubbies*.

This is now Iris on a good day: Iris, the author of twenty-six novels and five works of philosophy, including *Metaphysics as a Guide to Morals*. And you thought, Oh, the tragicomedy of brain death, the abysmal bathos of dementia . . . 'It will lift,' I had told her in 1995 or 1996. 'It *will* win,' says the young doctor in *Iris*. And he was right.

After the lights came back up I established that the only dry eyes in the house belonged to Professor Bayley. Perhaps he was seeing the film for the second time – or let's say the third time, in a certain sense. We only had to watch it, but John, in addition, had had to live it.

It won't be like that with Saul, I kept saying to myself, almost dismissively, throughout the autumn. He couldn't 'take in' September 11. Well who could?

It won't be like that with Saul.

The first crow

'Hitch, when did all this get going? Islamism. When did Muslims stop saying *Islam is the problem* and start saying *Islam is the solution*?'

'In the 1920s. Atatürk dissolved the Caliphate in '24, banned sharia, and separated church and state. The Muslim Brotherhood was founded four years later. *Islam is the solution* was the first clause in its charter.'

Then I asked him: when did jihadi attention turn from the *near enemy* to the *far enemy*? When did it turn from the Middle East to the West?

'I suppose 1979 is the date. Khomeini versus the Great Satan. Or 1989. First, the Ayatollah provokes an epic war with Iraq. And with that out of the way he –'

'And how many dead? I've read that Iran lost a million. Can that be true?'

'Nobody's really sure. But prodigious. And while the citizens of Persia are digesting that, the loss of an entire generation for *no gain*, Khomeini looks for a means to "re-energise the Revolution". I.e., to regather some legitimacy. He needs a *cause*. And he alights on . . . *The Satanic Verses*. And our friend.'

'Mm. Khomeini said Salman was paid a million dollars by world Jewry to write it . . . What did Salman call the *fatwa*?'

'Looking back, he called it the first crow flying across the sky.'

A day or two later Christopher said, 'Tell me about the feeling over there.'

'Well I did an event the other night. And for once you could mention America without the room freezing over. Instead you got a wave of sympathy and fellow feeling. I think it's like that all over Europe. Even in France.'

'It's worldwide. There were candlelit vigils in Karachi and Tehran. Both Shia of course. The Shias having always been slightly cooler than the Sunnis.'

I said, 'Quite a bit cooler . . . America's in Britain's good books for now. But of course the softening of mood doesn't extend to Israel.'

'Mm. Are they saying that all the Jews who worked in the Twin Towers called in sick on September 11?'

'No. That's conspiracy stuff, that is. In England, as you know, anti-Semitism is just another chore of snobbery. Though it does lend spice to their anti-Zionism.'

'It's the same here. I seem to be surrounded by people who think . . . They think that Osama would take off his trunks the minute there's a country called Palestine. Or the minute we lift the sanctions on Iraq. Et cetera. They don't understand. I think Osama probably does lose sleep about those GI "devils" polluting Mecca and Medina. But inasmuch as it's secular, his *casus belli* is about the end of the Islamic ascendancy. What bothers him is that the Muslim host was defeated at the gates of Vienna. The year was 1683 and the date was September 11.'

Later in the week he said,

'Mart, what do you hate about America? I don't mean its wars. I mean internally.'

'Oh, there's no end of things to hate. *America is more like a world than a country* – attributed to Henry James. And it's the best starting point. You can't say you love a *world* . . . Generally, what do I hate?' And I started out on the usual roster. Racism, guns, extreme inequality, for-profit healthcare . . . Oh yeah, and the Puritan heritage. I can't bear the way they love to say "zero tolerance". It means zero thought.'

'So all that. But what Osama hates about America isn't what we hate about it. It's what we love about it. Freedom, democracy, secular government, emancipated chicks driving around in *cars*, if you please.'

'And plenty of sex.* I was reading . . . in Islam, apparently, Satan, *Shaytan*, is first and foremost a *tempter*. Whispering to the hearts of men. They're *tempted* by America. Because a side of them fucking loves it.'

'Yeah, that's certainly in the mix. How *dare* America have the arrogance to tantalise good Muslims? Osama didn't include that in his list of wrongs.'

'With Osama I sometimes think fuck it, it's all to do with birth order. I mean, seventeenth out of fifty-three – that's a notoriously difficult spot.'

'And living proof that his dad, the illiterate billionaire, wasn't at all opposed to fornication. In Islam there's no free love till you're dead. With the virgins.'

---

* Bin Laden would have points of agreement with Noam Chomsky and Gore Vidal. His true soulmate, though, would be Jerry Falwell: 'the pagans, the abortionists and the gays and the lesbians . . . all of them have tried to secularise America. I point the finger in their face and say, "You helped this happen"' . . . This line of reasoning always makes me think of two lines from 'Leda and the Swan'. Yeats's sonnet begins with an act of bestiality and rape: Zeus in animal disguise ravishes and impregnates the nymph Leda; and that child will be Helen of Troy. 'A shudder in the loins engenders there / The broken wall, the burning roof and tower . . .'

'With the virgins. And on that cool white wine that makes you drunk without any impairment or hangover.'

'Mm, I sure could use a little of that. Yes, rightly did Khomeini call life, actual life as we know it, *the scum of existence*. Ah, Christ. This is a fight about religion, Mart. Don't let anyone tell you any different. And those fights never really end.'

Equinoctial

It was September 26, and he was vainly pleading with his wife. Elena had not weakened in her determination to go to Manhattan (and to Ground Zero).

'Don't do it yet awhile, El. Any day now they're going to start fucking up Afghanistan. And then we'll have another Walpurgis Night in New York. I hate it when you fly anyway. Don't do it yet awhile.'

She said, 'What'll they do there after they kill Osama?'

'Uh, kill Mullah Omar, the one-eyed cleric, and so get going on the Taliban.'

Elena and her husband, for their part, were walking at dusk along Regent's Park Road, heading for Camden Town and Pizza Express. Eliza and Inez would be waiting for them (minded by their faithful nanny, Catarina) . . . He looked around and sniffed the air. There was an instability in the weather, moist, brisk, rich, with a seam of something unsettling and arousing, like a welcome but careless embrace; the taste of it was familiar, too, though for now he couldn't tell why or how. It would come to him. Elena said,

'Well I'm off the day after tomorrow. Sorry, mate, but there it is. I have to.'

After a couple of moments he made it clear that he would accept this without much further complaint. At the same time he dimly consoled himself with the thought of a night or two of snooker and poker (and perhaps a night of darts with Robinson).

She said, 'Uh, how did it work itself out with Phoebe? You know. After you got back from your quid pro quo with Lily. Up north.'

'Oh.' They turned into Parkway and there across the road were the outdoor tables and the milk-bar lights of Pizza Express. 'Oh, we got past it somehow.'

But now they were within (and he could see the back legs of Inez's highchair just round the corner). There were greetings and hugs and kisses, and it was almost the same – almost the same as before.

'Four Seasons, me,' he said. 'And you?'

'American Hot,' said Elena.

As he drifted in and out of the small talk, doing more gazing than listening, his thoughts gingerly and discontinuously returned, not to the night of shame with Phoebe but to what followed it: i.e., the month of shame with Phoebe. During that time he very closely resembled Humbert Humbert in Part Two of *Lolita*.* As you get older you can of course remember what you went and did when you were younger; you can remember what you did. What you can't remember is the temperature of the volition – of the *I want*. You can remember why you wanted what you wanted. But you can't remember why you wanted it so much.

Their pizzas came, and while they ate Martin joined the conversation (a notably unstructured exchange about the dangers faced by somnambulists, especially those somnambulists who lived on aeroplanes, as Eliza planned one day to do). But it was not yet seven o'clock and he wasn't hungry enough, so he made what progress he could with the house red before slipping outside for a smoke . . .

It had never bothered him, morally – what he thought of as the transactional phase or blip in his time with Phoebe. All the haggling and counterbidding was conducted in a febrile, giggly, not to say mildly hysterical spirit; it was comic relief from the gravity of a wrecked childhood, and somehow allowing them to move sideways – into their earthly paradise . . . Martin ground out his cigarette under his shoe and went back to watch the girls primly wallowing in their ice creams.

*

* This comes in the seventh chapter – the one that begins: 'I am now faced with the distasteful task of recording a definite drop in Lolita's morals.' Humbert is instituting a regime of sexual bribes. Nabokov continues: 'O Reader! Laugh not, as you imagine me, on the very rack of joy noisily emitting dimes and quarters, and great big silver dollars like some sonorous, jingly and wholly demented machine . . .' Lolita is described as 'a cruel negotiator'. Phoebe was not a squeezer or a gouger; she was more like a cheerful auctioneer. And there were other differences. I wasn't a stepfather, I wasn't *in loco parentis*. And Phoebe was thirty-six, not thirteen.

'I need to see the ruin,' Elena said outside. The others had gone on a few yards ahead (Eliza shouldering her way through the wind). 'I want to see what's left.'

'They say it stinks . . . There's a couplet of Auden's daubed all over the city. *The unmentionable odour of death / Offends the September night*. And it does smell of death, apparently. And of liquefied computers. Hitch says he took all his clothes straight to the cleaner's.'

'I want to feel the weight of what came down . . .'

He took her arm. 'Are you going to write about it?'

'Maybe.' When Elena emphasised *maybe* on the first syllable, as here, she usually meant yes. 'Come on,' she said. 'Walk me to the Zoo and back. Come on.'

At the gate to the front garden they peeled off from their daughters and made their way in shared silence to the northern rim of Regent's Park. The taste of the air: it wasn't local, he realised, or even hemispherical, or even terrestrial. Yes, the equinox, when day and night went halves on the twenty-four hours; it happened twice a year (the third week in March, the third week in September), as the sun crossed 'the celestial equator'. So for an interlude you were subject not only to the home biosphere but also to the solar system and its larger arrangements. Did this explain the accompanying arrow shower of physical memories? You felt yourself as a multi-annual being; and instead of making you feel old, as you'd expect it to do, it made you feel young, precariously connecting you to earlier incarnations, to your forties, your thirties, your twenties, your teens and beyond, all the way from experience to innocence . . . The Child is Father of the man. True, O poet of the lakes; and twice a year, in March, in September, the man is father of the child.

. . . Standing at the railings near the Zoo's entranceway, they listened hopefully, and lingered long enough to pick up the odd neigh, whinny, roar, and trumpet.

They started back and after a few paces Elena said, 'For how long did she give you a hard time about Lily? Phoebe.'

He readjusted. Then he said, 'She didn't. She barely mentioned it. Maybe she was still nuts on Parfait Amour. Weird, because Phoebe wasn't one to forgive and forget. But she seemed to let it go. I wonder why.'

Elena tightened her grip on his arm and brought him to a halt. She turned full face, full face, and pale in the light of the conscious moon.

'Well now you know. That settles it, fool. She'd already got her own back – with your father.' Elena shook her head. 'You're as blind as a kitten sometimes.'

The manhole

On October 7 the first American cruise missiles struck Afghanistan, and on October 11 Elena flew safely back to London; and on October 31 I myself crossed the Atlantic. To spend a few days in Manhattan and then take the shuttle to Boston. I had hoped of course to see Christopher, but he was in the city of Peshawar on the Pakistani–Afghan border, at the head of the Khyber Pass . . .

'Some of them are really fired up about it – none more so than Norman.' *Them*, in this sentence, meant New York novelists, and Norman was of course Norman Mailer. 'He wanted to start writing a long novel about 9/11 on 9/12.'

The speaker was a young publisher friend, Jonas. We were drinking beer in an empty dive on 52nd Street.

I said, 'The urge soon passed, I bet. Norman's too wise about the ways of fiction. Have you read *The Spooky Art*? He'll wait. Something like this takes years to sink in.'

'I'm told that Bret' – Bret Easton Ellis, the rather blithely unsqueamish author of *American Psycho* – 'is struck dumb. For now.'

'Well. Everyone's responding in their, at their own . . .'

Jonas said, 'We have a lady in Publicity who does the press ads? She reads the book, she reads all the reviews, and she assembles and arranges the quotes. She's the best there is at that, and she's eighty-three. Totally on the ball. And you know something? She can't take it in. She was here – she saw what happened. But she doesn't *get* what happened. "I can't take it in," she says. "It's too big."'

'. . . It's too big.'

Three times I went downtown to what they were now calling the Pile.

204

My wife, in her piece,* wrote that Ground Zero made her think of *a steaming manhole*. A fourteen-acre manhole. When she was there, in late September, the double high-rise of the WTC had become a medium-rise – *a rusted steel and rubbish heap* stretching to twenty storeys (down from 110). Now, in early November, the medium-rise had become a low-rise, chewed at its periphery by excavators and various other mechanical dredgers and burrowers . . .

'The unmentionable odour of death' had lifted and dispersed. Later in Auden's poem we read:

> Into this neutral air
> Where blind skyscrapers use
> Their full height to proclaim
> The strength of Collective Man . . .

Down at the Pile the air was no longer neutral (it was redolent of doused flames, scorched electrics, and the dusty undertaste of a lost battle); but the strength of collective man was never more palpable. Here the colossal squid of American can-do, American will-do, was fully engaged, with ironworkers, structural engineers, plumbers, pipefitters, boilermakers, cement masons, with cognoscenti of asbestos, of insulation, of sheet metal, riggers, truckers, teamsters . . . Like millions of others, worldwide, I had seen the Towers collapse in real time; and before me now the hundreds of hardhats were testifying to the weight of what came down.

. . . West 11th Street (I was staying there at my in-laws', in the house where my wife was raised): on the corner of Sixth Avenue stood Ray's Pizza, on the corner of Seventh stood St Vincent's Hospital. When Elena was here both buildings were plastered with images of missing people: she read *several hundred legends typed or scrawled beneath a candid face* . . . '*Please call day or night if you have ANY information of ANY kind!!!!*' Elena wrote on:

> The posters give us many details: this daughter has a mole beneath her left buttock, this husband has a KO tattoo on his left arm, as if they are wandering around in a daze somewhere and don't know who they are. But they're not. It is we who are wandering around in a daze.

* Which ran in the *Guardian* on October 11. An expanded version appeared soon afterwards in the *American Scholar*.

And the lost will not be found. In total, three police officers, six firefighters, and eleven civilians were safely extracted from under the fused mass of the Pile, which contained approximately 2,700 dead bodies.

Chinatown

How was your trusted ex-girlfriend? asked Phoebe, drily, on the day of his return from Durham. *She was well,* he quietly answered. Lily was well in 1977 and she was well in 2001. They met for lunch on a Saturday in Chinatown.

Like Elena (and like Julia), Lily was an American who had spent much of her life in England. He had known her for forty years. So they talked about the past, and their marriages, and especially their children, and not just about September 11.

He had no reason to invoke that very congenial episode, up north. But he kept thinking of it while they ate. After the public event, the dinner, and the nightcaps in the hotel lounge, they went to her room and followed the dictates of muscle memory. Being faithful won't do a damn thing for me (he'd briefly reasoned): I'll be punished anyway . . .

Now they were talking about certain of their exes, and he said,

'Remember Phoebe? I never grilled you, but what was your impression?'

'Well I hated her at first of course because of her figure and the way she eats. But after that I took to her. She made me laugh.'

'Really? I'm glad, because she didn't get on that well with other women. And you're usually wary of those men-only types.'

'She made me laugh about your lunch with Roman Polanski. In Paris that time – when was that?'

'It was later on. I think it was '79. You know, Roman was born in Paris?'

'Was he? And you found him so charming.' Lily looked furtive and amused. 'Did you hear what happened there? . . . Well, when you went to the bathroom, he slid his hand between her thighs and said, *Get rid of him.*'

'. . . The dirty little bastard. What'd she say?'

'She said, or she said she said, *How can I get rid of him? He's writing a huge piece about you and we've only been here five minutes.* Then he gave her his phone number on a napkin and made her swear that she'd call him the next day.'

'And did she?'

Lily shook her head. 'That's what I asked her. And I remember exactly. She said, *Certainly not. He'd just jumped bail for drugging and buggering a thirteen-year-old. Perhaps I'm very old-fashioned, but I think that's* un peu trop, *don't you?*'

He said, 'You know, Polanski insisted that *everyone* wants to fuck young girls. The lawyers, the cops, the judge, the jury – they all want to fuck young girls. Everyone. I don't want to fuck young girls. Any more than I want to fuck a pet rabbit or a puppy.'

'But they do have a following, thirteen-year-olds.'

'I suppose. No, clearly they do. Ooh, that dirty little bastard. He waits till I go to the bathroom, then he . . .'

Now it was Lily's turn to go to the bathroom, and as Martin asked for the bill he thought about that breakfast in bed, at the Durham Imperial, and about the journey back by train: many hours to consider Phoebe's past warnings and threats (*Woe betide you*), which never materialised. Now he paid.

'What's she up to these days, Phoebe?' said Lily as they were heading out.

'I happened to see her niece the other day. Who told me Phoebe was rich. She gave up her business for a big cheque.'

'What was her business?'

'I was never really clear about that. Business business. Brokering. She took early retirement. With bonuses. Business.'

'She put the wind up me once. It was very soon after you saved my life in Durham. Phoebe gave me such a look. Like Lucrezia Borgia wondering how to flay me alive. Then she threw her head back and laughed and said, *Oh never mind.*'

Lily went south, and Martin walked north-west, through Chinatown and into Little Italy. The scents *of a dozen different cuisines*, as Elena had noted, and the sound of a dozen different languages: *You can't help thinking that the whole Taliban Council would go unnoticed walking down Canal Street* . . . Across Houston, past NYU, up Broadway as far as the Strand Bookstore, then left to Sixth Avenue. Ray's Pizza, no longer a would-be clearing house (no longer a kiosk thatched with photos and messages), but the locus of a neglected roadside shrine, keepsakes, scrawled farewells, and a little midden of petals, leaves, and stems.*

Roman Polanski, like Father Gabriel – men so stirred by violation that only children would do. Now that Martin had young daughters of his own all his thoughts and feelings about Phoebe were changed, recombined utterly. He used to imagine that he had weighed it and assessed its mass: the weight of the early betrayal, the weight of what came down. But now he knew he'd had *no idea*.

Long shadows

The mood of all New Yorkers just now, as Elena put it, *is of a huge self-help group* – cooperative, communitarian, even socialistic. But on November 7, in the paper, there was an informal interview with a civic-minded activist who every morning for eight weeks had stood on a corner nearby (with a score of others) bearing a sign that said SANITATION ROCKS.

'We were there to cheer the sanitation trucks as they passed by,' he told the reporter. 'But yesterday the truck passed by and when we cheered the driver gave us the finger. So I guess everything's slowly getting back to normal.'

And normal New York was still tumultuous. A true-blue Monday afternoon, and I stood on Sixth Avenue looking for a cab to take me to LaGuardia; under a lowered sun the long-shadowed moneymen and moneywomen of Manhattan streamed by, getting and spending in a spirit of sharp-elbowed devotion to gain. This was the Village, I knew, and not the South Bronx, but still: no fighting, no biting, and never mind the great gamut of castes and colours and alphabets. All the passions and hatreds of the multitude – all the bitter furies of complexity – were delegated to the metal beasts of the road: barbarously impatient,

---

* Flowers, somehow, are universally felt to propitiate death. Even Eliza, not quite five, understood this . . . On another autumn afternoon, in 2015, I stood outside the Bataclan in Paris: candles, letters ('Cher Hugo'), unopened bottles of wine, empty bottles of beer, and bushels of flowers, sheathed in sweating cellophane.

subhumanly short-fused, squirming and jostling to find their place in the Gold Rush.

Saul won't be like Iris, I was telling myself. Iris was slightly nuts in the first place (as was John Bayley).* Saul wouldn't be reduced to saying 'Where is?' and 'Must do go'. But why couldn't Saul absorb September 11? 'The history of the world', he used to say, not solemnly but not unseriously, 'is the history of anti-Semitism.' And there was plenty of anti-Semitism intertwined with September 11.† It was just 'too big': it was the *size* of the event that made it unwieldy, when Saul tried to contain it. That was what I kept telling myself.

I stared at the red traffic light to my left on 11th Street. It looked to me like a *Time* magazine illustration of some newsworthy virus or bacterium, faceted like an insect's eye, black-studded, and slightly hairy at the edges . . .

Repeatedly turning my head south, towards downtown (where the cabs were meant to be coming from), I saw that insistent void where the Twin Towers used to be. You wanted to avert your eyes from the helpless nudity of the air. Skyscrapers would never look the same, and planes would never look the same, and even the oceanic Manhattan blue, so intensely charged, would never look the same.

*

* They were the kind of people who like getting ill and like getting old. They preferred winter to summer and autumn to spring (yearning, as John wrote, for 'grey days without sun'). In company the Bayleys were both high-spirited and dreamy; their love of grey days was aesthetic, not neurotic . . . On the other hand, Iris and John were also truly incredible slobs. 'Single shoes [and single socks] lie about the house as if deposited by a flash flood . . . Dried-out capless pens crunch underfoot.' As for the housework: in the past 'nothing seemed to need to be done', and now 'nothing can be done'. At the Bayleys', the bath, so seldom used, has become 'unusable', and even the soap is begrimed . . . Saul was a Jew and not entirely non-observant (there were occasional prayers and rituals and I would don a beenie); and he was strict about cleanliness . . . No, I thought, Saul won't be like Iris. He wouldn't be out prospecting for pebbles and pennies in the gutters; he wouldn't be watching *Teletubbies*; he wouldn't be saying to his spouse, 'Don't hit me.'
† The right answer to the question 'How many Jews were in the WTC on September 11?' is 'Why do you want to know?' Among the wrong answers is 'None'. This was widely believed or at least touted by Judaeophobes, conspiracists, and huge pluralities in the Middle East. There were many Jews in the WTC and many died there. The numbers given seem to me surprisingly various (perhaps reflecting decent disquiet at the thought of any 'Jew Count'), but the median figure is 325.

In the end I was driven to the airport, at appalling speed, by a certain Boris Vronski. Fitfully I read, but kept looking up and out . . .

What exactly did 'political Islam' have in mind? World hegemony and a planet-wide caliphate. Attained how? Necessarily by defeating all the infidel armies, the British, the French, the Indian, the Japanese, the Chinese, the North Korean, the Russian, and the American – the infidel armies, with their aircraft carriers and their trillion-dollar budgets. The restored Caliphate: God willing. Yes, God would need to be willing. And able. That which political Islam had in mind made no sense at all without the weaponry of God.

I was coming to the end of my book, Norman Cohn's *Warrant for Genocide* (1967), a study of the Tsarist concoction *The Protocols of the Elders of Zion* (in the Middle East an evergreen bestseller, along with *Mein Kampf*). Now I turned to the foreword (added in 1995) and read:

> There exists a subterranean world where pathological fantasies disguised as ideas are churned out by crooks and half-educated fanatics [notably the lower clergy] for the benefit of the ignorant and the superstitious. There are times when this underworld emerges from the depths and suddenly fascinates, captures, and dominates multitudes of usually sane and responsible people, who thereupon take leave of sanity and responsibility. And it occasionally happens that this underworld becomes a political power and changes the course of history.*

At Delta Shuttle I climbed out, confirmed that the Trump Shuttle was no more, and bought a ticket for the forty-minute flight to Logan.

---

* In the fifteen years following 2001, about 750 Americans were killed by lightning strikes; in the same period, 123 Americans were killed by Islamists (accounting for one-third of 1 per cent of national murders: 240,000). Another database finds that 'over 80 per cent of all suicide attacks in history' have taken place since September 11; and the victims are very predominantly Muslim (estimates range 'between 82 and 97 per cent'). In 2015 there were 11,774 terrorist attacks worldwide, with 28,328 victims; that year in the US, Islamist terrorism killed nineteen people, two fewer than those killed by toddlers who got their hands on household guns . . . It would seem to follow that any generalised fear of Muslims – and all talk of a Third World War or even 'a clash of civilisations' – is caused either by delusion or by political opportunism. A terrorist WMD will remain a possibility, but September 11 is already unrepeatable (in other words, the culmination came first, and out of a clear blue sky). Islamism has indeed changed the course of history, by scarring it with additional wars. For the West the lesson is this: the real danger of terrorism lies not in what it inflicts but in what it provokes.

Chapter 5
France in the Time of Iraq
2: Shock and Awe

Jed Slot

Jed Slot was in the hotel bar – being interviewed. Himself a teetotaller, Jed did all his interviews in the hotel bar, and I'd arranged to do all my interviews in there too; but whereas Slot's sessions lasted all day long and well into the night, mine only accounted for teatime (so I often went in early and came out late, just to listen). The truth was that I had taken up Jed like a new hobby. I had even read him.

'*Eh bien*. Now tell me, if you would,' began the questioner (a shrivelled sage with a briar pipe), 'what is the difference between the novel and the short story – I mean compositionally, in terms of praxis?'

'Well, sir,' said Jed, 'the novel is more expansive. By contrast, the short story is more succinct.'

. . . The ceremonies involving Elena started at six-thirty; I was having a quick beer while she finished her preparations upstairs (having it out for the very last time with the bathroom mirror). I listened on.

'Does the prescriptive exiguity make so bold as to encroach on the causal nexus?'

After an unhappy silence Jed said, 'Excuse me? The causal . . . ?'

Jed Slot was a young American writer of *noir* novels, but his latest book was a collection of *noir* short stories (called *Court et noir*: short and black). Already a minor icon in genre book clubs across France, Slot was suddenly the author of an uncontrollable bestseller that was engaging the critics' deepest concern; and Slot's sudden promotion moved his publishers to fly him over from Buffalo, NY . . . In his early thirties, in a slightly dank charcoal suit, with flat brown hair parted at the side, with weak nose and weak chin: Elena had twice got chatting with Jed, and pronounced him *very polite but strangely charmless and uneasy-making*. She also remarked that he knew no French at all, not even *merci* or *bonjour*.

'Does the crystallisation process impel you in the direction of masque? Q-u-e?'

Jed consulted the thick sheath of his schedule. He said, 'I'm sorry uh, Professor Boysghellin, but could you –

'Boisgelin. But you can simply call me Jean-Ignace. Or plain Jean.'

Brightening, Jed said, 'I'm sorry, John, but could you explain the meaning of that last word? The one with the q-u-e?'

'No,' said Jean-Ignace, 'kabuki – the Shinto influence, but shorn of its fripperies, needless to add. In other words, Monsieur Slot – is the short story more abstract, more tropological if you prefer, more *conceptualised* than the novel?'

'. . . The short story is more *condensed* than the novel. The novel is uh, more extended, more –'

'Come *on* then,' urged Elena from the passageway. 'You're making us late.'

In the fresh air he said, 'Jed's going through it. As usual. His interviewers speak better English than he does, or than I do. And Jed's only got one thing to say.'

'Poor Jed. He told me some of them last two or three hours. He's here till May. Lyon is next. And it's his first trip abroad apart from Toronto.'

'Elena,' he said, halting and standing back from her. '. . . It would be a waste of breath to say how lovely, how intelligent, and how *young* you look.'

'Why a waste?'

'You know what I mean. It's obvious. Even a crowd of anti-American Jew-hounders could see it. In your own person you tell your own tale.'

Yes, and they linked arms . . . And it hit him in a rush – a sensation that was once very familiar, indeed almost routine. And this was the wrong time of day for it: the sensation of waking up happy.

As a result he felt slightly stoned. You know – strange to the earth.

High

'Imagine . . . Close your eyes,' said the salesman, 'and you can see the sailsmen of two centuries since, fighting the invader. Imagine.'

And I did imagine. Standing there with the French rep, Gilles (the dreamy, the faraway French rep), I looked down through leaded glass from an embrasure high up in one of the twin towers of the eviscerated castle, which now served as a convention centre, as a banqueting hall, and, this week in March, as Festival HQ. Below, the fists and claws of the jetty reached out into the North Atlantic, the ironwork rusted with blood and brine . . . At five foot six, I was getting further and further below average height (the average Dutchman was six foot one). In the developed West, Canada included, everyone was getting taller. Everyone except Americans – and no one knew why.* But I would've towered over the warrior-mariners of the 1800s, who were the size of modern twelve-year-olds (and famished and scrawny, too, unlike the twelve-stone twelve-year-olds currently rolling around the First World). So the pomp of inches might have made me brave, might have made me rather more inclined to stop, or momentarily impede, a cannonball for twenty centimes a day. I was beginning to be embrittled by age, and the thought of *combat* jarred my whole skeleton, as if all my bones were funny bones. I was shrinking, too. 'Mart, if you want to grow,' said my much taller brother (this was in early adolescence), 'sleep with your legs dead straight.' I tried it for a couple of years, and I didn't get much taller (and I didn't get much sleep).

'Will we go down?'

'You go ahead. Nice talking to you, Gilles. I'll be along directly.'

Elena was in a side room somewhere nearby, being interviewed by this medium and then by that medium and then by the other

---

* No, not even silver-spoon Ivy Leaguers were getting taller; and no one knew why. In a long and fascinating essay in the *New Yorker*, the scientist–writer, having exhausted all possible explanations, ended with what amounted to a poeticism. His guess was that the cause might be extreme inequality. Extreme inequality, we now know, has an adverse effect on every index of societal health – including economic health . . . Incidentally my height would have kept me out of the First World War; but not for long. In August 1914 you had to be at least five foot eight. By October it was five foot five (and soon after that it was five foot three). Similarly, twenty-twenty vision, as a requirement, soon degenerated; even basic bifocalism was waived, and you could join up with one eye.

medium, so I'd be all alone, without my wife – *ma femme, cicérone, et interprète* . . . As I came down the stone staircase I thought of something I'd read in a laddish American glossy on the Eurostar: *Who unties France from the tree and helps her find her panties every time the Germans are done with her? America, that's who.* This was from one of many articles in a whole special number endorsing Francophobia in all its forms. Another think piece, using charts and statistics, argued that the French were schlumps and slatterns, too, on top of everything else: for instance, barely half the men changed their underwear every day (the women were admitted to be rather cleaner – those panties that America was forever helping her find had a much better chance of being fresh out of the drawer). In the canyonlike reception room there were perhaps 300 of them, the French. And for a time I wandered around down there, trying to gauge these individuals with (for the occasion) a neurotically fastidious eye. And all right, there were unshaven chins and heads of unbrushed hair, and several wide smiles disclosed a seam along the gumline of last night's dessert (usually crème brûlée). But who cared? I was about as slovenly as the French, I reckoned, and I admired their lack of interest in how they looked. It freed them up for higher things, for the delirious pursuits of philosophy and art. Yes (I was deciding), France pullulated with poets and seekers (the 1954 census logged the existence of 1,100,000 avowed intellectuals, with thinkers and dreamers (like the rep in the high tower), with bohemians, in a word. At certain times and in certain moods (e.g., the present) I was a boho imperialist: bohemians, I believed, should rule the world, marching forth with sword and fire to conquer, colonise, and convert until . . .

I reached a glassed-off area, an internal conservatory or hothouse for the senior French writers, who were on exhibit but sequestered from the merchandisers, the publishers, the pundits, the conference bums, and of course the junior French writers. It now resembled one of those places compassionately reserved for smokers, still to be found in airports, even American airports . . . Was that one over there J. M. G. le Clézio? He was blondly haggard-handsome enough. In 1973 I reviewed a Le Clézio novel, *War*, and the piece was present in my mind because I'd recently collected it. *War* is an example of *choseisme*, or thing-ism; thus the author wanders about like a fact-finder from the planet Krypton (three pages on a department-store placard, four on a lightbulb) . . .* The senior French writers sat glazed and unsmiling (and among French intellectuals, I knew, it was considered trivial not to be clinically depressed). Did they find *anything* funny? One of the things that didn't make them laugh, clearly, was laughable pretension . . . In Nabokov's brightly mournful late novella *Transparent Things* (1972), flighty Julia takes the stolid hero, Hugh Person, to the avant-garde play that everyone is talking about: and when the curtain goes up Hugh is 'not surprised to be regaled with the sight of a naked hermit sitting on a cracked toilet in the middle of an empty stage'. Nabokov has elsewhere made the point that all writers who are any good are funny. Not funny all the time – but funny. All the lasting British novelists are funny; the same is true of the Russians (Gogol, Dostoevsky, and, yes, Tolstoy are funny); and this became true of the Americans. Franz Kafka, whatever your professor might have told you, is funny. Writers are funny because life is funny. Here's something else that is true: writers are life's eulogists. The *romanciers de grimace*, the woe specialists, the wound flaunters, the naked-hermit and cracked-toilet crowd have gone and made an elementary mistake, thinking that writers are life's elegists . . . Within the glass menagerie each scowlist was accompanied by an attractive young woman. And this was part of the trouble. In *Herzog* the hero calls for a sexual boycott of the professional melancholics – those who felt it was their duty to reject 'worldly happiness, this Western plague, this mental leprosy'. 'The world', writes Bellow, 'should love lovers; but not theoreticians. Never theoreticians! Show them the door.' Yes, that might do it. I noticed that one no doubt much-praised sourpuss (his baldy haircut, his nicotine-rich moustache, his mouth like a half-empty goody bag with its lumps of fudge and butterscotch) was warmly berating the meek little blonde at his side, who sat with her hands clenched and her head contritely bowed. Come on, darling, I thought (as I secured yet another glass of white wine), heed Moses Herzog. 'Ladies, throw out these gloomy bastards!'

Now Elena appeared. She looked combative, self-sufficient, and insanely cheerful. No, he couldn't go on evading it – he would have to sit down soon and come up with a definition of love.

*

* This kind of obsessiveness can be done funnily (as in early Nicholson Baker), but Le Clézio goes about it with a solemnity I found as leaden as his heroine's opening sally (oh, the falsity and boredom of that 'perhaps' and that 'simply' and that 'suddenly'): 'this girl blurted out, jokingly perhaps, or simply because it had suddenly become the truth: "I am nothing."' Well, it isn't the truth; and who could possibly take it 'jokingly'?

The presentation

'You're always saying I look insanely cheerful.'

'Well you always do,' he said. 'And it's particularly hard to miss around here. Elena – go and have a shriek and a cackle with J. M. G. le Clézio.'

'. . . What have you been up to?'

'Smirking at the scowl novelists – and mapping out my smirk novel. I'm committed to it, Pulc. I already feel it stirring within me.'

'Mm. That one'll go the way of *The Crap Generation*. You won't write a word.'

'Provably false. I've started it . . . Wait. Here we are. You're on.'

'. . . *Et le vainqueur*', intoned an amplified voice, '*du Prix Mirabeau de la Non-Fiction est –* Enterrez-moi debout: L'odyssée des Tziganes!*'*

'Careful now,' he said. 'Remember Jean-Jacques hates Sam.'

'Fuck Jean-Jacques. Here's my speech,' she said, passing him two photcopied pages, 'in English.'

Another kiss and she was away, striding forward and up on to the stage. As he watched her go, and watched her climb, he found that a little caesura had opened up in his mind: he knew why France hated America, but he had quite forgotten why America hated France. Elena was about to remind him.

'*Bonsoir*,' she began. '*En ce moment, les Français ne sont pas très populaires en America (et vice versa), parce que vous obstruez notre chemin vers la guerre.* Because you obstruct our path to war. *Mais vous*

---

* *Bury Me Standing: The Gypsies and their Journey*. That migration was from India to Eurasia, mainly to the countries of Eastern Europe. The title proper derived from a folk saying repeated to the author by a Bulgarian activist, Mustapha (at a conference in Slovakia): 'Bury me standing. I've been on my knees all my life.'

êtes très, très populaires avec cette Americaine. *Je vous remercie de tout mon coeur pour mon prix adorable . . .'*

She talked for another 105 seconds. During this time he followed the transcript but also looked around and became aware of the audience in the hall. Her unarguably, her ascertainably beautiful face filled half a dozen TV screens, like an electronic tutelary spirit. And the gradual smiles of the men and women gathered there slowly changed, from mildly reluctant to wholly unreluctant, even the smiles of the senior French novelists, as they acknowledged what was plain to see: a phenomenal concentration of blessings . . .

Well, one thing was clear. Martin didn't have a crap wife; he had a wife who was a blinding *embarras de richesses.* And the two of them dwelt harmoniously in a six-bedroom house near Regent's Park . . . So what was all this about suicide? But it was a fact; it was undeniably the case that he was always wondering why *everyone,* including all his children, even Inez (who was now three), didn't commit suicide. That's right: each time he laid eyes on them he was agreeably surprised to find that they were still in one piece. Well, here he was in the Holy Land of the counterintuitive. In the country of Gide, Sade, Genet, and Camus, everyone would automatically see the point of his psychological *acte gratuit.*

Why these thoughts – which, by the way, predated September 2001? . . . In 2010 or thereabouts (long after the phase had passed), he arrived at an explanation, partly trivial, partly universal (perhaps), and almost insultingly obvious.

He was fifty-two and he stood on a lowered drawbridge held flat and taut by burnished steel chains, smoking, and waiting for his wife. Ah, here she was . . .

Shock and Awe

'The novel is more capacious,' Jed Slot was saying. 'The short story, on the other hand, is more uh, more confined.'

'But yes,' said Jed's interviewer, a nervous, hard-living redhead of his own age, who tremblingly brandished a foot-long cigarette-holder and a tasselled rosary. 'The short story can be *plus pur*, no? . . . Uh, more purer. The reality uh, reality, is *atomisé*, no? *Granulaire. Et deffracté.* So is the short story somehow less *compromis*? Less uh, compromised than the novel?'

Slot pounced. 'The story is less *comprehensive* than the novel. In a short story you're more aware of limitations of space. So the story provides fewer . . .'

I paid the extras on the bill and went upstairs for the bag, into which Elena was forcing stray pairs of shoes. I said,

'It's a good job Jed brought his thesaurus with him from Buffalo. He might get through the whole six weeks without saying *shorter* or *longer*.'

'Don't be mean. We've got to say our fondest farewells to poor dear Jed.'

'You know that little nook to the side downstairs? They've got your book in there and my book, and the *complete* Jed Slot – in French and English. I did some browsing while you were having your massage. And there's no difference at all except the stories are shorter than the novels.'

'And the novels are longer than the stories.'

'And I'll tell you why he made you uneasy. Physically uneasy. He's a woman-hater, El. Whenever a chick walks in, his whole tone goes weird. He coolly "sees through her", he thinks, but it's all fantasy and paranoia. Very striking.'

She said, 'I don't think he's a woman-*hater*. More like a resenter. He's just sexually unlucky . . . Well things should perk up for him now. Now he's taken seriously.'

'Maybe. Yeah, maybe they will a bit.'

'But not by much. The trouble is he's still queasy and bitter. I booked our cab.'

'That's why he's sick enough to please the French. They don't mind writers being aggressive about women. Odd, when you think that political correctness was born and raised in France. They don't mind Beckett saying *So I kicked her in the cunt*. When's it coming, our cab?'

'Not till twelve.'

'Hitch must be on pins.'

'Why particularly?'

'It's almost upon us, Pulc. Six hours to go. Shock and Awe.'

*

218

Shock and Awe was the nickname of the doctrine officially entitled Rapid Dominance. The idea, according to military philosophers, military poets, and military dreamers, was to induce in the enemy a state of hysterical disorientation. High-tech 'precision engagement' would minimise civilian casualties while inflicting 'nearly incomprehensible levels of mass destruction'; US forces should also be ready to shut down communications, transport, food production, and water supply, in which case the Shock part of it would be 'national'.

'Given all that,' he said to his wife, 'at what point are they supposed to feel like dancing in the street?'

'They may do. No more Saddam. We'll see.'

Certain locations in Baghdad were being bombarded on March 19. March 20 saw boots on the ground and Running Start. On March 21 it would be the turn of Shock and Awe, scheduled for 17.00 GMT.

And March 21 was today.

'Did you ring the Jews?'

'Yes,' said Elena.

'And they're all right?'

'They're fine.' The Jews were their daughters (and they were full Jews too, by the ancient law of matrilinearity, and could simply walk into Israel as full citizens). Eliza and Inez were also known as the rats, the poems, the fools, and the flowers. 'Right. *Allons.*'

It would've made a better – and slightly longer – short story if the Hôtel Méridien was a citadel of swinish luxury; in fact it was a modest three-star (representing a 1950s vision of modernity: their room looked like the guest quarters of a Sussex polytechnic). But he for one was taking his leave with a heavy regret, lightened only by this dependable truth: being away from home makes home seem exotic (and at this stage the little girls seemed almost other-worldly). He wanted to get back to his house and his desk – but not to his silences and his circling thoughts . . .

While Elena was making her final inspection he opened the window and stuck his head out of it: under one vast and lonely cloud (as wispily flotational as an elderly combover), in freakish sunshine, little figures paddling, splashing, jumping, running . . . He remembered being a boy and running as fast as he could across sand;* a year or two ago he was able to remember this with his whole body, but now he just pictured it or half-imagined it. That boy was further away from him than he used to be, running across sand, running away from him across sand . . .

Looking out, he listened. 'The distant bathers' weak protesting trebles'; and he silently recited the closing lines of the poem:

> If the worst
> Of flawless weather is our falling short,
> It may be that through habit these do best,
> Coming to water clumsily undressed
> Yearly; teaching their children by a sort
> Of clowning; helping the old, too, as they ought.

Those last seven words. When he first read them (in the collection *High Windows* in 1979), he was thirty; and he considered it a right-minded and dignified conclusion; in March 2003 he saw their grim duteousness – and his eye kept straying left to the word *clowning*. The old fools, the old clowns. That would be years away. But it was limping ever closer . . .

What you see here is a man in his fifties. Your fifties – the Crap Decade.

'Now today we're going to have to have a change of heart.'

'Oh?' she said as she continued to look observantly out of the cab window.

'We're going to stop being against the war and start being for it. We're going to hope for total success and the best possible outcome. For Joe and Tommy and also of course for Kasim.'

'And Fetnab. Okay,' she said, now straightening up and searching for the tickets in her bag. 'Agreed. You don't want a disaster just to win an argument.'

'Exactly . . . I still can't see why Hitch is so keen. After all, it is a *war*, and war is hell. Oh, and guess what he told me on the phone. He said Hans Blix was on the take! Now *how* could Hitch swallow that. Imagine

* My early childhood in South Wales was dominated by the sea. Hilly needed no urging from Nicolas and me and later Myfanwy to go to the beach (there were several beaches) in any weather. Two hundred times a year I ran across sand with our big dogs. The dogs, prominent among them Bessie, then Flossie, then Nancy, also did their duty by the Amis children in giving us our first taste of death and grief. That's how you start.

it. Saddam says to this venerable Swede, *We're rolling in WMDs, but you keep your mouth shut and here's ten million quid.*'

'We'll have to hurry.'

'So will they, Elena. So will they. They're calling it the Race for Baghdad.'

Love songs in age and youth

On the slow, crowded, and companionably talkative train to Paris (full of all the people they'd met in St-Malo), he put aside his holiday reading (a book about Verdun and the battle that lasted for the entirety of 1916), and tried to be sociable; but then a headline on the cover of one of Elena's magazines took his fancy, and he was at once helplessly engrossed. The long article didn't squarely concern itself with mass death, though the days of its dramatis personae were obviouly numbered. No: it was about the lovelife fitfully enjoyed by the occupants of sunset homes.

There used to be a time, in sunset homes, when the old men and the old women were vigilantly kept apart (especially after dinner). Now that approach was considered old-fashioned. Why, these days, in sunset homes in Denmark, there were porno screenings every Saturday night, and assignations were cautiously encouraged. 'With many frail elderly,' the reporter allowed (echoing doctors' concerns), there was 'the risk of serious injury'; and 'questions of consent' could be complicated when one or both parties happened to be senile.

So far as Martin could tell, there was absolutely nothing to be said for lovelives in sunset homes; but lovelives in sunset homes there were, and they looked like the future. His future, too. He now had a vision of himself in the nodding, swaying, mumbling, drooling recreation room; there he sat, next to his latest girlfriend, as they watched the jolting tattoos of an adult video. A wattled cheek was pressed against his boneless jowl, and a crablike hand trembled on his wasted thigh; and he would be full of wonder. Wondering about serious physical injury; wondering where on earth he'd put his horn pills; and wondering whether she meant it when she said yes, and whether he meant it when he asked her to.

The train came to rest in a siding just before Chartres. A delay of fifteen minutes was announced, and at least half the passengers clambered out for a smoke (they were good little smokers, the French – another bohemian bond). When he was once more at Elena's side he said,

'My smirk novel – it's taking shape. I'll need your help with the title, El. I fancy a Rousseauesque intonation. How about *Confessions of a Sexually Irresistible Genius*? Bit of a mouthful, I agree. Or *Seer and Stud: His Confessions* . . . I know what you're thinking. You're thinking it'll make everyone hate me.'

'They hate you already.'

'Mm.' In the autumn of that year he would find out how true this was, when he published his eleventh work of fiction (which wasn't remotely a smirk novel). 'But that's the unavoidable consequence of smirk novels. How about something simpler. More direct and man-to-man. Like *I Fucked Them All*.'

She said patiently, 'Where's the genius element in *I Fucked Them All*?'

'Good point. We could partly fix it by having my name in really gigantic letters. But you're right. The title needs more work.'

'. . . You haven't really started it, have you.'

'Yes I have. At the moment I'm tackling the dedication. Which is going to run for about twenty pages. Girls' names in alphabetical order. Look. Aadita, Aara, Aba, Abba. The real fun starts with the Abigails. There'll be dozens of them. See? Abi, Abie, Aby, Abbi, Abbie, Abby. I'll round it off with a few Zuzis and Zuzannahs, then a Zyra, then an italicised note saying *And all the rest*. Or possibly *And all the others, God bless them*.'

'Christ,' said Elena. 'Read your book.'

He read his book. After a night of rain the ground at Verdun looked like the clammy skin of a monstrous toad. Then the battle resumed, the sky a thunderhead of iron and steel, the Mort Homme (as they called this eminence) a volcano of blood and fire, the smell of death thicker than the mustard gas, and the scarce water rations fouled by rotting flesh, the trench rats bloated like war profiteers, and everywhere the flies, huge, black, and silent. The Battle of Verdun was fought over a strip of land a little larger than the combined Royal Parks of London (and, once taken, opened up grave strategic risks). But the battle, *l'ogre*, seemed to shake off all human direction. Europe is mad. The world is mad. Man is mad. A bullet was *nothing*. What you feared was the pulping of your entire body: during bombardments, your leg was afraid, your back was afraid, your blood was afraid.

And where were the suicides? Where were they?

City of Light

'*Monsieur, s'il vous plaît. Donnez moi*', I said, holding up finger and thumb, '*uh, trois centimetres de vodka, avec uh, deux de Campari, et . . . un de Vermouth rouge.*'

'Mm,' said the waiter as he swivelled. 'Very esspensive drink.'

'And very fattening,' subtended Elena. 'And very damaging in every way.'

'Come now, Pulc. Here we are in the City of Man. Your prize. This spree. It's a special occasion.'

'Yes. And your funeral will be a special occasion.'

In Paris they'd changed stations. The capital was having one of its crimp-lipped strikes (because French unions were strong – a mere memory in England), and so the Amises' five-day idyll was puzzlingly marked by a ninety-minute traffic jam – ninety minutes of hurry up and wait, hurry up and wait for the red gold and green. Now, booked on a later train, they sat at a sticky and rickety café table across the way from the Gare du Nord.

'Elena, your health!' He drank. 'They also call it the City of Light. But Saul goes on about the gloom. Foggy, dripping . . .'

'*La grisaille.*'

'He called it one of the grimmest cities on earth.* I don't remember it like that.'

'I do. I was miserable here.'

'Come on, you've been to London, haven't you? Isn't London just a latitude worse? Anyway I remember the light here as painterly. You could always –'

'Painterly, my ass.'

'That's what Saul said. *Gay* Paris? Gay, my foot. But Anthony, that painter friend of mine, he said he never got as blue here as he did in London – because he could always go outside and get something from the light.'

---

* It was not because he shared Bellow's view of Paris that Hitler, in 1944, gave the order to destroy it (the order was disobeyed, as were other Führer Orders or 'Nero Orders' of his final year) . . . Saul was in Paris, with his first wife and his first child, from 1948 to 1950 on the GI Bill (and hating the French almost as much as Dostoevsky had hated them in 1862). 'Americans of my generation crossed the Atlantic . . . to look upon this human, warm, noble, beautiful and also proud, morbid, cynical, and treacherous setting.' 'My Paris', collected in *It All Adds Up*.

'With me it was simpler. I didn't know any people and I didn't know any French. Well it was better than Jed's, but I couldn't chat in it.'

They had both lived in Paris for the same few months in 1979/80, and in the same quarter (the Latin). They never met. Elena, at least at first, was wretchedly installed in la place Saint-Michel. Whereas Martin, flush with screenplay money, and writing his fourth novel, was renting a flat that belonged to the ex-wife of an Italian film star (Ugo Tognazzi), on rue Mouffetard, up by the Panthéon (and much of the time he was sharing it with Phoebe Phelps). He said,

'Your speech was perfect, and everyone *did* fall in love with you. You were very sweet to our hosts.' He rolled and lit a cigarette. 'Impossible to tell what they're going through, inside. Imagine. A great warrior nation. Charlemagne, Napoleon. They were *much* better than me in World War I. But it was *sauve qui peut* in 1940. Then – spontaneous collaboration. A joint effort – with the Nazis.'

'In other words, they banded together to round me up.'

'Too true, kid. As a way of embracing their humiliation . . . Where's that really murky part of Paris? The redlight-and-rentboy part. The gypsy part.'

'Pigalle. And we're in it. It's right across the street. Look.'

He looked – the heaps of rubbish, the shimmer of trespass and perversity . . .

'*Nostalgie de la boue*,' she said. 'Love of slime. The French love of rottenness.'

'Yeah, love of murk. Their writers have it too. I was thinking last night. There's hardly any murk in *our* literature, El. I have Lawrence and you have Kerouac and Burroughs and Bukowski – all of them the toast of Paris in their day. Here, murk is it. Murk's the Great Tradition. It's their history and their dirty conscience. In the soul of every French writer there's a . . .'

'There's a Quartier Pigalle.'*

---

* The last train to Auschwitz left France on August 22, 1944 (bringing the total of doomed deportees to about 76,000). August 22 was a Tuesday. The following Saturday de Gaulle officially inaugurated the Liberation of Paris. That same weekend Philippe Pétain and his crew were being forcibly transferred from one spa town to another, from Vichy in central France to Sigmaringen in southern Germany (in whose castle they gibbered to their defence lawyers while praying for a Nazi victory) . . . Now there is in world literature a venerable continuity of two-ply humanism in the form

'. . . Yes. But you're safe with me, my dear. You now enjoy the protection of my proud Nordic blood.'

'Nordic? You mean Celtic. You mean your proud Welsh blood.'

This was a frequent tease. According to Elena, he 'was born in the heart of Wales' (rather than in Oxford) and could trace his lineage back, on both sides, to Owen Glendower, or Owain Glyndŵr, who flourished in the fourteenth century.

'I'm no Taff. I'm no Gael. I'm a true-blue Anglo-Saxon. *Pur*, Elena.'

'Mm. Remember what Hilly said about you and Hitler? It's what made you right about him.* Guilt Anyway, all countries have done terrible things. You know what I did? I kidnapped and enslaved Africans to work the land I stole from the Indians.'

'No, put that way it doesn't sound very nice. But you didn't do all that in 1940.'

'I killed millions of South East Asians around 1970.'

'And I killed nearly a million Indian Indians in 1947. Breakneck partition. I did terrible things. But I didn't do them in England. Jean-Jacques did terrible things right here in the City of Light. While Fritz looted his shops and fucked his women.'

'Fritz fucked them all. Anyway I love Jean-Jacques because he gave me my prize.'

'Oh yeah, I meant to ask. Did he give you any money as well?'

'Yup. Five thousand euros. It's already spent.' And she frowned sorrowfully, saying, 'I bought a *hideous* dress last week.'

. . . For a year or two in the later 1970s, many women and quite a few men used to claim with a straight face that all men and all women were basically interchangeable (this was 'equalitarian feminism' in its idealist form). Now, no man has ever said or would ever say, *I bought a* hideous *suit last week*. He might very well have bought a hideous suit last week, but he wouldn't say it (because he wouldn't think it –

---

of writer–doctors: Rabelais, Henry Vaughan, Smollett, Goldsmith, Schiller, Chekhov, Bulgakov, William Carlos Williams. In Schloss Sigmaringen the goddess of history staged a negative epiphany. The writer–doctor in attendance there was the nth-degree nihilist and Judaeophobe, Louis-Ferdinand Céline. It was Céline's fate to listen to Pierre Laval's interminable self-vindications as he treated the old quisling's ulcer.

* By 2003 I had written a novel about the Third Reich, ten years earlier; and ten years later I would write another . . . 'When I'm at my desk, Mum,' I once or twice told her, 'I get at least as much from you as I get from Dad.'

because he wouldn't know it). I took Elena's hand and elongated its little finger.

'I am you and you are me. It's almost time, El. Pinkies clenched for Shock and Awe.'

'Pinkies clenched for Shock and Awe . . . Now let's read for a while.'

A fly was staring at me from the tabletop. Being a fly, it was in the heraldic posture we may call 'crappant' (this was the coinage of a certain contemporary poet famed among other things for his descriptions of urban dogs). The wet, viscid linoleum surface combined with the insect's suction pads to root it in place. Stale beer was probably of some interest to flies, but there was nothing here to engage their deepest fascination, no shit or blood or death.

Did they have 'horseholders' at Verdun? He remembered the horseholder from another book, and the night under shellfire: 'What can one man do with four terrified horses? If shells burst behind they lunge forward. If shells burst ahead they go back on their haunches, nearly pulling your arms out of their sockets. A week in the front-line trenches is better than one night as a horseholder under shellfire.' Eight million horses were killed in the First World War, and at Verdun 7,000 were killed in one day . . .

With every line of their bodies eloquent of innocence, the horses wouldn't have wanted to be there. But the flies, like the rats, were there of set purpose. Tensed on the tabletop, the fly in Pigalle continued to stare at him with its compound eyes. He waved it away but it returned and crouched and stared. Did he who made the horse make thee? Little lover of wastes and wounds and wars . . .

'I'm glad we never met here back then, El. I was thirty and you were what, eighteen? You needed to have your adventures. The timing would've been off.'

'Yes,' she said, 'but we could've made some sort of start.'

Which was exactly what he was thinking.

The power and the glory

The administrators of the Prix Mirabeau had seen fit to provide first-class tickets for the Eurostar, and so this attractive pair savoured a glass of champagne, and prepared themselves for red wine and red meat. He said,

'Is life worth living on these terms? You know, if I could speak French I would've gone into that glass booth and told the writers to stop writing the murk novel and start writing the smirk novel.'

'. . . I'm trying to think if there are any. Smirk novels.'

'There's plenty of smirk stuff in Nabokov. *My striking if somewhat brutal good looks. The crazed beauties that lashed my grim rock.* But it's all ironic.'

'There couldn't be a smirk novel that plays it straight.'

'I only know of one. By John Braine.' Like Kingsley, John Braine was a lower-middle-class Angry Young Man (a journalistic label derived from John Osborne's *Look Back in Anger*) who became increasingly reactionary as he got older and angrier (and richer). In his early and more successful years (*Room at the Top, Man at the Top*) he gained renown as an unusually noisy provocateur ('I want to go back to Bingley', South Yorkshire, 'in an open car with two naked ladies covered in jewels'), but towards the end he became a much-feared drunk and drag ('You ate me, daunt yer,' he once told a silenced lunch gathering, 'as I never went to university'). His smirk novel was his last, written as his dismal destiny loomed. Martin said,

'We used to have a lot of fun, me and Kingsley, elaborating on Braine's first page. We got it down to something like: *My ravishing young mistress, Lady Aramintha Worcestershire, pulled the top sheet over her bulging breasts, sighed happily, and said, "It's just not fair. You're a world-famous novelist, adored by millions of readers. You dine at the choicest restaurants with the cream of the intellectual elite. You make a fine living simply on the strength of your intellect and your talent. And yet you have the body, and the stamina, of a young boy. It's just not fair." "Thanks, loov," I said.* And going on like that for three hundred pages. *That's* a smirk novel.'

'I think you told me. Isn't there a good bit about bad reviews?'

'Yeah. At some snobbo cocktail party a titled connoisseur says to him, So the critics weren't very keen on your latest effort. And the hero says gruffly, Aye, no one was very keen on it – except the *pooblic*.'

'What happened to him?'

'Hang on.' He took his watch off and held a hand aloft. 'Baghdad is two hours ahead of Paris. When I slice my hand through the air we'll have Shock and Awe.' He sliced his hand through the air. 'Now it begins.'

They quietly returned to their books for an hour and then dinner started coming.

'Hans *Blix*,' he said, as they addressed their rather superior beefsteaks and quaffed the more than acceptable Bordeaux. 'You know what I reckon it was? Hitch got too close to power.' He chewed and sipped. 'It's dangerous stuff, power, and very infectious. And I wonder about his immunity to it.'*

'But now,' said Elena, 'we want our soldiers to be feted in the streets and pelted with rosebuds.'

'Definitely. I hope they get some frat, too.'

'Frat?'

'Frat. There's a funny footnote on frat in a Kingsley poem – about an army reunion. "'Fraternisation' between Allied troops and German women was forbidden by order of General Eisenhower in 1944. Phrases like 'a piece of frat' soon became current."'

'Well, there'll be no frat with Fetnab. And they're not allowed any alcohol either. You and I will be very careful not to offend our Muslim hosts.'

'Quite right too,' he said. 'But there's bound to be a vast black market. Not in frat but in booze. They'll find a way.'

'On TV last night Hitch was all blue-eyed and doubt-free.'

'Mm. People are saying he's gone neocon. But I don't think he's changed at all. People don't change. He's basically still a streetfighting Trot.'

'Then why's he considering Bush–Cheney in 2004?'

'I don't know. I think he thinks Kerry won't have his heart in it. Hitch wants regime change, but from the left. An anti-fascist crusade. He thinks Republicans are better at it. War.'

'. . . I'm trying to remember something. Yes, Barney and Spot.'

There would in the end be quite a fuss about Barney and Spot – the president's dogs. Or about the fact that he had been filmed playing with them. Bush quite testily complained that he shouldn't have been filmed on the White House lawn, playing with Barney and Spot. Playing? Well,

---

* In this area I knew myself to be rather frail. When I became back-half editor of the *New Statesman* I was assigned my own secretary. After a week I noticed a similar sort of expression on all the faces I knew best: a guarded reluctance to meet my eye. When I questioned them, I heard phrases like *unbearably grand* and *unrecognisably smug*. In short, I had gone insane. Because I had a secretary.

he wasn't going to roll around with them, not on the eve of the invasion. Bush played with Barney and Spot like a taskmaster, as if he was training them or testing them. He played with Barney and Spot without the slightest amusement. And who can be unamused by their dogs?

'He played with them as if he was saying, I can make you do this, I can make you do that. I can make this happen. Do you know what *else* I can make happen? Do you, Barney? Do you, Spot? Jesus, the way he walks. With his arse muscles tensed. The way he salutes – you know, when he gets off his helicopter. Bush doesn't drink any more but he's absolutely smashed on power. You'd think his dad might've had a word with him about that.'

'But he doesn't listen to his dad. He says he listens to a "higher father".'

'Great . . . Darling, it hurts me to say this, but you should've gone on calling it the axis of *hatred*. You were wrong to change it to the axis of evil. It might've helped you get used to the idea. Of being hated. Your trouble is that you keep expecting to be loved. Even in Iraq you expect it. Poor you. You keep expecting to be loved.'

Taking it personally

'He's steely enough, but Hitch could never be a politician. He'd have to give up smoking . . . I asked,' she said. 'There's a smoking car in second class – near the back. You might rock down there for a while.'

'That's kind in you, El. That's good in you.'

'But you're going to quit, right?'

'I hope to, yes.'

'You hope to. I told you what Eliza said. She said, *Daddy's going to die, and you'll get married again, and I'll have a stepfather.* She looked wretched. *That's what's going to happen next.*' Elena yawned and shuddered. 'Nap time. Bye.'

He kissed her and then with his book under his arm he picked up two miniatures of whisky as he headed south.

Where were the suicides?

Ah, here they were at last, the suicides. In the perpetual anguish and filth of the front line, during the gaps between the thunderbolts and the earthquakes, you could hear the wounded pleading for it, for oblivion; and in the field hospitals, under lamps black with airborne vermin, they hollered for it at the top of their voices (there was a French soldier who stabbed himself to death with a kitchen fork, clubbing down on the shaft with his fist). Martin drank a toast. Human beings, staked out on the soil of the Mort Homme, I honour you . . .

In the Middle East 'a cigarette' was a unit of time (about ten minutes), as in, Q: How long will he be gone? A (shrugging): Three cigarettes. Anyway, three cigarettes later Martin closed the book and, as he often did (with writers both living and dead), drafted a mental thankyou note to its author. The 'Crap Historians' segment of *The Crap Generation* would've made the following case: crap-generation historians were crap because they thought emotionlessness was a virtue. And Martin believed that you couldn't write history without emotion (however restrained and controlled). You had to take history personally. It produced you and it formed you. How else were you going to take it?

The book about the Battle of Verdun was old-school: it was beautifully emotional and therefore cathartic; terror and pity decisively deepened its prose. Dear Professor, he was murmuring to himself. And then he remembered something: in London, almost thirty years earlier, not for very long and with little success, he had paid court to the daughter, yes, she was the daughter – the daughter of the memorialist of Verdun . . .

Respected Professor, I am by now sympathetically aware that a father can be easily hurt by revelations about a daughter's lovelife, and I want to assure you, Sir, that she was a very good girl – in this case. She eventually allowed me to discompose her upper clothing; and that was all. Oh, we fooled around, Professor, but that was as far as she'd go. For my part, I was the perfect gentleman. A good pal of mine tried it on with her too, and when we later compared notes over a few drinks it turned out that his inroads were no less limited than mine. And I can say that her behaviour, Sir, was highly untypical of the mid-1970s, a time when young women would succumb even if they really didn't want to (that's generational ideology for you). With her patrician good looks and her authoritative bearing, she struck me as supremely well-equipped to negotiate the new freedoms, the new powers, that society was proposing to offer her (unlike my unfortunate sister, who was destroyed by these same freedoms and powers). I hope and trust that she remains healthy and happy. I congratulate you on your daughter, as I do on your fine book, which . . .

Yes, too many early deaths just now, I'm afraid, too many, too many for me, the poet Ian Hamilton at sixty-three, my teenhood friend Robinson at fifty-one, and my little sister Myfanwy at forty-six, each of them a horseholder, wrenched and jerked and tugged and racked by the horses of their own apocalypse.

The train dived underwater as the white cliffs neared.

True life

Elena's nap had been a clear success: he could tell by the warmed way she stretched her arms upwards to receive him.

'What's the matter? You look red-eyed.'

'You won't believe who I was moping about,' he said. 'That poor sod John Braine.'

'Why?'

'You asked what happened to him. He ended up in a bedsit with one spoon, one knife, and one fork. His last Christmas dinner was in a soup kitchen . . . That was the setting for his smirk novel.'

Braine's smirk novel, Martin had decided in the smoking section of the Eurostar, wasn't a smirk novel. It was a *wank* novel, a *roman de . . .*

'What's French for wank? W-a-n-q-u-e I suppose.'

'No.' And she told him.

'Feminine! How nice. Well then. A *roman de branlette*. A wank novel. Because there was no ravishing young mistress.' Martin had of course interviewed John Braine (for the *New Statesman* in 1975). And Braine looked like a guard in a prison or borstal, with a wide, full, strangely slack mouth, and his grey northern face coated with a thin Soviet sweat of difficulty. 'Not that bad a bloke, really. A funny sort of innocent. After a glass or two, though . . . Braine was just a crap drunk.'*

---

* As a non-reclusive man of letters from the British Isles, I could not but have encyclopedic experience of the effects of alcohol. Alcohol usually made people *more* this or *more* that – more high-spirited, more loud-voiced, more volatile, and so on. But the thing to look out for, as ever, is personality change. Those who undergo it are the dipsomaniacs, actual or potential. All else is just heavy drinking.

'He was probably pissed when he wrote his wank novel. It couldn't be true.'

'Mm. And his first novel was such a sensation. Unbelievably.' Indeed, you wondered what kind of shape the British imagination could have been in during the mid-1950s, to get itself 'captured' by *Room at the Top*. 'The paperback sold a million copies. They made a film of it. Starring Laurence Harvey – and Simone Signoret for Christ's sake. And then it all spiralled downwards. Like with Angus Wilson.'

'It couldn't happen to you.'

'Elena – don't tempt fate like that. Of course it could happen to me.'

'. . . How long did Braine live?'

'Till sixty-odd. His dates are the same as Larkin's.'

'Now don't you start.'

Loose London in the night was hurriedly and guiltily reassembling itself. The urban shapes thickened. And I could feel it about to resume – the unwelcome self-absorption, the slow twelve-bar blues of my thoughts . . . For suicide, the metaphysical model I favoured was that of Islam. In the Islamic afterlife, the self-slaughterer was on a loop, re-experiencing his death for ever and ever. But what was the loop's duration? If it was no more than a minute, then I would choke on my own vomit till the end of time. If on the other hand it was a fair bit longer, then a preliminary hour or two of drugged and drunken stupefaction, under a heap of vodka bottles and pill jars and tins of tobacco, seemed as good a way as any of getting through eternity . . . Suicide resembled the kind of marriage very frequently portrayed in art, where husband or wife or both just *had* to get out. Everyone on earth was married to life; and the suicides went because they couldn't stay, they just couldn't stay *another second*. I was married to life, but also to Elena. And I could stay, couldn't I? I could stay.

'What's French for short story?'

'Not sure. *Une conte* maybe.'

'I'm feeling sad about John Braine,' I said, as the train continued to loiter a mile or two south-east of Waterloo. 'And guilty about Jed Slot.'

'Guilty? About that little schnook?'

'Yes, guilty, Pulc – we should've come to his rescue. "Jed?" we should've said. "Let *us* handle this." We could've stepped in and talked about all the different types of short story. The parable. The squib. The anecdote. The sting in the tail. The slice of life.'

'Your voice has gone all gravelly.'

'I know. I can hear it . . . Ninety per cent of short stories are slices of life. And that's what life is like, in the end. Not a novel. A sliced loaf of short stories. But with different grains.' Different textures and thicknesses. Some as knotty as V. S. Pritchett, some as smooth as Alice Munro (some as cruel as 'Sredni Vashtar', some as tender as 'The Circular Ruins'). I said, '"St-Malo" qualifies as a smirk short story, El.' Actually it qualifies as a *conte de branlette* – but with one vital difference. Quite possibly unique in the soiled little archive of wank fiction, 'St-Malo' is true.

Interludial

Memos to my reader – 1

My American friends and relatives tell me I can't say they're nuts any more, not after Brexit. But I think I still can, up to a point. See, in the UK, no one had any idea what Brexit looked like. And in the US everyone knew exactly what Trump looked like. They'd been seeing little else for seventeen months. And if my British compatriots had known that Brexit looked like a hairy corn cob balancing on a Halloween pumpkin, then they would've voted Remain.

This brings us to the end of the first half.

. . . On the day after I got back from a book tour in Europe in October 2015 I said to Elena, 'Now I know I've got to get on with my real-life novel, but in Munich I walked straight into a real-life short story – and I'd better write it while it's fresh.' I did write it, and the story came out in the New Yorker *at the end of that year. The title was 'Oktober'; and it appears below.*

The novel I'd gone on the road for – my most recent – was set in Auschwitz in 1942–3. 'Oktober' makes no mention of the book about the Holocaust, so I'll add a few lines about the German response to it, which powerfully surprised me (and not because it was in any way positive).

I saw very many homeless nomads in Europe, most of them self-evacuees from the Middle East.

That was over a year ago, and now, for Christmas 2016, we're off to our house in the Sunshine State, me, Elena, and our two daughters, Eliza and Inez (to be joined, we hope, by my two sons, Nat and Gus) – before proudly returning, on New Year's Eve, to all the comfort and security of Strong Place . . .

'Oktober'

I

I sat drinking black tea in the foyer of the the Munich hotel. A lady in a lustrous purple trouser suit attended to the keys of the baby grand in the far corner, her rendition of *Hungarian Rhapsody* (with many graces and curlicues) for now unable to drown out the inarticulate howling and baying from the bar beyond the lifts. For it was the time of the Oktoberfest, and the city was playing host to 6 million visitors, thereby quintupling its population – visitors from all over Bavaria, and from all over Germany, and from all over the world. Other visitors (a far smaller contingent) were also expected, visitors who hoped to stay, and to stay indefinitely; they were coming from what was once known as the Fertile Crescent . . .

'Let's see if we can make a bit of sense of this,' an itinerant executive was stonily saying, bent over his mobile phone two tables away, with clipboard, legal pad, gaping laptop. He spoke in the only language I could understand – English; and his accent derived from northern regions, northern cities (Leeds, Doncaster, Barnsley). 'Yes yes, I should've rung two weeks ago. Three. All right, a *month* ago. But that doesn't affect the matter at hand, now does it. Believe me, the only thing that's kept me back's the prospect of having to go through all this with the likes of . . . Listen. Are you listening to me? We need to resolve the indemnity clause. Clause 4C.' He sighed. 'Have you got the paperwork in front of you at least? Quite honestly, it beats me how you get anything done. I'm a businessman, and I'm accustomed to dealing with people who have some idea of what they're about. Will you listen? Will you listen?'

The photographer arrived and after a minute he and I went out into the street. In great numbers the Oktoberfesters were parading past, the women in cinched dirndls and wenchy blouses, the men in suede or leather shorts laced just below the knee, and tight jackets studded with medals or badges, and jaunty little hats with feathers, rosettes, cockades. On the pavement Bernhardt erected his tripod and his tilted umbrella, and I prepared myself to enter the usual trance of inanition – forgetting that in this part of Eurasia, at least for now, there was only one subject, and that subject was of intense interest – to the entire planet. But first I said,

'What do they actually do in that park of theirs?'

'In the funfair?' Bernhardt smiled with a touch of sceptical fondness. 'A lot of drinking. A lot of eating. And singing. And dancing – if you can call it that. On tabletops.'

'Sort of clumping about?'

'The word is *schunkeln*. They link arms, and sway while they sing. From side to side. Thousands of them.'

'. . . *Schunkeln*'s the infinitive, right? How d'you spell that?'

'I'll write it down for you – yes, the infinitive.'

Our session began. Broad-shouldered and stubbly but also delicately handsome, Bernhardt was an Iranian-German (his family had come over in the 1950s); he was also very quick and courteous and of course seamlessly fluent.

'Last week I came by train from Salzburg,' he said, 'and there were eight hundred refugees on board.'

'Eight hundred. And how were they?'

'Very tired. And hungry. And dirty. Some with children, some with old people. They all want to get to this country because they have friends and family here. Germany is trying to be generous, trying to be kind, but . . . I took many photographs. If you like I'll drop some off for you.'

'Please do. I'd be grateful.'

And I remembered that other photograph from the front pages a few days ago: two or three dozen refugees arriving at a German rail station and being greeted by *applause*. In the photograph some of the arrivals are smiling, some laughing; and some are just breathing deeply and walking that much taller, it seemed, as if a needful thing had at last been restored to them. I said,

'Trying to be kind. When I was in Berlin the police closed a crossroads in the Tiergarten. Then bikes and a motorcade coming through. The Austrian prime minister. Faymann, for a little summit with Merkel. Hours later they announced they were sealing the border.'

'The numbers. The scale.'

'And the day before yesterday – I was in Salzburg and there were no trains to Munich. All cancelled. We came here by car.'

'Long wait at the border?'

'Only if you go on the highway. That's what the driver told us. He took the parallel roads . . . In Salzburg there were scores of refugees gathered at the roadsides. Girding themselves for the last leg.'

Bernhardt said, 'You know, they won't stop coming. They give up all they have – job, family, house, olive trees. They pay large sums of money to risk their lives crossing the sea, and then they walk across Europe. They *walk* across Europe. A few policemen and a stretch of barbed wire won't keep them out. And there are millions more where they came from. Unless Merkel yields to domestic pressure – you know, to the people who call them *aliens* – the flow's going to go on for years. And they won't stop coming. *Wir schaffen das*, she says – we can do this. But can we?'

II

It was two o'clock. I had forty-five minutes (my book tour was winding down, and this was not a busy day). In the bar I waited at the steel counter . . . When Bernhardt asked me how I was bearing up after three weeks on the road in Europe, I said I was well enough, though chronically underslept. Which was true . . . And actually, Bernhardt, to be even more frank with you, I feel unaccountably anxious, anxious almost to the point of formication (which the dictionary defines as 'a sensation like insects crawling over the skin'); it comes and goes . . . Home was 4,000 miles away, and six hours behind; pretty soon, it would be quite reasonable, surely, to return yet again to my room and see if there were any fresh bulletins from that quarter. For now I looked mistrustfully at my phone; in the email inbox there were over 1,800 unopened messages, but from wife, from children, as far as I could tell, there was nothing new.

The heroically methodical bartender duly set his course in my direction. I asked for a beer.

'Non-alcoholic. D'you have that?'

'I have – one per cent alcoholic.'

We were both needing to shout.

'One per cent.'

'Alcohol is everywhere. Even an apple is one per cent alcoholic.'

I shrugged. 'Go on then.'

The beer the Oktobrists were drinking by the quart was 13 per cent, or double strength; this at any rate was the claim of the young Thomas Wolfe who, after a couple of steins of it, acquired a broken nose, four scalp wounds, and a cerebral haemorrhage after a frenzied brawl (which he started) in some festival mud pit – but that was in 1928. These male celebrants in fancy dress at the bar had been drinking since 9 a.m. (I saw and heard them at breakfast) before setting off for the Biergarten, if indeed they ever went there. I saw them and heard them the night before, too; at that point they were either gesticulating and yelling in inhumanly loud voices, or else staring at the floor in rigid penitence, their eyes woeful and clogged. Then as now, the barman served even the drunkest of them with unconcern, going about his tasks with practised neutrality.

I was carrying a book: a bound review proof of the forthcoming *Letters to Véra*, by Véra's husband, Vladimir Nabokov. But the voices around me were insurmountably shrill – I could concentrate on what I was reading, just about, but I could extract no pleasure from it. So I took my drink back into the foyer, where the pianist had resumed. The businessman was still on the phone; as before we were sitting two tables from each other, and back to back. Occasionally I heard snatches ('Have you got any office *method* where you are? Have you?'). But now I was slowly and appreciatively turning the pages, listening to that other voice, VN's: humorous, resilient, boundlessly inquisitive and energetic. The letters to Véra begin in 1923; two years earlier he sent his mother a short poem – as proof 'that my mood is as radiant as ever. If I live to be a hundred, my spirit will still go around in short trousers'.

As January dawned in 1924, Vladimir (a year older than the century) was in Prague, helping his mother and two younger sisters settle into their cheap and freezing new apartment. ('Jesus Christ, will you listen? Will you listen?') These former boyars were now displaced and deracinated – and had 'no money at all'. ('5C? *No.* No, 4C. 4C for Christ's sake.') Vladimir himself, like his future wife, the *Judin* Véra Slonim, had settled in Berlin, along with almost half a million other Russian fugitives from October 1917. And in Berlin they would blithely and stubbornly remain. Their lone child, Dmitri, was born there in 1934; the Nuremberg Laws were passed in September 1935, and were expanded (and strictly enforced) after the Berlin Olympics of 1936; but not until 1937 did the Nabokovs hurriedly decamp to France, after a (never-ending) struggle with visas and exit permits and Nansen passports.

'No, I bet you don't. Okay, here's an idea. Why don't you pop on a plane and come and tell them that here in Germany? With your approach, so-called? They'd laugh you out of town. Because here they can handle the ABC and the two times two. Unlike some I could mention. Here they happen to understand a thing or two about *system*. And that's why they're the powerhouse of Europe. Go on, pop on a plane. Or is that beyond you too?'

The muted TV screen showed the chancellor in mid-explication, her face patient and reasonable and mildly beseeching . . . I put the book aside and briefly reminisced about Angela (with the hard *g*) – Frau Merkel.

I was introduced to her (a handshake and an exchange of hellos) by Tony Blair, in 2007, when she was two years into her first term (and I was spending several weeks on and off in the prime minister's entourage). We were in the top floor of the titanic new Chancellery: the full bar arrayed on the table, the (as yet spotless) ashtrays, Angela's humorous and particularising smile. The Chancellery was ten times the size of the White House – where Blair would also squire me a week or two later; but I had no more than a sudden moment of eye contact with President Bush, as he and Tony came up from the subterranean Situation Room (this was the time of the Surge in Iraq). And from Washington we went via London to Kuwait City, and to Basra, and to Baghdad.

Merkel was born in East Germany in the early days of the Cold War . . . So far, there have been several dozen female heads of state; and I thought then that Angela was perhaps the first who was capable of ruling *as a woman*. In the summer months of 2015, in the world's eyes she became the brutal auditress of the Greek Republic; by late September they were calling her *Mutti* Merkel, as she opened her gates as wide as she could to the multitudes of the dispossessed. *Willkomenskultur* was the word.

Blair was practically teetotal, but he was visibly charmed and stimulated by Angela Merkel (he was full of praise for her, adding with amused affection that she liked to sit up late and have a lively time), and on the Chancellery roof that evening the British premier could be seen with a beer in his hand, a beer perhaps of festival strength . . .

This is to some degree true of every human community on earth, but the national poet, here, said long ago of his Germans, with a strain of anguish: how impressive they were singly (how balanced, how reflective, how dry), and how desperately disappointing they were plurally, in groups, in cadres, in leagues, in blocs. And yet here they all were (for now), the Germans, both as a polity and a people, setting a progressive, even a futuristic example to the continent and to the world.

With the refugee crisis of 2015, 'Europe', Chancellor Merkel had said, was about to face its 'historic test'.

III

'Will you listen to me? Will you listen to me?'

But like a washing machine the businessman had moved on to a quieter cycle. Still tensed, still crouched, but reduced to a sour mutter. The pianist's shift was apparently at an end, and I was grimacing into a phone myself, trying to hear the questions of a studious young profilist I had talked to in Frankfurt. Eavesdroppers and those active in identity theft might have been tempted to draw near, but the foyer was practically deserted; the businessman and I had the space to ourselves.

'1949,' I said, 'in Oxford. Not Wales – Wales was later. Yes, go ahead. Why did my wife and I move to America? Because . . . well, it sounds complicated, but it's an ordinary story. In 2010 my mother Hilary died. She was on the verge of eighty-two. My mother-in-law, Betty, was also eighty-two at the time. So in response to that we moved to New York.' Yes, and Elena ended a voluntary and much-punctuated exile in London that had lasted twenty-seven years, returning to her childhood home in Greenwich Village. 'Us now? No. Brooklyn. Since 2011. You get too old for Manhattan.' We made our way to the final question. 'This trip? Six countries.' And ten cities. 'Oh definitely. And I'm reading all I can find on it, and everyone's talking about nothing else. Well, I haven't spent time with any experts – but of course I have impressions.'

Our call wound up. The businessman was going on in his minatory whisper,

'You know who you remind me of? The hordes of ragamuffins who're piling into this country even as I speak. You, you just can't stand on your own two feet, can you? You're helpless.'

*

An angular youth from the reception desk approached and handed me a foolscap Manila envelope. In it were Bernhardt's photographs. Registering this, I felt the rhythm of my unease slightly accelerate. I moved next door into the restaurant, and I fanned them out on the table.

The Europeans you talked to offered different views and prescriptions, but the underfeeling seemed to centre on an encounter with something, something not quite unknown but known only at a distance. The entity accumulating on the borders, the entity for which they were bracing and even rousing themselves to meet with goodwill and good grace, seemed amorphous, undifferentiated, almost insensate – like an act of God or a force of nature.

And it was as if Bernhardt's camera had set itself the task of individualisation, because here was a black-and-white *galère* of immediately and endearingly recognisable shapes and faces, bantering, yawning, frowning, grinning, scowling, weeping, in postures of exhaustion, stoic dynamism, and of course extreme uncertainty and dismay . . .

When you glimpsed them in the train stations, they were configured in narrow strings or little knots, always moving, moving, their gaze and gait strictly forward-directed (with no waste of attention, with no attention to spare). But in Salzburg two days earlier I saw seventy or eighty of them lined up on the street corner, very predominantly very young men, in international teenage gear, baseball caps, luminous windcheaters, dark glasses. Soon they would be approaching the German border (just a few miles away) – and then what? Theirs was a journey with charts and graphs and updates (those cell phones), but with no certain destination. Dawn had just arrived in Austria, and the buildings shone sheepishly in the dew. And you thought, How will all this look and feel a few weeks from now – after Oktober?

At four o'clock, as scheduled, I was joined by my penultimate interviewer, an academic, who began by reminding me of a salient historical fact. She was middle-aged, so it was not in her living memory; but it was in the living memory of her mother. In the period 1945–7 there were 10 million homeless supplicants on the periphery of what was once the Reich, all of them deported, ejected (in spasms of greater or lesser hatred and violence, with at least half a million deaths en route), from Poland, Czechoslovakia, Hungary, and Romania. And they were all Germans – the 'ethnic' Germans that Hitler claimed were so close to his heart.

'And your mother remembers that?'

'She was at the station. She was seven or eight. She remembers the iced-up cattle cars. It was Christmas.'

I had been gone for seventy-five minutes and the businessman was still in mid-conversation. By now his phone had a charger in it; and the short lead, plugged into a ground-level socket, required him to bend even tighter – he was jackknifed forward with his chin an inch from the knee-high tabletop.

'You carry on like this and you won't have a roof over your head. You'll be on the street and you'll deserve it. The wheels are coming off your whole operation. And I'm not surprised. Bloody hell, people like you. You make me sick, you do. Professionally sick.'

The pianist had gone but other noisemakers were on duty – a factory-size vacuum cleaner, a lorry revving and panting in the forecourt. I went back to my book. August 1924, and Vladimir was in Czechoslovakia again, holidaying with his mother in Dobřichovice. The hotel was expensive and they were sharing a (sizable) room divided in two by a white wardrobe. Soon he would return to Berlin, where Véra . . .

All ambient sounds suddenly ceased, and the businessman was saying,

'D'you know who this is? Do you? It's Geoffrey. Geoffrey Vane. Yeah, Geoffrey. Geoff. You know me. And you know what I'm like . . . Right, my patience is at an end. Congratulations. Or as you'd say, *Super* . . .

'Now. Get your fucking Mac and turn to your fucking emails. Do you understand me? Do you understand me? Go to the communication from the fucking agent. The on-site agent. You know, that fucking Argy – Feron. Fucking Roddy Feron. Got it? Now bring up the fucking attachment. Got it? Right – fucking 4C.'

The often-used intensifier he pronounced like *cooking* or *booking*. At this point I slowly went and slid on to the chair opposite me, so I could have a proper look at him – the clerical halo of grey hair, the head, still direly bowed and intent, the laptop, the legal pad.

'It's the fucking liability. Do you understand me? Now *say*. 4C. Does that, or does that not, square with Tulkinghorn's F6? It does? Well praise fucking be. Now go back to fucking 4C. And fucking okay it. Okay? Okay.' And he added with especial menace, 'And the Lord pity you if we have to go through this again. You fucking got that? Sweet dreams. Yeah, *cheers*.'

And now, in unwelcome symmetry, the businessman also moved to the seat opposite, though swiftly and without rising above a crouch; with his meaty right hand he appeared to be mopping himself down, seeing to the pink brow dotted with motes of sweat, the pale and moist upper lip. Our eyes met inexorably, and he focused.

'. . . Do you understand English?'

IV

Do I understand English? 'Uh, yeah,' I said.

'Ah.'

And I speak it, too. Like everyone else around here. Great Britain no longer had an empire – except the empire of words; not the imperial state, just the imperial tongue. Everyone knew English. The refugees knew English, a little bit. That partly explained why they wanted to get to the UK and Eire, because everyone there knew English. And it was why they wanted to get to Germany: the refugees knew no German, but the Germans all knew English – the nut-brown maid who was brushing the curtains knew English, the sandy-haired bellhop knew English.

'. . . You're *English*,' he announced with reluctant wonder.

I found myself saying, 'London, born and bred.' Not quite true; but this wasn't the time to expatiate on my babyhood – with the mother who was barely older than I was – in the Home Counties circa 1950, or to dream out loud about that early decade in South Wales, infancy, childhood, when the family was poor but still nuclear. For half a century after that, though, yes, it was London. He said,

'I can tell by the way you talk . . . That was a tough one, that.'

'The phone call.'

'The phone call. You know, with some people, they haven't got a fucking clue, quite honestly. You've just got to start from scratch. Every – every time.'

'I bet.' And I cursorily imagined a youngish middle manager, slumped over his disorderly workstation in a depot or showroom out by an airport somewhere, loosening his tie as he pressed the hot phone to his reddened ear.

'Look at that,' he said, meaning the television – the eternally silent television. On its flat screen half a dozen uniformed guards were tossing shop sandwiches (cellophane-wrapped) into a caged enclosure, and those within seemed to snap at them – and it was impossible to evade the mental image of feeding time at the zoo. The businessman said with contented absorption, as he made some calculations on the yellow page,

'Amazing the lengths people'll go to for a handout, in't it?'

The *in't it?* was rhetorical: his truism anticipated no reply. In Cracow and Warsaw (I recalled, as the businessman immersed himself in his columned figures) everyone was saying that Poland would be exempt: the only homogenous country in Central Europe, the only monoculture, blue-eyed Poland thought it would be exempt because 'the state gives no benefits'. I heard this from a translator so urbane that he could quote at length not only from Tennyson but also from Robert Browning; and in answer I nodded, and resumed work on my heavy meal. But when I was dropped off at the hotel (and stood on the square facing the antique prosthetic leg of Stalin's Palace of Culture), I shook my head. Someone who has trekked across the Hindu Kush would not be coming to Europe for a shop sandwich. The businessman said,

'Where are we. What country's this?'

He meant the country where dark-skinned travellers were being tumbled and scattered by water cannon (followed up with tear gas and pepper spray). I said,

'Looks like Hungary.'

'Eh, that bloke there's got the right idea.' He paused as he closed his eyes and the bloodless lips mimed a stretch of mental arithmetic. 'What's he called?'

I told him.

'Yeah. Orbán. We ought to be doing likewise in Calais. No choice. It's the only language they understand.'

Oh no, sir, the language they understand is much harsher than that. The language they understand consists of barrel bombs and nerve gas and the scimitars of incandescent theists. They're not in search of a nanny state, Mr Vane. It's more likely that they seek a state that just leaves them alone . . .

'Merkel,' he said. 'Frau Merkel should take a leaf out of Orbán's book. She won't of course. I know you shouldn't say this, but I think women are too emotional to be heads of state – too tender-hearted. By rights, Merkel should do an Orbán. Recognise what she's dealing with, namely illegal aliens. *Criminal* aliens. See? There you go.'

He meant the footage evidently posted by ISIS – a truck exploding in slow motion, three prisoners in orange jumpsuits kneeling on a sand dune, multipronged fighters tearing by in SUVs.

'Then there's *that*.' He achieved some climactic grand total on his pad, underlined it three times and circled it before tossing the pen aside. 'Jihadis.'

'Might be complicated,' I said.

'Complicated . . . Hang about,' he said with a frown. 'Silly me. Forgot to factor in the three point five. Give us a minute.'

Perhaps a better name for them, sir, would be *takfiri*. The *takfir* accusation (the lethal accusation of unbelief) is almost as old as Islam, but in current usage *takfiris*, Mr Vane, is sharply derogatory and it means, Muslims who kill Muslims (and not just infidels). And the logic of it goes on from there. If there are militants in the influx, and they act, Geoffrey, then it's the Muslims of Europe who will suffer; and the *takfiris* won't mind that because their policy, here, is the same as Lenin's during the Russian Civil War: 'the worse the better'. Is it fanciful, Geoff, to suggest that this lesson is the evil child of the witches in the Scottish play – 'Fair is foul, and foul is fair'?

'*Complicated?* That's the understatement of the year.'

Suddenly he became aware of the phone he had reflexively reached for. He inhaled with resignation and said, 'You know what gets me? The repetitions. You plod through the same things again and again. And it just doesn't sink in. Not with that one, oh no. Not with her.'

V

Her? I sat up straight.

'Tell me something,' he insisted. 'Why're they all coming *now*? They say despair. Despair, they say. But they can't all have despaired in the same *week*. Why're a million of them coming now? Tell me that.'

I regrouped and said, 'That's what I've been trying to find out. Apparently a safe route opened up. Through the Balkans. They're all in touch with each other and then there it was on Facebook.'

He went blank or withdrew for a moment. But then he returned. 'I'll give them bleeding Facebook. I'll give them bleeding Balkans.

They . . . They've turned their own countries into, into hellholes quite frankly, and now they're coming here. And even if they don't start killing us all they're going to want their own ways, aren't they. Halal, mosques. Uh, sharia, in't it. Arranged marriages – for ten-year-old first cousins . . . But let's uh be uh, "enlightened" about it. Okay. They'll have to adapt, and fucking quick about it and all. They'll have to bow their heads and toe the line. Socially. On the women question and that.'

He closed his computer, and gazed for a moment at its surface and even stroked his knuckles across it.

'You know, I'll have to call her back.' And there was now a sudden weak diffidence in his smile as he looked up and said, 'Well it *is* my mum.'

I had to make an effort to dissimulate the scope of my surprise . . . Shorn of context (the business hotel, the business suit – the expensive posture-pedic shoes, like velvet Crocs), his bland round white-fringed face looked as though it would be happiest, or at least happier, on a village green on a summer afternoon; that face could have belonged to anybody non-metropolitan, a newsagent, a retired colonel, a vicar. With a nod I reached for my electronic cigarette and drew on it.

'Eighty-one, she is.'

'Ah well.' After a moment I said, '*My* mother-in-law's eighty-six.' And you see, sir, it's a long story, but she was the reason we left England; and we never regretted it. The process felt natural for my wife, naturally, but it also felt natural for me. There must've been filial love left over after the death of Hilary Bardwell, and it had nowhere else to go. I said, 'Eighty-six – five years further on than yours.'

'Yeah? And what's the state of her then, eh? Can she hold a thought in her head for two seconds? Or is she all over the fucking gaff like mine. I mean, when your bonce goes, I ask you, what *is* the sense in carrying on?'

I gestured at the instrument he still held in his hand and said, 'Just wondering, but what was that – what was all that to do with?'

He sat back and grunted it out: *Lanzarote*. Sinking deeper, he reached up and eased his writhing neck. 'For her eightieth, see, I bought her a beautiful little timeshare in Lanzarote. Beautiful little holiday home. Maid looking in every morning. A bloke doing the garden. Good place to park her in the winter. Roof terrace overlooking the bay. And now she's meant to renew the insurance. That's all it is. The contents insurance and that. Shouldn't have taken but a minute.'

'Well. They do find it hard to . . .'

'You know, I've got four brothers. All younger. And not one of them'll touch her with a fucking bargepole. They won't have anything to do with her. It's true the old – she does drive you mad, there's no question. But you've got to grind it out, haven't you. And the four of them, they won't go near her. Can you credit it? They won't go near their own fucking mum. Pardon the language. Well, they haven't got my resources, admittedly. So answer me this. Where would she be without my support?'

With a glance at my wrist I said, 'Damn. I'd better pack. Early flight.'

'Here for a day or three yet, me. Take a well-earned rest. Look in at the gym. Room service. Uh, what's your destination?'

I took his offered hand. 'Home.'

VI

As I bunched and crushed various items into the splayed bag, I activated my computer. And saw that there was still no message from my wife (nor from a single one of my children). Yes, well, it was the same with Nabokov: 'Don't you find our correspondence is a little . . . one-sided?' And in my case it was curious, because when I was away like this I never fretted about my other life, my settled life, where everything was nearly always orderly and unchanging and fixed into place . . .

Otherwise I felt fine, and even quite vain of my vigour (health after all unbroken), and buoyant, and stimulated, and generally happy and proud; the tour had awakened anxiety in me but I have to say that even the anxiety was not unwelcome, because I recognised it as the kind of anxiety that would ask to be written about. At odd moments, though, I seriously questioned the existence of the house in Brooklyn, with its three female presences (wife, daughters), and I seriously questioned the existence of my two boys and my eldest daughter, all grown, in London – and my two grandchildren. So many! Could they, could any of them, still be there?

'Good morning, this is your wakeup call . . . Good morning, this is your wakeup call . . . Good morning, this is your –'

I had one final appointment: a radio interview with a journalist called Konrad Purper, destined to take place in what they called the Centre d'Affaires, with its swivel seats and cord carpets. When it was over Konrad and I stood talking in the foyer until my chaperone promptly but worriedly appeared. There had been many chaperones, many helpers and minders – Alisz, Agata, Heidi, Marguerite, Hannah, Ana, Johanna.

'There are no taxis!' said Johanna. 'They can't get near us. Because there's too many people!'

Normally I am very far from being an imperturbable transatlantic traveller. But at that moment I sensed that my watch was moving at its workaday pace; time did not start speeding up, did not start heating up. What was the worst thing that could happen? Nothing much. I said, 'So we . . .'

'Walk.'

'To the airport.'

'No – sorry. I'm not clear. To the train station. We can get there from there.'

'Oh and the station's close, isn't it.'

'Five minutes,' said Konrad. 'And every ten minutes a rail shuttle goes to Munich International.'

So with Johanna I started out, rolling my bag, and with Konrad perhaps coincidentally rolling his bike, and the three of us often rolling aside on to the carless tarmac in favour of the pageant of costumed revellers coming the other way. This narrow thoroughfare, Landwehrstrasse, with its negotiations between West and East – Erotic Studio, Turkish Restaurant, Deutsche Bank, Traditional Thai Massage, Daimler-Benz, Kabul Market . . .

We came out into the air and space of the Karlsplatz and the multitudes of Hansels and Gretels (many of the women, in the second week, decadently wearing the despised 'Barbie' alternative: a thick-stitched bodice and a much-shortened dirndl showing the white stocking tops just above the knee). How did it go in the Biergarten? According to Thomas Wolfe, they had merry-go-rounds, and an insane profusion of sausage shops, and whole oxen turning on spits. They ate and drank in tents that could seat 6,000, 7,000, 8,000. If you were in the middle of this, Wolfe wrote, Germany seemed to be 'one enormous belly'. Swaying, singing, linking arms: Germans together, en masse, objectively ridiculous, and blissfully innocent of any irony . . .

Now Johanna, I saw, was talking to a policeman who was stretched out in a parked sidecar. Konrad stood by. She turned and said to me,

'It's – you can't even get there by foot!'

For many years I lived in Notting Hill, and sat through many Carnivals (in earlier times often attending with my sons); I knew about cordons, police gauntlets, closed roads (for ambulance access), and panics and stampedes; once I was in a crush that firmly assured me that you could face death simply by means of a superfluity of life. Yes, there were affinities: Oktoberfest was like Carnival, but the flesh there was brown and the flesh here was pink. Hundreds of thousands of high-esprit scoutmasters – hundreds of thousands of festive dairymaids in their Sunday best.

'The only way is underground. One stop.'

Soon we were looking into the rosy deep of the stone staircase. Getting on for a month ago, in Brooklyn, while she was helping me pack, Elena remarked that my family-sized suitcase was 'not full enough'. Well it was certainly heavy enough, by now, with its sediment of gifts and autographed novels and poetry collections and things such as Bernhardt's portfolio in its stiff brown envelope. Humping a big load through the underground: I can do it, I thought, but I won't like doing it. And yet once again Konrad, having tethered his bike, was quietly at our side, tall, and calm, and my bag was now swinging easily in his grip.

In the Hauptbahnhof itself the crowd was interspersed with thin streams of dark-skinned and dark-clothed refugees, their eyes hagridden but determined, their tread leaden but firm, dragging their prams and goods-laden buggies, their children. Then came a rare sight, and then an even rarer one.

First, a mother of a certain age, a grandmother probably, tall, dressed in the rigid black of the full abaya, with her half-veiled face pointed straight ahead. Then, second, a lavishly assimilated young woman with the same colouring, perhaps the granddaughter of a Turkish *Gastarbeiter*, in tight white jacket and tight white jeans – and she had a stupendously, an unignorably full and prominent backside. For half a minute the two women inadvertently walked in step, away from us: on the right, the black edifice gliding as smoothly as a Dalek; on the left, the hugely undulating orbs of white.

When he had pointed us to our platform Konrad took his leave, much thanked, much praised. I turned to Johanna.

'The two women – did you see that?'

'Of course.'

'Well. She's not embarrassed by it, is she. Looking so cheerful. Swinging her arms. And dressed like that? She's not trying to hide it.'

'No.'

'I mean she's not shy about it.'

'No,' said Johanna. 'She likes it.'

VII

The Nabokovs were refugees, and three times over. As teenagers they independently fled the October Revolution; on her way out Véra Slonim passed through a pogrom in the Ukraine involving tens of thousands of mob murders. That was in 1919. They fled the Bolsheviks, horsemen of terror and famine, and, via the Crimea, Greece, and England, sought sanctuary – in Berlin. Then France; until the Germans followed them there; then the eleventh-hour embarcation to New York in 1940, a few weeks ahead of the Wehrmacht (on its next westbound crossing their boat, the *Champlain*, was torpedoed and sunk). VN's father (also Vladimir Nabokov), the liberal statesman, was murdered by a White Russian fascist in Berlin (1922); in the same city his brother Sergei was arrested in 1943 (for homosexuality), rearrested the following year (for sedition), and died in a concentration camp near Hamburg in January 1945. That was their Europe; and they went back there, in style and for good, in 1959.

Yes, and I met Véra too. I spent most of a day with her, in 1983, in the still centre of Europe, the Palace Hotel in Montreux, Switzerland (where they had lived since 1961), breaking only for lunch with her son, the incredibly tall Dmitri, whom I would meet again. Véra was a riveting and convivial goldenskinned beauty; on sensitive subjects she could suddenly turn very fierce, but I was never disconcerted because there was always the contingent light of humour in her eyes.

Vladimir died in 1977, aged seventy-eight. Véra died in 1991, aged eighty-nine. And Dmitri died in 2012, aged seventy-seven.

From Dmitri's funeral address in April 1991:

On the eve of a risky hip operation two years ago, my brave and considerate mother asked that I bring her her favourite blue dress, because she might be receiving someone. I had the eerie feeling she wanted that dress for a very different reason. She survived on *that* occasion. Now, for her last earthly encounter, she was clad in that very dress. It was Mother's wish that her ashes be united with those of Father's in the urn at the Clarens Cemetery. In a curiously Nabokovian twist of things, there was some difficulty in locating that urn. My instinct was to call Mother, and ask her what to do about it. But there was no Mother to ask.

I got to Munich International with an extra half hour to spare. And there in the terminal, bathed in watery early-morning light, behind the little rampart of his luggage (a squat gunmetal trunk, a suede briefcase with numerous zips and pouches), and leering into his cell phone, stood Geoffrey Vane. I hailed him.

'Why are you here? I thought you were going to take it easy.'

'Who, me? Me? Nah. No rest for the wicked. Her, her fucking *bungalow* burnt down last night. Electrics. It's always electrics. Burnt to a fucking crisp.'

'Really? She wasn't in it, was she?'

'Ma? No, at her sister's in Sheffield. It's muggins here that has to go and deal with the mess. See if we got any contents insurance. Or any insurance at all.'

'Will it be hard to get to Lanzarote?'

His face narrowed shrewdly. 'You know what you do when something like this happens? When you're a bit stranded? You go down under. Under here.' And he soundlessly tapped his padded shoe on the floor. 'That's where the airline *offices* are. Under here. Ryanair, easyJet, Germania, Condor. You go down and you go around and you sniff out the best deal.'

'Well, good luck.'

'Oh, *I'll* be all right. I'm not helpless. Because I've got the resources. Hey,' he said, and winked. 'Might even hop on a package. With all the old boilers. Cheers!'

So there was time for lots of coffee and for delicious and fattening croissants in the lounge. Then the brand-new, hangar-fresh Lufthansa jumbo took off, on schedule. Soon I was gorging myself on fine foods and choice wines, before relishing *Alien* (Ridley Scott) and then the sequel, *Aliens* (James Cameron). I landed punctually . . . Would-be immigrants and even asylum seekers often have to wait two years, but after two hours, in the admittedly inhospitable environs of Immigration, I was allowed into America.

VIII

And what I returned to still held, Elena, and the teenage daughters – who went far and wide, as they pleased, who boldly roamed Manhattan, where their grandmother (I now heard it confirmed) was still installed in that deluxe sunset home which, very understandably, she kept mistaking for a hotel . . .

How solid it all seemed, this other existence, how advanced, how evolved. It wasn't the middling-class comforts that amazed me: it was the lights, the locks, the taps, the *toilets*, all eagerly obedient to my touch. How tightly joined to the earth it all was with its steel and concrete, the brownstone on Strong Place.

Yes, the house felt ready to stay in one piece. But now its co-owner, in an unfortunate turn of events, suddenly fell apart.

In the tranquillity of middle-distance hindsight I easily identified the probable cause: a synergy of long-postponed exhaustion, air-travel lag and air-travel *bug* (a very ambitious flu), and anxiety. Which persisted. The anxiety in me was deeply layered and durable because it went back to before I was born.

My insomnia persisted too. Coming to terms with this involved mental labour, most of it done in darkness. I was home in America, the immigrant nation, stretching from sea to shining sea; and I couldn't sleep. 'Night is always a giant,' wrote the champion insomniac, Nabokov, in a late novella, 'but this one was especially terrible.' I had another book on my bedside table. It was a short and stylish study by the historian Mark Mazower called *Dark Continent*; and I would sometimes go next door with that for an hour before defeatedly returning.

When I closed my eyes I was met by the usual sights – an abstract battlefield or dismantled fairground at dusk, flowers in monochrome, figures cut out of limp white paper; and the thoughts and images verged encouragingly on the nonsensical. But no; my mind was in too low a gear for the cruise control of unconsciousness.

*

So many possible futures were queuing up and jockeying to be born. In time, one or other of them would break free and go surging clear of the rest . . .

They were coming here, the refugees, in the eye of a geohistorical convergence – themselves and their exodus on the one hand, and on the other al-Qaeda, and al-Shabaab, and Boko Haram, and the Taliban, and Sinai Province, and Islamic State.

And even now it was as if a tectonic force had taken hold of Europe and, using its fingernails, had scratched it open and tilted it, causing a heavy mudslide in the direction of old illusions, old dreams of purity and cruelty.

And that force will get heavier still, much heavier, immediately and irreversibly, after the first incidence of *takfir*. At which point Europe – that by now famously unrobust confederation – would meet another historic test.

And what they might be bringing, the refugees, was insignificant when set against what was already there, in the host nations, the spores and ash heaps of what was already there . . . *Dark Continent* is not a book about Africa. The rest of Mazower's title is 'Europe's Twentieth Century'.

Memo to my reader – 2

As well as Germany I went to Austria, Switzerland, Poland, France, and also Spain. I say 'also Spain' because that country wasn't implicated in the Holocaust, unlike all the others (very much including Switzerland – see in due course 'Afterthought: Masada and the Dead Sea').

Postwar Deutschland obviously had the sternest work to do in arriving at an unillusioned reckoning. And it is my amateur impression that its efforts deserve to be called, well, broadly commensurate – in itself a stupendous achievement.* Not only is Nazi criminality a part of the national conversation; highly significantly, in my opinion, the young want

---

* *The* Historikerstreit *('the historians' quarrel' of 1986–9) saw the last attempts to 'historicise' or 'relativise' (or somehow normalise) the Third Reich. From then on Nazism was firmly identified as a geopolitical 'singularity'; it stands alone.*

to talk about it. *And it has to be a 'talking cure', a long and nauseous iteration: what other way could there be? . . . And now Germany has become the first nation on earth to erect monuments to its own shame. So I expected the Germans to take my novel as a minor addition to the unresting debate.*

And they didn't do that. Nearly all of them (according to my publisher's laconic summary) rejected the book out of hand on literary principle: you see, I had on occasion applied to satire *('the use of ridicule, irony, sarcasm, etc., to expose folly or vice'); and the German reviewers all insisted that humour could not coexist with seriousness. This is a primitively literal-minded credo which, as I'm sure you've already sensed, more or less obliterates the anglophone canon. The fact is that seriousness – and morality, and indeed sanity – cannot exist at all without humour . . .*

What did I infer from this? That German literary criticism had at some point made a benighted category error and then stuck to it? Well there was nothing of much interest to think about there. But I went on to wonder if I'd touched on an unexpected sensitivity; it could be that the Germans, while fully accepting that National Socialism was atrocious, were somehow unwilling to admit that it was also ridiculous.

And it wasn't just the reviewers. After public events one or two old boys would shoulder their way to the signing table to air their objections, and a festival organiser, under his breath, made me really wonder at his vehemence: 'How can you presume to laugh *at Hitlerism?' I wanted to say, 'Mockery is a weapon. Why do you think it is that tyrants fear it and ban it, and why did Hitler seek to punish it with death?'*

I am familiar with the theory of 'Holocaust exceptionalism', which has a literary application: in its bluntest form it maintains that the Holocaust is a subject that historians alone have the right to address. This has emotional force – it is an appeal to decent reticence. But I believe that nothing, nothing whatever, should be shielded from the writer's eye. If this is the view of a literary fundamentalist, then that is what I am.

Oh. So you think they thought I was simply trespassing? Maybe that was part of it. And in that case another lesson beckons. In literature there is no room for territoriality. So politely ignore all warnings about 'cultural appropriation' and the like. Go where your pen takes you. Fiction is freedom, and freedom is indivisible.

On December 31, Inez and I – an advance guard – returned to Strong Place in late afternoon. Well before midnight we were out on the street. We too were homeless nomads. The house was a charred and sopping hulk.

I have crossed the equator and I'm now standing on the threshold of the second half . . .
   Life, as I said, is artistically lifeless; and its only unifying theme is death.

PART III

DISSOLUTIONS: ANTEPENULTIMATE

Chapter 1
The Shadow-Line

Embedment: The dismissal of shame

One evening in the late 1970s three baby boomers sought each other out at a drinks party in London: Christopher Hitchens and Martin Amis of the *New Statesman*, and Joan Juliet Buck of *Vogue*. Christopher had met her through his onetime girlfriend, Anna Wintour, then of *Harper's Bazaar*, and Martin had met her through his onetime girlfriend, Julie Kavanagh, the UK correspondent of *Women's Wear Daily*.

'Hello boys.'

Joan Juliet was a darkly imposing beauty, an editor, an actress (and later a novelist), whose first language was French.

'My dear, you look absolutely radiant.'

This was Christopher. He was of course already merciless in public debate, but his social manners were decorous and harmonial (and some of his embellishments look florid in print, unleavened by his smile). Hitch reserved especial courtliness for women. It is there in his writing, too. Descriptions of attractive girls have him reaching for words like 'poised', 'fragrant', and *'ravissant'*.

'Aglow with youth and vigour,' he went on with a bow. 'And forgive me for saying that I'm so pleased, because I heard you'd been in the wars. Those little uh, feminine ailments. If it wasn't one thing, it was the other. I trust that's all in the past?'

'Not quite,' said Joan Juliet. 'It's my fucking tits now.'

Candid, defiant, undiminished, and humorous: Christopher and Martin very much admired this remark, and for a while it was often quoted, joining the innumerable phrases and themelets and reference points that metronomically punctuated their conversation and their correspondence. Candour, humour, and above all a rejection of anything that could be mistaken for embarrassment or offended pride.* The dismissal of shame.

Boston, 2003: Something altogether new

'Tell me, how are Nat and Gus? How're they getting along?'

Saul and I were in the rear sitting room at Crowninshield Road, where we usually had our more earnest and more concerted chats, about politics, about religion, about literature. It was a comfortable room, a comfortable house: the habitat, you would say, of a senior Cambridge academic. 'Guys, I'm rich,' Saul announced to his friends in 1964, when *Herzog* was settling into its months as a bestseller (and publishers were splashing out on his backlist). 'Can I buy you something? Do you need any money?'† Saul, in 2003, had been through several costly divorces; he had everything he wanted, and a bit more in reserve, but he wasn't rich any more – not *rich*.

'Nat and Gus, they're fine, they're great. And they're *tall*, too.' I said. Although Saul was acquainted with my younger daughters, he and my sons went back fifteen years. 'They're still at that school Latymer in West London. It's not like St Paul's or Westminster, but it's solid enough. My mother's father went there – in the 1900s it must've been.'

Now a silence began to steal over us. It was a new kind of silence, one never heard before . . . I'd spent the entire winter in Uruguay, and one way or another I hadn't seen Saul for eighteen months: not since November 2001. And during that visit – to my surprise and relief – he was soothingly lucid (not at all like Iris. September 11, I concluded, was indeed just 'too

---

* I ran into Joan Juliet (at one of Tina Brown's summits at the Lincoln Center – 'Women in the World'); I hadn't seen her for at least thirty years, but I recognised her in an instant. This is another attribute of beauty: memorability. To adapt a coinage of Nabokov's, beauty is mnemogenic . . . Joan Juliet was in perfect health.
† The generosity was sincere, and lifelong. In Bellow's posthumous *Letters* (2010) we frequently see him offering to subsidise old friends, and with the gentlest tact: if you need it, he would typically write, 'I can spare it' . . . Gore Vidal was rich ('I'm the richest,' he said vis-à-vis his American peers). Philip Roth, it is safe to say, had a few bob (*Portnoy's Complaint* outsold *The Godfather*) . . . Incidentally, Vidal and Roth had no one obvious to leave their money to (they died without issue). The extreme Norman Mailer was in this respect a more typical American writer: six wives and nine children. The figures for Saul Bellow are five and four.

big'). But the silence around about us now was a frightening silence. I felt powerless to break it. Then Saul broke it, saying,

'Tell me. How are Nat and Gus?'

. . . Was he joking? Was I dreaming? With an unsteady hand I lowered my coffee cup, and went through it all again: fine, great, tall, Latymer in West London . . .

The silence returned. Crushing, smothering, and quite unbelievably *loud*. This wasn't forgetfulness – this was something altogether new. A shadow-line had been crossed. He said,

'Nat and Gus. Tell me, how are they?'

. . . Well, I can't claim I wasn't warned.

Long Island, July 2001

Through the open windows of his study Martin could hear his middle daughter in the garden below; she was five, she was alone, and she was singing. What was that – what was solitary childsong? Something like a ventilation of happiness. Eliza, for now, was not letting off steam (as she frequently needed to do), but letting off happiness. Imagine.

Her voice made him happy, and he was happy anyway, steady-state happy (mark the date), but not quite happy enough to add his voice to hers; similarly, when she skipped along the pavement, he felt no urge to keep in step. And when she did cartwheels, he stayed upright. Now why was that?

As for Eliza's little sister, Inez, well, she was twenty-five months. Not quite so many overflows of happiness for Inez, as yet. She had only just got here, only just touched down on the planet Earth; she was still feeling very shy, and there were all these new people – 8.5 billion of them. No wonder she sometimes hid her face and wept.

By a wonderful coincidence Inez shared a birthday (June 10) with her godfather, Saul – who was expected with his clan that afternoon. And it was a true coincidence, because Saul had accepted the appointment months before her birth . . .

Inez's eyes made Martin think of the Bellows' pond, over in Vermont, with its gradations of temperature. Gradations of trust, hope, uncertainty, and dread seemed to swim in Inez's eyes.

*

261

To get from East Hampton, NY, to Brattleboro, VT, you drove to North Haven and took the little ferry to Shelter Island, which you then cut across before taking another little ferry to Greenport; these little voyages (one of the adornments of North American life) lasted about ten minutes each, and the flat boats were old and low-slung, so you could stand on deck and briefly commune with the even ripples and wrinkles of the Sound.* From Greenport you drove to Orient Point and boarded the big ferry (the size of a liner, with a bar and a cinema) for the eighty-minute cruise to New London, CT. Then the final leg: a drive of 130 miles, due north, through Massachusetts to Vermont.

The Bellows would of course be coming the other way. Usually the journey went on for about seven hours, and today the temperature was very close to that of human blood. On June 10, 2001, in addition, Inez had turned two and Saul had turned eighty-six.

Then you step out the caw and the heat hits you like a brick . . . *Radger! Radger! Radger, get over here! The accent on that little girl! . . . I could listen to it all day lawng.*

This was the house imitation of the most vivid and expressive character the Amises had ever met on the ferry from New London to Orient Point (the little girl with the accent was Eliza). I said,

'And I got her name. Desirée Squadrino.'

Saul sipped his tea and said, 'Well she was right about the heat. Getting in and out of the hold was pretty rough, but apart from that . . . I didn't spot Desirée. All the people on board had spent the day playing craps and roulette. They'd just lost their shirts in a casino over the state line.'

'And the *scale* of them,' said Rosamund. 'Really unbelievable. As if they'd got that way on purpose. Through sheer willpower. And the *kids*.'

For a while they all talked about a report on the financial toll of pandemic childhood obesity. That generation would be sickly, true, and

---

* I could never make this trip without a visit from the following memory. Back in the late 1970s, when we worked at the *New Statesman*, Julian and I set a Weekend Competition in which contestants were asked to dream up organisations whose initials, in acronym form, were self-undermining – as in the Barnaby Rudge and Oliver Twist Hostel for Elderly Women: BROTHEL. That was a winning entry by Robert Conquest, who put inordinate energy into such things, and so was the Sailors', Yachtsmen's, and Pilots' Health Institute for Long Island Sound.

very expensive to treat; on the other hand, they would cost practically nothing to police, being too bulky and cumbrous to brawl, burgle, mug, rape, or flee. Elena said,

'I keep thinking the ferry's going to sink,' said Elena. 'It's the cheap food. Cheap food is drenched in what they call *saturated fats*.'

'We all know it's not their fault,' said Rosamund, 'but you still feel they couldn't get that way without buckling down to it.'

I said, 'Saul, your Sorella. In *Bellarosa*. She got that way on purpose. For a reason.'

'Yes, she did in a sense. And for a good reason.'

'A noble reason. Obeying a noble instinct.'*

In the kitchen other shapes and figures moved round about us, eating, slurping, tottering, lurching – namely Eliza and Inez Amis and Rosie Bellow (Eliza, five, was the eldest); also present were Catarina, the Amis nanny, and Sharon, the Bellow nanny, plus an auxiliary nanny, Rosamund's (very popular) niece, Rachael . . . Soon it would be time for baths, naps, and nappies – before the principals met again for evening drinks.

'If you'd come a week earlier,' said Elena, 'you'd've coincided with Hitch.'

Rosamund closed her eyes and said slowly, '. . . *Uch*.'†

'Well Rosamund,' I said, 'if it's any comfort I gave him a right slagging about that review. He didn't answer back. Which means he knew he'd done wrong.'

---

* Like Desirée Squadrino, Sorella Fonstein, the heroine of a late-period Bellow novel, is a girl from New Jersey; and she is fabulously fat: 'She made you look twice at a doorway. When she came to it, she filled the space like a freighter in a canal lock' . . . During the war Sorella stayed put in America, but her husband, club-footed Harry Fonstein, escaped only by a miracle from his appointment with Auschwitz, and crossed the Atlantic very comprehensively bereaved. The narrator respects and responds to Sorella's intelligence and integrity. 'I never lost sight of Fonstein's history, or of what it meant to be the survivor of such destruction. Maybe Sorella was trying to incorporate in fatty tissue some portion of what he had lost.' *The Bellarosa Connection* (1989).

† She wasn't still brooding about that disastrous dinner in 1989 (I drove Christopher to Vermont and we spent the night. He appeared at breakfast smoking a cigarette – but that was the least of it). What Rosamund was still brooding about was Christopher's review of *Ravelstein* (2000). And so was I. Christopher would go on to ridicule late novels by Philip Roth and John Updike, but only in Saul's case did he attribute the deficit to age and failing powers ('tired', 'thin', 'quavering') . . . 'You can't do that, man,' I told him. 'It's worse than insolent. It's *ungrateful*. I've forgiven you for 1989. You were getting divorced, and divorcees are allowed to go nuts for a year or two. But I haven't yet forgiven you for this.' It came up again in 2007, when he wrote a long, respectful,

Nobodaddy

Late morning the following day . . . I asked,

'Do you still believe in him, in it?'

'I do. I find that I still do.'

We were on the deck, with our heavily spiced Virgin Marys ('A *good* drink,' said Saul, weighing his glass) . . . Although he seemed to me to be intact and entire, there were differences. In earlier times our sessions resembled the best and friendliest kind of one-on-one tutorial – where the subject would've been RI or RK, and R would've stood for Reality (and there was no category shift when we turned to Saul's religious urges; they were part of *his* reality). The dialogue retained its slightly formal aspect but it was more like a panel or an 'in conversation with'. And he was dreamier, noticeably dreamier; unaccustomed pauses opened up, and I found myself doing more and more of the talking.

'It's impossible to justify,' he said. 'But I still do . . . believe.'

'Well it *is* uh, anomalous. "God's veil over everything." "Praise God – praise God." Arresting to see that in a work of high modernism.'*

Saul shrugged and smiled.

'A religious frame of reference', I persisted, 'comes naturally to poetry. Religion and poetry feel somehow co-eternal, don't you think? But the mainstream novel is a rational form . . . I think I know what you are, Saul. Technically. You're not a theist. You don't believe in a god that interferes with the world. You're a deist. You believe in a supreme being that minds its own business.'

and very interesting piece about *Augie March*. 'Good piece,' I said. 'But Saul's dead now, and you never thanked him for all the pleasure he gave you.' Christopher was longsufferingly silent – the closest he ever came to admitting the possibility of fault. In my view he was not a literary critic so much as a political critic of literature. The attack on *Ravelstein* was in essence an attack on Saul's turn to the right and on some of the positions of Saul's best friend Allan Bloom (the model for Abe Ravelstein). It was an attack on neoconservatism. *Ironically* is a word often misused to mean no more than 'oddly' or even 'by contrast'; but there would be irony in this for the Hitch – something to be revealed as contradictory.

* *Herzog* (1964) . . . What, or when, is modernism? Auden: 'At first critics classified authors as Ancients, that is to say Greek or Latin authors, and Moderns, that is to say every post-Classical author. Then they classified them by eras, the Augustans, the Victorians, etc., and now they classify them by decades, the Thirties, the Forties, etc. Very soon, it seems, they will be classifying them, like automobiles, by the year.' I think it is quite easy to give a date for the arrival of 'high' or developed modernism. 1922 –

• *Ulysses* and *The Waste Land*.

He said, 'Is belief the right word? There's no logical ground for it. Why should I do without proof in this one case? You reject scripture of course. You reject the idea that God writes books. Why would God write books? *We* write books.'

'So what's it look like, your supreme being?' I waited. Then I stepped in and paraphrased a couple of sentences from *Ravelstein*. Which are: *God appeared very early to me.* In childhood. *His hair was parted down the middle. I understood that we were related because he had made Adam in his image, breathed life into him.* 'I think that's lovely, but . . . Does he still wear his hair like that?'

Head back, chin up, Saul laughed (*uh, uh, uh*) – as he did not only at all jokes (however feeble) but at all quotes from his work (however sombre).

'I think,' he said, 'I think I was mingling him with my eldest brother. He wore his hair like that.'

'Maury. Rest in peace.'

'Those were early or primal impressions. And older brothers are as gods.'

'They are, they are.'

'God wouldn't look like Maury. God wouldn't look like anything we could imagine.'

'Agreed. No Nobodaddy.' Nobodaddy was William Blake's unimprovable epithet for the sky-god of Christianity: the phantom patriarch. 'And you, Saul, you still expect to re-encounter your father in the life to come . . .'

'It's not intellectually respectable, I know. It's an archaism. All I have are these persistent intuitions. Call them love impulses. I can't give up the feeling that I haven't seen the last of my parents and my sister and my brothers . . . When I die they will be waiting for me. I don't visualise any settings. And I don't know what they'll say. Very probably they'll tell me things I badly need to know . . . It's the power of early attachments. That's all.'

Now Rosamund and Elena, trailed by a child or two, came out to tell us that there was food on the table.

'We're coming.' And as I gathered my things I wanted to add, *Saul. Go on doing what you've always done. Trust the child in you. Trust the 'first heart'* (*as you once put it*). *Continue to see the world with your 'original*

265

eyes'. But all I said was, 'Hey, Saul. What's the difference between a Skoda and a Seventh-Day Adventist?'

'I don't know,' he said expectantly.

'You can close the door on a Seventh-Day Adventist.'

Back went the head, up went the chin . . . On the day my father died (in 1995) I rang Saul in Boston and told him the news. And we talked. And he told me what I badly needed to hear . . . He was never my 'literary father' (I already had one); and besides, he had his hands full with Gregory, Adam, and Daniel (and now Rosie). But I did say to him, a year or two later, 'As long as you're alive I'll never feel completely fatherless.' And after that, after Saul died, I would have – nobodaddy.

Laughter and the end of history

During lunch that day, at Elena's urging, Saul sang 'Just a Gigolo' in his soft and persuasive baritone. And at breakfast he'd given us 'K-K-K Katie' and, with Rosamund's equally pleasing harmonies, 'You Are My Sunshine'. Like me at that time, Saul tended to wake up happy. Alzheimer's would attack that happiness, and attack those harmonies. But not yet.

At some point in the afternoon I was sitting at the kitchen table with Rachael, Sharon, and Eliza; and Sharon was talking about her predecessor (as nanny to Rosie Bellow), saying,

'And she seemed such a nice girl on the surface. Very sensible and responsible.'

'Mm, I remember,' said Rachael.

'Very well brought up. No one dreamed she was such a . . .' Sharon checked herself and glanced at the attentive Eliza. 'No one dreamed she was such an ess el you tee.'

Eliza said, 'Why was she a slut?'

This was followed by a rush of laughter (and a second rush, when I passed it on to the others) . . . English is 'a *beautiful* language', I would later be told at a dinner party in Switzerland by a group of European writers; and this surprised me. Italian is beautiful, Spanish is beautiful, French is beautiful, and I'm prepared to accept that even German is or can be *jolie laide*. But English? It is impressively advanced, I knew:

no diacritical marks (no cedillas, no umlauts); 'natural' as opposed to 'grammatical' gender (cf. *das Mädchen*, where 'girl' is neuter); and an immense vocabulary.* Still, the thesaurus gets very thin when it comes to 'amusement'; it is very hard, in English, to describe laughter.

Which you need to do when you write about Saul. With him, laughter was essentially communitarian; and perhaps this is why he liked *all* jokes, however weakly punsome (and however dirty). Jokes are invitations to laughter; so he liked all jokes, and liked belonging to a species that liked telling them.

It was the cocktail hour, and I asked him, 'Now what can I get you?'

One day in the late 1990s Saul was told that he shouldn't drive any more – much resented, because he loved 'the little princess' (a recently acquired BMW). Not long afterwards he was told that he shouldn't drink any more (Updike would be told the same thing when his time drew nearer). On the day of his arrival Saul asked for a small Scotch – comprehensively deserved, I thought. Tonight he asked for a glass of red wine, and he nursed it through dinner and beyond.

We ate outside. After about an hour the conversation was veering in a certain direction and I saw my chance, saying,

'I want to tell you an anecdote about someone I hope to redeem in your eyes . . . You know who introduced me to your stuff, Saul? Without whom, perhaps, we wouldn't be sitting here tonight, under the stars, under the m-moonlight? Hitchens. In about 1975 he said, "Take a look at this." And gave me the red Penguin of *Herzog*.'

'You'd've got there on your own,' said Elena.

'Yes, I would – but when? And why fritter your life away?'

Rosamund was still lightly bristling, but Saul said genially, 'Tell your story.'

'Well here's what happened. He went to pick up a friend in the offices of *Vanity Fair*. And while he was waiting the photo editor staggered out of the darkroom, dropped his airbrush and his scalpel or

* By one calculation English comes top with 750,000 words, French second with 500,000, and Spanish third with 380,000. 'You use so many words for the verb *to walk*,' a Spanish translator once complained. 'To stroll, to saunter, to shuffle . . . Why can you not just say *andar*?'

whatever it was, sank into a chair, and said, *That's the biggest carve-down I've ever done in my entire life.'*

'What's a carve-down?'

'It's when they're trying to make somebody look less fat,' I said. 'And who was it? It was the much-maligned Monica Lewinsky . . . And Hitch had a realisation. America spent a year on O. J. Simpson, and another year on Monica Lewinsky. "Politics", said Hitch, "was once defined as 'what's going on'. And now there's nothing going on." He's nostalgic for the Cold War. There's nothing going on.'

Rosamund said, more leniently now, 'What's he miss about the Cold War?'

'. . . He's *ubi sunt* about the USSR. You know – where are they now? Where the utopian dream? Where the hard pure men like Lenin and Trotsky? But I think what he really misses is the *debate*. About an alternative to capitalism.'

'Well I was caught up in that too,' said Saul. 'Being a Trot made you feel you had a role in world history. Aiming for something higher than mere Mammon.'

'Exactly. Hitch loves America and he's committed to America. But he also wants something higher – and he lives for struggle. He says, "All the piss and vinegar's gone out of it." He says he's going to ease off politics and write more about literature.'

'Uh-oh,' said Elena.

And at last we did move on to Francis Fukuyama and his famous book.*

'History isn't over,' said Saul as we were beginning to move inside. 'Though it sometimes seems that way . . . History is never over.'

When September 11 happened Saul couldn't quite take it in. And soon, for him, history would indeed be over, in the sense that the past would be over, memory would be over. Laughter would be the last to go.

---

* *The End of History and the Last Man* (1992). Its thesis: history was over in the sense that 'mankind's ideological evolution' was over. Conflicts would of course continue, and there would continue to be events, possibly titanic events; but the only viable state model was capitalist democracy . . . As it happened, a titanic event was only seven weeks away – one supposedly heralding a different state model: that of a (worldwide) caliphate which would enforce Islamic law.

The convergence of the twain

One night there was an ultraviolent storm, many miles offshore (and reports of mountainous seas). What we saw of it – and how we all stood and stared – was economically evoked by Nabokov in *Pale Fire*: 'distant spasms of silent lightning' . . .

For some reason it was just me and Saul on the beach the next day. We had devoted the morning to a tour of East Hampton, with Elena at the wheel: visits to what were once the studios of two painters, old friends, Jackson Pollock and Saul Steinberg. 'You'd get there after breakfast, and he was already drunk,' said Bellow of the former. As a celebrated artist in America, Steinberg was insulated by his Jewishness and lived a long life; but Pollock was a helpless goy from Wyoming, and died while driving under the influence at the age of forty-six . . .

Saul said, 'Shall we swim?'

'Oh I don't know about that. Look at it. No – *listen* to it. But let's get our feet wet.'

Now normally, after one of its tantrums, its hysterical debauches, the North Atlantic would present itself as the picture of eirenic innocence, orderly, almost prim (a storm? What storm?), its waves quite lofty perhaps but unfolding reliably and negotiably towards the strand. Not today.

From a distance it looked flattened, stunned, though its surface raced crazily sideways (as if in desperate search of something), and when we entered up to our shins, then our knees, and found that the sea was . . . hideously hungover – but not as a human would be, not diffident, taciturn, and self-absorbed. All undertow, it seethed and hissed with hatred and hostility, snarling, sucking its teeth, smacking its chops, as ravenous as wildfire.

The experience was oxymoronic: a thrilling and perilous paddle, with the bright water careening past and tugging at our calves. It was a sea that refused pointblank to be swum in, but for half an hour we unsteadily ploughed through it, marvelling and laughing at its vehemence . . .

I was the first to turn and make for the shore, with Saul following; and I didn't see him go down. When I turned again he was flat on his back – in the shallowest shallows. He rose up. And he stood there and stared, stared out to sea. What was in that stare? . . . I moved to his flank and saw his face and his level eyes, which remained fixed. His eyes were eloquent of respect but also defiance and in themselves held an undertow of menace.

Saul never forgot a slight or an insult, and this ocean, as he would certainly admit, had just put him on his ass. If the Atlantic was a woman or a man, he could exact revenge by lousing it up in a novel. But the novels were over, like history.

All the same, during those two or three minutes it looked to me like a contest of equals. The sea was a force of nature. And so was Saul – so was Saul's prose. A force of nature.

Home movie

The Amises returned to London on Labor Day, which in 2001 fell on September 3. On September 6 or 7, there was a screening of the home movie (directed and presented by Elena) about the Bellows' visit to Long Island . . . That July I thought Saul was pretty much round and whole; but the camera, as all actors know, sees things that we don't see.

As the film began I was utterly absorbed by an Amis, not a Bellow: namely Inez. How very far she had come since June, the time of Christopher's stay: he couldn't go near her without inspiring a squall of tears ('Christ, how bad can it *be*?' he asked, after his fifth attempt to home in on her) . . . In what we might call the pre-credit sequence, Inez sprinted naked from the sitting room to the garden, and then, methodically using her rump, scaled the two or three steps to the raised deck where I, Saul, Rosamund, and Elena were drinking coffee, every now and then visited by Eliza, Rosie, Catarina, Rachael, Sharon . . . How happily and busily Inez moved among us, and with what soft attentiveness she heeded parental warnings when she picked up something heavy or went too near the edge. At one point she reflexively steadied herself, placing a hand on Saul's knee.* Saul's knee, Saul's eyes.

---

* Inez was horrified by Hitch in June, and was still capable of being horrified by me and by her brothers . . . Saul was undemonstratively sensitive to children and had a relaxing effect on them. I was always moved by the talent he had for it and the importance he attached to it. From a letter of June 1990: 'We loved seeing you and Julia. She served

'Look at his eyes,' said Elena.

'I am,' I said.

. . . Schizophrenia typically strikes when the victim is eighteen or nineteen: that's when the 'voices' start. But long before then the sufferer knows that something isn't right. And this was Saul's state, in July 2001. He could feel it coming on.

The home movie continued. Elena was priming him with general questions ('I'm sorry, I'm interviewing you,' she said), and Saul answered them with eloquence and ease. But his eyes weren't right – busy, flickering, over-alert. It was as if he was staring into his own brain and wondering what it would do to him next.

Typhoon

'Tell me,' he asked for the fourth or fifth time, 'how're Nat and Gus?'

By now all my efforts were aimed at dissimulating misery. And as I made my mechanical reply, I was thinking that Saul, in preparation for our talk, might even have written it down: *Ask about NAT and GUS* . . .

He did indeed ask about Nat and Gus. And I can't claim I wasn't warned.

I had arrived at the Bellow residence in Brookline ahead of schedule, at about eleven o'clock; the housekeeper, Marie, let me in. Rosamund was out somewhere, and Saul was in his study upstairs, and Rosie was with her minder in the front room. Marie gave me a cup of coffee and I slipped out of the kitchen and into the back garden for a smoke . . . I was in town as a guest of Boston University, and my mission was to lead a seminar alongside Professor Bellow. The book under discussion would be Joseph Conrad's *The Shadow-Line*. And as I sipped and puffed under the chestnut tree I wondered how Saul would react to a novella that formidably and thunderously excoriated religious belief. He would

us a dinner that made all the other dinners in Europe look sick. Also, Gus immediately recognised me as a friend which did much to restore my confidence in myself, none too firm these days.' With favoured male adults, Gus sped up to them and seized both their hands and proceeded to *climb* up their legs; he would then execute a reasonably neat backwards somersault and land on his feet. 'Just mind my dock,' cautioned Saul.

not rise up in zealous defence of his own inklings – about these he was always sweet and meek . . .

A faint rattling noise from behind – Rosamund, having returned, was coming out to join me. Her movements seemed hurried, yet she paused, and with almost pantomimic thoroughness she closed, she sealed, the double-layered door. Sealed it for sound. And even then – after the usual hug (or perhaps not so usual, more urgent, more heat-seeking) – she whispered,

'For this class – don't expect too much from him.' She said it almost entreatingly. 'He can't . . .'

I waited. And I remembered something she told me on the phone only a month or two ago: that one day when Saul was teaching he faltered (in mid-paragraph, in mid-sentence) and trailed off ('And normally he'd be *flying*'), and he gave a sudden frown, as if feeling a palpable occlusion.

'He can't . . .' Her eyes were downcast, directed at her shoes or the silky traces of April frost on the blades of grass. *My stepmother lowered her head when she spoke. It was her dyed and parted hair I had to interpret* (from *The Bellarosa Connection*). Except Rosamund's parted hair was undyed and grew with tangly force. She was forty-four, I was fifty-three, Saul was eighty-seven. 'He can't *read* any more.'

'*What?*' And I took a step away from her, to keep my balance.

She glanced over her shoulder. 'Each time he gets to the end of a sentence,' she said, or mouthed, 'he's forgotten how the sentence began . . .'

A line from *Herzog: Life couldn't be as indecent as that. Could it?*

And I thought incoherently of the times I'd found myself on the London tube without a book, or, worse, with a book but without glasses, or, worse still, with book and glasses but no light (power out) – but the book and the glasses will be found and the light will come back on, and I won't be sitting in the dark with a book on my lap for the rest of my life.*

---

* The writer's life is tripartite, divided between writing and reading and . . . oh yeah, living. Don't forget living. That has to be got done too. If you can't read then you clearly can't write, so all you can do is live. And then stop living. There's no avoiding that either. As James Last, the ailing hero of Conrad's *The Nigger of the 'Narcissus'*, puts it: 'I must live until I die, mustn't I?'

. . . Saul appeared and we embraced and he drank his coffee. The car that would drive us to the lecture hall was due at three, so there was plenty of time for the two of us to move into the rear sitting room for our talk.

Two-forty, and Saul was trussed up in his parka near the front door, waiting (waiting for the driver's knock), but just waiting. He had the Conrad under his arm; he wasn't looking at it. I said,

'Now why is your copy twice as thick as mine? May I?' I took it on to my lap. 'Ah. You've got *The Shadow-Line* but also *Typhoon*. That's a wonderful pairing, don't you think? *Typhoon* – the malevolence of the storm. And *The Shadow-Line* – the malevolence of the calm . . . D'you remember that sea in Long Island? The one that put you on your ass?' He smiled but said nothing. 'We were on the beach and we . . .'

And so I went on until the driver came. I had learnt my lesson.*

There is something going on in the sky

Our classroom contained about twenty-five students. Every other head of hair had the dark glisten, the mirrory radiance of our cousins from the distant end of Eurasia. As the cliché gears you to expect, the young Asians seemed inscrutable – but then so did the young westerners. This (a comparatively minor development of advancing years) is what had happened to me: youth itself seemed inscrutable. Youth, 'that mighty power', as Conrad repeatedly insists; but I could no longer feel its might. Only its strangeness.

---

* 'I just kept repeating myself,' I said to Rosamund, '– about Nat and Gus.' We were in the kitchen, where she was readying lunch. The radio was on, loud, and she was making as much noise as she could with blenders and gushing taps. 'I just kept repeating myself. I was as bad as *he* was!' All invention, all imagination, seemed to abandon me. 'You were probably in shock,' she said. '. . . That's probably true. I should've just babbled about *anything* – Uruguay, Elena, London, the girls. Conrad.' 'Don't feel bad about it. Maybe he wouldn't've wanted that. Because it's you.' I said, 'Rosamund, that's the gentlest comfort you could possibly give me. But no. I should've just filled the silences. Christ!' All the same, it *was* dumbfounding. Like being under the brow of an empty mountain – a mountain all hollowed out. So: fill the emptiness, fill the silence. It was the only thing you could do.

Keith Botsford, I was relieved to discover, would supervise the seminar.* I had known Keith for almost as long as I had known Saul; and I was relieved, not because he would share the burden of a ninety-minute talk about Conrad (I could manage that), but because he would share the burden of disquiet if Saul never once opened his mouth (a strong likelihood, according to Rosamund). We settled.

I was slow to feel it coming over me, but an unfamiliar – an unrecognisable – mental state was imposing itself; it was something like a surfeit of significance, with too many elements and arguments struggling to cohere. I couldn't control them – I had no idea what went where. It reminded me of the most painful gropings of authorship, when you're unmanned by sheer complexity – only here I was in real life and real time, facing an arduousness normally found only in pen and ink, and not in flesh and blood.†

There was some coughing and nose-blowing from the class. Saul sat there on the dais with his legs crossed, looking quiet and wise. The airy float of white hair, the broad mouth, the fine nose, the bicycle spokes of indentations on either temple (laugh lines) – eyes oystery with time but still rich and concentrated, full of things you badly needed to know . . . Handkerchiefs and tissues were put away, and replaced by pads and pens. Keith smoothly began.

The Shadow-Line was composed in the second year of the Great War and dedicated to Conrad's son Borys, who was about to enlist – at the

---

* Keith was a veteran literary maverick and boho; and his air of rakish irresponsibility had always fascinated Saul. For instance, Keith 'appears' in *Humboldt's Gift* (under the name of Pierre Thaxter), where he comes across as a flamboyant fantasist (with his debts, his wives, his innumerable children) and as something of 'a purple genius of the Baron Corvo type'. Recasting actual contemporaries in literature has consequences which some (including me) find uncomfortably worldly. I heard that Keith was asked to sign a libel waiver in the weeks before *Humboldt* appeared; he cheerfully obliged.
† Real life is almost always complicated, but it is hardly ever complex. When Freud called death 'the complex symbol', he meant that it contained many levels and many themes, all very hard to reconcile and combine. I'm now fairly sure that my singular mental state that day at BU was the result of a memento mori; it had been brought home to me that my mind, too, was mortal, and open to erasure . . . The Freud family (I feel moved to say) has left us with a complex symbol of the Holocaust. Sigmund died in London in 1939, aged eighty-three. His four younger sisters died differently: Pauline (aged eighty) and Marie (eighty-two) were murdered in Treblinka, Adolfine (eighty-one) in Theresienstadt, and Rosa (eighty-four) in Auschwitz.

age of seventeen. Borys would survive, and survive the Somme, gassed, wounded, and shell-shocked. Conrad, pained and agitated ('I am nearly driven distracted by my uselessness'), could at least assert paternal solidarity in this darkly autobiographical novella about the seminal crisis of his own life: his first command, in the South China Sea (the year was 1887, when Conrad was turning thirty). 'To Borys and all the others', runs the dedication, 'who like himself have crossed in early youth the shadow-line of their generation WITH LOVE.'

Non-coincidentally, *The Shadow-Line* is also one of the most aggressively godless testaments in the English language. From the introductory Author's Note:

> No, I am too firm in my consciousness of the marvellous to be ever fascinated by the merely supernatural, which (take it any way you like) is but a manufactured article, the fabrication of minds insensitive to the intimate delicacies of our relation to the dead and to the living, in their countless multitudes; a desecration of our tenderest memories; an outrage on our dignity.

And to add insult to insult, the author weaves a secularist taunt into the very structure of his tale.

Sailing south from Bangkok (for Australia), the narrator's sleek merchantman, the *Otago*, is very soon utterly becalmed in the Gulf of Thailand; one by one the hands are ailing (as if suffocated by the malarial miasmas gathering in the static air), and will be reliant for their survival on the quinine supposedly stored in the ship's medicine chest. Then the young captain makes his 'appalling discovery': the quinine is gone; it was sold by the old captain, his predecessor (a malign figure, now dead), to finance a pitifully gullible infatuation in the backstreets of Haiphong.

We glimpse the woman, who resembles 'a low-class medium', only in a photograph (characterised as 'an amazing human document'); and it is one of those moments when Conrad reaches for his most scathing register. There is the captain ('bald, squat, grey'), 'and by his side towered an awful, mature white female with rapacious nostrils and a cheaply ill-omened stare in her enormous eyes'. So honest men were stripped of their health, strength, sanity, and youth to foster a sordid mystic and her theatrical stare . . .

*

Keith ended his preamble and turned to me and Saul. 'Would you like to weigh in?' Saul shifted silently in his seat. 'Martin?'

I took out the draft I'd written a week ago, and I said, '*The Shadow-Line* is in the end a thrilling piece of work, but its structure is hopelessly inept. It has the shape, according to one critic, of a tiny teacup with a ludicrously large handle. All that harbourfront politicking and clubroom one-upping ashore. Very turgid, very dull, and very opaque. This goes on for *six-tenths* of the whole. Once the *Otago* gets out of port, the book at last spreads its sails and fills its lungs. Now Conrad draws himself up to his full height and looks you searchingly in the eye. And when he writes like this he is an honour to read. So with your permission – Keith, Saul – I suggest we go through a couple of passages . . .'

What were these components searching for unity in my head? I can try to list them. One: the malaise that enfeebles and deranges the officers and men on that voyage; this was of course painfully resonant. Two: Conrad's dismissal of religion – with the 'hereafter' treated with especial scorn – was resonant. Three: the question of auto-fiction, of 'life-writing', was resonant (the book is subtitled *A Confession*). And, four, our students themselves, or at least half of them, were roped into the argument because the book is set in their original longitudes – the Gulf of Siam (as it was then called) bounded by Thailand, Cambodia, and Vietnam; and the sickness smothering the crew, Conrad has his narrator suspect, is profoundly oriental in its mystery and power. All that, and also youth, war, isolation, sin, guilt, masculinity, madness, death . . .

'*There is something going on in the sky like a decomposition*,' I read out, '*like a corruption of the air . . . A great overheated stillness enveloped the ship, and seemed to hold her motionless . . . The punctual and wearisome stars reappeared over the mast-heads, but the air remained stagnant . . .*' I turned some pages and pressed on: '*The effect is curiously mechanical; the sun climbs and descends, the night swings over our heads as if somebody below the horizon were turning a crank. It is the pettiest, the most aimless . . .* And Conrad breaks off the sentence, as if defeated by fatuity, by futility, as if there's nothing worth saying, nothing worth thinking . . . *There were moments when I felt, not only that I would go mad, but I had gone mad already.*

'This is the shadow-line, the climacteric, the inner test that our narrator seems bound to fail. The loss of grip, the loss of connection, the weakening of consecutive thought. He succumbs to mere superstition, quailing at the local hexes and voodoos. He can't even . . .' Christ, I thought, how much more of this is there? I checked and saw there were two apparently gleeful paragraphs on the horrors and humiliations of the disintegrating mind. So I said, 'Now let's turn to the prose, and note the second-language writer's attraction to cliché. *In the twinkling of an eye* appears three times at ten-page intervals, *my head swam* twice in adjacent paragraphs. And how about this spare part of boilerplate: *The feeling seemed to me the most natural thing in the world. As natural as breathing.* On page ninety-nine we're told that *you could have heard a pin drop* in a silence *so profound that you* . . .'

But all occasions informed against me. As I toiled on, plausibly enough I suppose, I was thinking about the pure, the platonic Alzheimer's death, which happens when 'breathing' joins all the other activities that the patient forgets to do.

'It is the insistent Conradian crux,' said Keith, winding up. '*The Shadow-Line* is about nature's indifference to its most exotic creation – human consciousness.' He then shrugged and said, again fairly, 'But it's a mistake to ask what a novel's *about.*'

'Agreed,' I said. 'It's not something you can print on a T-shirt or a bumper sticker.'

'Yes. I mean, Saul, what's *Augie March* "about"?'

And Saul said, 'It's about two hundred pages too long.'

At the time, and given the circumstances, I thought this was perfect: aslant, athwart, and inspiring a burst of relieved laughter . . . A decade later I learnt that Saul's joke went all the way back to the time of *Augie's* publication in 1953. The long-term memories of the victims of Dr Alois, as I would go on to see, are more readily available than whatever it was that happened five minutes ago.

And I would still say that after half a century Saul's joke stood up pretty well. All the same, it was his only utterance of the afternoon.

Wrecking ball

He was becalmed in the doldrums of dementia – in windless stasis. That was one way of imagining it. What were the other ways? When he asked me about Nat and Gus, and went on asking me about Nat and Gus, I was stunned by the extent of the destruction already wrought; it was as if a host of Goths or Vandals had come and gone; everything that was beautiful or holy had been looted or wrecked. Yet here there was no human agency; the thing was insensible and indifferent . . . I eventually realised that Saul himself had come up with the most telling image, and he did it forty years ago, in *Herzog*.* From a famous paragraph:

> At the corner he paused to watch the work of the wrecking crew. The great metal ball swung at the walls, passed easily through brick, and entered the rooms, the lazy weight browsing on kitchens and parlors. Everything it touched wavered and burst, spilled down. There rose a white tranquil cloud of plaster dust.

And Dr Alzheimer's mission was not yet fully accomplished. The story wasn't over, any more than the day was over for Moses Herzog: 'The sun, now leaving for New Jersey and the west, was surrounded by a brilliant broth of atmospheric gases.'

James Bond and Captain Sparrow

'He likes James Bond,' said Rosamund on the phone.

'He likes James Bond?'

'Yes. If we could watch James Bond. With snacks. Little pastries and chocolates. I'll get all that.'

The idea was to appease Saul's frantic restlessness, at least for a couple of hours – to lull him with James Bond . . .

Rosamund said, 'He likes James Bond. We like James Bond.'

'Fine,' I said. 'Come around two. *I* like James Bond.'

*

* It seems curious – at least to me – that all the quotes in this chapter come from *Herzog*, a book that lies fairly low on the scale of my lecteurial love, coming in behind *Augie March*, the *Collected Stories* (with its five novellas), *Mr Sammler's Planet*, *Humboldt's Gift*, and *Ravelstein*. The only explanation I can come up with is that there must be a great deal of death awareness in its psychological cladding; and a fear of insanity, too, a fear much deeper than the crazily blithe first sentence allows: 'If I am out of my mind, it's all right with me, thought Moses Herzog.' It wasn't all right with Saul Bellow in 2001, when he felt its advent (his darting, flickering eyes). He would have echoed King Lear: 'O! Let me not be mad, sweet heaven! / Keep me in temper: I would not be mad.'

In the pre-credit sequence James Bond – or Pierce Brosnan – is arriving in some Far Eastern fleshpot by sea, having crossed a great stretch of the South Pacific, not by sailing ship like Conrad on the *Otago*, but by surfboard . . .

The three of us were crouched round the screen, eating the little snacks.

On the beach or the harbour shore the great Brosnan unzips his wetsuit to reveal a tuxedo – an *hommage* to the much more commanding and graceful Sean Connery in (perhaps) *From Russia with Love*. And pretty soon Pierce is closeted in the penthouse bedroom with a champagne bucket and a scheming beauty . . .

'Is this *it*?' said Saul.

'Apparently so,' I said.

During that visit I had prolonged my stay at a hotel that followed the all-suite format, and my rooms were chintzily *gemütlich*, as were the pastries and chocolates in their twirly wrappings. The pay-per-view service was efficient, the tea hot and fresh. The only distraction, I found, was the reproachful daylight beyond the wispy curtains, making me feel that I must've shirked some vital duty. The heavens that afternoon were interestingly split-level, baby blue below, but glowered down on by black smears and coalescing thunderheads.

By now Brosnan was kaleidoscopically involved with high-performance automobiles, mountain roads, manmade avalanches, hovering Predator drones.

Saul had stopped eating and was stiffly thrashing about in his seat. Suddenly he said with a touch of raggedness and even despair,

'Are we going to be here *all night*?'

In the evening of my last full day in Boston he and I companionably watched a video of *Pirates of the Caribbean: The Curse of the Black Pearl*. We exchanged words during the screening, words about the film, words about this and that. Rosie was of the audience, gazing up now and then from her other interests, toys, picture books; and Rosamund, who was making one of her expert dinners, passed through with appetisers and glasses of wine (for me).

'Unsentimental,' I said to Saul, after Captain Sparrow's forensic visit to a whorehouse – a whorehouse that evidently spanned a whole island.

The men were all drunkenly brawling and crashing around, and the women bore the vivid traces of maulings and batterings. 'You couldn't call it schmaltzy.'

'I guess not.'

'Christ, look at the size of the bruise on that blonde's cleavage.'

But now Captain Sparrow was once again on the high seas. His quest? To locate and reclaim his old ship, the *Black Pearl*, stolen from him by his onetime messmate Hector Barbossa . . .

'Pirates have been classified as terrorists,' I said, not really expecting any response. 'They were religious too, often – Muslim, Catholic, Protestant, though not Jewish, I don't think. And they were often all-gay . . . We're fond of pirates. We indulge them.'

'Bluebeard,' said Saul.

I had seen *Pirates of the Caribbean* before (sitting between Nat and Gus). Saul had also seen it before, last night, here at Crowninshield Road, and would be seeing it tomorrow, and the next day. We were actually seeing it again fifteen minutes later, because the tape mysteriously rewound and restarted. Now Captain Sparrow (Johnny Depp) was about to rescue Elizabeth Swann (Keira Knightley); he stood on the taffrail of the anchored galleon, and then he made the dive into the dark water.

In considered admiration Saul said, 'He's a brave boy.'

'He certainly is,' I said. 'A very brave boy.'

Brave was what we were all going to have to be from now on. None more so than Rosamund . . . The strangely dogged interconnectedness of that spell in Boston, the way reality seemed to have banished everything not strictly relevant (one way or another) to Saul's plight – the plight of the half-state, of half-being. Even Captain Sparrow made his contribution, discovering that Captain Hector Barbossa, and all his crew, had succumbed to the 'curse' of the *Black Pearl*: these men were now undead (deceased but technically animate). In Barbossa's words:

> For too long I've been parched of thirst and unable to quench it. Too long I've been starving to death and haven't died. I feel nothing. Not the wind on my face nor the spray of the sea, nor the warmth of a woman's flesh.

The mariners, the hands on the black-sailed *Black Pearl*, were exposed by moonlight. They were skeletons, frames of bone with the odd patch of skin and gristle . . .

Saul could still feel the warmth of a woman's flesh – and he could still transmit warmth (he was warm to be with on that last night). He always found Rosie's presence both soothing and strengthening. And perhaps he was beginning to feel the consolation that Alzheimer's carelessly throws your way. 'As the condition gets worse', wrote John Bayley in *Iris*, 'it also gets better': each new impoverishment reduces the awareness of loss.

But there were tropical deliriums yet to come. And I found it impossible not to keep thinking of Larkin's weighty lines in the early poem 'Next, Please':

> Only one ship is seeking us, a black-
> Sailed unfamiliar, towing at her back
> A huge and birdless silence: in her wake
> No waters breed or break.

Cross purpose: 'Go to your emails'

On June 29, 2010, I picked up the phone and said, 'Hello?'

'Martin.'

'Ian.'

'Bad news.'

'Yes,' I said, 'bad news. Oh, very bad. We had old friends here, and we were all having a warm and wonderful time, and then the call came through and I just – I just deliquesced.'

'. . . The call from?'

'From Spain. Nicolas's wife, saying she'd just died.'

'Sorry. Who'd just died?'

'My mother.'

'Oh no!'

And as Ian commiserated, with real feeling (Hilly had endeared herself to all my friends, and indeed to everyone she'd ever met, as the obituaries unanimously stressed), I felt the unspoolings and untwinings of cross purpose . . .

'Thank you, thank you,' I said. 'I flew back yesterday, from the funeral.' I breathed in. 'But that wasn't why you rang, was it. There's more bad news.'

'There's more bad news. Are you in your study? Go to your emails. I'll hang on, so take your time. It's to do with Hitch. I'll hang on.'

'Instant deliquescence' was about right: I turned to water; I was sixty, but I might as well have been six. And then, the next morning and beyond, a furtive disarray, like a relatively stable panic attack.* No, the death of the mother is unlike the death of the father – quite unlike.

On the night the clocks went back in 1995 I called Saul Bellow in Boston and after brief preliminaries I said,

'My father died at noon today . . . So I'm afraid you'll have to take over now.'

Towards the end of our talk I felt the truth of a (more or less) throwaway line in *Herzog*:

'It's as you say. *We are born to be orphaned and to leave orphans after us*. My mother's still there of course . . . I'll write. Goodbye.'

'Well, I love you very much . . . Goodbye.'

And those deep syllables got me through. Within three or four days of Kingsley's death I had the sense that I was moving, with my eyes wide open, from the reservists to the front line; the intercessionary figure was gone, and now I had to step up, I had to step forward. Again and again my body tingled with a sense of almost physical levitation; somewhere in the calves it seemed to hum . . .

The death of the father kicks the son upstairs. With the death of the mother, the son goes skyward too, clutching the banister, and more

---

* I found I seemed to do slightly better if I concentrated on specific memories (rather than simply weltering in woe). And it was this memory that gave the most dependable relief . . . I am seven, which makes Hilly twenty-eight, and we are walking along the seafront of a small town in South Wales. A man drives by – and on the instant mother and son are convulsed by laughter . . . The car was one thing (three-wheeled and roofless, and somehow entirely unserious, like an early and unaerodynamic attempt at a racer); and the man at the wheel, the lone occupant, in green tweeds and fawn scarf and porkpie hat, very round and red in the face with open mouth, the man at the wheel *exactly* resembled a prosperous pig smugly motoring through the pages of a children's book . . . After a few minutes, when we'd straightened up and quietened down, my mother and I turned to one another gasping and wiping our eyes in gratitude and faint disbelief, as if saying, *Well how could you possibly improve on that?* Then I looked round about me; and all the people I could see, townies, builders, a policewoman, a grocer, were wearing their everyday faces . . . Ah, I thought, so it's just the two of us – it's just her and me.

or less of his own volition – but he is seeking his childhood room and his childhood bed.

I went to my emails and there it was. From chitch9oo8, addressed to ianimcewan and martin.amis: and in his note Christopher gave a quiet forewarning of what they would all read in the papers the following day.*

'It's serious,' said Ian. 'I've talked to Ray.' Ray was Ray Dolan (Ian's very old friend and one of the most-cited neurobiologists in his field). 'He gave me the figures.'

I tried to listen. These figures or projections would fluctuate over time, but it seemed that our friend had a one-in-eight chance (or was it one-in-twelve) of living for another seven years. Or was it five?

'Soon we'll know more,' said Ian. 'So let's . . . I think that's very sad – I mean your mother. So let's be in constant touch.'

'Yes. Constant touch.'

The problem of re-entry

202 was the area code for Washington DC.

My grey house phone looked overworked and hard done by as I reached for it, all smudged and clammy with its owner's handprints, and it looked bilious, too, as if sick to its stomach of transmitting words about infirmity and ruin . . . I lifted the receiver, faltered (I was hopelessly unprepared), and laid it down again and tried to organise my thoughts.

For a start, it was 11 a.m. in London, and so . . . My crude aide-memoire for transatlantic time (why did I still need one?) went as follows: the UK was much *older* than the US, so it was always *later* in England. And that meant, in turn, that the sun was only squinting at America's east coast, and anyway Christopher seldom rose before ten. There were still five hours to go; and even after a long and necessary

* In this press release Christopher was officially curtailing a book tour (for his memoir *Hitch-22*). 'I have been advised by my physician that I must undergo a course of chemotherapy on my esophagus. This advice seems persuasive to me. I regret having had to cancel so many engagements at short notice.'

talk with Elena there were still four hours to go. I had nothing to do but sit there and smoke and wonder – What was Hitch going to *say*?

'The Hitch has landed,' he used to announce every time he called from Heathrow. As we know, the habit of referring to yourself in the third person is not always a sign of cloudless mental health. Such a habit, perhaps, is to be warily expected of iconic household faces – and in 2010 Christopher couldn't cross a city block anywhere in America without being recognised, greeted, praised, and buttonholed. And yet Christopher was the Hitch long, long before 2010.

In fact he referred to himself as the Hitch right from the start – in the early 1970s, when he and I were becoming friends. At that stage he was quite unknown beyond an inextensive circle of young Marxists and sympathetic young journalists (one of whom, I remember, singled him out as 'the meteoric Trotskyist'). In 1974, when we were both twenty-five, he came up to the literary department of the *New Statesman* in the late afternoon, and I said,

'You look very chuffed.'

'Yes, I had a rather "good" lunch with certain members of the board,' said Christopher. 'Tony' – Anthony Howard, the editor in chief – 'confirmed that they're going to start sending me abroad more.'

'How wonderful.'

'Belfast, Lebanon, Buenos Aires.' For a moment Christopher seemed to churn and sway with emotion, and then he said, 'This will soon be axiomatic for the whole planet. Wherever there is injustice and oppression, wherever the strong prey on the weak – then the pen of the Hitch will flash from its scabbard . . .'

'. . . Nor shall your sword sleep in your hand . . .'

'Till I have built Jerusalem. In this green and pleasant land.'

Everything he said was equivocal. Flippant and heartfelt, ironic and serious, whimsical and steely. Even his self-mythologising was also part of a project of self-deflation. 'Flash from its scabbard', for instance, is a decidedly high-style poeticism when applied to a drawn sword – but what is it when applied to a drawn pen?

*

A month or so later, on the stairs at the *New Statesman*, Christopher came out of the half-landing toilet and guiltily rocked to a halt. Some time ago, I should say, we had passed an edifying hour wondering what a bathroom would smell like after a visit from a dinosaur.

'Exit,' said Christopher, 'pursued by a brontosaurus.' He frowned. 'That needs more work. We want a carnivore, beginning with *b*.'

'Brachiosaurus. No, that's another herbivore. Hitch, where've you been all week?'

'Cyprus. Haven't you got my postcard? They love me in Cyprus.'

'Why, particularly?'

'Because I'm a true friend of the Cypriot people. Whenever I go to Cyprus there's a front-page headline in the *Nicosia Times* saying HITCH FLIES IN.'

'And what does the headline say when you leave?'

'HITCH FLIES OUT.'

. . . I would come to detect a logistical difficulty here. Christopher might very well see HITCH FLIES IN (as, say, he enjoyed his first breakfast at the hotel). But how would he ever see HITCH FLIES OUT? No, he'd be gone. Still, I'd constructed a tactical fantasy: Christopher on Cyprus Air's late flight to London, with a Scotch in one hand and a Rothmans in the other, looking forward to his dinner, and attending to an early edition of the *Nicosia Times* with the banner headline HITCH FLIES OUT.

It was now 3.45. What was Christopher going to *say*?

How would he usher in the new reality? A great deal would depend on his opening sentence. After hours of circular thought it was beginning to feel to me like a novelistic challenge: the fundamental challenge, which meets you twenty times a day, of *finding the right tone*.* And Christopher, with his extravagant idiolect . . .

The Hitch has landed; but now he was in mid-air, beginning another kind of journey, a 'deportation' (as he would soon write), 'taking me from

---

* Literary critics call it 'decorum'. In colloquial English decorum means 'in keeping with good taste and propriety'. Literary decorum means 'the concurrence of style and content', and is of course wholly inattentive to propriety and taste.

the country of the well across the stark frontier that marks off the land of malady'.*

I was sure he wouldn't be solemn, let alone lachrymose. He wouldn't be spiritless. But what would he be?

———————————

Mrs Christopher Hitchens, or Carol Blue (or simply 'Blue'), picked up.

'He knew you'd call,' she said. 'He's just getting out of the shower. I'll go and . . .'

For three or four minutes I sat with the silent mouthpiece in my hand. Then he came on.

'Mart.'

'Hitch.'

'. . . Dah,' he said. 'It's my fucking tits now.'

* All the relevant (i.e., 'medical') quotes in this chapter and the next derive from the series of columns Christopher wrote in *Vanity Fair* between September 2010 and October 2011; they were collected in a slim volume called *Mortality* (2012).

Chapter 2
Hitchens Goes to Houston

Tumortown, March 2011

The itinerary told me that my flight would take just over ten hours, and the boarding card told me that my seat was to be 58F, which was located just before – or even parallel with, or actually beyond – the Economy toilets. This was no cause for complaint. Far more conducive to puzzlement and unease was the fact that the PA system kept calling me a 'customer'. Passengers – on American Airlines and, I suspected, on American airlines in general – were now known as customers. *We are at full capacity so we do ask our customers to vacate the aisles as soon as . . .*

This was new, and it was policy (even the captain observed it, going on about *the comfort and safety of our customers*); and it struck the occupant of 58F as a clear demotion . . . I remember to this day how left wing, how ascetic, how anticapitalist – or, if you prefer, how short of money – I felt on that trip (the ticket alone cost thousands of pounds), and as a point of self-respect I wanted to stop being a customer and go back to being a passenger.

You see, I was in the process – now far advanced – of moving house, from the Land of the Rose to the Land of the Free.* When I was just a regular visitor I always felt at home in America; now that I would soon

---

* The news of Hilly's death came on a Thursday (June 24, 2010), the news of Christopher's cancer came on the following Tuesday, and on the following Monday Elena and I had (lesser) news of our own: we were moving from London to Brooklyn. It would take a year to bring this about, but meanwhile we were going back and forth . . . It was simple: Elena wanted to be near her mother, Betty (who was eighty-two, like Hilly), and I wanted to be near Hitch (who was sixty-one, like me).

be a resident, I felt like a visitor, and one from another planet. How very strange it was suddenly seeming – America.

––––––––––

It was March 2011 – a full nine months after diagnosis. I had seen Christopher regularly meanwhile, sometimes in New York but almost always in the District of Columbia. I would board the train from Penn Station to Washington Union, take a cab to the Wyoming apartment block off Dupont Circle, ride the elevator to the sixth storey, and brace myself while waiting for the door to open and reveal the latest changes in my friend. There always were changes – and in addition there always were sorties to hospital rooms and consulting rooms and treatment rooms and above all waiting rooms . . .

We knew early on that the cancer had metastasised (secondary tumours had colonised 'a bit of my lung as well as quite a bit of my lymph node'); the tumour on the collarbone was in addition 'palpable', to the touch and even to the eye. It took a little longer to determine the source and establish the verdict: Oesophageal Cancer, Stage Four. 'And', as he was never slow to add, 'there is no Stage Five.' The chemo had done what it could, and now, taking a more advanced and aggressive approach, Christopher enrolled as an outpatient at MD Anderson Cancer Center in Houston, Texas.

There I was aimed. On a flight marked by long interludes of riotous turbulence (with the plane's rear end waggling like that of a muscular bulldog on the point of being unleashed for a romp). As an experience, then, sitting there strapped into 58F was both expensive and uncomfortable – but not nearly as expensive and uncomfortable as being strapped into a Proton Therapy Synchrotron, which was to be Christopher's next recourse and ordeal.

First, the past, and the end of Yvonne

During that journey Martin had *Hitch-22* on his lap, and he was looking again at the pages about the fate of Mrs Yvonne Hitchens.

Hilly had a soft departure; she died in her farmhouse in rural Andalusia, attended by two devoted daughters-in-law (one of them a professional nurse); and she was in her early eighties. By contrast,

Yvonne died of unnatural causes in a Greek hotel, with a male cadaver in the adjoining room; and she was in her mid-forties. Hilly's death was in the newspapers – among the obituaries; Yvonne's death was on the front page.

As Christopher tells it, he was lying in bed one November morning 'with a wonderful new girlfriend' when he got a call from a (clearly quite wonderful) old girlfriend. She asked him if earlier that day he had listened to the BBC: there was a brief dispatch about a woman with his surname who had been found murdered in Athens. Having heard some particulars (clinchingly the full name of Yvonne's travelling companion), the old girlfriend said, 'Oh dear, then I'm very sorry but it probably is your mum.'*

That corpse next door was the man she had eloped with – a scrawny transcendentalist (and ex-priest) called Timothy Bryan.

Some historical imagination is necessary if we are to see the size of the calamity for Christopher's father, Eric, the stalwart naval officer. In one vital respect Commander Hitchens still lived in the culture of Trollope – the last of the great novelists to portray a world in which familial scandal led at once to social death. In his provincial and anxiously genteel milieu the commander had reconciled himself to the defection of 'an adored wife', but as *Hitch-22* goes on,

> [I]n the surrounding society of North Oxford, the two of them had a pact. If invited to a sherry party or a dinner, they would still show up together as if nothing had happened. Now, and on the front pages at that, everything was made known at once, and to everybody.

---

* I had an inkling of how this must have felt. In December 1974 my cousin Lucy Partington failed to return to her mother's house in the Gloucestershire village of Gretton (where I had spent many a childhood summer). She had disappeared, and there would soon be posters of her everywhere. Privately, over time, I managed to half-persuade myself of the following: 21-year-old Lucy – highly intelligent, artistic, and religious – had disappeared on purpose (for inscrutable reasons of her own). Two decades later, in March 1994, her body was exhumed, along with several other bodies, from beneath the 'house of horror', 25 Cromwell Street, Gloucester; she was one of the victims of Fred West, the serial murderer (and the complete, the perfect, the finished modern trog). When I opened the tabloid and saw her photograph, I felt as though a shaggy beast had brushed my face with its breath. I was Lucy's first cousin; Christopher was Yvonne's first son.

Eric Hitchens (also known as Hitch) was 'a man who for a long time braved death for a living'; and yet 'there was no question of his coming to Athens, and I myself, in any case, was already on my way . . .'

Already on his way. This will qualify as a theme: Christopher's compulsion to stride into his fears. It was the late November of 1973.

On November 17 of that year the regime of the Greek junta – a dictatorship, writes Christopher, 'of dark glasses and torturers and steel helmets' – was overthrown: the fascist colonel, George Papadopoulos, was replaced by a fascist general, Dimitrios Ioannidis, and the new junta was a dictatorship of massacre. This was the setting for the last days of Yvonne Hitchens.

And so we picture the youthful Christopher going through the motions with Athenian officialdom (the compromised coroner, the villainous police captain), and at the same time covertly mingling with the underground opposition (survivors of beatings, friends with bullet wounds who dared not go to any hospital). At one point, in a shabby student flat, he joined his comrades in an almost whispered rendition of 'The Internationale' . . .

At last Christopher was informed of the judicial verdict. It did not surprise him, and it must have consoled him. In London he had taken his mother and her lover out to dinner, and he had got a sense of Timothy Bryan: 'wispy', musical, an adherent of the Maharishi. No, not a murderer. And so not a murder-suicide. Yvonne had made a pact with her husband; she also made a pact with her lover – they used sleeping pills. In addition, Timothy, 'whose need to die must have been very great', had slit his wrists in the bath. And Christopher was obliged to absorb another fact (one destined to ramify for ever in his mind): according to the hotel telephonist's log, Yvonne had repeatedly tried to reach him in London. That was the penultimate shock – there was one more to come.

Christopher begins the two filial chapters of *Hitch-22* with a description of his first memory. In Athens he was twenty-four; and here he has just turned three. The scene is the Grand Harbour at Valletta (the capital of Malta, a British possession with a naval base where the commander serves). And Christopher is aboard a ferry, intoxicated by 'the discrepant yet melding blues' of the Mediterranean. His mother is with him, and although he is free to run around and explore she is always present and ready to take his hand.

The year is 1952. That is how it begins. And twenty-one years later,

> . . . [T]his is how it ends. I am eventually escorted to the hotel suite where it all happened. The two bodies had had to be removed, and their coffins sealed, before I could get there. This was for the dismally sordid reason that the dead couple had taken a while to be discovered. The pain of this is so piercing and exquisite, and the scenery of the two rooms so nasty and so tawdry, that I hide my tears and my nausea by pretending to seek some air at the window. And there, for the first time, I receive a shattering, full-on view of the Acropolis. For a moment, and like the Berlin Wall and other celebrated vistas when glimpsed for the first time, it almost resembles some remembered postcard of itself. But then it becomes utterly authentic and unique. That temple really must be the Parthenon, and almost near enough to stretch out and touch. The room behind me is full of death and darkness and depression, but suddenly here again and fully present is the flash and dazzle of the life-giving Mediterranean air and light that lent me my first hope and confidence. I only wish I could have been clutching my mother's hand for this, too.

I sent him a letter of condolence, in November 1973, on *Times Literary Supplement* notepaper; and he replied on the notepaper of the *New Statesman*. In his memoir he describes my letter as 'brief, well-phrased, memorable'. Not so memorable for me, but it began with an assertion of friendship; and quite suddenly we were no longer warm acquaintances. We were friends. I was his friend, and he was mine.

Christopher was perfectly willing to talk about his father (whom I got to know a bit: he always wore the same typhoon-proof thick-knit white rollneck); but I can't remember him saying anything about his mother, except this once . . . On a bright afternoon in early 1974 we were in his small chaotic office (the Hutch of the Hitch) gradually recovering from the midday meal; and for once the veins of our cigarette smoke were a beautiful, a Mediterranean blue, and I said,

'In Greece, was it really rough?'

With his eyes on the floor he tipped his head from side to side.

'No need to answer. I bet it was rough. I bet it wasn't boring, though, Hitch. You could give it that.'

His gaze was still downward. 'Let's just say I felt very alive.'

———————

It was 3 p.m. local time when the plane landed at George H. W. Bush Intercontinental Airport. The crew extended advice and courtesies to the passengers, who were hungry for a new kind of air, air they hadn't breathed ten thousand times already – virginal air. At the end of the very long line to the final checkpoint there was a sniffer dog, a beautifully groomed but insanely zealous Alsatian, with its uniformed master; it clambered all over me – but I ducked away and then I was clear. In the steamy open-air basement of the pick-up bays, I had a smoke, found a cab, and rode through gusty suburbs, heading for downtown and the Lone Star Hotel.

The five-stage theory

Where I failed to raise the Hitchenses. They were out, and neither Christopher nor Blue were picking up their phones. I fleetingly considered a tragic nap, but I never take naps, because all my naps are tragic naps . . .

And I was thinking of the two of them in hospital rooms and consulting rooms and treatment rooms and above all in waiting rooms. Sickness is itself a waiting room . . . Many, many people have written with great penetration on sickness, on the estrangement from the world of will and action, the indignity, the onerousness, but not many have evoked the boredom, as Christopher has: how really incredibly boring it is. 'It bores even me,' he wrote . . .

It would freeze my blood, for instance, to see an appointment-book entry that promised *morning with lawyers, afternoon with doctors*; but in Washington, when all this began, that was Christopher's daily routine. Now, later on, he was in Houston (that famous fortress on the medical frontier), and it was doctors all day long.

*

Half a year earlier Christopher wrote about the 'notorious' five-stage theory of Elisabeth Kübler-Ross – denial, rage, bargaining, depression, acceptance – and said that it 'hasn't so far had much application to my case'. 'The *bargaining* stage, though,' he went on. 'Maybe there's a loophole here.' The oncology wager presents itself as follows:

> You stick around for a bit, but in return we are going to need some things from you. These things may include your taste buds, your ability to concentrate, your ability to digest, and the hair on your head. This certainly appears to be a reasonable trade.

That bargain took effect, and quickly too.

'It's not just the rug,' he said as he greeted me at the Wyoming in the autumn of 2010 – meaning his hair, already reduced to a few grey strands and clumps. 'When I shave the razor glides down my chops and meets no resistance. Now that would be a grave affront to my virility – if I still had any. That went at once. Eros, Little Keith, goes immediately. Thanatos thinks, Mm, I'll be having that.'

'Christ. But it'll return, O Hitch. Now you're all lovely and slim.'

'I've shed fourteen pounds – a whole stone. And I don't feel any lighter.'

'That's weird. You used to say you felt lighter when you lost fourteen ounces.'

'I know. It's as if the tumour's made of . . . What's one down from a black hole? Or one up. When the collapse isn't so catastrophic.'

'A uh, a neutron star. A speck of a neutron star is heavier than a battleship.'

'That's the stuff. The tumour's made of neutrons.'

'Yeah, but you know, Hitch – this is *iatrogenic*. The result of medical treatment. It's not the disease that's doing it, it's the fucking doctors.'

'So far. Now – lunch. Where we'll talk about something less fucking *boring*.'

And at his favourite nearby restaurant, La Tomate (just down the slope from the Hilton where Reagan was shot), Christopher would now ask for a cushion – 'I haven't got an ass any more,' he'd explained. He was invariably feted in La Tomate, and the waiters had become almost rigidly attentive. And I realised that cancer sufferers, silently identified and singled out, wear a version of the Star. Singled out for respectful kindliness, and not for persecution; but they wear the Star. And hardly anyone recognised him in the street any more – or they did but they held back. Because he wore the Star . . .

Lunch with the Hitch was still lunch with the Hitch, in the sense that you got there around one, and left there while the place was filling up for dinner. His interest in food, never great, had now declined into indifference, but he drank his one or two Johnnie Blacks and his half a bottle of red wine ('sometimes more, never less' was his rule), and he talked with undiminished fluency and humour for six or seven hours – to such effect that it would be a sin, he said, not to round it off with some cognac.

Although I made no attempt whatever to match him in the daylight, it seems that I easily outdrank him after dusk. Pretty well every time I went to Union Station to get the train back to New York I was awed by the sheer desperation of my (compound) hangover. My hands would shake so violently that I often simply threw away the cigarette I was trying to roll and went within to buy a pack of Marlboros . . . For a few hours, then (and no longer), I would emulate my friend in gangrenousness. But my struggle would pass – but so would his, I truly and steadfastly believed.

Now, here in Texas, the neutrons that weighed him down were about to be attacked: powered by 250 million electron volts, a high dose of protons would be fired into his body at two-thirds of the speed of light, well over 100,000 miles per second. The protons would neutralise the neutrons and the patient would . . .

Make a full recovery. Denial, rage, bargaining, depression, acceptance. Looking back, it sometimes seems to me that I got off at the first stop and at once found satisfactory lodgings in Denial – and stayed there till the early afternoon of the very last day. Blind Denial, which wouldn't be at all out of character; but it proved to be slightly more complex than that.

Cadence, Trent, Brent, and the origins of the First World War

No word from anyone, so for an hour I strolled around among the billboards and parking lots of downtown Houston. And it had to be faced: I was an undocumented alien, like so many others down there, and very recently arrived. I was a stranger in a strange land.

As I was heading back into the hotel I paused in the forecourt for the usual ten-minute reason. Three discrete figures were warily converging at the taxi stand: a beautiful woman of about thirty, who was under four feet tall; a basketball player (a team of them had just checked in), inordinately long-limbed in navy-blue sweatshirt and sweatpants; and a man as four-cornered as a packing case, in a bouncer's charcoal suit, smoking, and then stretching out a burnished toecap and wiggling his leg with the fluidity of a dancer as he crushed the butt under his sole.

It was six-thirty. Time, I thought, to see what the hell was going on in the Lone Star Saloon. I stepped forward and paused as a stretch limousine streamed slowly by.

'Can I bum a cigarette?' said a voice from the street.

'Sure,' I said. 'But it's loose tobacco. Here, I'll roll one for you.'

'Thanks. But don't lick it,' he stipulated. 'Don't lick it. I'll lick it.'

In the Lone Star Saloon the lady said, 'So tell! Come on. Tell about Trent!'

The guy behind the teak counter said, '*I'm* Trent. You mean Brent. That's okay. People're always mixing us up.'

'*So* sorry, Trent. I meant Brent . . . I'm Cadence.' And she offered her hand.

'Cadence! An honour. Brent's told me all about you.'

'And Brent's told me all about *you.*'

Trent finished polishing a wine glass and slipped it into its slot. 'Brent? Well, Brent doesn't want to get his hopes up too much. But the signs are it's going to happen. You sense it, Cadence. You can sense when promotion's in the air.'

'Touch wood. So say!'

Cadence was a comfortably downy middle-aged blonde, softly swathed in fawn cashmere. She was one of those generous-hearted beings who, when staying in hotels and looking in on their cocktail lounges, develops a passionate interest in the welfare of certain members of the staff. Her interlocutor, Trent, cut a courtly figure in bow tie and ochre waistcoat. Two stools down from Cadence, and facing Trent, I sat slumped over a Coors Light; occasionally I stared without profit at my mobile phone . . . Swirling her rum–tonic in its ice, Cadence said,

'*Trent*. Don't keep me in suspenders! What's it going to be with Brent?'

'No one knows.' Trent added coyly, 'But possibly they're thinking Under Chef?'

'Under Chef?' Cadence frowned. 'Brent's a bartender. Can he cook?'

'Actually, Cadence, Under Chefs don't do a lot of cooking. They play more of an organisational role. On the other hand, he could make Catering Sales Coordinator?'

'Catering Sales Coordinator. Oh wow.'

I was back in the forecourt enjoying yet another fiery treat when my phone started to groan and throb. I was directed to a certain suite in 'the Tower'.

These reintroductions to Christopher's new world (always ominous and much previsualised): they usually began with the opening of a door. Usually the door opened inward or opened outward but this door split in two and opened sideways. And as I stepped from the elevator it was immediately clear that Christopher had moved on to another plane of distress. He was in the corridor that led to his rooms, reeling around on tiptoe as he struggled to contain it, to elongate himself and stay on top of it. A milky liquid burst upward from his mouth.

I embraced him (which these days I kept on reflexively doing). 'Don't worry,' I said. 'It's just a little accident. Don't worry.'

'The thing – the thing insists on getting out of me,' he said when he could.

'It's nothing, my dear. It's nothing.'

The sharply targeted weapon of proton treatment would begin on Monday. Today was Saturday, and the doctors had continued with the blunt instrument of chemotherapy, whereby 'you sit in a room with a set of other finalists', as Christopher put it, 'and kindly people bring a huge transparent bag of poison and plug it into your arm'. This is no metaphor: they transfuse quarts of 'intracellular poisons' – to inhibit 'milosis', or cell division. And the swarm of side effects includes, among much else, immunosuppression, anaemia, alopecia, impotence, fatigue, 'cognitive impairment', and (most dependably) the overpowering need to vomit.

Such had been the long afternoon of the Hitch. But now, in the hotel restaurant, he was giving a display of perfect equanimity (in the gaps between his uncomplaining visits to the bathroom), and paying affectionate and solicitous attentions to Blue and to their daughter Antonia (while rearranging the scraps of food he sometimes tried to swallow and keep down). Early on I lightly wondered,

'Has anyone noticed? On planes, they've started calling passengers customers.'

Blue, at least, had certainly noticed it, and thought it comical; and for a while we found some diversion in a word-replacement game of the kind we often played . . .

'"The passenger is always right." "Michelangelo Antonioni's sensitive study of alienation, *The Customer*". "He's an ugly passenger." "Only fools and customers drink at sea." "When you are –"'

'This won't work,' said Christopher. 'It's not subversive enough.'

I said, 'Mm. Insufficiently subversive. But why're they doing it? Who benefits?'

He said, 'Americans – that's who. You take it as an insult, Mart, but for an American it's a compliment. It's an upgrade.'

'How d'you work that one out? Jesus, I don't understand this goddamned country.'

'Well, here in the US, *passengers* might be freeloaders, you know, lying hippies and scrounging sleazebags. Whereas customers, with that discretionary income of theirs, are the lifeblood of the nation.'

'. . . All right. But doesn't it go against the grain of American euphemism? And uh, false gentility? Even in supermarkets they call us *guests*. Well here's one thing nobody'll ever say. *The plane crashed into Mount Fuji, with the loss of sixteen crew and just over three hundred customers.*'

'*The customers died instantly.* No. That *would* be subversive. If it kills you, I'd say – I'd say that once you're dead, you go back to being a passenger.'*

---

* A reasonable expectation, you might think. As it happens there were no fatalities on commercial US aircraft for almost ten years, beginning in 2009; but then in April 2018, on a flight from New York to Dallas, an engine exploded and a porthole window collapsed. Despite her fastened seatbelt, Mrs Jennifer Riordan (a youngish mother of two) was sucked out from the waist up and battered by debris before two men, a firefighter and 'a guy in a cowboy hat', managed to drag her back inside . . . A gruesome and freakish death, extraordinarily abrupt and arbitrary: a radical case of the instantaneous undeserved . . . 'This is a sad day,' intoned the CEO of Southwest Airlines, 'and our hearts go out to the family and loved ones of our deceased customer.'

The talk became general and familiar, and it went on being spirited. Looking back from seven years on, I see that there was some reason to be buoyant. The shadow was of course always there (the shadow on the negatives of Christopher's scans); but this weekend would mark the dethronement of that hated quackery, chemo, and the elevation in its place of radiotherapy in the futuristic form of the Proton Synchrotron. So we would put our faith, for now, in science fiction.

'That sad chemo,' I said. 'It feels antique. Like leeching.'

'Or like ritual sacrifice. Or like prayer.'

'Mm, like prayer.' The two of us were having a nightcap and a final smoke on a bench at the back entrance of the hotel. My body clock said 6 a.m., but I'd had a less tiring day than the Hitch. 'Months ago you were saying that it messed with your concentration.' And at dinner I noticed how he very slightly glazed over now and then, no doubt in suspicious communion with his viscera, just before disappearing for five or six minutes and then keenly returning and resuming. 'But you were great – you delighted the girls, and me too.'

He lifted a hand for silence and briskly threw up into the flower bed. He wiped his mouth and I said,

'You know how chemo got started? World War I. There were a couple of things about mustard gas that the medical boffins thought might be useful . . . Sorry, Hitch – let's get off anything medical.'

After a quiescence we drifted towards the summer of 1914 . . . Now I fancied I knew a thing or two about that, and I kept pace with him as we went through it – Franz Ferdinand murdered in Sarajevo in late June, the equivocations of Belgrade, the hardening of Vienna's position, Germany's assurance to Austria (known as the blank cheque), the Austrian ultimatum, the Russian mobilisation, the artillery of August . . .

All this had me sufficiently tested and stretched, but now Christopher said, 'Those were the precipitants. As for the *origins* . . .' And at that point I reached for my notebook and ballpoint.*

---

* For once I'd brought a notebook with me; it was the only time I ever made a written record *in situ*, and it was useful enough for the reconstruction of this particular exchange; but I'm glad I didn't make a habit of it. Many times I had seen and heard him, in public and on stage, 'opening up' to reveal no ordinary powers of retentiveness and mental orchestration. To have heard him performing – *in extremis*, with an audience of one – now feels like a peculiarly grievous privilege.

So: the savage regicide in Belgrade in 1903; the Austrian annexation of Bosnia and Herzegovina in 1908; the formation of the Serbian Black Hand (*Ujedinjenje ili smrt!* – 'Union or Death!') in 1911, and the Agadir Crisis four months later; the Italian attack on Libya in 1912; the gradual Ottoman retreat from Europe, and Germany's gradual displacement of England as the guardian of the Turkish Straits ('the Sublime Porte' being a permanent Russian obsession); the wild overestimation of Russian strength, fuelling German hastiness and fatalism . . .

'Of course,' he said, 'if you want to start nearer the beginning you'd have to go back to 1389.'

'1389?'

'1389, and the final humiliation of Serbian forces at the hands of the Turk. On the Field of Blackbirds in Kosovo.'

And I thought, If Hitch had time we could go all the way back to the beginning of everything – to Cain and Abel, to Adam and Eve.

'Kosovo Field. A wound in the Serbian psyche that Slobodan Milošević chose to reopen in 1989 in Kosovo, Little Keith – six hundred years later, to the day.'

Yes, or we could go forward. Through the Second World War, the Cold War, the Soviet invasion of Afghanistan, the end of Communism, September 11, the Iraq War, et cetera – all the way to where we were now (if we had time), sitting on a wooden bench at the back entrance of a Texan hotel in the third month of 2011.

During dinner Blue and I were briefly alone at the table and I said,

'The synchrotron – it doesn't hurt, right?'

'Not at the time . . . The truth is, they're nearly going to have to kill him to kill *it*.' She looked at me steadily. 'But he's an ox.'

I said, 'You're right. You're right. But he's an ox.'

Day of rest

Even the most dedicated Texan must see that the Lone Star is not a good name for an ambitious modern hotel. In fact the Lone Star was at least a four-star, and intensively money-absorbent, so my breakfasts there didn't last long: tea, juice, coffee, low-church anxiety precluding the twenty-dollar fruit platter, as well as the seventy-dollar eggs Benedict with smoked salmon and a celebratory glass of champagne . . .

Up in the Tower, Blue and Antonia, wearing white bathrobes and white slippers, moved swiftly past me – off to the spa for 'treatments' (non-invasive treatments – massage, pedicure). So I entered and made myself comfortable in the sitting room and waited for Christopher to stir. I noticed the extra bed, provided for Antonia, my god-daughter, whom I still thought of as a child, despite the recent memory of her driving us all out to an Indian restaurant in DC. She was sixteen but this is America.

Distant scouring and expectorating. As James Joyce put it: *Hoik!* . . . *Phthook!*

'I'm here,' I called out. 'But don't mind me.'

A pause, and then he called back, 'I may be some time.'

At length he appeared, in underpants and shirt; his calves, his thighs, had a whittled-down look; he clenched and reclenched his brow, trying to focus. Then he bent over the trolley and the mobile oven sent up by room service: coffee; a cautious bowl of porridge; a strip of bacon, a poached egg with hash browns; more coffee, sealed with a cigarette.

It was half an hour before noon on Christopher's day off.

'I'm feeling almost human,' he said wonderingly. 'I might even have a *Scotch* . . .'

Apart from the fact that he mixed his Johnnie Walker Black Label with Coca-Cola, as opposed to chilled Perrier water (no ice), this would have been the old pattern, the *status quo ante*, how it was before. And the normal pattern was a minimum of two American-sized whiskies starting at noon or a little earlier. Now they were English-sized whiskies, pub doubles, 'just a dirty glass', as he used to say . . .

Even when his intake was preternatural, even when lunch might last all day and dinner all night (and the interval between post-lunch wine and pre-dinner cocktails would be marked, not quite as often as not, by a hurried cup of tea), he never went to sleep unless he had produced 'at least a thousand words of printable copy' – without fail.

One evening in London in what must have been the spring of 1984, having varied his usual whiskies with the negronis I passed his way, Christopher was taken by me and Julia (who was pregnant with our first son, and therefore very continent) to a dancing party that might have qualified as a ball. The waiters were offering shot glasses of vodka, and Christopher and I went obediently from tray to tray. During the buffet dinner we both had about nineteen glasses of wine – nor, when they came, did we neglect the liqueurs, the Calvadoses, the Benedictines . . .

The expectant couple got home at about two. Three hours later, as I tried to balance on the *Medusa*'s raft of the bed, I heard Christopher let himself in. At about nine, during a spell of weary wakefulness, I heard Christopher let himself out, while a taxi rattled in the street – his destination, I knew, was a TV studio (where he assertively applied himself in the demanding company of Germaine Greer and Norman Mailer, and made a point of taunting Norman about his obsession with sodomy and homosexuality).*

'How are you feeling?' he asked me in the kitchen as he fixed himself a midday Johnnie Black.

'Truly dreadful. It's so bad I can't even smoke.'

He smiled with affectionate sadism and said, 'Mm. I don't get hangovers. Can't see the point of them.'

'The point of them, I suppose, is to make you vow you'll never drink again. Or at least to make you hold off for long enough to stay alive.'

'Try hair of the dog, Little Keith. Have a negroni. It's the best thing.'

'. . . Christ. Look at you. Sea breezes. You know, Hitch, you've got a naval constitution. Rum, bum, and baccy, and you fucking thrive on it. This morning. Did you get any sleep between when you got back and when you went out again?'

'No. I wrote a piece.'

'You wrote a *piece*?'

It took me a full minute to assimilate this. Then I got myself a beer and said,

'You know who you remind me of as a writer type? Anthony Burgess.' Christopher knew about my lunch with Burgess in Monaco, which made me seriously ill for three whole days and nights (and at six o'clock Burgess ordered a gin and tonic – as if to start all over again). 'And after that I bet I know what Burgess did. He went home and wrote

---

* Norman's answer was that his heterosexuality was so intense and impregnable that he was ideally placed to interpret its obverse. The story doesn't end there, of course, and Norman would strike back, saying in an interview that literary England was controlled by a gay cabal headed by Christopher Hitchens, Martin Amis, and Ian Hamilton. 'I think that's very unfair', said Christopher, 'to Ian Hamilton.'

a symphony and did all the housework and got back to his novel in progress. To you and him, it's just fuel.'

Blue had truth on her side. He's an ox.

Who's your worst-ever girlfriend?

We left the Lone Star and crossed the road and entered the mall. 'Over 30 Restaurants to Choose From,' said the sign. We chose Tex-Mex.

'Do you do this, Hitch?' I said. 'I think all men do it when they're turning sixty. I keep looking back on my uh – on how it went with women.'

'Oh yeah. Beginning at the beginning. And all the missed *chances* . . .'

'Missed chances are very bad. Still, I have to say I look back with broad satisfaction. Larkin must've looked back with horror. And what's the reason? Poets can pull.'

'Mm, remember Fleischer in *Humboldt's Gift*? He bangs on the girls' door and says, *Let me in. I'm a poet and I have a big cock.* Announcing his twin attractions.'

'Fleischer was overegging it. If you're a poet you don't need a big cock. You can look like Nosferatu and still pull. Poets get girls . . . A girl told me that. Not a poet.'

'Which girl?'

'Phoebe Phelps.'

'Ah. How is dear Phoebe? I'm sure no poets ever pulled her.'

'Well, definitely not when she was an escort girl. Poets can't afford escort girls. Or anything else. That's part of their spell.'

'Is it? I assumed poets got girls because they're supposed to be sensitive.'

'Not according to Phoebe. It's simpler than that. I can't quite remember. Something to do with female fairmindedness. Oddly enough. I can't quite . . .'

'Phoebe? Then she had hidden depths.'

'She was secretly . . . She read poets in secret. Or she read one poet.'

Christopher had with him a proof of Larkin's *Letters to Monica* (which he would review in the *Atlantic* in May; I had already reviewed *Letters to Monica* in the *Guardian*). My notebook records that Christopher decided on lentil soup and a BLT. It also records the following: *Hitch much quieter today (prospect of the synchrotron?). Making a visible effort not to seem too preoccupied. Like with Saul – found I was talking more.*

I tapped the cover of *Letters to Monica*. 'How're you finding it?'

He shrugged and said, 'I was expecting yet another layer of trex and mire. But so far it's not quite as dank as I'd feared.'

'It's pretty dank.'

Having ordered, they went out for a smoke. I said,

'The incidental stuff. Like their summer holidays. Sark. Mallaig. Poolewe. Who goes for a holiday on a crag in the North Sea? "Did you get my card from Pocklington?"'

'I've been to Pocklington.'

'You ought to be ashamed of yourself. Pocklington . . . But you like all that Middle England stuff that gives me the horrors.* And by Middle England I mean anywhere that's not in central London. Rustic towns, country houses, weekend cottages.'

'What could be more agreeable? You go for a long walk in the rain and then you drink yourself senseless in front of the fire.'

'. . . No, I'm touched by it – by the fact that you're touched by bourgeois yokels and their habitat. In *Hitch-22*, the rabbits on the lawn and all that. There *is* a kind of hick beauty there. And Larkin was its poet.'

'*And that will be England gone, The shadows, the meadows, the lanes . . .*'

'*The guildhalls, the carved choirs . . .*'

'*I just think it will happen, soon.*'

Two things were and would remain undiscussed. First, I wasn't going to tell Hitch about Phoebe and the Larkin complication (inactive for a while but quietly reignited by *Letters to Monica*); you think you keep no secrets from your closest friend, but no one tells anyone *everything*. Second, neither of us was likely to bring up the fact that Larkin died of

---

* From *Mortality*: 'I recently had to accept that I wasn't going to be able to attend my niece's wedding, in my old hometown and former university in Oxford. This depressed me for more than one reason, and an especially close friend inquired, "Is it that you're afraid that you'll never see England again?" As it happens he was exactly right to ask, and it had been precisely that which had been bothering me, but I was unreasonably shocked by his bluntness.' I wasn't that especially close friend (I think it was Ian McEwan). You see, it didn't occur to me that he would never see England again. Of course he would, when he was better.

oesophageal cancer at the age of sixty-three. And, for us, sixty-three was in plain sight – visible to the naked eye.

'With Monica,' I said when we were back at the table. '. . . Okay, here's a question for you. Who's your worst-ever girlfriend?'

'Mine? Worst in what sense?'

'You know, the least attractive and the most boring . . . Or put it this way. The least attractive, the most boring, the most embarrassing in company, the most garrulous, the most self-important, and the worst fuck. Because *that's* Monica.'

He said, 'You think? Maybe she was the best fuck. Look at the others.'

'No. Keep reading. Later on he says, *I can't tell whether you're feeling anything. You don't seem to like anything more than anything else* . . . That's not what you'd write to your best fuck. So go on – make a mental composite. Now. Imagine you went out with her, not for a week, not for six months, but for thirty-five years. Oh yeah, and this is a chick who votes Conservative. Confident and proud, she writes, of "my conservatism".'

'Christ.' For the first time he looked really shaken. '*My* conservatism.'

'Such was Monica. I last saw her in the uh, the early eighties. He brought her to dinner at Dad's. And I tell you, brother, I tell you, she was a real . . .'

'And so were all the others. Well I say *all*. All three or four of them.'

'He was a genteel poltroon – that's what I've come to think. Fastidious, prissy. He lacked courage, in all departments except poetry. Especially in the sack.'

'Is it . . . Do you *need* courage in the sack?'

'Have you come to the billet-doux where he says *all* sex is a form of male bullying – male "cruelty"? *Bending someone else to your will*, he says.'

'I don't think so. I'm on page . . . forty. I've skimmed ahead a bit. All those highminded excuses about his low sex drive.'

'Well it'll give you a twinge, this paragraph. There's no actual duress, but you can't help going through some of the same motions. You know – put your legs there. Flip over, darling. Now spin round . . . Decades ago I was in bed with Lily, uh, after the act, and she said, "Right. I'll show you what it's like being a girl." She's really strong, Lily, and she had me do the splits and hooked my feet round the back of my neck. All the time rutting breathily up against me. And it was certainly very forceful. And enlightening. And incredibly funny. I think I actually shat myself laughing . . . It's one of my most cherished memories.'

'He didn't have any cherished memories. Where's that bit? . . . Nothing *will be worth looking back on, I know that for certain.* For certain! *There will be nothing but remorse and regret for opportunities missed.* And he wrote that aged thirty-four.'

'Terrifying. I like looking back on my lovelife, and I'm sure you do too. But not everyone does. Maybe most people don't. The sexually unlucky, the sexually lonely. There's infinite misery in that.'

'How would you know? I mean, outside the crucible of your imagination. You've never been sexually lonely.'

'Oh yes I have. And a little goes a long way. And it was a lot, not a little. There was a whole year just before we became friends when I couldn't pull *anyone*. And you can feel all the yearning turn into bitterness. It's so corrosive, and so fast-acting. Your balance, your whole equilibrium . . . *Tina* got me out of that. When she was nineteen Tina rode into town and rescued me from Larkinland. If she hadn't I might still be there. Scowling at women and telling dirty jokes with a sick glint in my eye.'

'And if Tina hadn't intervened, you'd never have written about Stalin and Hitler.'

I said, 'Oi, that's a leap, isn't it? How d'you figure that?'

'What's that line in one of Julian's early novels? *How we are in the sack governs how we see the history of the world.* Or words to that effect.'

'I remember. Which sounds like a leap too, but there's definitely a connection.'

'And it might partly explain why Larkin never had a fucking word to say about the history of the world. His lovelife was a void, so he . . .'

'So he didn't know what the stakes were. Humanly. So he wasn't moved to speak.'

'Disgraceful, that. Or just pitifully stunted . . . You know what Trotsky called the Nazi–Soviet Pact? "The midnight of the twentieth century". But that's a good phrase for what followed – 1941 to '45. The midnight of the twentieth century.'

'. . . And we're midnight's children. But there's no reason why a poet should have strong views about it, or any views about it.'

'But you'd think they would.'

'Mm. Remember what Sebald said about the Holocaust? He said, as a dry aside, that no serious person ever thinks about anything else.'

'In that case, Little Keith,' said Christopher, 'we're serious about the history of the world. And does that mean we're serious in the sack?'

Chapter 3
Politics and the Bedroom

Not left wing enough

Is there a connection between your erotic life and the way you see history? And if there is, which of the two has precedence?

One day in 1974 I said, 'I don't understand you, Christopher Hitchens. Nadia, Nadia Lancaster goes and makes a pass – and you turn her down. Christ! Just like you did with Arabella West – and Lady Mab! Lady *Mab* . . .'

'I know. More lissom than any woman has the right to be. But that honking accent. She sounds as haughty, and inbred, as Princess Anne. It just puts me off.'

Christopher didn't make passes at girls; he waited for girls to make passes at him – and they did. The trouble was that they tended to be bluebloods.* He said,

'I think on some level it suffuses me with guilt. Nadia, Arabella, Lady Mab. Because if the arc of history holds true, in a couple of years I'll be stringing them all up.'

Oh, yes: the other revolution. He was smiling and so was I. 'Well then,' I said. 'Yet another reason to act now.'

'Ah. So you think I should sleep with Lady Mab *before* stringing her up. Or very soon after. Quick, lads, while she's warm . . . If I may say so, Mart, I find that typically uncouth.'

*

* 'You're upper class and you've got a very loud voice. Is it congenital?' I once asked an upper-class friend. 'Yes. It comes', he blared, 'from centuries of talking across very large rooms.' If upper-class girls were in the vanguard of the Sexual Revolution, which they were, it came from centuries of loudly asking for what they wanted and expecting to get it.

At some point in 1976 he said, 'Yes, but there's a catch. A drawback.'

'Now what?' The girl Christopher was having his doubts about, this time, was a young sociologist who wrote for the *New Statesman* (and when she delivered her pieces she was always asked to join us in the wine bar or the pub). Her name was Molly Jones. 'You won't be needing to string up Molly Jones. Her dad's a builder, so she's a uh, a hereditary proletarian. She's very nice and she looks very nice and she's very articulate and very good fun.'

'All true. And by the way she's subtly made it clear that she finds the Hitch not entirely repulsive. Still, there's an insufficiency in her.'

'And what's that?'

'She's not left wing enough . . . She's not *right* wing, it goes without saying. How many chicks do we know who're mad about flags and uniforms and squeaky black overcoats? She's not right wing, just insufficiently left.'

'So? . . . And I suppose you mean insufficiently Trotskyite.'

'Trotskyist.'

'Jesus. Trotskyist.'

'Only a Stalinist would call me Trotskyite.'

'What would a Stalinite call you? *Anyway*. I repeat my question. So? . . . She's attractive but insufficiently left. So? What's that got to do with anything?'

'Well, it's pretty basic. In the last election Molly voted Liberal. How do you laugh that one off?'

'That's not basic. What's basic about that?'

'You, you can respect incompatibility when it's physical. But every other kind of incompatibility, including political incompatibility, strikes you as footling.'

'That's right. Why drag all that stuff into the bedroom? Reaching the bedroom can be hard enough as it is. Why create another set of obstacles?'

'It's no use talking to you – you don't care what girls're like,' he said, 'as long as they're girls. That's dispositive. It settles it.'

'Hang on. I don't fancy *every* girl. Though they're nearly all fanciable once you get them to open up about themselves . . . There may be something in what you say. I just think, Let's get started and see how it goes.'

'Well, you would, wouldn't you. Because you've got no social conscience. That's the difference between us. I'm of that higher breed – those "to whom the miseries of the world Are misery, and will not let them rest". Keats, Little Keith.'

Inconceivable

In the late 1970s Christopher got started with Anna Wintour. The affair began with unrestrained elation (out together, they looked like the principals in the all-solving scene of a romantic comedy); so some friends and onlookers were powerfully surprised when things began to cool (when, it seemed, Christopher began to cool). I was not powerfully surprised – nor powerfully disappointed, I have to admit. Anna was the first Hitch girlfriend who aroused envy in me; and Envy is cruelly self-punitive, like the other Deadly Sins (very much including Anger, but with the admittedly unreliable exception of Lust).

So when they broke up I was relieved to be rid of it – of envy, and its skein of wasteful resentments. I also felt the pressure of an unsolved mystery. At the time, Anna told me not very much about the breakup, and Christopher told me nothing at all. But I thought I knew where the fault line lay. Not class: unlike Lady Mab, Anna wasn't provocatively high-born (in the shorthand of the day she was upper-middle). I assumed, then, that it was politics, or the absence of politics – as with Molly Jones. Anna at that stage was simply innocent of politics.

In his autobiography, *Interesting Times* (2003), the brilliant – and in my experience entirely amiable – Marxist historian Eric Hobsbawm wrote that, as a young man looking to settle down, marriage to a non-Communist was 'inconceivable'. (Eric secured his CP bride when he was twenty-six, in 1943; and they divorced in 1951.) But I continued to wonder at that adjective: *inconceivable* ('incapable of being imagined or grasped'). So they do exist: people for whom love is not blind; in their case, love is a keen-eyed commissar. Or maybe they are left wing in their very loins.

The young Hobsbawm (certainly), and the young Hitchens (arguably), would have been reluctant to get involved with the young Hilly, a mere Labour activist (who scandalised our Welsh neighbours in the 1950s not only by driving a car but by using it to ferry voters to the polls). Still, the taint was there: Hilly's parents were moneyed provincial bohemians (folk dancing, Esperanto, madrigals), and she had a tiny but lifelong private income (and I myself, along with my siblings and my innumerable cousins, inherited £1,000 on my twenty-first birthday).

In Princeton, New Jersey, in 1958, Hilly said to me,

'The thing is, the Republicans are . . . Is that warm enough? Or too hot?'

'Mum, I'll adjust it.' I could bathe myself by then (I was nine), but this was a shower: the first shower of my life. Earlier that week we had disembarked from the *Queen Mary* in New York Harbor . . . 'The Republicans are what?'

'In America, Mart, the Republicans are like the Tories. And the Democrats are like Labour. So we're for the Democrats.'

'. . . Yeah. We don't want to be for the *Tories*.'

'Definitely not.'

And her middle child never forgot that and, as it turned out, never strayed from it. I became a quietly constant ameliorative gradualist of the centre-left.*

'Did you have any luck last night?' I asked Christopher in the noonday pub. 'I mean sexually?'

'Yes.'

It was 1978 and we were in Blackpool, attending a Party Conference. He was there as a representative of the *Daily Express*, and I was there, with James Fenton, as a representative of the *New Statesman* (to which Christopher would return in 1979). The night before, I had left him in the bar of his hotel, the Imperial, at around twelve-thirty and walked with James to our rude boarding house on the outskirts of town, with its gravy-dinner smells and ticking deathwatch beetles . . .

I said, 'Who with?'

First breathing in, Christopher said grimly, 'I got off with the deputy treasurer of the Uxbridge Young Conservative Association.'

'. . . You lucky bastard. What was she like?'

'It was a bloke, actually.'

I thought about this. 'So then what?'

'Well. I kicked him out halfway through. Dah. I'm never going near that again.'

'You haven't gone near it in ages. You must've been drunker than I thought.'

'I was. I was as drunk as you've ever seen me.'

---

* So I never felt any correlation between politics and the bedroom. Come to think of it, though, my romantic CV was much more leftward than Christopher's. Nearly all the girlfriends of my later teens and early twenties were blue collar, and I was an internationalist too, courting a Ceylonese, an Iranian, a Pakistani, three West Indians, and a mixed-race South African who could *pass* in Johannesburg but not in Cape Town (her name was Jasmine Fortune, and she was by my side for six months; her usual endearment, very endearingly, was not 'honey' or 'sugar' but 'cookie') . . . Only about half of these multicultural involvements were consummated. Perrin, originally from Karachi, was a soulmate and we were close, but it never went beyond a single kiss – her first. Melody, originally from Antigua, was the telephonist at the *Statesman*. We had three dates. One night, when we were canoodling on the sofa at my flat, she seemed to snap out of herself and then she said soberly (of her often-mentioned long-term Antiguan boyfriend, who was religious, as was Melody), 'Joey'd never believe this. He wouldn't – even if I told him . . . He'd have to *see* it.'

'You hardly ever *look* drunk.' And he hardly ever looked hungover; but he looked hungover now, pressing against his brow the little tumbler of Bell's whisky with its two or three shreds of ice. 'What class was this Young Conservative?'

'Oh, the pits. Minor public-school with pretensions. He sounded the *t* in *often*.'

'Mm,' I said. 'Okay, he was a bloke and he can't help that, but it's certainly not a plus that he was a Young Conservative. Old Conservatives are bad enough, but young Conservatives . . .'

'Agreed. The pits.' Christopher assessed me with friendly exasperation. 'But if the deputy treasurer of the Uxbridge Young Conservative Association had been a *girl*, then no doubt you'd've been proud to make her acquaintance.'

'Uh, yeah. As long as she didn't actually goose-step into the bedroom . . . Did you hear the Thatcher speech?'

'I was there. Oh, she's a jade and a wanton. The sexual power of her.'

'But isn't she insufficiently left wing?'*

Almost thirty years later he rang me from the Wyoming in Washington DC, and asked for ideas about the title for his imminent autobiography, saying,

'I want it to point to the dual nature of the Hitch. You know, the business about the two sets of books. A socialist and, withal, a bit of a socialite.'

An hour later I rang him back and said, 'I came up with fuck all, I'm afraid. Just some dull play on the divided self.'

'What d'you think of this? *Hitch-22*.'

'. . . I think that's truly brilliant.'

---

* 'I was mad about him,' Anna told me, when the two of us had a Christopher-themed dinner in 2018. 'And he was mad about you,' I told her, 'and I never heard him say a less than reverent word about you – ever.' . . . Anna was inclined to pooh-pooh the notion that the cooling off had a political cause. She thought it had more to do with his general frenetic busyness (the fact that he was so in demand), and perhaps his sexual indeterminacies (which incidentally he never sought to hide; and as far as I could tell they were a thing of the past by 1980). Anna was not in the least resentful. She seemed on balance happy to have had her time with the Hitch, and she went down to spend more time with him, in Houston, just before he died.

'My dear Mart . . . I'm going to clear it with Erica Heller, just in case.'

'I've been meaning to ask you,' I said. 'What've you done about the chicks?'

'There's nothing about the chicks, just a bit each about the wives. Nothing about the chicks. No Jeannie. No Bridget. No Anna.'

'No Anna?'

'No chicks.'

Anna was upper middle, yet her voice was as pleasingly accentless as that of the Hitch himself; her face brimmed with freshness and generosity of spirit; and, as if that wasn't enough, she had a figure that belonged, not to the Olive Oyls of fashion, but to the shapely heroines of Hollywood. And don't forget that under-celebrated ingredient of allure, which is cheerfulness – which is happiness.

. . . Happiness, as a source of beauty. This somewhat tragic theory came over me slowly and much later on, after I'd taken my younger daughters to and from school a few thousand times. In the first year the girlchildren were almost without exception magical to look at. In the third year there was a significant minority whose eyes had lost much of their light (prideful fathers, angry mothers?). And by the fifth year a kind of apartheid had taken hold: the division between the happy and the not so happy, I came to think – as well as between the appealing and the not so appealing . . . Oh, this subject is as fiendishly complex as death. Which comes first? Are they happy because they're appealing or are they appealing because they're happy? Or is it that you can't be one without the other?

Luxury

People think they are seeing it in the Leader of Her Majesty's Opposition, Jeremy Corbyn; but they are only seeing its wraith. I mean the hard revolutionary left, which was Christopher's proper home. To belong there you needed three characteristics: a) fire, b) dogmatism, and c) humourlessness. Corbyn had hardly any a), but he had b), and he had c) in sumptuous profusion. Hitchens, on the other hand, had plenty of a) and quite enough b), but no c) whatever. It was as well that he was a divided self.

He developed this commitment independently, at school, through thought and reading. And as a very young man he paid all his dues: demonstrations (often violent), fistfights and exchanges of concrete missiles with enemy cadres, multiple arrests, occasional imprisonments. During his time at Oxford an average day

> might include leafleting or selling the *Socialist Worker* outside a car plant in the morning, then spray-painting pro-Vietcong graffiti on the walls, and arguing vehemently with Communists and Social Democrats or rival groups of Trotskyists long into the night.

And at Oxford he would continue to 'hope and work for the downfall of capitalism' – and the establishment of the socialist tomorrow.*

* And doing so with such a will that he 'neglected his studies', as the saying goes. In fact he did no work at all. Having bluffed and blustered his way through Finals (nine three-hour exams in the same week), Christopher was summoned to a viva – a supplementary interview. This meant he was on the margin between one grade and another. 'I thought the innate brilliance of the Hitch had somehow shone through,' he later told me, 'and I was being viva'd for a First. After a few minutes – "Mr Hitchens, does the year 1066 ring any kind of bell?" – I realised I was being viva'd for a *degree*.' He was not on the margin between a First and a Second. He was on the margin between a Third and a Fail. Like Fenton (like Auden), he got a Third.

This was in his Chris/Christopher period. In the daytime Chris might get himself roughed up by scabs on a picket line, but in the evening Christopher would slip into a dinner jacket (to address 'the Oxford Union debating society under the rules of parliamentary order'), and then go on to All Souls College,* where he would teasingly enthral a coterie of reactionary old queens (A. L. Rowse, Maurice Bowra, John Sparrow, et al.). Hitch called this 'keeping two sets of books'. In other words he was a romantic incendiary who also enjoyed the ambience of the beau monde.†

In general, Christopher chose not to avail himself of the new carnal freedoms of his era. The promiscuity that most of us were going in for he found . . . somehow not serious enough. There was I think a further scruple, less paradoxical than it at first seems, because he was someone in whom many cultural and historical strands combined. And one of those strands had to do with religion – or its residue.

Among the best things in *Hitch-22* is the description of the funeral of the author's father, the laconically Conservative and low-church Eric Hitchens. It was a very English occasion: the hilltop, the extreme cold, the 'misty churchyard' overlooking Portsmouth Harbour and the sweep of the Channel, the 'Navy Hymn', the 'gaunt Hampshire faces' ('these distant kinsmen gave a hasty clasp of the hand and faded back into the

---

* All Souls – rich, venerable, studentless. I ate there once, as a guest of Philip Larkin, who stayed a couple of terms as a visiting fellow in 1970 when he was editing *The Oxford Book of Twentieth-Century English Verse*. 'Today I read *all* of Alan Bold,' he said as he greeted me, referring to one of the many poets he omitted. 'And *all* of Alan Bold's no good.' The next year he would complete one of his greatest poems, 'Livings: I, II, III', which includes this evocation of All Souls (where the high-tabletalk is parodied with the technique of a light-verse maestro): 'Tonight we dine without the Master / (Nocturnal vapours do not please); / The port goes round so much the faster, / Topics are raised with no less ease – / Which advowson looks the fairest, / What the wood from Snape will fetch, / Names for *pudendum mulieris*, / Why is Judas like Jack Ketch?' ('Livings': III).
† So opening himself up to being called, among many alliterative variants (e.g., 'a limousine leftie'), 'a Bollinger Bolshevik'. Such were the phrases that wealthy right-wingers, between mouthfuls of Bollinger, used to think was enough to settle the hash of left-wingers who hypocritically failed to confine themselves to cheap drinks from the national cellar (Bristol Cream, barley wine, and room-temperature bitter). By this logic, your gustatory style had to conform to your politics – a remarkably undemanding task for a plutocrat.

chalky landscape'): all of it was 'stark enough to have pleased my father', and notable for the 'absence of fuss'. And then:

> I suddenly remembered the most contemptuous word I had ever heard the old man utter. Discovering me lying in the bath with a cigarette, a book, and a perilously perched glass [. . .], he almost barked, 'What is this? Luxury?' That this was another word for sin, drawn from the repertory of antique Calvinism, I immediately understood.

Hedonism was luxury. Anna in herself, in her physical person, was luxury. She was opulent, high church, sweet tooth.

After the collapse of Communism (1989), Christopher conceded that politics and religion in the twentieth century had got themselves weirdly intertwined. In my opinion that date also marks the birth of the Hitch as a writer.*

Utopianism is not the same thing as religion, but it is the same size, in the given individual. The two narratives are alike visionary, teleological (aimed at an *end*), and millenarian, and their followers have the same kind of temperament. Aggressively secular, the socialist utopians among them easily dispensed with the supernatural; but they certainly couldn't do without faith.

With them, politics engaged all the most intimate energies. The struggle went without sleep, it was consuming and immanent. With them, it wasn't a matter of letting politics into the bedroom. Politics was already there: wearing flannel pyjamas, and moodily recumbent on the faded patchwork quilt.

---

* It was an opinion that annoyed him, understandably, because it questioned everything he'd written before 1989. This much he conceded: 'It's a relief not to have to go on raising my scarred dukes to defend Trotsky' (though he went on defending – championing – Trotsky, in private and in public, for a further twenty years). What he didn't accept was my conviction that writing insists on freedom, absolute freedom, including freedom from all ideology.

Chapter 4
Hitchens Stays On in Houston

The synchrotron

The machine that was about to engulf him weighed nearly 200 tons.

On Monday morning Christopher, Blue, and I went by cab to the MD Anderson Proton Therapy Center. With its sleek surfaces and its tubular atrium, the place felt like the future – or like the very slightly dated future of the cinematic crystal ball. You thought of Kubrick's *2001*; and the synchrotron itself shared the heavy curves of the Enforcement Droid (ED 209) in Paul Verhoeven's *RoboCop*. This was also a future of padded footsteps and discreet whispers and inflexibly hopeful smiles . . .

'Are you claustrophobic, Hitch? I suppose they must've asked you that.'

'They did, and I'm not. Well, I was claustrophobic in North Carolina, but there I was trussed and hooded.'

'Also smothered and drowned.' In the spring of 2008 Christopher arranged to be waterboarded (by veterans of the Special Forces. See below). 'And those geezers weren't doing it for your health.'

'True, Little Keith,' he said, and without hesitation he readied himself for bombardment, removing the top half of his hospital smock. Christopher was always a rejectionist when it came to the beach or the swimming pool, and I realised that I hadn't seen him stripped to the waist for over thirty years – that time he danced topless, rather solemnly, at an incredibly drunken party in about 1975. Slimmed down by illness, his torso looked quite unchanged. The flesh was pale and marked by target crosses, true, but it touched me to see that the great tree-shaped thatch of shag on his chest* had largely survived the assault on his body hair, though parts of it had been 'shaved off for various hospital incisions'. He climbed on to the shelf or platform and the technician slid him in like someone closing a kitchen drawer . . . This technician would remain in touch (through a video link), but Christopher would otherwise be incommunicado for around an hour. I turned to Blue.

'Well?' I said as I reached for my Golden Virginia.

She hesitated, she frowned, she shrugged, she stood.

On our way out we paused in an alcove near the main entrance: this was the relatively sepulchral area reserved for framed photos and thankyou letters, plus engravings and plaques, sent by the Chosen – i.e., ex-patients. *Without you we, every morning when I, each time my husband smiles he.* This was meant to be encouraging: here were the sweepstake winners, the survivors, the saved, and in the MD Anderson promotional videos you could see them jogging and mountaineering and windsurfing and of course euphorically gambolling and snuggling with their families. I reviewed these beaming faces and their rapt descriptions of family treats and feasts with, I realised, an impatience that was moving slowly towards animus. Was there a quantity theory of cure – as the statistics certainly led you to believe? If so, then here were the spoilers, here were the roadhogs and me-firsters who squandered the good luck that so rightfully belonged to my friend.

The two of us went outside and lit up. Indifferent to alcohol, Blue was still passionately interested in tobacco. Old smoking campaigners, we stared in silence at the ups and downs of the Tumortown roofscape . . .

In the twenty-first century the average metropolitan hospital already does an excellent imitation of an airport, the signposted access roads, the medium-rise car parks (SHORT STAY, LONG STAY), the configured terminals and the buses shuttling between them. In Houston you very soon submit to the notion that the hospital was imitating not an airport but a city – and with equally startling success. The hospital is the size of Houston, no, it actually *is* Houston, with its administrative centres, its

---

* Described by him, without much exaggeration, as 'the toast of two continents', this was familiarly known as 'the pelt of the Hitch'. It insulated him so thoroughly that he seldom wore a sweater, let alone an overcoat, even in the cruellest winters.

gardens and malls, all the way out to the rest homes and recuperation dorms in its infinitely proliferating windblown suburbs.

. . . Escorted by Blue, Christopher smirkingly emerged. I asked him, 'Did it hurt?'

'Did what hurt? I couldn't even feel it,' he said. 'So I just had a restorative doze and then it was over.'

With some panache Christopher presented his care team with a bottle of champagne, and 'hopped', as he would later write, 'almost nimbly into a taxi'.

'The pain comes later. Or so we're told,' said Blue as we drove on to our next appointment.

In another district, another ward of the city, staked out on another flat surface, Christopher was being introduced to another oncologist.

'Forgive me if I don't stand up.'

'Oh, don't worry! . . . Our idea, now, is to catch the tumour off its guard. We suspect it's getting complacent. We've held off with the chemo for a while, so if we . . .'

As the three of us got ready to move on, Hitch said,

'More chemo. Fuck. You know, doctors take these things personally, so they personalise the tumours.'

And there was at least some solace in the fact that Christopher's tumour was considered both slow-witted and self-satisfied. But why personalise it, I thought – this thing of death, why grant it life?

'I wonder', he said, 'if they give the tumours names – you know, nicknames, pet names. Like Flip or Rover.'

. . . Much, much later the same day (long after dusk), in a shadowy warren of curtained cubicles, Christopher settled himself down on yet another flat white surface while a compassionate Filipina, breathing her soft breath, hooked him up to the two sacs of transparent fluid that ponderously dangled overhead – one containing nutrients, the other containing poisons . . . I had claimed the last watch: Blue, I hoped, was already asleep at the Lone Star, and her husband, too, was half curling up and murmuring about aches and pains – gut, shoulder . . .

All day I'd been casting about for a handful of parting words. Keeping my voice low but light (looking for the tone of a bedtime story or a prose lullaby), I said,

'You love what you call "the imagery of struggle", Hitch, but you don't feel you're in a fight, you don't feel you're "battling" anything. You feel "swamped with passivity, dissolving like a" – what was it? – "like a sugar lump in water". Now think how you've spent the last fifteen hours. That's a fight, by Christ. And you're still the Hitch, still utterly yourself, and *that's* a struggle, and it isn't just imagery. You're doing it. And it looks and feels like a battle to me . . . Now rest. Rest, O rest, perturbèd spirit.'

He slept. After a while I smoothed him and kissed him and, as instructed, left behind me on the bedside table a skeleton staff of cigarettes.

All the medical facilities in Houston have their own cab ranks, waiting for the next malignancy to come staggering out of the shadows. The lead driver inched forward and gave a conspiratorial wink of his lights. I held up a hand with fingers splayed. Five minutes would be needed – for a smoke, naturally, and also for the assimilation of pity, or sorrow, or sheer emptiness, which was how it took me, comparable, perhaps, to the sudden loss of faith in God or in Utopia, leaving you on a hopelessly soiled planet in a hopelessly soiled cosmos. My body remembered the times when late at night I used to leave my younger boy in the Peter Pan Ward of St Mary's in West London, fighting his breathlessness, when he was three.

I stepped towards the taxi while behind my back, behind the closed curtain, Christopher, like Gus, dreamed and drowsed. Lay your sleeping head, my love.

Rabbitism

The day before, on that placid Sunday afternoon, I sat reading in the Hitchenses' suite while Christopher applied himself to his desktop and his scattered mail. *I wonder*, he said, leaning back, *I wonder when I'll run out of* money . . .

You are, let us say, a citizen of the United Kingdom. And in your late forties you notice, with some sourness, how much of your social time is spent listening – or remaining silent – while your elders talk about health and its maintenance, about diet advisories and exercise regimes, about diagnoses and prognoses, about treatments, about surgical interventions, et cetera, et cetera. All this goes on for year after year after year until at a certain point – in your mid-fifties – you find that the health chat no longer sounds like a snore in another room. Is this mere habituation? No. The ugly truth is that you've started to find it all rather interesting. Mortality, when it's close enough to reveal its lineaments, turns out to be rather *interesting* . . .

Then, aged sixty-two (let us say), you emigrate from the United Kingdom to the United States. The conversation continues, but its terms have changed, and not subtly. Act V is what they're talking about in Great Britain (attitudes to it, mental strategies for it). In America they're talking about income-pegged tax credits, prefunded savings accounts, variable caps and ceilings for employer-provided 'plans', co-pay options, higher or lower deductibles, and out-of-pocket additionals . . . In the old country they seldom talk about the healthcare system – because it is free; in the new country they talk incessantly about the healthcare system – because it plays a part in about two-thirds of all individual bankruptcies.

While we were moving from Camden Town, London, to Cobble Hill, Brooklyn, there was much to do:* and Elena did almost all of it. At the outset she made it clear that by far the greatest obstacle we would face – the most time-consuming and labour-intensive, the most tediously labyrinthine, and the most extortionate – had to do with American healthcare. One afternoon I gingerly looked into it; and after an hour or two I thought, Well at least there'll be no ambiguity in our case: if any Amis gets so much as a headache or a nosebleed, it will be far simpler and thriftier for the four of us to fly first class to London, take a limousine each to the Savoy, and then, the next day, wander into one or another outlet of the NHS.

Stateside – and you learn all this by anecdote, atmosphere, and osmosis – adults of all ages imagine and anticipate illness or injury with a two-tier queasiness wholly unknown in Britain (and in all the other developed democracies except South Africa). On the question

---

* Before, during, and after my stay in Texas, 5 Regent's Park Road continued to denude itself of furniture. The house seemed well aware that we were forsaking it; the rooms, the gap-toothed bookcases, the stairs, the passages (even the garden) looked increasingly hurt and strained . . .

of healthcare, as on the question of guns, facts and figures lose their normal powers of suasion. It is no cause for embarrassment when the World Health Organization ranks America thirty-seventh in quality of service; and it may even be a point of pride that America comes a clear first, besting all rivals, in cost per capita.* On this question America will go on failing to put two and two together, and for a little clutch of very American reasons.

In the days leading up to the passage of Obamacare (the Affordable Care Act of 2010), I listened on the radio to 'a town hall'. 'I happen to be an American,' said a woman in the audience, her voice yodelling and hiccuping with emotion, 'and I *don't* want to live in a country like the Soviet Union!' Or, she might have said, a country (at last) beginning (at least) to emulate Canada, Australia, and all the constituent states of the EU. But in the US saying 'like Europe', or 'like England', or 'like France', or 'like Switzerland', is the rough equivalent of saying 'like the Soviet Union' – which disappeared for ever in 1991.

A marginally better-phrased version of the same distaste was put to me by John Updike, in the panoramic setting of Mass. Gen., or Massachusetts General Hospital, in Boston (the year was 1987). In the pre-interview chat I was absorbing the sight of hundreds of Updike's compatriots (and rough contemporaries) milling about the place in search of bargains (or good buys or sweet deals) on longevity, and I couldn't help saying,

'Look at them. Well, it's a shameful spectacle. To my eyes.'

'It's our system,' he said. 'Anything else would be unAmerican.'

Which was a tautology, as any truthful answer on this matter is bound to be.

It was not the highly individualised boho Updike who talked to me about healthcare in Mass. General; it was the lumpen bohunk Updike, the Rabbit Angstrom side of Updike – which is certainly there and is also the reason the Rabbit novels (particularly volumes three and four)

---

* You feel like a crazy professor for saying so, but the US spends about a fifth of its GDP on healthcare, while Sweden spends about a twelfth; and in life expectancy America comes in just behind Costa Rica. Here, free healthcare is never called 'free healthcare'; it is superstitiously known as 'the single-payer system' – where the single payer turns out to be the government. 'Free healthcare' doesn't sit well on the native tongue. It would confuse the sleep of a fully monetised society; every American subliminally accepts that, in the land of the free, absolutely nothing at all should be free of charge.

are so good and so inner. But Rabbit was saying what almost all Americans say, or whisper: the more you earn, the longer you deserve to live.* For-profit healthcare is such an obvious moral and economic fiasco that only ideology – in the form of inherited and unexamined beliefs – could possibly explain its survival.

Rabbitism is especially strident on the healthcare question because the basic aversion is to spending money on the poor – who, it is felt, got that way through moral unregeneracy. This was the prevalent view in mid-nineteenth-century England, and clarifies the meaning of Bumble the Beadle's repeated references (in *Oliver Twist*) to 'them wicious paupers'. Bumble, one of the vilest characters in all Dickens, hates and fears the poor – because he can so vividly see himself among them. But in America everyone hates and fears the poor, even the very rich.

An individualist, a libertarian, and a credulous believer in the underlying wisdom of the market, Uncle Sam, don't forget, is also a Puritan. Good, rich, clean-living Americans want to punish the unregenerate – as they would want to punish their own vulnerabilities, temptations, and nostalgias. The violent hypocrisy of *them wicious paupers* is of course an extreme manifestation of the urge. And perhaps Dickens, in creating Bumble, had in mind an even more savage exemplar.

---

* In the course of the (mainly literary) interview that followed I effusively praised 'The City', Updike's long short story about a man falling very ill on a business trip. Years later it occurred to me that Updike on American health had affinities with Gogol on Russian serfdom: as citizens they might have seemed to accept it, but as artists they rejected it *tout à fait*. See *Dead Souls*; and see 'The City' and much else, including Rabbit's lengthy hospitalisations . . . The theme of literary self-contradiction – meaning differences between the conscious and subconcious mind – cries out for a monograph. Dickens, in his 'editorial' voice, championed incarceration for bad language and flogging for bigamy, and approved the practice of strapping mutinous sepoys to the mouths of artillery pieces and firing cannonballs through them. All these positions are undermined by his fiction – and not just his fiction: in *American Notes*, Dickens (who elsewhere denounced black suffrage as 'a melancholy absurdity') writes hauntingly about passing from free territory into slave states, and declares that the ambient deformation is palpable in the very physiognomies of the whites . . . Updike, too, was capable of giving his inner hick access to the typewriter. In his memoir *Self-Consciousness*, the chapter called 'On Not Being a Dove' (i.e., on being a hawk on Vietnam) is unreconstructed – and self-pitying – Rabbit: 'It was all very well for civilised little countries like Sweden and Canada to tut-tut in the shade of our nuclear umbrella and welcome our deserters and draft-evaders, but the US had nobody to hide behind.' Updike continues this strophe by dully repeating, word for word, the number-one herd-think justification for prolonging the war: 'Credibility must be maintained.' Which is a dismal cliché even among bureaucrats.

This is from *Lear* – from one of the mad hero's great visionary fits
of perception in Act 4:

> Thou rascal beadle, hold thy bloody hand.
> Why dost thou lash that whore? Strip thine own back.
> Thou hotly lust'st to use her in that kind
> For which thou whipp'st her.

Then Lear continues, penetrating yet further:

> Through tattered clothes great vices do appear;
> Robes and furred gowns hide all. Plate sin with gold
> And the strong lance of justice hurtless breaks.
> Arm it in rags, a pigmy's straw doth pierce it.

With a groan he threw down his pen and sat back sharply . . .

'All agree', said Christopher, 'that paperwork is the bane of
Tumortown.'

'Yes, and everywhere else in America that has a hospital. Or a doctor.
In New York I went to get my ears sluiced and they handed me a ten-
page questionnaire.'

'They're just covering their asses,' he said, opening another bill. 'I
wonder when I'll run out of *money* . . .'

Christopher Hitchens was a bestselling author and a highly paid
columnist, with the unqualified support of a thriving magazine (and its
famously bountiful editor, Graydon Carter); he also had full insurance.
Yet there he was at his desk (in a gap between radio and chemo) with
a stack of mail and a chequebook, wondering when he'd run out of
money.*

I said, 'You're an American, Hitch.' True, as of 2007. 'And for now
you're a sick American. So you're not just a patient. You're a customer.
But you won't run out of money.' True again; the synchrotron treatment,
whose starting price (I'd learnt) was close to $200,000, would be duly
covered. 'You'll just worry about it. Money.'

---

* When I did some research into HIV/AIDS, in the early 1990s, an activist lawyer
told me that many sufferers were advised to render themselves sufficiently indigent to
qualify for federal assistance (Medicaid) – a process known as *spend down*.

It wasn't the time to elaborate on this, but I wanted to say, *American healthcare feels like an assault. Hasn't anyone here realised that money worries are bad for you? Bad* for your health? *Doesn't this partly explain why Americans don't live that long? Shelling it out while not bringing it in – the doublesqueeze of US healthcare* . . .

'What's bothering you', I said, 'is the enforced inactivity. It's the work ethic of the Hitch. You're not producing your thousand words per day, and you feel – what's that Larkin line? – you feel you've been pushed to the side of your own life.'

There was a lull; shadows moved. And I found myself telling Christopher everything about the Larkin complication and Phoebe Phelps.

Brent: life goes on

'Hi.'

'Hi. Who the hell are you? I'm sorry.'

'Grant. I'm sorry too, but who the hell are you?'

'Cadence. Grant, do you know what happened with Brent?'

'I'm just filling in here, Cadence. Who's Brent?'

'Jesus. Well where's Trent?'

Now about to take my leave, I realised I was at home in Houston; I knew how it went here. Grant was probably all right, and Trent and Brent were probably all right. And Cadence was apparently all right, for now. But her husband was not all right: a day or two ago, in the forecourt, I saw him being stretchered out of a hearselike limousine while Cadence looked fearfully on . . . Everyone in the bar was probably sick, or was at least the spouse or child or parent or sibling of someone who was sick. It was a developed local fact – like the staggering array of wheelchairs waiting like city bikes in Arrivals at Miami Airport.

'Trent's on at nine.'

'*Nine?* What's it now?'

'Six. Five after.'

'. . . I won't make it. I'll have a ministroke at the very least . . .'

In the Houston Center, with over thirty restaurants to choose from, Christopher chose the Hong Kong Cookery; and its ambience of neon lights and paper hats and party tooters suffused in us a mood that was no doubt quite common in Tumortown (and other warzones): the eerie euphoria of adversity.

That night Christopher wore the expression that his loved ones loved best. Blue called it 'his foxy face', crafty, greedy; to me it spoke of witty insubordination; and our friend Ian was not alone in maintaining that this particular smile went all the way back to his schooldays. 'Hitchens,' the masters kept telling him, 'take that look off your face!' From his memoir:

> 'Hitchens, report yourself at once to the study!'
> 'Report myself for what, sir?'
> 'Don't make it worse for yourself, Hitchens, you know perfectly well.'

It was a look nicely suited to (artful) protestations of innocence, while in reality giving flesh to the phrase *no whit abashed*. It was the look of a boy who (despite a regime of cold showers, caning, and prayers – with nothing private, and everything either compulsory or forbidden): a boy who is putting together an articulate, subversive, and indomitable inner life.

Oh, keep that look on your face, Hitchens. And don't ever take it off.

'Trent!'

'Cadence!'

My bags were packed, my goodbyes were said, my bill was paid; and I was having a final jolt in the Lone Star Saloon before heading off to George H. W. Bush Intercontinental – while also hoping, I admit, to hear tell of Brent.

'I talked with "Grant",' said Cadence, 'who didn't know squat. *Well?*'

'With Brent? Okay. Now take a deep breath, Cadence. Ready?'

'Ready. Catering Sales Coordinator? Under Chef?'

'Neither . . . *Banquets.*'

'Banquets,' Cadence whispered. 'Oh wow.' She sighed, and blinked tensely, squeezing two teardrops out of the corners of her eyes. 'I love to hear that.'

'Yep. Executive Comptroller of Banquets . . . Now easy, Cadence.'

'Oh I love to *feel* that. In this God-awful town. Oh I love to feel that. I just do.'

With my wheelie at my side I went into the fresh air. And for a moment I thought the hotel's fire alarm was out of service, and in American accordance with American regulations all the guests had been evicted from their rooms and sent outside (to sleep like tramps on the subway vents). No. It was just a queue for cabs – multitudinous but fast-flowing; nor did this massed exodus fail to include the basketballer (with four or five of his equally extensile teammates), the wonderfully pretty dwarf, and the cuboid bodyguard, stylishly wiggling his leg as he ground out a butt with a twirl of his shoe.

Escape velocity

What was it Cadence loved to hear, what was it she loved to feel?

As I tightened the belt round a gutful of relief, pity, guilt, and hope (and more than hope: belief), I knew what Cadence meant – and I felt what Cadence felt. Grateful submission to the force that wakes you up in the morning, lifts you to your feet, and impels you outwards into the world; the return of time and motion; the shaking off of thwartedness. Cadence loved what Christopher loved – life, life, which so famously *goes on* . . .

The plane pushed back, made its stately two-point turn, cruised forward in search of the exit chute – then lowered its head and began its desperate sprint. Escape velocity, lift-off, climb.

There he was aimed – at the stripped house on Regent's Park Road, where life, London life, was withering away. The work of resumption and renewal would need to be done here, in America.

And now the customers in their seats could gaze down from on high at the customers in their beds – fellow denizens of the strange land.

Chapter 5
And say why it never worked for me

'Now you can't ever ask her,' Elena had said one morning out of the blue, in 2010.

It was a few days after Hilly's death, so Martin could easily fill in the spaces: *Now you can't ever ask your mother if by any chance Philip Larkin knocked her up in December 1948.*

'That's right,' he said. And he was glad. It was the only solace he would ever get from his orphanhood. 'Now I can't ever ask her.'

———————

The book in your hands calls itself a novel – and it is a novel, I maintain.

So I want to assure the reader that everything that follows in this chapter is verifiably *non-fiction*.

The doll on the mantelpiece

1. 'Germany will win this war like a dose of salts, and if that gets me into gaol, a bloody good job too.' Philip Larkin, December 1940 (aged nineteen).

2. 'If there is any new life in the world today, it is in Germany. True, it's a vicious and blood-brutal kind of affair – the new shoots are rather like bayonets . . . Germany has revolted back too far, into the other extremes. But I think they have many valuable new habits. Otherwise how could D.H.L.* be called Fascist?' July 1942.

* D. H. Lawrence. What if anything does PL mean by this sentence? He means, I suppose, that if Lawrence ('so good I daren't really read him') can be called a fascist, then fascism must have its points. Was Lawrence a fascist? See below.

3. 'Externally, I believe we must "win the war". I dislike Germans and I dislike Nazis, at least what I've heard of them. But I don't think it will do any good.' January 1943 (aged twenty-one).

These sentences, notable for their moral defeatism (disguised in the first quote as gruff immunity to illusion), their ignorance, and their incuriosity, come from the early pages of the *Selected Letters of Philip Larkin* (1991). So here we confront a youth turning twenty who 'dislikes' Nazis (or at least what he's heard of them). By January 1943 he might have heard of what we now call the Holocaust ('probably the greatest mass slaughter in history', as the *New York Times* reported in June 1942). Did he hear of it later on? Neither in his correspondence nor in his public writings is there a single reference to the Holocaust – not one, in his entire life.*

Philip's father, Sydney Larkin, OBE, who somehow acquired a reputation for intellectual rigour, was a self-styled 'Conservative Anarchist'; he was also a zealous Germanophile. He went on being pro-German even after September 1939 – and even after November 1940, and even after VE Day in May 1945 . . . In November 1940 more than 400 German bombers descended on Sydney's hometown of Coventry, destroying the city centre, where he worked (as a senior municipal accountant), the fifteenth-century cathedral, nine aircraft factories, and much else; the raid wounded 865 and killed 380. The Luftwaffe raids began in August 1940 and continued until August 1942 (with a final death toll of over 1,200). And Sydney went on being pro-German.

Before the war, in 1936 and again in 1937, Sydney took his only son along with him on one of his regular pilgrimages to the Reich: consecutive summer holidays, the first in Königswinter and Wernigerode, the second in Kreuznach (so both trips saw a rare omission for Syd: no Nuremberg Rally, with its 140,000 kindred souls). As Philip wrote, much later (in 1980), when the facts of Sydney's affiliation were about to be drawn attention to in a PL *Festschrift*:

---

* There *is* a lone mention of Stalinism. It was forced out of him when that 'old bore' Robert Conquest sent him his 'whacking great book on Stalin's purges' (this is an allusion to its size). Conquest's book was the seminal, consciousness-shifting study, *The Great Terror* (1968). In his thankyou letter for the free copy, PL managed the following (this is an allusion to the Kremlin leadership): 'Grim crowd they sound . . .' And that was all – ever.

On the question of my father and so on, I do think it would be better to say 'He was an admirer of contemporary Germany, not excluding its politics.' In fact he was a lover of Germany, really batty about the place.

Nowhere is it written that Sydney was an anti-Semite.* But how could it have been otherwise, for an admirer of the politics of Nazi Germany?

One wonders what else he liked about the place. A serious and compulsive reader (with a particular affection for Thomas Hardy, on whom he once gave a public lecture), Sydney was not in any ordinary sense a philistine; and he would have felt the weight and glamour of German literature and German thought.

But the Third Reich immediately presented itself as a regime of book-burners. Old Syd lamely admired Germany's 'efficiency' and its 'office methods' (in fact the Nazi administration was always drowning in chaos). Did these supposed pluses outweigh the Reichstag Fire terror, the Jewish boycott, the gangsterish purge of the Brownshirts, the Nuremberg Laws, the state-led pogrom known as Kristallnacht, the rapes of Czechoslovakia and Poland, and the Second World War?

Although the discriminatory legislation was already in place, the summer of 1936 – when *père et fils* paid their maiden visit – saw a brief intermission for Germany's Jews. It was the year of the Berlin Olympics; and so the country Potemkinised itself for the occasion. Formerly there had been printed or painted signs, in hotels and restaurants and suchlike (NO JEWS OR DOGS) but also on the approach roads of various towns and villages, saying JEWS NOT WELCOME HERE. These were tastefully removed for the Games (the first ever to be televised). Afterwards, of course, the signs were re-emplaced.

It is said that Sydney had on his Coventry mantelpiece a moustachioed figurine which, at the touch of a button, gave the familiar salute. There was evidently nothing in the fascist spirit that Sydney didn't warm to: the menacing pageantry, the sweaty togetherness (he

---

* Or not until recently – with the publication in 2018 of Larkin's *Letters Home*, edited and introduced at illuminating length by James Booth. Here we learn that Sydney was indeed 'crudely anti-Semitic'. During the post-war revelations he never 'acknowledged Nazi barbarism', turning his guns, rather, on the Nuremberg Trials.

'liked the jolly singing in the beer cellars'), the puerile kitsch of the doll in the living room.

A sense of danger, a queer, *bristling* feeling of uncanny danger

In a diary entry for October 1934 Thomas Mann praised the 'admirably insightful letter by Lawrence, about Germany and its return to barbarism – [written] when Hitler was hardly even heard of . . .' D. H. Lawrence's 'Letter from Germany' was published, posthumously, in the *New Statesman*; but it was written six years earlier, in 1928, when the author was forty-two (and already dying).

Now Lawrence harboured many deplorable opinions and prejudices, including a cheaply unexamined strain of anti-Semitism: 'I hate Jews,' he wrote in a business letter; and even in the fiction Jewry is his automatic figure for cupidity and sharp practice. Indeed, the critic John Carey, in his essay 'D. H. Lawrence's Doctrine', concludes: 'the final paradox of Lawrence's thought is that, separated from his . . . wonderfully articulate being, it becomes the philosophy of any thug or moron.'

But that articulacy, that penetration, could sometimes approach the miraculous. Lawrence spoke German and was married to a German (Frieda von Richthofen); and he had a real grasp of the central divide in German modernity: the divide between the tug to the west and the tug to the east, between 'civilisation' and 'culture', between progressivism and reaction, between democracy and dictatorship (for a retrospective, see Michael Burleigh's *Germany Turns Eastwards*). Sydney went there in the late 1930s and had no sense that anything was wrong – at a time when most visitors found its militarised somnambulism 'terrifying'. Lawrence went there in 1928 and showed us what the human antennae are capable of:

> It is as if the life had retreated eastward. As if the German life were slowly ebbing away from contact with western Europe, ebbing to the deserts of the east . . . The moment you are in Germany, you know. It feels empty, and, somehow menacing . . .

[Germany] is very different from what it was two and a half years ago [1926], when I was here. Then it was still open to Europe. Then it still looked to Europe, for a sort of reconciliation. Now that is over. The inevitable, mysterious barrier, and the great leaning of the German spirit is once more eastward, towards Tartary.

. . . Returning yet again to the destructive East, that produced Atilla . . . But at night you feel strange things stirring in the darkness, strange feelings stirring out of their still-unconquered Black Forest. You stiffen your backbone and listen to the night. There is a sense of danger . . . Out of the very air comes a sense of danger, a queer, *bristling* feeling of uncanny danger.

1928, not 1933. Not 1939, and not 1940 – by which time the exiled historian Sebastian Haffner was writing *Germany: Jekyll and Hyde*, where he came to the following conclusion:

This point must be grasped because otherwise nothing can be understood. And all partial acquaintance is worthless and misleading unless it is thoroughly digested and absorbed. It is this: *Nazism is no ideology but a magic formula which attracts a definite type of men. It is a form of 'characterology' not ideology. To be a Nazi means to be a type of human being.*

And the National Socialist *Weltanschauung* 'has no other aim than to collect and rear this species': 'Those who, without pretext, can torture and beat, hunt and murder, are expected to gather together and be bound by the iron chain of common crime . . .'

And this is the ethos Sydney Larkin 'admired' or was 'really batty about'; this is the ethos his son cautiously 'disliked'.

And yet Philip Larkin, despite the crash in his reputation when the *Letters* and the Life came out ('racism', 'misogyny'), would deservedly – and inevitably – emerge as 'Britain's best-loved poet since the war'. It was a war, by the way, in which he played no part. In December 1941 PL was summoned to his medical. According to Andrew Motion, he 'made no secret of his hopes that he would fail'. And he did fail. Eyesight.

The PL of this period – a flashy dresser and a charismatic talent who for a while felt socially bold – was trying to sound insouciant; but

Eva, Philip, Sydney, Kitty

he was at all other times a sincere patriot, and so he felt humbled and unmanned and above all confused. Floundering and posturing to the last, showing every attribute of youth except physical courage (and now seeking safety in numbers), PL wrote, 'I was fundamentally – like the rest of my friends – uninterested in the war.'

Like the rest of his friends? Did he mean the ones who were in the army? Kingsley, for instance, who passed through France, Belgium, Holland, and Germany (in 1944–5), was interested in the war. For one thing he was interested in surviving it; and as a Communist as well as a

Britisher, he would have been ideologically and emotionally interested in winning it. (Kingsley was trained as an infantryman, but he was destined for the Signals and he never fired a shot.) In his version of *Machtpolitik*, KA hoped for the shoring up of Stalin. Now reread the three quotes with which this section began, and then try to evade the likelihood that PL hoped for the shoring up of Hitler.

Q: What could have steered the tremulous undergraduate into this morbid and forsaken cul-de-sac? A: Having a father like Sydney (and being very young).

When it was all so obvious. Even the most reactionary writer in the English canon, Evelyn Waugh, saw the elementary simplicity of September 1939. As Guy Crouchback, the hero of the WW2 trilogy *Sword of Honour*, puts it:

> He expected his country to go to war in a panic, for the wrong reasons or for no reason at all, with the wrong allies, in pitiful weakness. But now, splendidly, everything had become clear. The enemy at last was plain in view, huge and hateful, all disguise cast off . . . Whatever the outcome there was a place for him in that battle.

This much had long been clear to everybody: Naziism meant war (and for its enemies a just war par excellence). And, when war came, what type of young man would scorn a place in it – any place whatever?

Tyrants of mood don't hug and kiss

Sydney Larkin was 'unrepentant' about many things, including his views on women. 'Women are often dull, sometimes dangerous and always dishonourable' was a personal aphorism he cherrypicked for his diary. And this was another set of attitudes that his son, as a tyro adult, found himself dutifully echoing: 'All women are stupid beings'; they 'repel me inconceivably. They are shits.'

Larkin Sr made his daughter's 'life a misery', and over the years reduced his wife, Eva, to a martyred drizzle of anxiety and timorousness. 'My mother', PL wrote, 'is nervy, cowardly, obsessional, boring, grumbling, irritating, self pitying.' Sydney's life was short; Eva's was long. 'My mother,' PL resumed, decades later, 'not content with being motionless, deaf and speechless, is now going blind. That's what you get for not dying, you see.' Nevertheless, PL was thoroughgoingly filial, as we'll see.

In his office Sydney was always keen for a 'cuddle' with female subordinates, 'not missing an opportunity to put an arm round a secretary', as an assistant reminisced.* He was in addition the kind of patriarch, dourly typical of mid-century England, who set the emotional barometer for those around him — for all those within range.

As a child I had several friends with this kind of father. They were the mood tyrants. Brooding, frustrated, rancorous, intransigent, their will to power reduced to the mere furtherance of domestic unease. And these household gods all held sway over the same kind of household — the prized but intimidated sons, the warily self-effacing daughters, the mutely tiptoeing spouses, the cringeing, flinching pets . . .

Aged thirteen, after a weekend spent in the rain-lashed bungalow of just such a mood tyrant (the father of my best friend Robin), I cycled home to Madingley Road, Cambridge, parked my bike in one of the two outbuildings that housed our Alsatian, Nancy, and her recent litter, and our donkey, Debbie, then entered by the back door, stepping over one of our eldest cats, Minnie. Going in, I felt — I now suppose — like PL going out:

> When I try to tune into my childhood, the dominant emotions I pick up are, overwhelmingly, fear and boredom . . . I never left the house without the sense of walking into a cooler, cleaner, saner and pleasanter atmosphere.

But a happy child is no better than a gerbil or a goldfish when it comes to counting its blessings, and as I sauntered into the convivial kitchen I experienced no rush of gratitude towards my warmly humorous

---

* His workplace in City Hall was adorned with Nazi regalia — until the town clerk ordered him to get rid of it. We can just about imagine the scene: Sydney's bottom-pinching and nipple-twisting against a backdrop of swastikas and lightning bolts.

and high-spirited parents. I was home: that was all. I was in the place where – while it lasted – I was unthinkingly happy.

'They fuck you up, your mum and dad.' This is the most famous line in Larkin's corpus – partly, no doubt, because it was a near-universal tenet of the time (and seemed to be the starting point of all psychiatry). In principle Philip agreed that 'blaming one's parents' led nowhere, or rather led everywhere ('If one starts blaming one's parents, well, one never stops!'); but he went on:

> [Samuel] Butler said that anyone who was still worrying about his parents at 35 was a fool, but he certainly didn't forget them himself, and I think the influence they exert is enormous . . . What one doesn't learn from one's parents one never learns, or learns awkwardly, like a mining MP taking lessons in table manners or the middle aged Arnold Bennett learning to dance . . . I never remember my parents making a single spontaneous gesture of affection towards each other . . .

With PL, in any event, fondness failed to flow. 'I never got the hang of sex anyway,' he gauntly clarified in another letter to Monica Jones. 'If it were announced that all sex wd cease as from midnight on 31 December, my way of life wouldn't change at all.' That was written on December 15, 1954. 'Sexual intercourse began / In nineteen sixty-three,' runs Larkin's most famous couplet; but for him and Monica it was already withering away – in their early thirties. And yet they trundled on until 1985, when Philip died, aged sixty-three: his final *hommage* to Sydney.

PL never saw his parents hug and kiss. I and my siblings often saw our parents hug and kiss (and we responded with a mid-century version of what my younger daughters now say when they see their parents hug and kiss: 'Get a room'). But as I tittered, and blushed (blushed hotly and richly), a necessary transfusion was somehow taking place; I was seeing my mother and father as autonomous individuals, going through the rituals of their own affinity – their own affair. A child axiomatically needs to be the recipient of love; and a child also needs to witness it.

'I read your Larkin piece. Twice,' I said on the phone (New York–Washington, in the spring of 2011).* '*Full* of good things.' And I listed some of them. 'God, though, he's an impenetrable case, don't you find?'

'Oh, yeah. The poems, they're as clear as day, they're . . . pellucid, but humanly he's a labyrinth. You get lost in him.'

'That famous aside of his, you quote it – *deprivation is for me what daffodils were to Wordsworth.* So he liked deprivation because it stirred his muse.'

'Yes, and sometimes making you wonder whether he went looking for it.'

'But he means romantic deprivation. And how d'you go looking for that?'

'Especially when you've already got it. No one's *that* dedicated. And anyway, in this instance I'd say deprivation came from within.'

'You quote that other line he . . . Here it is. Sex is *always disappointing and often repulsive, like asking someone else to blow your own nose for you.* Blow your nose?'

'Blow your nose? Now there he shows real prowess of perversity.'

'You know, I get surer and surer that that's a big part of the Larkin fascination. The purity of the poems. And then the mystery story, the whodunnit of his – of his murk.'

'It's all Sydney, don't you think? That Komodo dragon in the living room.'

'Mm . . . Brother, we'll talk. Now. When are you getting here?'

'I'm aiming for Friday afternoon. Around drinks time.'

'What could be more agreeable?'

'Oh, tell me something. You miss the old country, I know. I don't expect to miss England but I'm sure I'll miss the English. It's that tone, that tone of humorous sympathy. Americans are nice too, individually, but you couldn't call them droll.'

'No. Tocqueville said that humour would be bred out of them by sheer diversity. Anything witty was bound to offend *someone*. He thought they'd reach the point where nobody'd dare say anything at all.'

---

* Christopher's essay on *Letters to Monica* had duly appeared in the *Atlantic* that May . . . This would be my last trip to the US as a visitor; thereafter I would be a resident. My friend was re-established at the Wyoming, and girding himself for the after-effects of his month in the synchrotron.

. . . This could wait for the weekend, but the Hitch was in fact under a serious misapprehension about Philip's father. He was right about the dragon in the living room: that was Sydney, a reliably unnerving man. What he got dead wrong was how Philip felt about him.

Every man is an island

During his time at Oxford (1940–3) Larkin briefly kept a dream journal, whose contents are summed up by Motion:

> Dreams in which he is in bed with men (friends in St John's [his college], a 'negro') outnumber dreams in which he is trying to seduce a woman, but the world in which these encounters occur is uniformly drab and disagreeable. Nazis, black dogs, excrement and underground rooms appear time and time again, and so do the figures of parents, aloof but omnipresent.

Excrement, black dogs – and Nazis . . . But as it happens Larkin's sexuality, seen from a safe distance, managed a reasonable imitation of normality. After a slow start, and many snubs and hurts, there was always a proven partner nearby, and we know a fair bit about what he got up to and with whom. All the same, the eros in him is still mysterious and very hard to infiltrate. It is indeed a maze, or a marshland with a few slippery handholds. And yet, as we wade through it all, we gratefully bear in mind that this – somehow or other – was Larkin's path to the poems.

To repeat: as a young man Larkin was intrigued, or better say fatally mesmerised, by the Yeatsian line about choosing between 'perfection of the life' and perfection 'of the work'. But that was a line in a poem ('The Choice'), not in a manifesto; no one was supposed to act on it (and Yeats certainly didn't). Larkin seized on the either/or notion, I think, as a highminded clearance for simply not bothering with the life, and settling instead for an unalloyed devotion to solitude and self. As he put it in 'Love' (1966): 'My life is for me. / As well ignore gravity.' Most crucially, the quest for artistic perfection coincided with his transcendent worldly goal – that of staying single.

'Sex is too good to share with anyone else,' Larkin half-joked, early on. Yet he found that the DIY approach to romance was always overcome by a prosaic need for female affection and support. And so there were lovers, five of them: Ruth, Monica, Patsy, Maeve, and Betty.* Larkin's affairs were not evenly spaced out over the thirty-odd years of his 'active life'. They came in two clusters: Monica overlapped with Ruth and Patsy, in the early 1950s, and she overlapped with Maeve and Betty, in the mid-1970s. This pair of triads represented the twin peaks of Larkin's libido, which was otherwise conveniently docile ('I am *not* a highly sexed person,' as he kept having to remind Monica).

Ruth was sixteen when he met her in 1945, 'a prim little small town girl', as she phrased it; two years later they became lovers and were briefly engaged. *Monica*, the mainstay, was an English don at Leicester (and we'll be spending an evening with her later on). *Patsy* was the only red squirrel in this clutch of grey Middle-Englanders; a highly educated poet and rather too thoroughgoing free spirit, Patsy died when she was forty-nine ('literally dead drunk', as PL noted). *Maeve*, a quasi-virgin of a certain age, a *faux naïf*, and a true Believer (who, post mortem, tried to enlist PL's godless spectre for the Catholic Church), was on the clerical staff at Hull. As was *Betty*, who, until Larkin made his sudden move, had been his wholly unpropositioned and unharassed secretary for the previous seventeen years.

Of the five, Betty had the considerable virtue of being 'always cheerful and tolerant': i.e., she was a good sport. Ruth, Patsy, Maeve, and overarchingly Monica were not good sports. According to my mother (and nothing in the ancillary literature contradicts her), these women were alike curiously unrelaxed and unrelaxing, oppressed – most likely – by class anxieties and inhibitions that we would now find merely arcane. In addition they all gave off a pulse of entitled yet obscurely injured merit, of vague and tetchy superiority – a superiority quite unconfirmed by achievement; Monica, a noisily opinionated academic all her adult life (but also a close reader, and now and then a trusted editor of Larkin's verse), never published a word . . .

---

* Or six, if you're inclined, as I was for a while, to believe Phoebe Phelps (whose candidate, my mother, would have come between Ruth and Monica). Phoebe can be doubted on optical grounds: if what she said was true, it would be as if Diana Dors had come bustling in on a singletons' knitting circle in somewhere like Nailsea. Anyway, the Hilly possibility is hereby dismissed.

Ruth Bowman

Monica Jones

Patsy Strang

Maeve Brennan

Betty Mackereth

Hilly Bardwell

As well as being rich and worldly (she studied at the Sorbonne) Patsy was artistic, and her prickliness took more highbrow form (Kingsley said she was 'the most uninterestingly unstable woman' he had ever met). Philip's liaison with her was manageable and brief (and he was touchingly grateful to have had it). But she scared the life out of him a decade later, drunkenly materialising in Hull – muzzy, weepy, utterly disorganised (wanting to stay the night and accusing him of 'not being continental') . . . As PL admitted, his women inclined towards the 'neurotic' and the 'difficult', and also the 'unattractive'. He summed them up himself, in four lines of wearily illusionless verse (quoted below).

Ruth, Patsy, Maeve, Betty – and Monica. His triangulations involved dramas, tears, scenes, twenty-page letters, and decathlons of guilt and reproach – more than enough grief, you'd have thought, to fuel a typical marriage. When Monica was told about Maeve she was physically sick, and soon lapsed into near-clinical depression. The best proof of how much his girlfriends meant to Larkin was his willingness to shoulder – or at least outwait – their episodes of suffering while he had his way.

All this was interspersed with a great deal of yearning, brooding, coveting, fuming, and dreaming, not to mention a great deal of 'wanking in digs' (as he put it to a ladyfriend). Larkin had an extra-strong passion for pornography and kept a cache of it in his office ('to wank to, or with, or at', as he put it to another ladyfriend). But he was far less blithe or brazen when he went foraging for the blue stuff in red-light London, no doubt because in Soho he was pursuing more specialised tastes (schoolgirls, flagellation). Often the size of the trespass overcrowed him; he would 'funk it', and just shuffle away.

The loss of nerve, the withdrawal: it gives us the flavour of the Larkin frustration and the Larkin thwartedness. With lowered head he slips out of the dark sex shop (the bachelors' bazaar) and into the rain, leaving that copy of *Swish* unmolested on its shelf as he creeps away, hugging to himself the familiar failure . . .

Invidia

In July 1959 Kingsley returned from an extended teaching job in America, and wrote to PL about his hyperactive success with the women of

Princeton, New Jersey. A few months later Philip completed 'Letter to a Friend About Girls' (which he never published). The 'friend' of the title is only approximately Kingsley, just as the narrator of the poem is only approximately Philip; but approximation can come very close. The poem begins:

> After comparing lives with you for years
> I see how I've been losing: all the while
> I've met a different gauge of girl from yours.
> Grant that, and all the rest makes sense as well:
> My mortification at your pushovers,
> Your mystification at my fecklessness –
> Everything proves we play in separate leagues.

More than once Kingsley said to Philip: it wasn't that they met different grades of girl; it was that they met *all* girls differently. They both had charm, but Kingsley's was the charm of confidence, and Philip's the charm of uncertainty; and it remains a maddening truth that both sexual success and sexual failure are steeply self-perpetuating. Philip knew all this, but in the poem the 'I' feigns ingenuousness, and evades the really embittering recognition: it wasn't a case of 'a different gauge of girl'; as Larkin acknowledged to Anthony Thwaite, it was a case of a different gauge of man. Still, the wretchedness he backs away from is quietly evoked.

Having listed some of the addressee's 'staggering skirmishes' with wives, students, and (it seems) passers-by, Philip goes on: 'And all the rest who beckon from that world . . . where to want / Is straightway to be wanted . . . A world where all nonsense is annulled, // And beauty is accepted slang for yes.' In honing that last line Larkin must have wondered what it was in himself that qualified as accepted slang for no.

There was another reason why Philip kept 'Letter to a Friend' in his bottom drawer. As he very reasonably wrote (again to Thwaite), 'it would hurt too many feelings'; 'If it were simply a marvellous poem, perhaps I might be callous, but it's not sufficiently good to be worth causing pain.' So it was only in 1988, with the publication of the rather overamplified – and of course posthumous – *Collected Poems*, that Ruth, Monica,

Maeve, and Betty came to read the following (note the resignedly slow rhythms of lines two to five), as the poet summons his women:

> But equally, haven't you noticed mine?
> They have their world, not much compared with yours,
> Where they work, and age, and put off men
> By being unattractive, or too shy,
> Or having morals – anyhow, none give in:
> Some of them go quite rigid with disgust
> At anything but marriage . . .
>   you mine away
> For months, both of you, till the collapse comes
> Into remorse, tears, and wondering why
> You ever start such boring barren games . . .

We can see why Philip was reduced to thinking that sex was too good to share with anyone else. Autoeroticism, for Larkin, wasn't just a stopgap, an improvised *faute de mieux*. It answered something fundamental not only in his life but also in the workings of his art. 'I *don't* want to take a girl out, and spend *circa* £5 when I can toss off in five minutes, free, and have the rest of the evening to myself.' And, as he wrote to his parents as early as 1947 (when Sydney was still alive), 'tonight I shall stay in and write. How beautiful life becomes when one's left alone!'

Something that might be described as 'positive' happened to Kingsley a year before he left for America. In response to it Philip wrote (to Patsy):

> [It] has had the obvious effect on me. I am a corpse eaten out with envy, impotence, failure, envy, boredom, sloth, snobbery, envy, incompetence, inefficiency, laziness, lechery, envy, fear, baldness, bad circulation, bitterness, bittiness, envy . . .

And what was this supposed coup of KA's? His 'appearance on Network 3 on jazz' – 'the first of six programmes', as Philip moodily adds.

If he felt that way about Network 3 (a radio subchannel devoted to hobbies), how would he feel about this? Just back from Princeton and his lucrative professorship in creative writing (July 1959), Kingsley writes to Philip and apologises for his year-long silence:

. . . I can plead that I wrote no more than four personal letters the whole time I was away . . . [and] that for the first half of my time there I was boozing and working harder than I have ever done since the Army, and that for the second half I was boozing and fucking harder than at any time at all. On the second count I found myself at it practically full-time.

By December of that year Philip had completed 'Letter to a Friend About Girls'.

'Empathy' is not as slimy a word as 'closure', but it still comes mincingly off the tongue. Even so, Kingsley, here, shows lack of empathy to an almost vicious degree; erotic success is a kind of wealth, after all, and here he is, fanning his wad at a pauper . . . As we turn to Philip we may say that envy is an offshoot of empathy: from L. *invidia*, from *invidere*, from *in-* 'into' and *videre* 'to see'. See into. Envy is negative empathy, it is empathy in the wrong place at the wrong time. Satisfyingly, too, 'envy' also derives from *invidere*, 'regard maliciously'. It is not surprising that PL, much of the time, hated KA.

By all means empathise with the less fortunate, and do so with every consideration. But be careful. Don't feel your way into the lives of the luckier. If you're Philip, don't 'see into' Lucky Jim.

We began with three snippets about politics; let's start winding up with three snippets about sex. The first comes from a letter to Monica, the second from a letter to Kingsley. To which of the two is the third letter addressed, would you say?

1. I think – though of course I am all for free love, advanced schools, & so on – someone might do a little research on some of the *inherent qualities* of sex – its *cruelty*, its *bullyingness*, for instance. It seems to me that *bending someone else to your will is the very stuff of sex* . . . And what's more, both sides *would sooner have it that way than not at all*. I wouldn't. And I suspect that means not that I can enjoy sex in my own quiet way but that I can't enjoy it at all. It's like rugby football: either you like kicking & being kicked, or your soul cringes away from the whole affair. There's no way of *quietly* enjoying rugby football. (1951)

2. Where's all this porn they talk about? . . . [In Hull] it's all been stamped out by the police with nothing better to do. It's like this permissive society they talk about: never permitted me anything as far as I recall. I mean like WATCHING SCHOOLGIRLS SUCK EACH OTHER OFF WHILE YOU WHIP THEM, or You know the trouble with old Phil is that he's never really grown up – just goes along the same old lines. Bit of a bore really. (1979)

3. It seems to me that what we have is a kind of homosexual relationship, disguised. Don't you think yourself there's something fishy about it? (1958)

In the first quote PL declares himself a sexual pacifist or vegan, and seems rather proud of his hypersensitivity (well 'I wouldn't'). In the second quote he gives a middleaged (and clearly very drunken) airing to his fantasy about caning schoolgirls, which dates back to his youth. The third quote appears in a letter to *Monica*. I've tried often, but I still don't understand it. What can it mean? That he, PL, wasn't very masculine and that she, MJ, wasn't very feminine? And that they were in-betweeners of the *same gender*?

Anyway, peculiar, eccentric, innovatory, without any known analogues – you might even call it *sui generis*.

In a late letter PL observed of the poetry critic Clive James, 'Just now and again he says something really penetrating: "originality is not an ingredient of poetry, it is poetry" – I've been feeling that for years.'

When poets go into their studies, they seek – or more exactly hope to receive – the original. Be original in your study. But not in your bedroom. It is like sanity: your hope, in these two departments, is to be derivative. You don't want to be out there all on your own.

Violence a long way back

In only one (very late) poem did Philip attempt an explanation of what we may call his erotic misalignment. It comes in the alarmingly gloves-off 'Love Again' (1979), which begins as a lyric of violent sexual jealousy – not sexual envy, sexual jealousy:

> Love again, wanking at ten past three
> (Surely he's taken her home by now?),
> The bedroom hot as a bakery . . .
> Someone else feeling her breasts . . .

But then just over halfway through this eighteen-liner the poet turns pointedly inward. 'Isolate rather this element', he soliloquises,

> That spreads through other lives like a tree
> And sways them on in a sort of sense
> And say why it never worked for me.
> Something to do with violence
> A long way back, and wrong rewards,
> And arrogant eternity.

The last three lines at first feel unyieldingly condensed. 'Arrogant eternity', we suppose, refers to the demands of art and to the brevity of the human span; 'wrong rewards', we suppose, refers to the haphazard allocation of luck, talent, sex, happiness, and (perhaps) literary recognition. But 'violence / A long way back'? Motion persuasively argues that PL is not referring to actual abuse but to the 'smothering nullity' of his parents' marriage: 'they showed him a universe of frustration [and] suppressed fury . . . which threatened him all his life, and which was indispensable to his genius.' All true; but I think we can go a little further than that.

In La Tomate off Dupont Circle I said (April 2011), 'You refer to Syd as Larkin's "detested father". Would it were so, O Hitch. That would've made for a much simpler story. But Philip loved him.'

'. . . Mart, you stagger me. That old cunt?'

'He loved and honoured that old cunt. It's all very fresh in my mind I'm afraid.'

'Mm, I suppose you know more about it than you want to know. Thanks to Phoebe.'

I sighed and said, 'I was having to think of Syd as my . . .'

'Christ, I do see . . . But there's nothing about Syd in *Letters to Monica*.'

'Just this – "O frigid inarticulate man!" So don't reproach yourself. It's all in the *Selected Letters* and the Life – twenty years ago. Get this.

When Syd died Larkin was so cut up he turned to the *Church*. Quote. "I am being instructed in the technique of religion"! And he describes his sessions with a twinkly old party called Leon.'

'When was this? How old was he?'

'Twenty-five. Quote, from Motion. *He had always looked up to his father, and they grew steadily closer. To lose him, Larkin thought, would be to lose part of himself.*'

'Christ. Well it was the part of himself he should've stomped into the gutter. Couldn't he see, couldn't he tell?'

'The day after the funeral he wrote, *I felt very proud of him*. Proud. And he started to write a fucking *elegy* for the old cunt.'

'Oh, where are they now, the great men of yore? Where the riding whip, where the jackboot? . . . Well all I can say is, It's amazing that the poems got out alive.'

The food came, and for the next hour we tried, with only partial success, to recite 'The Whitsun Weddings' (eighty lines); we did a little better with 'An Arundel Tomb' (forty-two).

'Something to do with violence / A long way back'. I think what we are seeing here is PL's unconscious mind (very tardily) beginning at least to register what he could never absorb. People can be violent non-kinetically; and Larkin Senior was an intensely violent man. Sebastian Haffner in 1940 identified the essence of National Socialism: it was a rallying cry for sadists. And Sydney heard that call.

How lastingly extraordinary it is. Larkin's fastidious soul was shaken by the Patsy visitation: 'it seemed a glimpse', he informed Monica, 'of another, more horrible world.' That world was bohemia, whose (sloppy but pacifistic) ethos repelled him all his life. As for the ethos of Bavaria and the Brown House and the Beer Hall Putsch – Larkin never seemed to mind that his father was a votary of the most organised and mechanised cult of violence the world has yet known . . .

'They fuck you up, your mum and dad, / They may not mean to, but they do.' Well, whether or not this dad meant to, here is a clear case of Mission Accomplished. As Philip's sister Kitty said after the cremation, 'We're nobody now. He did it all.'

*

Goodbye to the patriarchs, the little overlords, the goosers and gropers, the disseminators of disquiet, the wife crushers and daughter torturers, the fathers that everyone fears, the enemies of ease, the domestic totalitarians of the mid-twentieth century.

PART IV

PENULTIMATE

Preamble: The Fire on New Year's Eve

Now I suspect you wouldn't mind hearing a bit more about the fire, and of course I'll be glad to oblige. Not for the only time in these pages, a clear calamity leads to a relatively happy ending, one laid on by life, which moves in mysterious ways . . . 22 Strong Place didn't burn down – it burnt up. It was what they call a chimney fire.

A *chimney* fire? I thought chimneys were where fires were meant to be at home. Anyway, ours leaked. It had been leaking sparks for months . . .

It happened on New Year's Eve, remember, and it was all over by twelve. So – the fire was the farewell party thrown by 2016. First Brexit, then Trump, then no house and out on the street at midnight in midwinter.

Inez and I were there at the time, whereas . . . Hang on – some background. *We have a small house in West Palm Beach.* I can never say that without thinking of a cameo in Evelyn Waugh. Having introduced himself, a stranger on a train starts up a conversation with something like, *I have a small house in Antibes. Friends have been kind enough to say I have made it comfortable. The cook there, in his simple seaside way, is one of the best I have.*

There is no cook in West Palm, or anywhere else, but the fact remains that we have a small house in West Palm. And Nat and Gus were there for Christmas and it was great – reading by the pool all day and then noisy dinners in the soft warm air. Oh and most mornings Nat cycled off to Mar-a-Lago, to observe . . .

My wife and Eliza stayed on, but I came back to Brooklyn with Inez on December 31. We joined my younger brother, Jaime, my much younger half-brother, a whole generation younger, and his wife Isa.

She's Spanish and he's bilingual – he was born there. They'd spent the holiday in Thugz Mansion, and it was their first time in New York. And they'd had a thrilling week . . .

So the four of us, me and Inez, Jaime and Isa, were making a festive night of it. New Year's Eve. Drinks round the crackling hearth. And we were well into dinner when the doorbell rang.

It was a local posse. 'Look!' they said, pointing upwards. Cinders were streaming out of the cracked fifth-floor window. 911 had already been called.

There's a fleet of fire trucks pulling up outside the house, I told Elena on the phone. She seemed to be holding herself together, but poor Eliza was frantic, because it was happening in her room – all her clothes, all her drawings. I went up there with Jaime and it was just a sheet of asphyxiating white smoke.

That was the only dramatic part. Then came the only funny part. Elena rang back to say in a very calm and patient voice, *When the firemen come, could you ask them to take off their boots before they go upstairs?* She was thinking of her *runner* – the strip of carpet. She was in shock. I suppose we all were.

The firemen came. Ten huge Darth Vaders yelling, *GET OUTTA HERE! GET OUT! GO! GO! GO!* I got out, with the others. I didn't linger – didn't linger to ask them, in my ponciest English accent, to slip out of their boots. And up they stomped. We all got out and stood staring. Now there were *flames* up there. Flames up there like hyenas after a kill. So busy. So greedy. So much to do. So much to eat . . .

We spent the night as guests of kindly neighbours, Jaime and Isa across the road, Inez and I a couple of doors along. The two Amises had very temporarily joined the 60,000 homeless of New York City.

I know what you must be asking yourself. What's all this about a happy ending? Well it did come about. I can still feel its blessing, and I must gather such things to me, as I age, ever mindful of the destined mood . . .

Bright and early next morning we visited the scene. The FDNY, New York's Bravest, rightly so called, had to drown all those jackals – every last one of them. And quickly too – there were *babies* sleeping in numbers 20 and 24. So they strode to the top floor and humourlessly unleashed the regulation gigaton of water.

And yes, the fire was gone. But so was the house. Elena's precious runner, for example, was gone – and so were the banisters, the sidewalls, and the stairs.

Now as you're getting on in years, my reader, that kind of mishap can be conclusively discouraging. I'm certain, for example, that Kurt Vonnegut, having started a fire in his house – an ashtray fire – never recovered from it. In his *Letters* it's there as a totem. *Ever since the fire* . . . And it set the emotional tone of his Act V. I was uncharacteristically firm in my mind that we wouldn't get defeated by the fire. And we haven't been.

But the happy ending concerns Inez . . .

Now Inez, taking after me, is petite, is little. One day, aged fourteen or so, she stood in the hall in Strong Place and said, with adult clarity, 'What do I want? I want to *grow*.' You can imagine how helpless that made me feel. True helplessness – it's like finding yourself floating in water, without connection . . .

She was taken to a specialist who said she'd be lucky to reach five feet. Inez burst into tears. I'm glad I wasn't there for that (Elena was of course there for that). But I was there for much else. You see, I *know* short, I know all about being short. So I was rooting every day for Inez. I was her growth coach – I was with her every millimetre of her ascent to five feet. *You can do it, Bubba.* And she did it, she did do it.

'Now you're fine, you're safe,' I said at the impromptu party that developed on Sixty Inches Day. 'You made it.'

That was not very long ago. So I was hugely surprised when . . . Wait. Before we moved into my mother-in-law's place, we moved into my brother-in-law's place. Where we camped out under the January snows. Every day Elena returned to the dripping ruin of Strong Place, saving what she could. As seldom as I dared, I joined her, and stood in my study gathering scraps of paper and wringing out books.

So not a very festive time. And then one night, at the family table, Eliza nonchalantly revealed that *Inez had grown two more inches*.

I scraped my chair backwards and said, 'Two inches?'

'Not two inches,' said Inez. 'Two and a *half*.'

And for some reason no one had thought to tell me, me, the titch-in-chief, the oldtimer from Lilliput. And I was so glad I hadn't heard – because it was such overpowering news. Two and a half inches! When I was her age I'd hardly dare dream about two and a half inches.

It would've made me practically five foot *nine*. Even now my head spins . . .

And right then and there I thought, Fair enough! If God had said, *Inez will grow a bit more, but it'll cost you your house*, I'd've said, *Where do I sign?*

So that's my destined mood, maybe. Because something similar happened with regard to Hitch . . . My mother-in-law, Betty, is getting on for ninety years old, and at present she's in Battery Park at an assisted-living parlour called Brookdale and subtitled 'Senior Solutions'.

In a way that's an attractive American attitude (and selling point) – senior solutions. But it's a misnomer. Old age, as I'm coming to realise, is insoluble. There are *no* senior solutions. There *are* no senior solutions.

Christopher sought and found a senior solution. Only he wasn't a senior. He was sixty-two. Maybe that's it. Maybe you need to be comparatively junior, if you're going to find the senior solution.

Chapter 1
Christopher: Everyone Pray for Hitchens Day

'*Who else feels,*' I read out from the moist sheet of thin white paper on my lap, '*who else feels Christopher Hitchens getting terminal throat cancer was God's revenge for him using his voice to blaspheme him? Atheists like to ignore FACTS. They like to act like everything is a "coincidence". Really? It's just a "coincidence" [that] out of any part of his body Christopher Hitchens got cancer in the one part of his body he used for blasphemy? Yeah, keep on believing that, Atheists.*' I paused and Hitch said,

'As you may be starting to suspect, Mart, this chap isn't very bright.'

'I wondered . . . *Yeah, keep thinking that, Atheists. He's going to writhe in agony and pain and wither away to nothing and then die a horrible agonising death, and THEN comes the real fun, when he's sent to HELLFIRE forever to be tortured and set afire.*' I said, 'I'm beginning to see your point.'

'But at least he means well.'

'Also rather repetitive, wouldn't you say?'

'Mm. He plods through his premise. And then after he's done that, with that out of the way, he plods through it again. Besides, it isn't the only body part I've used for blasphemy.'

'. . . Sorry, Hitch, I don't get you. What other body parts?'

'Well, my dick, I suppose, and my brain and my tongue. But that's the least of it. Think what *sort* of god is being summoned. Literal-minded, thin-skinned, madly insecure, and wildly childish.'

'Especially childish . . . You know, when Nat wasn't quite two, I displeased him in some way, and he scowled at me fiercely as I left the room. A couple of minutes later I came back in – and he was astonished to see me.'

'That you'd survived. Because he'd wished you dead.'

'Dead or at least very fucked up. And there I was, bold as brass and still breathing, if you please. For about six months children think they're omnipotent.'*

'Boy children anyway. Alexander was like that, except he didn't want to use lightning bolts. He wanted to do the job himself. But not even children insist on being metronomically *praised*.'

I asked him, 'How would you feel, no, what would you think, if you got scanned in the morning and found you were miraculously cured. Miraculously.'

———————

This subsection is a flashback. Our talk about blasphemy took place in Washington DC, on Everyone Pray for Hitchens Day, which fell on September 20, 2010 (Houston and the synchrotron were still six months ahead of him).

Yes, Everyone Pray for Hitchens Day. So far as the religious community was concerned, the Christopher prognosis – made public that June – was the most newsworthy development in almost a decade. God hadn't had this kind of attention since September 11.

So Christopher at that point was on the receiving end of innumerable communications from the nation's churchgoers. And although a fraction of them were written by admirers and proponents of hellfire, the rest were expressions of solicitude – and love. One day earlier, in the hall, as I made my re-entry, he showed me some of it, or rather showed me some of the extent of it: hefty hardboard folders, in stacks. I said,

'That's the key thing about you, Hitch. You excite love.'

He said, 'My dear Little Keith . . .'

'Even among the puritans. Who don't know what a dirty little bastard you really are. But the love, Hitch – it's the key thing. When was an essayist last loved?'

* The godhead of boyhood doesn't last long: they grow out of it by the age of three. King Lear, whose infant delusion has been prolonged by the accident of kingship, is asked to grow out of it in his eighties. And he does. 'They flattered me like a dog . . . When the rain came to wet me once and the wind to make me chatter, when the thunder would not cease at my bidding, there I found 'em, there I smelt 'em out. Go to, they are not men o' their words: they told me I was everything; 'tis a lie . . .'

. . . Some correspondents said tenderly that they would refrain from praying for him (out of respect for his 'deepest convictions') and other correspondents said even more tenderly that they were going to pray for him anyway.

When two acquaintances, both of them evangelical clerics, reported that their congregations were praying for him, Christopher wrote back with the question: Praying, exactly, for what?

And of course it turned out that these letters weren't get-well-soon cards, or not in the normal sense. *We are, to be sure, concerned about your health, too, but that is a very secondary consideration.* While they'd be pleased enough if Christopher's body put itself right, their primary consideration was the fate of his soul.

Apart from all the religious (and all the secular) websites devoting themselves to the Hitch, a further online amenity encouraged you to place bets on whether or when he would lose his nerve – would crack, and hurriedly convert.

It was now nearly half past eleven. Hesitantly and of course drunkenly, I said,

'Put aside Pascal's Wager for now – Christ, how did *that* ever get itself capitalised? – and just think about Bohr's Tease.'*

It was five to twelve and Christopher said, 'If on the stroke of midnight I became cancer free I'd be overjoyed, but I wouldn't go down on my knees. I'd be delighted to thank a doctor. But I'm not saying *o gracias – aw, muchísimas gracias* – to no Nobodaddy.'

'. . . And anyway, prayer's so potent that it doesn't care if you don't believe in it.'

---

* Blaise Pascal's pitiful dates are 1623 to 1662 (far back enough for his Wager to sound challenging). He was a spiritual prevaricator, and a sickly one; and I don't know how well he was feeling when he put together his famous proposition. In it he argued that a rational (and presumably cynical) unbeliever, faced with the choice between God and godlessness, would in the end opt for God: if he wins the bet, he gains eternity in heaven as opposed to eternity in hell, and if he loses, the cost is nothing more than a minor sacrifice of some last-hour hedonism (and, we might add, a major sacrifice of last-hour dignity) . . . In a recent bulletin from the land of the sick Christopher had juxtaposed Pascal's Wager with Bohr's Tease – Niels Bohr, the Nobelist pioneer of the subatomic world. Bohr had a horseshoe suspended over his doorway; and when a fellow scientist incredulously asked him if he believed this would bring him good luck, Bohr answered: *No, of course I don't. But apparently it works whether you believe in it or not.*

'Still, it would be a very irritating coincidence . . . Our blogger friend – the Hellfire artist. If he thinks God awards the appropriate cancers, what does he make of childhood leukaemia? *They* haven't blasphemed, they haven't sinned. And they haven't spent forty-five years living like there's no tomorrow, let alone no eternity.'

Everyone Pray for Hitchens Day was a Monday. Christopher and his entourage were not especially disheartened to find him unrecovered on Tuesday morning.

At this point he was no longer living as if there was no tomorrow. He was still smoking and drinking (up to a point), and he was still eating, and he was still talking (all four habits would soon be in serious question). He was still writing his thousand words a day and he was still engaging in public debates. And he was still giving time to pundits and profilists: open a paper or a magazine, and there'd almost always be something about the Hitch.

Once or twice Christopher described these pieces as gun-jumping obituaries, but the ones I saw were careful to avoid the slightest suggestion of finality. His younger fans and followers, in particular, always signed off rousingly, with something like *If anyone can beat cancer, it's Hitchens* or *Up against Hitchens, cancer doesn't have a chance.* Although I approved and concurred, I could tell that these codas were to some degree expressions of hope – rhetorical hope.

My hope wasn't rhetorical. It was actual. Christopher, I was sure, would win his fight, whether anyone prayed for him or not. But I must have known – mustn't I? – that cancer at least had a chance.

Texas: Come again another day

The word went forth from the state house in Austin. Governor Rick Perry announced with no little pomp ('I do hereby proclaim') that April 22–24, 2011, Good Friday through Easter Sunday (Crucifixion through Resurrection), were to be known as the Days of Prayer for Rain . . .

It was a tense weekend for Christians. It was a tense weekend for atheists, too. And in our daily communications (between New York and Houston), Christopher and I had to admit that it was a tense weekend for Texans, after three months of drought, high winds, and no humidity, and with a million acres already on fire. We sympathised, semi-hypocritically, but the truth was we hoped for continued or even intensified dehydration: we wanted no April showers in Texas, not over Easter and not for at least a month or two after that. We wanted a decent interval so that no one could run away with the idea that the Prayer for Rain had actually worked.

I flew there on May 4; and the Lone Star state was incorrigibly parched.*

That night Hitch and I and Blue were settling down to dinner. Not in the Lone Star Hotel, and not in a party-hat Chinese restaurant, but on a broad lawn, attended to by loyal retainers and surrounded by fish ponds and fountains, statues and sculptures, flowers and bowers. And our hostess, Nina Zilkha (*née* Cornelia O'Leary), with her honeysuckle vowels, lent the occasion an antebellum air – the gracious South. Well, Texan Nina was gracious (and literary), but Texas itself, with its heritage of lawlessness, slavery, revolt, defeat, Jim Crow, big oil, packed churches, weekly death sentences, and its enduring thirst for secession?

Still, that evening it would have been quite reasonable to say (as Herzog said in the Berkshires), *Praise God* – in the sense of *praise nature*, or *praise life*. The Hitch was home from MDA. And on top of that we were looking forward to some harmless knockabout fun on TV: the first (of nine) Republican presidential debates.†

Meanwhile the plates of melon and prosciutto were being laid out, and the bottles of wine. And this spread must have seemed almost abstract to Christopher, who had been nil-by-mouth for some while. I looked his way. Downward-averted, his face expressed something I recognised, and with fellow feeling: unwelcome self-absorption. The causes and symptoms of it in me were usually idly psychological; but in Christopher, just now, they seemed to be of the body.

---

* In fact after Easter Sunday the crisis steadily worsened. At that point only about 16 per cent of Texas was affected; the figure would go on rising to about 70 per cent in mid-August. By then our sympathy for the South would be hypocritical no longer . . . The skies finally opened on October 9, almost six months after the Days of Prayer for Rain.

† At this stage in the primaries there were only five participants (and the last two were about to creep back into obscurity): Ron Paul, Herman Cain, Rick Santorum, Tom Pawlenty, and Gary Johnson. So no Mitt Romney, no Newt Gingrich, no Michele Bachmann, and no Rick Perry – not yet; but it was an encouraging start.

He couldn't eat, he couldn't drink – and not so long ago (though that was over now) he couldn't speak. What else couldn't he do?

Christopher suddenly raised his arm upright and we fell silent.

He said faintly, 'I can't . . .'

———————

That expanse of real estate – tended by six or seven gardeners – belonged to an old friend of Christopher's and mine, Michael Zilkha.* One of the many remarkable things about Michael, who is rich, left, and green (his business at the time was biofuel), is his habit of personally transporting you to and from the airport – a gallantry nowadays unthinkable even for newlyweds. The very first time I met him, at Anna Wintour's apartment in 1979, he ended up personally transporting me to JFK (for my return flight to London). And when I arrived at Bush Intercontinental on May 4, 2011, Michael was waiting outside Arrivals in his new electric car. That day he dropped me at the hospital and took my suitcase on to his guest house, where the Hitchenses were already installed . . .

At MD Anderson I rode up to the eighth floor, as instructed, and a passing orderly pointed to Christopher's room or wardlet. Which was empty. Returning to the central bay I asked the registrar.

'Sorry,' I said, thinking I must've misheard, '– he's gone where?'

'To the gym.'

'The *gym*?'

Hitch had never gone to a gym in his life (though I suppose they might have made him look in there once or twice at boarding school). Nowadays he would hardly know how to *say* the word 'gym' . . . In normal life Christopher was willing to take a long stroll now and then, a country walk with a pleasant destination in mind (a country pub, say),

———————

* The Zilkhas were originally a banking family based in Baghdad – something like the Rothschilds of Mesopotamia. I had always assumed that Selim Zilkha, Michael's father, had emigrated as a result of Iraqi anti-Semitism; but Michael has informed me, in his soft Oxonian tones, that Selim went into exile (his first stop was Lebanon) when he was forty days old, in 1927, during the British mandate (he came to the UK in 1960, and founded Mothercare). Iraqi Judaeophobia became proactive in the 1940s, with the rise of Zionism; and after the establishment of Israel it assumed the character of a semi-permanent pogrom. Indigenous since the sixth century BCE, the Jewish community numbered 130,000 in 1948; today there aren't enough Jews in Baghdad to form a *minyan*, for which the quorum is ten males over the age of thirteen.

but readers can rest assured that he never, ever, took any exercise for the sake of it – and in gyms that was all anybody did. Frowning, I said,

'What gym?'

'The hospital gym. In the elevator press minus one.'

On the way down I thought about the first wedding of the Hitch, when we all went to Cyprus. Hitch flew in, and so did friends and relations, and we stayed in a beachside Nicosia four-star (where the toilets in the public spaces were designated Othellos and Desdemonas). Christopher never went near the sea or even the pool – where I, along with others of his coterie or clan, lay bronzing myself between dips and lengths (and sets of tennis). Whenever he came near us out there, often wearing a dark two-piece suit (but no necktie), his stride was dismissively brisk: he was heading for the shaded outdoor bar to meet some journalist or terrorist or Greek Orthodox archbishop. The near-naked torsos on lilos and loungers – it was all distastefully frivolous to him, this business with the body and its lotions and unguents, its narcissism, its hubris . . .

'Well, Hitch,' I said as we embraced. 'Here you are in a gym.'

'I know. I'm doing this under orders but guess what, I'm feeling almost keen.'

Blue and I sat on a plastic bench and watched. The vast space was occupied not by unsmiling young strivers in T-shirts and sweatpants but by vague wanderers in light gowns and pyjamas, who moved among the various contraptions (rowing machine, punchbag) sceptically, like cautious shoppers. Among them Christopher cut a relatively dynamic figure, mounting a fixed bike and going at it with real will and evident pleasure, his pale, thinned legs gamely whirring.

'Look at him,' we said. 'He's really on for it.'

A little later he approached a wooden contrivance in the shape of a freestanding staircase, cut off by a latticed paling on the fourth step. He mounted it, climbed it, backed down, climbed it, backed down; and after that he could do no more. He seemed surprised, puzzled, almost offended. Blue said quietly,

'There's a long way to go. But he'll get there.'

'Of course he will. A hospital gym,' I went on, 'it's a contradiction – like a Young Conservative. Anyway, he'll be back in the guest house tomorrow.'

We went over. Christopher sat resting, sober faced, on the ground floor of the little stairway that led nowhere.

'You'll be out of here tomorrow,' said Blue.

And I said, 'In time for the Republican debate. Think of all you'll learn at the feet of Herman Cain and Rick Santorum.'

'Cat, you ought to lie down for a while,' said Blue. 'Rest up for your homecoming.'

––––––

It was the evening of May 5, and he was home. At the dinner table in the garden he raised an arm for silence and said,

'I can't . . . I can't breathe.'

'What?'

'I can't breathe.'

The speed of time

This took place at around seven-thirty. Blue, Christopher, and I got back to the Zilkha annex at three in the morning.

He could survive without eating and drinking and (more doubtfully) without speaking, but he couldn't survive without breathing. Christopher was under attack from 'dyspnoea', to use the typically melodious medical name for it: a condition best understood as *air hunger*. To Joseph Conrad the exercise of captaincy seemed the 'most natural thing in the world. As natural as breathing'. What was breathing as natural as? 'I imagined I could not have lived without it.' As natural, then, as living.

Within minutes Blue was steering us towards the looming heights of MD Anderson . . . Christopher stayed silent, slightly hunched over in his seat with a concentrating look on his face, and now and then his eyes would swell and widen.

There was no waiting-room period. The three of us were at once ushered into a warren of cubicles and labs, and a stream of specialists came and bent over him one after the other, and then sailed off again; and nobody was there when his air hunger suddenly increased.

Dyspnoea brings with it mortal fear, a clinical condition in its own right. Christopher was facing it without obvious physical strain. But I wasn't – I was in fact making something of a spectacle of myself, pacing the floor and waving my arms and yelling out, 'He can't *breathe!*'

And from then on there was always someone sticking an instrument down his throat or sticking another instrument up his nose or kneading his neck and shoulders or making him cough or sniff or snort or stand or sit . . .

'This can't be right,' I said, staring at my watch and pouring myself a huge glass of wine. 'I thought it was about ten-thirty at the latest. Unbelievable how quickly that all seemed to go . . .'

We were settling down on the porch in the dusty Dixie night.

'I bet it didn't feel that way to you, Hitch.'

'No.' He drew on his Rothmans. 'From my point of view there were certain uh, longueurs. But I see what you mean – in the sense of never a dull moment.'

Exhaustively and exhaustingly pinched and poked, Christopher now looked battered, and spiritually battered, too. The medics went about their work with impressive vocational drive; but it was the pathology that interested them, exclusively, and not the patient. Hitch himself was no more than a delivery boy or a beast of burden, bearing this savoury load, this disease, for their delectation.

'Many strange divestments', he said, 'await you in the land of the sick . . . Now if you'll excuse me, I have some catching up to get done – in the rethink parlour.'

Meaning the toilet . . . 'Blue,' I said ruminatively, 'have you heard about the new money spinner in the healthcare business – the Walk-In Medical Centers? You show up off the street, you get dealt with, and you pay your bill. The great thing about Walk-Ins is this. Having walked in, you can then walk out. Hitch can't walk out. I can walk out whenever I want, and even you, you get some . . . respite if just for ten minutes. But he doesn't, he never does. He's always in it, he's never not in it.'

She faced me levelly, not drinking but levelly smoking. She said,

'He can't get out, not for the duration. He says it isn't like a war, but it is, even if you're a civilian. All you can do is wait for it to end.'

'Wait for it to roll through villages. But he's a warhorse. And he's still an ox.'

'He's still an ox.'

Christopher returned. We stayed up till dawn, with our computers on YouTube, laughing and weeping at the songs of our youth.

Mortal combat

'Christ, Chreestophairr,' I said (this was the way Eleni Meleagrou used to say it), 'for a while you were as bad off as *Japan*. Earthquake, nuclear accident, tsunami.'

'Well, when sorrows come, Little Keith, they come not single spies . . .'

'True, O Hitch. It's much better now, your voice.* You're perfectly audible. You just sound a bit like Bob.' A reference to Whispering Bob Conquest, who was *piano* all his life. 'Only much louder.'

'Good. The trouble is, I keep thinking it's going to come back again. I mean go away again . . . Let's do one more.'

'Two more.'

Some days had passed and the out-patient was an in-patient all over again. I don't think he was often seen in the hospital gym, but twice a day he would do 'laps' in the Texan-scale atrium, and I or Blue would accompany him as his personal trainer. Each circuit took ten or fifteen minutes, and we always did two or three of them. Now in his dressing gown he moved slowly by my side, not a shuffler, more like a wader, making steady progress through a countervailing medium – through an element that never sleeps and never tires. He said,

'How did the idea of combat get itself attached to cancer? They never say, So and so pegged out after a long battle against heart disease or brain death. Or old age.'

'You won't remember, but I lectured you about this one night here in Houston when you were half asleep.' And I repeated some of what I'd said.

---

* 'Most despond-inducing and alarming of all [negative developments, or nasty surprises], so far, was the moment when my voice suddenly rose to a childish (or perhaps piglet-like) piping squeak. It then began to register all over the place, from a gruff and husky whisper to a papery, plaintive bleat. I used to be able to stop a New York cab at thirty paces.' But one day, in Washington, 'I made an attempt to hail a taxi outside my home – and nothing happened. I stood, frozen, like a silly cat that had abruptly lost its meow.' In the space of a few lines Christopher compares himself to a child, a piglet, a goat, and a cat – all of them defenceless beings.

'Yeah, but you can't make war when you're this bad off. It just seems absurd to me. How can you fight when you're flat on your back?'

'By maintaining your spirit and your courage.'

He sighed. 'I think the struggle stuff is there just to trick you into thinking you've got a part to play in all this. To stop you blacking out from sheer inanity. No one ever says how *null* it is, cancer. Boring. Boring *avec*. Don't forget boring.'

'And you evoke it. You're at your desk. You're not snivelling in a corner.'

'No, I'm staggering round in circles. Good try, Mart, but it's not a fight. Who or what am I fighting? My past life, my body, me myself? That's the whole trouble with it. The patient can't ever get away from the patient. One more lap.'

'. . . Two more laps.'

He said, 'I hope this isn't a chore for you.'

'Not at all. I love it.'

And I did love it. I was back with Gus (not quite three, and very consciously the younger brother), circumnavigating the roundabout in his first leather shoes. And just a week before he had been in despair about ever growing up, prostrate under the kitchen table and slowly pounding the floor with his fists (*I'll always be doing silly phings . . . I'll always be with little childs*), and now here he was, a few days later, Gus, mightily shod as he paced the darkening city, with his smile seeming to say, At last – at last I'm getting somewhere.

The man of God

There was a knock on the door, which was in itself quite unusual – a knock on the door to Christopher's single-occupancy ward at MDA. Usually they swept straight in with stethoscopes flying. I answered it, and then returned to the bedside.

'Who was that?'

'Oh just some goddamned man of God. By the way, Hitch, I know you like decapitalising the word God, as in *god is not great*. Looks very iconoclastic. But you really ought to capitalise it in all talk about monotheisms. Where they're referring to a definite bloke.'

'. . . So where is he?'

'Who?'

'Him with a small aitch.'

'Oh the wowser. *I* don't know. Maybe he's still out there.'

'Well we must . . . What kind of wowser?'

'*I* don't know. You mean what denomination?'

'No. What kind of bloke.'

'Oh. The standard peanut. All aglitter. What should I do with him? I know. I'll tell him his faith stinks and kick him down the stairs.'

'No, Mart, ask him if he'd be good enough to step inside . . . Go on. What the hell. Sling him over.'

'Are you sure? All right, then I'm off to get a coffee.'

In the central bay I attended to the hot-drinks machine. Nurses and doctors, men and women in jumpsuits holding clipboards, launderers and caterers, the conditioned and sanitised air, the tubfuls of medical waste, the cloudwracks of used linen . . . After at least twenty minutes the man of God slipped out, looking pleased.

'Jesus, he took his time. Was he after your soul?'

'Of course. All in a day's work.'

'Well I hope you sent him on his way with a few choice words.'

'No, I let him meander on a bit. You sidetrack them. Steer them towards points of doctrine. I got him going on redemption.'

'Doesn't that just lead to conversion? Well, the Hitch is big game. Maybe he'd get a bounty or a finder's fee. I'm amazed you can spare the patience.'

'I'm just endlessly riveted by the religious mind. Religion really is the most interesting thing on earth.'

'Except when the other chap believes in it. Then at the flick of a switch it becomes the least interesting thing on earth.'

'That isn't so. It's far more interesting than cancer. And it's not about me.'

I turned my head and looked out. Here, even the sky seemed enclosed. The totems of MDA, their darkened and treated windows filled with one another's reflections . . .

'Did he talk about hellfire and targeted cancers?'

'No. He wasn't of that chapter.'

'Did you ask him about childhood leukaemias and infantile tumours?'

'No. I didn't have the energy. I couldn't be fucked. Come on. Let's do our laps.'

God is not impressed by death

You saw them as they were coming in or going out, the little childs, accompanied by one parent or another or by both. Now and then, if you looked through the wrong passageway porthole, you saw them in groups, gathered round a rec-room table. The in-patients and out-patients of Pediatric Oncology were all boys (they're 'almost entirely boys. No one knows why'); and so all the bald children 'look like brothers'.* Hairless heads, and enormous, startled, blinking eyes – as if blinking off the effects of a flashbulb. And they seemed to me to be asking themselves the same question their parents were asking. 'When a baby gets cancer, you think, Who came up with *this* idea? What celestial abandon gave rise to *this*?'

There's the Peter Pan Ward, and there's the Tiny Tim Lounge:

> The Tiny Tim Lounge is a little sitting area at the end of the [Pediatric Oncology] corridor . . . On one of the lounge walls there is a gold plaque with the singer Tiny Tim's name on it: his son was treated once at this hospital and so, five years ago, he donated money for the lounge. It is a cramped little lounge, which, one suspects, would be larger if Tiny Tim's son had actually lived. Instead, he died here, at this hospital, and now there is this tiny room which is part gratitude, part generosity, part *fuck-you*.

And, if you're a capitaliser of pronouns, then that would have to be 'part *fuck-You*'.

Why does God preside over the deaths, by cancer, of the very young? The many televangelists in the neighbourhood had an answer. Namely, it's because 'He wants them with Him right away'. (Does He? What for? And as regards their parents, what does He want?) And the answer of the writers is no more satisfying. 'You cannot understand, my child, nor can I, nor can anyone,' says the priest at the conclusion of Graham Greene's *Brighton Rock*, 'the appalling strangeness of the mercy of God.'

---

* The quotes are from Lorrie Moore's 'People Like That are the Only People Here: Canonical Babbling in Peed Onk', as are all the unattributed quotes in the rest of this section. Moore's story is to be found in *Birds of America* (1998). It is – or it feels like – an example of life-writing that firmly elevates this rather dubious genre.

Oh, it's *mercy*, is it – yeah, keep believing that, Believers . . . Greene was a theist. Saul, a deist, had the best answer, the only answer: *God is not impressed by death*. Yes, and also this. God never grieves.

There he goes, the boy aged four or five, led by the orderly in the blue smock. The colour blue: *the surgeon, the anaesthesiologist, all the nurses, the social worker. In their blue caps and scrubs, they look like a clutch of forget-me-nots* . . . 'Children often become afraid of the color blue' . . . Then don't go outside, little ones, don't even look outside, because it's all blue there, nothing but blue.

Later in the afternoon Michael Z drove me to the airport, and soon enough I was up in it, in the blue of the careless Southern sky.

How to Write
The Mind's Ear

'He wasn't just angry. He was beside himself.'

Modern readers would more or less skim the second sentence while perhaps casually noting the cliché. But *beside himself* is a startlingly vivid image, and all credit to whoever used it first (probably a late-medieval translator who vivified the French phrase *hors de soi*, or 'out of self'). The same is true of another image, *the mind's eye*, which had been knocking around for at least as long – but in this case everyone knows who gathered it in and made it immortal:

> Ham.: My father – methinks I see my father.
> Hor.: Where, my lord?
> Ham.: In my mind's eye, Horatio.

*

If you're struggling to describe a face or a landscape, try this: close your eyes and describe what your mind's eye sees. The mind's eye is a tool. And so is the mind's ear.

I want to talk about the mind's ear, but before I do that I want to say a few more words about Vonnegut. His ear, his prose, his fire, and his destined mood.

There really are such things as destined moods. At a certain point, usually in late middle age, something congeals and solidifies and encysts itself – and that's your lot, that's your destiny. You're going to feel this way for the rest of your life. You have found your destined mood, and it has found you, too.

You know, Kurt Vonnegut is statistically the favourite writer of very many of your peers; and I bet you have an affection for his stuff, as do I – its originality and charm. All right, his flights of inventiveness sometimes felt undercontrolled, and he was too strongly attracted to what Clive James called 'gee-whiz writing' ('So it goes'); but what is inarguable is the quality of his *ear*. And I don't just mean an ear for dialogue (an eavesdropper's attention to varying rhythms of speech), though he excelled at that too. I mean the *mind's* ear – your mind's ear, which as we'll see is the conductor, the musical director, of your prose.

Kurt was an effervescently affable man who, in his final decade, lost all his mirth, turning away from the world and starting to fold inwards. My first encounter with the Later Kurt left me slightly shocked – and slightly hurt (I realised at that moment how fond I'd grown of him). We were in the antechamber of a function in New York; formerly he had always greeted me with his characteristically spluttering enthusiasm, but that night he just nodded distantly and gazed elsewhere. His face seemed drained of its responsiveness; it was resignedly static. And his bearing was different too: stolid, erect, even soldierly – no longer donnishly gangly and loose. He was on duty. And at that gathering his wheezily breathless laugh went unheard.

Now Kurt did describe himself as a hereditary 'monopolar depressive' (his mother was a suicide); but psychological disorder, as an explanation, tends to frustrate all human curiosity; and besides he had lived with that for most of his adult life. In his *Letters*, it should be duly noted, he went on being affectionate, generous, and playful with relatives and old friends, right up until his death;* but with everyone else he could offer only a distant civility.

As I see it (and I am only a remote observer), there were two other elements. His amatory timeline – a crucial determinant here – almost exactly corresponds to that of my father: born in 1922, early marriage and early children, divorced in his forties, second marriage terminated by second wife (after he discovered that 'she had stockpiled a guy' in her studio next door), and, thereafter, celibacy. And as Kingsley told me,

---

* In January 2000, as I mentioned, Vonnegut sleepily upended an ashtray overflowing with butts of the untipped Pall Malls he always smoked, torching a fire in his Manhattan townhouse. He was rushed to hospital (smoke inhalation) and briefly listed as 'critical'. His bodily recovery, it turned out, was swift; but he had lost his clothes, his bed, and all his books and papers. Four years later he wrote to Robert Weide (who did the screen adaptation of *Mother Night*) and the letter ended: 'I have scarcely had a day worth living since the fire, am bored absolutely shitless by myself. Cheers – Kurt.'

late on, 'it's only half a life without a woman'. Bear in mind too that Kurt was far more uxorious (and monogamous) than Kingsley. Still, the result was the same: romantic defeat and an internal 'snarl of disappointment'.

The other component, for Kurt, had to do with literary pride. For writers, this is the rule of thumb: those who sell a lot want to be taken seriously, and those who are taken seriously want to sell a lot (and the latter ambition is clearly the more ignoble). Kurt, who sold a lot, wanted to be taken seriously; he felt under-esteemed. And don't ever forget that the authorial ego is – and has to be – vulgarly and queasily vast. Probably not that many novelists and poets, argued Auden, would like to be the only novelist or poet who has ever lived; but most of them wouldn't mind being the only novelist or poet who is living *now*.

'I have to keep reminding myself that *I* wrote those early books,' he said to me (in the course of an interview in 1983). Those early books – pre-*Slaughterhouse* 5 – were the ones he thought were the most cruelly skimped. 'The only way I can regain credit for my early work is – to die.' The very last time I saw Kurt was at a literary gala in the very early 2000s: he mounted the stage to receive a career-achievement award – and also to receive by far the longest and loudest ovation of the night. His response was dignified and subdued. I very much hoped that some alleviation and even some pleasure managed to filter through to him.

Like Elmore Leonard,* Vonnegut was a popular – or demotic – artist gifted with an exceptional inner ear. Which meant that his prose was almost wholly free of 'false quantities' (in the non-technical sense): free of rhymes, chimes, repetitions, toe-stubs, letdowns, free of anything, in short, that makes the careful reader *pause without profit*. A near-

---

* And the last time I saw Elmore was at another literary gala in New York (November 2012), where he in his turn won an award for Lifetime Achievement. That night I gave an introductory speech, praising *inter alia* Leonard's wholly original and swingeingly effective way with *tense*. He uses not the past tense ('he lived in'), not the imperfect ('he was living in'), not the historic present ('he lives in' – the present tense used to vivify completed actions, as in Updike's Rabbit books), and not quite the present tense; he uses – or he invents – a present tense indefinitely suspended ('Warren Ganz III, living up in Manalapan', 'Bobby saying', 'Dawn saying'). In *Riding the Rap* a louche character at a louche party is said to be 'burning herb' and (prudently) 'maintaining on reefer'. And it is a kind of marijuana tense, vague and creamy, opening up a lag in time . . . After the presentations Elmore and I went outside (twice) for a smoke and a discussion of another seminal crime writer, George V. Higgins. Later we parted with embraces and warm words. His destined mood appeared to be one of slightly agitated high spirits. He was eighty-seven. And he never saw eighty-eight.

frictionless verbal surface is usually the result of much blood, toil, tears, and sweat. I'll be giving you a few tips on how to streamline the process.

*

For example, when I am reading – this applies to fiction especially but not just to fiction – I partly imagine that what I have on my lap is a provisional draft of something that might have been written by me. So I'm thinking, Mm, I wouldn't put it quite like that, I'd avoid that repetition, this phrase isn't precise enough, that word should've been tucked in earlier in the sentence, and – again and again – is that rhyme/half-rhyme/alliteration intended or is it unintended? Et cetera.

Going on being a writer while you are reading becomes second nature and helps train the ear. As for getting the prose to flow smoothly – that's more mysterious. But certitude of rhythm can be cumulatively acquired. With Kurt, and with Elmore, it seemed to be innate. So we can marvel at them, but we can't learn from them.

*

Let me assure you that you do have an inner ear – everybody does; and it is a vital instrument (and helpmate), almost as vital as your subconscious. But before you can bond with it, you first have to find it. So let's find yours. We can do that by setting your mind's ear two modest – indeed fairly lowly – tasks.

Number one: the 'I or me?' business. People often get this wrong in speech (I have heard well-known novelists and also professors of literature get this wrong), but it's rare to see it in published prose. Here is a quote from Bill McKibben's would-be green bible, *The End of Nature*: 'A ten-minute walk brings the dog and I to the waterfall.' Now, take out the 'the dog and' bit – lose the dog – and silently rehearse that sentence: 'A ten-minute walk brings I to the waterfall'? Whether it's the dog and I, or John and I, or the other board members and I, put the 'I' first for a moment, and your ear will guide you. Ditto, obviously, with 'John and me met up with Mary' . . . Personally I find this less irksome than 'Mary met up with John and I', which is not only an illiteracy but also an attempted genteelism.

Some people think that 'myself' is there to help them out. 'John and myself met up with', 'brings the dog and myself': it may not be an illiteracy, but it certainly sounds like one. *Myself* is just a crap word, that's all, though some constructions – notably reflexive verbs – force it on you. The other day, as Elena was lamenting one of her supposed character flaws, she said, 'I hate me'; and I thought that was a definite improvement.

Number two: the 'who or whom?' business. This is very slightly trickier. 'John, whom I know to be an honourable man' is right; 'John, whom I know is an honourable man' is wrong. Here's what you do: you mentally recast the subclauses as main clauses – 'I know him to be an honourable man', 'I know he is an honourable man' – and your ear will guide you: 'him' demands 'whom', and 'he' demands 'who' . . . In conversational prose be wary of *whom*. In the closing pages of *Herzog*, Bellow writes, 'Whom was I kidding?' This is grammatically correct; it also leaves the sentence up on one stilt. 'Whom the fuck d'you think you're looking at?' Or even worse, 'At whom the fuck d'you think you're looking?' Never worry about ending a sentence with a preposition. 'That rule', Churchill famously said, 'is the kind of pedantry up with which I will not put.'

These are rather menial exercises; but having established a relationship with your mind's ear (your aural imagination), you can then go on to cultivate it. I spend a large fraction of my working day saying whole sentences again and again in my head. What I'm doing is probing for dissonances, for false quantities. And I never get them all, no, you never get them all . . .

The thing is, literature differs from the other arts in one glaring particular. Not everybody can paint or sculpt, not everybody can act or sing. But everybody can write. So you're in the position of a trainee pilot in a world where everybody – from the age of four or five – can fly an aeroplane.

Words lead a double life, and so far as I can see what this means is that you have to become something of an expert on them – an expert on words; and I spend another large fraction of my day looking them up. I find it stabilising and also salutary. Every time I do it I feel a grey cell being born – while no doubt a billion are blindly dying off. Check the exact definition, check the origin. That word is then more firmly yours.

*

. . . For a whole decade I was brimful of foreboding about my destined mood. That decade was my fifties (your fifties are spent coping with the negative eureka of your forties: no, you are not an exception to the rule of time). Is it going to be a fair mood or a foul mood? Well, guess who took care of that. Mr Christopher Hitchens, that's who. I'm not even sure how he did it. But he did it.

If your destined mood is your final mood, which it would seem to be, then it is part of your preparation for death. During this period, as you lie dying, there may be physical hardships and humiliations to get through; so long as you're good and old, though (seventy-something will just about do), it's philosophically straightforward. Remember. Time is a river that carries you away; but you are the river.

*

By now of course 'my mind's eye' is categorically unusable. Not, or not only, because it belongs to someone else. Immature writers imitate, said Eliot, and mature writers steal: you can pocket the odd phrase, but only if you then do something with it, something 'mature'. The rightful owner is Shakespeare – so you'd get caught, and quickly, too. This is the Plagiarist's Dilemma: your writers have to be worth stealing from, and their stuff is famous for that reason . . .

You can't use 'the mind's eye' because you'd be violating a master law of writing, which is: Never use a form of words which is in any sense *ready made*. A form of words like *stifling heat* or *biting cold* or *healthy scepticism* or *yawning gap*; adjective and noun, long-married couples who ought by now to be sick of the sight of each other. And the same goes for shopworn novelties: rapidly ageing newlyweds of the kind we'll be looking at in twenty pages or so, when we turn to the matter of Decorum.

For now, I'll leave you with a quote, which (conveniently) offends on both counts: 'In business, I don't actively make decisions based on my religious beliefs, but those beliefs are there – big time.' Donald J. Trump, *Crippled America: How To Make America Great Again* (2015). In this instance, Trump is also peddling a consummate untruth (for targeted electoral gain). But let other pens dwell on that.

Chapter 2
Saul: Idlewild

Wind chimes

'*Rage,*' said Rosamund.

Does it make any sense to talk about Saul's destined mood? Think for a moment . . . Well, does it?

'Rage,' said Rosamund.

The two of us were sitting at the half-cleared lunch table in Vermont. Saul, Elena, and the children were for now elsewhere.

'All the time he's in a rage. Sometimes a quiet rage, sometimes not so quiet, but always in a rage.'

I hadn't found him much altered since the interlude of *Pirates of the Caribbean* and *The Shadow-Line* and James Bond. But what was settling in me was an incremental disbelief: to see him so often sitting there with no book on his lap, just sitting and gazing. I never got used to it; every exposure mystified me. And I had to drag myself back through the story all over again, as if in plodding homage to one of Saul's (many) difficulties. I said,

'Sometimes when I come into the room he looks at me with a jolt of surprise. Slightly affronted surprise. He recognises me, I'm almost sure, but it's as if he had no idea I was in the house . . . I haven't seen any rage.'

'No,' she said. 'It's aimed at me.'

'. . . You? What for?'

With her eyes lowered she said, 'I don't know if I can bring myself to tell you.'

But she didn't have to tell me, not then, because all the others were returning from the pond.

. . . We all used to swim – Saul included – in the little round pond, which was endowed with an alerting range of temperatures; even in high summer your calves tingled to the cooler currents . . . In a Bellow essay of 1993, Vermont, pastoral Vermont is called 'the good place'. Pastoral Vermont, poor Vermont, with its tunnels of flora and its roadside syrup stalls, its backyards almost blotted out by old tyres and fenders and eviscerated cars and trucks and tractor-trailers and even excavators, its book barns, its patio wind chimes.

The would-be forgotten

I never saw the point of the Americanism 'off of' (surely the 'of' is always redundant) until I had children; and then I absorbed its accuracy and justice.

When I first started coming to stay at this house, in the late 1980s, I was accompanied by my first wife and our two very young sons, and I spent the entire time wiping shit off of everything. Later, when I came to stay in the late 1990s, I was accompanied by my second wife and our two very young daughters, and I spent the entire time wiping shit off of everything. In the early 2000s, when we paid our last two or three visits, I spent some but by no means all of my time wiping shit off of everything in a nearby hotel, rather than in the house, where the Bellows had a newcomer of their own, Naomi Rose, and where Rosamund at least was no doubt similarly and simultaneously engaged.

. . . While we're here we should again salute the unsung heroism of babies – of babyhood and infancy. And of parents, who perhaps deserve a double honour, having once been babies themselves (and knowing exactly what they're in for). Of course human beings forget all that: this welcome loophole is confusingly called 'childhood amnesia' – whereby memory remains quiescent until the age of three and a half, which just so happens to coincide with emancipation from the nappy.*

In fact it is difficult, here, not to see a beneficent hand at work. Memory, in my theory of it, holds back – is loth to form – until the individual has attained mastery of the commode. Yes, memory has the everyday decency to recuse itself, to look the other way, during this awkward transition, sparing us that indignity. Over these things Mother Nature or some such genius erects her all-absolving screen; in ordering the scope of human remembrance, this mother takes the trouble to wipe the shit off of memory.

Saul (b. 1915) was always known to wield exceptional powers of recall.

Mnemosyne operations got under way when he was two – so perhaps he remembered his dealings with the non-disposable nappies of World War I; certainly, his retrievals from 1917 have been corroborated by relatives. 'Herzog persecuted everyone with his memory. It was like a terrible engine.' And again: 'all the dead and mad are in my custody, and I am the nemesis of the would-be forgotten.'

How was the engine now, in 2002/3/4? Its short-term capabilities, as we have seen, were much reduced. Nevertheless he could still

---

* One afternoon in London in 1999 I was minding Eliza in her room. She wore a dark brown Babygro; she was not quite three. We both had books on our laps (*Mrs Dalloway* for me, *Mr Silly* for her). A sudden and very loud noise caused me to look up. '. . . Oh,' I said with resignation. 'Well I suppose we ought to make a start. Would it be simpler if I just ran a bath?' In a dignified voice and without raising her eyes from the page, Eliza said, 'That was just an enormous fart, Daddy.' She was thirty-four months . . . A small percentage of infants ('potty prodigies') are fully trained by the age of two; the median age is three and a half (though there will still be 'oopsies' up to year five). Three and a half is when memory begins. Girls are potty-trained earlier than boys; and their memory begins earlier, too; in both cases the difference is about three months – not long enough, I suppose, to explain why little girls are measurably brighter than little boys.

sometimes make contact with the long-ago. It was as if, in the sea cave of his brain, there were ledges and air pockets that the waters hadn't yet breached. Yesterday night (for instance) he had given us a fascinating twenty minutes on the Norwegian writer and fascist Knut Hamsun, an influential admirer of the Third Reich who (via Goebbels) managed to bring about a (disastrous) tête-à-tête with Hitler.*

*

Saul and I were drinking tea on the deck of the nearby hotel – reminding me of the time, just a couple of years ago, when we had resumed our ongoing talks about deism and the supernatural and the life to come . . . Now, in my one-on-one sessions with Saul, I was testing the uses of silence. If his memory could no longer get him through a written sentence, then concerted duologue (I reckoned) must surely be a torment. It felt as though it didn't fit, this silence; but by sharing in the unnatural constraint I could join him in his vacancy. We sat side by side, staring out; his visage was illegible, but every minute or so it gave a punctual flinch . . . He never had 'the lion face', as gerontologists call it: that top-of-the-food-chain impassivity. Saul always seemed to be thinking, or trying to.

Torment. And rage. I was remembering Rosamund's words in the kitchen; and remembering the look in her eyes – one never seen before. I thought it was a look of terminal exasperation (which it wasn't, not exactly), and it frightened me, because if Rosamund – savagely protective, barbarically loyal Rosamund – was weakening . . . *Rage*, she said. I never witnessed any of that, not once, though I knew it to be ever-present in him. Herzog again, with his 'angry heart'.

---

* 'A warrior for mankind, a preacher of the gospel of justice for all nations': this is from Hamsun's 'eulogy' published after Hitler did away with himself on Walpurgisnacht (April 30) in the ruins of Berlin. Then again old Knut was in his mid-eighties at the time, and probably dementia contributed to his clinching *trahison*. The long-lobbied-for audience with the Führer, which came to fruition in June 1943, is in retrospect pretty satisfying. Confronted by a garrulous critique of his Norwegian policies (during which Hamsun touted the merits of Vidkun Quisling), Hitler tried to shout Hamsun down, but found for once that he couldn't just rely on a hollered monologue, couldn't just activate 'the usual gramophone record' (Mussolini) – because Hamsun was deaf. Recent scholarship, from Oslo, tells us that Hamsun, by the end of this great meeting of minds, was in tears, and Hitler's post-interview tantrum, as his press officer tells it, took three days to subside.

If Saul consulted his long-term memory, there were good reasons to be furious, reasons both avocational* and romantic. Five marriages meant four divorces; I had been divorced once, and I weakly attempted to quadruple that alp-weight of pain, emotional violence, and above all *failure*. And to persist, to persist, to try again in the face of so much disappointment. With Rosamund the disappointment was solved and salved; she represented the triumph of innocence over experience. So why was this rage of his directed at her? Of all people – her.

Now I turned, and poured more tea from the pot, Saul assenting with a quarter-smile and a tolerant grunt; words of mild approbation were exchanged about the weather . . . Did his mood have something to do with hurt intelligence, with intellectual hurt? Was he thinking, Why am I just listening all the time, and not talking? Why am I following the conversation (with difficulty) and not leading it? And if you went back a way: his brothers – Samuel possibly, Maury certainly – and his father and almost everybody else in Chicago despised his type of intelligence; but his type of intelligence proved to be at least as effective (and far more remarkable) than theirs – and that includes you, Maury, and never mind your 'suburban dukedom' and your 300 suits. And now Saul, the lone survivor, was met by a design flaw, manifesting itself from within. Did it hurt? Was it a negative tingle in the brain? Did it itch? Couldn't we depend on the Murdoch Law, as promulgated by John Bayley? *Every new incapacity diminishes the awareness of loss* . . .

I gave it up, I disembarked from this train of thought (and actually I was getting it all wrong, because I couldn't free myself from the linear world of *sequiturs*), I gave it up and directed my citified, my townie eyes to the scene spread out in front of us. New England, or the New England I was used to (Connecticut, Long Island), had a beauty-parlour sheen to it, freshly primped and pared; but Vermont always

---

* He had got the Jewish-American novel up and running, making a start with *Dangling Man* in 1944: 1944, a time when anti-Semitism in the US was at its historical apogee, with desecrations, beatings, daubed swastikas. Nonetheless, the Jewish-American novel survived and endured; it dominated the national literature for over half a century. During that emergence many wounds were given and received. And how ironic, and how tragic, it is that the Judaeophobic fulmination should exactly coincide with the Holocaust; and the weight of public opinion inevitably moved Roosevelt to restrict Jewish immigration. In 1941–5, no Jew was murdered in America; the attendant butcher's bill was paid in Europe. One example. In 1939 the steamship *St Louis*, from Hamburg, was denied permission to land in Florida; of the 980 passengers, 254 are known to have died in the Holocaust.

looked as though it had just woken up and climbed out of bed, tousled, balding, indigent, guileless, and here before me were the crazy fairy queens of the trees sprouting up at all angles from the green and flaxen luminescence, and the minutely pullulating carpet meadow. Yes, the bumpy flatland seemed to writhe and live, and I lost myself in it to such effect that I re-experienced – or helplessly flashed back to – the least disastrous of the four or five acid trips I took during my second summer at university, when I was turning twenty-one.

'Time to go?' I said (apart from anything else I wanted a drink). Saul nodded.

He was the one who looked at nature as an established mystic and scholar, who sensed God's veil over everything, who could give names to the things I saw, the shagbark hickory, and all that. And I liked to think he still sensed it. Saul got to his feet smoothly with no tremors or winces; he never lost his bodily solidity; mentally absent, he was physically present, warmly, influentially present . . .

'I have invented a new genre,' said Isaac Babel, to his writer friends in Stalin's USSR, '– that of silence.' A good remark and a good idea, though it didn't save him. Of another writer, Boris Pasternak, Stalin said, 'Do not touch this cloud dweller.' Like Babel, Bellow was a Jew and a Trotskyite. But now you would look at him and say to yourself, No. Do not touch this cloud dweller.

Wandering off

A textbook hazard of advanced dementia is something called 'wandering off'. This is not a reference to the sufferers' conversational style. Wandering off means going missing; it means escape.

Iris wandered off. She was usually to be found in a neighbour's garden, says Professor Bayley in *Iris and the Friends*, or patrolling the familiar stretch of pavement opposite the house.* One day – this was

---

* Iris would collect things. 'Old sweet wrappings, matchsticks, cigarette-ends' – a Coca-Cola tin, a rusty spanner, a single shoe. Bayley pictures her 'fiddling incessantly with her small *objets trouvés* – twigs and pebbles, bits of dirt, scraps of silver foil, even dead worms'. Bayley (in common with most readers) quietly accepts this as a continuation of Iris's necessary dreaminess. John and Iris were authentic and uninhibited bohemians, low-bohemian in the life, like hippies or tramps, and high-bohemian in the mind – until, in her case, there was no mind.

easily the most dramatic instance – she burst through the unattended front door and disappeared for two hours (the police were called); eventually she was spotted by a vigilant academic in the far precincts of North Oxford . . . Now North Oxford is a quaintly prelapsarian Toytown, but streets are streets and cars are cars. A family friend 'happened to see her – nearly at the top of Woodstock Road', writes Bayley tensely (and many well-disposed readers will regret that he suppressed an exclamation mark).

When Saul wandered off, one time, he didn't just go for a stroll and a potter around Crowninshield Road. After all, he was an American; he had absorbed the principles of mobility and self-reliance. So he took a cab to the airport and got on a plane. I was reminded of this incident out in Vermont when Saul's secretary, a handsome and humorous BU graduate (cheerful, head-in-air) called Will Lautzenheiser, made one of his regular runs from Boston to bring the mail and a thick wedge of invitations and requests. He had been the point man when Saul went missing.

Will spent his couple of hours with Saul, and everyone had lunch, and then I walked him out to his car. We had met several times before and I always thought how lucky the Bellows were to have found such a congenial Boy Friday. Will was a hardened Joycean, by the way, with an unfeigned appetite for the avant-garde; he would save up and travel great distances to attend, say, a futuristic mime in Los Angeles or an atonal opera in Austin. I particularly liked Will's attitude to his job and to his charge. *It's as if I'm making life a bit easier for Shakespeare,* he told me. *You're proud to get the chance to do it.* I now said in the driveway,

'Rosamund described it to me but I'm hazy on the . . . Saul flew from Boston to New York – is that right?'

'No. He flew from Toronto to Boston. He *attempted* to fly to New York – he bought a ticket to New York, he thought he was still living there. But he must've realised his mistake, or they . . .'

'Mm, you have to do a lot of talking to get in and out of Canada. Customs, Immigration. Maybe they put him right. Wait. When did it happen?'

It happened surprisingly long ago: August 2001 (just after the visit to East Hampton and just before September 11). Saul had gone with Rosamund to Toronto, where she was speaking at a conference on *Under Western Eyes* (Conrad's second consecutive novel about terrorism, following *The Secret Agent*). They brought Rosie with them, counting on the support of two very capable Torontoans, Harvey and Sonya Friedman, Rosamund's parents.

'So where exactly did Saul do a runner from?'

'The hotel. They were going to pick him up for dinner, but he checked himself out and . . . That night I got home late.' That night Will had characteristically sat through a six-hour screening of Lars von Trier's *The Kingdom*. 'There was a message from Saul saying he was on his way in from Logan. Astounding.'

'Yes he was uh, very bold.'

'Very bold.'

And we laughed, shaking our heads.

'It did seem kind of funny once we knew he was safe. When I called Rosamund in Toronto she was beside herself. The police were out. *I* was beside myself.'

And Will, I bore in mind, had a twin . . . He sprinted the mile to Crowninshield Road. Saul was there, tired, calm, lucid, and mainly just sad and anxious.

'He thought Rosamund was about to leave him.'

'. . . You're kidding.'

'I told him no, no, Rosamund loves you. And he said, *Well that's what I've always thought. But I'm not sure. I'm not sure today.*'

'He doubted *Rosamund* . . . Well he's getting things wrong. Like he thought he lived in New York. He's getting big things wrong.'

'Yeah, he is.' Will opened the car door, saying, 'That night he talked on the phone with an old friend, who reassured him. So I got him to bed. And I stayed over.'

'Good for you.'

In Will climbed. I told him to take care and I waved as he reversed into the lane.* For a while I stood on the drive, tangentially wondering if Saul, when he arrived at Toronto International, had asked for a ticket to Idlewild, which was what Herzog and everybody else called it, back in 1960.

---

* And I would see him again in Boston, where he remained on board right to the end. Will Lautzenheiser's later story can be found online; it tells of phenomenal calamity – and phenomenal resilience. He is now forty-something.

Idlewild. There was much to admire in that name, that word. I always thought it derived from a flower, but it was just an inheritance from Idlewild Beach Golf Course, on which New York's main airport was built in 1947 (to be rechristened JFK in 1963). 'Idlewild' is a familiar American place-name – there's one in Michigan – but its origin is obscure. Some say it comes from a proverb or ditty: 'idle men and wild women' . . .

Rosamund said, 'He keeps accusing me. Accusing me of . . .'

We were taking a turn in the garden (Eliza was up the slope and busy on the swing).

'He keeps thinking I'm . . .'

The Alzheimer's literature alerts relatives and carers to the sort of behaviour, or behaviours, considered 'inappropriate'.* There are also pages and pages about infuriated (and of course delusive) sexual jealousy, among other concomitants. So I wasn't completely astounded to learn the following: Saul was under the impression that Rosamund was interesting herself in other men.

'Ah – poor you,' I said. 'How very awful.' I clenched my eyes shut and groaned. And poor him, too. 'I know this is asking a lot but you mustn't take it personally. It's just a symptom.' Was that any better? Saul deindividualised, lost in a mess of symptoms and syndromes? I said feebly, 'It's like Elena's mother. She wakes up every day thinking she's been robbed in the night.'

'He doesn't think that.'

---

* Even back then, in the earliest years of the century, I marvelled at the illustrious future assembling itself at the feet of this word. Up until the renovation of 'inappropriate', 'offensive' and 'potentially offensive' were rather desperately holding the fort; but now Americans (and some others) at last had a multisyllabic euphemism that meant 'the kind of thing that some individual or other might not like' . . . Less woollily it can also mean 'the kind of thing that certain people should by definition be spared'. In 2010 or so Inez (eleven) was entertaining two family friends aged seven and five; the three of them were watching a show about teen romance, and after a few minutes Inez reached protectively for the remote control, mouthing at me: 'Inappropriate.' In 2017, in the course of defending Judge Roy Moore of Alabama, President Trump conceded that the accusation (molesting underage girls), 'if true', would be 'incredibly inappropriate'.

'No, but he does think this.'

Again her frown, her defeated look. There was hurt in it all right, and lost patience. And another element, I saw: a self-accusing reassessment of her own strength. She believed she was up to it; now, facing daily insult and (truly definitive) injustice, she was wondering if that was true.

'With the sexual stuff, when it recrudesces like this . . . You know it could be worse.' What kind of comfort was that? And besides – it could very well *get* worse all by itself . . . I thought of the advice offered in the Alzheimer's updates and downloads. In a case I'd read about, where the husband was wandering around half naked and fondling himself, the wife was told *to learn how to distract and redirect him to more appropriate activities*. Would that work on Saul? I said, 'Well, the doctors do tell you to try not to bridle. And not to argue the point. Just make a simple statement to the contrary . . . Interested in other men. *What* men? *Which* men?'

'The old guy fixing the roof. The fat kid delivering the groceries.'

'Jesus.'

'I know.' She frowned sadly. 'It's never with anyone nice.'

Literature and madness

Saul's affliction, his variant of dementia, was officially listed as a 'mental illness' – provoking great disgust among health professionals (mainly because it complicates the stigma). But Alzheimer's does have an organic cause, distinguishing it from neurosis (which is inorganic and doesn't involve a 'radical' loss of touch with reality). Like schizophrenia and like manic depression, Alzheimer's (like religion) tends to involve a passionate belief in things that aren't there.

Psychologists can do practically nothing with organic insanity (except give it drugs); and writers – perhaps not entirely noncoincidentally – can't do much with it either. Neuroses, compulsions, repressions, and especially obsessions are the bread and butter, the meat and drink, of fiction. But it may be that organic insanity – like dreams, like religion, like sex – is fundamentally impervious to literary art.* Among writers there is one great exception – indeed, we might as well call him the Great Exception, the Singularity. As Matthew Arnold announces in the first line of his short poem, 'Shakespeare': 'Others abide our question. Thou art free.'

———

'Internally, in itself, madness is an artistic desert. Nothing of any general interest can be said about it. But the effect it has on the world outside it can be very interesting indeed. It has no other valid literary use. [The subject of my book] was just how well or, mostly, how badly writers have described madness.†

'Shakespeare got it right. Lear, of course. Cerebral atherosclerosis, a senile organic disease of the brain. Periods of mania followed by amnesia. Rational episodes marked by great dread of the renewed onset of mania. That way madness lies – let me shun that – no more of that.

'Perhaps even more striking – Ophelia. In fact it's such a good description that this subdivision of schizophrenia is known as the Ophelia Syndrome even to those many psychiatrists who have never seen or read the play. It's very thoroughly set up – young girl of meek disposition, no mother, no sister, the brother she depends on not

---

* I once had a long talk about this with a writer friend who has made notable efforts in the sphere of madness, Patrick McGrath (*The Grotesque, Spider, Asylum*), at a time when I was wondering how mad I ought to make the anti-hero of my thirteenth novel. The essential difficulty, we agreed, was this: a work of art needs to cohere ('together' + 'to stick') and organic madness is the sworn enemy of coherence. So the author faces an unfamilar hazard, namely a surfeit of freedom: as in dreams, anything at all can happen . . . Mad characters, therefore, have to be surrounded – and constantly challenged – by sane characters; madness must never be allowed to take centre stage. So no mad heroes or mad heroines and no mad narrators (of the sort you too often find in the early work of Elena Ferrante). It is like nonsense verse: a very little goes a very long way.
† The speaker is Dr Alfred Nash, a character in Kingsley's novel of 1984, *Stanley and the Women*. Nash's monologue was based on, or made possible by, Jim Durham, a learned and literary psychologist and a close family friend . . . When I was in my early twenties Jim effortlessly cured me of what felt like a serious mental condition – incapacitating panic attacks on the London Underground ('Just remember', he said, 'that no harm can come to you'). And I would have gone to him with the confusions induced by Phoebe Phelps in 2001; but by then he had repatriated himself to Australia, where he runs a psychiatric hospital in Sydney.

available, lover apparently gone mad, mad enough anyway to kill her father. Entirely characteristic that a girl with her kind of upbringing should go round spouting little giggling harmless obscenities when mad.

'The play's full of interesting remarks about madness. Polonius. You remember he has a chat with Hamlet, the fishmonger conversation, and is made a fool of – the very model of a dialogue between stupid questioner and clever madman as seen by that, er, that unusual person R. D. Laing. Polonius says, I will take my leave of you, my lord. And Hamlet says, You cannot take from me anything I would more willingly part withal, except my life, except my life.

'Very clever, very droll. But actually Hamlet's only *pretending* to be mad, isn't he. Polonius gets halfway to the point. How pregnant sometimes his replies are, he says, a happiness that often madness hits on, which reason and sanity could not so prosperously be delivered of – as it happens, a remarkably twentieth-century view. Hamlet in general very cleverly behaves in a way that people who've never seen a madman, a madman *fresh* and unmedicated, expect a madman to behave.

'In my view, though, Polonius is a rather underrated fellow. Earlier in the same scene he comes up with a very good definition of madness, not a complete definition, but an essential part of it, excluding north-north-west madness. He says, To define true madness, what is it but to be nothing else but mad?'*

———————

Saul was never close to that, not remotely (though Iris was close by the end). In any case the tragic hero Saul resembled during this phase of his was of course Othello. Wild imaginings ('Goats and monkeys!'), but imaginings skilfully conjured up by a third party – Iago. And Saul's Iago was an Iago of the mind.

Why does Iago destroy Othello, what is his 'motive'? He has none. He invents grievances (Othello has thwarted my rise to the officer class, Othello has slept with my wife), but these are flimsy pretexts. He is like Claggart in *Billy Budd* (a very conscious iteration of the theme of

———————

* Kingsley had an obviously very memorable encounter with somebody who was nothing else but mad: a middle-aged woman on a bus. She was mad, he wrote, *mad to the ends of her hair.*

motiveless malice). Iago allows us a brief glimpse of the truth when he talks, not about Othello, but about the bland prettyboy Cassio: 'He hath a daily beauty in his life / That makes me ugly.' And this is why Claggart destroys Billy, the Handsome Sailor. The two destroyers are vandals; they vandalise beautiful souls.

And dementia is the vandal within. You cannot reason with it or distract it or soften it. All you can do is hate it. In *Othello* the most telling verdict on Iago belongs not to the Moor or to Desdemona or even to the keenly perceptive Emilia. It belongs to the well-gulled fop, Roderigo. These are his last words, addressed to the murderer crouching over him with the blade: 'O, damned Iago. O, inhuman dog.'

And that's what I say to Dr Alois Alzheimer.

O, damned Alois. O, inhuman dog.

'Tis the god Hercules

The night before we left he gave us an aural pen portrait of John Berryman. In 1972 Saul wrote a farewell address to John Berryman and the words were still in him (though when I later reread 'John Berryman' I found that the dinner-table version included many newly surfaced memories and details). Then we exchanged quotes and there were a couple of short readings from *Dream Songs*.

He was pretty close to his very best, and when he again fell silent, I said rather impulsively, hoping to keep him in it (and also rather drunkenly),

'The guy, the college janitor who found Berryman's body' – on the river shore under the bridge in Minneapolis – 'had an interesting name. Art Hitman . . . Saul, aren't you weary of the line *reality is stranger than fiction*? Or that it's becoming stranger? I think it's always been stranger. *Ooh, you couldn't put Art Hitman in a novel!* Well you couldn't – because you wouldn't want to. Reality is stranger than fiction. And it's crasser than fiction too.'

I felt Elena's shoe on my shin, a jab and then a steady pressure. I readjusted. She was right: I was talking as if to the old Saul, the ever-renewing Saul, and there he was, across the table, fading, withdrawing . . .

'Mm,' he said, 'I'm just feeling . . . I miss Delmore. I miss Hart Crane. I miss poor John Berryman.'

Well at least he knew they were gone. Rosamund told me that he kept forgetting that the dead were dead, and, when reminded, was bereft all over again . . .

Later, as I sought sleep (early departure, get the girls in the car, New London, ferry to Orient Point, ferry to Shelter Island, ferry to North Haven and Sag Harbor), I was thinking about what Philip Roth said to Andrew Wylie (Philip's agent, Saul's agent, my agent), 'He's depressed? You'd be depressed if *that* universe was shutting down on you.'

Shutting down. In Act 4, Scene 3 of another Shakespearean tragedy, on the night before the sea battle of Actium (and the conclusive defeat, and the paired suicides), four soldiers are patrolling the grounds of the Alexandrian palace:

> [*Music of the hautboys – oboes – as under the stage.*]
> Fourth Soldier: Peace! what noise?
> First Soldier: List, list!
> Second Soldier: Hark!
> First Soldier: Music i' the air.
> Third Soldier: Under the earth.
> Fourth Soldier: It signs well, does it not?
> Third Soldier: No.
> First Soldier: Peace, I say! What should this mean?
> Second Soldier: 'Tis the god Hercules, whom Antony loved,
>   Now leaves him.

How to Write
Decorum

We are living, you and I, through a kind of Counter-Enlightenment. Popularly known as 'populism', it is a movement supposedly attentive and responsive to 'the interests and opinions of ordinary people'. Another word for populism is 'anti-elitism'. Ordinary people know best; crowds are wise. 'I love the undereducated,' said Trump at a rally. 'We're the really smart ones.'

Every now and then there's an urge to apply the same emphasis to the arts; and the most vulnerable is literature – literature in prose. To populists, the novel is especially inviting because it is already the most populist of the forms, the most egalitarian and democratic: it asks for no special tools or training. All you need is what everyone automatically has – a ballpoint and a scrap of paper.

So we saw the anti-Great Books movement, the anti-Dead White Males movement, and the like. In Britain twenty years ago there was a movement that called itself the New Simplicity; it was anti-metaphor, anti-polysyllable, anti-adverb, and anti-subordinate clause. The New Simplicity, I thought, was a secular version of the vow of poverty. Or even the vow of silence.

I confess that I don't understand the impulse (though I can see that it's entirely sociopolitical and not at all literary). Do you know any *reflexive* anti-elitists – I don't mean the bookish types so much as the rank and file? . . . Fascinating. Are these anti-elitists, I wonder, feeling anti-elitist, feeling anti-expertise, when they go to the doctor? Or when they board a plane? Or when they hire a lawyer – or an electrician or indeed a hairdresser? Show me a sphere where we exalt the 'ordinary', the inexpert, the amateurish, the average.

389

Well, there's always that leisure-class boondoggle known as fiction. Here the lit-crit sociopoliticians have found an endeavour so unserious that no one need bother about levels of competence. Who listens to literature? Who cares what it says?

*

The good reader cares, of course, and listens. And the good reader automatically expects high proficiency – which is achievable by anyone willing to put in the time. It is possible, and pleasurable, to learn more about words and how they go together. If writing is your job, then it's just a matter of self-respect.

You're not trying to set yourself up as an exquisite or a mandarin. The modest goal is to leave the reader in as little doubt as possible that *you know what you're doing.* As you negotiate this task, you will realise, very early on, that elitism has got to start somewhere. And I think I know just the place.

On the table there are three recent historical studies, all of them by apparently genuine scholars, all of them reviewed at deferential length. The top one (on the American Revolution) tells me, inter alia, that early readers of Jonathan Swift, unused to the genre of satire, must have been 'gobsmacked' by A Modest Proposal (which was published in the early eighteenth century); the middle one (on the Third Reich) tells me that Hitler was feeling 'upbeat' when he returned to Berlin after a holiday in the Bavarian Alps; the bottom one (on Stalin) tells me that Kaiser Wilhelm I, in delegating foreign affairs to Otto von Bismarck, showed 'smarts'.

What kind of reader does this kind of writer think he's pleasing? 'Smarts' (for instance) derives from 'street-smart', and Kaiser Wilhelm never went near a street in his life; but this writer considers that 'acuity', say, or 'good sense', would be a wasted opportunity or a missed trick, given the availability of 'smarts'. I suppose there must be one reader in a hundred who will greet this or any other stop-press colloquialism with an approving leer (and forget about that reader, never mind that reader, you don't want that reader). And there must be many more, presumably including all the reviewers I read, who don't mind or just don't notice.

When the context is historical, you see at once how ruinously these vulgarisms distort the tone. Here, toadying to the contemporary is not just resoundingly anachronistic; it also does violence to decorum, to literary decorum, which has nothing to do with etiquette and simply means *conformity of style to content*. I resent being told that Hitler was at any point feeling 'upbeat', which chummily accords him a human status that was never his. I find this *inappropriate*. And as for the idea of readers being 'gobsmacked' in 1729 . . .

From here a larger lesson follows.

*

To re-emphasise: never use any phrase that bears the taint of the second-hand. All credit to whoever coined *no-brainer* and (I suppose) to whoever coined *go ballistic* and *Marxism lite* and *you rock* and *eye-popping* and *jaw-dropping* and *double whammy* and all the rest of them. Never do it – not even in conversation. Never say (let alone write) *You know what?* or *I don't* think *so* or *Hello?* or *Hey* (jocularly, as in 'But hey, we all make mistakes'). Even in a quite handy-looking little tag like *anytime soon* you can hear the bleats and the cowbells. Don't write, don't say, and don't think *Whatever* (this is probably the most counter-literary item in the entire lexicon).* Shun all vogue phrases, shun all herd words; detect them early on and shun them. Been there, done that, took the selfie, got the T-shirt . . .

Clichés have in their time put in some honest toil for the canon – Evelyn Waugh's foreign-correspondent journalese in *Scoop* ('The body of a child, like a broken doll'), the placid but maddening catchphrases in the cabman's shelter in *Ulysses* ('the acme of first class music as such, literally knocking everything else into a cocked hat'). These are venerable clichés, solidified by time. The clichés of the moment are evanescent; even in the impoverished lodgings of platitude they are mere transients.

In a work of fiction, 'gobsmacked', 'upbeat', and 'smarts' could achieve decorum – just about and not for long – if put into the mouth of a minor character, a representative (in Saul's phrase) of 'the mental rabble of the wised-up world'. Such speech would lose its threadbare

---

* I know an American teenager who holds up the thumbs and index fingers of either hand – forming the shape of a W – to spare herself the effort of saying *Whatever*. This in its way is self-parody of considerable wit.

legitimacy in a year or two, and the character would himself become an anachronism.

So cleanse your prose of anything that smells of the flock and the sheep dip. Your prose, obviously, should come from you, from you yourself – purpose-built, and not mass-produced.

*

'The hidden work of uneventful days' . . . That's Saul's marvellous evocation of the subconscious, the subconscious hard at it, trying to clarify and modulate. And it also evokes the process of writing, writing something long: writing a novel.

John Banville has described the mental atmosphere of composition as a dreamy or a dreamlike state, and so it is. And yet Banville intended no paradox when on another occasion he said with some vehemence, 'The most important thing? *Energy, energy, energy.*' Abstraction combined with exertion, producing a thrilled and thwarted tingle, like an ungratified need to sneeze; it is the tingle of creative life. That sensation, that feeling of pregnant arrest, was what Saul, at the last, was mourning.

Bellow Sr, Abraham Bellow, who died in 1955, always described Saul as a desperate sluggard, the only son 'not working only writing'. Not working? From *Augie March*:

> All the while you thought you were going around idle terribly hard work was taking place. Hard, hard work, excavation and digging, mining, moling through tunnels, heaving, pushing, moving rock, working, working, working, working, working, panting, hauling, hoisting. And none of this work is seen from the outside. It's internally done . . . [I]n yourself you labor, you wage and combat, settle scores, remember insults, fight, reply, deny, blab, denounce, triumph, outwit, overcome, vindicate, cry, persist, absolve, die and rise again yourself! Where is everybody? Inside your breast and skin, the entire cast.

'It's the same idea, isn't it,' I said to Rosamund. 'The hidden work of uneventful days.'

'This time given the bravura treatment,' she said. 'But it's the same idea.'

We had the book out on the kitchen table at Crowninshield Road. Rosie was nearby, of course, and so were Rosamund's parents, Sonya and Harvey. It was April 2005, just a few days – a few uneventful days (the quiet visits to the synagogue, the quiet procession of friends and neighbours dropping off cooked meals, mostly stews or thick soups, in tureens and engraved samovars) – after the funeral.

*

Phoebe Phelps is about to revisit us, but before we open the door and let her in . . . You know, every now and then, as I age, I discover a fresh refinement in 'the complex symbol', which is also the complex reality – meaning death.

It's like this. There I am, staked out in the Boca Raton hospice; until recently I was retching and whimpering away with some brio, but now I'm in the Critical Care Unit and trussed up with tubes and pumps and catheters. I imagine that Elena, Bobbie, Nat, Gus, Eliza, and Inez were all there, all round about me. But they're not. Together with my brothers and my friends and everyone alive whom I have ever loved – they're in mid-air on a chartered jet, coming to Florida to say their goodbyes. And halfway through the flight (JFK to West Palm Beach), the plane suffers what they call *a failure cascade*, and by the time it crosses from South Carolina to Georgia it has no hydraulics, no flaps, no spoilers, no reverse thrust, and no brakes.

I have entered a light coma and my vital signs are flickering, and the plane is busy dumping fuel just east of Savannah as it prepares to ditch at, say, Brodie Air Force Base, a few miles north of the Sunshine State (also known, remember, as the Seniors' State). Brodie has a runway of 12,000 feet, and they need twenty, thirty . . . As my medical team applies the jump leads, hoping to hot-wire me for a final half hour, the plane comes yawing through the lower air, smashes down on the Brodie tarmac, tears along its length, bursts through the barricade of foam, bubble-wrap, and bouncy castles, shinnies up the grassy knoll at the far end, and explodes.

So they die at exactly the moment I die.

In actuality, needless to say, I die and they live, and are bereaved of me. But I am bereaved of them – all of them, all my loved ones, all my pretty ones.

The only consolation I can see in this is that there won't be any time to miss them and wish they were here.

*

The end of a sentence is a weighty occasion. The end of a paragraph is even weightier (as a general guide, aim to put its best sentence last). The end of a chapter is seismic but also more pliant (either put its best paragraph last, or follow your inclination to adjourn with a light touch of the gavel). The end of a novel, you'll be relieved to learn, is usually straightforward, because by then everything has been decided, and with any luck your closing words will feel preordained.

Don't let your sentences peter out with an apologetic mumble, a trickle of dross like 'in the circumstances' or 'at least for the time being' or 'in its own way'. Most sentences have a *burden*, something to impart or get across: put that bit last. The end of a sentence is weighty, and that means that it should tend to round itself off with a *stress*. So don't end a sentence with an *–ly* adverb. The *–ly* adverb, like the apologetic mumble, can be tucked in earlier on. 'This she could effortlessly achieve' is smoother and more self-contained than 'This she could achieve effortlessly'.

Literary English seems to want to be end-stressed. Maybe it's the iamb. With the exception of Housman and not many others, the meter of serious poetry is ti-*tum*.

*

A longlasting sonic charge is packed into any word that directly precedes a punctuation mark – most especially a full stop. Look at this quote from Updike's final collection of stories, *My Father's Tears* (published posthumously in 2009):

> . . . Craig Martin took an interest in the traces left by prior owners of his land. In the prime of his life, when he worked every weekday and socialised all weekend, he had pretty much ignored his land.

So we have '. . . his land' full stop, and then '. . . his land' full stop. The word preceding a full stop is invested with treacherous stamina: as a result, 'land' and a fortiori 'his land' are effectively unusable for at least half a page – until the sonic charge wears off, and the ear forgets.*

For a whole other order of inadvertency, contemplate this: 'The grapes make a mess of the bricks in the fall; nobody ever thinks to pick them up when they fall.' (The most ridiculous thing about that sentence, somehow, is its stately semicolon.) And what follows here is not a sample quatrain of Updikean light verse:

> ants make mounds like coffee grounds . . .
> except for her bust, abruptly out-thrust . . .
> my bride became allied in my mind . . .
> polished bright by sliding anthracite . . .

No, not poetry, not doggerel. Those are just four separate snippets of deaf prose.

*

Ian became friends with John; they corresponded, and Mr and Mrs McEwan went to stay with Mr and Mrs Updike in Massachusetts in the late-middle 2000s – anyway not long before the death. And what was Updike's destined mood? You can tell from *My Father's Tears*, which contains a fair amount of life-writing, that the 'uncanny equanimity' Updike once laid claim to was in the end replaced by mild but unalleviated depression. And did Updike *know* he was losing his inner ear? Clearly not, I would say. How else could the clangers quoted above survive the two or three rereadings he must unavoidably have given them?

In 1987 I spent most of a summer day with Updike. We started off in the enormous cafeteria at Massachusetts General Hospital (where he faced a minor procedure that was belatedly postponed). At one point I asked if he would mind a brief interlude in the smoking section, and he said, 'Not at all. I envy you. I quit.' He quit in his early thirties. But oncologists call lung cancer 'the long-distance runner', and it came for him in his mid-seventies.

---

* The sonic charge is strangely uneven when it comes to common prepositions and other nuts and bolts. 'With', 'to', and 'of' – these are almost instantly forgotten by the inner ear. But 'up' (perhaps flexing its status as an adverb) has real staying power. It takes two or three hundred words before the mind forgets an 'up'.

Literary talent has perhaps four or five ways of dying. Most writers simply become watery and slightly stale. In others the subtraction is more localised and more conspicuous. Nabokov lost his sense of moral delicacy and reserve (the last four novels are heedlessly infested with twelve-year-old girls). Philip Roth lost the ability to imbue his characters with a convincingly independent life. Updike lost his ear – his mind's ear; he forgot how to use it in the formation of his prose . . .

The body, on the other hand, confronts a multiplicity of exit routes. And Updike's lungs remembered, and neither did the cancer forget.

Chapter 3
Philip: The Love of His Life

The bod from Realisations

'What d'you think I should wear?' said Phoebe on the phone (it was late morning). 'I'm not asking for your advice. I just want to hear your opinion.'

'One of your summer dresses.'

'That's no good. I want to sex him up.'

'Oh.' Phoebe meant Larkin. 'That might be a tall order . . . Wait, I know. Just keep your business suit on. You won't have to change after work, if you're rushed. It starts early, remember. Or just put on a different business suit.'

'Why would that sex him up?'

'Lots of reasons.' Martin didn't go on about the work ethic and men of a certain era and fear of the poorhouse and the blacking factory and all that. 'In his case it comes down to cold cash. The idea of a woman who might go Dutch – that'd sex him up.'

Phoebe said, 'Well I think that's too, what d'you call it, that's too generic. I want something more – more customised. Now. Larkin likes . . . Oh sorry Mart, but the bod from Acquisitions wants a word. Shall I ring back or can you wait for two minutes?'

He said he'd wait. When he called her at Transworld Financial Services there was always some bod wanting a word – the bod from Deacquisitions, plus the bods from Revendications, Encashments, Subreptions, Transmittals, and (his favourite) the bod from Realisations. He, Martin, was at present a bod from Realisations. He realised something was wrong, something was missing, something was not as it should be. He went on thinking about it, but he had no idea what it was.

'Are you still there?' she said. 'Now. Larkin likes schoolgirls.'

'Well he likes daydreaming about schoolgirls.'

'What was the bit in the letter to your dad? You know, about schoolgirls plating each other.'

'Mm.' The quote Phoebe was after went WATCHING SCHOOL-GIRLS SUCK EACH OTHER OFF WHILE YOU WHIP THEM. 'So, Phoebe? How're you going to manage that?'

'It's a challenge, I admit. But I'll see what I can do . . . Hang on. Acquisitions wants yet another word. When're you picking me up? Sixish?'

It was September 1980. The Night of Shame (July 1978), then the period of costly debauchery, then the biennium of perfect love. It can now be revealed that the time of perfect love (it in fact lasted twenty-five months and twenty-five days) had about ten hours to go.

Apollo 1

'They're not dreads and dreams, Hitch, they're more like . . . more like strange dissatisfactions. I can't describe them, I can't even identify them. Maybe it's just to do with not going to an office any more. Phoebe gets up early, so I do too. I'm at my desk by nine, and I write till one or one-thirty. And then what?'

'Mm, it's meant to be why writers are such pissers, isn't it. You do your four or five hours, then you're no good any more, so you slope off down the drinker.'

It was two o'clock on a Monday afternoon and we were in the Apollo, a West Indian bar and onetime music hall near Christopher's flat on Golborne Road. The West Indians, all of them tall and muscular young men, were sipping Sprites and Lucozades; they glanced with perfunctory pity at my pint of lager and the double Scotch of the Hitch, and at our steadily filling ashtray. I said,

'I'm in a drinker, true, but this is an exception. Boozing in the afternoon . . . it fucks up boozing in the evening. We're not all like you. We can't take it – pissed all day.'

'Pissed all week. It's my new unit. Fresh as a daisy till Tuesday afternoon when I do my column. Not too clever by Thursday. And completely tonto by Friday . . . Oh, this is going to be a heavy sacrifice when I cross the Atlantic.'

'Heavier than being ruled by Reagan?'

'Personally much heavier. Alcohol's suddenly uncool over there – even in New York. No more nine-Martini lunches. They're all on iced tea. Or fucking Sanka.'

I got more drinks and he said,

'How does it hit you, the dissatisfaction? Tell.'

'It comes on me when I stop work and feel alone. A restless vacancy, a sense of – what's the next thing? Where is it?' I arched my back. '*When* is it?'

'Maybe it's because around now everyone seems to be settling down. Ian's settling down with Penny. Julian's settling down with Pat.'

'And you're settling down with Eleni.'

'As I said, she loves the Hitch, she wants to marry the Hitch . . . It's a pity about the timing. Because I finally got the hang of promiscuity – thanks to America.'

'How's that?'

'Well, first off, you know my besetting weakness, don't you. It's a sort of timidity, or a fear of giving offence – or a fear of rejection. And in America it's the chicks who make all the moves.'

'Oi. What about Lady Mab and the others? They made all the moves and you still didn't come across. Because you'd have to string them up the next morning.'

'That's the other half of it. There are no chicks worth stringing up in America. None of them sound like Lady Mab. Even the heiresses' dads were at some point poor. I know there are dynasties, but very few US chicks are *born* entitled, which is what I can't stand. They have a different class system over there.'

'And it's just race and money. But you say it's also very weird.'

'One example. The poor whites, the hookworm-and-incest crowd, have made an unspoken deal with the rich whites. You can sneer at us so long as we can both sneer at the blacks. And then there are little fripperies like the Boston Brahmins.'

'. . . Julia's dad's a Boston Brahmin. Not at all rich but very *Mayflower*.'

'Any developments there?'

'With Julia? Don't talk stupid. It's at least a year too soon.'

'When was it again?'

'Just over a month ago. Cancer. At *his* age . . . So Hitch. Who am I going to settle down with? Phoebe's finite. She loves Little Keith, I think, but she doesn't want to marry Little Keith. Or anybody else. She's completely reconciled to it. And I always sort of knew I shouldn't marry Phoebe. She isn't the love of my life.'

'You just want to get to the end of her sexually.'

'Yes – while I'm at it. And I keep thinking I'm nearly there. But on the phone with her this morning I had a sick bonk throughout – the whole half an hour.'

'Still. In the nature of things Phoebe will end. So then who?'

'Remember Miri, Miriam Gould? I find myself mooning a lot about Miri. Our little thing should've been a big thing – that's another form of the missed chance. And I wouldn't mind settling down for a while with Janet Hobhouse.'

'Ah. A surprising omission of yours I always thought. Wait.'

He got more drinks and I said,

'Not a total omission. We've had a night or two together. Oh yeah. During the act, Hitch, Janet does something quite rare. Don't look so intent – it's nothing dirty. Real feminists aren't dirty. Logically enough. No. She's a smiler. She smiles. During.'

'How incredibly sweet.'

'Now I come to think of it, just like Germaine . . . With Miri there was some other fucking bloke in the background. Same with Janet.'

'You mean her husband. Janet's great, I agree. But the one you're really interested in, Mart – and yes I know the complications – is Julia. I can tell.'

'Mm. I ought to go. Oh, and don't you be late tonight,' I said. 'Dad told me that Larkin's not bringing his bird, he's not bringing Monica. So Phoebe's planning some kind of sex tease on him – and it should be good.'

'I'll be there. Janet's a major chick.'

'Miri's a major chick. And as for Julia . . . I had a drink with her the other night and she made me feel like a teenager. Or a child. She's so evolved.'

'It's death does that.'

*

And looking back, now, from here, I see how busy death always is, and what great plans it always has.

Julia's first husband – incandescently vigorous, it seemed, in body and mind – died in August 1980 at the age of thirty-four. Miri, Miriam Gould, killed herself in Barcelona in 1986 at the age of thirty-seven. And Janet, Janet Hobhouse, the novelist (and life-writer), died in 1991 at the age of forty-two.

What lesson, what moral, can be drawn from this?

One had better be quick.

Bobby socks

Phoebe buzzed him in and Martin climbed the stairs. He had his own set of keys, but (as instructed) he still used the intercom to give a polite warning. The bedroom door was open and he went straight through . . . She was semi-naked in the chair before the dressing table with her legs at a familiar elevation and with her crossed feet reflected in the three mirrors. Her hands held an eyeliner pencil and a slim volume.

She said, 'That's what he'll think the moment we walk in. *When I see a couple of kids And guess he's fucking her and she's Taking pills or wearing a diaphragm, I know this is paradise // Everyone old has dreamed of all their lives.* That's exactly what he'll think when he sees us walk in.'

'Yeah, and he'll envy me. With good reason. I think he's a powerful envier anyway.'

Martin went and kissed her and each of them said a few things about their day.

'I'll fetch a beer while you get dressed.'

'No I'm ready.' She bounced to her feet. 'Let's go.'

Phoebe was back in her mansion flat and was once again prosperous and broadhanded. TFS let her do more trading now, and so her need for gaming was confined to the turf (a recreational fiver once or twice a week). And purdah never lasted more than a single night. Their erotic life was emotional, carnal, innovational, and – most signally – habitual. When acknowledging that this was indeed the case, Phoebe always said, *You realise it'll be the end of us.* And Martin always thought, Yes, and so do you – and why isn't it already? . . . The cause of his disquiet, he would've said and would've meant, was not to be found in the bedroom.

As far as he knew he had never felt more thoroughly slaked. He now said,

'You're not going out dressed like that, young lady. You've to stop home.'

'What're you talking about?'

He looked at her from top to toe and then from toe to top. The feet (as yet unshod), the long coppertone legs, the pink tutu or ra-ra skirt sticking out practically at right angles to the cinched waist, the shortsleeved pale-pink singlet with its bra-less orbs and staring nipples, the pigtails, and the black beret with a sprawling gold crest on it saying, RICHMOND ACADEMY FOR GIRLS.

'Have a heart, Phoebe. Come on, think. He's never written a word about schoolgirls. Not in public. Dad's going to be there too, and he'll know at once I squealed.'

She said, 'And did Kingsley swear you to secrecy? Of course he didn't. So it's just a bit of insider dealing, and very much to be expected. Stop fussing. Bloody hell.'

'. . . Are you going to wear sandals? Or just gyms.'

'Bobby socks and spike-heeled red booties. No *gyms*. And no navy-blue knickers either.' She turned a half circle. 'Can you just about see the undersides of my arse?'

'Yeah, just about. And I can just about see the undersides of your pants.'

'That's because you're a shrimp. He's tall. If it comes to it I may have to . . .'

He said, 'Phoebe, you've finally put my mind at rest. May have to what?'

The drinks party was being thrown by Robert Conquest, who lived on Prince of Wales Drive, Battersea (an area that estate agents had started calling Lower Chelsea). As they drove over the sunshot, the sheet-metal River Thames, Phoebe, her mouth stiffened to receive lipstick, said in a distorted voice,

'Do you like schoolgirls at all?'

'In that sense? No, not a bit. I mean I liked schoolgirls when I was a schoolboy. But even then the girls I really fancied were grownup women. Teachers, movie stars, Aunt Miggy. Mum's friends. Especially the one called Rhona.'

'Remember Polanski?' Phoebe squished her lips together and straightened her mouth. That off-centredness, that loutish asymmetry – it was gone, long gone (together with her aversion to Anglosaxonisms); love, or quasi-love, had wiped it from her face. This gratified his ego and his honour (even though he missed it). 'According to him,' she said, '*all* men want to fuck young girls.'

'Yeah, as if it's "only human". I wouldn't want to even if it wasn't against the law.'

'You don't like them till they're eighteen.'

'I like them older than eighteen. Twice as old. You, for instance, Phoebe.'

'Youth is pretty, you claim, but it's not interesting. Oh yes it is. It commands plenty of interest. Haven't you noticed? Look around.'

'I'm not just saying it, I mean it, I feel it. I don't like schoolgirls, not in your sense.'

'Mm. I don't like schoolboys. What do men like about schoolgirls – those who do? What is it they like the idea of?'

These days, when it came up, they talked about paedophilia 'normally', as if it was just a subject like any other. He found himself saying,

'There was a schoolgirl Dad had a crush on.' They were waiting at a red light – parkland on one side, gabled and churchy Victorian houses on the other . . . Martin now recalled Kingsley's puzzled and diffident late-night confession. In some semi-rustic earlier life – Eynsham, perhaps – a pretty fourteen-year-old in the market square gave him a smile that he went on thinking about all day. And there might have been another smile or two. Anyway, the last time he saw her their eyes met and she looked straight past him; and for a whole month he despaired. 'Yeah, my dad liked a schoolgirl,' he said. 'Though of course he never did anything about it.'

'Father Gabriel liked a schoolgirl,' said Phoebe, and said nothing more.

Poets can pull

'The US edition of *High Windows* is out,' wrote Larkin in 1974, 'with a photograph of me that cries out for the headline, FAITH HEALER?

OR HEARTLESS FRAUD?' In common with all PL's self-descriptions, this was unsparingly apt: 'And then my sagging face, an egg sculpted in lard, with goggles on.' He looked antique, stranded in time; his was one of those forgotten figures from the 1930s (a minor politician, a senior civil servant). Then there was his figure, which was also ovoid – tall, cumbrous, and unhappily heavy. 'None of my clothes fit either: when I sit down my tongue comes out.' As he headed off for one of his pseudo-holidays in Eigg or the Isle of Mull ('one couldn't call this spot anything but desolate, or the weather anything but wet'), Larkin's bathroom scales would be stowed in his luggage . . .

Phoebe and I used the lift then went within. Conquest's sitting room and contiguous dining area contained about three dozen people (some of them faintly familiar, a poet, a knighted journalist), and the Hermit of Hull was over in the far corner, his head bent forward as he listened to the kind of man who, to paraphrase Kingsley (also present), looked like the kind of woman who played Sir Toby Belch in sorority productions of *Twelfth Night*. I said,

'That geezer seems to be slipping away. I'll slip away too after I've introduced you.'

'No,' she said, 'slip away now. I'll do it.'

'Okay, but don't scare him, Phoebe.'

With a twirl and a glide she was there in front of him and brightly saying, 'Dr Larkin, good evening. I'm Phoebe, I'm Martin's girlfriend.'

He politely inclined his head and took her offered hand.

'I'm a big fan.'

'Are you now. Everyone's saying that, suddenly. "I'm a big fan." Making me wonder, Where are all the medium-sized fans? Where are all the *little* fans?'

'Yes, where are all the dear little fans? But I'm not a little fan. I'm a big fan.'

He was smiling. 'All right. Quote me a line.'

'All right. *When I see a couple of kids / And guess he's* . . . No, that won't do. Uh, *He married a woman to stop her getting away / Now she's there all day, // And the money he gets for wasting his life on work / She takes as her perk / To pay for the kiddies' clobber and the drier / And the electric fire* . . .'

'That *is* quite impressive.'

'Paying for the kiddies' clobber and the electric fire – it's hardly her *perk*, is it? I mean, the kiddies can't go around naked, and the husband gets warm too. But that just makes it funnier somehow. Why are you so funny, Dr Larkin?'

'. . . Why?'

Their duologue was now lost in ambient murmurs, and I moved off to get a drink and say hello to Bob and find my dad. This I did, without losing sight of Phoebe; and from this distance, in this company, she looked like a peacock let loose in a senior common room.

Kingsley said, 'What's the point of that get-up?'

I shrugged. 'She wanted to give him a thrill.'

'No harm in that I suppose.'

'In which case,' said Bob (b. 1917), 'she should've worn one of her business suits.'

Within its staid limits the party was getting thicker and louder. After a few minutes I got hold of another drink and went and attached myself to an elderly and unvoluble foursome to Larkin's rear, and Phoebe (who still held his full attention) was saying,

'. . . and you're *famous*. As well as being funny and the rest of it. So you might as well have some fun along the way. Because poets can pull, you know.'

Larkin straightened up. 'Now how is it that this evident truth has passed me by?'

'Perhaps you haven't chanced your arm enough. Poets can pull. I've seen it, mate.'

'Ah. You're referring to rugged brutes like Ted Hughes and Ian Hamilton.'

'No. When I was a little girl we had a so-called poet living across the street. And he looked like Quasimodo – you know, one eye here, one eye there. I don't think he'd ever published a line – all he did was *say* he was a poet. And he had this permanent gaggle of bints lining up to muck out his bedsit and bring him his pale ales and his hot dinners. That was in the bungalow belt. And as for what I've seen in town . . . It's one of those laws of nature. Women like poets.'

'Mm, I've heard rumours to that effect. Women like poets. Why d'you think the ones that do do? Is it because we're meant to be in touch with our feelings? With a well-developed feminine side?'

'Well, getting, uh securing the interest of a poet – that makes women feel interesting. But I think it's simpler than that. Correct me if I'm wrong, Dr Larkin, but poets don't get much in the way of rewards, do they. Compared to dramatists and even novelists.'

'That at least is incontrovertible.'

'And women sense it. Poets don't get much, so women make sure poets get women. God bless them.' Phoebe clutched her bag and gazed about her. 'Ah, Christopher's here. He's a definite Christopher, isn't he – not a Chris. Now Dr Larkin, I can't hog you all night. There's a press of admirers dying to give you a pinch and a punch.'

She meant the two young men and the one old lady who were hovering disconnectedly nearby.

'Now you won't vanish, will you,' said Larkin, 'without bidding me farewell?'

'Oh I promise.'

———————————

That particular poet took the late train back to Hull, while Martin, his girlfriend, and his father had a noisy dinner in a local tratt with Bob and Liddie (wife number four) plus Hitch and Eleni. Also present were a couple of young academics from San Francisco, who became increasingly entranced by the sheer bulk of what Phoebe was putting away; they fell silent after she ordered a second veal chop and a further hamper of bread; and when at last she got nimbly to her feet (after two custard pies and two fruit salads), they stared at one another and shook their heads . . .

Then there was Kingsley to be driven home and dropped off in Hampstead. The house was still lit, at twelve-fifteen; and something told Martin that the white sheen from the sitting room – it had a coldly watchful look in the warm summer night – would be reproduced in Jane's waiting face . . . Now Kingsley climbed heavily from the car, heavily aware that he would not be going straight to bed.

Unlike his middle child. In fact it started on the moonlit landing, in Hereford Mansions; as he followed Phoebe up the stairs, giving himself a shadowy eye-level view of the enormous bra of her underpants, he reached up and she went still and widened the set of her legs, saying,

'Give me your hand.'

And even as the reptilian glaze came down on him, he was thinking, no, this isn't quite right, something is not as it should be.* But it will do beautifully for now . . .

Later – but not very much later – she said, 'That was quick.'

'I know. I'm sorry. I just lost concentration . . . It won't happen again.'

There was a silence – a silence he urgently wanted to break. He said,

'Uh Phoebe, did you manage to say goodbye to the old boy?'

'Oh yes,' she said (unhuffily and even with some enthusiasm). 'We had a whole other chat. And we got on to death I'm afraid. I told him I was just as messed up about it as he was. I even told him about the lav.'

'You didn't.'

'I did. And I asked him if he felt the same way.'

'You didn't,' I said. 'And did he? Does he?'

Phoebe's fear of death, or her type of death awareness, somehow extended to her morning visits to the bathroom. These visits were always preceded by a hectic demand for absolute sequestration (even at her place, with its remote second toilet, she sent him out to buy a paper). *I thought only blokes were like that*, he once said – because in his experience girls just went in there, without locking or even closing the door, and just came out again as if nothing had happened. Yet Phoebe argued the other way. *You'd* expect *a bloke to need a shit now and then. But not girls. How're you meant to think of yourself as even halfway pretty*, she said, *when you're responsible for that, that swamp of hot muck? Every day? No wonder I'm neurotic about it.*

'And was he? Is he the same way?'

'No. He said he regards it as "communing with nature". Which I thought was slightly nuts too. Still, he doesn't see it as a visit to hell.

'On one thing we saw absolutely eye to eye. The kiddies. I said, *I take a lot of pride in my figure. It's my one great blessing. And I won't stand for some grasping little bleeder ruining my midriff and my tits*, which he

* This obscure unease – it felt like a sin of omission, as yet undisclosed but always on the point of revealing itself. And there was a spiritual edge to it. I imagined that the religiously inclined would know how it felt: a fear of falling short, of missing out on something transformative – the Resurrection, the Rapture . . .

kept trying not to stare at, *and God knows what else*. And on that he was with me all the way . . .

'I was planning to give him a flash before I went off. There was hardly anybody there by then, so I thought I'd drop my compact and then bend right over to pick it up. Then he'd be able to structure a wank around it when he got back up north. I mean, with him that's the point of it all, isn't it? Wanks. There's no boring bit before and after with wanks, not like fucks. And wanks are free.

'It seemed so *lame*. But I couldn't think what else to do. So I did it. And stayed down an extra minute fiddling with my boot buttons. Then I straightened up with a silly-me smile . . . And I think I *did* scare him, because he had a frail look on his face, like an old woman. He *is* an old woman. And he said, *You oughtn't to be allowed.*'

'Oughtn't. That's very him.'

She said, 'Martin. Earlier on. It was as if you came as quickly as you could.'

'. . . I'm sorry, Phoebe. It won't happen again.'

Not long after, when she went quiet and then still, I carefully got out of bed and groped my way to the balcony and had a shivery smoke, saying to myself, Christ. Even the *sex* has suddenly got something wrong with it . . .

Knowing and accepting that 'the moronic fraternity of sleep' (Nabokov) would be closed to me that night, I went inside and turned on the table lamp and ran my eye over Phoebe's sparse bookshelves. A paperback bestseller called *The Usurers*, Jane Howard's *After Julius*, a legal thriller, Ian's first collection of stories, a romance set in the Paris Bourse, my third novel, and – wedged between *Principles of Accountancy* and *The Crash* – the four volumes of Larkin (barely an inch thick), 1945, 1955, 1964, 1974 . . .

1964 contained the poem I'd been meaning to look out, 'Dockery and Son', in fact a B-grade PL poem famous for its last four lines.* But the bit I wanted came in the stanza before . . . Funereally dressed for the occasion ('death-suited'), the poet-narrator, who is forty-one (and wifeless and childless), pays a visit to his old college and learns that a

---

* 'Life is first boredom, then fear. / Whether or not we use it, it goes, / And leaves what something hidden from us chose, / And age, and then the only end of age.'

contemporary of his, Dockery, already has a son enrolled there. And the stunned 'I' wonders at how

> Convinced he was he should be added to!
> Why did he think adding meant increase?
> To me it was dilution.

And I thought, No. To me it wouldn't be dilution, and not addition, either. Something more impersonal. Continuation: so that when the only end of age at last arrives, your story doesn't just stop – doesn't just stop dead.

Children, that was the thing (that was the next thing): you needed children. Because (or so I later came to believe) they were the ones who embodied the ordinary, the average, the near-universal push for a kind of immortality. Or so I later came to believe. I would say it out loud, gropingly, several times a day – *I just want to see a fresh face* . . .

Julia, then (I hoped), let it one day be Julia.

Apollo 2

'They're used to us in here now,' I said (it was six months later – March 1981). 'I don't even feel particularly white.'

'Nor me,' he said. 'I just feel particularly alcoholic. And particularly *gay*.'

'I know what you mean . . . Yeah, but they don't mind us.'

'No. We're just those two pissed little queers.'

'Exactly . . . Hitch, I thought only chicks felt broody.'

'Me too. But maybe it's just that blokes never own up to it.'

'Or don't know they're feeling it. Are you feeling broody do you think?'

'No. I'm feeling open to experience, but I'm not feeling broody.'

'Mm. Talking of not feeling broody, how did you find Larkin that time? Did you talk? I can't remember.'

'I only had a couple of minutes with the old buzzard. And he just went on and on about his *bills*. His bills. Especially as they related to his car.'

He got more drinks and I said,

'Didn't he say something about black people?'

'About foreigners in general. He said he didn't like London because of all the foreign germs . . . You know, that's the one thing that really daunts me about America. Race. And now Ronnie's stirring it up with that guff about welfare queens and strapping young bucks buying T-bone steaks with food stamps.'

'All plain *invented*. "I'm not smart enough to tell a lie" – remember that?'

'He's too thick to make any up, but he's happy to repeat all the ones he hears. He'll even tell the same lie twice! They've worked out he tells a lie, in public, every single day. Can you imagine?'

'Unbelievable. Yeah. "Eighty per cent of acid rain is caused by *trees*." He's not just pig-ignorant, it's as if he's anti-knowledge. He's actually anti-science!'

'Did you see that quote from Andy Warhol? Saying it was "kind of great", so American – having a Hollywood actor as president. Yeah, but what next?'

I said, 'Ronnie's still an actor, and quite good at it too. Don't forget I travelled with him for nearly a week last year, and I heard him tell the same long anecdote nine times – with identical intonations. That's what actors do.'

'And now he's an actor playing the part of an aw-shucks goodie. He's not a goodie. You're meant to think there's no harm in the old boy, but I sense . . . Oh, the pen of the Hitch'll have some warm work to do in America.'

'It'll be okay. The First Lady's a distinguished astrologer. She'll keep him steady.'

I got more drinks and he said,

'Tell me, Little Keith. I've just reread *Lucky Jim*. Is it true that Margaret Peel was based on the old buzzard's bird? On Monica?'

'Absolutely. And with the old buzzard's enthusiastic collaboration. And no disguise – not even an alias. Monica's full name is Margaret Monica Beale Jones. But Larkin drew a line. He made Kingsley change *Beale* to *Peel*.'

'Ah, so chivalry isn't dead . . . Christ, that Margaret. Dirndls and weird jewellery, and not only always tedious but always absolutely excruciating.'

PHILIP: THE LOVE OF HIS LIFE

'. . . Monica *can't* be that bad. Or she can't *still* be that bad. They've been together since we were one. Imagine that.'

'Mm, well that's how it happens. No kids. So you get stalled in your status quo.'

'That's what Mum says. Childlessness dooms you to childishness. Having kids isn't the trap – not having them's the trap . . . Right, that's it, I've decided. Which means farewell to Phoebe.'

'You're always saying that. Then you creep back to your sick bonk . . .'

'That's stopped working. Now even the sex is fucked up. All the time, while we're writhing around, I'm thinking, What's sex *for*?'

'What's it for? Well, pleasure, morale. And an escape from thought.'

'And also the little matter of procreation. I can't go on evading it, Hitch. I need to see a fresh face. One unmarked by the world. I need to see an innocent.'

In conversation with Monica Jones

'THEN THE *RECTOR*,' she said, 'BY WHICH HONORIFIC I DO *NOT* REFER TO THE INCUMBENT OF A PARISH AND THE RECIPIENT OF THE TITHES THEREOF IN THE GOOD OLD CHURCH OF ENGLAND, *OH* NO. I MEAN THE HEAD OF ONE OF OUR VENERABLE SEATS OF *LEARNING*.'

'Do you mean Leicester University, Monica?' I asked.

'WELL DONE THAT MAN! NONE OTHER, GRACIOUS SIR! . . . OUR MOST HONOURABLE *RECTOR*! NOW, AT THIS JUNCTURE, SAID RECTOR PERMITS HIMSELF A COPIOUS DRAUGHT OF SHERRY AND THEN LOOKS ME UP AND DOWN AND ENQUIRES, "HELLO. WHO ARE YOU THEN?"'

'And what did you say?'

'"RECTOR!" I BEGIN, TURNING TO SAME, "I TEACH ENGLISH LITERATURE HERE IN YOUR HALLOWED HALLS." TO WHICH, IN HIS STENTORIAN TONES, HE EXPOSTULATES THUSLY . . . "MADAM," QUOTH HE. "*IT IS NOT A FUNCTION OF MY OFFICE TO COMMIT TO PHOTOGRAPHIC MEMORY EACH AND EVERY . . .*"'

The speaker was Monica Beale Jones (whose mouth was perhaps a centimetre away from mine): Monica, a burly sixty-year-old in gunmetal satin tank top, thick brown trousers (my memory vacillates between crushed velvet and leatherette), and slablike black shoes with steel buckles; she also sported horn-rimmed glasses, earrings the size of horseshoes, and cropped tufty hair . . . In early photographs, from the late 1940s, her face is intelligent and shapely, and expresses a touching, striven-for self-possession. By May 1982 that face was fuller and squarer and naturally coarser. And it wasn't just masculine; it was male. Rowdily, pugnaciously male, like her voice. When I visualise her now, I see an *urka* out on the razzle.* At this point Larkin had been with Monica for over thirty years.

And let's have a look at *him* while we're at it. I said that at Oxford he dressed with some flamboyance, but the cravats and the crimson flannels were put aside soon after graduation. And that evening in London he simply passed for what he'd eventually become – a fairly senior provincial archivist and administrator (who, most counterintuitively, also happened to be the widely beloved national poet). From the moment they entered the house,† PL exuded not benevolence so much as utter harmlessness, prim, timorous, and demure, as if content to hope that nothing would go too gravely awry. His demeanour, in short, was that of the politely longsuffering wife of a notoriously impossible husband.

In the early 1980s I knew nothing much about Philip and Monica. I know a lot about them now. And nothing stands out as starkly as the letter quoted below.

They met in September 1946; by the summer of 1950 PL 'had come to me', as Monica quaintly put it; and in October 1952 he wrote to her with this advice:

---

* Dating back to Russia's Time of Troubles in the 1600s, the *urkas* or *urki* constituted a dynamic subculture of hereditary criminals. In the Bolshevik Gulag they were classified as Socially Friendly Elements and were given the status of trusties; the *urkas* were thus empowered and encouraged to torment the *counters* and the *fascists* – i.e., the intellectuals, very much including the poets.

† They had spent the day at Lord's Cricket Ground in St John's Wood, watching a Test match between England and Pakistan. Monica immediately started putting everyone right about the visiting team's spin bowlers. 'IT *WASN'T* ABDUL QADIR! IT WAS IQBAL QASIM!'

Dear, I must sound very pompous . . . It's simply that in my view you would do much better to revise, drastically, the amount you say and the intensity with which you say it . . . I *do* want to urge you with all love and kindness . . . I'd even go so far as to make 3 rules.

One. *Never* say more than two sentences, or *very rarely* three, without waiting for an answer or comment from whoever you're speaking to; Two, abandon *altogether* your harsh didactic voice, & use *only* the soft musical one (except in special cases); & Three, don't do more than *glance* at your interlocutor (wrong word?) once or twice while speaking. You're getting a habit of *boring* your face up or round into the features of your listener – don't do it! It's most trying.

Now this is the kind of therapeutic routine that would need to be rehearsed at least twice a week. Rehearsed with all love and kindness, and also high moral energy (a smattering of sexual legitimacy would have been useful too – they were both about thirty). But it was an effort never made by him, and never made by her. In the early 1980s the Monica idiolect was just as PL described it in the early 1950s.

So they had their world, with its cosy jokes and whimsies, its pet names and imagined menageries, its confidences and indulgences, its childlike attempts at the physical ('I'm sorry to have failed you!'). That was their own business. But when they mingled with others Philip was inflicting on the company what he had somehow managed to inflict on himself: unignorable proximity to a deafening windbag. And she wasn't his weird sister or his crazy cousin: she was the woman you would have to call the love of his life.

A female observer of Saul Bellow's amatory ups and downs remarked that he 'was the kind of man who thought he could change women . . . And he couldn't. I mean who can? You don't.' That's right, you don't: they don't change you and you don't change them. But it is surely a sacred obligation – to go on trying to impede, or at least retard, your lover's journey into monstrousness.

I said my goodbyes and then steered the black Mini to the significant house on the street off Ladbroke Grove, a street quite thickly flanked by trees of cherry blossom and apple blossom . . .

'After she told the very long story about the rector,' I said with my face in my hands, 'she told a very long story about an alderman. A remarkably similar story. From which she also emerged with obscure credit.' I looked up, blinking. 'And you know, I sort of warmed to Monica at least to start with. I told myself, Relax – it's only another boho evening. But she isn't at all boho, and neither is he. No, they're anti-boho. They're bourgeois fogeys, the pair of them.'

Julia said, 'Now sit back and have a big whisky. Is she mentally ill d'you think? I hate mad people.'

'So do I. I couldn't decide. Dad says she is. What's the word, Asperger's.'

'It can't be that. Asperger's is meant to be mild.'

'Well. She thoroughly enjoyed herself – she thought she was in wonderful form . . . That's what I couldn't get over. The gurgling.'

'What gurgling?'

'Are you very tired?'

'No, not very. Go on. And have another big whisky. And talk. Talk now, or you'll never sleep a wink.'

. . . Well, Julia, at dinner, in the intervals between one dumbfounding soliloquy and another dumbfounding soliloquy (a soliloquy, in which a stage character gives vent to thoughts 'when alone or regardless of hearers'), Monica took little breaks or breathers; and during these she audibly gurgled, a continuous series of breathy gulps and grunts and swallows. What did this sound express? I was on Monica's left, and it sounded to me like a stupor of self-satisfaction . . .

'And I'd heard that same gurgling before. You know Robinson. He's got a demented aunt who lives in a small manor house in Sussex. Surrounded by hopeful young relatives like Robinson – more or less patiently awaiting her death. And Aunt Esme, she seems all right, but she has this fatal flaw. She refuses to believe it isn't May 16, 1958. Every day.

'Rob told me to avoid, on pain of death, the slightest suggestion that it *wasn't* May 16, 1958. When I was there it was a summer afternoon, and Auntie Esme was already on her guard because it was ninety-five degrees. "Rather unseasonal for May," she kept saying. Which is apparently what she keeps saying whenever they get snowed in . . . Then after lunch the old nutter found the milkman's bill on the doormat, and it was firmly stamped August 1, 1977. So she was fainting and having seizures and everyone was saying, *Get the mail! Where's the mail?* What they meant was the specially preserved *Daily Mail* of May 16, 1958.

'They finally found it and presented it to her, and she immediately went all smug and serene – at last a bit of *sense* . . . She curled up with it on an armchair, the yellowing, crackling relic of the *Daily Mail*. The headline was USSR LAUNCHES SPUTNIK III. And for half an hour Auntie Esme gurgled, exactly like Monica. And she gurgled *gloatingly*.'

'. . . Mad but *right*.'

'Vindicated, finally. Right all along. As if telling herself, "See? Some have said I'm a bore – but I'm not! I'm hugely entertaining!" . . . Ah well. There was a sweet moment early on. Nicolas spontaneously embraced his godfather, and Larkin embraced him back. For a moment he looked very fond and very gentle. And very happy. I could see what Dad meant when he called his manner "sunlit".'

'Sunlit. That's a nice word to use,' said Julia. 'Come on, finish that and let's go up.'

When he left the house the next morning a summery windstorm was in boisterous operation and having it all its own way – spelling the end of the spring blossoms, the cherry blossom, the apple blossom, for another year. And now the pink and the white buds and petals surged and swirled in reckless celebration, as if all the trees were suddenly getting married.

The fireside chat

In May 1982 I was thirty-two and Larkin was fifty-nine. In December 1985 I was thirty-six (with a wife and a son, and another child on the way) and Larkin was dead.

. . . Haemorrhoids, neck-ache, an enlarged liver, giddiness, and other familiar complaints; and then some difficulty in swallowing. A 'barium meal' disclosed a tumour in his alimentary canal. His oesophagus would have to come out.

The night before the operation he summoned Monica from the kitchen to the sitting room. She was very poorly too: acute inflammation of the nerve endings (shingles). Beyond in the hall their walking sticks hung side by side . . .

The two of them settled in front of the gas fire. He said,

'Suppose I've got cancer. Suppose I've got this. How long would you give me?'

Monica felt that 'she couldn't lie to him', not then. So she said, rightly or wrongly but very accurately,

'Six months.'

Larkin said, '. . . Oh. Is that all?'

How to Write
Impersonal Forces

Human beings are essentially social animals, and the anglophone novel is essentially a social form; it is in addition a rational form and a moral form. So one shouldn't be surprised by the fact that, on the little planet called Fiction, social realism is the lone superpower. And although most modern writers, once or twice in their writing lives, will want to get out from under it and go off somewhere else, social realism still stands as their primary residence – their fixed address.

Literary experimentalists can do anything they want – indeed, they have already done just that by confronting you with a literary experiment. Literary social realists are temperamentally drawn the other way: they embrace solid conventions, and then work within and around them; and as they embark on a novel they reflexively accept that certain social norms will still apply. Readers are your guests, after all, and they come to your house as strangers; so you reassure them and make them feel at home, and then you start warming them up . . .

Now, if you ever paid a call on Anthony Trollope, the master social realist, I'm sure you'd be suavely received. Trollope was proud of his professional facility (he spent only three hours a day in his study, and produced over forty novels), and he would want to regale you with the fruits of his success (the house, the grounds, the dining room, the cellar, and other incidentals). Far more importantly, though, he would greet you with an alert and inquisitive eye, and would want to stimulate you into vividness . . . We now ask ourselves, What would James Joyce, the master experimentalist, be like to pay a call on?

The cryptic directions you were given lead you to a house that does not exist, or, rather, to a vast and gusty demolition site through whose soot and grit you can glimpse, in the middle distance, one unrazed building. And so you slither and hurdle your way down there and squelch through the mud and somehow activate the elaborate gong, and after a lengthy and soundless wait the door is wrenched open to reveal a figure who is angrily arguing with himself in several languages at once – before he again slips away, to be found an hour later in a distant scullery, where he gives you a jamjar of brown whey and a bowlful of turnips and eels.

*

So don't do that: don't be baffling and indigestible. The good, the thoughtful host doesn't do that. And he doesn't do this: he doesn't overwhelm you. Don't, for example, harass your visitor with a multitude of fresh acquaintances, as Faulkner tends to do, beginning a short story with something like *Abe, Bax, Cal, and Dirk were sitting up front, so I got in back with Emery, Fil, Grunt, Hube, and J-J (who used to be called Zoodie), and out on the flatbed I could see Keller, Leroy, Mo, Ned, Orrin* . . . Even Muriel Spark, often the very deftest of writers, can quickly exhaust your powers of retention (there are far, far too many girls of slender means in *The Girls of Slender Means*). At the outset, before things loosen up, introduce only one character or maybe two, or possibly three, or at the very most four.

Take the earliest opportunity to give the readers a bit of typographical *air* – a break, a subhead, a new chapter. As I remember it, the first of Updike's Rabbit books, *Rabbit, Run*, trundles on for thirty or thirty-five pages before we get so much as a line-space – long enough, at any rate, to establish an impression of fathomless garrulity. Don't do that: don't keep them waiting too long for a stretch of clear white paper. They will be grateful for a chance to catch their breath and to brace themselves for more; and so will you.

This is yet another example of the strange co-identity of writer and reader. Just as *guest* and *host* have the same root – from Latin *hospes, hospit-* ('host, guest') – readers and writers are in some sense interchangeable (because a tale, a teller, is nothing without a listener). And readers are artists, too. Each and every one of them paints a different mental picture of Madame Bovary.

Asked to sum up the pleasures of reading, Nabokov said that they exactly correspond to the pleasures of writing. I for one have never read a novel that I 'wished I'd written' (that would be simultaneously craven and brash), but I certainly and invariably try to write the novels I would wish to read. When we write, we are also reading. When we read (as noted earlier), we are also writing. Reading and writing are somehow the same thing.

'I can't start a novel', my stepmother Jane used to say, 'until I can jot down its theme on the back of an envelope. Just a few words – and it doesn't matter how trite they are. *Appearances are deceptive. Cheats never prosper. Look before you leap* . . . Then I'm ready to begin.'

'That would be impossible for me,' my father Kingsley used to say. 'I don't *know* what its theme is. I've got a certain situation or a certain character. Then I just feel my way.'

'Well I feel my way too. Once I've got going. But I can't get going until I can at least fool myself that I know what I'm getting going *on*.'

. . . For me it's a journey with a destination but without maps; you have a certain place you want to get to – but you don't know the way. As you near that goal, though (one year later, or two, or four, or six), you can probably do what Jane did: you can formulate its gist in a single phrase; and that commonplace motto can serve as a touchstone during your final revisions. This is when you begin to sense the salutary pressure to *cut* . . . Particular sentences and paragraphs will feel strained and unstable; they seem to be hinting at their own expendability. And now's the time to consult the back of that envelope: if the passage that disquiets you has no clear bearing on the stated theme – then (with regret, having saved what you can for another day) you should let it go. What you are after, at this stage, is *unity*.

Writing a novel is a . . . is a learning experience. In the old days I would get to the end of a first draft and then flip the whole thing over, and stare at it in wonder; and then start reading. And I was always astonished and embarrassed by how little I knew about that particular fiction, how larval it seemed, and how approximate. That's the first page. By the last page you are back where you were (and confirming that, yes, the entire cast without exception has been transformed en route: their names, their ages, even sometimes their genders) . . . A much milder reprise of the same experience can be expected when you come to the end of draft two.

In writing this or that novel, you are learning – you are uncovering information – about this or that novel.

*

I knew at once what he meant. 'Mart,' said my brother Nicolas on the phone. 'It's happened.' In other words, Jane had bolted from the house on Flask Walk.

It wasn't at all unexpected. Here was a marriage audibly pleading to be put out of its misery . . . Kingsley was hurt, romantically hurt (he came close to writing a poem about it – until his feelings fiercely hardened); and there was a great deal of disruption.* But there was no surprise and no censure. Everybody understood.

Still, I am forced to conclude that there was some resentment on my part (filial protective solidarity, perhaps), because I exacted a small but interesting revenge on Jane – strangely mean-spirited, as I now judge it. She ceased to be my legal stepmother in 1983, but she continued to be my confidante and mentor until her death (in 2014 at the age of ninety). It was a writerly revenge. I didn't stop seeing her; I just stopped reading her.†

*

There are three impersonal forces – three guardian spirits – hovering over the theme park of fiction; they are there to help you; they are your friends.

First: genre. If you write Westerns, you will have the tacit support of all those who are attracted to Westerns. If you write historical romance, you will have the tacit support of all those who are attracted to historical romance. If you write social realism, you will have the tacit support

---

* It was of course the disruption, and not the hurt, that (feebly) agitated Philip Larkin. 'Sorry to hear about your misfortunes. To me the loss of a loved one (in this sense) would be nothing at all compared to the consequent throes of MOVING – I think I hate moving almost more than anything. Are you really going to have to do all that?' So Phoebe was right. 'He's never going to move to London, he's never going to move out of Hell. He couldn't. He couldn't move *next door*.'

† And this half-conscious retaliatory flail cost me far more than it cost Jane Howard. It postponed my engorged encounter with her five-volume magnum opus, the Cazalet Chronicles. And it deprived Jane of the many hours of detailed praise I would've given it, face to face (and she needed detailed praise, in life and in art). To hear that would have pleased her, and to voice it would have pleased me. Of course, it's too late now. She no longer needs that praise. Nevertheless, the omission, and all the attendant regret, is lastingly mine.

of all those attracted to society and reality – a rather larger quorum. And you have the ballast of the familiar and the everyday; you have the ballast of human interaction and the way we live now.

Second: structure. If it has energy, fictional prose will tend to be headstrong. Structure is there to keep it in line. It's a question of chopping up the narrative and parcelling it out in a satisfying pattern. Once the pattern is formed, you can be confident that the building won't fall apart overnight; the scaffolds are in place.

Third: the subconscious.

On this subject I hesitate to say too much – because I don't want to spook you. The mysterious contribution of the subconscious, in particular, *is* spooky (it's why Norman Mailer called his collection of his very perceptive 'thoughts on writing' *The Spooky Art*). The business of compiling a novel puts you in near-daily contact with a force that feels supernatural (and duly gives rise to superstitions).

I'd been writing fiction for twenty years before I was personally aware of its existence, let alone its power. In the old days when I was young, if I came up against a difficulty, a stretch of prose that bloodymindedly went on resisting me, I would simply redouble my attack on it; after a nasty couple of weeks I would grind out something that never satisfied me (a little later I came to recognise these dead bits and to jettison them, after only a couple of wasted days). If I can spare you one such session of pointless struggle, then . . .

No one will ever understand the subconscious; but you can learn to humour it. Nowadays, when the obstruction announces itself, I don't bang my head against the wall; rather, I stroll off and do something else. This has become instinctual and even crudely physical: my legs straighten up and bear me away from the desk, usually from hard chair to easy chair, where I sit and read while I let time pass. It may take an hour, it may take a day, a night, two days, three nights, until I find myself again in the hard chair, because my legs have delivered me there, just as my legs, earlier on, drew me away. It means that the path is now clear.

A sinister process, but benign: a type of holistic white magic (and I'm convinced, incidentally, that 'writer's block' simply describes a failure in the transmission belt: an internal power cut). One of the several hindrances in life-writing is that it gives the subconscious so little to do. With fiction, you often have to *sleep on it* – to rejoin the world of dreams and death, from which, many believe, all human energy comes.

Life-writing (the facts, the linear reality of things that went ahead and happened) doesn't leave much room for the subliminal. And this cannot be anything but a loss.

Most fictions, including short stories, have their origin in the subconscious. Very often you can feel them arrive. It is an exquisite sensation. Nabokov called it 'a throb', Updike 'a shiver': the sense of pregnant arrest. The subconscious is putting you on notice: you have been brooding about something without knowing it. Fiction comes from there – from silent anxiety. And now it has given you a novel to write.

*

A few minor points.

Dialogue should be very sparely punctuated. Just use the comma, the dash, and – above all – the full stop. People talk in short sentences (however many of them they string together). For centuries it was a convention to represent (say) rural labourers as saying things like *Arr, the master lived over there: beyond them hillocks; he used to loik coming over the* . . . Despite what some novelists still seem to believe, no one *talks* with colons and semicolons – not farmers, and not phoneticians.

If you want to show a moment of hesitation, use the ellipsis, the dot-dot-dot (which has many other very civilised uses); it will save you the indignity of typing out such makeweight formulations as 'She paused for thought, and then continued'. Otherwise, in dialogue, confine yourself to those marks that have some kind of aural equivalent: the comma (a short pause), the full stop (a rounded-off statement followed by a longer pause), and the dash.

The dash is a versatile little customer – but a word of warning. A single dash will do as an informal colon (among many other functions). Two dashes signal a parenthesis, like brackets (though without their slight *sotto voce* effect). But never present your reader with three dashes in the same sentence (as some highly distinguished writers persist in doing), typically with two serving as brackets and one as a colon. This is a sure formula for syntactical chaos.

Last and also least (so far as I'm concerned), there is the subjunctive, the verbal mood that deals in conjecture ('if I were a carpenter'). Well, I'm pleased to report that it's on its way out. The subjunctive, in English, used to swan around the place with some freedom. No verb was safe from it. *If she have a fault. I recommend that Mrs Jones face a sentence of no less than* . . . But for some time the subjunctive has been confined to one verb and one verb only: *to be*. Yes, *to be* is the last man standing (note too those rusting trinkets *as it were* and *albeit*). So for a little while longer it's just a question of *if she were* or *if she was*.

And which is it? . . . That question has inspired huge volumes of linguistic philosophy, full of graphs and equations. No doubt it is all nauseatingly complicated. I stick to a simple rule. If I'm writing in the present tense I use it, and if I'm writing in the past tense I don't. So it's *she wishes she were* and it's *she wished she was*. The present can go either way. The past is settled. I really think that's all you need to know. *He wishes his friend were alive. He wished his friend was alive.* Is that at least reasonably clear?

Chapter 4
Beelzebub

Xalapa

As for how Christopher might be amusing himself *otherwise*, if he hadn't been pushed to the side of his own life, the subject never came up. It never came up because it so obviously groaned with frustration and futility. But there was this one time, in Texas in the fall of October 2011, brought about by happenstance . . .

It was then seventeen months since onset and a full year since he published his first report from the land of the stricken (it would become Chapter 1 of *Mortality*), where he wrote, 'I had real plans for my next decade and felt I'd worked hard enough to earn it.'* What he was most immediately looking forward to, Blue told me, was a leisurely circuit of various universities with their daughter Antonia, who was then seventeen, and by October 2011 that window had closed.

The missed opportunity I was about to present him with was in comparison vanishingly slight. But minor wounds, too, can hurt and connect ('once one has got used to the big wrongs of life,' wrote V. S. Pritchett, 'little ones wake up, with their mean little teeth'). We were in the Zilkhas' garden, among its statues and butterflies, and I said as casually as I could,

---

* In the context of premature mortality, all talk of *earning* this or *deserving* that, all talk of justice and injustice, is understandable but delusive self-pity, which Christopher instantly recognised: that same paragraph ends, 'To the dumb question, "Why me?" the cosmos barely bothers to return the reply: Why not?' . . . Larkin never grasped this and never got beyond it. 'I really feel', he maintained, in the last paragraph of the last letter he ever wrote, '[that] this year has been more than I deserve.'

424

'When I leave tomorrow I'll be heading south. Over the Rio Grande.'

'Oh? To what end?'

'Just a festival. By air to Veracruz, then by road to Xalapa.'

And it struck me: I couldn't think of an adventure he would find more powerfully enticing. The late flight out of Houston, the midnight landing in violent Veracruz, the drive to the complimentary hotel, the international cast of thinkers and drinkers, the fresh audiences of upturned faces – in Mexico, with its voluptuous flora, its tangily effectual margaritas and mojitos, its scorching spices, land of revolution and of knifepoint anti-clericalism, land of the implacable rebel, of Álvaro Obregón, of Pancho Villa, of Emiliano Zapata . . .

'Sorry, Hitch.'

'What for?' he said without any sign of disappointment in his open face. 'Someone's got to do it. They did ask me, if I remember.'

'Of course they asked you. I saw your picture in one of the programmes.' Instead of going to Mexico, Christopher would be going to MD Anderson, most days – for monitoring and therapy. I thought of the past summer, when he returned to Washington and a) waited out a throat-to-navel radiation rash (caused by thirty-five days under the synchrotron),* and b) was admitted to a DC hospital which gave him 'a vicious staph pneumonia (and sent [him] home twice with it)'; during that time – certainly, confessedly – he came very close to despair and to surrender; but then there were 'intervals of relative robustness' marked by nothing much worse than 'annihilating fatigue'. I now said, 'But I'm changing my ticket. I'm coming straight back here. By the weekend, Hitch, I'll once again be in your arms.'

On Tuesday evening as I climbed into the yellow cab (Michael Z was unaccountably elsewhere), Christopher came to see me off, out on the driveway, in shirtsleeves, cheerfully and lovingly . . . And then the flight south through the darkness, and the long bus ride to Xalapa with a score of other attendees, and the meal break en route at a roadside bodega, where I had a stimulating talk with the historian Niall Ferguson (husband of Ayaan Hirsi Ali, on whom the Hitch had long had a crush).

---

* 'To say the rash hurt would be pointless. The struggle is to convey the way it hurt *on the inside*. I lay for days on end, trying in vain to postpone the moment when I would have to swallow. Every time I did swallow, a hellish tide of pain would flow up my throat, culminating in what felt like a mule kick in the small of my back.'

He, Christopher, might've had all this happen to him too, together with me, in the alternate world of health.

———————————

'I didn't want to be discouraging, but now you're back safe and sound, Little Keith, I can tell you a very crunchy story about Mexico City. It's a good one.'

'Please.'

Out of hospital for a while, Christopher, by now very much used to being in and out of hospital, was in hospital. Up in the Tower and in his own room – the scattered notebooks and typescripts, the beeping monitors, the high bed standing to attention.

'A Nordic theologian,' said Christopher, 'a gentleman and a scholar, landed at the airport and took a taxi to his hotel. Before he could get inside he was snatched and bundled into a car. They had him humped over on his knees in the back and they kept jabbing his arse with their awls and skewers – as he told them all his passwords and pin numbers. Then they drove him around to various ATMs and had great fun with his bank account. And you'd think that'd be the end of it. But no . . . Now the narrative takes on a tragic complexion.'

A tap on the door was instantly followed by a flight attendant pushing a drinks trolley – or so for an instant I thought. It was in fact a wheeled tray of vials and tubes steered by a nurse who sang out,

'Good afternoon!'

'Good afternoon,' said Christopher. 'Ah. Blood work. I used to tell my visitors, *This'll only take a minute and it doesn't hurt.* Both claims are no longer true.' He looked to his left. 'And how are you, my dear?'

'Great! And how are you doing today?'

'Medium cool, thank you . . . Mart, this young lady's prepping me for a PIC line, which is a uh, a peripherally inserted catheter. Once that's in, there'll be no more probing around for usable veins. Ten minutes. Go and have a quick burn.'

. . . Outside on the plant-lined pathway I lit up and strolled back and forth. *Has all this put you off smoking?* asked Alexander on one of his recent visits. *No,* I said. *What it's done is put me off medical treatment.* So I dragged and puffed and stared at the dusty flora, each little bush and shrub on its midden of cigarette ends, which looked almost decoratively organic, like thick white catkins . . .

'Success?' I said, as the blood lady was rattling off to her next customer.

'Yeah, as far as it went. For the actual insertion, the blood lady said she'll need the help of at least one or two blood blokes. Where were we?'

'Our tragic Scandinavian. Then what?'

'Ah. Well once they'd cleaned him out the droogs took him off into the wilderness and left him naked in a paddy field miles from town. They beat him up of course – but get this. They smeared him with *dogshit*. All over his face and hair.'

'. . . What was that in aid of? Why?'

'Why. A very interesting question. Which I'm sure he asked himself – accustomed as he was to balancing divine providence against the existence of evil. Anyway, he flew without incident back to Stockholm or Oslo. That was three years ago. And, it's a funny thing, but he hasn't said a word since.'

'Christ.'

'Mm. Most unfortunate. He's in a darkened room in some cackle-factory up in the tundra. But wouldn't you agree, Little Keith, that Mexico's much maligned? You'd never guess that the murder rate in Mexico City is much lower than St Louis.'

I said, 'From what I saw they're a lovely people. And you know, I was in a two-hour traffic jam in Xalapa and I didn't hear a single horn.'

He and I talked of Mexico until the arrival of Blue, and then Alexander, and we got ready to go. Here was another thing Christopher would have been doing otherwise: joining us that night for rounds of cocktails and a three-course meal. We all commiserated in our different ways. I said,

'You awe me, Hitch. You don't have an issue with us going off to a snazzy grill? You don't find it uh, concerning? You're comfortable with that?'

'Of course,' he said, picking up his book. 'I'd much rather think about you doing it than think about you not doing it. I do like to feel it's getting done.'

'That's good in you, Hitch. And listen, Xalapa's on every October and we'll go there together a year from now. Let's shake on it. Xalapa, in 2012.'

*

The examined death

The Hitchenses, as a couple, were returning to Michael's guest house less and less often. Blue slept there (except during crises), and so did I whenever I flew down: waking up to a leisurely breakfast with Blue on the sunny porch, both of us eating cereal laced with berries, and getting through enormous quantities of caffeine and tobacco. Blue and I, we were calm and companionable; when we talked about Christopher's condition, we scoffed at his cringeing tumours and his punily curable pneumonias. Around noon we would climb into one of Michael's cars and make the brief journey to the Tower.

And there would be Christopher, for whom 'every passing day represents more and more' — as he wrote that same month — being 'relentlessly subtracted from less and less'.

Denial, rage, bargaining, depression, and, finally, acceptance.

Christopher summarised 'the notorious stage theory' in his first dispatch from the sickroom (September 2010). And only the other day, eight years later, did I learn that Elisabeth Kübler-Ross's subject was not mortal illness; it was bereavement.

Which of course changes everything. In the case of bereavement, you are negotiating psychic terms with someone who is already dead — and not with someone who may yet survive.

So the stages would have to be revised. It wasn't *denial* that ensnared us, all three of us, Blue, me, and (to an unknowable but I think lesser extent) the patient himself. It was more like hardened hope, or blind faith, or adamantine wishfulness.

About six months after the diagnosis I wrote a long piece about Christopher; in the London *Observer*, and I cleared it with him and with Blue, and also with Ian, who said (I am conflating emails and phone calls),

'Here and there you're too severe, I think. When you quote the more minor Hitch. I mean you're not wrong, but . . .'

'Well he and I have a tradition of being hard on each other not in person but in print. If it didn't have some vinegar in it he'd find it — oily.'

'I agree with your general point. And I agree about puns. But a couple of the examples you give, and what you say about them. Does he need to see that now?'

'Now?'

'Now he's dying.'

I felt a jolt and had a strong impulse to say, with real indignation, 'But he's *not* dying' . . . I didn't say it. I just thought it. I just thought: But he's *not* dying.

A minute later I rolled a cigarette and went outside to the stone-paved garden behind the house on Regent's Park Road, where the cold sun was staring down through huge voids and tunnels in the covering cloud. I was reminded of how it feels to be an expectant father in the days immediately before the birth – the infinite restlessness and the sense of being almost criminally underemployed. As Prince Hal says in ambivalent mockery of Hotspur: 'He that kills me some six or seven dozen of Scots at a breakfast, washes his hands, and says to his wife: "Fie upon this quiet life! I want work."' Oh, what to do with all this stoppered energy. Release me. Let me go and rearrange heaven and earth with my bare hands . . . Is that what religion is, the groping of the powerless?

As Blue understood it, Christopher's chances of 'cure' or long remission were between '5 to 20 per cent'. But Ian told me that even the lower figure was too high – and about medical science he was never wrong. Oesophageal Cancer, Stage Four. And yet, as Carol Blue wrote in her exemplary afterword to *Mortality*:

> Without ever deceiving himself about his medical condition, and without ever allowing me to entertain illusions about his prospects for survival, he responded to every bit of clinical or statistical good news with a radical, childlike hope.

Blue was right: 'His will to keep his existence intact, to remain engaged with his preternatural intensity, was spectacular.' But there was also this, from a piece about Nietzsche's dictum 'Whatever doesn't kill me makes me stronger', which he showed me that October:

> . . . it seemed absurd to affect the idea that this bluffing on my part was making me stronger, or making other people perform more strongly or cheerfully either. Whatever view one takes of the outcome being affected by morale, it seems certain that the realm of illusion must be escaped before anything else.

'Nietzsche was perhaps mistaken,' added Hitch, 'don't you think? Whatever doesn't kill you makes you weaker, and kills you later on.'

'I do want to die well . . . But how is it done?'

So says Guy Openshaw, a character in the Iris Murdoch novel *Nuns and Soldiers* (1980). Guy expires overleaf (and – for clear artistic reasons – offstage), but we are on page 100 by now, and the reader has had time to see what dying well, at least as an aspiration, might be supposed to mean. This is a novel by Iris Murdoch, so everyone is implausibly articulate, and 'dying well' is considered above all as a task for the intellect. Guy therefore involves himself in many testing dialogues with his closest male friend – about leavetaking, about non-existence – in an attempt, as Saul had put it in *The Dean's December*, to make 'sober, decent terms with death' and so move on to 'the completion of your reality'.

For a long time after it was all over I thought that this was the clearest flaw of my see-no-evil approach to a potentially fatal illness: death could not be talked about. But now I think, Talk about *what*, exactly? The famous aphorisms about death – Freud's, Rochefoucauld's – maintain the intrinsic impossibility of facing up to it. 'Philosophy' means 'love of wisdom', and philosophers have further defined it, more explicitly, as 'learning how to die'; but the fruits of this learning have never been passed on to us . . . Noticing the first marks of age on an ex-lover's face, Herzog identifies 'death, the artist, very slow'. Death brims with artistic complexity, but its philosophical content is slight. Death is an artist, not an intellectual.

Death is nothingness. So talk about what, exactly? If you multiply a number, any number, by zero, the result is still zero; the answer is always zero. Christopher and I could have had long talks about nothingness. Would this have helped him? I still wonder. There is a particular photograph (which I'll duly disclose) that makes me still wonder.

Torture in North Carolina

The historian Timothy Snyder has recently said that African Americans are all experiencing a form of PTSD – post-traumatic stress disorder (an ancient concept with many names). Snyder's premise will no doubt be challenged, but to me it has the power of 'a truth goose' (the phrase is Tim O'Brien's).

Christopher, in the autumn of 2011, came to think that he now qualified as a sufferer. His episode of traumatic stress didn't last long and was self-inflicted (also self-regulated). It took place on 'a gorgeous day' in May 2008 in North Carolina.

'You know, I still can't believe you did that,' I said at his bedside in Houston. 'Why'd you let it happen? No, why'd you bring it about? Why'd you *seek* it?'

'Curiosity. And there's the pro bono aspect, Little Keith.'

'Oh, sure. I fail to understand you, Christopher Hitchens. Jesus Christ, you must fucking love it.'

He couldn't and wouldn't claim that he didn't know what he was getting into. The 'agreement' Christopher signed beforehand was quite specific, noting that the experience he was procuring for himself

> is a potentially dangerous activity in which the participant
> can receive serious and permanent (physical, emotional, and
> psychological) injuries and even death due to the respiratory and
> neurological systems of the body.

The 'due to' clause in that sentence looks woolly and equivocal, but there is no mistaking a later warning: 'safeguards' would be in place during the 'process', but 'these measures may fail and even if they work properly they may not prevent Hitchens from experiencing injury or death'.

To book himself in for this, Christopher made a number of calls. The first 'specialist' he talked to asked his age (fifty-nine), then 'laughed out loud and told me to forget it'. Instead of forgetting it, though, instead of deciding not to risk experiencing death, Hitch persevered. Along the way he 'had to produce a doctor's certificate assuring them that I did not have asthma' – 'but I wondered if I should tell them', he continues, 'about the 15,000 cigarettes I had inhaled every year for the last several decades' (which is more than forty a day). And then he got on a plane and betook himself to a remote dwelling or 'facility' at the end of a long and tapering country road in the hills of western North Carolina.

If you want to, you can watch the whole thing on YouTube . . .

We are in what looks like an orderly suburban garage (there is a fridge, and a mower or motorbike under tarps); orderly and ordinary, although it would serve perfectly well, cinematically, as the lab or rec room of some relatively unpretentious serial murderer. After a while heavyset men are purposefully busying themselves, while the viewer concentrates on a two-plank table of bare pine, supported by A-frames and tilting slightly downwards to the right, where a bucket lurks. The Hitch appears, under escort and black-hooded as if for execution (no eye-slits), and is helped into a seated position. Fade. Now he is strapped down on the sloping board so that his heart is higher than his head (and his loafers higher still). A hunched operative leans over him and says, with the plodding and patronising menace that marks the voice of American officialdom (do I *make myself clear?*),

'All right, listen up. I'm going to give you some instructions . . . Do you understand me?'

'Yes, I do.'

'We're going to place metal objects in each of your hands. These objects are to be released if you experience unbearable stress . . . Do you understand?'

'Yes, I do.'

'You have a code word you can use for distress. That word is *red*. R-E-D. Say the word.'

'Red.'

'Again, what is the word?'

'Red.'

'That is correct.'

Now the Special Forces veterans go about their work with ominously practised movements of their gloved hands. One of them aligns and steadies the subject's body while another folds a white towel over the subject's mouth and nose, and produces . . . a plastic jug of Poland Spring. And then the towel – a white mask upon a black mask – is assiduously drenched.

Seventeen seconds later the metal objects (which look like steel batons) are dashed to the ground. The men at once desist, the straps are loosened, and the hood is whipped off to reveal a face both flushed and tumid, as if about to burst.

'All right, are you breathing?'

The live footage soon fades. What we don't see is Christopher asking 'to try it one more time' . . . When he did, the specialists, after a by-the-book interval with repeated and elaborated warnings ('racing pulse', 'adrenaline rush'), duly obliged.

The most difficult position

I glanced out of the window at the familiar towers of MD Anderson, as odiously changeless as the daily Tex-Mex blue. *For I don't understand you, Christopher Hitchens*: this was more, now, than an often-used conversational flourish. I said,

'You wanted another go to see if you could last longer.'

'Of course. You know, family honour.' He was sitting in his dressing gown on the padded chair beside the bed – the hospital bed, with his computer open on its detachable meal tray. 'You seem to want me to spell it out. My ancestors, Little Keith, who faced peril on the sea. When they struggled in an alien element, their courage did not desert them.'

'Mm.' No one who knew him at all well would discount Christopher's reverence for the 'Navy Hymn' and the no-nonsense fortitude of Commander Hitchens and all the rest. In his torture piece he talked of the 'shame and misery' he felt after his prompt capitulation in North Carolina ('shame' could be merely gestural, but 'misery' feels authentic, and peculiar – peculiar to him). 'All right, you struck a blow for your ancient mariners. And as a result you've got PTSD.'

'So it would seem,' he said. 'PTSD. Yes, I know, I used to sneer at those abbreviations and so did you. When the kindergarten shrinks were raring to drug Alexander, I'd think, Attention Deficit Disorder – these are just fancy names for the little sins of childhood. Messy Eater Syndrome. Won't Sit Still Spectrum. But PTSD . . . I think it's a real condition.'

'So do I.* But the point is you went looking for it. You went cruising for a bruising, mate. Twice.'

---

* I had recently read Philip Caputo's famous Vietnam memoir *A Rumor of War*, published in 1977 (when PTSD was first recognised and described). After nearly a year of front-line combat, Caputo rises from his cot on 'a quiet day, one of those days when it was difficult to believe there was a war on. Yet my sensations were those of a man actually under fire . . . Psychologically, I had never felt worse . . . a feeling of being afraid when there was no reason to be'; and of dissociation (sometimes known as 'doubling') – a feeling of being there and also not being there.

'Yes yes, Mart, but it was worth doing. Now we know that waterboarding's not a "simulation" of torture. It's an enactment.'

'Someone had to do it – maybe – but not you. Your history ruled you out. On several counts.' And I ticked them off: lifelong fear of drowning, waking up with air hunger (plus 'acid reflux'), acute breathlessness after mild exertion . . . He said nothing. I said, 'I don't understand you, Christopher Hitchens.'

And it was true. I didn't – and I don't – understand him. And I reduced my thoughts, that night in Houston, to stupefied silence as I tried and failed to understand Christopher Hitchens.

. . . His attraction to perversity was familiar enough to everyone. In the journalistic narrative the adjective of first resort – 'contrarian' – was now something like Christopher's middle name. And he did seem to covet the disapproval, even the ostracism, of his peers. Time and again I watched him do it, watched him seek *the most difficult position*, difficult anyway and quite exceptionally difficult for Christopher Hitchens.*

This trait of his was always mysteriously self-punitive. Still, though – to go out of your way to volunteer for torture? In all other cases it was his intellectual reputation he put at risk, not his physical instrument – not his life.

He was obscurely compelled to embrace complication, to test his courage, to walk into his doubts and fears. And so it was that in 2008 he decided that the most difficult position, for him, was lying on his back (with his face under two layers of sopping cloth) on a narrow board that sloped downwards, so that his heart was higher than his head.

Courage

'It is so very difficult for a sick man not to be a scoundrel,' observed Dr Johnson, as he embarked on one of his most magisterial paragraphs:

---

* There was nothing blithe or heedless about it. 'Oh, man. I'm living in a world of pain,' he said when I reached him on the phone, in the late 1990s, during an intense but transient furore. While never, ever admitting he was wrong, Christopher suffered quietly but sharply for his errancies. Above all, naturally, he was tormented by the proliferating disaster of Iraq – a neocon experiment that he supported (no, championed) from the standpoint of the hard left . . .

It may be said that disease generally begins that equality which death completes. All distinctions which set one man apart from another are very little perceived in the gloom of the sick chamber, where it will be vain to expect entertainment from the gay, or instruction from the wise; where all human glory is obliterated, the wit is clouded, the reasoner perplexed, and the hero subdued . . .

Of all the literary genres, panegyric is easily the dullest. Yet I must now praise the Hitch. It was courage, and it was more than courage; it was honour, it was integrity, it was character. In any event, not one of the Johnsonian deficits was ever visible in him . . . And when you consider how swiftly even a routine illness – a potent flu, say – exhausts your reserves of patience, tolerance, civility, warmth, and imaginative sympathy, despite the tacit assurance that the miseries of the present will soon join the forgotten miseries of the past. Christopher knew no such assurance, and he had been immured in the land of the sick for seventeen months.

'The blood squad's due around now,' he said.

'Oh,' I said, 'is this for the catheter? Well I'll go and get a coffee.'

'No, Mart, you'll need your book. Ten minutes, they claim. Or they used to. But it'll take longer than that.'

Christopher was proud of his 'very rare blood type', and would often 'give', spontaneously, for the public weal (as he twice did in Vietnam, in 1967 and 2006). He used to find the process absurdly easy: the clasping squeeze of the tourniquet, the brisk little stab – and then the cup of tea and the ginger biscuit (in South East Asia he also got 'a sustaining bowl of beef noodles'). It was different now.

That same month he described it in writing:

The phlebotomist would sit down, take my hand or wrist in his or her hand, and sigh. The welts of reddish and purple could already be seen, giving the arm a definite 'junkie' look. The veins themselves lay sunken in their beds, either hollow or crushed . . . I was recently scheduled for the inserion of a 'PIC' line, by means of which a permanent blood catheter is inserted in the upper arm . . . It can't have been much less than two hours until, having tried and failed with both arms, I was lying between two bed-pads that were liberally laced with dried or clotting blood. The upset of the nurses was palpable.

When it was over, when the 'life-giving thread' had begun 'to unspool in the syringe' ('Twelve times is the charm!' cries a medic), and the smeared bed-pads had been cleared away, that's what the half-conscious patient felt moved to think about: the upset of the nurses.

Susceptibility to emotion is not encouraged in a hospital dedicated to profit. In Britain we have the famous NHS; and despite its wartime feel (as everyone somehow bootstraps along with what they've got), you are always seeing the kind of vocational ardour that silently declares, *This is my talent – the alleviation of suffering is what I'm good at*. In America the ardour has been selected out. Hence that frostily elfin politeness that envelops you all the way from the reception desk to the intensive care unit . . . Invariably and effortlessly Christopher moved past the robotic spryness that surrounded him, and developed relationships that included sensitivity and humour and trust – with the oncologists, the blood-extraction teams, the caterers, and the cleaners, even as he took up the most difficult position of all.

So let me praise him, let us praise the Hitch: *contra* Dr Johnson, he seemed to find it the easiest thing in the world to be the very opposite of a scoundrel. In the gloom of the sick chamber, all the distinctions that set one man apart from another were unforgettably perceived; he kept hold of his gaiety and his sagacity, his wit was unclouded, his reason unperplexed. His human glory was not obliterated, and the hero was unsubdued.

 I do so want to die well . . . But how is it done?

 That is how it is done.

The occasion of sin – 1

But of course we didn't accept that that was what he was doing – dying.

 And I myself was no doubt exorbitantly encouraged by a fresh development. During the last month or so, in our hours together,

Christopher wanted to talk about – and to hear about – *sex*. And this was new; indeed, the subject had gone unmentioned for over a year . . . Very early on in his medical exile (it comes on page 8 of *Mortality*), Christopher owned up to a sudden and sweeping indifference to feminine allure. 'If Penelope Cruz had been one of my nurses, I wouldn't even have noticed. In the war against Thanatos, the immediate loss of Eros is a huge initial sacrifice.' And now here it was again, eros, nature's strongest – and most ineffable – force: the one that peoples the earth.

'I've got a good one for you, Hitch,' I began. 'And one you've never heard before. When Phoebe stripteased my cock plum off in the bathroom at the flat . . . Actually she didn't tease it off, not this time. She *tempted* it off. Gaw, she –'

A knock, then a nurse. Who acknowledged my presence, and indulgently withdrew.

'Late summer 1981. Thirty years ago to the month, and you were packing your bags for America. I was too ashamed to tell you at the time.'

'Too ashamed? You? This sounds very promising. So in your prenuptial period.'

'Exactly. And you were giving me those pep talks about monogamy. You were very serious and very impressive.'

'Well it's vitally important, monogamy, when you're squaring up to wedlock. Or else you lose the moral glow. Christ. I mean, is this or is this not an exception?'

'Perfectly true, Hitch. And I needed to hear it.'

'You did. Steeped in promiscuity as you were. You were a right little slag, Mart, if you'll forgive me for saying so. And now you had before you a shining prize. Julia.'

'Yes, and I was grateful, and I listened. You said a lot of good things. *Avoid the occasion of sin, Little Keith* . . . What's that from?'

'It's a Catholic teaching, strange to say. Insultingly obvious, really, but nicely phrased. Avoid the things you know will tempt you. Avoid being alone with ex-girlfriends – that's what it comes down to. Avoid being alone with canny and talented ex-girlfriends with a point to prove.'

'And avoid it is exactly what I didn't do. Oh, and I can tell you now why it always is ex-girlfriends. I mean, you wouldn't go after someone new, would you. You don't want any surprises. But with an ex, a long-serving ex, whose body you know as well as you know your own . . . It's weird. The familiarity, the snugness, the sameyness – it flips. It goes all heady and hot.'

'And there's no fear of failure . . . Well Mart, you listened, but you didn't learn. What were you *doing* in the bathroom with Phoebe Phelps?'

'I know. That's what I was ashamed of. You cautioned me, and the very next *day* I . . . I embraced an occasion of sin – of blazing crime.' I said, 'The trouble was I found the prospect of being tempted tempting in itself. I was irresistibly tempted by temptation. Because I felt sure I could deal with it. How was I to know she'd come on so, so Grand Guignol?'

'How was I to know. See? That's *precisely* the wrong attitude. Okay. I want the long version. Concentrate. It's amazing the persistence of sexual memories, don't you find? And the clarity of contour. I suppose, I suppose the memory's so sharp because those are the times when you're most alive. Begin.'

'Well. There I was in my new flat, Leamington Road, minding my own business. And she rang from the airport and –'

A knock, and another hairdo round the door.

'Ah,' said Christopher. 'Good afternoon, my dear.'

This was the pain lady, or the painkiller lady (something of a cult figure at MDA; and Christopher's neck, I knew, was hurting, and so were his arms, and so were his hands and his fingers). And he was now readying himself for relief ('a sort of warming tingle with an idiotic bliss to it'). As I was edging my way out she said,

'Mr Hitchens! Good afternoon! And how are we today?'

'Well, Cheryl, you're obviously in top form. As for me, I have some uh, discomfort, as they call it here. But I felt twice the price the moment I saw your face . . . Ten minutes, Mart. Then the long version.'

The cancer pincer

Out on the main deck I was beckoned into an alcove and found myself in an informal, water-cooler symposium convened by Christopher's carers – or perhaps convened by Blue, who was asking many questions. By now she was up to PhD standard on Oesophageal Cancer, Stage Four (she knew the names and doses of all the drugs), and so the talk was mostly above my reach. But I soon fell into a whispered exchange with the blue-smocked figure called Dr Lal . . . Dr Lal was the most attractive of all the MDA oncologists – a lean Indian gentleman with a poet's face, full of sadness and humanity, a face formed over many decades and many bedsides: Dr Lal was that increasingly rare kind of specialist, one who engaged with the patient, and not just with the patient's disease. He said in an undertone,

'Mr Hitchens is now faced with a choice. To stay here or to go home.'

I said, 'You mean home to Washington? . . . No, I suppose not, or not yet. Home to our friends' house ten minutes away? He *could* do that, could he?'

'Theoretically, yes. He has the, the option of going home. Let me briefly explain.'

Christopher was caught in the double bind of his sickness: the doublecross of cancer. The tumours had been shrunken, scorched, and effectively cauterised by chemicals and protons; but the patient too was much reduced (and his immune system ravaged). Dr Lal went on,

'He is without defences. And if he stays here, a secondary infection will certainly follow. It's not if or when. It's when.'

'Then I don't . . . What could be the reason for staying here?'

On the one hand, home, Michael's: the material and emotional comfort, the padded density, the numerous staff (including the two security men who courteously and affectionately materialised to help Christopher from the car to the house, and then rematerialised to help him upstairs to his bedroom). On the other hand, MDA: the stasis, the locked windows, the false smiles and false sparkle, the hairless children – and the invisible but inevitable gigabugs, biding their time in sinks and drains . . .

Dr Lal arched his back, saying, 'You see, there is the psychological element. And the fact remains that Mr Hitchens doesn't want to leave.'

Why? What possible counterforce would make him want to stay?

The answer was that he somehow felt *less threatened* in hospital. And here we have to imagine a sense of limitless frailty – unquantifiably worsened by a state of mind always characterised, first and foremost, as one of overwhelming fear. It was a double bind within a double bind.

. . . Another, older name for *battle fatigue* is *soldier's heart*. And whenever I try to evoke that fear I think of what soldiers say (and write)

about the hours before battle. The heart is full of love, but the physical instrument, the outward being, is full of fear; my neck is afraid, my shoulders are afraid, my arms are afraid, my hands are afraid, my fingers are afraid.

Lord of the Flies

You housefly, you horsefly – did he who made the lamb make thee?

There were no insects at MDA, not even in its slightly frowsy cafeterias at the close of a long weekend. No insects. So what lay in my view was without doubt an illusion; solemnly, stonily, I sat through it, waiting.

First, though, let us make terms with the actual. There was Christopher in his dressing gown, and he was already ill, additionally ill, as ill as I'd ever seen him, as ill as I'd ever seen anyone. Coughing, stiffly twisting in his chair, rocking from side to side, tipping himself forwards, his face wearing a light sheen of silvery sweat in the afternoon grey: that was the actual. He wasn't groaning, he wasn't complaining, he wasn't swearing, he wasn't even saying *Christ*. No, he was using his voice to respond to the tautened needs and nerves of his loved ones, more specifically to intercede in a row between his son and his second wife (in itself a most difficult position); the row was logistical (to do with Alexander having to foreshorten his stay), and it was unrestrained. Don't forget that they, we, had had eighteen months of this, Blue (much the most proximate), Alexander, and I too. None of us were really ourselves: we were all someone else. And Christopher mediating and moderating, and turning aside now and then to get on with the business of being very ill. Meanwhile I sat silent in the corner with my suitcase and my plane ticket, feeling strange, feeling strange to the world. That was also actual.

What wasn't actual was this: the room was full of flies.

All the way back to Brooklyn – all the way, from the hospital cab rank to the blue front door of 22 Strong Place – the usually reliable narrator, Martin, tried to make sense of his hallucination: a trick of the ear as well as the eye, for the flies thronged like bumblebees, as fat, as hairy, and also as noisy, purring, fizzing, sizzling. In his imagination and in his novels flies had always represented necrosis: *little skull and crossbones, little gasmasked survivalists, little flecks of death* – little shiteaters, little admirers of trash, wounds, battlegrounds, killing fields, abattoirs, carrion, blood, and mire.

Watch the vermin swarm for long enough, stand among them for long enough when they swarm (I used to do this in our Brooklyn woodshed), and you feel in their triumphal excitement the undoing of the whole moral order . . . In demonology the little flecks of death owe fealty to the Seventh Prince of Hell, who excites lust in priests, who excites jealousies and murders in cities, who excites in nations love of war – Beelzebub, Lord of the Flies.

How to Write
The Uses of Variety

I'll be in London all next week, as I'm sure I told you. Well, mostly to see my eldest daughter Bobbie and her clan – her husband Mathew and their little boy and their little girl – my pretty grandchildren . . . I'm also due to have an audience, over afternoon tea, with Phoebe Phelps. Now I haven't seen Phoebe for thirty years. All this was brokered by the niece, Maud. Who seems to confine herself to briskly merciless hints. For instance she casually mentioned that Phoebe *never goes out*. Outside. She never goes outside . . .

Nothing can prepare you in any way for that kind of meeting. Certainly not literature, which is curiously incapable of helping you through the critical events of an average span (for example, the deaths of parents). I suppose the lesson is that you have to enter into it and see for yourself . . . At Larkin's funeral my father talked of 'the terrible effects of time on everything we have and are'. So I'm expecting some of that, vivified and enriched by the fact that she and I were lovers for five years, in our prime and in our pomp. Our meeting impends before me like the worst kind of medical examination. Which it is, in a sort of sense. An hour with Doctor Time.

*

Now . . . Oh before I forget – a few words about paragraph size.

Many eminent writers don't seem to sense that paragraphs are aesthetic units; so they'll give you a short one, then a long one, then a very long one, then a medium one, then another medium one, then a short one, then a very short one, etc. Paragraphs should be aware of their immediate neighbours, and should show it by observing a flexible uniformity of length: usually medium, though retaining the right to become uniformly long or uniformly short as you vary the rhythm of the chapter. Going from short to long (and back again) resembles a change of gear. Long paragraphs are for the freeway, short paragraphs for city traffic.

*

'There is only one school of writing,' said Nabokov, 'that of talent.' And talent can't be taught or learned. But technique can be; and so can the foundations of palatable prose. All it asks of you is a reasonable commitment of time and trouble.

Nabokov's *Invitation to a Beheading* (1938) was originally – and very briefly – entitled 'Invitation to an Execution'. Now why do you think he changed it?

'. . . The repeated suffix?'

Exactly. Invitashun to an execushun. It sounds like doggerel. So keep an eye on the suffixes; maintain a safe distance between words ending (say) with -*ment*, or -*ness*, or -*ing*; and the same goes for prefixes, for words beginning (say) with *con*-, or *pre*-, or *ex*-. Try it. You'll notice that the sentences feel more aerodynamic. Oh yes. Can you use the same word twice in a sentence? This is arguable (see below). But do try not to use the same *syllable* twice in a sentence (which can only be the result of inattention): 'reporter' and 'importance', 'faction' and 'artefact', and so on.

When I'm at my desk I spend most of my time avoiding little uglinesses (rather than striving for great beauties). If you can lay down a verbal surface free of asperities (bits of lint and grit), you will already be giving your readers some modest subliminal pleasure; they will feel well disposed to the thing before them without quite knowing why.

*

As you compose and then revise a sentence, repeat it in your head (or out loud) until your ear ceases to be dissatisfied – until your tuning fork is still. Sometimes, along the way, you'll find you want a trisyllable instead of a monosyllable, or the other way round, so you look for a more congenial synonym. It's the rhythm, not the content, that you're refining. And such decisions will be peculiar to you and to the rhythms of your inner voice. When you write, don't forget how you talk.

It is here that you'll need the thesaurus – whose function is much misunderstood, especially by the young. When I was about eighteen, I used to think that the thesaurus was there to equip me with a vocabulary brimming with arcane sonorities: why would you ever write 'centre of attraction' or 'arid', given the availability of 'cynosure' and 'jejune'?

Although the passion for fancy words (and the more polysyllabic the better) is a forgivable phase or even a necessary rite of passage, it soon starts to feel like an affectation. So for years my thesaurus went unconsulted, scorned as a kind of crib. But now I use it as often as once an hour – just to vary the vowel sounds and to avoid unwanted alliterations. It sits on my desk alongside the *Concise Oxford Dictionary*, and I often spend twenty minutes going from one to the other, making sure that the word I'm tracking down still passes the test of precision.

*

Mark this well. There is a need for elegance and, to that end, there is a need for variation. There is never any need for what is called Elegant Variation (EV) – where the adjective is of course ironic and sour.

My favourite example of EV comes from a thoroughly average biography of Abraham Lincoln: 'If the president seemed to support the Radicals in New York, in Washington he appeared to back the Conservatives.' Thus 'seemed to support' becomes 'appeared to back' – without the slightest variation of meaning. And yet you can almost hear the author's little cluck of contentment: he has avoided repetition, and done it with style.

'The fatal influence', writes the great usage-watcher Henry Fowler, 'is the advice given to young writers never to use the same word [or phrase] twice in a sentence . . . Such writers are 'first terrorised by a misunderstood taboo, next fascinated by a newly discovered ingenuity, & finally addicted to an incurable vice . . .'

Christopher, eccentrically enough, was for a while a dogged exponent of EV. I tormented him about it for a decade and a half. I would say,

'Ooh, you won't catch the Hitch using *use* twice in a sentence – the second time it comes up, he employs *employs*. He's that elegant.'

'Yes, well,' he said without much irritation (these were early days), 'that's what they taught me at school.'*

A few years later (having not let up in the interval) I said, 'You did it again! You employed *used* and used *employed*.'

He sighed. 'I tell myself to stick to *use* and not be tempted by *employ*. But I can never quite bring myself to follow through . . . Do me a favour, Mart. Stop going on at me about Elegant Variation.'

I said, 'Okay. I'll stop reproaching you for Elegant Variation. From now on I'll uh, I'll upbraid you for Gracious Dissimilitude.'

'Christ . . . I suppose I could just swear off it.' Which he did (pretty much). 'And start denying myself that – what was it? That little cluck of contentment.'

. . . Eliot said that poetry 'is an impersonal use of words': it has no designs on the reader, or eavesdropper, because poets are not heard – they are overheard. To a lesser extent this applies to the novelist. Sickeningly rife in discursive prose, EV is comparatively rare in fiction – though it regularly vandalises the 'beautiful' sentences of Henry James (in which 'breakfast' becomes 'this repaste', 'teapot' becomes 'this receptacle', and 'his arms', pitiably, becomes 'these members').

The little cluck of contentment: in general, something has gone very wrong when one finds oneself picturing the fuddled toilers at their desks; the reader, in effect, becomes conscious of the writer's self-consciousness; with a blush, the reader becomes the reader of the writer's mind.†

*

* Early advice, or early commandments, can be pernicious. I love the short stories of Alice Munro; but someone must have told her, when she was little, to shun everyday contractions like 'couldn't' and 'wouldn't' and 'hadn't' (for example, '[Enid had to tell Rupert] that she could not swim. And that would not be a lie . . . she had not learned to swim'). It makes for a choppy, counter-conversational forward flow. But in the end all those *nots* only amount to a flesh wound: bits of buckshot on the body of Munro's prose . . . Whoever introduced Henry James to the joys of EV (see below) has systemic ills to answer for – among them gentility and evasiveness.

† As we say goodbye to this shaming topic, let's spare a thought for perhaps the most pathetic noun in the English language: 'missive' (and its plural). Having no life of its own, it dawdles on street corners, waiting for some dim bulb – in his or her riff about 'letters' – to exhaust the usual EVs ('communications', 'dispatches', 'items of correspondence', and of course 'epistles') and finally make a long arm for 'missives'. Then for a little while the shivering wretch creeps in from the cold.

Your path as a writer will be largely determined by temperament. Are you cautious, buoyant, transgressive, methodical? It is temperament that decides the most fundamental distinction of all: are you a writer of prose or a writer of verse?

On this matter Auden's sonnet 'The Novelist' wields great authority. 'Encased in talent like a uniform', the poet is pure royalty, to the manner born, tolerating no distractions or competing voices; the poet sings as the sole begetter. By contrast the novelist is a putschist upstart, and cannot aspire to such purity (or any purity at all), and must become 'the whole of boredom', 'among the Just / Be just, among the Filthy filthy too'. The novelist is partly an everyman – and partly an innocent.

'Everything is to be viewed as though for the first time,' advised Saul Bellow (in one of his essays); accept Santayana's definition of that discredited word *piety* – 'reverence for the sources of one's being'; reawaken the childhood perceptions of your 'original eyes' and trust your 'first heart'; and never forget that the imagination has its own 'eternal naivete'.

I'll be needing to say more about innocence, at the very end. But now I have to *pack*. It's one of those dawn departures. They're meant to be good, Elena says, because you only lose a day, and not a night; but once I've got up at five in the morning it feels as though I'm losing both . . .

When I come to write the next chapter (which I hope to do while I'm there) I'll be able at some point to slip into something more comfortable – namely the light armour of the third person. Before I write it, though, I'll first have to live it. And when I reach Phoebe's room, and when the room opens up to let me in, there'll be no third person. It'll just be me – and her.

Chapter 5
London: Phoebe at Seventy-Five

On a midweek afternoon I took the tube from Marble Arch to Bayswater, walked down the little cosmopolis of Queensway, turned left into Kensington Gardens Square, and paused outside number 14 . . . I was thinking back, thinking back to the times when (after a certain sort of phone call) I used to sprint – sprint – the half mile from here to Phoebe's flat and to her waiting human shape. Now, in 2017, my senses could look forward to a rather different kind of feast – and how nice it would be, I thought, to turn around and sprint or at least scuttle in the opposite direction. But no, of course I shuddered on, north for a block, then left into Westbourne Grove, where Hereford Mansions soon loomed.

As I approached the building I saw two once-familiar figures stepping out from under the porch and into the September sunshine, Lars and Raoul, squinting and chuckling as they furled their off-white silk scarves round their throats . . . I was early, and had time to consider them. Lars and Raoul resembled their long-ago selves in the same kind of way that 'Beijing' resembles 'Peking', that 'Mumbai' resembles 'Bombay': cognately. The same went for Martin, of course: I only *derived* from the Martin I used to be.

'Ah, Mr Amis! It's all our yesterdays!'

'*Martin*. So – a blast from the past!'

'Raoul, Lars,' I said, lighting the pre-ordeal cigarette and asking them how they were . . . Up close, I had to admit, they seemed scandalously unchanged, Lars still the wiry beachcomber, Raoul still the ample maître d'; unchanged too were the inexplicably clean whites of their idle eyes. After a while I said,

'Well, gentlemen. Nice to see you. I'd better go in. How's her mood?'

'Up and down, obviously,' said Lars. 'Though really not *that* bad. Considering.'

'Great blow to her pride of course,' said Raoul. 'Her father.'

I said, 'What about him?'

'She never got over his death, you see. Sir Graeme popped off – ooh, ten years ago. At a hundred and six, God bless him. And he *was* a baronet, Martin,' Raoul went on with a priestly air. 'The centuries-old connection to the nobility severed, with Lady Dallen long gone and no male line. And I happen to believe that kind of thing matters dreadfully. A huge blow to her social self-esteem. Her entrée.'

'You really think so? Is that when she stopped going out? . . . Maud told me. When I last saw Phoebe I'd just turned thirty-two. And now I'm more than twice that.'

'In which case,' said Raoul, smiling at Lars, 'you may find her slightly *changed*.'

Phoebe was in her old apartment block, but she wasn't in her old apartment. She had moved, from A (2) to g (vii), from the second floor to the eighth: to 'the attic of grannies and widows', as she used to call it, 'and old maids'. The name tag no longer promised 'Kontakt' – just 'Miss P. Phelps'. I pressed the steel nub and within a couple of seconds the lock buzzed and weakly rattled.

In the lift I tried to arrange my face in accordance with the politesse of late-phase reunions: bland, all-forgiving. But the door to g (vii) was already open and the woman peering through the gap couldn't possibly be Miss P. Phelps. This was ruled out not by her hair (tufts of caramel blonde with a neglected streak of mauve), nor, at least in theory, by her wipeable nylon jumpsuit and her chunky yellow gyms; it was ruled out by her age (she wasn't even sixty). In a rustic singsong she said,

'Hello there, Martin. I'm *Meg*. Now have a seat here whilst I fetch you a tea. I'm told you like it as it comes, no milk, no sugar? She won't be long. Her helper, Jonjon – he's with her at the minute. Why don't you have a seat and read some of those books?'

. . . Like its predecessor six floors down, Phoebe's living room made you think of a doctor's vestibule; in here, though, you would be waiting to see a different kind of doctor, an older doctor, not a Harley Street specialist but an enfeebled GP with a surgery on, say, Cold Blow Lane (one plugging along with his little backlist of patented remedies).

Dormer windows, grey carpet, low ceiling . . . By *books* Meg meant the waiting-room magazines: a few tousled glossies that had long lost their shine, *House and Garden, Country Life* . . .

The day seemed to darken. It was ten past four. Meg entered stage left, placed the mug on a tablemat, and continued across the room; she dipped into an alcove or passageway in the far right corner, and I could hear the squeak of her soles getting softer, then pausing, then getting louder again; she re-entered stage right, and announced with a chastened look,

'Whew, she'll be a fair while yet I fancy! Are you all right there, Martin?' She turned and gazed towards the shadowy chute of the window. 'Thank heavens for that Jonjon is all I can say. It beats me how he does it.'

I drank the tea, endorsing it with near-continuous infusions of nicotine and water vapour from my e-pen (brandname: Logic).* Out on the street Lars had gone on to say, *Getting on for forty years?* And he looked pained and protective when I told him the year. *Oh, Mart,* he murmured, *that's half a lifetime away* . . .

Yes, Lars. The summer of 1981. We'd already broken up, and I was more or less engaged to someone else. But then she called me from the airport and she . . .

The occasion of sin – 2

She called him from the airport and she said,

'Ah, there you are. It's me. Listen. Merry and I've just got off a plane and we find ourselves in a bit of a predicament. We're at Gatwick, and we –'

He listened on. The phone was busily telling him some story about door keys, or mortise locks, and how Merry (you know Merry), as forgetful as ever, had left the spare set in the beachbag that they . . .

'*Meaning*', she summarised, 'can I come over for an hour? Till this gets sorted out?'

---

* Life can be very simple. When I turned sixty I cut my carcinogen intake by about 80 per cent. It was no doubt far too little and far too late – but it instantly cured me of thinking about suicide. Probably because my death is no longer something I'm so actively engaged in bringing about. As I say, life can be very simple.

'Let me think,' he said. 'Uh, where did you fly in from?'

'Corsica. So I'm lovely and brown . . . Go on, Mart. I won't disturb you, honest. You can go on working. I'll take a quick tour of your new place and then I'll curl up with my *Daily Mail* and won't make a sound.'

As he drew in breath to answer he felt again the burden of the advice passed on to him just the night before by that earnest *fiancé*, C. E. Hitchens: advice about 'error-likely situations' . . . But Martin felt he needn't worry: he was fine, he was safe. Solemnly and gratefully committed to Julia, settled and steadied by the promise of marriage and fatherhood, he had moved beyond the old compulsiveness (no more man-pleasers and man-teasers, no more walking-talking aphrodisiacs, no more illuminati of boudoir and garter belt) . . . Also to be considered was the fact that Phoebe, a very old friend, was in a bit of a fix (and she was lovely and brown, and there was the – quite harmless – peepshow element, and a temptation was better than nothing at all). So he shrugged and said,

'An hour? Yeah sure.' It was all right. He was safe.

Then what you might ask was that strained protuberance doing on his lap? What was that sullen pulse? What was that transmission from his lower heart?

Just an echo, a reverberation. Or so he told himself ninety minutes later as he sauntered down the single flight to let her in.

Martin slid the bolt and pulled the door open – and immediately had to deal with another reflex. He gagged.*

Copper-coloured Phoebe was wearing white – a sheer summer dress. With her white handbag slung over her shoulder. And kitten-heeled white sandals with thin white bands that curled up around her copper-coloured calves . . .

'No suitcase?' he asked as he kissed her cheek.

---

* Not quite a retch but somewhere between an abrupt gulp and a stoppered hiccup . . . I'd like to have a look at the technical literature on sexuality and the gag reflex. In my own male circle it was occasionally discussed, but only in the context of going to bed with two girls at once (what we called a 'carwash') – something never achieved by any of us; it had to do, then, with the vision of carnal gluttony . . . The reflex is not exclusively male; Janet Malcolm, the biographer of Sylvia Plath, acknowledged it when she first laid eyes on the husky Ted Hughes.

'I parked it at Merry's. Where I also had a quick bath first.' She stepped past him. 'Is it up here?'

'Let me lead the way,' he said, suddenly reluctant to follow in her wake. Phoebe, seen from the rear, always reminded him that even the slenderest girls held untold power in their back saddles, patiently ticking over; nor did he want to see all that western light come flooding through her inner thighs, forming a candleflame in her core, as he knew it would, like a wavering question mark . . . Phoebe said,

'It's freestanding and a nice shape.' She meant the house. 'What was it before?'

'A rectory. There's still some kind of tabernacle across the backyard.'

'How many flats?'

'Three. I'm the middle one – here.'

Once inside, she twirled to the doorway of the sitting room, then to the doorway of the study (where the balcony windows were open to the breeze), then to the doorway of the underused kitchen, which had another room off it, with its signs of everyday kitchen life – a kitchen table and a couple of kitchen chairs . . .

She said, 'And the bathroom. Which is quite a decent size, I see. Ooh and with a chaise longue no less. And that's the way to the bedroom? I'll just take a quick scan of it.' Which she did, without comment. 'Mm, if we'd lived here, maybe we wouldn't've broken up. So *airy* . . . Right. Back to your desk! I'll curl up with my paper in there. Oh, are you still single by the way?'

'Uh, yes, officially. For a little while longer.'

'So you haven't uh, tendered your vows? You haven't yet foresworn all others?'

Sinking back on the sofa, she gave a quiet laugh of settled condescension, as if enjoying a private joke, as if saying, *Really, the notions some people get about themselves*, and rounding it all off with a decidedly asocial grimace. Yes, the brutish off-centredness had had time to reappear (and we regret to say that he was additionally stirred to see it). 'Look at that mosquito bite on my thigh. It itched, so I scratched it. Go on, back to the grindstone with you. Don't shut the doors the whole way, Mart. That'd be unfriendly. But I promise, you won't know I'm here . . .'

*

Oh, he knew she was there – even in the silence barely a heartbeat passed when he didn't know she was there. Then came sounds. The kitchen tap. The fizz of the TV (quickly extinguished). The fumble with the telephone, then her voice. Then her voice, closer, saying, 'Forty-five minutes . . . Can I have a bath before I go?'

'I thought you'd had a bath.'

'I did, but it was only a whore's bath. On Merry's bidet.' The study door opened. 'I'm rather achey from the flight.' Her arms were wing-shaped and her hands were occupied behind her back. 'What I need is a good soak.' A shoulder was bared, and a section of intricate clavicle. 'A good soak. Don't you agree?'

'. . . Well go on then.'

'Thanks.' As she moved off he heard a sigh and a soft whoosh as she vacated her dress. '. . . Mart,' she called, 'the plug. Does the thingy go up or down?'

He waited a moment; he gripped the desk and levered himself to his feet.

'. . . You needn't look so shocked,' she said with an affronted frown, 'just because I'm wearing a bra. Don't tell me you've forgotten *already* that planes make my breasts swell up. Well they do. They keep their shape but they go all heavy and feel as though they're about to burst. See for yourself. See?' She stepped back and looked down. '. . . Ah, and there we have it. Tycoon Tanya. She has curves in places where other girls don't even have places. Shall I get it out? . . . Here. Give me your hand.'

He opened his eyes and sat up straight. And there before him was a male strongman in a fishnet singlet who was wiping his armpits with a pink J-cloth.

'How do,' he said. 'All right?'

'Not so bad. And yourself, Jonjon?'

He yawned, and a transient rainbow of saliva wafted from his mouth. 'Miss Phelps is ready for you now. She's good for half an hour, I'd calculate. Through there.'

. . . The etiquette of reunions – how did it go? No words, just a fond flat smile that said, I've changed, and you've changed, that is our world and our condition, that is the nature of time, but don't concern yourself, my dear, in your case it's nothing, it's absolutely nothing at all . . .

He entered the alcove and walked the length of the passage to a waiting door, past a low window (treetops and rooftops and the unbounded city), past a wheelchair with a green shawl athwart the back of it. He knocked.

'Ah, come and sit here, Martin, if you would. The visitor's chair. Sit here and get your bearings . . . Did you happen to read about that unbelievable berk in – Hounslow? Peckham? One of those. He managed to wedge himself in his own bedsit. He outgrew it while he was still inside it. They had to demolish two walls and half a roof before they could winch him out. Dozens of people were involved, doctors, firemen, sappers, navvies. The whole operation came to six figures. He was seventeen and he weighed fifty-eight stone . . .'

Lying at a shallow angle with just her head propped up (framed by a thick headboard of deep-green velvet, and further braced by a pair of bunched duvets, and garnished with wispy shawls and neckerchiefs), she looked like a prodigious equatorial bloom, perhaps centuries old . . . She went on, in her bodiless falsetto,

'I suppose I could claim I've got Cushing's Syndrome or hyper-cortisolism or something like that. But my thing's much simpler. Weight gain, Martin, occurs when energy consumed – in the form of food – exceeds energy expended. And the only time I expend any energy at all is when I eat. A slowing metabolism doesn't help. And depression, depression doesn't help.

'You know, I don't fear death any more . . . The other highlight of my exercise regime is going to the bathroom. That's where the irresistible Jonjon comes in. Jonjon's an orderly at the bariatric unit in St Swithin's, where they have to weigh people in a kind of *lift*. As you know, I've always had a soft spot for the loo, and it's even more fun with Jonjon there. And after a session with him, and another one to look forward to the next day, who gives a, who gives a shit about death . . .

'So how about it, Mart? Shall I slip into a pair of cool pants? Or a pair of scanties I picked up cheap in the sales? Then I'll book a table somewhere for what, nine-thirty? And then we'll have all the time in the world.'

*

Holy father

'These helpers of yours, Phoebe. Jonjon, and Meg, who told me about the night nurse – Beth, is it? And you can afford them? . . . Mm, Maud told me you were flush. What was it you sold off exactly? Did you have a kind of fief at TFS? . . . You know, Transworld Financial Services. The skyscraper in Berkeley Square.'

'Oh *that*. I only set foot in TFS when I was meeting you in the lobby. Or Siobhan or Mum. I didn't bother when it was just Daddy, because he . . .' She yawned without opening her mouth. 'Bit of a chore, all this, but it has to be done.

'Right. What I sold off was Ess Es. I sold off Essential Escorts, plus the Mayfair maisonette I ran it from, plus all the files. It was a huge business by the time I left, thousands of girls and not just young ones either. Merry was sixty-two when she finally hung up her trunks. Lars and Raoul were my top panders, Lars for the actual escorts, Raoul for the clients, mostly Saudis and Chechnyans. Now they deal in trafficked labour – you know, with ganghouses of Latvians licking out cellars in Notting Hill. Scum of the earth, the pair of them, but quite loyal in their way. Okay. I expect you'll want to ask me a question or two. Beginning with your father.'

Her face was still there, and still pretty, too (same lean lips and strong teeth, the eyes rather more domelike and unblinking), but you had to seek all this out within the face that had subsumed and imprisoned it (the original chin seemed no bigger than a thimble). And now as he neared the foot of the bed, both faces disappeared, blotted out by the hard fact of her mass (and it *was* hard, her mass. There was no give in it). He sat, and they smiled. Yes, Phoebe was a novelistic kind of character; and she knew that such people had their allotted tasks . . . She wouldn't give him closure – because that comes only with death (and nobody ever gets over anything). Still, she would do what she could with what she had and with what she was.

He said, 'Well, my dear old friend. There's my father.' And there's yours, he thought.

'Okay. You went off to Durham to betray me with that Lily. Consider my situation. I was trapped in Kingsley's house and I obviously had to sleep with *someone*. And who else was there? So what could I do

454

except get flopsy on Parfait Amour and squirm around till he made a pass. In the end he did give a rather flowery speech – that bit was true. And I immediately complied. There.' She stared at him with growing accusation. 'Don't you mind?'

He said, 'Nah, I really don't. When it's safely in the past, who cares about infidelity?'

'Women do.'

'So I'm told. You can smell them.'

'Yes, we can smell them. And we remember that smell for the rest of our lives.'

'Mm. With men, or with me anyway, now, I just think – the more the merrier. A contribution to the gaiety of nations. *La ronde*, Phoebe. Here's another example. I wish to Christ I'd slept with you and your suntan when you got back from Corsica. That time. It would've made a nice memory. To add to all the others.'

She acknowledged his words with dissimulated pleasure, though she said, 'Oh, I *hated* you for that.'

'I hated me too. Why didn't I? Chances are I'd've got away with it.'

'You can put your mind at rest on that one, Martin. You would *not*'ve got away with it. Trust me.'

'Oh well. But you looked so . . . I should've made a real pig of myself.'

'And you didn't! Absolutely inexcusable. Apart from Lily it was the main reason I spun you that line about Larkin. Uh, did it work, by the way?'

'You mean did it bother me? Oh yes.'

She said fervently, '*God*, what a relief. How long did it work for?'

'Five years. Ridiculous. And it worked in a way I'm sure you didn't reckon on. For five years all it did was darken my . . . See, Phoebe, when I look back on my lovelife I mainly feel happy and proud, and grateful, and incredibly lucky. All those episodes of passionate fascination. All those wonderful women, very much including you – or even starring you. But for five years what I remembered was all my sins. My conscience turned on me, Phoebe. Every last instance of ruthlessness and coarseness – even just insensitivity, even plain bad manners. I . . .'

'Do you good,' she said. 'Uh no, I didn't reckon on that. I suppose you were just reliving it with the thought that you were useless with women. All thumbs and getting everything wrong . . . Don Juan in Hull. Five years. What made it stop?'

'It hasn't stopped, not entirely. Things keep emerging. Like a very flirtatious, even salacious, letter to Philip from Mum. Dated 1950.'

'When you were safely born.'

'Mm. And recently I've come to *like* the idea of them having a little affair. Do them good. Anyway. One day, in 2006, I saw a photo of Dad not long after the war, and I looked across the room at Nat – my older boy – and I thought, Jesus, they're the same person. The continuity. Essence and aura, and not just looks.'

'*You* look just like Kingsley too, you bloody fool. And you *are* a bloody fool. It's what stops you being a total pill . . . You see, Martin, the thing is – you're in the flow, you're in the tide. You loved your parents and now you love your children. And I hate you for it. I'm like some nutter on the internet. Because me, I'm outside the flow. I'm outside. *I'm* the one that's like Larkin. Fetch the book, if you would. It's on the fridge. And while you're at it bring me two choc ices, the ones in the dark wrappers. I want four but they melt.'

'I'll bring a couple more before I go . . . Which poem? Is it "Love Again"?'

'No. "Faith Healing". Here. "In everyone there sleeps / A sense of life lived according to love." Which is all there is to say. "That nothing cures. An immense slackening ache . . . " He was an unusually determined man, Father Gabriel.'

'Mm. I suppose they all are, people like him.' After a silence he said, 'I think the consequences of that are entitled to be infinite. I think you've had a very hard road, Phoebe.'

'Ah, so someone's finally said it. Unusually determined, and unusually exacting too. *Don't loll, girlie, keep your hands busy, keep working little one* . . . He even tried it on again later, after that thing with Timmy. He was rearoused, you see, by the idea of teachers and pupils. That's when I got my first inkling of the other half of it.'

'The other half of it.'

Don't even change my name

There was a knock. Meg, with a tray: white wine, steel ice bucket, a single glass. It was six o'clock.

'Jonjon'll be here till seven, Miss Phelps. If you should . . .'

'Thank you, Meg. I'll ring if need be.'

Phoebe kept her gaze on the closing door, saying, 'Graeme. Oh *come* on. There was my perfectly nice, perfectly weak, perfectly bedridden mother. And there was Sir Grae, the househusband, giving me my bath and then shooing me into the Jag. He didn't hate money. Money was the love of his life. He just couldn't earn any. And whenever he got his hands on a few quid he went and pissed it away at the Ritz. Graeme let it happen for money. So much a week. When the Timmy business happened, and Father Gabriel stirred, Daddy tried to coax me into it.'

Another silence. 'A compound crime,' he said, 'giving you a compound wound – Graeme orphaned you, Phoebe.'

'Yes. Jane was right. And not just that. He widowed me too. That's how it feels. And now I'm Widow Twankey, up in her spinster pad. God's blood.' Another silence. 'Sir Grae, when he was finally dying he clutched my arm and said, *I'm sorry, I'm sorry. Can you forgive me?* I said not a word. Then he coughed with a huge splat and he was gone. Gone to Hell . . . Then I *really* started to eat.

'Notice all the books, Mart? I used to spend the whole time reading. Then I stopped. I didn't want to be interested in anything. You know, that's what I thought when I saw Christopher'd died. I thought, Oh and he was interested in *so* many things . . . Me, I could go any time. I've got a suicide *pact*'s worth of pills stored away. Any time at all.

'There was a thing about you in the *Mail*. You and your tell-all novel. I want you to know that you can say anything you like about me. Anything. Don't even change my name. And Martin. Did you love me? I think you must've, or how else did you stick it? I felt love coming at me, and I liked it, and I pretended a bit, but I couldn't do it back. It's like asthma. You can breathe in but you can't breathe out. I'm sorry I couldn't.'

'Don't be. I never said the words, but there was love. There was definitely love.'

'Oh no . . . I was planning to be mean to you but I find I've gone and let you off. Give me your hand. I just want to kiss it goodbye. And then leave.'

'One other kiss.' He gazed down at her and imagined the full-length figurehead of a pagan sailing ship, carved out of the heaviest redwood and all swollen in the sun. Her face – he pressed his lips to it. 'There.'

'Thank you. Now let me sleep. Goodbye. Let me sleep now.'

PART V

ULTIMATE: DOING THE DYING

It seemed that out of battle I escaped

Those flies I thought I saw in Christopher's room. Were they 'death receptors'?

Death receptors actually exist – they occupy the surfaces of living cells. The science of it I find impenetrable, but I was haunted at once by the imagery. Death receptors are 'signalling pathways' from a cytoplasmic region known as 'the death domain', and may be imagined as ghostly groundsmen and chambermaids: their mission is to prepare the body to accommodate its strange new guest.

The swarming vermin in the sickroom were death receptors, given flesh and blood and a smear of hair by my eyes.

'She died instantly'. Oh no she didn't. I have never believed for a moment that anyone dies instantly. It takes a while to die; even the wallshadows of Hiroshima and Nagasaki took a while to die. I have similar objections to 'he died in his sleep'. Oh no he didn't. He had to wake up first, just long enough to do the dying. Or maybe he had a certain kind of bad dream: the kind that under-anaesthetised patients are said to have during surgery . . .

The chapter heading above is the first line of Wilfred Owen's 'Strange Meeting' (1918). Our narrator, our warrior poet, *has* escaped from battle, but only by being killed on its field. He has passed from life to death, and the immense and solemn toil of the crossing, with all it asks of you, is beautifully and terrifyingly rendered by means of high technique. The combination of the stately pentameter and the grating half-rhymes or slant rhymes (or, in Owen's virtuoso use of them, dissonant assonances):

It seemed that out of battle I escaped
Down some profound dull tunnel, long since scooped,
Through granites which titanic wars had groined,
Yet also there encumbered sleepers groaned . . .

Escaped, scooped, groined, groaned: the slant rhymes, the dissonant assonances that will roll through you when you do the dying.

The Poet
December 1985

In the latter months of 1984, the year before his body went over the waterfall, Philip Larkin was unprecedentedly overweight (sixteen stone), 'terribly deaf', and 'drinking like a fish'. He would start the day with a glass or two of port – though he was disciplined enough to keep the bottle elsewhere, 'so I have to get out of bed'. Within a few months he was subsisting on 'cheap red wine' and Complan (while Monica – recovered from shingles but recently diagnosed with Parkinson's – relied on tomato sandwiches and gin). On the phone my mother made a suggestion: 'Why don't you try some *nice* red wine?' But Philip persisted with cheap.

And his destined mood? The road outside the house (194 Newland Park, Hull, Yorks) was not much travelled, and in its spare time served as a bike track for local children; they sorely irritated Larkin, who objected not to their cries and chatter so much as their 'presence'. He wrote to a very old friend about them, the ever-gruff Colin Gunner (now a misanthropic old swine – and Catholic convert – living in a caravan). 'I had the pleasure', he regaled Gunner, 'of seeing one fall off his new tricycle, and set up a howl.' I find I'm unwilling to imagine that pleasure taking facial form; anyway, he wasn't pleased for long. 'Instead of cuffing him about the ears the father walked him up and down in his arms. Grrr.' Cheered to see a child in distress, enraged to see a sympathetic parent: Larkin's destined mood was a candid and (slightly) playful inversion of the human norms.

In less than a week it would be New Year's Day. 'Happy '85 – hope we stay alive,' he said in a note to Conquest. Bob (b. 1917) had thirty years yet to come; Philip had eleven months.

The poet's familiar, steady-state ailments – insomnia, hay fever, piles, constipation, pre-thrombotic leg, pre-arthritic neck – were joined by 'cardio-spasms', confirmed by a Dr Aber, who also thought it worth noting that Larkin had 'cancer phobia and fear of dying'. The most ominous development, it turned out, was 'a funny feeling' in the back of the throat. Sydney Larkin – he of the golden eagle and the paired lightning shafts – died at sixty-three (cancer). This portent now became a fixed idea. Philip was sixty-two.

His oesophagus was removed on June 11, 1985; it contained 'a great deal of unpleasant stagnant material', according to a Dr Royston; it was cancerous (and there were secondary tumours). Monica's pre-operative forecast – 'six months' – was thus confirmed. She decided Larkin should not be told; and he never asked ('felt I had enough to worry about', he meekly informed a penpal).

In the post-operative period a never-identified visitor to the ICU at the Nuffield gave Larkin a bottle of Scotch. On June 19 he drank 'most of it' and flooded his lungs; he was unconscious for five days. Three weeks later a friend drove him back to Newland Park. At the end of August he fell backwards down the stairs.

By November he was 'deathly thin', and of course 'intensely depressed'. He told Monica, in what she called his 'lugubrious' mode, that he felt he was 'spiralling down towards extinction'. 'He said it with a fascinated horror' – looking as though he 'was about to burst into tears'. After completing what he called 'a wasted life', he had 'nothing to live for'. Now he was bearing the full weight of the closing sentence of 'The View' (1972), whose third and last stanza runs:

> Where has it gone, the lifetime?
> Search me. What's left is drear.
> Unchilded and unwifed, I'm
> Able to view that clear:
> So final. And so near.

'I've been telling him this for – for forty years,' said Kingsley. 'Listen, you bloody fool, we *all* fear death, you bloody fool. But what we fear is *dying*. And you, you bloody fool, *you* fear *being dead*. You bloody fool.'

I said, 'I bet he fears dying too. He says so. " . . . yet the dread / Of dying, and being dead, / Flashes afresh to hold and horrify".'

'Yes, but once you've got the dying out of the way, what's wrong with being dead?'

Jane, who was leaving the kitchen (for her lie-down), paused at the doorway. 'Did he mind it – all those centuries before he was born?'

'Exactly,' I said. 'That's what's wrong with the poem. He can't make not being alive sound horrifying. Or even irksome.'

It was mid-afternoon on Christmas Day, 1977, and on December 23 'Aubade' had appeared, with some fanfare, in the *TLS* (we had an open copy on the table, staked out with wine bottles and chutney jars). I was twenty-eight and Kingsley, as ever, was the same age as Larkin.

'He's answering *you* here, Dad. "And specious stuff that says *No rational being / Can fear a thing it will not feel* . . . " Specious. Attractive but suspect.'

'I know what it means.'

'So he's . . . he's finding rationality suspect. And trusting in his superstition.'

'Which is de-universalising, don't you find? I mean, how many readers are bloody fools about being dead . . . Look. Even his technique wanders off. " . . . *Can fear a thing it will not feel*, not seeing / That this is what we fear – no sight, no sound, / No touch or taste or smell, nothing to think with, / Nothing to love or link with . . . " Listen, mate. If there's nothing to think with, you won't know or care if there's nothing to link with, you bloody fool. Pitiful rhyme, that.'

'Pitiful. And two *fear*s, and two *not*s in one line . . . Quite a poem, though. *You* used to be like that, Dad, didn't you. Jelly-kneed and pant-wetting about being dead?'

'Balls,' he said, not lifting his eyes from the page. 'Only about dying. I never gave a toss about being dead.'

In his early thirties Larkin tried – in my view with considerable success – to imagine 'the moment of death'. And I'm bearing in mind that he was already an admirer of Wilfred Owen (and would go on to write two essays on him, in 1963 and 1975). That final moment, he imagined, 'must be a little choppy, a fribbling [stammering] as the currents of life fray against the currents of death'.

But then too the moment of death takes more than a moment; a full-grown human being is among other things a great *fait accompli* of aggregation; and all those experiences and memories need a while to disperse.

Still, in Larkin's case . . . 'The Life with a Hole in it' is the title of a poem of 1972; Larkin's was a hole with a life in it. He kept it very thin, lenten, and gaunt, with nothing 'worth looking back on'. So maybe the scattering, the fraying of the currents, was quickly over.

June 20, 1985. At this time (following the episode with the whisky) the *Guardian* was publishing daily bulletins on PL's health. I called my father and said, 'Are you going up there?'

'I offered. With Hilly. But he . . . Anyway, they're saying he's out of danger.'

'You offered. And he what, he didn't fancy it?' Kingsley wasn't really inclined to talk but I pressed him. 'Why, do you think?'

'. . . Because he might lose his nerve and he doesn't want us to see him gibbering.'

October 5. 'And you still read him every night,' I asked. 'Really every night?'

'Yeah, one or two. Last thing. As the other half of my nightcap.'

'Any good stuff in that?' I meant the letter on the kitchen table. 'Is he still off solids?'

'Uh . . . *I can't fuckin eat fuck all. It really is scaring . . . Three months ago my doctors said I should slowly get better. To my mind I am slowly getting worse.* Here's a quite funny bit. *The GP listens to all this sympathetically, but rather as if he were the next door neighbour – without suggesting that it has any special relevance to his own knowledge or responsibilities.* He signs off by saying he's "not long for this world". But he's been saying that since he was twenty. Nothing about Monica.'

'Christ,' I said wonderingly. 'How *is* Monica? . . . I mean to live with.'

'Christ. How d'you think?'

December 3. 'When are you going up there?' Philip had done the dying. Now he was being dead (and awaiting burial). 'Are you expected to speak?'

'It's on the ninth. Yes.'

The dying took place on December 2 – on a Monday, in the small hours.

On November 29, at home, he collapsed twice, in the sitting room, and then in the downstairs toilet, wedging the door shut with his feet. This is Motion:

> Monica was unable to force the door open. She couldn't even make him hear her – he had left his hearing aid behind – but she could hear him. 'Hot! Hot!' he was whispering piteously. He had fallen with his face pressed to one of the central heating pipes that ran round the lavatory wall.

She enlisted a neighbour and managed to haul Philip into the kitchen. He asked for some Complan; while she prepared it she rang for an ambulance. 'I'll see you tomorrow, Bun,' he said as he was being stretchered back to the Nuffield . . . And he did see her on Saturday, and again on Sunday, but he was too thoroughly tranquillised to make any sense. On Sunday evening she went home to wait for the phone call, which came at half past one.

Michael Bowen, a recent addition to the circle (a fellow jazz buff and one of life's willing hands), ferried Monica back and forth on that last weekend. 'If Philip hadn't been drugged, he would have been raving,' Bowen told Motion (in 1991): 'He was that frightened.' Well, maybe the drugs neutralised what there was of his courage, too, as well as much of his fear; and the fact remains that he wasn't raving. 'Why aren't I screaming?' he said in a letter, back in January – picking up on a line in 'The Old Fools' (1973): 'Why aren't they screaming?'

Yes, why *aren't* they screaming? Because one doesn't, because people don't. His middle-class inhibitions saw him through, along with his middle-class conscientiousness. Like a good boy he amended his will and turned up for all his appointments (including one with his dentist); he left clear instructions on the disposal – the shredding – of his voluminous (and reportedly 'desperate') diaries and notebooks; and he wrote, or rather dictated, a lengthy, calm, generous, and conspicuously graceful letter to Kingsley, the only male friend who excited in him anything that resembled love.

His last letter was in due course followed by his last words. At the very end he was sufficiently composed to deliver them, faintly, to the nurse who was holding his hand. He said, 'I am going to the inevitable.'

December 9. 'How was it up there?'

'It was all *right*, I suppose.'

Kingsley poured a huge glass of Macallan's and took it off to bed. That was one part of his nightcap. Would he be reaching for the other half? . . . To him it was more than the loss of a poet, as he told Conquest in a letter – the loss of a presence.

I sat on with my mother.

'How was that Monica?'

'She didn't come. Too shattered, apparently. Poor old thing. What's she going to do now? . . . Your father can't *stand* her of course.'

'Gaw, his women. Mum, you used to say he was scared of girls.'

'I always respected Philip very much. He was the nicest of Kings's friends. But think. He had a stutter, and then early baldness . . .'

'And early deafness, and inch-thick specs since childhood. But what I mean is, if he was frightened of girls, why were his girls so frightening – in themselves?'

'They were all frightening, the ones I knew. Even little Ruth. Very proud . . . You know, don't you, that he *dreaded* the thought of imposing himself. And probably the girls who were drawn to him thought, Well it's up to me to do the imposing.'

I tried to weigh this. Then I said, 'A long day in Hull. Mum, you must be exhausted. Did it smell of fish?'

'Not particularly. It was far too cold to smell of anything. They say it smells of fish just before it rains . . . Your father was very lowered by it all.'

'Well Dad did love him.'

'On the train there he kept saying, "Why have I never been here before? Why've I never been to his house?" And on the train back he said, all disappointed like a child, "It's very strange. I feel I never really knew him."'

Maybe nobody really knew him. Except Margaret Monica Beale Jones. She knew what he was as a man (she was tough enough to sustain that) and she knew what he was as a poet.

My father's aversion to Monica survived Larkin's death – largely because she fell into the habit of ringing him up, most nights, to reminisce drunkenly and interminably about the love of her life. 'Grief?' said Kingsley after an eighty-minute session. 'No. She's glorying in it.'

But in truth Monica had little else to glory in, and less and less as the years went by. In 1988 she had the *Collected Poems* and 'Letter to a Friend About Girls' (in which she and the others 'have their world . . . where they work, and age, and put off men / By being unattractive'), and in 1992 she had the *Selected Letters*, where she saw the most elaborate belittlement of all.* Monica lived on in Newland Park, alone and semi-bedridden, until 2001. 'Oh, he was a bugger,' she told Andrew Motion. 'He lied to me, the bugger, but I loved him.'

During a stay in hospital (one of many in his final year), he was visited by Monica, of course, and also by Maeve and also by Betty (his 'loaf-haired secretary'). 'I didn't want to see Maeve,' he told Betty. 'I wanted to see Monica to tell her I love her' . . . Is it merely sentimental to fantasise about a deathbed wedding (perhaps the only kind of wedding he could honestly respect)? In which case Monica would have passed her remaining sixteen years as Larkin's widow, and not just as one of the spinsters he left behind.

'When I was young', he said in an interview, 'I thought I hated everybody, but when I grew up I realised it was just children I didn't like . . . Children are very horrible, aren't they? Selfish, noisy, cruel, vulgar little brutes.'

As he got older Kingsley, too, devoted some leisure to the defamation of children. 'This anti-child routine of yours,' I once said to him (as a freshly smitten parent). 'It's very occasionally quite funny. And I know it's intentionally mean-spirited. But is it meant to be fatuous?' Asked by his tightened lips to elaborate, I said, 'Well – hark at the pot calling the kettle black. What d'you think *you* were until you were twelve?'

And this at least gave him pause. Larkin, though, would have had his answer ready. 'You know I was never a child,' he announced in a letter

---

* Of his (never-finished) third novel Larkin wrote to Patsy in 1953: 'You know, I *can't* write this book: if it is to be written at all it should be largely an attack on Monica, & I *can't* do that, not while we are still on friendly terms, and I'm not sure it even interests me sufficiently to go on.'

of 1980. Was this a prelude to some paedophobic refinement, perhaps? No. He soberly continued: 'my life began at 21, or 31 more likely. Say with the publication of *The Less Deceived*' . . . That is, November 1955, when he was thirty-three. But actually February 1948, when he was twenty-five, has greater explanatory power: 'I am in bad spirits because of my father' – who had only weeks to live. 'I feel I have got to make a big mental jump – to stop being a child and become an adult . . .'

This was a serious recognition, and one that might have led to some serious thought about that adult known as Sydney Larkin. Instead, Philip responded to the death as follows: he underwent religious instruction; he got himself engaged to Ruth (an avowedly 'provisional' engagement, though one solemnised with a ring); and he moved in with his widowed mother for a 'frightful' twenty-five months. He didn't jump into adulthood. During this time his romantic life sagged and his artistic life ceased.

And yet: 'Deprivation is for me what daffodils were for Wordsworth.' I find this epigram fishy on more than one level. Alliterative and 'eminently quotable', it was clearly long premeditated; but in retrospect it sounds like a (failing) attempt to glory in gloom. That vein of stubborn persistence was instantly identified by Wystan Auden (they met just once, at a dinner party given by Stephen Spender, in 1972).

Auden: 'How do you like living in Hull?'

Larkin: 'I'm no unhappier there than I should be anywhere else.'

Auden: 'Naughty naughty! Mother wouldn't like it!'

Telling the story years later (in the *Paris Review*), Larkin said he found the remark 'very funny', which it is; but it is alarmingly salient, too. What Auden saw was a defensive façade – and one so obvious that he could greet it only with amicable satire.

The façade was shakily defending Larkin's failure to construct so much as a remotely and minimally convincing life. And he knew it, he 'viewed it clear': this deciding truth, like death itself, stays 'on the edge of vision, / A small unfocused blur, a standing chill', but a blur that regularly 'flashes afresh to hold and horrify'. And as we know, it was a fate that he had prearranged (with some loftiness of spirit) in his early twenties; prompted by Yeats, he bowed to a transparently false opposition between 'the life' and 'the work' (as if the two were somehow mutually exclusive). And when the work, the poems, duly retreated from him (the date he gives is 1974), he found himself helplessly marooned in 'a fucked up life'. 'My life seems stuffed full of nothing'; 'What an absurd, empty life!'; 'I suddenly see myself as a freak and a failure, & my way of life as a farce.'

Together with its almost sinister memorability, and its unique combination of the lapidary and the colloquial, the key distinction of Larkin's corpus is its humour: he is by many magnitudes the funniest poet in English (and I include all exponents of light verse). Nor, needless to say, is his comedy just a pleasant additive; it is foundational . . . Was he helped in this – was he somehow 'swayed on' – by living a hollow life, 'a farce', 'absurd', and 'stuffed full of nothing'? Well, not nothing; his life was stuffed full of the kind of repetitive indignities that make us say, If you didn't laugh, you'd cry. Yes, and if you didn't cry, you'd laugh. This is the axis on which the poems rotate. His indignities were his daffodils.

As we take our leave let us recall a very late poem (1979) that captures some of his personal pathos, his muted benignity, and his exquisitely tentative tenderness. One day he was mowing the lawn and ran over a hedgehog in the taller grass. 'When it happened,' said Monica, 'he came in from the garden howling. He was very upset. He'd been feeding the hedgehog, you see – he looked out for it . . . He started writing about it soon afterwards.' The result was 'The Mower' (closely related, here, to the Reaper), which ends:

> Next morning I got up and it did not.
> The first day after a death, the new absence
> Is always the same; we should be careful
>
> Of each other, we should be kind
> While there is still time.

The Novelist
April 2005

On June 10, 1995, I rang him in Vermont and said,

'Happy birthday. And congratulations.'

'Thank you,' he said. 'But what exactly are the congratulations for?'

'You're eighty – you've made old bones. You should be feeling very proud and grand. Old bones is a great thing. A very great thing.'

I said it more or less unreflectingly, just to buck him up and give him heart, and I was pleased to hear him laughing ('Uh – uh – uh'); but a little reflection informs me that old bones is indeed a very great thing.

'Strange Meeting', the last poem written by Wilfred Owen (1893–1918), proceeds:

> Yet also there encumbered sleepers groaned,
> Too fast in thought or death to be bestirred.
> Then, as I probed them, one sprang up, and stared
> With piteous recognition in fixed eyes,
> Lifting distressful hands, as if to bless.
>
> 'Strange friend,' I said, 'here is no cause to mourn.'
> 'None,' said that other, 'save the undone years . . .'

Old bones will give you plenty of causes to mourn, naturally, but you wouldn't linger long on the undone years. Old bones has the power to enervate death, depriving it of its tragic complexity. Dying two months short of your ninetieth birthday: this may call for any number of adjectives, but not *tragic*.

I was at my desk in the coastal village of José Ignacio, in the province of Maldonado, in the country of Uruguay: Uruguay: civically, socially, and humanly the princess of the nether America.

When we were down there – and we were down there, with intermissions, from 2003 to 2006 – I worked in a separate building a hundred yards from the house (it had a bedroom and a bathroom, and would in fact soon serve as the self-contained *cabana* of the Hitch, who was coming south for a long weekend). To get to my study, Elena would climb down the external steps from the balcony and walk past the swimming pool, which in April was in my opinion already unusably cold. Because in Latin America, below the latitude of Equador, April is the beginning of fall. Elena was coming by to tell me something.

This study of mine was glass-fronted and gave you a horizon-wide vista of the sea, which surged about us on all three fronts of the peninsula – the South Atlantic Ocean, with its occasional whales and daily cloud-shadows (and the cloud-shadows always looked like whales idling or basking just beneath the foam); the distinctively pale blue sky issued its weather forecasts, redder than fire when the sun went down, or else racked at dawn by portents of coming *tormentas* – thunderstorms – that were prehistoric in their power . . . A human shape now encroached on the stillness, and I knew by her tread and her blank face exactly what she had come to tell me.* Elena stood there outside the window slowly shaking her head.

'How did you hear?' I said as I stepped out into the air.

'It was on the news. The funeral's tomorrow.'

'Tomorrow?' I said. 'Well that's that. There's nothing I can do.' I waved an uncommunicative and even accusatory arm at her and went back inside.

---

* No, it wasn't unexpected. Saul's ebbing was twofold, first the mind, then the body. For the past year he had been increasingly unmoored in time. As an eerie consequence of this, he was freshly devastated, bereaved again and again, by the deaths of contemporaries who had already predeceased him, for example his soulmate Allan Bloom (d. 1992) and his sister Jane (d. 2003). All the dead were in his custody, and he couldn't let them go . . . He was unmoored in space, too, wondering where he was (on a train, on a boat?), and mistaking his own bedroom for a hotel ('I want to check out. Give me ten dollars and get me out of here') . . . The somatic trajectory was more conventional, marked by pneumonias, falls, a series of minor strokes, followed by difficulty in swallowing, then in breathing. He slept much of the time, but his death receptors were just waking up.

. . . Saul, then, had desisted, desisted from living, stopped being alive. So I went back inside and tasted the ancient flavours of desistence and defeat. And helplessness. Also a kind of terrestrial disaffection: the paradise around me didn't become infernal or purgatorial; it just became ordinary . . .

An hour later I was still muttering it – *There's nothing I can do* – when Elena reappeared on the far side of the glass. You see, Elena, as well as being Elena, was an American, and unresigned. She was smiling now and the red-foiled ticket she was holding streamed and palpitated in the wind.

. . . So Carrasco Airport in Montevideo, then Ministro Pistarini Airport (known as Ezeiza) in Buenos Aires, then (eleven hours and five minutes later) Kennedy Airport in New York, then Logan Airport in Boston; and I got to Crowninshield Road just as the first of the towncars was leaving for the cemetery in Brattleboro, Vermont – a distance of a hundred miles, to add to my five and a half thousand; and meanwhile, here, winter was stepping aside for spring.

In the little reception area of the local synagogue there was a cardboard box full of beanies – black skullcaps, yarmulkes. Rosamund took one, and when she saw me hesitate she said,

'*You* needn't bother.'

'I don't mind. And I'm married to a Jew.'

'Well take it, but you won't have to put it on.'

Just as the two of us settled in our seats (while the rabbi ululated) an elderly woman turned and with a stiffly and rapidly jutting hand pointed to the crown of her head.

Rosamund whispered, 'She wants you to put it on.'

I put it on.

. . . Earlier that day, in the Jewish section of Morningside Cemetery, a black cloth with a white Star of David was drawn away from the coffin just before it was lowered, and at the same time the black ribbons we had been issued were torn up (not just a rite, this, but an enactment – for many did it frowningly, almost scowlingly, as if in great bitterness), to symbolise grief and loss . . .

Religion. When I was a child (in a household where that kind of thing just never came up), other children's parents sometimes took me along to church on Sunday mornings; and I sat through it all in perplexity, estrangement, and, after five or ten minutes, heartfelt and then passionate boredom. But now I was half a century older, and – let's be fair – the Judaic faith was twice as old as the Christian; so I was intrigued and perhaps minutely solaced by the strength of these continuities and observances.

By one in particular. On the brink of the grave stood a considerable pyramid of earth intermixed with orange sand. In Jewish lore it is felt that the dead should not be inhumed by strangers – that this work belongs to the near and dear, to the loved and loving, to family and friends. Rosamund went first, getting right down on her haunches and emptying the shovel gently and almost soundlessly; followed by the three sons (the three half-brothers), Gregory, Adam, Daniel; followed by all able-bodied mourners, in their turn . . . When it came to Philip Roth, he gave the shovel a dismissive glance and reached into the grit with his bare right hand, raised his arm, and splayed his fingers over the rectangular cavity in the ground.* Most of the real spading, and the conscientious levelling of the surface, fell to Mr Frank Maltese, the local man who built Saul's nearby house, back in 1975.

And death is still death, whenever it comes – death is always death. Chaucer, *The Knight's Tale*:

> What is this world? what asketh man to have?
> Now with his love, now in his cold grave,
> Alone, withouten any company.

---

* I thought this gesture – the handful of dust – was both dignified and intimate. Almost at once several different mourners sought to amuse me with a deflating explanation: Roth did it that way to spare his bad back. Well, if you like. It was also said that Roth spent the occasion gaping (and stumbling) with grief. To me he looked sombre but also humorous – his usual disposition . . . After a death, as Zachary Leader notes in the second volume of his definitive *Life of Saul Bellow*, there is a short pause and then the world floods back in 'with its animosities, anxieties, importunities' – and its long-cherished resentments. Leader takes us through them, with their strange instances of cattiness and scepticism. Unsensed by me at the time, many grievances (amatory and literary) were reopened at the graveside (funerals no doubt have a way of encouraging recrudescences); but all the second-hand and unworthy rancour, I bet, was confined to its natural home – the periphery.

Shiva, the prescribed period of mourning, starts immediately after interment and lasts seven days. I stayed in Boston for about that long, putting up at a downtown Marriott and presenting myself at Crowninshield Road before lunch and leaving after dinner. I was just present and around, autonomous but available, along with Rosamund's parents, her sister, her niece, and other friends and helpers, and of course Rosie – we were the circled wagons of Rosamund's train.

That week there were further attendances at shul, and there were other rituals. At Crowninshield Road life solidified around the kitchen table, where we talked and reminisced, and although there was a great deal of eating there was hardly any cooking. Every day at dusk a family group would appear on the front doorstep: neighbours, in this Judaeo-academic enclave, bearing those tubs and tureens heavy with thick stews and thick soups . . . You could hear a laconic exchange of words but there was no ingress, no intrusion. And always, it seemed, a companionable little party was in progress on the front path, people coming or going, bearing meals or bearing away various rinsed containers and utensils, and modestly reminding you that food is love.

In 2005 I was the son of a dead writer, Kingsley (1922–95). I ought to have known better than anyone that writers survive their deaths. A sceptic might say that only their books survive; but their books were and are their lives, and this was most pointedly true of Saul, the master of the Higher Autobiography – the Life-Writer.

The table in that spacious kitchen had an additional strength and virtue: it featured stacks of Saul – the novels, the stories, the essays and reportage – and they were often consulted during the week-long wake. There was one especially intensive session involving Rosamund and me plus the critic–novelist James Wood and his wife, the novelist–critic Claire Messud, and when it was over I thought – yes, the trick really *works*. I felt as stimulated, as stretched, and as satisfied as I used to feel after a long evening with Saul.* I hoped and trusted that Rosamund

---

* Perhaps recalling Adam Bellow at the graveside (and his involuntary aria of tearful distress), I read out the last paragraph of 'A Silver Dish', a story that describes a very singular parting of father and son. The father, Pop, is an ancient Chicago grifter (and 'consistently a terrible little man'); Woody, 'practical, physical, healthy-minded, and experienced', is his remarkably – even perversely – loving son . . . I think it may be the best thing in all Bellow: 'After a time, Pop's resistance ended. He subsided and

felt as I did. This transfusion from the afterlife of words must surely hasten another of the projects of grief: finding the space to step back, to step back and see the whole man (and in his fullest vigour), rather than simply the poor bare forked creature under your care, confused by the struggle to complete his allowance of reality.

'I didn't know what to expect,' said Eugene Goodheart (literary theorist and the author of *Confessions of a Secular Jew*). 'Would Saul be awake? Would he recognise me? So I decided to be brusque. I marched in there and . . . Saul was fully conscious and he looked – meditative, on that raised bed.* I even felt I might be disturbing his train of thought. Anyway I kept to my plan.'

Eugene: 'Well, Bellow – what have you got to say for yourself?'

Saul: '. . . Well, Gene, it's like this. I've been wondering. Wondering, Which is it? Is it, There goes a man? Or is it, There goes a jerk?'

Eugene (firmly): 'There goes a man.'

'Which was the right answer,' I said. 'If he'd asked me that . . .' If he'd asked me that, I would've honestly (and I now see romantically) added, *Saul, don't worry about a thing. You never put a foot wrong.*

But I also took note. In the end, it's not your Nobel Prize you're thinking of, it's not your three National Book Awards, and all that. It's your sins of the heart (real or imagined), it's your wives, your children, and how things went with them.

subsided. He rested against his son, his small body curled there. Nurses came and looked. They disapproved, but Woody, who couldn't spare a hand to wave them out, motioned with his head toward the door. Pop, whom Woody thought he had stilled, had only found a better way to get around him. Loss of heat was the way he did it. His heat was leaving him. As can happen with small animals while you hold them in your hand. Woody presently felt him cooling. Then, as Woody did his best to restrain him, and thought he was succeeding, Pop divided himself. And when he was separated from his warmth, he slipped into death. And there was his elderly, large, muscular son, still holding and pressing him when there was nothing anymore to press. You could never pin down that self-willed man. When he was ready to make his move, he made it – always on his own terms. And always, always, something up his sleeve. That was how he was.'

* I had an audience with Saul in the same setting in 2003, where I read out a piece I'd written for the *Atlantic*. Its argument was that Saul was the greatest American novelist. 'What should he fear?' I quoted. 'The melodramatic formularies of Hawthorne? The multitudinous facetiousness of Melville? The murkily iterative menace of Faulkner? No. The only American who gives Bellow any serious trouble is Henry James.' Up to this point I still wasn't sure Saul was listening (rather than sleeping). But now his head jolted on the pillow and he said, 'Jesus Christ!'

477

*

Saul's last day on earth.

I heard about it from each of the three witnesses, Rosamund, Maria (the sweet-looking but incredibly strong Latina maid, who used to gird her spine, reach out her arms, and *carry* the forward-facing Bellow to the top of the stairs), and also from the devoted and indispensable factotum, Will Lautzenheiser.

That morning Saul woke up believing he was in transit – on a ship, perhaps? 'He didn't really know who I was,' said Will. Saul wanted nothing to eat or drink (he was perhaps observing the traditional fast of the moribund – abstinence, with a garnish of penitence). Then he went back to sleep, or rejoined the light coma which, in his final weeks, patiently shadowed him. Time passed. His breathing became slow and effortful. Rosamund had an hour alone with him, and when the others came back into the room she was stroking his head, and she was talking to him, saying, 'It's okay, my baby, it's okay.' Saul opened his eyes and gazed at her in awe, a gaze from the heart, an ardent gaze; and then he died.

. . . When the last day began Saul thought he was at sea on a transatlantic voyage. That was a venture, that was a crossing, of about the right size – the mighty waters, the great deeps, the unknowable doldrums and *tormentas*.

Spring now reverted to fall, but Uruguay had largely regained its confidence and colour. Jorge Luis Borges, in Buenos Aires, used to imagine Uruguay as an Elysian Field where hard-pressed Argentinians, on expiration, were transformed into angels; they could then unobtrusively hobnob with the angels that were already in residence . . . Still, to my eyes, something was missing, something wasn't there.

In the mid-period novella *Him With His Foot in His Mouth* Bellow's elderly (and unnamed) narrator is languishing in British Columbia as he awaits extradition to Chicago – the fallguy for financial crimes committed by his family. Meanwhile there is no one to talk to except the landlady, Mrs Gracewell, a widowed mystic who likes to expatiate on Divinity:

The Divine Spirit, she tells me, has withdrawn in our time from the outer, visible world. You can see what it once wrought, you are surrounded by its created forms. But although natural processes continue, Divinity has absented itself. The wrought work is brightly divine but Divinity is not now active within it. The world's grandeur is fading. And this is our human setting . . .

Well, that was how the world looked to me, when I was reinstalled in José Ignacio. The world was merely itself, for now, and had to get along without Saul Bellow – who had worked so fervently 'to bring back the light that has gone from these molded likenesses'.

The Essayist
December 2011

In 'that sullen hall' which Owen calls 'Hell', the dead soldier from England listens as his 'strange friend' – the dead soldier from Germany – explores certain memories and regrets ('For by my glee might many men have laughed, / And of my weeping something had been left, / Which must die now'), and speaks of war and 'the pity of war'. Finally 'that other' gently confronts the poet with a grievous revelation:

> 'I am the enemy you killed, my friend.
> I knew you in this dark: for so you frowned
> Yesterday through me as you jabbed and killed.
> I parried, but my hands were loath and cold.
> Let us sleep now . . .'*

Sleep – death's brother . . . Wilfred Owen was killed in action soon after dawn on November 4. He was twenty-five, like Keats, and already, like Keats, a poet of Shakespearean pith. His mother Susan – who was Wilfred's one essential intimate – received the telegram while all the bells of Salisbury were wagging and tumbling in celebration of Armistice Day – November 11, 1918.

———————

At noon on December 15, 2011, as I walked out into the enclosed forecourt of Bush Intercontinental (its low roof dripping with the tepid

---

* 'I am the enemy you killed, my friend' has strong claims to being the greatest line of war poetry ever written. And incidentally it could have been 'I am the enemy you killed, my love'. See 'Shadwell Stair', which opens, 'I am the ghost of Shadwell Stair', and closes, 'I walk till the stars of London wane / And dawn creeps up the Shadwell Stair. / But when the crowing sirens blare / I with another ghost am lain.'

sweat of cars), Michael Z was as usual waiting for me. He had a book spread flat against the steering wheel, and he started like a guilty thing when I tapped lightly on the glass.

I got aboard and as usual we embraced. Then he straightened up.

'. . . This is a dreadful thing to have to tell you, Martin,' he said. 'But basically it's all over.'

Come here about me, you my Myrmidons . . . I had a sensation of nakedness, including a sensation of cold. That lasted for three or four seconds. Then I managed to lose myself in a finical linguistic question prompted by Salman's email a day or two ago, addressed to Elena, in which he asked her, 'Is it true that Christopher has died?' Not 'is dead', I noticed, but the slightly softer 'has died'. Slightly softer? Actually very much softer; there seems to be an inherent metrical stress on the word *dead*, imparting something decisive: not a process but a fact . . . Elena wrote back, saying it wasn't true, he hadn't died. But that was a day or two ago.

The car moved through the Houston suburbs (Christopher, now, was sleeping, deeply, and wasn't expected to reawake) and as we drove the slowly melting igloo I'd been living in – the one with its name, Hope (or Denial), on a little plaque just above the entry tube – turned to slush. *Come here about me* was a summons: to my myrmidons, my praetorian guard of hormones and chemicals. That was my strategy, it turned out – blind negation, followed by clinical shock.

'I was up there this morning,' said Michael. Now we were in the different forecourt, under the shadow of the high-rise. 'So I won't . . . I think I'll just go home.'

After a moment I said, 'Yes, go home and be with Nina. How is Nina?'

'The truth is we're both very numb.'

Numb was something I understood. It seemed I was almost legless with internal sedatives and painkillers, but I was awake, I was above all alive, and I got out of the car and I walked into MD Anderson.

Christopher was lying on his back with his head at an angle, his face averted, his eyes closed. I went straight to him and kissed his cheek and said in his ear, 'Hitch, it's Mart, and I'm at your side.' His lashes, his eyelids, didn't flicker . . . When after a minute I turned, I saw that there were seven others in the room. I registered them one by one: Blue, Blue's father Edwin, Blue's cousin Keith, Blue's daughter Antonia, Christopher's other children, Alexander and Sophia, and Blue's very old friend Steve Wasserman. No doctors, no nurses: help from that quarter was at an end. The death-adoring flies, too, had sizzled off elsewhere; their work done, they had moved on elsewhere, they had moved on to another bed in another room.

And so had Christopher – because this wasn't the familiar wardlet on the eighth floor. His possessions were there, half stowed or half packed, but this wasn't the billet of an active being, no books or papers, no keyboard on the meal tray, no work in progress. A halfway house, a waiting room.

I quite soon realised what it was we were there to do. So I went round quietly greeting everyone, took a chair, folded my arms, and joined the death watch.

How young and handsome he was. How calmingly young and handsome. He looked like a thinker, a hard thinker, taking a brief rest, his neck bent back – to ease the strain of prolonged and testing meditations . . . Now reason slept, now the sleep of reason; he looked like Keats on his white bedding in Rome; he looked twenty-five.

From what Michael Z had said (and what Blue had let slip), I was beginning to understand. The disease that Christopher's death would cure was not the emperor of all maladies, cancer; it was instead 'the old man's friend' – that old tramp, pneumonia. Yes, yet another hospital infection (his fourth, his fifth?), and for this particular bout he had waived all remedy.

Entirely typically, it had always been Christopher's intention 'to "do" death in the active and not the passive sense, and to be there and look it in the eye' ('wishing to be spared nothing that properly belongs to a life span'). Had it worked? Had he, in some sense, already done the dying?

Well, he was insensible now, he was oblivious now. Which, I supposed, was a necessary condition for any death watch. How could it be effected otherwise? You could watch death come, but you couldn't watch your own death watch. Not even Christopher would contemplate something so terrible . . .

Indeed, his eyes were closed and his face averted, as if to make doubly sure he wouldn't see us all gathered there – all those faces that would soon conclusively disappear.

*

*'[H]e gradually sank into death,' wrote Joseph Severn, the portraitist,
'so quiet, that I still thought he slept.'*

There he lay . . .

Two hours had churned by, and we sat in place like art students in class, sizing up a model.

. . . Not long before I was born my teenage mother used to 'sit' at the Ruskin in Oxford. She told me that she passed the hours by 'pretending to be dead' – not that she felt at all embarrassed or uncomfortable (she regularly posed nude); no, she relayed the information just to equip me with a trick, or a spell, to make time go fast.

There were muted comments and whispered asides – but nothing that resembled conversation; every now and then one or other of us stealthily and briefly slipped away, to go to the bathroom, to make a phone call, to stretch the legs, to taste some variation in the air . . .

Around seven I had a smoke with Blue, out in the dusty shrubbery. She struck me as someone quite different from the woman I knew, decidedly reserved or even bashful, but neutrally and unaffectedly so, as if that was her real nature, and all the forthright liveliness I was used to merely belonged to an absent twin.

Days earlier, she told me, Christopher was as usual being prodded and tested and shifted and hoisted, and he said (in a very forceful tone), 'That's enough. No more treatment now. Now I want to die.' He had run out of dry land, and recognised that the time had properly come to make the crossing. These weren't his last words, not in any formal sense; his last words were a day or two away . . .

In Houston, even in the winter months, the diurnal temperature seldom drops below sixty-five. Before us, before Blue and me, stretched a fine December evening, and one that looked set to last till midnight . . . We hurried back up and took our places, as in a gallery or a playhouse, to gaze at a portrait or a motionless mime.

Blue had spoken about Christopher's coming end dispassionately, almost dismissively. She was getting through it by pretending to be cold.

There was another presence at the death watch, inorganic and at first unregarded, but by now wholly dominant – the point at which all our stares converged.

It was the tall contraption glowering over the far right-hand corner of the bed, and it looked like the innards of an elderly robot, a Bakelite and metal organ tree (stickled together, it seemed, at Crazy Eddie's discount store): lit-up computer screens, mobile phones, clock radios, pocket calculators, walkie-talkies – each of them heaped one on top of the other, and then studiously titivated, here at MDA, with sacs and vials of nutrients and medicaments. Blood-red, sharp-shouldered digits flashed out their readings.

At eight the blood pressure said 120/80. At nine it said 105/65. It kept on going down.

. . . Nineteen months ago, when all this began, I used to think, with fearful anticipation, of Auden's Icarus: 'the splash, the forsaken cry . . .

Something amazing, a boy falling out of the sky'. But now the moment had come I thought of Eliot's Christ-figure (in 'Preludes'): 'I am moved by fancies that are curled / Around these images, and cling: / The notion of some infinitely gentle / Infinitely suffering thing.'

The chest continued to rise and fall, but shallowly now.

The breathing weakened smoothly – visibly but not audibly. No wheezing, no gasping and gulping, no choking: no struggle, no tremor – nothing sudden.

The continuously undulating line at the base of the heart monitor, like a childish representation of a wavy sea, now stretched itself out into a dead calm.

The widow, after a silence, briskly began to assemble her things, and she rose to her feet, saying,

'Come on. There's nothing there now. That,' she whispered to me, meaning the body, 'there's nothing in it any more. It's just – rubbish.' As we headed into the corridor she turned and saw something among his belongings that for just a moment made her stride falter. With a sharp intake of breath she gasped out,

'His . . . *shoes!*'

Mortality, which appeared in early 2012, lies on my desk in Brooklyn, here in 2018, and I can say with certainty that it is a valiant and noble addition to the literature of dying.

Christopher's last words were formulaic (though also in my view characterologically superb). But why are Last Words in general so predominantly second-rate? And I mean the last words of our greatest poets, thinkers, scientists, leaders, visionaries, our supermen and our wonderwomen: why can't the *ne plus ultra* of articulate humanity, faced with this defining moment, do a little better?

Henry James (1843–1916) came up with 'So it has come at last, the distinguished thing.' This is rhetorically very splendid – last words in the high style. He claimed that his valedictory flourish was spontaneous (his 'first thought' as his leg gave way and he embarked on a fall). But the high style, by definition, is never spontaneous – and what's 'distinguished' about falling over? I'd say that James had been working on his last words since about 1870.

The best last words known to me belong to Jane Austen (b. 1775) who was dying (of lymphoma) in unalleviable pain at the age of forty one. Asked what she needed, she said, 'Nothing but death.' This sounds impulsive, unbidden, perhaps even serendipitious; it also sounds both weary and resolute, both impatient and stoical. Not content with that Austen's crystallised poeticism – even the 'but' plays its part – dramatises a fell reality, because 'nothing' and 'death', here and elsewhere, are synonyms. 'Nothing but nothing' was her meaning.

Otherwise, last words are dross, like the defunct human body. And the words that precede death could hardly be as feeble as they are unless something about death rendered them so. Being impenetrable, death defeats the expressive powers, and our best and our brightest can do nothing with it. Well, *ne plus ultra* – 'the most perfect or most extreme example' – derives from the mythological KEEP OUT sign inscribed on the Pillars of Hercules: 'not further beyond'.

We got back from MDA round about midnight and sat untalkatively in the kitchen and on the patio of the guest house (untalkatively joined by Michael Z). Although my mental state was obscure to me, my body after its saturnalia of chemicals (now reinforced by Chardonnay), felt familiar: the comedown would soon be followed by the hangover, and a hangover of the spiritual category, strongly featuring remorse and regret. Christopher wrote that *regret* was for things you did and *remorse* was for things you didn't do – sins of commission as against sins of omission . . . Everyone stayed up, trying to de-coagulate. And around noon the next day most of us went in groups to the airport, and defeatedly boarded flights to San Francisco, Washington DC, New York, and perhaps other cities.

. . . Christopher's last words, unlike James's (and unlike Larkin's), were unrehearsed. Also inadvertent, because he lost consciousness in mid-thought: his last words – there were only two of them – were simply the words he said last. They were rhetorically primitive, barely more than a slogan or a chant. Yet anyone who knew him is sure to find them full of meaning and affective force. It was Alexander who described the scene to me, over a paper cupful of coffee a few hours before the death; and we both smiled and closed our eyes and nodded.

Yesterday Christopher was lying there alive but unstirring, with his mind in that region between deep sleep and light coma, and he softly articulated something. Alexander (and Steve Wasserman, also in attendance) drew closer and urged him to repeat it. He did so: 'Capitalism.' When Alexander asked him if he had anything to add, he said faintly, '. . . Downfall.' That was the Hitch, comprehensively unconverted – except when it came to socialism, and utopia, and the earthly paradise. Crossing the floor to death: and yet he never changed.

'Alexander, your father's *not* dying at sixty-two. He's about seventy-five, I'd say – because he never, ever went to sleep.' We sat there with our paper cups. 'Christ, it's so radical of him to die,' I said. 'It's so *left wing* of him to die.'

. . . There it lurks before me, under the angle lamp, *Mortality* – droll, steadfast, and desperately and startlingly *short*. Usually I pick it up and put it down with the greatest care, to avoid seeing the photo that fills the back cover; but sometimes, as now, I make myself flip it over and I stare. We never talked about death, he and I, we never talked about the probably imminent death of the Hitch. But one glance at this portrait convinces me that *he* exhaustively discussed it – with himself. Those are the eyes of a man in hourly communion with the distinguished thing; they hold a great concentration of grief and waste, but they are clear, the pupils blue, the whites white. Christopher, long before the fact, mounted his own death watch. *Prepared for the Worst* was the title of his earliest collection of essays (1988), and it was his lifelong stance and slogan. He felt the compulsion to go looking for the most difficult position, and here he is, in the most difficult position of all – the most difficult position for him, and for everyone else on earth.

On the day D. H. Lawrence stopped living (at the age of forty-four) he said three interesting things. His antepenultimate sentence was 'Don't cry' (addressed to Frieda); his penultimate sentence was 'Look at *him* in the bed there!'; his ultimate sentence was 'I feel better now' (the last words of many a waning murmurer). Lawrence got the order wrong: he should've signed off with *Don't cry* . . .

Don't cry. They weren't Christopher's last words – but they were his legacy, and in the strangest way. He himself was very open to emotion, he was quickly and strongly moved by poetry (literary and political), and he was unalarmed by the sentimental and even the spiritual; but he wouldn't have anything whatever to do with the supernatural. And so I now say to his ghost,

'After you died, Hitch, something very surprising happened . . . It wasn't supernatural, obviously. Nothing ever is. It only *felt* supernatural.'

'How supernatural?'

'Mildly supernatural. Only a bit supernatural.'

'And are you suggesting that I brought this about from beyond the grave? Or from beyond the incinerator, because as you know my grave is in the sky.'

'True – the mass grave of so many of your blood brothers and your blood sisters. No I'm not saying that. It was all your own work – but the work was done when you were alive.'

'Explain.'

'I will explain, and I'll try to make you understand.'

Postludial

Christopher once wrote of 'the light, continuous English rain' that was part of his 'birthright'. I know that rain, I know that island rain, which hardly has the weight to fall and comes on tiptoe, as if trying to pose as the silent element; and it is not the silent element.

Snow is the silent element. It is also the informative element: silently snow tells you, at great length and with great precision, how old you are, how old in body, how old in mind. And how does snow communicate this?

When I was a boy in winter I used to go to sleep tearfully praying for snow, tearfully imploring the heavens to send me snow. And I can still taste the deliciously mentholated pang in my throat whenever I jerked up from sleep, two-handedly wrenched open the curtains on the side of my bed – and saw a world of white . . . Snow loves the young (giving them snowballs and snowmen together with many other treats); and the young love it back.

But in recent years a world of white does no more than replenish my loathing and dread. After a night of snowfall, when snow has heavily but silently settled, I winch up the blinds in the morning and face an antagonist who I half-hoped had forgotten me . . . Snow hates the old.

There are gradations, true. To this day, reluctantly and with thorough ill grace, I still have to hand it to snow. I don't want to go out into it (I want to stay indoors with a rug on my lap), and I don't want it to tell me how old I am; but I do still want to marvel at it, while it's white and new. The silent element, snow falls silently, and has the other-worldly power to silence a city . . .

But all that's over for another year, thank God; and then came spring, and here is summer.

Hello again, thank you for coming, and welcome back . . . All right, not *back* exactly. After a year as wandering freeloaders, as passengers, we're customers again, and this is our new place, up on the twentieth floor (my sons call it the *skypad*). And yes thanks, you find me in fairly resilient spirits – for three reasons.

First, my Green Card finally came through, after however many years it's been. So no more staggering from office to office at the hateful Department of Homeland Security. Tax cuts for the rich don't trickle down, but moral squalor in high places is the Steamboat Geyser; and the atmosphere in and around the Immigration Court is now one of smug and insolent contempt. On your way into Federal Plaza you can witness teenage doormen jeering at bewildered Hispanic couples because they *can't even speak* English . . .

Second, Trump is in trouble as the mid-term elections loom. Of course, he's always in trouble, and always will be, for this simple reason: he honestly can't tell the difference between right and wrong . . . No, even if he finagles his way to a second term, we have no plans to move to Canada. Trump's not a reason to leave; he's a reason to stay. Later tonight I'm joining my immediate family and about two dozen of our American cousins. And that's what Americans are – my cousins.

Three, the last page of *Inside Story* is now visible to the naked eye. Finishing a novel is usually the cause of grim satisfaction with a trace of tristesse. But just now the emotions feel rather differently configured . . .

Anyway, I suppose, my friend, that this will be goodbye. We've been through a lot together, and you've shown incredible patience and constancy. So let's mark the occasion by taking an ice bucket and a bottle of wine out on to the roof, where we can watch the sunset.

. . . Have we got everything? This staircase has no handrail, not yet, and I've learnt that approximately 100 per cent of elderly disasters happen on stairs. And even you should be careful, carrying all that. Just two short half-flights and we'll be there.

You know, in Uruguay, very near our house, there was a nightclub on a sloping lawn and all these young people used to gather at dusk to see the show. And when the sun at last disappeared over the far brim of the South Atlantic they would *applaud*, every night, with sincerity and gratitude. Very Uruguayan, that, and very sweet we always thought. And vaguely ancient as well as vaguely postmodern. Hang on. Mind the . . .

New York Harbor.

With Liberty Island in the middle of it. Behold . . . Lady Liberty often makes me think of Phoebe Phelps – physically, at seventy-five, enormous and weighty, and seemingly without an ounce of superfluous tissue, *hard* to the touch, like a rubber dinghy stiffly – maximally – inflated. But what's the opposite of liberty? Subjection. Encumbrance. Thraldom. Lifelong *liability* (from French *lier*, 'to bind'). Well then – Lady Liability . . .

Whenever I look out there at the whole field of view I find I've got myself trapped in a metaphor, because I keep imagining it as a kind of urban Serengeti. Look at all the cranes, the near ones and the ones over there, in New Jersey, look at the exact angle of their necks, and don't you think for a moment that they're herds of mechanical giraffes? And those various beasts in and around the water, the hippos of the storage tugs, the great stretching crocs of the barges, the Jurassic diehards of the . . . Et cetera, et cetera, with further correspondences rather too readily suggesting themselves. It's known as an 'epic simile'. But let's cast off its shackles . . .

See that plane approaching so low over the water – at helicopter height. It's a widebody, what the industry calls a *heavy*. Now to my sensorium it is homing in – with every sign of vicious determination – on Freedom Tower, there, One World Trade Center, the tallest structure in your sight . . . This trick of the eye is a 'parallax illusion', having to do with perceptions of depth. All will right itself the moment the plane passes safely beyond its target. As it does – now . . . A trick of the eye, and the reflex of a mind conditioned by 2001 – when you were a child. I really should be able to tell the difference, because the planes of September 11 were going about three times faster than that sedate and blameless 767 . . .

Our whole section of downtown Brooklyn is a martyr to the US system of criminal justice. Courthouses and lockups and parole-board fora, and all the go-betweens – bailbondsmen, shyster lawyers, bent attorneys – who work the interface between freedom and its opposite. As well as busloads of police, who then fan out on motorbikes and in squadcars, and they've even got one of those pathetic two-seaters, with NYPD emblazoned on it . . .

See that fortified rooftop right in front of us? I tell you, that there's the exercise yard of Brooklyn Detention Complex on Atlantic Avenue . . . It's an encaged basketball court, and through the mesh you glimpse these lithe figures bobbing around within. Not much to see but plenty to hear. There was a ringing *Fuck you* followed by the usual six-letter salutation, but it was black-on-black – and friendly, even admiring, in tone, as if in recognition of some successful stunt or feint beneath the hoop . . .

They're all black. The queues outside the seats of trial and correction, they're all black. Last year Elena toured a high-security prison upstate – they're all black. And we spent half a day together on the vast holding pen of Rikers Island – and they're all black. It feels like a dogged answer to the African-American 'question'. In about 1985 someone suddenly said, I know – let's just lock them all up . . . No, really. Have a look at Michelle Alexander's *The New Jim Crow*.

See that massive orange brick powering through the water? It could be a prison hulk on its way to Alcatraz, couldn't it, but it's only the Staten Island ferry, full of commuters and a few daytrippers in funny hats. I love that ferry now. So ingenuously, so loyally ploughing its furrow . . .

Yes, it was strange, it was passing strange with the Hitch. I don't live in fear of being thought sentimental, as you know, but even I find it a shade embarrassing. Anyway, let's save that for last.

. . . Look at Lady Liberty there, holding her golden torch aloft. She's actually staring right at us, though we can't clearly see that face of hers, with the Roman nose and the sneer of cold command – a conqueror's face. And genderless too. It was always thought that the sculptor, Bartholdi, modelled her on his mother, but a recent view has it that he modelled her on his *brother* . . .

I went there, I went inside her, back in 1958, when I was nine. In her left hand she holds a tablet with a date in Roman numerals – July 4, 1776. At her feet lies a broken chain . . .

Far, far and away the most hateful thing about DJT is his – well, let me put it this way.

Picture in your mind the four black college students who in mid-afternoon ordered four cups of coffee at the wrong Woolworth's lunch counter (Whites Only) on Monday, February 1, 1960, in Greensboro, North Carolina; they were denied service and directed to the Colored Section, heckled by incredulous locals. But they stayed in their seats, reading, until the store closed. This taut ritual was re-enacted the next day, and the next, and the next, in ever-strengthening numbers on both sides. By the end of the week, over 1,000 black protestors were faced by an equal number of whites . . .

Picture in your mind Ruby Bridges, who in the same year walked to school accompanied by four federal marshals, in New Orleans, a slender six-year-old in white bobby socks, clutching a satchel and a yellow ruler; she crossed the cordon of hollering, gesticulating citizens with her head unbowed and with firm steps entered William Frantz Elementary. All the other children had been spirited away by their parents, and all the teachers had left their posts and were on strike, all except one . . .

As we know and have always known, there is in this country a vast and inveterate minority (about 35 per cent) whose sympathies lie not with the silently studious protestors, in Greensboro, but with the rejectionists yelling in their ears and pouring sodas on their heads and then beating them to the ground; not with six-year-old Ruby Bridges, in New Orleans, but with the hate-warped face of the housewife in the picket line brandishing a black doll in a toy coffin.

. . . Is Trump a genuine white supremacist – or did he surmise, early on, that white supremacism was his only path to power? Is he an entirely unreflecting barbarian or is he an unusually scurvy opportunist? He is surely both. In any case, he thought it worth doing: to take the great American stain/taint/wound/block/blight/shame/crime – hate crime – and give it another season in the sun.

On clear mornings she looks at her very best, she looks as she's supposed to look, an iconic beacon lighting the way to a glorious idea. When the clouds are low and the mist thickens, she looks like the remaining stub of a civilisation that has come and gone: two vast and trunkless legs of stone, in the soiled remnants of a robe.

. . . Fog, the other silent element, joining everything to everything else in a night of grey. Though it can't silence a city, fog can subdue it, fog can talk it down and make it tamer – but mere rain, mere darkness is capable of that . . .

Look! I've never seen this before. Out in the estuary, yes, but not so close, not in the stretch before Governors and Liberty. The Staten Island ferries are about to *cross*.

One incoming, one outgoing. It's like an eclipse. Two become one, just for a moment – and then become two again.

———————————

Yes, now you ask, I do think about death, almost constantly in the sense that it's always in my thoughts, like an unwanted song. That's why I take it very kindly that you're so young. Because you'll be reading me every now and then at least until about 2080, weather permitting. And when you go maybe my afterlife, too, will come to an end, my afterlife of words.

And I'll join the unknown German soldier in 1918. *For by my glee might many men have laughed / And of my weeping something had been left, / Which must die now.* That'll be the third death: first my urge, then my life, then my written words.

Fair's fair, and a promise is a promise. And we'll come to the bequest of the Hitch very soon. But first . . .

We've talked about immortality. Have you heard about the 'transhumanist' movement? It's for people who not only wouldn't mind being mechanical (like that herd of giraffes over there), with carbon-fibre 'blades' instead of legs and so on; they also wouldn't mind being electronic, equipped for instance with *bat* radar . . . How many of these questing Prometheans, I wonder, are on the minimum wage. No, unlike literature, transhumanism isn't open to everybody . . .

I mean, who cares, but transhumanism sounds to me like an offshoot of cryonics – the live-forever scam. Had not the presidency intervened, Trump Immortality might well've been Donald J.'s next business move, after Trump Faith School and Trump Meatloaf . . . Obedient to cryonic guidance, you get your corpse bedded down in a vatlike icebox, and then you wait. Online I saw one of the ads: the photo of a man who looked like – who looked like a coiffed American sumo wrestler, in a tweed jacket and a huge equilateral tie knot, grinning in front of his fridge – empty, I'll bet, except for a yoghurt and a couple of beers.

Under this individual's care, your remains will look forward to a far-future society that for some reason will feel the need to defrost and revive a squad of self-infatuated and fatally diseased old dupes – ailing hoarders who did whatever they could to linger on in the counting house . . .

The dead-body freeze costs about $200,000, but it's just 80,000 if you opt for 'the neuro' – the head-only package.

As on the question of the earthly utopia, so with eternal life: literature is unanimous in regarding human perfection or indefinite perpetuation as essentially horrific. Try this instead.

'The woods decay, the woods decay and fall, / The vapours weep their burden to the ground, / Man comes and tills the field and lies beneath, / And after many a summer dies the swan.' Tennyson, 'Tithonus'. I've noticed again and again that it is poetry, and poetry alone, that can face death on anything like equal terms.

Prose is too fast-moving. To face death it has to be slowed down to almost a processional pace. Jorge Luis Borges (who wrote a terrifying story called 'The Immortal') elsewhere surmised that 'Time is the substance I am made of. Time is a river which sweeps me away, but I am the river; it is a tiger which destroys me, but I am the tiger; it is a fire which consumes me, but I am the fire.' Suggesting that death is not an intruder but a resident; the river, the tiger, the fire – they're already there.

It is right, it is fitting, it is as it should be, that we die. 'Death is the dark backing a mirror needs before we can see anything,' wrote Saul Bellow. And without death there is no art, because without death there is no interest, or to be more precise there is no *fascination* (a fine word, that, and as Nabokov said of a different sort of fine word, 'a welcome guest to my prose'). *Fascination* means, one, the tendency to engross irresistibly, and, two (semi-archaically), the ambition 'to deprive (prey) of the ability to resist or escape the power of a gaze' . . .

Why is dying so hard, physically? That's what I want to know. Oh, the toil, the slave labour of dying. Oh, the great sweat of death . . .

Time is the enemy of the writer as an individual, in that the longevity of talent hasn't kept pace with other advances; but immortality, like utopia, is the enemy of writing *tout à fait* – root, bole, branch, and twig. Writers used to die young, remember (in common with absolutely everyone else) . . . Christopher had already outlasted Shakespeare, the Immortal, by a whole decade when I joined his death watch in Houston on December 15, 2011. My best friend was sixty-two. That is not right, that is not fitting, that is not as it should be.

On December 16 I flew back from Houston to New York. Funnily and mistakenly enough, the weather was fresh and bright. But I was undeceived by the blue skies, or so I thought. This is a disaster, I kept telling myself again and again. This is clearly an absolute disaster . . .

I woke up the next morning in a state of puzzled self-exploration. Then I lived another day, December 17, at home with my family. And then another day, walking out once or twice in my neighbourhood and enjoying the customary interactions in the shops and outlets of Cobble Hill; and the morning after that I woke up changed. The feeling didn't merely loiter – it had established itself. But I couldn't trust it; I felt I just couldn't trust it.

Then Blue, in one of our written exchanges, revealed that *she* had it too! Now, I'd lost a beloved friend; but Blue had lost a beloved spouse . . . When we met up for dinner in Manhattan we had a gripped and gripping exchange – like patients comparing symptoms, or more like a pair of hikers sharing notes about the same journey. We had both experienced it: an infusion, an invasion of overpowering happiness. Happiness: the delight of sentience. I asked her,

'He wouldn't be hurt, would he? Hurt that we're not lying around ruined for ever?'

'No! He'd be thrilled.'

'. . . That's true. Of course he would. He'd be thrilled.'

All right, this is what seemed to have taken place. The love of life of the Hitch – the existential *amour fou* of the Hitch, the 'uncontrollable or obsessive passion' – had in part transferred itself to us. And henceforth, we agreed, it would be our solemn duty to maintain it and to honour it.

After seven and a half years the happiness is still there, weakened or let's say qualified by the narrowing stretch of time before I *join him* – as they used to put it. The happiness is also, I have to confide, slightly but persistently wrinkled by guilt. What am I guilty of, apart from surviving and living longer? It comes from a structural peculiarity of the death watch.

In an early poem, 'Wants', Larkin spoke of 'the costly aversion of the eyes away from death'. But the fixed stare is also costly – prohibitive. Halfway through an eight-hour death watch, you stop wanting them to wake up, and start wanting them to sleep for ever: in other words, you wish them gone. The death watch forces this treason on you – you just can't get out of the way of it . . .

I watched my little sister die, in the year 2000; and in her case I didn't have time to wish her gone. Myfanwy was dead within half an hour and I never even knew it. Because she was still breathing, lustily breathing, until the nurse came back in and compassionately pointed to the flat line. Seeing my astonishment, she pointed to the respirator, the machine that was doing Myfanwy's breathing . . . So there was my sister, a panting corpse at the age of forty-six. Surely, surely, I could've done something about that. Couldn't I?

Anyway, down with the death watch, to hell with the death watch, death to the death watch.

Bracingly but also demandingly, it turns out that there is a moral order, and that we are moral beings. Our big transgressions of course stay with us, but so do all the little ones. Each of our sins of commission and omission, every instance of cruelty and neglect, every snub – every slight: every brick we've ever dropped lands on our own foot, in the end, and goes on smarting till we die.

Now there is the sun, and we can stare at it . . . Jesus, it looks like a real *star*, don't you think? Not the twinkle-twinkle type but a star as it actually is – a steady-state fusion bomb of boiling gas, with in this case a diameter of a million earthling miles. I have the greatest respect for the prince of our solar system, but I've never seen it look more like a furious cosmic zit getting ready to burst. And to the eye it's almost as smooth as glass . . . There it goes, there it goes. And now it's gone.

A final piece of vocational advice.

Temperament (as I've said) is vital. You need an unusual appetite for solitude, and a strong and durable commitment to the creative form (you have to want to be in it for life). These are qualities that the dedicated reader already has. You will also need this strange affinity with the reader – unendingly complex though almost entirely unconscious. Then there is a fourth element . . .

One night in my twentieth year Kingsley Amis and Elizabeth Jane Howard and I watched a TV play about a poet. Not a historical poet. It didn't begin, 'John Clare grew up in a rural setting', and then give you a shot of a sheep saying *baa*. No, the poet was contemporary, and it seemed uncomplainingly minor, getting on in years now, and pottering about in and around his suburban semi-detached. The play was called *He Used to Notice Such Things*, and it was narrated by the poet's wife.

'Cuthbert would take an orange from the fruit bowl and weigh it in his hands and examine the tiny stipples on its surface with a smile of childish wonder.' That kind of thing. Old Cuthbert was the same in the street, like a medieval village idiot airdropped into a metropolis – utterly confounded by the sight of a bus, a letterbox, a telegraph pole . . . Jane was quietly sceptical, but Kingsley and I writhed and swore and sneered our way through the whole ninety minutes.

For a long time now I've been wanting to get hold of Kingsley's spirit and say, *Dad, I'm sorry about this, but do you remember the TV play about that fucking old fool of a poet? Cuthbert? He Used to Notice Such Things? Well listen. It was trite and corny and thoroughly and comprehensively ballsaching – but it wasn't wrong. Not wrong. To be a poet, to be a writer, you have to be continuously surprised. You have to have something of the fucking old fool in you.*

Borges, in his long conversation with the *Paris Review*, at one point spoke with bafflement about all the people who simply fail to notice the mystery and glamour of the observable world. In a sentence that stands out for its homeliness, he said, 'They take it all for granted.' They accept the *face value* of things . . .

Writers take nothing for granted. See the world with 'your original eyes', 'your first heart', but don't *play* the child, don't *play* the innocent – don't examine an orange like a caveman toying with an iPhone. You know more than that, you know better than that. The world you see out there is *ulterior*: it is other than what is obvious or admitted.

So never take a single speck of it for granted. Don't trust anything, don't even dare to get used to anything. Be continuously surprised. Those who accept the face value of things are the true innocents, endearingly and in a way enviably rational: far too rational to attempt a novel or a poem. They are unsuspecting – yes, that's it. They are the unsuspecting.

*

As a counterpoise this too remember. You are a stranger in a strange land – but you come to it with a . . .

All right. Nabokov's first novel, *Mary*, was written in a Berlin boarding house, when both the author and the century were about twenty-five. His situation was as follows: having fled the Bolsheviks, he and his Jewish bride now awaited the Nazis (the NSDAP was formed in 1920); his father had been shot dead by a (Russian) fascist in 1922; his mother and his sisters were penniless in Prague. Vladimir was deracinated, declassed, and destitute. And yet *Mary* bears not the slightest trace of melancholy, let alone alienation or *nausée*. Indeed, the only angst Nabokov ever suffered from had to do with 'the impossibility of assimilating, swallowing, all the beauty in the world'. And his first novel ends with his promise to meet that world with 'a fresh, loving eye'. That's your situation. You are a stranger in a strange land; but you come to it with a fresh and loving eye.

Saul Bellow was a phenomenon of love; he loved the world in such a way that his readers reciprocated and loved him in return. The same goes for Philip Larkin, but more lopsidedly; the world loved him and he loved the world in his way (he certainly didn't want to leave it), but so far as I can tell he didn't love a single one of its inhabitants (except, conceivably, my wholly unfrightening mother: 'without being in the least pretty', she was, he wrote in his last letter, 'the most beautiful woman I have ever seen'). Anyway, the love transaction has always operated, to various degrees, with each and every repeatedly published novelist and poet. With essayists, the love transaction was more or less unknown until Christopher Hitchens came along – until he came along, and then went away again.

This is literature's dewy little secret. Its energy is the energy of love. All evocations of people, places, animals, objects, feelings, concepts, landscapes, seascapes, and cloudscapes: all such evocations are in spirit amorous and celebratory. Love gets put into the writing, and love gets taken out . . .

———————

Now I must get ready to go, I'm afraid. Come on, I'll see you to the door. Pick up that glass there, if you would, and follow me down.

. . . Did you bring anything, a coat, a bag, a hat? Now my parting words to you would normally be: *I'll see you – or some slightly different version of you – in due course, in 2021, say, or soon thereafter.* But next August I enter my seventieth year. There are a good few short stories I mean to get done (most of them about race in America), and I have in mind a third fiction about the Third Reich – a modest novella. You see, another full-length fiction, let alone another long fiction, now seems unlikely. Time will tell. Maybe towards the end I'll just shut up and read . . . In which case, oh, I'll miss it, I'll grieve for everything about it, even its pains, trifling and fleeting compared to its pleasures, but formidable in their way. With every work of fiction, with every voyage of discovery, you're at some point utterly becalmed (like Conrad on the *Otago*), and you drop overboard and sink through the fathoms until you reach the following dual certainty: that not only is the book you're writing no good, no good at all, but also that every line you've ever written is no good either, no good at all. Then, when you're deep down there, among the rocks and the shipwrecks and the blind and brainless bottomfeeders, you touch sand, and can start to gird yourself to kick back up again.

I'll miss that. And I'll miss you too, your warmth, your encouragement, your clemency. Here we are.

'Well, goodbye.'

Goodbye, my reader, I said. Goodbye, my dear, my close, my gentle.

Afterthought
Masada and the Dead Sea

I scaled Masada in 1986 and I scaled it again in 2010. For some reason (and no one has yet told me why), it was much more difficult the second time. It would seem that during the passage of that quarter-century certain processes were at work . . . Nevertheless, I hope to scale Masada a third time, one of these days. Perhaps (you never know) it will be even more difficult in, say, 2035.

. . . At this point I'd like to steal a fluent and assured three-liner from DJT. Asked on British radio about David Cameron calling his Muslim ban *divisive, stupid, and wrong*, Trump said, *Number one, I'm not stupid, okay? I can tell you that right now. Just the opposite.* Well I'm not stupid either, and I do know I'm getting older. But it seems that being in Israel can make it hard to face the obvious.

In 2010 I holidayed there with Elena and our daughters, Eliza and Inez, and we stayed in Tel Aviv-Yafo (Jaffa) with Michael C and his American wife, Erin, and *their* daughters, Noa, Maia, and Edie . . . At this stage Larkin had been dead for twenty-five years and Saul for five, and in fifteen months Christopher, too, would be dead.

Whereas Michael Z emerged from Iraq, Michael C (a prosperous executive based mainly in London) is a Sabra, that is to say a native-born Israeli: the word comes from modern Hebrew – it means 'cactus fruit'. And Michael C does have certain affinities with the prickly pear.

For instance, he is uninhibitedly sympathetic to most of the views of the secular hard right and is thus an all-out territorial maximalist. But there's drollery in it somewhere, I suspect. Whenever there's the slightest political reverse or retardation in his schema, Michael C just waves a hand and says brightly, 'Well – build more settlements!' Such a line goes down frictionlessly in Israel (where the left, everyone says, has shrunk to next to nothing), but naturally causes heated bewilderment in Britain. Michael C dutifully and wryly shoulders the ill fame.

I have known and liked Michael for many years, and have always been grateful for his generosity both as a host and as a correspondent (he is my man in Tel Aviv). But I still can't decide what I make of him and the positions he holds. Does the abrasive rind conceal something softer and sweeter? I felt closest to an answer when I carefully raised the subject of his mandatory three-year service in the Israel Defense Forces – 1980–83 (seeing him through from eighteen to twenty-one).

He talked about this period sombrely and again dutifully – the same spirit he brought to his national service, where he was mostly a kind of jailer. Michael's very blue blue eyes admitted to a degree of humiliation, the humiliation he imposed and the humiliation he himself suffered in being its instrument. Onerous, grievous, even injurious, to be sure; but it had to be done. A Jew in Israel has no business being sweet and soft.

One time at a dinner in Regent's Park Road, in the earliest days of the Arab Spring, Michael caused our friend Roger Cohen (of the *New York Times* and one of nature's true optimists) to say, with dignified indignation ('dignant' is how more than one novelist has described the familiar stiffening), 'I find that offensive.' What he found offensive was Michael's remark: 'I don't think the Egyptians are ready for democracy.' *Optimism* originally denoted a character trait (rather than a mood one might occasionally adopt); Roger is an *optimist* . . .

Another time, in the summer of 2014, Michael's eldest girl stormed out of a noisy kitchen-cabinet debate on the Palestinian question with the words, 'You're a fucking racist!' But there is a sheen of stoical irony in Michael C's habitual half smile. And he and I enthusiastically went on, that evening, to compare notes on Ari Shavit's *My Promised Land: The Triumph and Tragedy of Israel*, a book riven by patriotic pride in tandem with patriotic distress . . .

Michael is aware that Israel's situation is almost certainly finite in time. He suspects that global disfavour will assume more and more tangible forms; he suspects that America, as its influence retreats, will one day retreat from Israel (DJT's recent sheath of blank cheques notwithstanding); but he knows for a fact that the projectiles of Hamas (and Hezbollah) will continue to evolve in their accuracy and range.

'I'm waiting for a voice on the other side,' says Michael. A voice that seems desirous – or more frankly capable – of negotiation (the Arab administrators, he says, 'couldn't run a shop'). For now, the Palestinian Authority is moribund with corruption; and what can you do with the wild and childish rejectionism of the Zealots of Gaza ('Hamas', remember, means *zeal*)? Their very charter solemnly and gullibly cites *The Protocols of the Elders of Zion*,* and, in addition, lays claim to 'every inch' of historical Palestine, to be secured by means of jihad.

Christopher said, 'Mart, you try to be sympathetic to the Israelis, because they're surrounded by about two billion mortal enemies. A tribute to the evenhandedness of Little Keith . . . I know, I know, but their location is hardly ideal, is it. I often idly imagine how things might be if they'd settled somewhere else.'

'Yeah, me too. But where?'

'I keep thinking – what if the Allies had forced a spacious Jewish homeland on the razed Germany of the later 1940s? A deindustrialised and ruralised and, I stress, an exhaustively humbled Germany. Serve it fucking well right. So. What's wrong with Bavaria?'

This conversation took place on adjacent Greenwich Village barstools in the summer of 2010 (about three months after diagnosis). Christopher, tonight (all things considered), was at his ease. When you are ill in America you are also, and automatically, sick with worry about

---

* This 'document' was exposed as a fabrication almost a century ago, in 1921. It is curious that the word 'forgery' has attached itself to the Protocols (a word used pretty well invariably by even the most serious and well-intentioned historians). As Hitchens often pointed out, with deepening weariness, 'a forgery is at least a false copy of a true bill'. What were the Protocols a copy of? The adhesive epithet slanderously implies that there was once an original, whereas of course the whole fantasy was conjured out of nothing, in the early 1900s, by the Okhrana, the Tsarist secret police, to defame Russian Jews and so justify the coming pogroms . . . The Hamas charter. Though intransigently unrevised for thirty years, the Hamas Covenant (1988) is now considered to be something of a relic. But the updated version (2017) still demands the entire territory 'from the river to the sea' and still insists that the 'establishment of "Israel" is entirely illegal'. 'There shall be no recognition of the legitimacy of the Zionist entity' – that is, of its right to exist.

paying for it. Christopher was in New York to give an outlandishly well-paid speech; he would then have dinner with his wife and with me and my wife, sitting outside, at Graydon Carter's restaurant in Bank Street, before going on to a party at Anna Wintour's, where there would be many other friends and familiars . . . He was happy tonight, rediscovering how much he loved being in America, loved being with intimates, loved being the expositor and explicator, loved being himself, and loved being alive. He said,

'As you recline in the Bavarian homeland, what would be the worst that could happen? An occasional Molotov cocktail lobbed in by some leather-shorted, feather-hatted Xerxes from the BLO?'

'. . . But Germany. Germany might've gone nuts again.'

'It was invaded and occupied. It couldn't've gone nuts again. And it *fears* going nuts again. Germany fears itself. Could I have a Xerox of that,' he said to the barman, and pointed at his double Johnnie Black. 'I do see that the Bavaria solution, Zion in the Reich, was of course impossible for the Jews. It had to be the Holy Land.'

'I suppose so. And at least it's aesthetically right, don't you think? If the whole thing was just dramaturgy, you know, a heroic poem or an opera, the artist wouldn't even consider Bavaria. What about Bavaria? What about Madagascar? It had to be the Holy Land.'

'Mm. But the Holy Land makes them messianic.'

'The Six Day War made them incredibly messianic. But I'm told the Yom Kippur War gave them back the old fear.'

'For a while. We Jews did do our atonement in 1973. Then what did we get? Likud, in 1977. That's the durably significant date. Messianism is back and will never go away. They'll be needing divine intervention – because the Islamist rockets will soon become cruise missiles. And the Fertile Crescent isn't going to suddenly get over being anti-Semitic, now is it. Not in this millennium.'

'. . . What the hell *is* anti-Semitism?'

'Come on, Mart, you've read the books. The last time I saw you you finished *The Oldest Hatred* and picked up *The Longest Hatred* in the same afternoon.'

'But I still don't get it. You say it's a neurosis, Saul said it's a psychosis. Tony Judt – have you read him?' I didn't add that Tony Judt had died just a couple of weeks earlier, here in Manhattan, aged sixty-two. 'Judt was talking about anti-Semitism in Russia and Eastern Europe, and he said the causes need no analysis, because in that part of the world *anti-Semitism is its own reward.* Maybe that's what I can't grasp.'

'That anti-Semitism is enjoyable?'

'Yeah. Like self-righteousness. Look at people when they're being self-righteous, look at their eyes. They fucking love it. It's like cocaine. Anti-Semitism – *mmmm.*'

'Same with messianism. For them it's like a wonderful wank. As you'll see.'

'. . . And there's something in the air of the Holy Land – it makes you fragile against illusion.'

'When are you going?'

'Late September. Just a family holiday . . . Your eyelashes, Hitch. They remind me of Jett Travolta's. They're about an inch long.'

'I know. It's just some fool of a side effect from the chemo . . . Well, take your notebook with you. I'll want a full report.'

So we ate our dinner at the Waverly Inn, and went on to Anna's party, and then in a group of eight or nine we cruised around the spontaneous block parties in the strips and rinks of downtown. As Blue would write in her afterword to *Mortality* (2012), evoking June 8, the day of diagnosis,

> It was the sort of early summer evening in New York when all you can think of is living . . . Everything was as it should be, except that it wasn't. We were living in two worlds. The old one, which never seemed more beautiful, had not yet vanished; and the new one, about which we knew little except to fear it, had not yet arrived.

The new world lasted nineteen months.

I scaled Masada in 1986 and I scaled it again in 2010. The crest of this dramatic chunk of rock is only a couple of hundred feet above sea level, but the ambient Judaean Desert is the most sunken area on earth, adding another 1,300 feet to the climb. So it takes at least an hour, and that afternoon the temperature was around ninety-five.

Elena and Eliza forged ahead on their powerful brown legs, while I was in the rear with Inez (b. 1999). About a tenth of the way up, as the slope became much steeper, she went all floppy and weepy and begged to go back down and take the cable car. I said,

'Courage, Bubba. Onward. Just think. Hitch can't climb Masada – but you can. And once you're up there you'll remember this day for the rest of your life.'

She rallied. The young collapse suddenly and rally suddenly. About a tenth of the way from the summit I paused in a patch of shade for a breather (and a gasper), and Inez said imperiously,

'*Come* on, Daddy! We haven't come this far to give up now!'

'I'm not giving up.'

'Then come on!'

Ten minutes later we were all looking down at the beautiful and painfully ancient desert and the Dead Sea. And there too, on the horizon, you could just make out in the bright air the distant mirage of Jerusalem and its vague devotional silhouettes.

The Masada movement started in January 1942. It was a time when the Jews were engaged in a spasm civil war with the Palestinians, who had recently formed an official alliance with the Third Reich (their Grand Mufti met with Hitler in Berlin in November 1941). At this point, too, Erwin Rommel was rampant in North Africa (and the Holocaust had been under way – as covertly as it could, given that the Germans were using bullets, not gas – for about six months). As the crises gathered there was a concerted campaign to mythologise and centralise, in effect to nationalise, Masada, or the spirit of Masada, or 'the way of Masada', in Shavit's phrase.

Why? What happened there? This is the story.

By 73 CE, after the Roman sacking of Jerusalem, the Great Revolt of the Jews was close to its crushing end. Masada, which Herod had turned into a near-unbreachable bastion a hundred years earlier, was the locus of the last stand of the self-styled Zealots, the most extreme of the rebel forces. Up on the rock there were just under a thousand men, women, and children when Flavius Silva's Xth legion began its final assault. With defeat inevitable, the remaining Zealots put themselves to the sword. The men killed the women and children, then drew lots to see who would start killing the men.

So: a nihilistic tale of bloody fanaticism and bloody downfall was re-engineered into the regnant symbol of the new Jewish identity.

This had immediate popular appeal; but even Zionists, and David Ben-Gurion himself, found the associations of the historical event repellently grim. The men of fighting age on Masada faced execution, but the women faced not death but probable rape and certain enslavement, and the children faced enslavement only. Five of the latter group survived by hiding in a pothole and were captured. Making you wonder how many other women and children, given the choice, would have joined them.

Nevertheless, the campaign, dreamed up and spearheaded by the scholar, archaeologist, and trekker Shmaryahu Gutman (who, affectingly, was by birth a Glaswegian), shifted the emphasis: 'Masada shall not fall again.' And this shaping vow – the absolute refusal to yield – was very quickly emplaced as the defining Jewish truth . . . There are always many chains of boy scouts and girl scouts and school groups and platoons of IDF inductees streaming their way up and down Masada.

'Only the young Hebrews willing to die will be able to ensure for themselves a secure and sovereign life,' as Shavit summarises the meaning and the moral of Masada. 'Only their willingness to fight to the end will prevent their end.'

We came down from the fortress on the *mesa* and went and immersed ourselves in another emblem of Israel and its political life.

I almost typed, *We swam in the Dead Sea.* But you cannot swim in the Dead Sea – swim in the sense of propelling yourself through water. Because the water of the Dead Sea (the Sea of Death) is ten times saltier than brine.

You can wallow in it – you can more or less sit in it, or even on it. When you try anything else you become aware that you have no weight, no ballast, and are soon upended by the whimsical physics of zero gravity, as in space. Then the head goes under and you savour the glutinous liquid – like the spoiled anchovies from the Sea of Azov that Stalin's organs used to give to parched prisoners heading for the camps.

But look at what surrounds you. The festive daytrippers of Israel (some of them daubing themselves with the reputedly wholesome black sand), the cheap-and-cheerful snackbar (where Eliza and Inez devoured their burgers and fries), the scuttled waste of Judea, the dramatic eminences of Masada, and Jerusalem, twenty miles away, under its encrustation of curses.

The historian Tony Judt – late, lamented, and (for the record) Jewish – closed his monumental *Postwar: A History of Europe Since 1945* (2005) with an epilogue entitled 'From the House of the Dead: An Essay on Modern European Memory'. Thirty-odd pages long, and shored up by the 800 pages that precede it, Judt's *tour d'horizon* chastens the reader with its force:

> As Europe prepares to leave World War Two behind – as the last memorials are inaugurated, the last surviving combatants and victims honoured – the recovered memory of Europe's dead Jews has become the very definition and guarantee of the continent's recovered humanity.

Though still far from complete, the psychic work of reckoning, country by country, has typically taken two generations – or roughly fifty years.

Never mind, for now, about the countries with the most obvious burdens of guilt: Germany, and then (in no particular order) Romania, Hungary, Austria, Croatia, Slovakia, and France, all of which Judt inspects. France famously developed its 'Vichy syndrome' (amnesia and evasion), but as Judt says, every Nazi-occupied country 'developed its own "Vichy syndrome"' – including Holland and, yes, Sweden (only Denmark escaped the taint of collaboration). All the occupied countries, and all but one of the countries that remained neutral throughout; Ireland played no part in the German war effort, but the others did, Spain (supplying manganese), Portugal (tungsten), Sweden (iron ore); and as for Switzerland . . .

We remember that during the occupation of France 'Marshal Pétain's Vichy regime played Uriah Heep to Germany's Bill Sikes' (as Judt witheringly notes). But consider the supposed Little Nell of Switzerland:

1) Not until 1994 did the Swiss government concede that it had petitioned Berlin (in 1938) 'for the letter "J" to be stamped on the passports of all German Jews – the better to keep them out . . .'

2) 'In 1941 and 1942, 60 per cent of Switzerland's munitions industry, 50 per cent of its optical industry and 40 per cent of its engineering output was producing for Germany, remunerated in gold' – and it 'was still selling rapid-fire guns to the Wehrmacht in April 1945'.

3) Over the war years 'the German Reichsbank deposited the gold equivalent of 1,638,000,000 Swiss francs in Switzerland' – for channelling and laundering.

4) 'Swiss banks and insurance companies knowingly pocketed indecently large sums of money belonging to Jewish account holders or to the claimants of insurance policies on murdered relatives.'

5) 'In a secret post-war agreement . . . Bern even offered to assign the bank accounts of dead Polish Jews to the new authorities in Warsaw in return for indemnity payments to Swiss banks and businesses expropriated after the Communists' takeover.' (And the Poles 'happily agreed'.)

All this surfaced in the 1990s, and Switzerland's 'burnished reputation', writes Judt, 'came apart'. The piecemeal disclosures racked the country for a decade.

By the end of the twentieth century, it is fair to say, the murder of Europe's Jews was a Western *idée fixe*. Every population affected by the Nazis was thinking and talking about the murder of Europe's Jews. Every population except that of Israel.

'It's like a family tragedy that you don't discuss,' said Michael C. 'It's taught in schools and it's publicly commemorated. But privately you don't talk about it.'

'The Shoah? It just never comes up,' you get quite cheerfully told again and again. This fact, and it is a fact, seems to me fathomable but psychologically very ominous. If you're not talking about it then you're not actively thinking about it. We can deduce from this that the subconscious of Israel is in a state of acute and chronic turmoil.

'The denial of the Palestinian disaster', writes Shavit (using 'denial' as a psychiatrist might), 'is not the only denial the Israeli miracle of the 1950s is based upon. Young Israel also denies the great Jewish catastrophe of the twentieth century.'

Holocaust denial, here, means Holocaust inertia. Not out of the bitter disgust expressed by a Bellow character – 'First those people murdered you, then they forced you to brood on their crimes. It suffocated me to do this.' It was, rather, an effort of cultural will. The two calamities – the Palestinian, the Jewish – have been consigned to the storage unit of the unarticulated inner life.

In response to the Palestinian disaster, the Israelis subvocalise as follows: What's 700,000 displaced compared to 6 million displaced for the purpose of execution? In response to the Jewish disaster, the Israelis tell themselves, in Shavit's words, 'The Holocaust is only the low point from which the Zionist revival rose. The Israeli continuum rejects trauma and defeat and pain and harrowing memories.' Here, the 'survivors are expected *not* to tell their stories'.

'It is highly likely that this multilevel denial was essential,' Shavit goes on. 'Without it, it would have been impossible to function, to build, to live . . . Denial was a life-or-death imperative for the nine-year-old nation into which I was born.'

———————

In Washington a month later Christopher said,

'How am I? Well at the moment I'm being filleted by people offering *advice*. Fly today to Kyoto and consult Dr . . . Eat only wild fartleberries and raw kale until you . . . My aunt had cancer of the G-spot but as soon as she . . .

'I did get quite a funny note from a Native American friend. Whoff fucking Native American friend? She's Cheyenne-Arapaho and a fine comrade. And she wrote to say that everybody who's taken a tribal cure died almost instantly.

'Oh, and I did go to the palatial clinic of one celebrated quack, who leadenly told me what I already knew and then, as I was paying, gifted me a bugbite that doubled the size of my left hand. But fuck all that. How was Tel Aviv-Jaffa?'

This happened as October became November in 2010. The Wyoming, in the District of Columbia, late afternoon, under a cover of cloud. I said,

'Jaffa . . . For days on end it's like any Mediterranean city. You know, sun, sea – lunch with the children under a canopy on the beach. You have your delicious seafood salad and your lovely glass of white wine. Then on the way back Erin, that's Michael's very nice wife, points to the hulk of the uh, the Dolphinarium Disco.'

'I remember. Suicide bombed in when?'

'Around 2000. The Second Intifada. And there it still is, like a punk skull. Twenty-one dead. Most of them teenagers, most of them girls, and most of them Russian. That's the other thing. It's more Russian now. Not an unqualified plus. And the Foreign Minister – what's his name?'

'Avigdor Lieberman. The perfect choice to take control of a delicate equipoise. He'll bring in some Russian finesse.'

'People go on about demographics, but the worst push is self-inflicted. Only around a third – a third – of Jewish schoolchildren are getting a secular education.'

'. . . I know what it'll be like. It'll be like the distorted age structures in the West. A shrinking middle class will have to pay for all the drones who spend their time frowning at the Torah or nutting the Wailing Wall. So. The state will eventually cease to be majority-Jewish, cease to be democratic, and cease to be secular. A racial theocracy. Just what we all hoped for. Like many a Red Sea pedestrian I feel, I feel *let down* by Israel.'

'Judt's the same. So's Hobsbawm . . . What was it you imagined?'

'I don't know, somewhere full of interest and subtlety and testing intelligence. A friend of Victor Klemperer's called the Jews "a seismic people". They stir things up, but it should give rise to something original. A load of weightlifters from Queens buying second homes in Fort Condo – I suppose that's original. But I wanted something, something more . . .'

The room was now dark, but I could see that this was becoming one of Christopher's great political sadnesses. Like his sloughing of hope in socialism, like his sloughing of hope in the outcome of the war in Iraq . . .

Christopher stayed silent so I said,

'What I couldn't shake off was the sense of unreality. Michael says it's like living with a permanent low-level flu. Manageable, but with flare-ups and fevers . . . Unreal. And humankind, Hitch, cannot bear very much unreality.'

'I would never write this, but Israel should call itself Unrael. It's utopian in the literal meaning. *Not place.*'

The capital P has no bearing on the PTSD of Israel. The dread of extinction is the white noise the people continuously try to ignore – continuously, because the dread of extinction is punctually refreshed. Following the Holocaust, within three years of the Holocaust, what starts to happen?

Independence Day was proclaimed on May 15, 1948, and on May 16, 1948, five Arab armies launched what was avowedly a *Vernichtungskrieg*, a war of annihilation (its failure was the original Arab *nakba* – 'catastrophe'). The same applied in June 1967 (the Six Day War) and in October 1973 (the Yom Kippur War) . . . In January 1991 the existential threat came from Saddam Hussein; during the first Gulf War, Tel Aviv was bombarded by Iraqi missiles, and Israeli families sat in sealed rooms with German-made gas masks covering their faces. In March 2002, with the Second Intifada, the threat came from the Palestinians. Now the threat comes from Gaza, and from the overarching prospect of nuclear weapons in Iran . . .

To understate the obvious, this is not a formula for radiant mental health. And if there's a scintilla of truth in the notion that countries are like people, then it is vain to expect Israel to behave normatively or even rationally. The question is not, How can you expect it, after all that? The question is, After all that, *why* do you expect it?

Fifty-one years on, it is clear at least that the Occupation – as exactly foreseen by Abba Eban – was a social, moral, and political *nakba* for the Jews. Let us close with these incantatory lines from James Fenton's 'Jerusalem' (December 1988):

III
  This is your fault.
  This is a crusader vault.
The Brook of Kidron flows from Mea She'arim.
  I will pray for you.
  I will tell you what to do.
 I'll stone you. I shall break your every limb.
   Oh I'm not afraid of you
But maybe I should fear the things you make me do.

VII
  . . . Have you ever met an Arab?
  Yes I am a scarab.
I am a worm. I am a thing of scorn.
  I cry Impure from street to street
And see my degradation in the eyes I meet.

And finally:

    X

Stone cries to stone,
Heart to heart, heart to stone.
These are the warrior archaeologists.
This is us and that is them.
This is Jerusalem.
These are the dying men with tattooed wrists.
Do this and I'll destroy your home.
I have destroyed your home. You have destroyed my home.

Addendum
Elizabeth Jane Howard

'You know your father's got a fancy woman in London,' said Eva García, with her thick Welsh accent ('Ewe gnaw ewe father') and her thick Welsh *Schadenfreude* (the simple pleasure of relaying bad news). 'Fancy man', according to the dictionary, is 'a woman's lover'; 'fancy woman', far more specifically, is 'a married man's mistress'. I didn't know that then. I was thirteen. But I took Eva's meaning.

Celt-Iberian Eva García had served as our nanny-housekeeper during the family's decade in Swansea, South Wales; and she was now summoned down to Cambridge to help keep things steady during an undefined domestic crisis (my father, Kingsley, was elsewhere, and no one had told me why). I found Eva's words completely unabsorbable, and I cancelled them from my mind. Simultaneously I intuited that her intervention was spontaneous and unauthorised, and this damaged my trust in it. But it still awakened fear in me.

A week later, as my mother, Hilly, dropped me off at school, she said that she and Kingsley were embarking on 'a trial separation' ('we're just not getting on any more'). What I remember feeling at the time was numbness, pierced only by a weak hope. I was not yet aware, of course, that trial separations were nearly always a resounding success. But I never doubted that my father still loved my mother. (And it was true.) At the same time the fear awakened by Eva now filled the sky like a mushroom cloud: was this the end of everything? Yet it seems that even a pre-adolescent gets hormonal support (adrenaline? testosterone?), allowing him to contemplate the disaster with an imitation of pragmatic calm.

That night I lay there in the dark pining for the return of my brother Nicolas from boarding school, which I knew would strengthen me.

I also made one adjustment to my internal plot summary. The fancy woman was removed from the cast.

During the summer break Hilly took her three children – Nicolas, Martin, and Myfanwy, now fifteen, fourteen, and ten – to a rented house near Sóller, Mallorca, for an indefinite stay. My brother and I were enrolled at the International School in Palma; Myfanwy attended classes, in Spanish, at a local nunnery (and very soon became fluent). By November the boys were feeling the loss of their father so sharply that they spent at least an hour every morning waiting for the postman to stop by on his motorbike; and once in a while there was a brief, jaunty, and uninformative paternal letter, or more usually a paternal postcard.

So sharply (I repeat) that when half term came Hilly immediately put Nicolas and me on a plane to Heathrow, equipped with the address of Kingsley's 'bachelor flat' in Knightsbridge. I think both the brothers at this point believed in the first word of the quoted phrase. I for one certainly had daydreams about Dad having his tea and toast alone in a modest kitchen, and perhaps making the bed or even doing a bit of dusting . . .

The flight was delayed, and it was well past midnight when we rang the bell in Basil Mansions, London SW3. My father, wearing striped pyjamas, opened the door and rocked back in astonishment (Hilly's telegram had not arrived). These were his first words: 'You know I'm not alone here.' We shrugged coolly, but we were now as astonished as he was. Silently the three of us filed into the kitchen. Kingsley disappeared and then reappeared. Then Jane appeared . . .

A modern youth would have thought, simply, *Wow*. But this was 1963, and what I thought was more like *Cor* (with the slightly reluctant rider, *Say what you like about him, but Dad can't half pull*). Tall, erect, calm, fine-boned, and with the queenly bearing of the fashion model she once was, in a spotless white bathrobe and with a yard of rich blonde hair extending to her waist, Jane straightforwardly introduced herself and set about making us bacon and eggs.

Our five-day visit was a saturnalia of treats and sprees – Harrods fruit-juice bar every morning, restaurants, record shops, West End cinemas (55 *Days at Peking*, with Kingsley lying down on the floor at our feet every single time Ava Gardner appeared on screen), punctuated by several agonising and tearful heart-to-hearts between father and sons (during one of which Nicolas – very impressively, I've always thought – called Kingsley a cunt). But there it was: he had made up his mind and he wasn't coming back.

On the last night, in the middle of a small dinner party, the telephone rang and my father answered; he listened for a moment, and shouted out, 'No!' Then he looked out at us and said four words. Jane quietly began to weep. And one of the guests, George Gale (or, as *Private Eye* called him, George G. Ale), grimly fetched his overcoat and headed off to Fleet Street and the *Daily Express*. It was November 22. Kennedy had been assassinated.

Over the next three or four years my lovelorn mother's homestead in the Fulham Road – so bohemian that it was never locked – steadily disintegrated; and by the time the two boys went to live with Kingsley and Jane I was a semiliterate truant and waster whose main interest was hanging around in betting shops (where, tellingly, I specialised in reversible forecasts on the dogs). The move was Jane's idea.

She always had a pronounced philanthropic bent, and was strongly drawn to strugglers and lost souls – to those who, as she put it, 'had such terrible lives'. She wanted goals, tasks, projects; unlike either of my parents, she was proactive and she was *organised*. Nicolas, far bolder and more rebellious than I was, didn't last very long in the elegant and mannerly house in Maida Vale (and by his own efforts he went on to the Camberwell College of Arts). But I liked it there. So I swallowed the guilt of disloyalty (to my mother) and I responded to my stepmother's interest and advice.

When Jane took me on I was averaging an O level a year, and I read nothing but comics, plus the occasional Harold Robbins and – for example – the dirty bits in *Lady Chatterley*; I had recently sat an A level in English (the only subject in which I'd ever shown any promise) and was awarded an F: I failed. After just over a year under Jane's direction (much of it spent in a last-ditch boarding crammer in Brighton), I had another half-dozen O levels (including Latin from scratch), three A levels, and a second-tier scholarship to Oxford. None of this would have happened without Jane's energy and concentration.

The process also had its intimacies. One day, early on, she presented me with a reading list: Austen, Dickens, Scott Fitzgerald, Waugh, Greene,

Murdoch, Golding, Spark. I began, leerily, with *Pride and Prejudice*. After an hour or so I went and knocked on Jane's study door. 'Ah Mart,' she said, taking off her glasses and leaning back from her desk. I said, 'Jane, I've got to know. Does Elizabeth marry Mr Darcy?' Jane hesitated, looking stern, and I expected her to say, 'Well you'll have to finish it and find out.' But she tenderly relented and said, '*Yes*' (and in addition she put my troubled mind at rest about Jane Bennet and Mr Bingley). Long afterwards we agreed that this was the simple secret of Austen's narrative force, and of the reader's abnormally keen desire for the happy ending: she slowly unites heroes and heroines who are literally made for each other, and made with all her intelligence and insight and art.

In the early years at least, Kingsley and Jane seemed made for each other. It was an unusual and unusually stimulating ménage: two passionately dedicated novelists who were also passionately in love. Their approach to the daily business of writing formed a clear contrast, one from which I derived a tentative theory about the difference between male and female fiction. Kingsley was a grinder; no matter how he was feeling (sickly, clogged, loth – or plain hungover, if you prefer), he trudged off to his desk after breakfast; there was a half-hour lunchbreak, and that was that until it was time for evening drinks. Jane was far more spasmodic and compulsive. She would wander from room to room, she would do some cooking or some gardening, and plenty of smoking as she stared out of the sitting-room window with arms folded and an air of anxious preoccupation. Then she would suddenly hasten to her study, and you'd hear the clatter of her typewriter keys. Quite soon she would shyly emerge, having written more in an hour than my father would write in a day.

The great critic Northrop Frye, in a discussion of Milton's elegy 'Lycidas', made the distinction between real sincerity and literary sincerity. When told of the death of a friend, poets can burst into tears; but they cannot burst into song. I would very cautiously suggest that there is more 'song' in women's fiction – more real sincerity, and less tradition-haunted contrivance. This is certainly true of Elizabeth Jane Howard. She was an instinctivist, with a freakishly metaphorical eye and a sure ear for rhythmically fast-moving prose. Kingsley once 'corrected' one of Jane's short stories, regularising her grammar. All his changes were technically sound; and all of them, in my view, were marked disimprovements (and later on I privately said so).

Later on, because by this time mutual hostility was clearly building; and an attentive reader of Kingsley's novel, *Girl, 20* (1971), could feel pretty sure that all hope was already lost. At the outset, one of the qualities that attracted my father to Jane was her well-travelled (and twice-married) worldliness, her confident social presence – her class, in a word. England in the sixties and seventies was stratified to an extent that now seems barely credible; and it is naive to expect artists or intellectuals to be immune, in the living of their lives, to the stock responses, the emotional clichés, of their time.

The daughter of a prosperous timber merchant, Jane was educated by governesses and grew up in a large house full of servants in Notting Hill. The son of a clerk at a mustard manufacturers, Kingsley was a South London scholarship boy and the first Amis to attend university (he was also a card-carrying Communist until the ridiculously advanced age of thirty-five). That gulf in status was part of the attraction, on both sides; there is bathos as well as pathos in the fact that in the end it proved unbridgeable.

Kingsley would later write that many marriages adhere to a familiar pattern: the wife regards the husband as slightly uncouth and ill-bred, and the husband regards the wife as slightly over-refined and stuck-up. And it was as if Kingsley set himself the task of broadening that divide.

To take a relatively trivial example (while remembering that marriages are measured by relative trivialities), among her other accomplishments Jane was a culinary expert who expended a lot of time and trouble in the kitchen; Kingsley did not go so far as to smother her soufflés with HP Sauce, but with increasing frequency he reached for the pickles, the chutneys, and the jams, muttering that he had to make this or that venison terrine or smoked-fish mousse 'taste of *something*'. In a well-meaning marriage the principals soon identify each other's irritabilities and seek to appease them. Jane and especially Kingsley did the opposite. As he got coarser, she could not but seem snootier. The antagonisms proliferated and ramified; it became a cold civil war.

Jane was a self-confessed 'bolter'. Maybe, in her two earlier marriages. But no one was even mildly surprised when, in 1980, she did a medium-paced runner on Kingsley. Nicolas called me and said, 'Mart. It's happened'; and I knew in a heartbeat what he meant. Her disappearance seemed punitive, and certainly gave rise to great complication, due to my father's lavish array of phobias (he couldn't drive, he couldn't fly, and he couldn't be alone after dark). This necessitated a system of 'Dadsitting' by his three children – until we hit upon an unlikely arrangement involving my mother and her third husband, which to everyone's consternation lasted till Kingsley's death in 1995. A man who abandons his first wife and is then himself abandoned by her successor loses everything: he becomes an amatory zero. But as soon as Kingsley was reunited with Hilly (though only platonically and prudentially) he stopped 'feeling cut-up about Jane'. And thereafter, it still pains me to report, he never had a good word to say for her.

During their early years together Kingsley and Jane practised a curious ritual. Before dinner they would in turn read out to each other the results of their day's labour. I always found this incomprehensible: after all, the prose is unrevised, raw, contingent; and besides fiction is there to be read, not listened to. I once rather snidely asked my father if he had yet regaled Jane with the penultimate paragraph of *Jake's Thing* (1978). He looked furtive, and this is why:

> Jake did a quick run-through of women in his mind, not of the
> ones he had known or dealt with in the past few months or years
> so much as all of them: their concern with the surface of things,
> with objects and appearances, with their surroundings and how
> they looked and sounded in them, with seeming to be better
> and to be right while getting everything wrong, their automatic
> assumption of the role of injured party in any clash of wills, their
> certainty that a view is more credible and useful for the fact that
> they hold it, their use of misunderstanding and misrepresentation
> as weapons of debate, their selective sensitivity to tones of voice,
> their unawareness of the difference in themselves between
> sincerity and insincerity, their interest in importance (together
> with noticeable inability to discriminate in that sphere), their
> fondness for general conversation and directionless discussion,
> their pre-emption of the major share of feeling, their exaggerated
> estimate of their own plausibility, their never listening and lots of
> other things like that, all according to him.

The blanket condemnation became outright misogyny in *Stanley and the Women* (1984). In that long sentence I can see glimmers of Jane; but I can see nothing of Hilly, whose presence in the house cured

Kingsley of his aversion, and thereby rescued his artistic sense, which was in the end redoubtable. In 1986 he won the Booker Prize for his longest and most satisfying novel, *The Old Devils*.

After Jane separated herself from Kingsley, it never occurred to anyone that I should separate myself from Jane. But I naturally saw far less of her. She wanted more from me – more than I felt able to give. It was always that way. From the very start I sensed emanations of love from her. I was very grateful and very attached and very admiring. But your father's 'other woman', I fear, is doomed to love her stepson without full requital. The blood tie to the blood mother is simply too potent and too deep.

With a secretive look Jane said to me in 1965, just after she and Kingsley got married, 'I'm your wicked stepmother.' And it was true: she was wicked in the sense of 'exceptionally *good*'. In my last letter to her, written in December 2013, I saluted Jane for her artistic longevity (she had just published *All Change*, volume five of the Cazalet Chronicles, at the age of ninety); and I cited the example of the skilled historical yarner Herman Wouk, who had just published *The Lawgiver* at the age of ninety-seven. I hoped and more than half expected Jane to duplicate Wouk's feat. But she died on January 2, 2014, barely a month after her younger brother Colin, an unsung hero of this saga (charming, witty, not very happily gay, universally adored, and one of the most sweet-natured people I have ever known), who lived with Jane before Kingsley and went on living with her through the lion's share of the Kingsley years.

For reasons that no doubt go back to a dismal childhood (with a cold mother and an intrusively intimate father), Jane was always restless for affection; and at the same time she remained a calamitous chooser of men. Indeed, my father – by any standards a mixed blessing – was probably the pick of the bunch, standing out (there were other, briefer exceptions) from a ghastly *galère* of frauds, bullies, and rogues. One of Jane's finest books was a collection of stories called *Mr Wrong*. So maybe in the end it is Colin – always known by everyone as Monkey – who will have to serve, and serve honourably, as the love of Elizabeth Jane Howard's life.

Postscript

I spent that Christmas and New Year with my wife and younger daughters in Florida, where I heard of Jane's death and wrote the first version of this personal obituary. On the plane back to New York I said to my wife, 'I wonder if Jane answered my letter.' And she had; the envelope, eerily, with her slightly shrunken but unmistakable hand, was waiting on the mat in Brooklyn (postmarked December 16). Inside it were two single-spaced typed pages. She included a resilient account of Colin's funeral, a stoical (and amusing) catalogue of the sort of disabilities you'd expect as you enter your tenth decade, some kind remarks about my last novel, and news about her work in progress (she was a third of the way through). There was not the slightest hint that she felt herself to be fading or ailing. Indeed, she approved my suggestion that we resume the quite diligent correspondence we kept up during my years as a student, half a century ago.

Jane's authorised biographer, Artemis Cooper (and at that stage hers was another work in progress), told me that Jane had a full and active Christmas (she was always a generous and ingenious buyer of presents), and duly answered all the letters lamenting her younger brother. With that done, her appetite began to fail, and her body seemed to be 'shutting down'. Medical science has only recently recognised the condition – but we have all seen it at work. The spouse, the companion, the close relative goes, and often with terrifying speed the soulmate follows. With good reason did Saul Bellow entitle one of his later novels *More Die of Heartbreak*. Jane's final morning came on January 2; and she 'serenely' ceased to be in the early afternoon.

Post-postscript

Telling a dream, we all know by now, impedes a novel or a story. But this is not fiction. In early February I dreamt I was very young again, and I and my brother and sister heard that Jane's dog Rosie was in great distress (a 'ruby' Cavalier spaniel, Rosie was put to sleep with much sorrow in the mid-1970s); and we set off to find her, as if on a quest in an idealistic children's book. Nicolas asked, 'What shall we do when we find her?' 'Cuddle her,' Myfanwy firmly answered. We found Rosie, who was the wrong colour but was certainly suffering, and we set about giving her comfort. Then I woke up. Later that day I realised why, in dream logic, Rosie was crying. She was crying because her mistress was dead.

Illustration Credits

p.6 Saul Bellow on the New York subway in 1975 © Neal Boenzi / New York Times / Redux / eyevine; p.57 Elizabeth Jane Howard © John Hedgecoe / TopFoto; p.80 Bellow and Kollek in 1987 © Max Jacoby, used by permission of the Special Collections Research Center, University of Chicago Library; p.86 The Bellows on their wedding day, used by permission of the Saul Bellow Estate; p.195 Eliza's drawing of the 9/11 attacks, author's own; p.216 Isabel Elena Fonseca © Marion Ettlinger; p.306 Christopher Hitchens, Martin Amis and Tina Brown © Photograph by Dafydd Jones; p.309 Christopher Hitchens and Anna Wintour, used by kind permission of Gully Wells; p.314 Christopher Hitchens under arrest © Billett Potter, Oxford; p.333 Larkin family portrait, used by permission of The Society of Authors as the Literary Representative of the Estate of Philip Larkin; p.340 Ruth Bowman, used by permission of The Society of Authors as the Literary Representative of the Estate of Philip Larkin; p.340 Hilly with pet dogs in 1958 © Daily Mail / Shutterstock; p.376 Saul Bellow and Martin Amis, used by permission of the Saul Bellow Estate]; p.456 Kingsley and Hilly Amis at the time of their marriage; p.483 *John Keats in His Last Illness*, from 'The Century Illustrated Monthly Magazine', May to October, 1883 (engraving) © Bridgeman Images; p.488 Christopher Hitchens © Brooks Kraft / Getty Images

Quotation Credits

The quotations from 'Aubade', 'Annus Mirabilis', 'This Be the Verse', 'The Trees', 'To the Sea', 'Vers de Société', 'Next, Please', 'Going, Going', 'Love Again', 'High Windows', 'Self's the Man', 'Dockery and Son', 'The Mower' and 'The View' are from *The Complete Poems* © Philip Larkin, used by permission of Faber & Faber Ltd.; The quotation from 'Letter to a Friend about Girls' is © Philip Larkin, used by permission of Faber & Faber Ltd.; The quotations from 'In Memory of W.B. Yeats' and 'September 1, 1939' are from *Another Time* © 1940 by W.H. Auden, renewed. Reprinted by permission of Curtis Brown, Ltd.; The quotation from 'Preludes' is from *Collected Poems 1909–1962* © T.S. Eliot, used by permission of Faber & Faber Ltd.; The quotation from 'Jerusalem' is from *Yellow Tulips: Poems 1968–2011* © James Fenton, used by permission of Faber & Faber Ltd.

Index